THE YEAR'S
BEST SCIENCE
FICTION

THE YEAR'S BEST SCIENCE FICTION

**ELEVENTH
ANNUAL
COLLECTION**

Gardner Dozois, Editor

ST. MARTIN'S PRESS   NEW YORK

For Jane Jewell
and Peter Heck—
fellow travelers

Library of Congress Catalog Card Number: 85-645716

ISBN 0-312-11105-3 (paperback)
ISBN 0-312-11104-5 (hardcover)

First Edition: August 1994

10 9 8 7 6 5 4 3 2

Acknowledgment is made for permission to print the following material:

"Papa," by Ian R. MacLeod. Copyright © 1993 by Bantam Doubleday Dell Magazines. First published in *Asimov's Science Fiction*, October 1993. Reprinted by permission of the author and the author's agents, Owlswick Literary Agency.

"Sacred Cow," by Bruce Sterling. Copyright © 1993 by Omni Publications International Ltd. First published in *Omni*, January 1993. Reprinted by permission of the author.

"Dancing on Air," by Nancy Kress. Copyright © 1993 by Bantam Doubleday Dell Magazines. First published in *Asimov's Science Fiction*, July 1993. Reprinted by permission of the author.

"A Visit to the Farside," by Don Webb. Copyright © 1993 by TSR, Inc. First published in *Amazing Stories*, April 1993. Reprinted by permission of the author.

"Alien Bootlegger," by Rebecca Ore. Copyright © 1993 by Rebecca Ore. First published in *Alien Bootlegger and Other Stories* (Tor Books). Reprinted by permission of the author.

"Death on the Nile," by Connie Willis. Copyright © 1993 by Bantam Doubleday Dell Magazines. First published in *Asimov's Science Fiction*, March 1993. Reprinted by permission of the author.

"Friendship Bridge," by Brian W. Aldiss. Copyright © 1993 by Brian W. Aldiss. First published in *New Worlds 3* (Gollancz). Reprinted by permission of the author.

"Into the Miranda Rift," by G. David Nordley. Copyright © 1993 by Bantam Doubleday Dell Magazines. First published in *Analog Science Fiction and Fact*, July 1993. Reprinted by permission of the author.

"Mwalimu in the Squared Circle," by Mike Resnick. Copyright © 1993 by Bantam Doubleday Dell Magazines. First published in *Asimov's Science Fiction*, March 1993. Reprinted by permission of the author.

"Guest of Honor," by Robert Reed. Copyright © 1993 by Mercury Press, Inc. First published in *The Magazine of Fantasy & Science Fiction*, June 1993. Reprinted by permission of the author.

"Love Toys of the Gods," by Pat Cadigan. Copyright © 1993 by Pat Cadigan. First published in *Omni Best Science Fiction Three* (Omni Books). Reprinted by permission of the author.

"Chaff," by Greg Egan. Copyright © 1993 by *Interzone*. First published in *Interzone*, December 1993. Reprinted by permission of the author.

"Georgia on My Mind," by Charles Sheffield. Copyright © 1993 by Bantam Doubleday Dell Magazines. First published in *Analog Science Fiction and Fact*, January 1993. Reprinted by permission of the author.

"Cush," by Neal Barrett, Jr. Copyright © 1993 by Bantam Doubleday Dell Magazines. First published in *Asimov's Science Fiction*, November 1993. Reprinted by permission of the author.

"On the Collection of Humans," by Mark Rich. Copyright © 1993 by Mark Rich. First published in *Nova 5*. Reprinted by permission of the author.

"There and Then," by Steven Utley. Copyright © 1993 by Bantam Doubleday Dell Magazines. First published in *Asimov's Science Fiction*, November 1993. Reprinted by permission of the author.

CONTENTS

ACKNOWLEDGMENTS

The editor would like to thank the following people for their help and support: first and foremost, Susan Casper, for doing much of the thankless scut work involved in producing this anthology; Michael Swanwick, Janet Kagan, Ellen Datlow, Virginia Kidd, Sheila Williams, Ian Randal Strock, Scott L. Towner, Tina Lee, David Pringle, Kristine Kathryn Rusch, Dean Wesley Smith, Pat Cadigan, David S. Garnett, Charles C. Ryan, Chuq von Rospach, Susan Allison, Ginjer Buchanan, Lou Aronica, Betsy Mitchell, Beth Meacham, Claire Eddy, David G. Hartwell, Bob Walters, Tess Kissinger, Jim Frenkel, Greg Egan, Steve Pasechnick, Susan Ann Protter, Lawrence Person, Dwight Brown, Chris Reed, Dirk Strasser, Michael Sumbera, Glen Cox, Darrell Schweitzer, Don Keller, Robert Killheffer, Greg Cox, and special thanks to my own editor, Gordon Van Gelder.

Thanks are also due to Charles N. Brown, whose magazine *Locus* (Locus Publications, P.O. Box 13305, Oakland, CA 94661, $38.00 for a one-year subscription [twelve issues] via second class; credit card orders [510] 339-9198) was used as a reference source throughout the Summation, and to Andrew Porter, whose magazine *Science Fiction Chronicle* (Science Fiction Chronicle, P.O. Box 022730, Brooklyn, NY 11202-0056, $30.00 for a one-year subscription [twelve issues]; $36.00 first class) was also used as a reference source throughout.

SUMMATION
1993

This was a generally quiet year, and whether you considered it to be a depressing year or a hopeful year depended largely on which omens you chose to read, for certainly every negative omen was counterbalanced by a positive one, or vice versa.

The traditional game of Editorial Musical Chairs, which started up again last year, went through a couple of additional rounds *this* year, with John Silbersack, who had moved to Warner from Roc in 1992, moving from Warner to HarperCollins in 1993, and being replaced at Warner by former Bantam editor Betsy Mitchell; former Legend (U.K.) editor Deborah Beale, who had moved to Millennium a couple of years back, decided to quit the publishing world (or at least to semiretire), and was replaced at Millennium by Caroline Oakley. Lou Aronica, deputy publisher of Bantam, moved to The Berkley Publishing Group as senior vice president and publisher, succeeding Roger Cooper, who moved to St. Martin's Press last year, and being succeeded as deputy publisher at Bantam by Nita Taublib. In the vacuum left behind by the departure of Lou Aronica and Betsy Mitchell, Jennifer Hershey was promoted internally to executive editor, and Tom Dupree was moved internally to help coordinate the Bantam Spectra SF line. Susan Allison remains editor-in-chief of Ace and executive editor of Berkley, while Ginjer Buchanan is still executive editor of Ace and senior editor of Berkley. Christopher Schelling left Roc early in 1994 and joined HarperCollins as an executive editor. Amy Stout replaced him at Roc as executive editor.

On the downhill side, editor Michael Kandel parted ways with Harcourt Brace, killing their very promising SF line; there were cutbacks at several publishing houses, including at Bantam Spectra, where they've cut to an average of three titles per month from a previous average of five or six titles per month in 1992; the fate of the AvoNova SF line remains uncertain, as contradictory rumors continued to circulate right up until press time about whether or not Avon and Morrow would be sold (and if so, to whom, and what would *happen* to them there); the Poseidon Press line from Simon & Schuster was canceled after the dismissal of editor Ann Patty; we probably have lost one of the major SF magazines, and the imminent death and vanishing of the *rest* of the SF magazines was predicted once again, as it has been predicted nearly every year since the late 1960s.

On the other hand, on the *up*hill side, John Silbersack is starting a major new SF line, HarperPrism; Betsy Mitchell is "relaunching" Warner Questar as the Warner Aspect line (essentially creating a whole new line); Tor launched two new lines, Orb and Forge; Ellen Key Harris launched the successful "Del Rey Discoveries" line at Del Rey; Jeanne Cavelos launched a new "Dell Edge" line at Dell to publish less genre-oriented books that don't fit into her "Dell/Abyss" line; book sales held reasonably steady throughout the field (the loss in some places being offset by gains in *other* places); the small-press market continued to expand, and not only did the SF magazines manage to survive the year again, there are a flock of *new* ones pushing to be born, including a couple that look near to establishing themselves successfully.

So, as I say, whether you sum these omens and decide that 1993 was a discouraging or an encouraging year for science fiction depends largely on *which* omens you decide to consider, and how much weight you decide to give them. As I mentioned last year, though, it *does* seem to me as though there's more gloom and pessimism around about the Future of Science Fiction than is really *justified* by the year's events. Some critics, such as Barry N. Malzberg, John Clute, and others, have even gone so far as to say that, with the death of older writers such as Isaac Asimov, the field has lost its "center," that science fiction is in a much worse state now than it was in a few years ago, and that the outlook for the future is very gloomy, that science fiction is now doomed either to extinction or at least to a long, slow dwindling-away into eventual obscurity where less and less of real merit will be published every year—that, in other words, SF's best days are *behind* it.

I must say that I don't believe this. It's easy to see where this kind of depression comes from, as SF *has* suffered terrible losses in the last few years, with the death of major figures such as Isaac Asimov, Fritz Leiber, Robert Heinlein, Theodore Sturgeon, Avram Davidson, Alfred Bester, and dozens of others. Nevertheless, to conclude that SF's best days are behind it is to view the evidence with a very selective eye, and to distort historical perspective by creating a wistfully utopian version of a past that never really existed—and then holding the present up to that imaginary past and judging the present as lacking.

For one thing, I doubt that there ever really *was* a "center" to the field—it has *always* been a matter of what (and who) you choose to look at, and what you choose to ignore, of selective viewing of the evidence. To say, for instance, that John Campbell's *Astounding* was once the center of the field is to ignore all those writers who couldn't really fit *into* it comfortably, such as Frederik Pohl and C. M. Kornbluth and Damon Knight, who later went on to become the mainstay of *Astounding*'s chief rival, *Galaxy*; and even if you then widen the definition of "center" of the field to include both *Astounding* and *Galaxy*, that still ignores those writers such as Ray Bradbury, Jack Vance, Charles Harness, Leigh Brackett, and a number of others, who mostly didn't fit into *either* magazine. And it has *always* been true, and still is, that major works of substance and high literary ambition are published side-by-side with trooping legions of bottom-of-the-barrel, lowest-common-denominator hack books . . . and that sometimes posterity ends up remembering the ''hack'' books as major work, and forgets about the supposedly ''major'' novels altogether! Gene Wolfe and Jerry Pournelle are displayed on the same racks in the same bookstores, and which of them you choose to say represents the ''center'' of the field is largely a subjective matter, and depends largely on who *you* are inthe first place. The field probably has quite a different ''center'' for each of us.

For another thing, science fiction has *always* depended on the work of the new young writers coming along as much (or more) as it depended on the work of the Big Name Writers at the top, and *that's* the work that often determines the overall quality of a period, not the work of the Famous Authors at the top of the best-seller lists—and this was just as true when the new young writers coming along were Isaac Asimov and Robert Heinlein as it is today. And new young writers of quality have definitely *not* stopped coming into science fiction; if anything, they are coming into the field in *increasing* numbers as the nineties progress. Isaac Asimov himself would certainly have dismissed the idea that science fiction was finished, or at least that some essential quality had gone out of it, because *he* was gone; in fact, he probably would have been offended by the idea. He knew that science fiction depends on new writers for its continued evolution, and drew comfort from the idea that they would go on building on the foundations of his own life's work long after he was dead, just as he in his time had built upon the work of those who came before *him*. He would have laughed to scorn the idea that science fiction had died *with* him.

Finally, I must question the idea that science fiction as a genre has seen better days. I've been here, observing it, for at least the past thirty years, and I must say, when *was* this Terrestrial Paradise? *I* don't remember it. (I've heard both the New Wave days of the late-sixties and the post–New Wave days of the mid-seventies put forward as the Time When Things Were So Much Better, by young critics like t. Winter-Damon and K. J. Cypret, and others . . . and if you could go back in a time machine and tell *that* to writers living through either period, they'd fall on the ground laughing.) A lot of this is nostalgia, and a lot of it is selective memory. In fact, for all of our very real problems, it seems to me as if the genre has never been in a *better* position, either commercially or artistically.

Consider: When I first became professionally involved in the field, in the early sixties, very few SF novels were *allowed* to be longer than 50,000 words; almost nobody, including most of the Big Names, was getting more than three or four thousand dollars per book; almost nobody could make a living from writing SF, unless he or she was prolific enough to turn out five or six books a year; the total number of SF books published every year was *immensely* smaller than it is today, and, even so, few bookstores carried more than a smattering of SF titles (most carried no titles at all); SF was an academically taboo topic, and admitting that you read it was often enough to get you ostracized from Decent Society—you might even be openly berated and publicly humiliated for reading SF, by total strangers, if you happened to be caught reading it on a bus or in a laundromat. Artistically, things were even *worse*, both in the novel market and the short fiction market. You were not allowed to write about sex, for instance—in many cases, you were not allowed to even *say* that your characters had *had* sex, let alone to describe the sex act in any sort of detail. You were not allowed to use "dirty" language—which, in many cases, extended even down to the word "damn," which an editor of one of the major SF magazines of the time systematically changed to "darn" every time I used it. You were not allowed very much, if any, latitude in the matter of political controversy, either, and in most cases, religious and racial issues were taboo, as was any really "disturbing" view of society, or any adopting of values that weren't those of the straightest mainline society. You were even discouraged from using certain kinds of *characters*, since the SF audience wasn't supposed to be interested in reading about women or black people (I got that last one, about the SF audience not being interested in reading about black people, as late as *last year*, when I was trying to sell my *Under African Skies* anthology), let *alone* gay or lesbian people or "political extremists," and, of course, any kind of *stylistic* experimentation, even of the most basic sorts, was totally out of the question. Worse, in many markets you were *required* to be "upbeat" and "positive," and more than one writer, including myself, routinely had their stories rejected for not being "optimistic" enough. Few readers or even writers who entered the field after the "New Wave revolution" of the late sixties realize how bad things really and routinely *were* back then, or how badly the "New Wave revolution" was *needed*.

In fact, I'd be willing to bet that at least 70 percent of the SF novels published in 1993—and probably closer to 90 percent of the short fiction, even that from the most conservative of markets—*could not have been published* in 1963; *most* of it still could not have been published in 1973, and probably a considerable percentage of it still couldn't have been published in *1983*, either. This is why I find it hard to conclude that SF's Best Days are behind it. In spite of the flood of sharecropper novels and choose-your-own-adventure books and gaming and media-related tie-in titles on the shelves, there is more good SF and fantasy of many different kinds being published today, across an amazingly wide aesthetic spectrum, and by writers of all generations, from the surviving Golden Age giants to the newest of new writers, than there has ever been before—and most of it could not even have *been* published just a few decades back. If you want to see the Golden Age, don't look to the past—look around you.

This kind of thinking is not unique to the science fiction world, of course. I run into it every time I hear some young person say despairingly that no progress at all has been made in combating racism or sexism in the past few decades—something that those of us who actually *remember* living in the fifties *know* is not true—and that therefore there's no point trying to fight to make things better in the future, either. I strongly recommend Otto Bettman's book *The Good Old Days—They Were Terrible!* as an antidote for such thinking. Because, of course, in science fiction or out of it, the danger in painting the past as having been better than it was is that it encourages people to think that the present is worse than it *is*, and that therefore there's no hope, and no viable future to struggle toward, and *that* generates apathy and despair. Let's not give up on the future

before we reach it, and especially not because we're judging the present by the standards of a past that never was.

It was another gray year in the magazine market, and although most of the magazines at least managed to hold their ground, the year did see the probable loss of a major magazine, and some serious problems at a few others; on the uphill side, it *also* saw a few new magazines successfully complete their first full year of publication, and a number of even newer magazines struggled to be born, with rumor of even more to come.

The big story of the year in this market was *Amazing*, which went "on hiatus" toward the end of 1993 while TSR Publishing decides what they want to do with the magazine. As of this writing, no one seems really sure whether or not this means that *Amazing* has died. It seems certain, however, that at the very least, the end of *Amazing*'s incarnation as a large-size, slick-format monthly has come. This incarnation proved ruinously expensive to produce, since production costs are much *much* higher for a large-size magazine than they are for a digest-sized magazine, which drives profitability down; the last large-size issue, scheduled to be the December issue, was published at the end of the year as the "Winter 1994" issue instead (we've listed stories from that issue in this year's Honorable Mentions list for convenience's sake, in spite of the 1994 cover date, since the magazine did come out in 1993). *Amazing*'s circulation had plummeted disastrously in 1992, down 61.6 percent from the previous year, at the worst possible time, since sales were dropping just as profitability was declining (due to the rising costs demanded by the shift from a digest-sized to a large-size format); circulation did come up 21.4 percent this year, with most of the gain in newsstand sales, but it was too little too late to save a magazine that was rumored to have been losing almost $50,000 per issue. Initial reports in early 1994 were that the magazine *was* dead, and that its unused inventory would be used up in two original anthologies for Tor. Later, rumors began to circulate that *Amazing* would be reborn as a monthly digest-sized magazine, back to its old format, sometime in 1994. Then there were rumors that it would *not* be reborn, or, perhaps, would be reborn in some other format, such as an original anthology series or even in an "illustrated" version similar to "graphic novel" format. The last report I've seen claims that *Amazing* will "temporarily resume publication" as a digest-sized magazine (although the two Tor original anthologies of inventory stories apparently will still appear as well), publishing three issues which are scheduled to appear in Spring 1994, Fall 1994, and Winter 1995; I suppose that this is being done largely to test the waters, and, if sales don't climb very significantly on those issues, I expect that TSR will finally pull the plug on *Amazing* for good, in any format. TSR is still talking supportively about *Amazing*, with associate publisher Brian Thomsen quoted by the newszine *Locus* as saying "*Amazing Stories* is the oldest, and longest-running, magazine in the field, and TSR has no desire to go down in history as the company who killed it." . . . But he *then* goes on to say that TSR "will by no means rule out the sale of the

magazine to another party'' as one of the options they're considering. I've pronounced *Amazing* dead several times before during the eighteen years that I've been editing Best of the Year anthologies, only to see it come to life again each time, so I'm reluctant to go out on a limb again *this* time—but I suspect that, unless a new buyer for the magazine *can* be found (always a possibility, of course), *Amazing* may finally have run out of lives. We'll see. In the meantime, let's wish it well.

Aboriginal SF had another rocky year in 1993, losing a further 37.8 percent in overall circulation, most of those losses coming in subscriptions, which have declined a whopping 45 percent overall since 1992—this is bad news, since almost all fiction magazines depend on their subscription list to survive, far more so than they do on their newsstand sales, which have been weak throughout the industry for several years now, even for magazines such as *Omni*. On the other hand, they managed to keep to their quarterly schedule this year, unlike last year, producing all four issues they were supposed to produce, and they *did* manage to convince the IRS to grant them the nonprofit status they'd been seeking, which ought to help them continue to publish, so it may be that *Aboriginal SF* is past the hump as far as its troubles are concerned, for the moment, anyway. It was also a tough year for *Pulphouse: A Fiction Magazine*, as money problems at Pulphouse Publishing (which came very close to going under in 1992 and struggled to recover throughout 1993) continued to affect the magazine adversely. Last year, Pulphouse published only six out of a scheduled thirteen issues of *Pulphouse: A Fiction Magazine*—not even keeping to their announced every-four-week publication schedule, let alone to their original ambitious but unrealistic intention of making it a *weekly* magazine—and in 1993 they managed to publish only *two* issues. On the other hand, there are signs that the worst of the crisis at Pulphouse Publishing may be past, and publisher Dean Wesley Smith has pledged to devote more resources and time to the project, now that the situation at Pulphouse is stabilizing, so perhaps the magazine will finally achieve a reliable publication schedule in 1994. Former editor Smith stepped down in 1993, to be replaced by Jonathan E. Bond, who seems to have taken *Pulphouse: A Fiction Magazine* even further in the direction of ''dark suspense'' and non-supernatural ''psychological horror,'' so that very little in the magazine even qualifies as fantasy anymore, let alone science fiction.

Weird Tales also had problems this year, once again managing to publish only two issues out of a scheduled four. On the other hand, there were also some *encouraging* signs for *Weird Tales* this year—it's now being carried by most of the nationwide bookstore chains, and the circulation did rise in 1993, up 14 percent overall, with direct sales up 11 percent and subscriptions up 16 percent. Winning a World Fantasy Award, which they did this year, could probably also be legitimately counted as an ''encouraging sign,'' and can certainly only help their reputation; let's hope it helps their sales as well. *Omni*'s circulation was down 10.3 percent from last year, down 30 percent overall from their high point in 1988. Rumors circulated in the spring of 1993 that *Omni* was up for sale, but figures at *Omni* quickly denied these rumors, and I must say that I don't put

much credence in them myself. What should be remembered is that, even with a 30 percent decline, *Omni*'s circulation remains *immensely* higher than any other magazine we'll discuss here, more than 700,000 copies per year, and I don't think they'll run out of gas anytime soon, especially as the internal reorganization they went through in 1992 and the consequent changes in format and production methods should make the magazine considerably cheaper to produce than it once was, which, of course, probably *increases* its profitability. I'd be very surprised to see *Omni* either sold or folded any time in the foreseeable future (although, of course, in the publishing business, anything *can* happen).

Analog and *Asimov's Science Fiction* went through their first full year as part of the Dell Magazine stable. Overall circulation was up slightly at *Asimov's*, up by 1.4 percent, with all of the gain coming in subscriptions; newsstand sales remained unchanged from last year, in spite of an increased effort to put more of both magazines out on the newsstands. Longtime *Asimov's* book reviewer Baird Searles died, and was replaced by a "rotating" three-man reviewing staff consisting of Peter Heck, Paul Di Filippo, and Moshe Feder, joining Norman Spinrad, whose column will continue as usual. Starting in mid-1994, Robert Silverberg's "Reflections" column, which has been running in *Amazing* for a number of years, will transfer to *Asimov's* as a regular monthly feature. Overall circulation held steady at *Analog*, which lost a thousand newsstand sales but gained a thousand new subscribers. Artistically, *Analog* had one of its strongest years in some time in 1993, placing several stories on this year's Nebula Ballot. Overall circulation at *The Magazine of Fantasy & Science Fiction* was up slightly, 2.5 percent higher than last year, with an 8 percent gain in subscriptions but an 18 percent drop in newsstand sales. Newish editor Kristine Kathryn Rusch, who took over from longtime editor Ed Ferman in mid-1991, seems to be doing a good job, and *F&SF* placed more stories on this year's Nebula Ballot and *Locus* Recommended List than it has for some time. Charles de Lint will be replacing Orson Scott Card as one of *F&SF*'s rotating book reviewers, the others being John Kessel and now Robert Killheffer. Gregory Benford and Bruce Sterling continue as the rotating science columnists, although there are rumors that Sterling is about to quit. The British magazine *Interzone* completed its third full year as a monthly publication, and managed to weather a crisis caused by the failure of its perhaps ill-advised attempt to create a companion nonfiction and critical magazine, called *Million*, which has subsequently died and been "incorporated" into *Interzone*. Circulation remained steady in 1993, and literary quality is still high, although they seemed to publish a good deal more fantasy this year than they usually do, which may account in part for the fact that they placed fewer stories on the *Locus* Recommended List this year than they did the year before.

Two *new* SF magazines successfully completed their first full year of publication in 1993, each putting out their scheduled six issues—*Science Fiction Age* and *Tomorrow*. *Science Fiction Age*, a large-size full-color magazine, was not *quite* as instantly successful as it had been reported to be last year, when it was rumored to have achieved a circulation of over 100,000, but it did manage to establish a solid overall circulation of about 61,000, which is very impressive for a brand-new magazine; unusually, the bulk of that was in newsstand sales. *That* is probably because, now that *Amazing* is nearly dead (at least in its large-size format), *Science Fiction Age* is the best-*looking* SF magazine on the newsstands—it's a very slick-looking magazine, with nice art and layout, interior color, and high production values. This, in turn, probably explains why it is attracting some advertisers who have rarely if ever bothered with SF magazines before. It also carries an interesting mix of nonfiction and criticism, with columns covering the worlds of books, movies, comics, games, science, and fantastic art. *Science Fiction Age* has been successful enough that they are reported to be about to launch both a companion fantasy magazine (entitled *Realms of Fantasy*) and the *Sci-Fi Channel* magazine in similar formats, which worries me a little, since these might be premature moves; because, of course, the downside of *Science Fiction Age*'s slick format is that it must be very expensive to produce, which means they need a higher level of profitability than a digest-sized magazine just to break even; it's also expensive to maintain the kind of prominent rack-display that it has been getting so far in many of the national bookstore chains, often as much as ten dollars per register *per store*. All of which makes me wonder if the magazine is really profitable *enough* at a circulation of 61,000, even with all the advertising they're getting, to balance the expenses—which in turn makes me wonder if it wouldn't be more prudent of them to wait another year or so to see before launching *another* new magazine. *Tomorrow*, the year's other new magazine, is an interesting contrast to *Science Fiction Age*: *Tomorrow* is not a particularly slick or "upscale"-looking magazine, and they're obviously getting little advertising—the paper-stock and production values are considerably inferior to *Science Fiction Age*, the layout is dull, there's no interior color, the interior illustrations are often crude, and there's very little nonfiction or criticism about any topic in the magazine, except for editor Algis Budrys's continuing how-to-write column. On the other hand, the *fiction* that *Tomorrow* has published this year has by and large been livelier and more substantial than that published by *Science Fiction Age*, which so far has tended to publish a lot of solid professional stuff of the second rank, but little that's really exceptional or exciting. *Tomorrow* has yet to publish anything of absolutely first-rank quality either, or it would be in this anthology, but the magazine does have a certain panache, and several stories from it came closer to making the cut this year than did most of the stories from *Science Fiction Age*; *Tomorrow* publishes quite a few long stories, while *Science Fiction Age* doesn't publish many novelettes or novellas, which may have helped to give *Tomorrow* the edge in "substantial" stories. In spite of *Tomorrow*'s claim that they publish only Good Old-Fashioned science fiction, both magazines published a good deal of fantasy, but *Science Fiction Age* was perhaps willing to move further away from the core of the field, and seemed more open to literary experimentation. (It's fascinating to see the editorial personalities of these two magazines developing right before our eyes!) Hard to tell yet what *Tomorrow*'s chances of survival are. *Tomorrow* must be considerably cheaper to produce than *Science Fiction Age*, but, on the other hand, Budrys, who is publishing the magazine himself, probably has considerably shallower pockets than the company backing *Science Fiction Age*, which might make it harder for him to deal with a crisis or a cash-flow crunch if it occurs. The field needs *both* of these magazines, and both of them deserve to survive.

Several other new fiction magazines were struggling to be born, including *Expanse*, *Crank!*, *Offworld*, a reborn version of *Galaxy*, and others, but as yet they barely qualify even for the semiprozine category, and it's very hard to tell which of them, if any, have any chance of survival.

As most of you probably know, I, Gardner Dozois, am also the editor of a prominent SF magazine, *Asimov's Science Fiction*. And that, as I've mentioned before, does pose a problem for me in compiling this summation, particularly the magazine-by-magazine review that follows. As the editor of *Asimov's*, I could be said to have a vested interest in the magazine's success, so that anything negative I said about another SF magazine (particularly another digest-sized magazine, my direct competition) could be perceived as an attempt to make my own magazine look good by tearing down the competition. Aware of this constraint, I've decided that nobody can complain if I only say *positive* things about the competition . . . and so, once again, I've limited myself to a listing of some of the worthwhile authors published by each.

Omni published good fiction this year by Terry Bisson, Bruce Sterling, Harlan Ellison, Simon Ings, Carol Emshwiller, and others. *Omni*'s fiction editor is Ellen Datlow.

The Magazine of Fantasy & Science Fiction featured good work by Walter Jon Williams, Jack Cady, Robert Reed, R. Garcia y Robertson, Nina Kiriki Hoffman, D. William Shunn, Bridget McKenna, Valerie J. Freireich, Lisa Goldstein, Jack Williamson, Jane Yolen, and others. *F&FS*'s editor is Kristine Kathryn Rusch.

Asimov's Science Fiction featured good work by Ian R. MacLeod, Connie Willis, Nancy Kress, Steven Utley, Maureen F. McHugh, Mike Resnick, Mary Rosenblum, Brian Stableford, Michael Swanwick, R. Garcia y Robertson, Jonathan Lethem, Neal Barrett, Jr., Robert Reed, and others. *Asimov's* editor is Gardner Dozois.

Analog featured good work by G. David Nordley, Charles Sheffield, Rob Chilson, L. Sprague de Camp, Harry Turtledove, Stanley Schmidt, Michael Flynn, Geoffrey A. Landis, Bud Sparhawk, Phillip C. Jennings, and others. *Analog*'s longtime editor is Stanley Schmidt.

Amazing featured good work by Ursula K. Le Guin, Don Webb, Brian Stableford, J. R. Dunn, Jack Dann, Ian McDowell, Howard Waldrop, Eleanor Arnason, Phillip C. Jennings, Jack McDevitt, Eric T. Baker, and others. *Amazing*'s editor is Kim Mohan.

Interzone featured good work by Greg Egan, Stephen Baxter, Nicola Griffith, Chris Beckett, Brian Stableford, Lawrence Dyer, Jamil Nasir, Paul Di Filippo, Astrid Julian, Kim Newman, Paul J. McAuley, and others. *Interzone*'s editor is David Pringle.

Tomorrow published good work by M. Shayne Bell, Avram Davidson, Gene Wolfe, Kandis Elliot, Robert Reed, Valerie J. Freireich, Kathleen Ann Goonan, Virginia Baker, Norman Spinrad, and others. *Tomorrow*'s editor is Algis Budrys.

Science Fiction Age published good work by Rick Shelley, Charles Sheffield, Barry N. Malzberg, Tony Daniel, Phyllis Gotlieb, Allen Steele, and others. *Science Fiction Age*'s editor is Scott Edelman.

Aboriginal Science Fiction featured good work by Valerie J. Freireich, Patricia Anthony, Howard V. Hendrix, Alexander Jablokov, Jamil Nasir, and others. The editor of *Aboriginal Science Fiction* is Charles C. Ryan.

Weird Tales published good work by Tanith Lee, Ian Watson, John Brunner, Nina Kiriki Hoffman, and others. *Weird Tales*—which has just changed its name to *Worlds of Fantasy and Horror*—is edited by Darrell Schweitzer.

Pulphouse: A Fiction Magazine published good work by Ray Vukcevich, Lawrence Watt-Evans, Sonia Orin Lyris, Carrie Richerson, and others. *Pulphouse: A Fiction Magazine*'s editor is Jonathan E. Bond.

As usual, short SF continued to appear in many magazines outside genre boundaries, from respectable literary magazines all the way to an odd combination cyberpunk/porno magazine called *Future Sex. Playboy* in particular continues to run a good deal of SF, under fiction editor Alice K. Turner, this year publishing stories by Joe Haldeman, Robert Silverberg, Dan Simmons, and others.

(Subscription addresses follow for those magazines hardest to find on the newsstands: *The Magazine of Fantasy & Science Fiction*, Mercury Press, Inc., 143 Cream Hill Road, West Cornwall, CT, 06796, annual subscription—$26.00 in U.S.; *Asimov's Science Fiction*, Dell Magazines Fiction Group, P.O. Box 5130, Harlan, IA, 51593-2633—$34.95 for thirteen issues; *Interzone*, 217 Preston Drove, Brighton BN1 6FL, United Kingdom—$52.00 for an airmail one-year [twelve issues] subscription; *Analog*, Dell Magazines Fiction Group, P.O. Box 5133, Harlan, IA, 51593-2633—$34.95 for thirteen issues; *Tomorrow*, the Unifont Company, Box 6038, Evanston, IL 60204—$18.00 for a one-year [6 issues] subscription; *Pulphouse: A Fiction Magazine*, P.O. Box 1227, Eugene, OR 97440—$26.00 per year [13 issues] in U.S.; *Aboriginal Science Fiction*, P.O. Box 2449, Woburn, MA 01888-0849—$18.00 for 6 issues in U.S.; *Weird Tales*, Terminus Publishing Company, 123 Crooked Lane, King of Prussia, PA 19406-2570—$16.00 for 4 issues in U.S.)

The semiprozine market was in a state of flux, particularly in the fiction area, where we have lost several of the established fiction semiprozines over the last couple of years, while a host of new ones struggled to be born. There were two issues of Steve Pasechnick's *Strange Plasma* this year, but it has subsequently announced that its next issue will be its last, and I have to assume that *New Pathways* and *Whispers* are dead as well, since nothing has been heard from either of them in several years. *Midnight Zoo* was reported to be in serious trouble, and its future may be questionable. We lost *Science Fiction Review*, *Midnight Graffiti*, and *Iniquities* the year before last. *Grue, 2 A.M., Deathrealm, Weirdbook*, and *The Leading Edge* produced only single issues this year, while

Tales of the Unanticipated, *Next Phase*, and *Xizquil* produced two. It was hard to tell from this remove exactly what was happening in the confusing British semiprozine scene, but I believe that *Back Brain Recluse*, *REM*, *Nexus*, and *Strange Attractor* are still alive, and I saw a copy of *Nova*, *Nova 5*, which apparently is the last issue. *Marion Zimmer Bradley's Fantasy Magazine* published four issues this year, but continued to remain unimpressive in quality.

Of the already established fiction semiprozines, your best bets in SF are the Canadian magazine *On Spec*, and two Australian magazines, *Aurealis* and *Eidolon*. All of these seem to be fairly firmly established, so there's a decent chance that they'll still be around next year, and all of them publish fiction a lot closer to professional level than 90 percent of what you'll see in most of the other SF fiction semiprozines. In horror, as far as I've been following it, *Cemetery Dance* seems to have established itself as the most prominent of the horror semiprozines, and is now available on many large newsstands.

As I mentioned above, there are a lot of new fiction semiprozines struggling to establish themselves, especially in SF: *Crank!*, *Expanse*, *Offworld*, *Harsh Mistress Science Fiction Adventures*, the revamped version of *Galaxy*, *Argonaut Science Fiction*, and so on. At this point, it's almost impossible to say which of these magazines will even survive to produce a second issue—if *any* of them do—let alone which will have a shot at eventually establishing themselves as professional magazines, which makes it hard to recommend any of them with confidence. By the measuring-stick of literary quality, the most sophisticated and professional of these magazines by a considerable margin—although perhaps also the one the furthest out on the fringes of science fiction—was *Crank!*, which featured good professional-quality work by A. A. Attanasio, Gwyneth Jones, Michael Blumlein, Garry Kilworth, and others, and which is probably the only one of these magazines I'd really feel comfortable with recommending so far. (A second issue of it appeared as I was finishing this Summation.)

As always, Charles N. Brown's *Locus* and Andrew I. Porter's *SF Chronicle* remain your best bet among the semiprozines if you are looking for news and/ or an overview of what's happening in the genre. *The New York Review of Science Fiction* (whose editorial staff includes David G. Hartwell, Donald G. Keller, Robert Killheffer, and Gordon Van Gelder) has firmly established itself as by far the most reliably published of the "criticalzines," keeping to its twelve-issue schedule once again this year; it also is highly eclectic, publishing a far-ranging and sometimes downright *odd* mix of different types of material, and I find that there is something to annoy, educate, entertain, bore, and enrage me in almost every issue, which I'm sure is as the editors intended. Stephen P. Brown's *Science Fiction Eye* only published one issue, early in 1993, but when it *does* publish an issue, that issue is usually a fat one stuffed full of interesting, eclectic, and (sometimes deliberately) controversial material. *Nova Express*—edited by Lawrence Person, Glen Cox, and Dwight V. Brown—is also entertaining, when you can find it, although they too only produced one issue this year, in early 1993. The long-running *Quantum* (formerly *Thrust*) published one last issue this year and then "merged" with *SF Eye*, although it's unclear as yet just what that's going to mean in practical terms. There was a new criticalzine called *Non-Stop Magazine* that published some interesting stuff in its premiere issue, although, in spite of a good deal of self-congratulatory rhetoric about how Hip, Cool, and utterly Cutting-Edge they are; by far the *most* interesting item here was an autobiographical article by L. Sprague de Camp about his early days as a writer in the thirties and forties (they also publish some fiction, including, for some reason, a reprint of a Paul Di Filippo story that appeared in *New Worlds* a few years back). There was also a new magazine devoted to the reviewing of short fiction, *Tangent II*, edited by David A. Truesdale, and although the quality of the criticism varied widely from competent professionalism to inept amateurism, it's a welcome addition to the critical scene, and an important one, since very little short fiction gets reviewed anywhere in the genre during the course of the year, with the almost single exception (until now) of Mark Kelly's column in *Locus*. A third issue of the Damon Knight–edited *Monad* seemed to receive poor distribution, as *I* never saw a copy of it and have to rely on my editor's good word to believe *he* saw it.

(*Locus*, Locus Publications, Inc., P.O. Box 13305, Oakland, CA 94661— $38.00 for a one-year subscription, 12 issues; *Science Fiction Chronicle*, Algol Press, P.O. Box 022730, Brooklyn, NY 11202-0056—$30.00 for 1 year [12 issues], $36.00 first class; *The New York Review of Science Fiction*, Dragon Press, P.O. Box 78, Pleasantville, NY 10570—$30.00 per year; *Science Fiction Eye*, Box 18539, Asheville, NC 28814—$10.00 for one year; *Nova Express*, White Car Publications, P.O. Box 27231, Austin, Texas 78755-2231—$10.00 for a one-year [four issues] subscription; *Tangent II*, 5779 Norfleet, Raytown, MO 64133—$18.00 for one year, six issues; *Non-Stop Magazine*, Box 981, Peck Slip Station, New York, NY 10272-0981—$18.00 for one year, four issues; *Monad*, Pulphouse Publishing, Box 1227, Eugene, OR 97440—$5.00 for single issues or $18.00 for four issues; *Aurealis, the Australian Magazine of Fantasy and Science Fiction*, Chimaera Publications, P.O. Box 538, Mt. Waverley, Victoria 3149, Australia—$24.00 for a four-issue [quarterly] subscription, "all money orders for overseas subscriptions should be in Australian dollars"; *Eidolon, the Journal of Australian Science Fiction and Fantasy*, Eidolon Publications, P.O. Box 225, North Perth, Western Australia 6006—$34.00 [Australian] for 4 issues overseas, payable to Richard Scriven; *On Spec, the Canadian Magazine of Speculative Writing*, P.O. Box 4727, Edmonton, AB, Canada T6E 5G6— $18.00 for a one-year subscription; *Crank!*, Broken Mirrors Press, P.O. Box 380473, Cambridge, MA 02238—$12.00 for four issues; *Back Brain Recluse*, P.O. Box 625, Sheffield S1 3GY, United Kingdom—$18.00 for four issues; *REM*, REM Publications, 19 Sandringham Road, Willesden, London NW2 5EP, United Kingdom—£7.50 for four issues; *Xizquil*, P.O. Box 2885, Reserve, New Mexico, 87830—$10.00 for three issues; *SF Nexus*, P.O. Box 1123, Brighton BN1 6EX, United Kingdom—$25.00 for four issues; *Strange Attractor: Horror, Fantasy, & Slipstream*, 111 Sundon Road, Houghton Regis, Beds. LU5 5NL, United Kingdom—£7.75 for four issues; *Cemetery Dance*, P.O. Box 858, Edgewood, MD 21040—$15.00 for four issues [one year], $25.00 for eight issues [two years], "checks or money orders should be payable to Richard T. Chizmar only!"; *Grue Magazine*, Hells Kitchen Productions, Box 370, Times Square Sta., New York, NY 10108—$13.00 for three issues; *Expanse*, P.O. Box 43547, Baltimore, MD 21236-0547—$16.00 for four issues; *Galaxy Magazine*, P.O. Box 370, Nevada City, CA 95959; *The Leading Edge*, 3163 JKHB, Provo, UT 84602—$8.00 for three issues; *Harsh Mistress Science Fiction Adventures*, P.O. Box 13, Greenfield, MA 01302—three issues for $12, all checks payable to "Harsh Mistress SFA"; *Argonaut Science Fiction*, P.O. Box 4201, Austin, TX 78765—$8.00 for two issues.)

This was a decent but unexceptional year for original anthologies, with a couple of solid volumes of SF anthology series and the start of a promising new fantasy series, but also with a flock of average-to-weak "theme" anthologies—with a few exceptions, the really first-rate stories, the potential award-winners, were not published in the original anthology market this year, although there *was* a great deal of good solid second-rank work published there.

Turning to the series anthologies, *Full Spectrum 4* (Bantam Spectra—edited by Lou Aronica, Amy Stout, and Betsy Mitchell) was greeted with the same kind of rave reviews that other *Full Spectrum* volumes have received, but I was disappointed by it nevertheless, and personally consider it to be the weakest in overall quality of any book in the series, containing no really outstanding stories, and a good number of weak ones; still, the book is so large, and contains so *many* stories, most of them competent and entertaining, that it's a fairly good value for the money anyway. The best story here, by a good margin, is by new writer L. Timmel Duchamp, although *Full Spectrum 4* also features good work by Martha Soukup, Dave Smeds, Bonita Kale, Gregory Feeley, Elizabeth Hand, Kevin J. Anderson, Danith McPherson, and others. It'll be interesting to see what happens to the *Full Spectrum* series now that all of its founding editors have left Bantam Spectra for editorial jobs elsewhere; supposedly the series *will* continue, and I understand that work is being done on volume 5 even a I type these words, but who the new editors will be on the project, and what kind of a job they will *do* with it, remains to be seen; let's wish them luck, since this has been an important anthology series for the field, and it would be good to see it continue for many years to come. *New Worlds 3* (Gollancz), the third volume in the British anthology series edited by David Garnett, is considerably stronger than last year's disappointing *New Worlds 2*; there are still a few weak stories here, but *New Worlds 3* also features a first-rate story by Brian W. Aldiss, and good work by Gwyneth Jones, Paul J. McAuley, Paul Di Filippo, Simon Ings and Charles Stross, and others, enough to make it probably the strongest volume of a series anthology this year. Its only real rival for that title, and another very good anthology, is *Omni Best Science Fiction Three* (Omni Books), edited by Ellen Datlow. *Omni Best Science Fiction Three* is the best volume of this series to date, by a considerable margin, and they've all been strong—it features first-rate work by Ian McDonald and Pat Cadigan, and good work by Simon Ings, Pat Murphy, Bruce McAllister, Scott Baker, and others. *Pulphouse: The Hardback*

Magazine: Issue Twelve, The Last Issue (Pulphouse), edited by Kristine Kathryn Rusch, finally came out this year after having been delayed for a couple of years. As the self-explanatory subtitle says, this is the last issue of the long-running hardcover anthology series, and they've gone out on a fairly high note, not the best of the series but not the worst, either, and certainly somewhere on the high end. It's the usual *Pulphouse* anthology mix of fantasy, soft science fiction, and mild horror, and while there's no really outstanding stuff here, there is good work by Rick Wilber, Rob Chilson, Lawrence Watt-Evans, William F. Wu, Norman Spinrad, Janet Kagan, Steve Rasnic Tem, Robert Frazier, and others. (Most of the other anthologies covered here are trade books, but *Pulphouse 12* is small-press, and may be hard to find in the bookstores, so here's an address for it: Pulphouse Publishing, Box 1227, Eugene, OR 97440). The editorship of *L. Ron Hubbard Presents Writers of the Future* (Bridge) has changed hands, from longtime editor Algis Budrys to Dave Wolverton, but Volume IX, the latest volume, remains about what you'd expect—mostly minor stories from writers who someday may—or may not—be Big Name Authors in the future, some of the stories pleasant, most very slight, all novice work. There was no volume in the *Synergy* anthology series out in 1993, for the third year in a row, although series editor George Zebrowski continues to assure me that the series is not dead, but will be published on an irregular basis, whenever he's assembled enough worthwhile material.

There seemed to be fewer shared-world anthologies this year than there have been in previous years. Those that were published included: *Bolos: Honor of the Regiment* (Baen), edited by Bill Fawcett; *Blood and War* (Baen), edited by Gordon R. Dickson; *The Further Adventures of Superman* (Bantam Spectra), edited by Martin H. Greenberg; *The Further Adventures of Wonder Woman* (Bantam Spectra), edited by Martin H. Greenberg; and *Battlestation Book Two: Vanguard* (Baen), edited by David Drake and Bill Fawcett.

Turning to the nonseries anthologies, it was a moderately weak year for them in science fiction. The best original SF nonseries anthology of the year was probably *Alternate Warriors* (Tor), edited by Mike Resnick; the two strongest stories here are by Kristine Kathryn Rusch and Resnick himself, first-rate stuff, and there's also good work here by Michael P. Kube-McDowell, Kathe Koja, Maureen F. McHugh, Barry N. Malzberg, Judith Tarr, Beth Meacham, and a number of others. Having *said* that, though, I also feel constrained to add that *Alternate Warriors* is a good deal weaker overall than last year's excellent *Alternate Presidents*, the first in this series, and is even weaker than the *second* volume in the sequence, *Alternate Kennedys*, which was weaker than the first . . . all of which makes me wonder if we're into diminishing returns here, and also makes me somewhat concerned for the quality of upcoming volumes, of which there are several in the works. *Alternate Presidents* was, for the most part, solid science fiction speculation on legitimate Alternate History themes, things that really *could* have happened, but by the time we get to *Alternate Warriors*, three books down the line, a good deal of the stories feature scenarios so far-out and improbable (if not downright silly) that many of them function almost as self-parody . . . as, in fact, does the cover, which, featuring a muscle-bound Ramboesque Mahatma Gandhi ferociously brandishing a missile launcher, could easily have functioned as the cover of a *parody* of a book such as *Alternate Presidents*. In fact, I can't help but wonder if there aren't readers out there who are going to be *offended* by the cover, to say nothing of stories featuring Martin Luther King, Mother Teresa, Gandhi, Saint Francis of Assisi, and even Jesus Christ Himself as violent, bloody-handed, gun- or sword-toting revolutionaries, mercenaries, and assassins. None of this particularly bothers *me*, personally, but this *is* the age of Political Correctness and of fundamentalist religious intolerance of many different stripes, and they're certainly running the risk of offending *some*body with this book; let's hope that Resnick doesn't end up in hiding, roommates with Salman Rushdie. Resnick's other original "theme" anthologies this year are considerably less controversial, but also more innocuous. *Dinosaur Fantastic* (DAW), edited by Resnick and Martin H. Greenberg, is a fun read, but the writers in it, for the most part, content themselves with working clever but superficial variations on the theme, often broadly comedic or satirical ones, and there is very little weight or (excuse the unconscious pun I see rushing down upon us even as I type) bite here; no major work in this one, but there is entertaining stuff by Frank M. Robinson (one of the few stories with some heft to it), Judith Tarr, Pat Cadigan, David Gerrold, Susan Casper, Barbara Delapalce, Gregory Feeley, and others. *More Whatdunnits* (DAW), also edited by Resnick, the follow-up to last year's *Whatdunnits*, is even more minor; the gimmick here is that various authors write science fiction mystery stories from plot-ideas provided by Resnick himself, solving the mystery scenarios that he throws out to them; the best work here is by Martha Soukup, Ginjer Buchanan, Susan Casper, and George Alec Effinger, but few of the stories in the book manage to be much more than competent at best; this is another good, entertaining light read, a good volume to take on a bus trip with you, but you'll have forgotten most of the stories in it by the next day. Much the same could be said of *Journeys to the Twilight Zone* (DAW), edited by Carol Serling, although there are a few more substantial stories here, including good work by Jack Dann, Susan Casper, Charles de Lint, Pamela Sargent, and others. *Swashbuckling Editor Stories* (Wildside Press, 37 Fillmore Street, Newark, NJ 07105—$7.95), edited by John Gregory Betancourt, is minor enough to make even the slightest of these other anthologies look weighty; some minor chuckles, but, after a story or two, the central conceit quickly palls, and the book become repetitive.

I wonder if the seeming decline in "shared-world" anthologies is linked to the *increase* in these original "theme" anthologies, which have proliferated greatly in the last couple of years, with Resnick and Greenberg, either alone or in collaboration, having produced at least a dozen of them, with more to come. I suspect, though, that the peak for the original "theme" anthology may already be past, as it looks to me as if the market is becoming oversaturated with them, and soon there'll be a bust. We'll see.

Continuing a trend from last year, a trend I find very encouraging, there were several strong original fantasy anthologies this year; in fact, pound for pound, the fantasy anthology market (as distinguished from horror) may have been stronger than the science fiction anthology market. The biggest news here this year was the founding of a new annual original series called *Xanadu*, the first such annual anthology series for some time; I believe, in fact, that this is the first regular non-theme original annual fantasy anthology series to be published in the United States since the death of Terri Windling and Mark Alan Arnold's *Elsewhere* series in 1984 (there was another such series published later in the decade in Great Britain, *Other Edens*, edited by Christopher Evans and Robert Holdstock, but that has since died as well). Edited by world-renowned fantasy writer Jane Yolen, the first volume, *Xanadu* (Tor), is a strong and pleasingly eclectic anthology, featuring a number of different *types* of fantasy (high fantasy, urban fantasy, humorous fantasy, mystical fantasy, etc.), a few poems, some mild (*very*, by today's standards) horror, and even, somewhat incongruously, a pure-quill science fiction story (Eleanor Arnason's ''The Hound of Merin''—although it appears on the back cover as ''The Hound of Merlin,'' a very telling typo! And perhaps the reason no one in the science fiction field seems to have looked at it closely enough to notice that it *is* SF). The strongest stories here are the above-mentioned Eleanor Arnason story and Ursula K. Le Guin's ''The Poacher,'' but *Xanadu* also features strong stories by Tanith Lee, Lisa Tuttle, Nancy Kress, Esther M. Friesner, Mike Resnick, Pamela Dean, and others. A very promising series debut, and another indication, along with the rumored new fantasy magazine from the *SF Age* people, that the market for short fantasy stories is expanding. The year's other first-rate original fantasy anthology is *Snow White, Blood Red* (AvoNova/Morrow), edited by Ellen Datlow and Terri Windling. This book of ''updated'' fairy tales told with modern sensibilities could almost as validly be looked at as a horror anthology, and there is a strong streak of the grotesque here (much more so than in *Xanadu*), but the tone varies nicely from story to story, and you get an eclectic variety of types of fantasy here as well; there is powerful work here by Kathe Koja, Susan Wade, Tanith Lee, Melanie Tem, Jack Dann, Nancy Kress, Elizabeth A. Lynn, Neil Gaiman, Esther M. Friesner, Lisa Goldstein, Leonard Rysdyk, Patricia A. McKillip, and others, and it makes a nice companion piece to Tanith Lee's similar short story collection from 1983, *Red As Blood*. (In fact, the Lee collection and the Datlow/Windling anthology, taken together with other books this year such as the reprint anthology *The Oxford Book of Modern Fairy Tales* and the nonfiction studies *Off with Their Heads!: Fairy Tales and the Culture of Childhood* and *The Trials and Tribulations of Little Red Riding Hood* seem to indicate a sharp resurgence of interest in fairy tales on the part of the modern fantasy audience.)

Along somewhat similar lines, *The Dedalus Book of Femmes Fatales* (Dedalus), edited by Brian Stableford, is a mixed collection of ''classical'' reprints and original stories examining the very old folk tradition (going all the way back to the Old Testament's Lilith, if not before) of the ''femme fatale,'' the supernatural seductress (and often destroyer) of hapless men. ''La Belle Dame Sans Merci'' is an archetypical figure which is still very current in the pages of modern horror fiction, where it has been given a new lease on life by the seductive the fantasy anthology market (as distinguished from horror) may have been stronger than the science fiction anthology market. The biggest news here this year was the founding of a new annual original series called *Xanadu*, the first such annual anthology series for some time; I believe, in fact, that this is the first regular non-theme original annual fantasy anthology series to be published in the United States since the death of Terri Windling and Mark Alan Arnold's *Elsewhere* series in 1984 (there was another such series published later in the decade in Great Britain, *Other Edens*, edited by Christopher Evans and Robert Holdstock, but that has since died as well). Edited by world-renowned fantasy writer Jane Yolen, the first volume, *Xanadu* (Tor), is a strong and pleasingly eclectic anthology, featuring a number of different *types* of fantasy (high fantasy, urban fantasy, humorous fantasy, mystical fantasy, etc.), a few poems, some mild (*very*, by today's standards) horror, and even, somewhat incongruously, a pure-quill science fiction story (Eleanor Arnason's "The Hound of Merin"—although it appears on the back cover as "The Hound of Merlin," a very telling typo! And perhaps the reason no one in the science fiction field seems to have looked at it closely enough to notice that it *is* SF). The strongest stories here are the above-mentioned Eleanor Arnason story and Ursula K. Le Guin's "The Poacher," but *Xanadu* also features strong stories by Tanith Lee, Lisa Tuttle, Nancy Kress, Esther M. Friesner, Mike Resnick, Pamela Dean, and others. A very promising series debut, and another indication, along with the rumored new fantasy magazine from the *SF Age* people, that the market for short fantasy stories is expanding. The year's other first-rate original fantasy anthology is *Snow White, Blood Red* (AvoNova/Morrow), edited by Ellen Datlow and Terri Windling. This book of "updated" fairy tales told with modern sensibilities could almost as validly be looked at as a horror anthology, and there is a strong streak of the grotesque here (much more so than in *Xanadu*), but the tone varies nicely from story to story, and you get an eclectic variety of types of fantasy here as well; there is powerful work here by Kathe Koja, Susan Wade, Tanith Lee, Melanie Tem, Jack Dann, Nancy Kress, Elizabeth A. Lynn, Neil Gaiman, Esther M. Friesner, Lisa Goldstein, Leonard Rysdyk, Patricia A. McKillip, and others, and it makes a nice companion piece to Tanith Lee's similar short story collection from 1983, *Red As Blood*. (In fact, the Lee collection and the Datlow/ Windling anthology, taken together with other books this year such as the reprint anthology *The Oxford Book of Modern Fairy Tales* and the nonfiction studies *Off with Their Heads!: Fairy Tales and the Culture of Childhood* and *The Trials and Tribulations of Little Red Riding Hood* seem to indicate a sharp resurgence of interest in fairy tales on the part of the modern fantasy audience.)

Along somewhat similar lines, *The Dedalus Book of Femmes Fatales* (Dedalus), edited by Brian Stableford, is a mixed collection of "classical" reprints and original stories examining the very old folk tradition (going all the way back to the Old Testament's Lilith, if not before) of the "femme fatale," the supernatural seductress (and often destroyer) of hapless men. "La Belle Dame Sans Merci" is an archetypical figure which is still very current in the pages of modern horror fiction, where it has been given a new lease on life by the seductive self-parody . . . as, in fact, does the cover, which, featuring a muscle-bound Ramboesque Mahatma Gandhi ferociously brandishing a missile launcher, could easily have functioned as the cover of a *parody* of a book such as *Alternate Presidents*. In fact, I can't help but wonder if there aren't readers out there who are going to be *offended* by the cover, to say nothing of stories featuring Martin Luther King, Mother Teresa, Gandhi, Saint Francis of Assisi, and even Jesus Christ Himself as violent, bloody-handed, gun- or sword-toting revolutionaries, mercenaries, and assassins. None of this particularly bothers *me*, personally, but this *is* the age of Political Correctness and of fundamentalist religious intolerance of many different stripes, and they're certainly running the risk of offending *some*body with this book; let's hope that Resnick doesn't end up in hiding, roommates with Salman Rushdie. Resnick's other original ''theme'' anthologies this year are considerably less controversial, but also more innocuous. *Dinosaur Fantastic* (DAW), edited by Resnick and Martin H. Greenberg, is a fun read, but the writers in it, for the most part, content themselves with working clever but superficial variations on the theme, often broadly comedic or satirical ones, and there is very little weight or (excuse the unconscious pun I see rushing down upon us even as I type) bite here; no major work in this one, but there is entertaining stuff by Frank M. Robinson (one of the few stories with some heft to it), Judith Tarr, Pat Cadigan, David Gerrold, Susan Casper, Barbara Delapalce, Gregory Feeley, and others. *More Whatdunnits* (DAW), also edited by Resnick, the follow-up to last year's *Whatdunnits*, is even more minor; the gimmick here is that various authors write science fiction mystery stories from plot-ideas provided by Resnick himself, solving the mystery scenarios that he throws out to them; the best work here is by Martha Soukup, Ginjer Buchanan, Susan Casper, and George Alec Effinger, but few of the stories in the book manage to be much more than competent at best; this is another good, entertaining light read, a good volume to take on a bus trip with you, but you'll have forgotten most of the stories in it by the next day. Much the same could be said of *Journeys to the Twilight Zone* (DAW), edited by Carol Serling, although there are a few more substantial stories here, including good work by Jack Dann, Susan Casper, Charles de Lint, Pamela Sargent, and others. *Swashbuckling Editor Stories* (Wildside Press, 37 Fillmore Street, Newark, NJ 07105—$7.95), edited by John Gregory Betancourt, is minor enough to make even the slightest of these other anthologies look weighty; some minor chuckles, but, after a story or two, the central conceit quickly palls, and the book become repetitive.

I wonder if the seeming decline in ''shared-world'' anthologies is linked to the *increase* in these original ''theme'' anthologies, which have proliferated greatly in the last couple of years, with Resnick and Greenberg, either alone or in collaboration, having produced at least a dozen of them, with more to come. I suspect, though, that the peak for the original ''theme'' anthology may already be past, as it looks to me as if the market is becoming oversaturated with them, and soon there'll be a bust. We'll see.

Continuing a trend from last year, a trend I find very encouraging, there were several strong original fantasy anthologies this year; in fact, pound for pound,

novels published (down somewhat from last year's estimate of 278), and 175 new horror novels (up some from last year's 165 in spite of sharp cutbacks in the adult horror novel market because of an explosion of Young Adult horror novels, which nearly doubled in 1993, to 30 percent of the overall horror novel total).

Even if we ignore the fantasy and horror novels, it has obviously become just about impossible for any one individual to read and evaluate *all* of the more than 200 new science fiction novels that come out every year, or even a really significant fraction of them. Certainly with all of the reading I have to do at shorter lengths for *Asimov's* and for this anthology, *I* don't have the time to read all the novels anymore; in fact, I can't even come close.

This year, I seemed to have even *less* time for novels than usual, so I'm going to limit myself to listing those novels that have received a lot of attention and acclaim in 1993, including: *Beggars in Spain*, Nancy Kress (Morrow/AvoNova); *Virtual Light*, William Gibson (Bantam Spectra); *Ring of Swords*, Eleanor Arnason (Tor); *The Drylands*, Mary Rosenblum (Del Rey); *Timelike Infinity*, Stephen Baxter (Roc); *The Innkeeper's Song*, Peter S. Beagle (Roc); *Moving Mars*, Greg Bear (Tor); *Cold Allies*, Patricia Anthony (Harcourt Brace Jovanovich); *Growing Up Weightless*, John M. Ford (Bantam Spectra); *Hard Landing*, Algis Budrys (Warner Questar); *Ammonite*, Nicola Griffith (Del Rey); *Assemblers of Infinity*, Kevin J. Anderson and Doug Beason (Bantam Spectra); *Nightside the Long Sun*, Gene Wolfe (Tor); *The Hammer of God*, Arthur C. Clarke (Bantam Spectra); *Nimbus*, Alexander Jablokov (Morrow/AvoNova); *Kalifornia*, Marc Laidlaw (St. Martin's Press); *High Steel*, Jack C. Haldeman II and Jack Dann (Tor); *Godspeed*, Charles Sheffield (Tor); *Harm's Way*, Colin Greenland (AvoNova); *Purgatory: A Chronicle of a Distant World*, Mike Resnick (Tor); *A Plague of Angels*, Sheri S. Tepper (Bantam Spectra); *Chimera*, Mary Rosenblum (Del Rey); *The Call of Earth*, Orson Scott Card (Tor); *Glimpses*, Lewis Shiner (Morrow); *Forward the Foundation*, Isaac Asimov (Doubleday Foundation); *Kingdoms of the Wall*, Robert Silverberg (Bantam Spectra); *Dream of Glass*, Jean Mark Gawron (Harcourt Brace & Co.); *Warpath*, Tony Daniel (Tor); *Rainbow Man*, M. J. Engh (Tor); *Brother Termite*, Patricia Anthony (Harcourt Brace & Co.); *Vanishing Point*, Michaela Roessner (Tor); *A Clear Cold Light*, Gregory Frost (AvoNova); *Virtual Girl*, Amy Thomson (Ace); *Harvest of Stars*, Poul Anderson (Tor); *Glory Season*, David Brin (Bantam Spectra); *Strange Devices of the Sun and Moon*, Lisa Goldstein (Tor); *Icarus Descending*, Elizabeth Hand (Bantam Spectra); *Deerskin*, Robin McKinley (Ace); *Elvissey*, Jack Womack (Tor); *Throy*, Jack Vance (Tor); *The Destiny Makers*, George Turner (Morrow/AvoNova); *The Broken God*, David Zindell (Bantam Spectra); *The Golden*, Lucius Shepard (Bantam); and *Against a Dark Background*, Iain M. Banks (Bantam Spectra).

My subjective opinion, gathered to a large extent from reading the reviews and listening to reader reaction, was that 1993 was a good solid year for novels, but that none of the individual titles has whipped up the kind of excitement that 1992's strongest books, like Connie Willis's *Doomsday Book* and Kim Stanley Robinson's *Red Mars*, had received the year before; even Gibson's *Virtual Light*

did not receive the kind of wholehearted rave reviews that Gibson's books usually get, although it, and Nancy Kress's *Beggars in Spain*, seem to have stirred up the most excitement overall among this year's novels, with Eleanor Arnason's *Ring of Swords* perhaps sneaking in as a dark horse (many sources didn't review it at all, but those that did tended to like it a lot). The field lost a very promising line with the dismissal of Michael Kandel at Harcourt Brace & Co., and, with the fate of Avon up in the air, no one seems at all sure what's going to happen with the AvonNova line. On the other hand, new editors (although, as the game of Editorial Musical Chairs plays itself out once again, they're mostly *familiar* faces) are now in authority at Bantam Spectra, Roc, and Millennium while others are starting new lines for houses like HarperCollins and Warner, and it will be interesting to see what they can do with these lines in the years ahead. It'll also be interesting to see what Tor can do with the new Orb ''classic reprint'' line, another very promising line. As should be obvious from the list above, Tor had another solid year, as did Bantam Spectra.

This was another strong year for first novels—in fact, in some ways the best of the first novels stirred up as much excitement as the novels by more experienced hands . . . *more*, in some cases. Among the strongest of the first novels, and among those that have aroused the most enthusiastic response, are: *Ammonite*, Nicola Griffith; *The Drylands*, Mary Rosenblum; *Cold Allies*, Patricia Anthony; and *Warpath*, Tony Daniel; the prolific Rosenblum and Anthony had each turned out a well-received *second* novel (Rosenblum's *Chimera* and Anthony's *Brother Termite*) before the end of the year! Other good first novels included: *Virtual Girl*, Amy Thomson; *Mutagenesis*, Helen Collins (Tor); *The Rising of the Moon*, Flynn Connolly (Del Rey); *CrashCourse*, Wilhelmina Baird (Ace); *The Well-Favored Man*, Elizabeth Willey (Tor); and *Flying to Valhalla*, Charles Pellegrino (Morrow/AvoNova). As can be seen, the new ''Del Rey Discovery'' line, edited by Ellen Key Harris, has scored big this year, and, if it can keep it up, may turn out to be one of the most important ''first novel'' lines since the demise of Terry Carr's (all-too-briefly) revived ''Ace Special'' line, which introduced at book length the work of such (at the time) new authors as Kim Stanley Robinson, William Gibson, Lucius Shepard, and Michael Swanwick. Michael Kandel's now-defunct line for Harcourt was also turning up a lot of new talent (Patricia Anthony's first and second novels this year, Jonathan Lethem's and J. R. Dunn's first novels coming up in 1994), as Tor, AvoNova, and Ace have been doing as well. All of these editors should be congratulated, as should every editor who dares to take a chance on untested new talent in a novel market that grows ever more cautious and addicted to ''the sure thing'' (not that such a thing actually *exists*, mind you, but editors and publishers are a superstitious lot, and like to *believe* that it does—the alternative, that you can never *really* tell what's going to sell well, no matter whose name is on the cover and how much you spend promoting it, is too horrible to contemplate, and makes such people wake up screaming in the dead of night).

It's hard to see any clear favorite here for this year's Hugo Award, and it's even harder to handicap the race for the Nebula Award, since, due to SFWA's

bizarre "rolling eligibility" rule, several prominent novels from 1992, such as Robinson's *Red Mars* and Budrys's *Hard Landing*, are eligible for *this* year's award as well; we'll just have to wait and see what ends up winning what—I won't even venture a guess.

There were several novels this year that came very close to functioning as straight historical novels, with only slight (and sometimes almost subliminal) fantastic elements, or, sometimes, with minor Alternate History tropes: Parke Godwin's *Robin and the King* (Morrow), Harry Harrison's *The Hammer and the Cross* (Tor), Diana L. Paxson's *The Wolf and the Raven*, Judith Tarr's *Lord of the Two Lands* (Tor), and others. This really shouldn't be surprising, I guess, since many genre authors such as L. Sprague de Camp, Keith Roberts, Poul Anderson, Tanith Lee, and others have written well-received historical novels, and many other authors, like Judith Tarr and Harry Turtledove, have academic backgrounds in historical scholarship. I wonder if *enough* of these borderline fantasy/historical novels will actually be written every year to split this sort of thing off eventually into a separate subgenre. There is a parallel in the mystery field with the phenomenal rise of so-called "historical mysteries"—originally sometimes called "medieval mysteries," but the time periods used have broadened out—which have increased mightily in numbers during the past few years. Some fantasy and SF writers, such as John Maddox Roberts and David Drake, also work in the "historical mystery" field, and some of the novels published there also have fantastic elements—for instance, to what genre does a mystery novel set in ancient Rome which features historical characters tracking down a vampire belong? Such novels have so far been classified as mysteries, but surely it would be just as valid to consider them fantasy novels with historical settings, or, for that matter, historical novels with fantastic tropes. It's interesting to watch how the boundaries between *all* fictional categories (what about a mystery, published as a hardcore mainline mystery, in which one of the main characters is a ghost, for instance? [*In the Electric Mist with Confederate Dead*, mentioned below.] Where do you list *that*?) is blurring more and more frequently as the 90s progress.

Associational items and obscurely published novels that might be of interest to SF readers this year included: Samuel R. Delany's *They Fly at Çiron* ($25.00 plus $3.00 shipping and handling from Incunabula Press, P.O. Box 20146, Seattle, WA 98103-0146); John Calvin Batchelor's *Peter Nevsky and the True Story of the Russian Moon Landing* (Holt); and Octavia E. Butler's *Parable of the Sower* (Four Walls, Eight Windows); Paul Voermans's *The Weird Colonial Boy* (Gollancz) probably never will have an American edition, but is worth seeking out. Mystery novels of associational interest or by known genre authors include: *Justice for Some*, Kate Wilhelm (St. Martin's Press); *In the Electric Mist with Confederate Dead*, James Lee Burke (Hyperion—mystery with fantastic elements); *The Long-Legged Fly* (Carroll & Graf) and *Moth* (Carroll & Graf), both by James Sallis; *Growing Light*, Marta Randall (under the pseudonym "Martha Conley") (St. Martin's Press); and a reissue of a long out-of-print mystery by H. Beam Piper, *Murder in the Gunroom* (Old Earth Books, $15.00 plus $3.00 shipping and handling).

Nineteen ninety-three was another good year for short-story collections. The best collection of the year, and one of the best *in* years, is the posthumous retrospective collection *The Rediscovery of Man: The Complete Short Science Fiction of Cordwainer Smith* (NESFA Press). The subtitle says it all—Smith was one of the greatest short story writers ever to work in the genre, and this immense (672 pages) collection manages to gather almost every science fiction story he ever wrote, plus an interesting array of associational material. Sadly, Smith is almost unknown these days to many contemporary readers, even though he is a giant of the form, someone who was essential to the evolution of modern science fiction; maybe, with luck, the NESFA collection will help to redress this injustice, and reintroduce Smith's work to new generations of readers. This is a collection that belongs in every complete science fiction library. As does also a reissue of Samuel R. Delany's landmark *Driftglass* collection, one of the best collections of the 60s, now reissued with a few added stories, and with the title slightly altered, as *Driftglass/Starshards* (Grafton).

Among the more modern masters, the best collections of the year were: *Impossible Things*, Connie Willis (Bantam Spectra); *The Aliens of Earth*, Nancy Kress (Arkham House); *Dirty Work*, Pat Cadigan (Mark V. Ziesing); *Bears Discover Fire*, Terry Bisson (Tor); *Antiquities*, John Crowley (Incunabula); *LoveDeath*, Dan Simmons (Warner); and *Alien Bootlegger and Other Stories*, Rebecca Ore (Tor). Also first-rate were: *Vietnam and Other Alien Worlds*, Joe Haldeman (NESFA Press); *Rivers in Time*, L. Sprague de Camp (Baen); *Departures*, Harry Turtledove (Del Rey); *Dancing with Myself*, Charles Sheffield (Baen); *Rude Astronauts*, Allen Steele (Old Earth Books); *Nightmares & Dreamscapes*, Stephen King (Viking); *Sam Gunn, Unlimited*, Ben Bova (Bantam Spectra); *Challenges*, Ben Bova (Tor); *Maureen Birnbaum, Barbarian Swordsperson: The Complete Stories*, George Alec Effinger (Swan Press); *Identifying the Object*, Gwyneth Jones (Swan Press); *Bunch!*, David R. Bunch (Broken Mirrors Press); and *Hogfoot Right and Bird-hands*, Garry Kilworth (Edgewood Press). *Nightshades*, Tanith Lee (Headline), is an interesting package that contains a novel by Lee plus twelve stories; the novel, *Nightshade*, is published there for the first time, but the stories, while reprints, take up the bulk of the book, so I've decided to list it here under collections. Also of interest were several collections that straddled the uneasily defined borderlines between SF, fantasy, and mainstream "Magic Realism": *The Return of Count Electric and Other Stories*, William Browning Spencer (The Permanent Press); *Evolution Annie and Other Stories*, Rosaleen Love (The Women's Press); and *The Seventh Day and After*, Don Webb (Wordcraft of Oregon).

As has been true for several years now, with a few exceptions (Tor was fairly active this year, for instance), the bulk of the best collections continue to come from small-press publishers instead of by mainline trade publishers. The most unfortunate thing about this—other than the fact that the authors probably don't get *paid* as much for a collection by a small press as they would have been paid by a trade publisher—is that it makes it harder for the average reader, with the average reader's resources, to *find* short story collections than it was a few decades ago. And *that*, I think, is, in the long run, bad for the field. It makes it harder for writers to build their reputations, particularly writers who work primarily at short fiction length, and the knowledge of how hard it is to sell a trade collection these days must certainly be yet another economic factor to discourage writers from doing short work in the *first* place . . . and, since, as I've said before, most of the really important evolutionary work that gets done, work that's going to change the shape of the field, gets done at the short-story level, that certainly hampers the development of the genre. Lack of access to short fiction also makes it more difficult for a reader to develop any kind of systematic overview of the state of the field, and contributes to the dismaying loss of historical memory and historical continuity that is now endemic among younger audiences. Perhaps most importantly, it also hurts the readers because it keeps them from easy access to material that they might otherwise *enjoy*.

For those readers interested enough to seek out some of the short-story collections listed above, all but a very few of which will *not* easily be found in the average bookstore, or even the average chain store; your best bet is probably to go to a well-stocked SF specialty bookstore, or to the dealer's room at a large science fiction convention, or, failing that, to one of the new chain "superstores," or to a store in one of the more "literary" chains such as *Borders*. For many of the titles above, though, even these resources will prove to be insufficient (and many people will just not have access to them)—and then you have no choice other than to turn to mail-order, either by contacting a general mail-order catalog company such as Mark V. Ziesing, DreamHaven Books, or Barry R. Levin, or by writing directly to the small-press publishers themselves with your orders. (Mark V. Ziesing—address below; DreamHaven Books & Art, 1309 Fourth St. SE, Minneapolis, MN 55414; Barry R. Levin, SF & Fantasy Literature, 726 Santa Monica Blvd., Suite 201, Santa Monica, CA 90401.)

All this may seem like a lot of trouble—but it's worth it, because it's a way to find material that you're otherwise just *not* going to find anywhere else in these days of Big Commercial Publishing and timid corporate conformity. So, just in case you *are* interested, I'm going to list the addresses of some of these small-press publishers, especially the hardest-to-find ones: NESFA Press, P.O. Box 809, Framingham, MA 07101-0203—$24.95 for *The Rediscovery of Man: The Complete Short Science Fiction of Cordwainer Smith*, and $17.00 for *Vietnam and Other Alien Worlds*; Mark V. Ziesing, P.O. Box 76, Shingletown, CA 96088—$29.95 for *Dirty Work*; Arkham House, P.O. Box 546, Sauk City, Wisconsin 53583—$20.95 for *The Aliens of Earth*; Incunabula Press, P.O. Box 20146, Seattle, WA 98103-0146—$25.00 for *Antiquities*; Headline Book Publishing, Headline House, 79 Great Titchfield Street, London W1P 7FN—£16.99 for *Nightshades*; Swan Press, P.O. Box 90006, Austin, TX 78709—$10.00 for *Maureen Birnbaum, Barbarian Swordsperson: The Complete Stories*; Edgewood Press, P.O. Box 264, Cambridge MA 02238—$10.00 for *Hogfoot*

Right and Bird-hands; Broken Mirror Press, P.O. Box 380473, Cambridge, MA 02338—$8.95 for *Bunch!*; Old Earth Books, P.O. Box 19951, Baltimore, MD 21211—$13.00 plus $3.00 shipping and handling for *Rude Astronauts*; The Permanent Press, Sag Harbor, NY 11963—$22.00 for *The Return of Count Electric and Other Stories*; The Women's Press, 34 Great Sutton Street, London EC1V 0DX—£6.99 for *Evolution Annie and Other Stories*; Wordcraft of Oregon, P.O. Box 3235, La Grande, OR 97850—$7.95 for *The Seventh Day and After*.

This was a good solid year in the reprint anthology market, although hardly an exceptional one. As is usually the case, the best bet for your money were the various "Best of the Year" anthologies, and the annual Nebula Award anthology, *Nebula Awards 27* (Harcourt Brace), edited by James Morrow (I wonder what effect the recent shakeups at Harcourt will have on the annual Nebula Award anthology? None, I hope). Science fiction is still being covered by only one anthology series, the one you are holding in your hand at this moment, and reviewers sometimes get grumpy about that when reviewing this series, but, hey, it's not *my* fault! In fact, I agree that it would be healthier for the genre as a whole if it were being covered from more than one individual perspective; certainly in such a wide and various field, there should be room for volumes representing different tastes than my own, even *radically* different tastes. Now all someone has to do is convince the *publishers*. There are still three Best of the Year anthologies covering horror: Karl Edward Wagner's long-established *Year's Best Horror Stories* (DAW), now up to volume XXI; a newer British series called *Best New Horror* (Carroll & Graf), edited by Ramsey Campbell and Stephen Jones, up to volume 4 this year; and the Ellen Datlow half of a mammoth volume covering both horror *and* fantasy, *The Year's Best Fantasy and Horror* (St. Martin's Press), edited by Ellen Datlow and Terri Windling, this year up to its Sixth Annual Collection. In spite of the fact that the short fiction fantasy market continues to expand, with a new annual anthology series in place and a new professional fantasy magazine being planned, fantasy, as distinguished from horror, is covered only by Terri Windling's half of the Datlow/Windling anthology—a situation that I think cries out to be changed even more than does the situation in the science fiction field. Publishers have to be convinced here, too, though, and so far no one has been, in either cse.

The most controversial reprint anthology of the year was probably a big "historical overview"-type retrospective anthology called *The Norton Book of Science Fiction* (Norton), edited by Ursula K. Le Guin and Brian Attebery, the publication of which stirred up fierce arguments in the fannish press and several "flame wars" on the various computer networks over whether its canonical selection of the most important stories of the last few decades was "valid" or "representational," and whether or not it provided an accurate impression and overview of the science fiction field. This seemed largely to be a false controversy to me. The *Norton Book* is, of course, idiosyncratic and subjective in its selections, but so what? So is every book of this type, including the one you hold in your hands. The *Norton Book* is certainly not the book *I* would have put together, but then, why *should* it be? *Le Guin and Attebery* are the editors, and the book naturally reflects *their* tastes. I could argue with some of their historical judgments and evaluations, especially as to the relative merits of different kinds of science fiction, but it seems pointless to argue that one person's taste is more "valid" than someone else's. And what this argument obscures is the fact that, regardless of whether the book is "representational" or not, this is a massive anthology jammed with good stories by a large number of good writers, and certainly well worth the money; pound for pound, it's quite a good value, in fact. Other good values for your money of the "historical overview" type were *The Mammoth Book of Modern Science Fiction Short Novels of the 1980s* (Carroll & Graf), edited by Isaac Asimov, Martin H. Greenberg, and Charles G. Waugh; *The Oxford Book of Modern Fairy Tales* (Oxford University Press), edited by Alison Lurie; and *The Lifted Veil: The Book of Fantastic Literature by Women* (Carroll & Graf), edited by A. Susan Williams.

It was also possible to argue with, or at least to question, the selections in what was probably the best one-shot reprint anthology of the year, *Strange Dreams* (Bantam Spectra), edited by Stephen R. Donaldson. The title makes it seem like a "theme" anthology, but, as you soon realize, there's really no theme here, and not even really any easily discernible rationale for what is selected; the book is a hodgepodge of science fiction, fantasy, and horror of different types and moods, covering a variety of different topics. Once you realize, however, that the book *isn't* a theme anthology at all, and really should have been called something like *Stephen R. Donaldson's Favorite Stories . . .* that, in other words, in spite of Donaldson's heroic efforts to come up with one in the introduction, there *is* no connecting rationale or basis for selection other than the simple fact that Donaldson *liked* them, then it is possible to relax and accept the book on its own terms. And, *on* those terms, and looked at in that way, *Strange Dreams* is quite a good anthology, well worth the cover price, a massive anthology containing first-rate stories (of many different sorts) by writers such as R. A. Lafferty, Jack Vance, Rudyard Kipling, Edward Bryant, Edgar Pangborn, Michael Bishop, John Varley, and many others. Also very eclectic was *Elvis Rising: Stories on the King* (Avon), edited by Kay Sloan and Constance Pierce, which mixes science fiction, fantasy, "magic realist," and straight mainstream stories about (of course) Elvis; unfortunately, the overall quality of the anthology is not as high as that of the Donaldson book, since some of the stories are quite weak, but it does feature strong work by T. Coraghessan Boyle, W. P. Kinsella, Howard Waldrop, William Hauptman, Elizabeth Hand, Michael Swanwick, Jack Dann, and others. Also worthwhile were *Omni Visions One* (Omni Books), edited by Ellen Datlow, a collection of reprints (with one original) from *Omni* magazine; *Simulations: 15 Tales of Virtual Reality*, edited by Karie Jacobson (Citadel Press), which is just what the title says, with reprints, excerpts, and one original story centered on the subject of virtual reality; *Animal Brigade 3000* (Ace, edited by Martin H. Greenberg and Charles G. Waugh; and *Sword & Sorceress X* (DAW), edited by Marion Zimmer Bradley.

Noted without comment are: *Future Earths: Under African Skies* (DAW), edited by Mike Resnick and Gardner Dozois; *Future Earths: Under South Ameri-can Skies* (DAW), edited by Mike Resnick and Gardner Dozois; *Invaders!* (Ace), edited by Jack Dann and Gardner Dozois; *Dragons!* (Ace), edited by Jack Dann and Gardner Dozois; *Isaac Asimov's SF Lite* (Ace), edited by Gardner Dozois; and *Isaac Asimov's War* (Ace), edited by Gardner Dozois.

This was a strong year in the SF-oriented nonfiction and reference-book field, if only because it saw the publication of the long-promised and long-awaited update of Peter Nicholls's 1979 *Science Fiction Encyclopedia*, finally reissued in updated format and at nearly twice the length this year as *The Encyclopedia of Science Fiction* (St. Martin's Press), edited by John Clute and Peter Nicholls. It was worth the wait. This is a magnificent reference work, the best to appear in the field since the original Nicholls's *Encylcopedia*, which had *not* been adequately replaced as a reference tool by the subsequent attempts of others to create a comprehensive SF encyclopedia. Yes, there are errors in the Clute/Nicholls book (although St. Martin's has assembled an errata sheet to be used to update the forthcoming paperback and CD-ROM versions), I doubt that such a work could be produced *without* them, and there are omissions (a few months ago, one of the computer networks was full of messages from writers complaining that they'd been left out of the book), but it seems to me that this *Encyclopedia* probably is as nearly accurate and as nearly complete in its mention of newer writers as it is humanly possible to be, and the immense effort that has gone into making it so is obvious. At any rate, it is *far* more complete, more accurate, and more useable *as* a real encyclopedia than either of its most recent rivals, Gunn's *The New Encyclopedia of Science Fiction* or Watson and Schellinger's *Twentieth-Century Science Fiction Writers*, and I doubt that it will be superseded any time soon. Clute and Nicholls's *The Encyclopedia of Science Fiction* is likely to remain *the* single most valuable science fiction reference source well into the twenty-first century; it belongs in every library, and, in spite of the steep cover price, in every serious private collection as well, where it will replace a three-foot shelf of other reference titles.

Elsewhere, your best bets for SF reference works this year (although they are all somewhat specialized) included: *Science Fiction and Fantasy Reference Index: 1985–1991* (Libraries Unlimited), edited by Hal W. Hall; *Reginald's Science Fiction and Fantasy Awards, Third Edition* (Borgo Press), edited by Daryl F. Mallett and Robert Reginald; and *Hawk's Author's Pseudonyms for Book Collec-tors* (Pat Hawk), edited by Pat Hawk. For those interested in SF history, *PITFCS: Proceedings of the Institute for Twenty-First Century Studies* (Advent Publish-ers), edited by Theodore R. Cogswell, offers a fascinating look at the kinds of things that were being talked about in professional SF circles in the fifties and early sixties; it's a collection of articles and exchanges of letters from what essentially amounted to a fanzine for professional SF writers (today we'd call it a "criticalzine") that the late Cogswell published in that era, and contains commentary from and occasionally some sharp infighting among most of the major professional figures of the day. Also of interest here, although in somewhat more specialized areas, might be *Vultures of the Void: A History of British Science Fiction Publishing 1946–1956* (Borgo Press), by Philip Harbottle and Stephen Holland; *The Magic That Works: John W. Campbell and the American Response to Technology* (Borgo Press), by Albert I. Berger; *The Search for E.T. Bell, Also Known as John Taine* (Mathematical Association of America), by Constance Reid; *Once Around the Bloch: An Unauthorized Autobiography* (Tor), by the irrepressible Robert Bloch; and *Argyll*, an interesting, posthumously published autobiographical study by Theodore Sturgeon (The Sturgeon Project, Box 611, Glen Ellen, CA 95442—$12.00 postpaid).

In the critical studies field, there was an interesting examination of the roots of horror fiction, *The Monster Show: A Cultural History of Horror* (Norton), by David J. Skal; a couple of scholarly examinations of fairy tales, *Off with Their Heads!: Fairy Tales and the Culture of Childhood* (Princeton University Press), by Maria Tatar; and *The Trials and Tribulations of Little Red Riding Hood, Second Edition* (Routledge), edited by Jack Zipes; a study of comic book art, *Understanding Comics: The Invisible Art* (Tundra Publishing), by Scott McCloud; *The John W. Campbell Letters with Isaac Asimov & A. E. van Vogt*, edited by Perry Chapdelaine, Sr. (AC Projects, 5106 Old Harding Road, Franklin, TN 37064); and several rather heavy works of SF criticism, including *Styles of Creation: Aesthetic Technique and the Creation of Fictional Worlds* (University of Georgia Press), edited by George Slusser and Eric S. Rabkin; *Terminal Identity: The Virtual Subject in Postmodern Science Fiction* (Duke University Press), by Scott Bukatman; *Ultimate Island: On the Nature of British Science Fiction* (Greenwood Press), by Nicholas Ruddick; *Flame Wars: The Discourse of Cyberculture* (Duke University Press), edited by Mark Dery; and *A New Species: Gender and Science in Science Fiction* (University of Illinois Press), by Robin Roberts.

Turning to the year's art books, there was nothing to rival the charm and imagination of last year's *Dinotopia* (which, as I predicted, won James Gurney a Hugo), but there *were* some impressive art books out this year, the best of which probably were: *The Art of Michael Whelan* (Bantam Spectra), Michael Whelan; *Dreamquests: The Art of Don Maitz* (Underwood/Miller), Don Maitz; and *Pastures in the Sky* (Pomegranate), Patrick Woodroffe. Also good were: *Carl Lundgren: Great Artist* (Gator Press), Carl Lundgren (which is a partial autobiography as well as an art book); *Virgil Finlay's Phantasms* (Underwood/Miller), Virgil Finlay; *Virgil Finlay's Strange Science* (Underwood/Miller), Virgil Finlay; and *A Hannes Bok Treasury* (Underwood/Miller), Hannes Bok—these last three of considerable historic interest as well.

In the general genre-related nonfiction field, the choice was clear for *me*, although I may be in a minority—for my money, the best general nonfiction book of the year, and the best book of its type since the death of Willy Ley, was the late Avram Davidson's last book, the ornate and fascinating *Adventures in Unhistory: Conjectures on the Factual Foundations of Several Ancient Legends* (Owlswick Press). This is a collection of the "Adventures in Unhistory" essays that Davidson published here and there throughout the field, mostly in *Asimov's*

Science Fiction and *Amazing*, during the last decade or so, essays exploring little-known backwaters of folklore and natural history, and covering subjects as diverse as Mermaids, Dragons, Prester John, Medieval Industrial Espionage (the pirating of the silk industry from the Far East), Mandrakes, the life of Aleister Crowley, the history of and the techniques used in the practice of shrinking human heads, Extinct Flightless Birds, and much else. I freely admit that this book will not be to everyone's taste—although anything but stuffy or pretentiously scholarly (in fact, it's often very funny), these essays are nevertheless written in Davidson's eccentric, flavorful, and sometimes almost unbelievably discursive style, with digression leading to digression to further digression until the main thread of thought is *almost* lost (it never quite *is*), and people schooled to the "quick read" may not have the patience to deal with this. If so, that's a shame, because there's information and shrewd speculation here that you will find nowhere else, no matter how many *other* books you read, and fascinating areas examined in a way that you may never see them examined again, because Davidson was one of the few people in recent times to have the depth of eclectic erudition and the breadth of interests needed to make the connections that he makes here between widely disparate subjects, connections that seem obvious once he has made them, but that no one else ever would have made. And for those who can respond to his quirky and eloquent style, the book is a joy to read. Certainly, reading these essays made me laugh out loud dozens of times, and moved me almost to tears on one or two occasions, and it's hard to think of too many *other* nonfiction books you can say that about. (Owlswick Press, P.O. Box 8243, Philadelphia, PA 19101-8243—$24.75 for *Adventures in Unhistory*.) Almost as flavorful and quirky in its own weird way is an odd item called *The Cartoon Guide to (Non) Communication: The Use and Misuse of Information in the Modern World* (HarperPerennial), by Larry Gonick, author of the classic *The Cartoon History of the Universe* (which, by the way, is intelligent and erudite and amazingly well-researched, and which I would recommend for the library of anyone interested in science fiction or scientific/historical subjects, in spite of it being a lowly "comic book"). Gonick's *Cartoon Guide to (Non) Communications* is very funny and often remarkably insightful, and I think that it will appeal to anyone who is interested in computers, the rapidly evolving "electronic community," information theory, the impact of electronic communications on the human mind, perceived reality, the coming "information superhighway," the roots of aggression and territoriality, symbolic logic, the evolution of the brain, and much else. And it's got *pictures*, too! Who could ask for anything more?

Well, of course, the big story of the year in genre films was the immense success of Stephen Spielberg's *Jurassic Park*, the largest-grossing film of all time (I'm tempted to say that it was a monster hit—ha ha—but I'll restrain myself), which had people waiting in line for hours to see it during the first few months of its release. There is little doubt what accounted for *Jurassic Park*'s success: the awesome special effects, which, when they worked well (and there *were* a few places in the film where they *didn't* work well—but only a few), gave you the hair-raising feeling that you were watching *living dinosaurs* in action on the screen, prompting more than one person to joke that they'd watched the credits for a reference to the ''Dinosaur Wrangler'' who certainly must have been in charge of the beasts. It's a good thing for Spielberg that the effects worked as well as they did, however, because *other* than the mind-blowing special effects, and a few fairly suspenseful chase scenes, the movie really had little to recommend it artistically, with only competent or worse performances from everybody except the dinosaurs, very slow pacing except for the chase scenes, clumsy scripting (including a paleontologist soberly explaining the theory that dinosaurs might have been warm-blooded to a group of *paleontology students* in the field, who listen raptly, apparently never having heard of this before), sloppy editing, including the raising of several subplots that are subsequently dropped and never heard from again (and the significance of which—and they are, or *should* be, quite significant—you will understand only if you happen to have read Michael Crichton's novel), and numerous holes in the plot-logic large enough to drive an Ultrasaurus through (for instance, to name only one, how can the huge *Tyrannosaurus rex*, who is shown earlier as being so heavy that his footsteps literally shake the ground, like an earthquake, manage to *sneak up* on them without a sound later on, especially inside a building?). I was also disappointed that the human characters didn't manage to figure out some way to *defeat* the smart little killer dinosaurs and save themselves by their *own* efforts (which it certainly seemed like they could have done, with all the equipment lying around for them to work with), rather than having to be rescued at the last moment by a Deus-Ex-Tyrannosaurus ending—but I guess that's a lost cause; a low-budget sleeper called *Tremors* is the only monster movie I can think of in recent years in which the characters defeat the monsters fair-and-square by out*thinking* them, by using their brains; everyone else seems to rely on being in good with the scriptwriter. There will, of course, be a sequel, but it's the development of the special effects technology necessary to film *Jurassic Park*, advancing various forms of computer animation even beyond the high point that *Terminator 2* had taken them to a couple of years back, that will continue to be of significance to the film industry long after the movie itself is only a nostalgic curiosity. For instance, one of the action sequences in the film featured not only Special Effects Dinosaurs, but a Special Effects *Jeff Goldblum* as well, executed well enough that it's hard to tell the effect from the real actor; few people seem to have noticed the significance of this, but the implications for the future are staggering, and, if I were a member of the Screen Actors' Guild, I'd be starting to worry about technological unemployment right about now. It won't come to that—computer animation producing footage of actors indistinguishable form the real actors— to any really major extent for quite some time yet, of course, but probably, sooner or later, come to that it *will*—and why bother to hire temperamental *human* actors when you can get Bogart or Mel Gibson or Cary Grant for any feature you want them for, and you can make them *do* anything you want them to do, any way you want them to do it, and you *don't* have to pay them a salary, and you don't have to provide dressing rooms for them, and you don't have to feed them lunch?

Meanwhile, what tends to be covered to some extent by the immense success of *Jurassic Park* is that it was *not* really a very successful year for genre films overall, with many of them being commercially disappointing, and some of them being outright bombs. Next to *Jurassic Park*, although considerably down the scale, the most successful genre movie of the year commercially was *Groundhog Day*; it was probably the most successful artistically as well, a pleasant and well-meaning little fantasy with an engaging performance from Bill Murray . . . although I did keep wondering why he didn't try to get out of his Möbius-strip predicament by doing something like staying up all night or going somewhere else, dodges that will occur immediately to any experienced genre reader, but never seem to occur to Murray's character. *Hocus Pocus* was a classic *dumb* fantasy, as opposed to a reasonably intelligent fantasy like *Groundhog Day*; it featured a trio of comic-book witches, and didn't arouse much enthusiasm in anybody. Tim Burton's *The Nightmare Before Christmas* did have some intelligent touches, and some wonderfully creative animation, but, in spite of that, the audience didn't seem to warm to it either. Nor did *Demolition Man* really do all that well at the box office, in spite of the presence of Sly Stallone, although it did feature some welcome humor and some nice satirical touches, mixed in with the usual shoot-'em-up ultraviolence (maybe that's *why* it didn't do all that well, come to think of it!). And even the presence of the Mighty Schwarzenegger, king of the action movies, Big Arnold himself, couldn't save *The Last Action Hero*, which bombed disastrously at the box office, especially when you factor in how much it *cost* to make in the first place. *Super Mario Brothers*, *Coneheads*, *Addams Family Values*, and *Robocop 3* were all box-office disappointments as well.

All in all, not much of a year, once you get by *Jurassic Park*.

On the horizon: a theatrical *Star Trek: The Next Generation* film, perhaps with cast members from the original *Star Trek* thrown in, a new SF movie called *AI* directed by Stanley Kubrick, a new *Indiana Jones* movie, and three new *Star Wars* movies, prequels to the original three.

Turning to television, it was a year of mixed success there, too, although at least a lot was happening.

Of last year's new shows, "Time Trax" has survived, although I still don't like it much, as has the animated "Batman" show (although a spinoff animated theatrical film called *Batman: Mask of the Phantasm* didn't do well at the box office), and, unsurprisingly, "Star Trek: Deep Space Nine." "Babylon 5" looked like it was going to go down the tubes last year, but it has gotten a new lease on life, and is back to compete with its direct rival, "Deep Space Nine"—both shows being similar enough in concept and format that probably only one of them can survive (so far, it looks like "Deep Space Nine," which enjoys an enormous spinoff audience from the other *Star Trek* shows, will be the one, but we'll see). George R.R. Martin's proposed new series, *Doors*, never made it to the screen.

There were also several new genre shows this year. "SeaQuest DSV" started out with a big initial audience, probably attracted by the Spielberg name, but has sunk slowly on a Voyage to the Bottom of the Ratings ever since; it's a weak and derivative show creatively, and its future is probably in doubt. "The X-Files"—FBI agents fight UFO aliens, killer computers, and various sorts of weird occult beasties—has gathered an enthusiastic cult following, and is a good deal more fun to watch than the dull "SeaQuest DSV," but is also shaky in the ratings, and faces an uncertain future. "Lois and Clark," a slick postmodern take on Superman, seems to be doing fairly well, as does "The Adventures of Brisco County, Jr.," a comic western with fantastic elements, reminiscent of "The Wild, Wild West." "Beavis and Butthead" are *this* year's "Ren and Stimpy," which in turn were the year *before*'s "Simpsons," but I can't work up much enthusiasm for any of them, *especially* "Beavis and Butthead." There was a muddled and confusing "cyberpunk" mini-series called "Wild Palms," featuring William Gibson in a cameo walk-on as himself, which mostly reminded me of how much better the original British version of *Max Headroom* handled this kind of material almost a decade ago. And, in spite of a lot of self-conscious, self-referential, self-satirizing, postmodern tropes (trying, for instance, to make it all a Metaphor for Feminist Rage), a remake of *Attack of the 50 Foot Woman* turned out to be just about as dumb as the *original* version.

Elsewhere, the writing has slipped another notch or two on "Northern Exposure," alas (and they no longer seem to be doing many shows with fantastic elements in them), and I don't much like Joel's replacement on "Mystery Science Theater 3000" (the more modern movies they're doing now are also no longer as Classically Bad as some of the unbelievably awful movies from the fifties they used to do, and so not as entertaining to roast, and I have to wonder if this show isn't reaching the end of its natural life span). Since last year, our local cable company has started carrying the *Sci-Fi Channel*, and I have had a chance to watch it—and, I must say, I am not impressed; for the most part, it seems to be an endless parade of all the awful old monster movies and all the inept old "Sci-Fi" television shows you suffered through in the fifties and sixties, and what original programming there *is* is pretty lame. For a look at the sort of thing that *could* be done with such a format, check out the Canadian program about science fiction and the science fiction field, "Prisoners of Gravity," which has been running here and there this year on various PBS stations around the United States, and which (in spite of a few annoyingly self-indulgent stylistic tropes) is considerably more intelligent than any of the original programming I've seen so far on the "Sci-Fi Channel."

The two most popular genre shows on the air are "Star Trek: The Next Generation" and "Star Trek: Deep Space Nine," and although the writing *does* seem to have slipped a bit this year, "Star Trek: The Next Generation" is probably still the best science fiction show on television. It surprises me to say this, since I didn't much like "Star Trek: TNG" when it first aired, but it has snuck up on me over the last few years, and a few seasons back I even found myself enjoying most of the episodes. I wondered if I'd been unfair to the show originally, and I've recently gone back and rewatched many of those old episodes, and, nope, I was right—they really *did* stink. "Star Trek: TNG" was terrible for the first few seasons, and probably deserves some sort of award for Most Dramatic Improvement in Quality. Starting from the Usual Old Tripe, "Star Trek: TNG" progressed to the point where, at its peak a season or two back, they were doing shows such as the sequence of episodes about the Klingon Civil War that were almost as valid *as* science fiction as, say, one of Poul Anderson's spacefaring political/military adventure novels of the early sixties (the matte-paintings of the Klingon capital city even *look* like an Ed Emshwiller cover for one of Anderson's Dominic Flandry novels; not accidentally, I suspect). A few episodes, such as the thoughtful one in which Captain Picard goes back to France to visit his brother, even progressed beyond adventure tropes to something approaching post-sixties, post–New Wave print SF values and aesthetics—which is considerably closer to having caught up with where the print SF genre is today than most media SF I can think of (with a few exceptions, such as *2001: A Space Odyssey* or *A Clockwork Orange*), and *especially* SF on televison—and all you have to do to prove *that* is to turn to the Sci-Fi Channel and catch an episode of "Lost in Space." I suspect that most of the credit goes to Rick Berman, who took over as producer when Gene Roddenberry went into his final illness, and to the writers, of course, and to the fact that the cast featured a few people such as Patrick Stewart who actually could *act* well enough to handle more sophisticated material with conviction.

Next year is rumored to be the last season for "Star Trek: TNG," since they're anxious to move the cast on to theatrical films, but I wonder if that isn't a mistake. I still haven't warmed to "Star Trek: Deep Space Nine," which strikes me as a dull and woodenly acted show, and I wonder if it's really strong enough to hold the Star Trek empire together once "Star Trek: TNG" is gone. Certainly most of the "Star Trek: TNG" fans I know are not really all *that* enthusiastic about "Star Trek: Deep Space Nine"—they watch it because it follows "Star Trek: TNG," and it's easier not to change the channel . . . but will they *continue* to watch it for long once "Star Trek: TNG" is gone? I suppose that a lot will depend on how strong the *new* Star Trek spinoff planned for next year, "Star Trek: Voyager," actually turns out to be. One of the things that helped to save "Star Trek: TNG" during its shaky first few seasons was that Patrick Stewart proved to be surprisingly forceful and charismatic in the role of Captain Picard, actually making the role much more central to the show, by sheer force of character, than had originally been intended by the show's producers. So far, "Star Trek: Deep Space Nine" lacks an actor with that kind of charismatic presence—in fact, Captain Picard's counterpart in "Deep Space Nine" is one of the *dullest* performers in a generally lackluster ensemble cast. Let's hope they can ship somebody with a little more flamboyance aboard "Star Trek: Voyager."

disclaimer to protect it from attacks by religious fundamentalists, we may *all* end up hiding out with Salman Rushdie!

I'm not following the horror field as closely as I used to, since it's now being covered by three separate Best of the Year anthologies, but there the big original anthologies of the year seem to have been *Confederacy of the Dead* (Roc), edited by Richard Gilliam, Martin H. Greenberg, and Edward E. Kramer, and *Borderlands 3* (Avon), edited by Tom Monteleone. (It should be pointed out, though, that *Snow White, Blood Red*, which I've chosen to consider as a fantasy anthology here, could also be considered to be a horror anthology, and a major one, if you squint at it a bit differently . . . and that anthologies such as *Pulphouse Twelve*, *Christmas Ghosts*, and *Christmas Forever* also carried a pretty high percentage of horror stories in them. Deciding whether to list these books as horror anthologies or fantasy anthologies was a subjective call on my part, and a case could be made for either categorization.)

As far as literary quality is concerned, 1993 seemed to be another pretty strong year for novels, although perhaps not as strong overall as last year . . . but it was a good year for first novels. As far as the numbers are concerned, the newsmagazine *Locus* estimates 1173 original books and 647 reprints, for an overall total of 1820 SF/fantasy/horror books published in 1993, declining by only 1 percent from 1992's total, in spite of much grim recessionary talk during the last couple of years; original SF/fantasy/horror *novels* make up 705 titles in that overall total. As usual, there were gains in some areas, balanced by losses in others, the kind of thing that makes it hard to predict whether next year's numbers will be down due to factors such as the cancellation of the Harcourt Brace line or up due to factors such as the launch of the new HarperCollins line and the revamped Warner line. Hardcover numbers were up 13 percent, according to *Locus*, with hardcover reprints up 11 percent, fueled in part by an increase in small-press hardcover titles, while mass-market paperbacks were down 10 percent, with paperback originals down 5 percent and paperback reprints down 15 percent; paperback originals are down 23 percent overall since 1991. This decline in mass-market paperback totals is partially due to cutbacks, but also because some publishers have begun to publish books as hardcovers or trade paperbacks that they would have published as mass-market paperbacks in previous years; Tor, for instance, now does 76 percent of its original titles as hardcovers. This may have interesting implications for the future, since it seems to support the theory that much of the general public now feels that books are too expensive, perhaps particularly mass-market paperbacks, which, after all, used to have as their main (if not only) selling-point the fact that they were "cheap"—perhaps the buying public now feels that they come closer to "getting their money's worth" when they purchase a more-permanent hardcover or a "classier"-looking trade paperback, since the gap between the price of those formats and the price of a mass-market paperback is no longer as wide as it once was. *Locus* estimates that there were 263 new SF novels published last year (up from 1992's estimate of 239, although down somewhat from 1991's estimate of 308), 267 new fantasy

female vampire, and one which—oddly, given the inevitable sexist undertones—
is quite popular with women writers (disappointingly, only one woman writer
appears in this particular anthology, although Tanith Lee, to name just one
example, has written a great number of stories that would have fit in very
nicely). The classic reprints consist of poetry and prose by John Keats, Charles
Baudelaire, Edgar Allan Poe, Algernon Charles Swinburne, and others; the
modern original section contains an excellent story by Ian McDonald, and good
work by Kim Newman, Thomas Ligotti, Steve Rasnic Tem, Storm Constantine,
Stableford himself, and others. It's a curious anthology that is worth seeking
out, as much for the historical information it contains on the figure of the *femme
fatale* in art and literature as for the fiction.

There were two new additions this year to the sleighload of Christmas anthologies that have been produced in the last few years, both original anthologies.
The better of the two was *Christmas Forever* (Tor), edited by David G. Hartwell,
a mixed anthology of fantasy, horror, and some science fiction, featuring good
work by Damon Knight, Dave Wolverton, Gene Wolfe, Maggie Flinn, Paul C.
Tumey, Janet Kagan, Bruce McAllister, James P. Blaylock and Tim Powers,
and others—don't expect a jolly lightweight read, here, though: Seasonal Theme
or not, most of the stories are somewhat somber, and a few, though powerful,
are depressing and downright grim (appropriate, I guess, since many people find
Christmas depressing and downright grim!). *Christmas Ghosts* (DAW), edited
by Mike Resnick and Martin H. Greenberg, is considerably lighter in tone, but
also less substantial, for the most part—a tradeoff. There is some good work
here, by Maureen F. McHugh, Alan Rodgers, Judith Tarr, Barry N. Malzberg
and Kathe Koja, and others, but *Christmas Ghosts* is hampered by being too
specialized—the editors were specifically requested to create a book of stories
about the Ghosts of Christmas Past, Present, or Future, from the classic Dickens
story—so that many of the stories end up being just jokes about or demythifying
satirical takes on Dickens's *A Christmas Carol* (taking us through the familiar
story from someone else's point of view, say—that of one of the Ghosts, perhaps—or reversing things so that the Ghosts *don't* reform Scrooge but he corrupts
them, and so forth) and after a while it all becomes too familiar. This is probably
a book that you should read a story from every once in a while, rather than try
to read all the way through at once; approached that way, it would probably be
worthwhile light reading.

There was also a book of pleasant but mostly minor funny fantasy stories,
Betcha Can't Read Just One (Ace), edited by Alan Dean Foster and Martin H.
Greenberg; another anthology of stories about Frankenstein's Monster (there was
one out a couple of years ago), *Frankenstein: The Monster Wakes* (DAW), edited
by Martin H. Greenberg; and two more in the somewhat lackluster "Ultimate"
anthology series, *The Ultimate Witch* (Dell) and *The Ultimate Zombie* (Dell),
both edited by John Gregory Betancourt and Byron Preiss. I was horrified to see
that *The Ultimate Witch* bears a disclaimer stating that the anthology is not meant
to endorse the practice of witchcraft! Boy, if we're far enough gone in this
country that a fantasy anthology can't be published without running such a

The 51st World Science Fiction Convention, ConFrancisco, was held in San Francisco, California, from September 2 to September 6, 1993, and drew an estimated attendance of 7,100. The 1993 Hugo Awards, presented at ConFrancisco, were: Best Novel (tie), *A Fire Upon the Deep*, by Vernor Vinge and *Doomsday Book*, by Connie Willis; Best Novella, "Barnacle Bill the Spacer," by Lucius Shepard; Best Novelette, "The Nutcracker Coup," by Janet Kagan; Best Short Story, "Even the Queen," by Connie Willis; Best Nonfiction, *A Wealth of Fable: An Informal History of Science Fiction Fandom in the 1950s*, by Harry Warner, Jr.; Best Professional Editor, Gardner Dozois; Best Professional Artist, Don Maitz; Best Original Artwork, *Dinotopia*, by James Gurney; Best Dramatic Presentation, "The Inner Light," from *Star Trek: The Next Generation*; Best Semiprozine, *Science Fiction Chronicle*; Best Fanzine, *Mimosa*, edited by Dick and Nicki Lynch; Best Fan Writer, David Langford; Best Fan Artist, Peggy Ranson; plus the John W. Campbell Award for Best New Writer to Laura Resnick.

The 1992 Nebula Awards, presented at a banquet at the Holiday Inn Crowne Plaza in New Orleans, Louisiana, on April 18, 1993, were: Best Novel, *Doomsday Book*, Connie Willis; Best Novella, "City of Truth," James Morrow; Best Novelette, "Danny Goes to Mars," Pamela Sargent; Best Short Story, "Even the Queen," Connie Willis; plus the Grand Master Nebula to Frederik Pohl.

The World Fantasy Awards, presented at the Nineteenth Annual World Fantasy Convention in Minneapolis, Minnesota, on October 31, 1993, were: Best Novel, *Last Call*, by Tim Powers; Best Novella, "The Ghost Village," by Peter Straub; Best Short Story (tie), "Graves," by Joe Haldeman and "This Year's Class Picture," by Dan Simmons; Best Collection, *The Sons of Noah & Other Stories*, by Jack Cady; Best Anthology, *Metahorror*, edited by Dennis Etchison; Best Artist, James Gurney; Special Award (Professional), Jeanne Cavelos, for the Dell/Abyss line; Special Award (Nonprofessional), Doug and Tomi Lewis, for Roadkill Press; plus a Life Achievement Award to Harlan Ellison.

The 1993 Bram Stoker Awards, presented on June 19, 1993, at the Warwick Hotel in New York City by The Horror Writers of America, were: Best Novel, *Blood of the Lamb*, by Thomas F. Monteleone; Best First Novel, *Sineater*, Elizabeth Massie; Best Collection, *Mr. Fox and Other Feral Tales*, by Norman Partridge; Best Novella/Novelette (tie), *Aliens: Tribes*, by Stephen Bissette and "The Events Concerning a Nude Fold-Out Found in a Harlequin Romance," by Joe R. Lansdale; Best Short Story, "This Year's Class Picture," by Dan Simmons; Best Nonfiction, *Cut!: Horror Writers on Horror Film*, edited by Christopher Golden; plus a Life Achievement Award to Ray Russell.

The 1992 John W. Campbell Memorial Award–winner was *Brother to Dragons*, by Charles Sheffield.

The 1992 Theodore Sturgeon Award was won by "This Year's Class Picture," by Dan Simmons.

The 1992 Philip K. Dick Memorial Award–winner was *Through the Heart*, by Richard Grant.

The 1992 Arthur C. Clarke award was won by *Body of Glass*, by Marge Piercy (published in the U.S. as *He, She and It*).

The 1992 James Tiptree, Jr. Award was won by *China Mountain Zhang*, by Maureen F. McHugh.

Once again—and how terrible that we now have to say this, year after year—Death took a heavy toll from the science fiction field in 1993 and early 1994, claiming a number of major figures. Among the dead were: **Avram Davidson**, 70, Hugo, Edgar, and World Fantasy Award–winner, one-time editor of *The Magazine of Fantasy & Science Fiction*, and one of the greatest short story writers of modern times (he has been compared to Saki and John Collier, among others), author of *The Adventures of Doctor Esterhazy*, *Or All the Seas with Oysters*, *The Phoenix and the Mirror*, *Masters of the Maze*, *Rork!*, and many others; **Lester del Rey**, 77, a Golden Age giant who wrote more than forty books and scores of short stories, including the classic "Nerves" and "Helen O'Loy," and worked as a magazine editor and book reviewer, but is perhaps best-known as the editor who (along with his late wife, Judy-Lynn del Rey) cofounded Del Rey Books, and who is often credited with creating the modern fantasy field as a viable commercial genre; **Frank Belknap Long**, 90, last surviving member of the famous Lovecraft Circle, winner of the World Fantasy Convention Life Achievement Award, and primarily a writer of supernatural horror (although he did write some SF), author of *The Hounds of Tindalos* and the critical study *Howard Phillips Lovecraft: Dreamer on the Night Side*; **Chad Oliver**, 65, anthropologist and SF writer (he also wrote Western novels, for one of which he won a Western Writers of America Spur Award), often credited with popularizing anthropological themes in science fiction, author of *Shadows in the Sun*, *The Winds of Time*, *Unearthly Neighbors*, *Giants in the Dust*, and *Shores of Another Sea*, among others; **Sir William Golding**, 81, Nobel Prize winner who was also the author of one of the most famout SF novels of the last half of the twentieth century, *Lord of the Flies*, as well as associational SF novels such as *The Inheritors*; **Anthony Burgess**, 76, well-known author of more than fifty books, perhaps best-known to the genre audience for his highly influential SF novel *A Clockwork Orange*, although he also produced SF novels such as *The Wanting Seed*, *1985*, and *The End of the World News*, and fantasies such as *The Eve of Saint Venus* and *Any Old Iron*; **John Hersey**, 78, who won the Pulitzer Prize for his novel *A Bell for Adano* and was famous for his nonfiction study, *Hiroshima*, but who also wrote SF novels such as *White Lotus*, *The Child Buyer*, and *My Petition for More Space*; **Leslie Charteris**, 85, best known as the creator of the long-running series of mysteries (later adapted to movies and television) about "The Saint," some of which had fantastic elements; **Fletcher Knebel**, 81, author of the borderline SF political thriller, *Seven Days in May*; **Robert Westall**, 63, author of more than thirty Young Adult novels, as well as ghost stories for adults, author of *The Scarecrows*, *The Wild Eye*, *The Watch House*, and *The Devil on the Road*, among others; **Walter Kubilius**, 74, SF writer and Futurian; **Claire Parman Brown**, 28, beginning SF writer and SF fan; **William C. Brinkley**,

76, author of eight novels of the sea, including the post-holocaust thriller *The Last Ship*; **Ron Nance**, SF writer; **Robert E. Gilbert**, SF writer and fan artist; **L. Jerome Stanton**, 80, once assistant editor of *Astounding*; **Baird Searles**, 58, longtime reviewer of SF/fantasy books and films and regular columnist for places such as *Asimov's Science Fiction* and *The Magazine of Fantasy & Science Fiction*, also the cofounder of one of the earliest and most successful of SF specialty bookstores, New York City's *The Science Fiction Shop*; **Thomas D. Clareson**, 66, SF scholar, winner of the Pilgrim Award, cofounder of the Science Fiction Research Association and founder and longtime editor of the scholarly journal *Extrapolation*; **Chris Steinbrunner**, 59, longtime mystery and SF fan, co-editor of *The Encyclopedia of Mystery and Detection*; **Harvey Kurtzman**, 68, well-known cartoonist, one of the founders of *Mad* magazine; **Jack Kirby**, 77, famous comic book artist and occasional script author, one of the true giants of comic book illustration, the original artist for *The Fantastic Four* and *Thor*, among many other superhero titles; **Vincent Price**, 82, distinguished film and stage actor, best known to the genre audience for a long sequence of roles in campy horror movies from the early 50s on, including *House of Wax*, *The Raven*, and *The Abominable Dr. Phibes*; **Don Ameche**, 85, film actor, best known to the genre audience for roles in *Heaven Can Wait* and *Cocoon*; **Fred Gwynne**, 66, underappreciated and underutilized film actor, best known for his roles in television's *The Munsters* and *Car 54, Where Are You?*; **Bill Bixby**, 59, actor, best known for his television work in such genre shows as *My Favorite Martian* and *The Incredible Hulk*; **Christian Nyby**, 80, film director, best known to genre audiences as the director of the original version of *The Thing*; **Bruce C. Herbert**, 41, son of SF writer Frank Herbert; **Lenore Marie Nier**, 48, wife of SF writer F. Gwynplaine MacIntyre; **Robert McSwiggin**, 73, uncle of SF editor Gardner Dozois; **Dr. Richard Van Gelder**, 65, author and a curator of the American Museum of Natural History, father of SF editor Gordon Van Gelder; and **John L. Mitchell**, 64, energy economist and chemical engineer, father of SF editor Betsy Mitchell.

PAPA

Ian R. MacLeod

▼

British writer Ian R. MacLeod has been one of the hottest new writers of the nineties to date, and, as the decade progresses, his work continues to grow in power and deepen in maturity. MacLeod has published a slew of strong stories in the first years of the nineties in *Interzone, Asimov's Science Fiction, Weird Tales, Amazing*, and *The Magazine of Fantasy & Science Fiction*, among other markets; several of these stories have made the cut for one or another of the various "Best of the Year" anthologies, including appearances here in our Eighth, Ninth, and Tenth Annual Collections. In 1990, in fact, he appeared in *three* different Best of the Year anthologies with three different stories, certainly a rare distinction. He has yet to produce a novel, but it is being eagerly awaited by genre insiders, and in the meantime he remains pleasingly prolific at shorter lengths, with his first story collection in the works. MacLeod is in his late thirties, and lives with his wife and young daughter in the West Midlands of England.

Here he offers us a compassionate, powerful, and richly imaginative study of the ultimate Culture Shock gap, the abyss between the Young and the Old, and how that gap might *widen* in the future, in strange and unexpected ways. . . .

My grandchildren have brought time back to me. Even when they have gone, my house will never be the same. Of course, I didn't hear them when they arrived—on this as on many other mornings, I hadn't bothered to turn on my eardrums—but a tingling jab from the console beside my bed finally caught my attention. What had I been doing? Lying in the shadowed heat, watching the sea breeze lift the dappled blinds? Not even that. I had been somewhere distant. A traveler in white empty space.

The blinds flicker. My bedhelper emerges from its wallspace, extending mantis arms for me to grab. One heave, and I'm sitting up. Another, and I'm standing. The salt air pushes hot, cool. I pause to blink. Slow, quick, with both eyes. A moment's concentration. Despite everything Doc Fanian's told me, it's never become like riding a bicycle, but then who am I, now, to ride a bike? And then my eardrums are *on*, and the sound of everything leaps into me. I hear the waves, the sea, the lizards stirring on the rocks, distant birdsong, the faint whispering trees. I hear the slow drip of the showerhead on the bathroom tiles, and the putter

I

of a rainbow-winged flyer somewhere up in the hot blue sky. I hear the papery breath and heartbeat of an old man aroused from his mid-morning slumbers. And I hear voices—young voices—outside my front door.

"He *can't* be in."

"Well, he can't be *out* . . ."

"Let's—"

"—No, you."

"I'll—"

"—listen. I think . . ."

"It's him."

Looking down at myself, I see that, yes, I am clothed, after a fashion: shorts and a T-shirt—crumpled, but at least not the ones I slept in last night. So I *did* get dressed today, eat breakfast, clean up afterward, shave. . . .

"Are you in there, Papa?"

My granddaughter Agatha's voice.

"Wait a moment," I croak, sleep-stiff, not really believing. Heading for the hall.

The front door presents an obstacle. There's the voice recognition system my son Bill had fitted for me. Not that anyone mugs or burgles anyone else any longer, but Bill's a worrier—he's past eighty now, and of that age.

"Are you all right in there?"

Saul's voice this time.

"Yes, I'm fine."

The simple routine of the voicecode momentarily befuddles me. The tiny screen says *User Not Recognized*. I try again, and then again, but my voice is as dry as my limbs are until the lubricants get working. My grandchildren can hear me outside, and I know they'll think Papa's talking to himself.

At last. My front door swings open.

Saul and Agatha. Both incredibly real in the morning brightness with the cypressed road shimmering behind them. I want them to stand there for a few moments so I can catch my breath—and for the corneas I had fitted last winter to darken—but I'm hugged and I'm kissed and they're past me and into the house before any of my senses can adjust. I turn back into the hall. Their luggage lies in a heap. Salt-rimed, sandy, the colors bleached, bulging with washing and the excitements of far-off places. *Venice. Paris. New York. The Sea of Tranquillity.* Even then, I have to touch to be sure.

"Hey Papa, where's the *food*?"

Agatha crouches down on the tiles in my old-fashioned kitchen, gazing into the open fridge. And Saul's tipping back a self-cooling carafe he's found above the sink, his brown throat working. They're both in cut-off shorts, ragged tops. Stuff they've obviously had on for days. And here's me worrying about what I'm wearing—but the same rules don't apply. Agatha stands up, fills her mouth with a cube of ammoniac brie from the depths of the fridge. Saul wipes his lips on the back of his hand, smiles. As though he senses that the hug on the doorstep might have passed me by, he comes over to me. He gives me another. Held tight, towered over, I feel the rub of his stubbled jaw against my bald head as he murmurs *Papa, it's good to be here*. And Agatha joins in, kisses me with cheese crumbs on her lips, bringing the sense of all the miles she's traveled to get here, the salt dust of a million far-off places. I'm tempted to pull away when I feel the soft pressure of her breasts against my arm. But this moment is too sweet, too innocent. I wish it could go on forever.

Finally, we step back and regard each other.

"You should have let me know you were coming," I say, wondering why I have to spoil this moment by complaining. "I'd have stocked up."

"We tried, Papa," Agatha says.

Saul nods. "A few days ago at the shuttleport in Athens, Papa. And then I don't know how many times on the ferry through the islands. But all we got was the engaged flag."

"I've been meaning," I say, "to get the console fixed."

Saul smiles, not believing for one moment. He asks, "Would you like me to take a look?"

I shrug. Then I nod Yes, because the console really does need reprogramming. And Saul and Agatha were probably genuinely worried when they couldn't get through, even though nothing serious could happen without one of my implant alarms going off.

"But you don't mind us coming, do you, Papa? I mean, if we're getting in the way or anything. Just say and we'll go." Agatha's teasing, of course, just to see the look on Papa's face.

"No, no." I lift my hands in surrender, feeling the joints starting to ease. "It's wonderful to have you here. Stay with us as long as you want. Do whatever you like. That's what grandparents are for."

They nod sagely, as though Papa's spoken a great truth. But sharp-eyed glances are exchanged across the ancient kitchen table, and I catch the echo of my words before they fade. And I realize what Papa's gone and said. *We. Us.*

Why did I use the plural? Why? When Hannah's been dead for more than seventy years?

An hour later, after the hormones and lubricants have stabilized, I'm heading down to the port in my rattletrap open-top Ford. Off shopping to feed those hungry mouths even though I want to hold onto every moment of Saul and Agatha's company.

White houses, cool streets framing slabs of sea and sky. I drive down here to the port once or twice a week to get what little stuff I need these days, but today I'm seeing things I've never noticed before. Canaries and flowers on the window ledges. A stall filled with candied fruit and marzipan mice, wafting a sugared breeze. I park the Ford in the square, slap on my autolegs and head off just as the noonday bells begin to chime.

By the time I reach Antonio's, my usual baker, the display on the fat-wheeled trolley I picked up in the concourse by the fountains is already reading *Full Load*. I really should have selected the larger model, but you have to put in extra money or something. Antonio grins. He's a big man, fronting slopes of golden crust, cherry-nippled lines of iced bun. Sweaty and floured, he loves his job the way everyone seems to these days.

I'm pointing everywhere. Two, no, three loaves. And up there; never mind, I'll have some anyway. And those long twirly things—are they sweet?—I've always wondered. . . .

"You've got visitors?" He packs the crisp warm loaves into crisp brown bags.

"My grandchildren." I smile, broody as a hen. "They came out of nowhere this morning."

"That's great," he beams. He'd slap my shoulder if he could reach that far across the marble counter. "How old?"

I shrug. What is it now? Bill's eighty-something. So—nearly thirty. But that can't be right. . . .

"Anyway," he hands me the bags, too polite to ask if I can manage. "Now's a good time." My autolegs hiss as I back out toward the door. The loaded trolley follows.

But he's right. Now *is* a good time. The very best.

I drop the bags of bread on my way back to the square. The trolley's too full to help even if I knew how to ask it, and I can't bend down without climbing out of the autolegs, but a grey-haired woman gathers them up from the pavement and helps me back to the car.

"You *drive*?" she asks as I clank across the square toward my Ford and the trolley rumbles behind in attendance. It's a museum piece. She chuckles again. Her face is hidden under the shadow-weave of a straw sunhat.

Then she says, "Grandchildren—how lovely," as nectarines and oranges tumble into the back seat. I can't remember telling her about Saul and Agatha as we walked—in my absorption, I can't even remember speaking—but perhaps it's the only possible explanation for someone of my age doing this amount of shopping. When I look up to thank her, she's already heading off under the date palms. The sway of a floral print dress. Crinkled elbows and heels, sandals flapping, soft wisps of grey hair, the rings on her slightly lumpen fingers catching in sunlight. I'm staring, thinking. Thinking, if only.

Back at the house, hours after the quick trip I'd intended, the front door is open, unlocked. The thing usually bleeps like mad when I leave it even fractionally ajar, but my grandchildren have obviously managed to disable it. I step out of my autolegs. I stand there in my own hall, feeling the tingling in my synthetic hip, waiting for my corneas to adjust to the change in light.

"I'm back!"

There's silence—or as close to silence as these eardrums will allow. Beating waves. Beating heart. And breathing. Soft, slow breathing. I follow the sound.

Inside my bathroom, it looks as if Saul and Agatha have been washing a large and very uncooperative dog. Sodden towels are everywhere, and the floor is a soapy lake, but then they're of a generation that's used to machines clearing up after them. Beyond, in the shadowed double room they've taken for their own, my grandchildren lie curled. Agatha's in my old off-white dressing gown—

which, now I've seen her in it, I'll never want to wash or replace. Her hair spills across the pillow, her thumb rests close to her mouth. And Saul's stretched on the mattress facing the other way, naked, his bum pressed against hers. Long flanks of honey-brown. He's smooth and still, lovely as a statue.

There's a tomb-memorial I saw once—in an old cathedral, in old England—of two sleeping children, carved in white marble. I must have been there with Hannah, for I remember the ease of her presence beside me, or at least the absence of the ache that has hardly ever left me since. And I remember staring at those sweet white faces and thinking how impossible that kind of serenity was, even in the wildest depths of childhood. But now it happens all the time. Everything's an everyday miracle.

I back away. Close the door, making a clumsy noise that I hope doesn't wake them. I unload the shopping in the kitchen by hand, watching the contents of my bags diminish as if by magic as I place them on the shelves. So much becoming so little. But never mind; there's enough for a late lunch, maybe dinner. And my grandchildren are sleeping and the house swirls with their dreams. It's time, anyway, to ring Bill.

My son's in his office. Bill always looks different on the console, and as usual I wonder if this is a face he puts on especially for me. In theory, Bill's like Antonio—working simply because he loves his job—but I find that hard to believe. Everything about Bill speaks of duty rather than pleasure. I see the evening towers of a great city through a window beyond his shoulder. The lights of homeward-bound flyers drifting like sparks in a bonfire-pink sky. But which city? Bill's always moving, chasing business. My console finds him anyway, but it isn't programmed to tell you *where* unless you specifically ask. And I don't know how.

"Hi, Dad."

Two or three beats. Somewhere, nowhere, space dissolves, instantaneously relaying this silence between us. Bill's waiting for me to say why I've called. He knows Papa wouldn't call unless he had a reason.

I say, "You look fine, son."

He inclines his head in acknowledgment. His hair's still mostly a natural red-brown—which was Hannah's color—but I see that he's started to recede, and go grey. And there are deep creases around the hollows of his eyes as he stares at me. If I didn't know any better, I'd almost say that my son was starting to look old. "You too, Dad."

"Your kids are here. Saul and Agatha."

"I see." He blinks, moves swiftly on. "How are they?"

"They're—" I want to say, great, wonderful, incredible; all those big stupid puppy dog words. "—they're fine. Asleep at the moment, of course."

"Where have they been?"

I wish I could just shrug, but I've never been comfortable using nonverbal gestures over the phone. "We haven't really talked yet, Bill. They're tired. I just thought I'd let you know."

Bill purses his long, narrow lips. He's about to say something, but then he holds it back. *Tired. Haven't talked yet. Thought I'd let you know.* Oh, the casualness of it all! As though Saul and Agatha were here with their Papa last month and will probably call in next as well.

"Well, thanks, Dad. You must give them my love."

"Any other messages?"

"Tell them I'd be happy if they could give me a call."

"Sure, I'll do that. How's Meg?"

"She's fine."

"The two of you should come down here."

"You could come *here*, Dad."

"We must arrange something. Anyway, I'm sure you're—"

"—pretty busy, yes. But thanks for ringing, Dad."

"Take care, son."

"You too."

The screen snows. After a few moments' fiddling, I manage to turn it off.

I set about getting a meal for my two sleeping beauties. Salads, cheese, crusty bread, slices of pepper and carrot, garlicy dips. Everything new and fresh and raw. As I do so, the conversation with Bill drones on in my head. These last few years, they can go on for hours inside me after we've spoken. Phrases and sentences tumbling off into new meaning. Things unsaid. Now, I'm not even sure why I bothered to call him. There's obviously no reason why he should be worried about Saul and Agatha. Was it just to brag—Hey, look, I've got your kids!—or was it in the hope that, ringing out of the blue in what were apparently office hours in whatever city he was in, I'd really make contact?

Slicing with my old steel knives on the rainbow-wet cutting board, I remember Bill the young man, Bill the child, Bill the baby. Bill when Hannah and I didn't even have a name for him two weeks out of the hospital. As Hannah had grown big in those ancient days of pre-birth uncertainty, we'd planned on Paul for a boy, Esther for a girl. But when he arrived, when we took him home and bathed him, when we looked at this tiny creature like some red Indian totem with his bulbous eyes, enormous balls, and alarmingly erect penis, Paul had seemed entirely wrong. He used to warble when he smelled Hannah close to him—we called it his milk song. And he waved his legs in the air and chuckled and laughed at an age when babies supposedly aren't able to do that kind of thing. So we called him William. An impish, mischievous name. In our daft parental certainty, even all the dick and willy connotations had seemed entirely appropriate. But by the time he was two, he was Bill to everyone. A solid, practical name that fit, even though calling him Bill was something we'd never dreamed or wanted or intended.

In the heat of mid-afternoon, beneath the awning on the patio between sky and sea, Papa's with his offsprings, sated with food. I feel a little sick, to be honest, but I'm hoping it doesn't show.

"Your dad rang," I say, finding the wine has turned the meaning of the sentence around—as though, for once, Bill had actually made the effort and contacted *me*.

"Rang?" Agatha puzzles over the old, unfamiliar phrase. Rang. Called. She nods. "Oh yeah?" She lifts an espadrilled foot to avoid squashing the ants who are carrying off breadcrumbs and scraps of salad. "What did he say?"

"Not much." *I'd be happy if they'd call.* Did he mean he'd be unhappy otherwise? "Bill seemed pretty busy," I say. "Oh, and he wanted to know where you've been these last few months."

Saul laughs. "That sounds like Dad, all right."

"He's just interested," I say, feeling I should put up some kind of defense.

Agatha shakes her head. "You know what Dad gets like, Papa." She wrinkles her nose. "All serious and worried. Not that you shouldn't be serious about things. But not about *everything*."

"And he's so bloody possessive," Saul agrees, scratching his ribs.

I try not to nod. But they're just saying what children have always said: waving and shouting across a generation gap that gets bigger and bigger. Hannah and me, we put off having Bill until we were late-thirties for the sake of our careers. Bill and his wife Meg, they must have both been gone fifty when they had these two. Not that they were worn out—in another age, they'd have passed for thirty—but old is old is old.

The flyers circle in the great blue dome above the bay, clear silver eggs with the rainbow flicker of improbably tiny wings; the crickets chirp amid the myrtled rocks; the yachts catch the breeze. I'd like to say something serious to Saul and Agatha as we sit out here on the patio, to try to find out what's really going on between them and Bill, and maybe even make an attempt at repair. But instead, we start to talk about holidays. I ask them if they really have been to the Sea of Tranquillity, to the moon.

"Do you want to see?"

"I'd love to."

Saul dives back into the house. Without actually thinking—nearly a century out of date—I'm expecting him to return with a wad of photos in an envelope. But he returns with this box, a little VR thing with tiny rows of user-defined touchpads. He holds it out toward me, but I shake my head.

"You'd better do it, Saul."

So he slips two cool wires over my ears, presses another against the side of my nose and drops the box onto the rug that covers my lap. He touches a button. As yet, nothing happens.

"Papa, can you hear me?"

"Yes. . . ."

"Can you see?"

I nod without thinking, but all I'm getting is the stepped green lawns of my overly neat garden, the sea unfolding the horizon. Plain old actual reality.

Then, Blam!

Saul says, "This is us coming in on the moonshuttle."

I'm flying over black and white craters. The stars are sliding overhead. I'm falling through the teeth of airless mountains. I'm tumbling toward a silver city of spires and domes.

"And this is Lunar Park."

Blam! A midnight jungle strung with lights. Looking up without my willing it through incredible foliage and the geodome, I see the distant Earth; a tiny blue globe.

"Remember, Ag? That party."

From somewhere, Agatha chuckles. "And you in that getup."

Faces. Dancing. Gleaming bodies. Parakeet colors. Someone leaps ten, fifteen feet into the air. I shudder as a hand touches me. I smell Agatha's scent, hear her saying something that's drowned in music. I can't tell whether she's in VR or on the patio.

"This goes on for ages. You know, Papa, fun at the time, but . . . I'll run it forward."

I hear myself say, "Thanks."

Then, Blam! I'm lying on my back on the patio. The deckchair is tipped over beside me.

"You're okay? Papa?"

Agatha's leaning down over me out of the sky. Strands of hair almost touching my face, the fall of her breasts against her white cotton blouse.

"You sort of rolled off your chair. . . ."

I nod, pushing up on my old elbows, feeling the flush of stupid embarrassment, the jolt on my back and arse and the promise of a truly spectacular bruise. Black. Crimson. Purple. Like God smiling down through tropical clouds.

Agatha's helping me as I rise. I'm still a little dizzy, and I'm gulping back the urge to be sick. For a moment, as the endorphins advance and re-group in my bloodstream, I even get a glimpse beyond the veil at the messages my body is really trying to send. I almost feel *pain*, for Chrissake. I blink slowly, willing it to recede. I can see the patio paving in shadow and sunlight. I can see the cracked, fallen box of the little VR machine.

"Hey, don't worry."

Strong arms place me back in my deckchair. I lick my lips and swallow, swallow, swallow. No, I won't be sick.

"Are you okay? You . . ."

"I'm fine. Is that thing repairable? Can I have a look?"

Saul immediately gives the VR box back to me, which makes me certain it's irretrievably busted. I lift the cracked lid. Inside, it's mostly empty space. Just a few silver hairs reaching to a superconductor ring in the middle.

"These machines are incredible, aren't they?" I find myself muttering.

"Papa, they turn out this kind of crap by the million now. They make them fragile 'cos they want them to break so you go out and buy another. It's no big deal. Do you want to go inside? Maybe it's a bit hot for you out here."

Before I can think of an answer, I'm being helped back inside the house. I'm laid on the sofa in the cool and the dark, with the doors closed and the shutters down, propped up on cushions like a doll. Part of me hates this, but the sensation of being cared for by humans instead of machines is too nice for me to protest.

I close my eyes. After a few seconds of red darkness, my corneas automatically blank themselves out. The first time they did this, I'd expected a sensation of deep, ultimate black. But for me at least—and Doc Fanian tells me it's different for all of his patients—white is the color of absence. Like a snowfield on a dead planet. Aching white. Like hospital sheets in the moment before you go under.

"Papa?"

"What time is it?"

I open my eyes. An instant later, my vision returns.

"You've been asleep."

I try to sit up. With ease, Agatha holds me down. A tissue appears. She wipes some drool from off my chin. The clock in the room says seven. Nearly twilight. No need to blink; my eardrums are still on. Through the open patio doors comes the sound of the tide breaking on the rocks, but I'm also picking up a strange buzzing. I tilt my head like a dog. I look around for a fly. Could it be that I've blinked without realizing and reconfigured my eardrums in some odd way? Then movement catches my eye. A black-and-silver thing hardly bigger than a pinhead whirs past my nose, and I see that Saul's busy controlling it with a palette he's got on his lap at the far end of the sofa. Some new game.

I slide my legs down off the sofa. I'm sitting up, and suddenly feeling almost normal. Sleeping in the afternoon usually leaves me feeling ten years older—like a corpse—but this particular sleep has actually done me some good. The nausea's gone. Agatha's kneeling beside me, and Saul's playing with his toy. I'm bright-eyed, bushy tailed. I feel like a ninety-year-old.

I say, "I was speaking this morning to Antonio."

"Antonio, Papa?" Agatha's forehead crinkles with puzzlement.

"He's a man in a shop," I say. "I mean, you don't know him. He runs a bakery in the port."

"Anyway, Papa," Agatha prompts sweetly, "what were you saying to him?"

"I told him that you were staying—my grandchildren—and he asked how old you were. The thing is, I wasn't quite sure."

"Can't you guess?"

I gaze at her. Why do she and Saul always want to turn everything into a game?

"I'm sorry, Papa," she relents. "I shouldn't tease. I'm twenty-eight and a half now, and Saul's thirty-two and three-quarters."

"Seven-eighths," Saul says without taking his eyes off the buzzing pinhead as it circles close to the open windows. "And you'd better not forget my birthday." The pinhead zooms back across the room. "I mean you, Ag. Not Papa. Papa never forgets. . . ."

The pinhead buzzes close to Agatha, brushing strands of her hair, almost touching her nose. "Look, Saul," she snaps, standing up, stamping her foot. "Can't you turn that bloody thing off?"

Saul smiles and shakes his head. Agatha reaches up to grab it, but Saul's too quick. He whisks it away. It loops the loop. She's giggling now, and Saul's shoulders are shaking with mirth as she dashes after it across the room.

Nodding, smiling palely, I watch my grandchildren at play.

"What is that thing, anyway?" I ask as they finally start to tire.

"It's a metacam, Papa." Saul touches a control. The pinhead stops dead in the middle of the room. Slowly turning, catching the pale evening light on facets of silver, it hovers, waiting for a new command. "We're just pissing around."

Agatha flops down in a chair. She says, "Papa, it's the latest thing. Don't say you haven't seen them on the news?"

I shake my head. Even on the old flatscreen TV I keep in the corner, everything nowadays comes across like a rock music video. And the endless good news just doesn't feel *right* to me, raised as I was on a diet of war and starving Africans.

"What does it do?" I ask.

"Well," Saul says, "this metacam shows the effects of multiple wave-form collapse. Look . . . ." Saul shuffles toward me down the length of the sofa, the palette still on his lap. "That buzzing thing up there is a multilens, and I simply control it from down here—"

"—that's amazing." I say. "When I was young they used to have pocket camcorders you couldn't even get in your pocket. Not unless you had one made specially. The pockets, I mean. Not the cameras. . . ."

Saul keeps smiling through my digression. "But it's not *just* a camera, Papa, and anyway you could get ones this size fifteen years ago." He touches the palette on his lap, and suddenly a well of brightness tunnels down from it, seemingly right through and into the floor. Then the brightness resolves into an image. "You see? There's Agatha."

I nod. And there, indeed, she is: three-dee on the palette screen on Saul's lap. Agatha. Prettier than a picture.

I watch Agatha on the palette as she gets up from the chair. She strolls over to the windows. The pinhead lens drifts after her, panning. I'm fascinated. Perhaps it's my new corneas, but she seems clearer in the image than she does in reality.

Humming to herself, Agatha starts plucking the pink rose petals from a display on the windowledge, letting them fall to the floor. As I watch her on Saul's palette screen, I notice the odd way that the petals seem to drift from her fingers, how they multiply and divide. Some even rise and dance, seemingly caught on a breeze although the air in the room is still, leaving fading trails behind them. Then Agatha's face blurs as she turns and smiles. But she's also still in profile, looking out of the window. Eyes and a mouth at both angles at once. Then she takes a step forward, while at the same time remaining still. At first, the effect of these overlays is attractive, like a portrait by Picasso, but as they build up, the palette becomes confused. Saul touches the palette edge. Agatha collapses back into one image again. She's looking out through the window into the twilight at the big yacht with white sails at anchor out in the bay. The same Agatha I see as I look up toward her.

"Isn't that something?" Saul says.

I can only nod.

"Yes, incredible, isn't it?" Agatha says, brushing pollen from her fingers. "The metacam's showing possible universes that lie close to our own. You do understand that, Papa?"

"Yes. But . . ."

Agatha comes over and kisses the age-mottled top of my head.

Outside, beyond the patio and the velvety neat garden, the sea horizon has dissolved. The big white-sailed yacht now seems to be floating with the early stars. I can't even tell whether it's an illusion.

"We thought we'd go out on our own this evening, Papa," she murmurs, her lips ticklingly close to my ear. "See what's going on down in the port. That is, if you're feeling okay. You don't mind us leaving for a few hours, do you?"

A flyer from the port comes to collect Saul and Agatha. I stand waving on the patio as they rise into the starry darkness like silver twins of the moon.

Back inside the house, even with all the lights on, everything feels empty. I find myself wondering what it will be like after my grandchildren have gone entirely, which can only be a matter of days. I fix some food in the kitchen. Usually, I like the sense of control that my old culinary tools give me, but the buzzing of the molecular knife seems to fill my bones as I cut, slice, arrange. Saul and Agatha. Everything about them means happiness, but still I have this stupid idea that there's a price to pay.

I sit down at the kitchen table, gazing at green-bellied mussels, bits of squid swimming in oil, bread that's already going stale. What came over me this morning, buying all this crap? I stand up, pushing my way through the furniture to get outside. There. The stars, the moon, the faint lights of the port set down in the scoop of the darkly gleaming coast. If I really knew how to configure these eardrums, I could probably filter out everything but distant laughter in those lantern-strung streets, music, the clink of glasses. I could eavesdrop on what Saul and Agatha are saying about Papa as they sit at some café table, whether they think I've gone downhill since the last time, or whether, all things considered, I'm holding up pretty well.

They'll be taking clues from things around this house that I don't even notice. I remember visiting a great aunt back in the last century when I was only a kid. She was always punctilious about her appearance, but as she got older she used to cake her face with white powder, and there was some terrible discovery my mother made when she looked through the old newspapers in the front room. Soon after that, auntie was taken into what was euphemistically called a Home. These days, you can keep your own company for much longer. There are machines that will do most things for you: I've already got one in my bedside drawer that crawls down my leg and cuts my toenails for me. But when do you finally cross that line of not coping? And who will warn you when you get close?

Unaided, I climb down from the patio and hobble along the pathways of my stepped garden. Since Bill decided that I wasn't up to maintaining it any longer and bought me a mec-cultivator, I really only wander out here at night. I've always been a raggedy kind of gardener, and this place is now far too neat for me. You could putt on the neat little lawns, and the borders are a lesson in geometry. So I generally make do with darkness, the secret touch of the leaves, the scents of hidden blooms. I haven't seen the mec-cultivator for several days now anyway, although it's obviously still keeping busy, trundling along with its silver arms and prettily painted panels, searching endlessly for weeds, collecting seedheads, snipping at stray fingers of ivy. We avoid each other, it and I. In its prim determination—even in the flower displays that it delivers to the house when I'm not looking—it reminds me of Bill. He tries so hard, does Bill. He's a worrier in an age when people have given up worrying. And he's a carer, too. I know that. And I love my son. I truly love him. I just wish that Hannah was alive to love him with me. I wish that she was walking the streets of the port, buying dresses from the stalls down by the harbor. I just wish that things were a little different.

I sit down on the wall. It's hard to remember for sure now whether things were ever that happy for me. I must go back to times late in the last century when I was with Hannah, and everything was so much less easy then. We all thought the world was ending, for a start. Everything we did had a kind of twilit intensity. Of course, I was lucky; I worked in engineering construction—all those Newtonian equations that are now routinely demolished—at a time when rivers were being diverted, flood barriers erected, seas tamed. I had money and I had opportunity. But if you spend your life thinking Lucky, Lucky, Lucky, you're really simply waiting for a fall. I remember the agonies Hannah and I went through before we decided to have Bill. We talked on and on about the wars, the heat, the continents of skeleton bodies. But we finally decided as parents always do that love and hope is enough. And we made love as though we meant it, and Bill was born, and the money—at least for us—kept on coming in through the endless recessions. There were even inklings of the ways that things would get better. I remember TV programs where academics tried to describe the golden horizons that lay ahead—how unraveling the edges of possibility and time promised predictive intelligence, unlimited energy. Hannah and I were better equipped than most to understand, but we were still puzzled, confused. And we knew enough about history to recognize the parallels between all this quantum magic and the fiasco of nuclear power, which must once have seemed equally promising, and equally incomprehensible.

But this time the physicists had got it largely right. Bill must have been ten by the time the good news began to outweigh the bad, and he was still drawing pictures of burnt-out rainforest, although by then he was using a paintbox PC to do it. I remember that I was a little amazed at his steady aura of gloom. But I thought that perhaps he just needed time to change and adjust to a world that was undeniably getting better, and perhaps he would have done so, become like Saul and Agatha—a child of the bright new age—if Hannah hadn't died.

I totter back through the garden, across the patio and into the house. Feeling like a voyeur, I peek into Saul and Agatha's bedroom. They've been here— what?—less than a day, and already it looks deeply lived in, and smells like a gym. Odd socks and bedsheets and tissues are strewn across the floor, along with food wrappers (does that mean I'm not feeding them enough?), shoes, the torn pages of the in-flight shuttle magazine, the softly glowing sheet of whatever book Agatha's reading. I gaze at it, but of course it's not a book, but another game; Agatha's probably never read a book in her life. Whatever the thing is, I feel giddy just looking at it. Like falling down a prismatic well.

Putting the thing down again exactly where I found it, I notice that they've broken the top off the vase on the dresser, and then pushed the shards back into place. It's a thing that Hannah bought from one of those shops that used to sell Third World goods at First World prices; when there was a Third and First World. Thick blue glaze, decorated with unlikely looking birds. I used to hate that vase, until Hannah died, and then the things we squabbled over became achingly sweet. Saul and Agatha'll probably tell me about breaking it when they find the right moment. Or perhaps they think Papa'll never notice. But I don't mind. I really don't care. Saul and Agatha can break anything they want, smash up this whole fucking house. I almost wish they would, in fact, or at least leave some lasting impression. This place is filled with the stuff of a lifetime, but now it seems empty. How I envy my grandchildren this dreadfully messy room, the way they manage to fill up so much space from those little bags and with all the life they bring with them. If only I could program my vacuum cleaner not to tidy it all up into oblivion as soon as they go, I'd leave it this way forever.

Saul's stuffed the metacam back into the top of his traveling bag on the floor. I can see the white corner of the palette sticking out, and part of me wants to take a good look, maybe even turn it on and try to work out if he really meant that stuff about showing alternate realities. But I go cold at the thought of dropping or breaking it—it's obviously his current favorite toy—and my hands are trembling slightly even as I think of the possibilities, of half worlds beside our own. I see an image: me bending over the metacam as it lies smashed on the tiled floor. Would the metacam record its own destruction? Does it really matter?

I leave the room, close the door. Then I open it to check that I've left things as they were. I close the door again, then I pull it back ajar, as I found it.

I go to my room, wash, and then the bedhelper trundles out and lifts me into bed, even though I could have managed it on my own. I blink three times to turn off my eardrums. Then I close my eyes.

Sleep on demand isn't an option that Doc Fanian's been able to offer me yet. When I've mentioned to him how long the nights can seem—and conversely how easily I drop without willing it in the middle of the afternoon—he gives me a look that suggests that he's heard the same thing from thousands of other elderly patients on this island. I'm sure a solution to these empty hours will be found eventually, but helping the old has never been a primary aim of technology. We're flotsam at the edge of the great ocean of life. We have to make do with spin-offs as the waves push us further and further up the beach.

But no sleep. No sleep. Just silence and whiteness. If I wasn't so tired, I'd pursue the age-old remedy and get up and actually do something. It would be better, at least, to think happy thoughts of this happy day. But Saul and Agatha evade me. Somehow, they're still too close to be real. Memory needs distance, understanding. That's what sleep's for, but as you get older, you *want* sleep, but you don't need it. I turn over in shimmering endless whiteness. I find myself thinking of gadgets, of driftwood spindrift spinoffs. Endless broken gadgets on a white infinite shore. Their cracked lids and flailing wires. If only I could kneel, bend, pick them up and come to some kind of understanding. If only these bones would allow.

There was a time when I could work the latest Japanese gadget straight out of the box. I was a master. VCR two-year-event timers, graphic equalizers, PCs and photocopiers, the eight-speaker stereo in the car. Even those fancy camcorders were no problem, although somehow the results were always disappointing. I remember Hannah walking down a frosty lane, glancing back toward me with the bare winter trees behind her, smiling though grey clouds of breath. And Hannah in some park with boats on a lake, holding baby Bill up for me as I crouched with my eye pressed to the viewfinder. I used to play those tapes late at night after she died when Bill was asleep up in his room. I'd run them backward, forward, freeze-frame. I'd run them even though she wasn't quite the Hannah I remembered, even though she always looked stiff and uneasy when a lens was pointed at her. I had them re-recorded when the formats changed. Then the formats changed again. Things were redigitized. Converted into solid-state. Into superconductor rings. Somewhere along the way, I lost touch with the technology.

In the morning, the door to the room where my grandchildren are sleeping is closed. After persuading my front door to open, and for some stubborn reason deciding not to put on my autolegs, I hobble out into the sunlight and start to descend the steps at the side of my house unaided. Hand over rickety hand.

It's another clear and perfect morning. I can see the snow-gleam of the mainland peaks through a cleft in the island hills, and my neighbors the Euthons are heading out on their habitual morning jog. They wave, and I wave back. What's left of their greying hair is tucked into headbands as though it might get in the way.

The Euthons sometimes invite me to their house for drinks, and, although he's shown it to me many times before, Mr. Euthon always demonstrates his holographic hi-fi, playing Mozart at volume levels that the great genius himself can probably hear far across the warm seas and the green rolling continents in his unmarked grave. I suspect that the Euthons' real interest in me lies simply in the fascination that the old have for the truly ancient—like gazing at a signpost: this is the way things will lead. But they're still sprightly enough, barely past one hundred. One morning last summer, I looked out and saw the Euthons chasing each other naked around their swimming pool. Their sagging arms and breasts and bellies flapped like featherless wings. Mrs. Euthon was shrieking like a schoolgirl and Mr. Euthon had a glistening pink erection. I wish them luck. They're living this happy, golden age.

I reach the bottom of the steps and catch my breath. Parked in the shadow of my house, my old Ford is dented, splattered with dust and dew. I only ever take it on the short drive to and from the port nowadays, but the roads grow worse by the season, and extract an increasingly heavy price. Who'd have thought the road surfaces would be allowed to get this bad, this far into the future? People generally use flyers now, and what land vehicles there are have predictive suspension; they'll give you a magic carpet ride over any kind of terrain. Me and my old car, we're too old to be even an anachronism.

I lift up the hood and gaze inside, breathing the smell of oil and dirt. Ah, good old-fashioned engineering. V8 cylinders. Sparkplugs leading to distributor caps. Rust holes in the wheel arch. I learnt about cars on chilly northern mornings, bit by bit as things refused to work. I can still remember most of it more easily than what I had for lunch yesterday.

A flock of white doves clatter up and circle east, out over the silken sea toward the lime groves on the headland. Bowed down beneath the hood, my fingers trace oiled dirt, and I find myself wishing that the old girl actually needed fixing. But over the years, as bits and pieces have given out and fallen away, the people at the workshop in the port have connected in new devices. I'm still not sure that I believe them when they tell me that until they are introduced into the car's system, every device is actually the same. To me, that sounds like the kind of baloney you give to someone who's too stupid to understand. But the new bits soon get oiled-over nicely enough anyway, and after a while they even start to look like the old bits they've replaced. It's like my own body, all the new odds and ends that Doc Fanian's put in. Eardrums, corneas, a liver, hips, a heart, joints too numerous to mention. Endless chemical implants to make up for all the things I should be manufacturing naturally. Little nano-creatures that clean and repair the walls of my arteries. Stuff to keep back the pain. After a while, you start to wonder just how much of something you have to replace before it ceases to be what it is.

"Fixing something, Papa?"

I look up with a start, nearly cracking my head on the underside of the hood. Agatha.

"I mean, your hands look filthy." She stares at them, these gnarled old tree roots that Doc Fanian has yet to replace. A little amazed. She's in the same blouse she wore yesterday. Her hair's done up with a ribbon.

"Just fiddling around."

"You must give me and Saul a ride."

"I'd love to."

"Did you hear us come back last night, Papa? I'm sorry if we were noisy— and it *was* pretty late." Carved out of the gorgeous sunlight, she raises a fist and rubs at sleep-crusted eyes.

"No." I point. "These ears."

"So you probably missed the carnival fireworks as well. But it must be great, being able to turn yourself off and on like that. What *are* they? Re or inter-active?"

I shrug. What can I say . . . ? I can't even hear fireworks—or my own grandchildren coming in drunk. "Did you have a good time last night?"

"It was nice." She gazes at me, smiling. Nice. She means it. She means everything she says.

I see that she's got wine stains on her blouse, and bits of tomato seed. As she leans over the engine, I gaze at the crown of her head, the pale skin whorled beneath.

"You still miss Grandma, don't you, Papa?" she asks, looking up at me from the engine with oil on the tip of her nose.

"It's all in the past," I say, fiddling for the catch, pulling the hood back down with a rusty bang.

Agatha gives me a hand as I climb the steps to the front of the house. I lean heavily on her, wondering how I'll ever manage alone.

I drive Saul and Agatha down to the beach. They rattle around in the back of my Ford, whooping and laughing. And I'm grinning broadly too, happy as a kitten as I take the hairpins in and out of sunlight, through cool shadows of forest with the glittering race of water far below. At last! A chance to show that Papa's not past it! In control. The gearshift's automatic, but there's still the steering, the brakes, the choke, the accelerator. My hands and feet shift in a complex dance, ancient and arcane as alchemy.

We crash down the road in clouds of dust. I beep the horn, but people can hear us coming a mile off, anyway. They point and wave. Flyers dip low, their bee-wings blurring, for a better look. The sun shines bright and hot. The trees are dancing green. The sea is shimmering silver. I'm a mad old man, wise as the deep and lovely hills, deeply loved by his deeply lovely grandchildren. And I decide right here and now that I should get out more often. Meet new strangers. See the island, make the most of the future. Live a little while I still can.

"You're okay, Papa?"

On the bench, Agatha presses a button, and a striped parasol unfolds. "If we leave this here, it should keep track of the sun for you."

"Thanks."

"Do you still swim?" She reaches to her waist and pulls off her T-shirt. I do not even glance at her breasts.

Saul's already naked. He stretches out on the white sand beside me. His penis flops out over his thigh; a beached baby whale.

"Do you, Papa? I mean, swim?"

"No," I say. "Not for a few years."

"We could try one of the pedalos later." Agatha steps out from her shorts and underpants. "They're powered. You don't have to pedal unless you want to."

"Sure."

Agatha shakes the ribbon from her hair and scampers off down the beach, kicking up the sand. It's late morning. Surfers are riding the deep green waves. People are laughing, splashing, swimming, drifting on the tide in huge transparent bubbles. And on the beach there are sun-worshippers and runners, kids making sandcastles, robot vendors selling ice cream.

"Ag and Dad are a real problem," Saul says, lying back, his eyes closed against the sun.

I glance down at him. "You're going to see him. . . . ?"

He pulls a face. "It's a duty to see Mum and Dad, you know? It's not like coming here to see you, Papa."

"No."

"You know what they're like."

"Yes," I say, wondering why I even bother with the lie.

Of course, when Hannah died, everyone seemed to assume a deepening closeness would develop between father and son. Everyone, that is, apart from anyone who knew anything about grief or bereavement. Bill was eleven then, and when I looked up from the breakfast table one morning, he was twelve, then thirteen. He was finding his own views, starting to seek independence. He kept himself busy, he did well at school. We went on daytrips together and took foreign holidays. We talked amicably, we visited Mum's grave at Christmas and on her birthday and walked through the damp grass back to the car keeping our separate silences. Sometimes, we'd talk animatedly about things that didn't matter. But we never argued. When he was seventeen, Bill went to college in another town. When he was twenty, he took a job in another country. He wrote and rang dutifully, but the gaps got bigger. Even with tri-dee and the revolutions of instantaneous communication, it got harder and harder to know what to say. And Bill married Meg, and Meg was like him, only more so: a child of that generation. Respectful, hardworking, discreet, always ready to say the right thing. I think they both dealt in currency and commodities for people who couldn't be bothered to handle their own affairs. I was never quite sure. And Meg was always just a face and a name. Of course, their two kids—when they finally got around to having them—were wildly different. I loved them deeply, richly. I loved them without doubt or question. For a while, when Saul and Agatha were still children and I didn't yet need these autolegs to get around, I used to visit Bill and Meg regularly.

Agatha runs back up the beach from her swim. She lies down and lets the sun dry her shining body. Then it's time for the picnic, and to my relief, they both put some clothes back on. I don't recognize most of the food they spread out on the matting. New flavors, new textures. I certainly didn't buy any of it yesterday on my trip to the port. But anyway, it's delicious, as lovely as this day.

"Did you do this in the last century, Papa?" Saul asks. "I mean, have picnics on the beach?"

I shrug Yes and No. "Yes," I say eventually, "But there was a problem if you sat out too long. A problem with the sky."

"The *sky*?"

Saul reaches across the mat to re-stack his plate with something sweet and crusty that's probably as good for you and unfattening as fresh air. He doesn't say it, but still I can tell that he's wondering how we ever managed to get ourselves into such a mess back then, how anyone could possibly mess up something as fundamental as the sky.

Afterward, Saul produces his metacam palette from one of the bags. It unfolds. The little pinhead buzzes up, winking in the light.

"The sand here isn't a problem?" I ask.

"Sand?"

"I mean . . . getting into the mechanism."

"Oh, no."

From the corner of my eye, I see Agatha raising her eyebrows. Then she plumps her cushion and lies down in the sun. She's humming again. Her eyes are closed. I'm wondering if there isn't some music going on inside her head that I can't even hear.

"You were saying yesterday, Saul," I persist, "that it's more than a camera. . . ."

"Well," Saul looks up at me, and blanks the palette, weighing up just how much he can tell Papa that Papa would understand. "You know about quantum technology, Papa, and the unified field?"

I nod encouragingly.

He tells me anyway. "What it means is that for every event, there are a massive number of possibilities."

Again, I nod.

"What happens, you see, Papa, is that you push artificial intelligence along the quantum shift to observe these fractionally different worlds, to make the waveform collapse. That's where we get all the world's energy from nowadays, from the gradient of that minute difference. And that's how this palette works. It displays some of the worlds that lie close beside our own. Then it projects them forward. A kind of animation. Like predictive suspension, only much more advanced. . . ."

I nod, already losing touch. And that's only the beginning. His explanation carries on, grows more involved. I keep on nodding. After all, I do know a little about quantum magic. But it's all hypothetical, technical stuff; electrons and positrons. It's got nothing to do with real different worlds, has it?

"So it really *is* showing things that might have happened?" I ask when he's finally finished. "It really isn't a trick?"

Saul glances down at his palette, then back up at me, looking slightly offended. The pinhead lens hangs motionless in the air between us, totally ignoring the breeze "No," he says. "It's not a trick, Papa."

Saul shows me the palette: he even lets me rest the thing on my lap. I gaze down, and watch the worlds divide.

The waves tumble, falling and breaking over the sand in big glassy lumps. The wind lifts the flags along the shore in a thousand different ways. The sky shivers. A seagull flies over, mewing, breaking into a starburst of wings. Grey comet-tailed things that might be ghosts, people, or—for all I know—the product of my own addled and enhanced senses, blur by across the shore.

"You've got implant corneas, haven't you, Papa?" Saul says. "I could probably rig things up so you could have the metacam projected directly into your eyes."

"No thanks," I say.

Probably remembering what happened to the VR, Saul doesn't push it.

I look down in wonder. "This is . . ."

What? Incredible? Impossible? Unreal?

"This is . . ."

Saul touches the palette screen again. He cancels out the breaking, shattering waves. And Agatha calls the vendor for an ice cream, and somehow it's a shock when she pushes the cool cone into my hand. I have to hold it well out of the way, careful not to drip over the palette.

"This is . . ."

And my ice creams falls, splattering Saul's arm.

Agatha leans over. "Here, let me. I'll turn that off, Papa."

"Yes, do."

There's nothing left on the palette now, anyway. Just a drop of ice cream, and the wide empty beach. The screen blanks at Agatha's touch, and the pinhead camera shoots down from a sky that suddenly seems much darker, cooler. Immense purple-grey clouds are billowing over the sea. The yachts and the flyers are turning for home. Agatha and Saul begin to pack our stuff away.

"I'll drive the car home, Papa," Agatha says, helping me from the deckchair just as I feel the first heavy drops of rain.

"But . . ."

They take an arm each. They half-carry me across the sand and up the slope to the end of the beach road where I've parked—badly I now see—the Ford.

"But . . ."

They put me down, and unhesitatingly unfold the Ford's complex hood. They help me in.

"But . . ."

They wind up the windows and turn on the headlights just as the first grey veils strike the shore. The wipers flap, the rain drums. Even though she's never driven before in her life, Agatha spins the Ford's wheel and shoots uphill through the thickening mud, crashing through the puddles toward the hairpin.

Nestled against Saul in the back seat, too tired to complain, I fall asleep.

That evening, we go dancing. Saul. Agatha. Papa.

There are faces. Gleaming bodies. Parakeet colors. Looking through the roof-tops of the port into the dark sky, I can see the moon. I'm vaguely disappointed to find that she's so full tonight. Since I've had these corneas fitted, and with the air nowadays so clear, I can often make out the lights of the new settlements when she's hooded in shadow.

Agatha leans over the café table. She's humming some indefinable tune. "What are you looking at, Papa?"

"The moon."

She gazes up herself, and the moon settles in the pools of her eyes. She blinks and half-smiles. I can tell that Agatha really does see mystery up there. She's sat in the bars, slept in the hotels, hired dust buggies and gone crater-climbing. Yet she still feels the mystery.

"You've never been up there, have you, Papa?"

"I've never left the Earth."

"There's always time," she says.

"Time for what?"

She laughs, shaking her head.

Music is playing. Wine is flowing. The port is beautiful in daylight, but even more so under these lanterns, these stars, this moon, on this warm summer night. Someone grabs Saul and pulls him out to join the dance that fills the square. Agatha remains sitting by me. They're sweet, considerate kids. One of them always stays at Papa's side.

"Do you know what kind of work Bill does these days?" I ask Agatha—a clumsy attempt both to satisfy my curiosity, and to raise the subject of Bill and Meg.

"He works the markets, Papa. Like always. He sells commodities."

"But if he deals in things," I say, genuinely if only vaguely puzzled, "that must mean there isn't enough of everything. . . ?" But perhaps it's another part of the game. If everything was available in unlimited supply, there would be no fun left, would there? Nothing to save up for. No sense of anticipation or pleasurable denial. But then, how come Bill takes it all so seriously? What's he trying to prove?

Agatha shrugs So what? at my question anyway. She really doesn't understand these things herself, and cares even less. Then someone pulls her up into the dance, and Saul takes her place beside me. The moment is lost. Saul's tapping his feet. Smiling at Agatha as her bright skirt swirls. No metacam tonight, no Picasso faces. She doesn't dissolve or clap her hands, burst into laughter or tears, or walk back singing to the table. But it's hard not to keep thinking of all those tumbling possibilities. Where does it end? Is there a different Papa for every moment, even one that sprawls dying right now on these slick cobbles as blood pumps out from fragile arteries into his brain? And is there another one, far across the barricades of time, that sits here with Saul as Agatha swirls and dances, with Hannah still at his side?

I reach for my wine glass and swallow, swallow. Hannah's dead—but what if one cell, one strand of double helix, one atom had been different . . . ? Or perhaps if Hannah had been less of an optimist? What if she hadn't ignored those tiny symptoms, those minor niggles, if she'd worried and gone straight to the doctor and had the tests? Or if it had happened later, just five or ten years later, when there was a guaranteed cure . . . ?

But still—and despite the metacam—I'm convinced that there's only one real universe. All the rest is hocus pocus, the flicker of an atom, quantum magic. And, after all, it seems churlish to complain about a world where so many things have finally worked out right. . . .

"Penny for them."

"What?"

"Your thoughts." Saul pours out more wine. "It's a phrase."

"Oh yes." My head is starting to fizz. I drink the wine. "It's an old one. I know it."

The music stops. Agatha claps, her hands raised, her face shining. The crowd pushes by. Time for drinks, conversation. Looking across the cleared space of the square, down the shadowed street leading to the harbor, I see a grey-haired woman walking toward us. I blink twice, slowly, waiting for her to disappear. But my ears pick up the clip of her shoes over the voices and the re-tuning of the band. She's smiling. She knows us. She waves. As my heart trampolines on my stomach, she crosses the square and pulls a seat over to our table.

"May I?"

Agatha and Saul nod Yes. They're always happy to meet new people. Me, I'm staring. She's not Hannah, of course. Not Hannah.

"Remember?" She asks me, tucking her dress under her legs as she sits down. "I helped carry your bags to that car of yours. I've seen it once or twice in the square. I've always wondered who drove it."

"It's Papa's pride and joy," Agatha says, her chest heaving from the dance.

The woman leans forward across the table, smiling. Her skin is soft, plump, downy as a peach.

I point to Saul. "My grandson here's got this device. He tells me it projects other possible worlds—"

"—Oh, you mean a metacam." She turns to Saul. "What model?"

Saul tells her. The woman who isn't Hannah nods, spreads her hands, sticks out her chin a little. It's not the choice she'd have made, but . . .

"More wine, Papa?"

I nod. Agatha pours.

I watch the woman with grey hair. Eyes that aren't Hannah's color, a disappointing droop to her nose that she probably keeps that way out of inverted vanity. I try to follow her and Saul's conversation as the music starts up again, waiting for her to turn back toward me, waiting for the point where I can butt in. It doesn't come, and I drink my wine.

Somewhere there seems to be a mirror—or perhaps it's just a possible mirror in some other world, or my own blurred imagination—and I see the woman whose name I didn't catch sitting there, and I can see me, Papa. Propped at an off-center angle against the arms of a chair. Fat belly and long thin limbs, disturbingly pale eyes and a slack mouth surrounded by drapes of ancient skin. A face you can see right through to the skull beneath.

Not-Hannah laughs at something Saul says. Their lips move, their hands touch, but I can't hear any longer. I've been blinking too much—I may even have been crying—and I've somehow turned my eardrums off. In silence, Not-Hannah catches Saul's strong young arms and pulls him up to dance. They settle easily into the beat and the sway. His hand nestles in the small of her back. She twirls in his arms, easy as thistledown. I blink, and drink more wine, and the sound crashes in again. I blink again. It's there. It's gone. Breaking like the tide. What am I doing here anyway, spoiling the fun of the able, the happy, the young?

This party will go on, all the dancing and the laughing, until a doomsday that'll never come. These people, they'll live forever. They'll warm up the sun, they'll stop the universe from final collapse, or maybe they'll simply relive each glorious moment as the universe turns back on itself and time reverses, party with the dinosaurs, resurrect the dead, dance until everything ends with the biggest of all possible bangs.

"Are you all right, Papa?"

"I'm fine."

I pour out more of the wine.

It slops over the table.

Saul's sitting at the table again with Not-Hannah, and the spillage dribbles over Not-Hannah's dress. I say fuck it, never mind, spilling more as I try to catch the flow, and I've really given the two of them the perfect excuse to go off together so he can help her to clean up. Yes, help to lift off her dress even though she's old enough to be his—

But then, who cares? Fun is fun is fun is fun. Or maybe it's Agatha she was after. Or both, or neither. It doesn't matter, does it? After all, my grandchildren have got each other. Call me old-fashioned, but look at them. My own bloody grandchildren. Look at them. Creatures from another fucking planet—

But Not-Hannah's gone off on her own anyway. Maybe it was something I said, but my eardrums are off—I can't even hear my own words, which is probably a good thing. Saul and Agatha are staring at me. Looking worried. Their lips are saying something about Papa and Bed and Home, and there's a huge red firework flashing over the moon. Or perhaps it's a warning cursor, which was one of things Doc Fanian told me to look out for if there was ever a problem. My body is fitted with all sorts of systems and alarms, which my flesh and veins happily embrace. It's just this brain that's become a little wild, a little estranged, swimming like a pale fish in its bowl of liquid and bone. So why not fit a few new extra pieces, get rid of the last of the old grey meat? And I'd be new, I'd be perfect—

Whiteness. Whiteness. No light. No darkness.

"Are you in there, Papa?"

Doc Fanian's voice.

"Where else would I be?"

I open my eyes. Everything becomes clear. Tiger-stripes of sunlight across the walls of my bedroom. The silver mantis limbs of my bedhelper. The smell of my own skin like sour ancient leather. Memories of the night before. "What have you done to me?"

"Nothing at all."

I blink and swallow. I stop myself from blinking again. Doc Fanian's in beach shorts and a bright, ridiculous shirt; his usual attire for a consultation.

"Did you know," I say, "that they've installed a big red neon sign just above the moon that says Please Stop Drinking Alcohol?"

"So the cursor *did* work!" Doc Fanian looks pleased with himself. His boyish features crinkle. "Then I suppose you passed out?"

"Not long after. I thought it was just the drink."

"It's a safety circuit. Of course, the body has got one too, but it's less reliable at your age."

"I haven't even got a hangover."

"The filters will have seen to that."

Doc Fanian gazes around my bedroom. There's a photo of Hannah on the far wall. She's hugging her knees as she sits on a grassy bank with nothing but sky behind her; a time and place I can't even remember. He peers at it, but says nothing. He's probably had a good mooch around the whole house by now, looking for signs, seeing how Papa's managing. Which is exactly why I normally make a point of visiting him at the surgery. I never used to be afraid of doctors when I was fitter, younger. But I am now. Now that I need them. . . .

"Your grandchildren called me in. They were worried. It's understandable, although there was really no cause. None at all." There's a faint tone of irritation in Doc Fanian's voice. He's annoyed that anyone should doubt his professional handiwork, or think that Papa's systems might have been so casually set up that a few glasses of wine would cause any difficulty.

"Well, thanks."

"It's no problem." He smiles. He starts humming again. He forgives easily. "If you'd care to pop into the surgery in the next week or two, there's some new stuff I'd like to show you. It's a kind of short-term memory enhancement. You know— it helps if you forget things you've been doing recently."

I say nothing, wondering what Doc Fanian has encountered around the house to make him come up with this suggestion.

"Where are Saul and Agatha?"

"Just next door. Packing."

"*Packing?*"

"Anyway." He smiles. "I really must be going. I'd like to stay for breakfast, but . . ."

"Maybe some other universe, eh?"

He turns and gazes back at me for a moment. He understands more about me than I do myself, but still he looks puzzled.

"Yes," he nods. Half-smiling. Humoring an old man. "Take care, you hear?"

He leaves the door open behind him. I can hear Saul and Agatha. Laughing, squabbling. Packing.

I shift myself up. The bedhelper trundles out and offers arms for me to grab. I'm standing when Saul comes into the room.

"I'm sorry about getting the doc out, Papa. We just thought, you know. . . ."

"Why are you packing? You're not off already, are you?"

He smiles. "Remember, Papa? We're off to the Amazon. We told you on the beach yesterday."

I nod.

"But it's been great, Papa. It really has."

"I'm sorry about last night. I behaved like an idiot."

"Yes." He claps his hands on my bony shoulders and laughs outright. "That was quite something." He shakes his head in admiration. Papa, a party animal! "You really did cut loose, didn't you?"

Agatha fixes breakfast. The fridge is filled with all kinds of stuff I've never even heard of. They've re-stocked it from somewhere, and now it looks like the horn of plenty. I sit watching my lovely granddaughter as she moves around, humming.

Cooking smells. The sigh of the sea wafts through the open window. Another perfect day. The way I feel about her and Saul leaving, I could have done with grey torrents of rain. But even in paradise you can't have everything.

"So," I say, "you're off to the Amazon."

"Yeah." She bangs the plates down on the table. "There are freshwater dolphins. Giant anteaters. People living the way their ancestors did, now the rainforest has been restored." She smiles, looking as dreamy as last night when she gazed at the moon. I can see her standing in the magical darkness of a forest floor, naked as a priestess, her skin striped with green and mahogany shadows. It requires no imagination at all. "It'll be fun," she says.

"Then you won't be visiting Bill and Meg for a while?"

She bangs out more food. "There's plenty of time. We'll get there eventually. And I wish we'd talked more here, Papa, to be honest. There are so many things I want to ask."

"About Grandma?" I ask. Making an easy guess.

"You too, Papa. All those years after she died. I mean, between then and now. You'll have to tell me what happened."

I open my mouth, hoping it will fill up with some comment. But nothing comes out. All those years: how could I have lived through so many without even noticing? My life is divided as geologists divide up the rock crust of Earth's time: those huge empty spaces of rock without life, and a narrow band which seems to contain everything. And Saul and Agatha are leaving, and time—that most precious commodity of all—has passed me by. Again.

Agatha sits down on a stool and leans forward, brown arms resting on her brown thighs. For a moment, I think that she's not going to press the point. But she says, "Do tell me about Grandma, Papa. It's one of those things Dad won't talk about."

"What do you want to know?"

"I know this is awkward, but . . . how did she die?"

"Bill's never told you?"

"We figured that perhaps he was too young at the time to know. But he wasn't, was he? We worked that out."

"Bill was eleven when your Gram died." I say. I know why she's asking me this now: she's getting Papa's story before it's too late. But I'm not offended. She has a right to know. "We tried to keep a lot of stuff about Hannah's death away from Bill. Perhaps that was a mistake, but that was what we both decided."

"It was a disease called cancer, wasn't it?"

So she does know something after all. Perhaps Bill's told her more than she's admitting. Perhaps she's checking up, comparing versions. But, seeing her innocent, questioning face, I know that the thought is unjust.

"Yes," I say, "it was cancer. They could cure a great many forms of the disease even then. They could probably have cured Hannah if she'd gone and had the tests a few months earlier."

"I'm sorry, Papa. It must have been awful."

I stare at my lovely granddaughter. Another new century will soon be turning, and I'm deep into the future; further than I'd ever imagined. Has Agatha ever even known anyone who's died? And pain, what does she know about pain? And who am I, like the last bloody guest at the Masque of the Red Death, to reveal it to her now?

What *does* she want to know, anyway—how good or bad would she like me to make it? Does she want me to tell her that, six months after the first diagnosis, Hannah was dead? Or that she spent her last days in hospital even though she'd have liked to have passed away at home—but the sight of her in her final stages distressed little Bill too much? It distressed me, too. It distressed *her*. Her skin was covered in ulcers from the treatment that the doctors had insisted on giving, stretched tight over bone and fluid-distended tissue.

"It was all over with fairly quickly," I say. "And it was long ago."

My ears catch a noise behind me. I turn. Saul's standing leaning in the kitchen doorway, his arms folded, his head bowed. He's been listening, too. And both my grandchildren look sad, almost as if they've heard all the things I haven't been able to tell them.

Now Saul comes and puts his arm around my shoulder. "Poor Papa." Agatha comes over too. I bury my face into them, trembling a little. But life must go on, and I pull away. I don't want to spoil their visit by crying. But I cry anyway. And they draw me back into their warmth, and the tears come sweet as rain.

Then we sit together, and eat breakfast. I feel shaky and clean. For a few moments, the present seems as real as the past.

"That car of yours," Saul says, waving his fork, swapping subjects with the ease of youth. "I was thinking, Papa, do you know if there's any way of getting another one?"

I'm almost tempted to let him have the Ford. But then, what would that leave me with? "There used to be huge dumps of them everywhere," I say.

"Then I'll come back here to the island and get one, and get all that incredible stuff you've had done in that workshop down in the port. I mean," he chuckles, "I don't want to have to stop for gas."

Gas. When did I last buy *gas*? Years ago, for sure. Yet the old Ford still rattles along.

"Anyway," Agatha says, standing up, her plate empty although I've hardly even started on mine. "I'll finish packing."

I sit with Saul as he finishes his food, feeling hugely un-hungry, yet envying his gusto. He pushes the plate back, glances around for some kitchen machine that isn't there to take it, then pulls a face.

"Papa, I nearly forgot. I said I'd fix that console of yours."

I nod. The engaged flag that prevented him and Agatha getting through to me before they arrived must still be on: the thing that stops people from ringing.

Saul's as good as his word. As Agatha sings some wordless melody in their room, he goes through some of the simpler options on the console with me. I nod, trying hard to concentrate. And Hannah holds her knees and smiles down at us from the photo on the wall. Saul doesn't seem to notice her gaze. I'm tempted to ask for his help with other things in the house. Ways to reprogram the mec-gardener and the vacuum, ways to make the place feel more like my own. But I know that I'll never remember his instructions. All I really want is for him to stay talking to me for a few moments longer.

"So you're okay about that, Papa?"

"I'm fine."

He turns away and shouts, "Hey, Ag!"

After that, everything takes only a moment. Suddenly, they're standing together in the hall, their bags packed. *Venice. Paris. New York. The Sea of Tranquility.* Ready to go.

"We thought we'd walk down to the port, Papa. Just catch whatever ferry is going. It's such a lovely day."

"And thanks, Papa. Thanks for everything."

"Yes."

I'm hugged first by one, then the other. After the tears before breakfast. I now feel astonishingly dry-eyed.

"Well. . . ."

"Yes. . . ."

I gaze at Saul and Agatha, my beautiful grandchildren. Still trying to take them in. The future stretches before us and between us.

They open the door. They head off hand-in-hand down the cypressed road. "Bye, Papa. We love you."

I stand there, feeling the sunlight on my face. Watching them go. My front door starts to bleep. I ignore it. In the shadow of my house, beside my old Ford, I see there's a limp-winged flyer; Saul and Agatha must have used it last night to get me home. I don't know how to work these things. I have no idea how I'll get rid of it.

Saul and Agatha turn again and wave before they vanish around the curve in the road. I wave back.

Then I'm inside. The door is closed. The house is silent.

I head for Saul and Agatha's room.

They've stripped the beds and made a reasonable attempt at clearing up, but still I can almost feel my vacuum cleaner itching to get in and finish the job. Agatha's left the dressing gown she borrowed on the bed. I lift it up to my face. Soap and sea salt—a deeper undertow like forest thyme. Her scent will last a few hours, and after that I suppose I'll still have the memory of her every time I put it on. The vase that Hannah bought all those years ago still sits on top of the dressing table: they never did get around to telling me that they broke the thing. I lift it up, turning the glazed weight in my hands to inspect the damage. But the cracks, the shards, have vanished. The vase is whole and perfect again—as perfect, at least, as it ever was. In a panic, almost dropping the thing, I gaze around the room, wondering what else I've forgotten or imagined. But it's still there, the fading sense of my grandchildren's presence. A forgotten sock, torn pages of the shuttle magazine. I put the vase gently down again. When so many other things are possible, I suppose there's bound to be a cheaply available gadget that heals china.

Feeling oddly expectant, I look under the beds. There's dust that the vacuum cleaner will soon clear away. The greased blue inner wrapper of something I don't understand. A few crumpled tissues. And, of course, Saul's taken the metacam with him. He would; it's his favorite toy. The wonderful promise of those controls, and the green menus that floated like pond lilies on the screen. REVISE. CREATE. EDIT. CHANGE. And Agatha turning. CHANGE. Agatha standing still. REVISE. Ghost-petals drifting up from her hands, and a white yacht floating with the stars on the horizon. If you could change the past, if you could alter, if you could amend . . .?

But I'd always known in my heart that the dream is just a dream, and that a toy is still just a toy. Perhaps one day, it'll be possible to revisit the pharaohs, or return to the hot sweet sheets of first love. But that lies far ahead, much further even than the nearest stars that the first big ships will soon be reaching. Far beyond my own lifetime.

The broken VR machine sticks out from the top of the wastebin by the window. I take it out, wrapping the wires around the case, still wondering if there is any way to fix it. Once upon a time, VR was seen as a way out from the troubles of the world. But nobody bothers much with it any longer. It was my generation that couldn't do anything without recording it on whatever new medium the Japanese had come up with. Saul and Agatha aren't like that. They're not afraid of losing the past. They're not afraid of living in the present. They're not afraid of finding the future.

I stand for a moment, clawing at the sensation of their fading presence, dragging in breath after breath. Then the console starts to bleep along the corridor in my bedroom, and the front doorbell sounds. I stumble toward it, light-headed with joy. They're back! They've changed their minds! There isn't a ferry until tomorrow! I can't believe . . .

The door flashes USER NOT RECOGNIZED at me. Eventually, I manage to get it open.

"You *are* in. I thought . . ."

I stand there, momentarily dumbstruck. The pretty, grey-haired woman from yesterday evening at the café gazes at me.

"They're gone," I say.

"Who? Oh, your grandchildren. They're taking a ferry this morning, aren't they? Off to Brazil or someplace." She smiles and shakes her head. The wildnesses of youth. "Anyway," she points, "that's my flyer. Rather than try to call it in, I thought I'd walk over here and collect it." She glances back at the blue sea, the blue sky, this gorgeous island. She breathes it all in deeply. "Such a lovely day."

"Would you like to come in?"

"Well, just for a moment."

"I'm afraid I was a little drunk last night. . . ."

"Don't worry about it. I had a fine time."

I glance over, looking for sarcasm. But of course she means it. People always do.

I burrow into my hugely overstocked fridge. When I emerge with a tray, she's sitting gazing at the blank screen of my old TV.

"You know," she says, "I haven't seen one of those in years. We didn't have one at home, of course. But my grandparents did."

I put down the tray and rummage in my pocket. "This," I say, waving the broken VR machine in my gnarled hand. "Is it possible to get it fixed?"

"Let me see." She takes it from me, lifts the cracked lid. "Oh, I should think so, unless the coil's been broken. Of course, it would be cheaper to go out and buy a new one, but I take it that you've memories in here that you'd like to keep?"

I pocket the VR machine like some dirty secret, and pour out the coffee. I sit down. We look at each other, this woman and I. How old is she, anyway? These days, it's often hard to tell. Somewhere between Bill and the Euthons, I suppose, which makes her thirty or even forty years younger than me. And, even if she were more like Hannah, she isn't the way Hannah would be if she were alive. Hannah would be like me, staggering on ancient limbs, confused, trying to communicate through senses that are no longer her own, dragged ever-forward into the unheeding future, scrabbling desperately to get back to the past, clawing at those bright rare days when the grandchildren come to visit, feeling the golden grit of precious moments slipping though her fingers even before they are gone.

And time doesn't matter to this woman; or to anyone under a hundred. That's one of the reasons it's so hard for me to keep track. The seasons on this island change, but people just gaze and admire. They pick the fruit as it falls. They breathe the salt wind from off the grey winter ocean and shiver happily, knowing they'll sit eating toast by the fire as soon as they get home.

"I don't live that far from here," the woman says eventually. "I mean, if there's anything that you'd like help with. If there's anything that needs doing."

I gaze back at her, trying not to feel offended. I know, after all, that I probably do need help of some kind or other. I just can't think of what it is.

"Or we could just talk," she adds hopefully.

"Do you remember fast food? McDonalds?"

She shakes her head.

"ET? Pee-Wee Herman? Global warming? Ethnic cleansing? Dan Quayle?"

She shakes her head. "I'm sorry. . . ."

She lifts her coffee from the table, drinking it quickly.

The silence falls between us like snow.

I stand in my doorway, watching as her flyer rises and turns, its tiny wings flashing in sunlight. A final wave, and I close the door, knowing that Saul and Agatha will probably be on a ferry now. Off this island.

I head toward my bedroom. Assuming it's time for my morning rest, my bedhelper clicks out its arms expectantly. I glare at it, but of course it doesn't understand, and I've already forgotten the trick Saul showed me that you could do to disable it. The house is already back to its old ways, taking charge, cleaning up Saul and Agatha's room, getting rid of every sign of life.

But I did at least make an effort with the console, and I do know now how to make sure the engaged flag isn't showing. Child's play, really—and I always knew how to call my son Bill's number. Which is what I do now.

Of all places, Bill's in London. The precise location shows up on the console before he appears; it was just a question of making the right demand, of touching the right key. Then there's a pause.

I have to wait.

It's almost as if the console is testing my resolve, although I know that Bill's probably having to put someone else on hold so he can speak to me. And that he'll imagine there's a minor crisis brewing—otherwise, why would Papa bother to ring?

But I wait anyway, and, as I do, I rehearse the words I'll have to say, although I know that they'll come out differently. But while there's still time, I'll do my best to bridge the years.

At least, I'll start to try.

SACRED COW

Bruce Sterling

▼

One of the most powerful and innovative talents to enter SF in recent years, Bruce Sterling published his first story in 1976, and has since sold stories to *Universe*, *Omni*, *Asimov's Science Fiction*, *The Magazine of Fantasy & Science Fiction*, *Lone Star Universe*, and elsewhere. He first attracted serious attention in the eighties with a series of stories set in his exotic ''Shaper/Mechanist'' future (a complex and disturbing future where warring political factions struggle to control the shape of human destiny), and by the end of the decade had established himself, with novels such as the complex and Stapeldonian *Schismatrix* and the well-received *Islands in the Net* (as well as with his editing of the influential anthology *Mirrorshades: the Cyberpunk Anthology* and the infamous critical magazine *Cheap Truth*) as perhaps the prime driving force behind the revolutionary cyberpunk movement in science fiction (rivaled for that title only by his friend and collaborator, William Gibson), and also as one of the best new hard science writers to enter the field in some time. His stories have appeared in our First, Second, Third, Fourth, Fifth, Sixth, Seventh, and Eighth Collections. His other books include the novels *The Artificial Kid, Involution Ocean*, and a novel in collaboration with William Gibson, *The Difference Engine*, and the landmark collection *Crystal Express*. His most recent books are a new collection, *Globalhead*, and a critically acclaimed nonfiction study of First Amendment issues in the world of computer networking, *The Hacker Crackdown: Law and Disorder on the Electronic Frontier*, and he has just completed a new novel. He lives with his family in Austin, Texas.

In the unsettling story that follows, he takes us to a not-too-distant future in which the sun most definitely *has* set, undeniably and unequivocally, on the British Empire. . . .

He woke in darkness to the steady racket of the rails. Vast unknowable landscapes, huge as the dreams of childhood, rumbled behind his shocked reflection in the carriage pane.

Jackie smoothed his rumpled hair, stretched stiffly, wiped at his moustache, tucked the railway blanket around his silk-pajama'd legs. Across the aisle, two of his crew slept uneasily, sprawled across their seats: Kumar the soundman, Jimmie Suraj his cinematographer. Suraj had an unlit cigarette tucked behind one ear, the thin gold chains at his neck bunched in an awkward tangle.

The crew's leading lady, Lakshmi "Bubbles" Malini, came pale and swaying down the aisle, wrapped sari-like in a souvenir Scottish blanket. "Awake, Jackie?"

"Yaar, girl," he said, "I suppose so."

"So that woke you, okay?" she announced, gripping the seat. "That big bump just now. That bloody lurch, for Pete's sake. It almost threw us from the track."

"Sit down, Bubbles," he apologized.

" 'Dozens die,' okay?" she said, sitting. " 'Stars, director, crew perish in bloody English tragic rail accident.' I can see it all in print in bloody *Stardust* already."

Jackie patted her plump hand, found his kit bag, extracted a cigarette case, lit one. Bubbles stole a puff, handed it back. Bubbles was not a smoker. Bad for the voice, bad for a dancer's wind. But after two months in Britain she was kipping smokes from everybody.

"We're not dying in any bloody train," Jackie told her, smiling. "We're filmwallas, darling. We were born to be killed by taxmen."

Jackie watched a battered railway terminal rattle past in a spectral glare of fog. A pair of tall English, wrapped to the eyes, sat on their luggage with looks of sphinxlike inscrutability. Jackie liked the look of them. Native extras. Good atmosphere.

Bubbles was restless. "Was this all a good idea, Jackie, you think?"

He shrugged. "Horrid old rail lines here, darling, but they take life damn slow now, the English."

She shook her head. "This country, Jackie!"

"Well," he said, smoothing his hair. "It's bloody cheap here. Four films in the can for the price of one feature in Bombay."

"I liked London," Bubbles offered bravely. "Glasgow too. Bloody cold but not so bad . . . But Bolton? Nobody films in bloody Bolton."

"Business, darling," he said. "Need to lower those production costs. The ratio of rupees to meter of filmstock exposed . . ."

"Jackie?"

He grunted.

"You're bullshitting me, darling."

He shook his head. "Yaar, girl, Jackie Amar never bounce a crew cheque yet. Get some sleep, darling. Got to look beautiful."

Jackie did not title his own movies. He had given that up after his first fifty films. The studio in Bombay kept a whole office of hack writers to do titles, with Hindi rhyming dictionaries at their elbows. Now Jackie kept track of his cinematic oeuvre by number and plot summary in a gold-edged fake-leather notebook with detachable pages.

Jackie Amar Production #127 had been his first in merrie old England. They'd shot #127 in a warehouse in Tooting Bec, with a few rented hours at the Tower of London. No. 127 was an adventure/crime/comedy about a pair of hapless expatriate twins (Raj Khanna, Ram Khanna) who cook up a scheme to steal back the Koh-i-noor Diamond from the Crown Jewels of England. The Khanna brothers had been drunk much of the time. Bubbles had done two dance numbers and complained bitterly about the brothers' Scotch-tainted breath in the clinch scenes. Jackie had sent the twins packing back to Bombay.

No. 128 had been the first to star Jackie's English ingenue discovery, Betty Chalmers. Betty had answered a classified ad asking for English girls 18–20, of mixed Indian descent, boasting certain specific bodily measurements. Betty played the exotic Brit-Asian mistress of a gallant Indian military-intelligence attaché (Bobby Denzongpa) who foils a plot by Japanese yakuza gangsters to blow up the Tower of London. (There had been a fair amount of leftover Tower footage from film #127.) Local actors, their English subtitled in Hindi, played the bumbling comics from Scotland Yard. Betty died beautifully in the last reel, struck by a poisoned ninja blowdart, just after the final dance number. Betty's lines in halting phonetic Hindi had been overdubbed in the Bombay studio.

Events then necessitated leaving London, events taking the shape of a dapper and humorless Indian embassy official who had alarmingly specific questions for a certain Javed "Jackie" Amar concerning income-tax arrears for Rupees 6,435,000.

A change of venue to Scotland had considerably complicated the legal case against Jackie, but #129 had been born in the midst of chaos. Veteran soundman Wasant "Winnie" Kumar had been misplaced as the crew scrambled from London, and the musical score of #129 had been done, at hours' notice, by a friend of Betty's from Manchester, a shabby, scarecrow-tall youngster named Smith. Smith, who owned a jerry-rigged portable mixing station clamped together with duct tape, had produced a deathly pounding racket of synthesized tablas and digitally warped sitars.

Jackie, despairing, had left the score as Smith had recorded it, for the weird noise seemed to fit the story, and young Smith had worked on percentage—which would likely come to no real pay at all. Western historicals were hot in Bombay this year—or at least, they had been, back in '48—and Jackie had scripted one in an all-night frenzy of coffee and pills. A penniless Irish actor had starred as John Fitzgerald Kennedy, with Betty Chalmers as a White House chambermaid who falls for the virile young president and becomes the first woman to orbit the Moon. An old film contact in Kazakhstan had provided some stock Soviet space footage with enthusiastic twentieth-century crowd scenes. Bubbles had done a spacesuit dance.

Somewhat ashamed of this excess—he had shot the entire film with only five hours sleep in four days—Jackie gave his best to #130, a foreign dramatic romance. Bobby Denzongpa starred as an Indian engineer, disappointed in love, who flees overseas to escape his past and becomes the owner of a seedy Glasgow hotel. No. 130 had been shot, by necessity, in the crew's own hotel in Glasgow with the puzzled but enthusiastic Scottish staff as extras. Bubbles starred as an expatriate cabaret dancer and Bobby's love interest. Bubbles died in the last reel, having successfully thawed Bobby's cynical heart and sent him back to India. No. 130 was a classic weepie and, Jackie thought, the only one of the four to have any chance in hell of making money.

Jackie was still not sure about the plot of No. 131, his fifth British film. When the tax troubles had caught up to him in Scotland, he had picked the name of Bolton at random from a railway schedule.

Bolton turned out to be a chilly and silent hamlet of perhaps sixty thousand English, all of them busy dismantling the abandoned suburban sprawl around the city and putting fresh paint and flowers on Bolton's nineteenth-century core. Such was the tourist economy in modern England. All the real modern-day businesses in Bolton were in the hands of Japanese, Arabs, and Sikhs.

A word with the station master got their rail cars safely parked on an obscure siding and their equipment loaded into a small fleet of English pedalcabs. A generous offer to pay in rupees found them a fairly reasonable hotel. It began to rain.

Jackie sat stolidly in the lobby that afternoon, leafing through tourist brochures in search of possible shooting sites. The crew drank cheap English beer and bitched. Jimmie Suraj the cameraman complained of the few miserable hours of pale, wintry European light. The lighting boys feared suffocation under the mountainous wool blankets in their rooms. Kumar the soundman speculated loudly and uneasily over the contents of the hotel's "shepherd's pie" and, worse yet, "toad-in-the-hole." Bobby Denzongpa and Betty Chalmers vanished without permission in search of a disco.

Jackie nodded, sympathized, tut-tutted, patted heads, made empty promises. At ten o'clock he called the studio in Bombay. No. 127 had been judged a commercial no-hope and had been slotted direct to video. No. 128 had been redubbed in Tamil and was dying a slow kiss-off death on the southern village circuit. "Goldie" Vachchani, head of the studio, had been asking about him. In Jackie's circles it was not considered auspicious to have Goldie ask about a fellow.

Jackie left the hotel's phone number with the studio. At midnight, as he sat sipping bad champagne and studying plot synopses from ten years back in search of inspiration, there was a call for him. It was his son Salim, the eldest of his five children and his only child by his first wife.

"Where did you get this number?" Jackie said.

"A friend," Salim said. "Dad, listen. I need a favor."

Jackie listened to the ugly hiss and warble of long-distance submarine cables. "What is it this time?"

"You know Goldie Vachchani, don't you? The big Bombay filmwalla?"

"I know Goldie," Jackie admitted.

"His brother's just been named head of the state aeronautics bureau."

"I don't know Goldie very well, mind you."

"This is a major to-do, Dad. I have the news on best private background authority. The budget for aeronautics will triple next Congress. The nation is responding to the Japanese challenge in space."

"What challenge is that? A few weather satellites."

Salim sighed patiently. "This is the Fifties now, Dad. History is marching. The nation is on the wing."

"Why?" Jackie asked.

"The Americans went to the Moon eighty years ago."

"I know they did. So?"

"They polluted it," Salim announced. "The Americans left a junkyard of crashed machines up on our Moon. Even a junked motor car is there. And a golf ball." Salim lowered his voice. "And urine and feces, Dad. There is American fecal matter on the Moon that will last there in cold and vacuum for ten million years. Unless, that is, the Moon is ritually purified."

"God almighty, you've been talking to those crazy fundamentalists again," Jackie said. "I warned you not to go into politics. It's nothing but crooks and fakirs." The hissing phone line emitted an indulgent chuckle. "You're being culturally inauthentic, daddyji! You're Westoxicated! This is the modern age now! If the Japanese get to the Moon first they'll cover it with bloody shopping malls."

"Best of luck to the damn fool Japanese, then."

"They already own most of China," Salim said, with sinister emphasis. "Expanding all the time. Tireless, soulless, and efficient."

"Bosh," Jackie said. "What about us? The Indian Army's in Laos, Tibet, and Sri Lanka."

"If we want the world to respect our sacred cultural values, then we must visibly transcend the earthly realm. . . ."

Jackie shuddered, adjusted his silk dressing gown. "Son, listen to me. This is not real politics. This is a silly movie fantasy you are talking about. A bad dream. Look at the Russians and Americans if you want to know what aiming at the Moon will get you. They're eating chaff today and sleeping on straw."

"You don't know Goldie Vachchani, Dad?"

"I don't like him."

"I thought I'd ask," Salim said sulkily. He paused. "Dad?"

"What?"

"Is there any reason why the Civil Investigation Division would want to inventory your house?"

Jackie went cold. "Some mistake, son. A mixup."

"Are you in trouble, daddyji? I could try to pull some strings, up top. . . ."

"No no," Jackie said swiftly. "There's bloody horrid noise on this phone. Salim—I'll be in touch." He hung up.

Half an anxious hour with the script and cigarettes got him nowhere. At last he belted his robe, put on warm slippers and a nightcap, and tapped at Bubbles' door.

"Jackie," she said, opening it, her wet hair turbanned in a towel. Furnace-heated air gushed into the chilly hall. "I'm on the phone, darling. Long distance."

"Who?" he said.

"My husband."

Jackie nodded. "How is Vijay?"

She made a face. "Divorced, for Pete's sake! Dalip is my husband now, Dalip Sabnis, remember? Honestly, Jackie, you're so absent-minded sometimes."

"Sorry," Jackie said. "Give Dalip my best." He sat in a chair and leafed through one of Bubbles' Bombay fan mags while she cooed into the phone.

Bubbles hung up, sighed. "I miss him so bad," she said. "What is it, okay?"

"My oldest boy just told me that I am culturally inauthentic."

She tossed the towel from her head, put her fists on her hips. "These young people today! What do they want from us?"

"They want the real India," Jackie said. "But we all watched Hollywood films for a hundred bloody years . . . We have no native soul left, don't you know." He sighed heavily. "We're all bits and pieces inside. We're a jigsaw people, we Indians. Quotes and remakes. Rags and tatters."

Bubbles tapped her chin with one lacquered forefinger. "You're having trouble with the script."

Mournfully, he ignored her. "Liberation came a hundred bloody years ago. But still we obsess with the damn British. Look at this country of theirs. It's a museum. But us—we're worse. We're a wounded civilization. Naipaul was right. Rushdie was right!"

"You work too hard," Bubbles said. "That historical we just did, about the Moon, yaar? That one was stupid crazy, darling. That music boy Smith, from Manchester? He don't even speak English, okay. I can't understand a word he bloody says."

"My dear, that's English. This is England. That is how they speak their native language."

"My foot," Bubbles said. "We have five hundred million to speak English. How many left have they?"

Jackie laughed. "They're getting better, yes. Learning to talk more properly, like us." He yawned hugely. "It's bloody hot in here, Bubbles. Feels good. Just like home."

"That young girl, Betty Chalmers, okay? When she tries to speak Hindi I bust from laughs." Bubbles paused. "She's a smart little cookie, though. She could go places in business. Did you sleep with her?"

"Just once," Jackie said. "She was nice. But very English."

"She's American," Bubbles said triumphantly. "A Cherokee Indian from Tulsa Oklahoma, USA. When your advert said Indian blood, she thought you meant American Indians."

"Damn!" Jackie said. "Really?"

"Cross my heart it's true, Jackie."

"Damn . . . And the camera loves her, too. Don't tell anybody."

Bubbles shrugged, a little too casually. "It's funny how much they want to be just like us."

"Sad for them," Jackie said. "An existential tragedy."

"No, darling, I mean it's really funny, for an audience at home. Laugh out loud, roll in the aisles, big knee-slapper! It could be a good movie, Jackie. About how funny the English are. Being so inauthentic like us."

"Bloody hell," Jackie marvelled.

"A remake of *Param Dharam* or *Gammat Jammat*, but funny, because of all English players, okay."

"*Gammat Jammat* has some great dance scenes."

She smiled.

His head felt inflamed with sudden inspiration. "We can do that. Yes. We will! And it'll make a bloody fortune!" He clapped his hands together, bowed his head to her. "Miss Malini, you are a trouper." She made a pleased salaam. "Satisfaction guaranteed, sahib."

He rose from the chair. "I'll get on it straightaway."

She slipped across the room to block his way. "No no no! Not tonight."

"Why not?"

"None of those little red pills of yours."

He frowned.

"You'll pop from those someday, Jackieji. You jump like a jack-in-box every time they snap the clapperboard. You think I don't know?"

He flinched. "You don't know the troubles of this crew. We need a hit like hell, darling. Not today, yesterday."

"Money troubles. So what? Not tonight, boss, not to worry. You're the only director that knows my best angles. You think I want to be stuck with no director in this bloody dump?" Gently, she took his hand. "Calming down, okay. Changing your mind, having some fun. This is your old pal Bubbles here, yaar? Look, Jackieji. Bubbles." She struck a hand-on-hip pose and shot him her best sidelong come-on look.

Jackie was touched. He got into bed. She pinned him down, kissed him firmly, put both his hands on her breasts and pulled the cover over her shoulders. "Nice and easy, okay? A little pampering. Let me do it."

She straddled his groin, settled down, undulated a bit in muscular dancer's fashion, then stopped, and began to pinch and scratch his chest with absent-minded Vedic skill. "You're so funny sometimes, darling. 'Inauthentic.' I can tap dance, I can bump and grind, and you think I can't wiggle my neck like a natyam dancer? Watch me do it, for Pete's sake."

"Stop it," he begged. "Be funny before, be funny afterward, but don't be funny in the middle."

"Okay, nothing funny darling, short and sweet." She set to work on him and in two divine minutes she had wrung him out like a sponge.

"There," she said. "All done. Feel better?"

"God, yes."

"Inauthentic as hell and it feels just as good, yaar?"

"It's why the human race goes on."

"Well then," she said. "That, and a good night's sleep, baby."

Jackie was enjoying a solid if somewhat flavorless breakfast of kippers and eggs when Jimmie Suraj came in. "It's Smith, boss," Jimmie said. "We can't get him to shut up that bloody box of his."

Jackie sighed, finished his breakfast, dabbed bits of kipper from his lips, and walked into the lobby. Smith, Betty Chalmers, and Bobby Denzongpa sat around a low table in overstuffed chairs. There was a stranger with them. A young Japanese.

"Turn it off, Smithie, there's a good fellow," Jackie said. "It sounds like bloody cats being skinned."

"Just running a demo for Mr. Big Yen here," Smith muttered. With bad grace, he turned off his machine. This was an elaborate procedure, involving much flicking of switches, twisting of knobs, and whirring of disk drives.

The Japanese—a long-haired, elegant youngster in a sheepskin coat, corduroy beret and jeans—rose from his chair, bowed crisply, and offered Jackie a business card. Jackie read it. The man was from a movie company—Kinema Junpo. His name was Baisho.

Jackie did a namaste. "A pleasure to meet you, Mr. Baisho." Baisho looked a bit wary.

"Our boss says he's glad to meet you," Smith repeated.

"*Hai*," Baisho said alertly.

"We met Baisho-san at the disco last night," Betty Chalmers said. Baisho, sitting up straighter, emitted an enthusiastic string of alien syllables.

"Baisho says he's a big fan of English dance-hall music," Smith mumbled. "He was looking for a proper dance hall here. What he thinks is one. Vesta Tilly, ta-ra-ra-boom-de-ay, that sort of bloody thing."

"Ah," Jackie said. "You speak any English, Mr. Baisho?"

Baisho smiled politely and replied at length, with much waving of arms. "He's also hunting for first editions of Noel Coward and J. B. Priestley," Betty said. "They're his favorite English authors. And boss—Jackie—Mr. Baisho *is* speaking English. I mean, if you listen, all the vowels and consonants are in there. Really."

"Rather better than *your* English, actually," Smith muttered.

"I have heard of Noel Coward," Jackie said. "Very witty playwright, that Coward fellow." Baisho waited politely until Jackie's lips had stopped moving and then plunged back into his narrative.

"He says that it's lucky he met us because he's here on location himself," Betty said. "Kinema Junpo—that's his boss—is shooting a remake of *Throne of Blood* in Scotland. He's been . . . uh . . . appointed to check out some special location here in Bolton."

"Yes?" Jackie said.

"Said the local English won't help him because they're kind of superstitious about the place," Betty said. She smiled. "How 'bout you, Smithie? You're not superstitious, are you?"

"Nah," Smith said. He lit a cigarette.

"He wants us to help him?" Jackie said.

Betty smiled. "They have truckloads of cash, the Japanese."

"If you don't want to do it, I can get some mates o' mine from Manchester," Smith said, picking at a blemish. "They're nae scared of bloody Bolton."

"What is it about Bolton?" Jackie said.

"You didn't know?" Betty said. "Well, not much. I mean, it's not much of a town, but it does have the biggest mass grave in England."

"Over a million," Smith muttered. "From Manchester, London—they used to ship 'em out here in trains, during the plague."

"Ah," Jackie said.

"Over a million in one bloody spot," Smith said, stirring in his chair. He blew a curl of smoke. "Me grandfather used to talk about it. Real proud about Bolton they was, real civil government emergency and all, kept good order, soldiers and such . . . Every dead bloke got his own marker, even the women and kids. Other places, later, they just scraped a hole with bulldozers and shoved 'em in."

"Spirit," Baisho said loudly, enunciating as carefully as he could. "Good cinema spirit in city of Boruton."

Despite himself, Jackie felt a chill. He sat down. "Inauspicious. That's what we'd call it."

"It was fifty years ago," Smith said, bored. "Thirty years before I was born. Or Betty here either, eh? 'Bovine Spongiform Encephalopathy.' Mad Cow Disease. So what? B.S.E. will never come back. It was a fluke. A bloody twentieth-century industrial accident."

"You know, I'm not frightened," Betty said, with her brightest smile. "I've even eaten beef several times. There's no more virions in it. I mean, they wiped out scrapie years ago. Killed every sheep, every cow that might have any infection. It's perfectly safe to eat now, beef."

"We lost many people in Japan," Baisho offered slowly. "Tourists who eated . . . ate . . . Engrish beef, here in Europe. But trade friction protect most of us. Old trade barriers. The farmers of Japan." He smiled.

Smith ground out his cigarette. "Another fluke. Your old granddad was just lucky, Baisho-san."

"Lucky?" Bobby Denzongpa said suddenly. His dark gazelle-like eyes were red-rimmed with hangover. "Yaar, they fed sheeps to the cows here! God did not make cows for eating of sheeps! And the flesh of Mother Cow is not for us to eat. . . ."

"Bobby," Jackie warned.

Bobby shrugged irritably. "It's the truth, boss, yaar? They made foul sheep, slaughterhouse offal into protein for cattle feed, and they fed that bloody trash to their own English cows. For years they did this wicked thing, even when the cows were going mad and dying in front of them! They knew it was risky, but they went straightaway on doing it simply because it was cheaper! That was a crime against nature. It was properly punished."

"That is enough," Jackie said coldly. "We are guests in this country. We of India also lost many fellow countrymen to that tragedy, don't you know."

"Moslems, good riddance," Bobby muttered under his breath, and got up and staggered off.

Jackie glowered at him as he left, for the sake of the others.

"It's okay," Smith said in the uneasy silence. "He's a bloody Asian racist, your filmstar walla there, but we're used to that here." He shrugged. "It's just— the plague, you know, it's all they talk about in school, like England was really high-class back then and we're nothing at all now, just a shadow or something. . . . You get bloody tired of hearing that. I mean, it was all fifty bloody years ago." He sneered. "I'm not the shadow of the Beatles or the fucking Sex Pistols. I'm a working, professional, modern, British musician, and got my union papers to prove it.''

"No, you're really good, Smithie,'' Betty told him. She had gone pale. "I mean, England's coming back strong now. Really.''

"Look, we're not 'coming back,' lass,'' Smith insisted. "We're already here right now, earning our bloody living. It's life, eh? Life goes fucking on.'' Smith stood up, picked up his deck, scratched at his shaggy head. "I gotta work. Jackie. Boss, eh? Can you spare five pound, man? I gotta make some phone calls.''

Jackie searched in his wallet and handed over a bill in the local currency.

Baisho had five Japanese in his crew. Even with the help of Jackie's crew, it took them most of the evening to scythe back the thick brown weeds in the old Bolton plagueyard. Every half meter or so they came across a marker for the dead. Small square granite posts had been hammered into the ground, fifty years ago, then sheared off clean with some kind of metal saw. Fading names and dates and computer ID numbers had been chiselled into the tops of the posts.

Jackie thought that the graveyard must stretch around for about a kilometer. The rolling English earth was studded with plump, thick-rooted oaks and ashes, with that strange naked look of European trees in winter.

There was nothing much to the place. It was utterly prosaic, like a badly kept city park in some third-class town. It defied the tragic imagination. Jackie had been a child when the scrapie plague had hit, but he could remember sitting in hot Bombay darkness, staring nonplussed at the anxious shouting newsreels, vague images, shot in color no doubt, but grainy black and white in the eye of his memory. Packed cots in European medical camps, uniformed shuffling white people gone all gaunt and trembling, spooning up charity gruel with numb, gnarled hands. The scrapie plague had a devilishly slow incubation in humans, but no human being had ever survived the full onset.

First came the slow grinding headaches and the unending sense of fatigue. Then the tripping and flopping and stumbling as the nerves of the victim's legs gave out. As the lesions spread, and tunneled deep within the brain, the muscles went slack and flabby, and a lethal psychotic apathy set in. In those old cinema newsreels, Western civilization gazed at the Indian lens in demented puzzlement as millions refused to realize that they were dying simply because they had eaten a cow.

What were they called? thought Jackie. Beefburgers? Hamburgers. Ninety percent of Britain, thirty percent of Western Europe, twenty percent of jet-setting America, horribly dead. Because of hamburgers.

Baisho's set-design crew was working hard to invest the dreary place with proper atmosphere. They were spraying long white webs of some kind of thready aerosol across the cropped grass and setting up gel-filtered lights. It was to be a night shoot. Macbeth and Macduff would arrive soon on the express train.

Betty sought him out. "Baisho-san wants to know what you think.''

"My professional opinion of his set, as a veteran Indian filmmaker?'' Jackie said.

"Right, boss."

Jackie did not much care for giving out his trade secrets but could not resist the urge to cap the Japanese. "A wind machine," he pronounced briskly. "This place needs a wind machine. Have him leave some of the taller weeds, and set up under a tree. We've fifty kilos of glitter dust back in Bolton. It's his, if he wants to pay. Sift that dust, hand by hand, through the back of the wind machine and you'll get a fine effect. It's more spooky than hell."

Betty offered this advice. Baisho nodded, thought the idea over, then reached for a small machine on his belt. He opened it and began to press tiny buttons.

Jackie walked closer. "What's that then? A telephone?"

"Yes," Betty said. "He needs to clear the plan with headquarters."

"No phone cables out here," Jackie said.

"High tech," Betty said. "They have a satellite link."

"Bloody hell," Jackie said. "And here I am offering technical aid. To the bloody Japanese, eh."

Betty looked at him for a long moment. "You've got Japan outnumbered eight to one. You shouldn't worry about Japan."

"Oh, I don't worry," Jackie said. "I'm a tolerant fellow, dear. A very secular fellow. But I'm thinking, what my studio will say, when they hear we break bread here with the nation's competition. It might not look so good in the Bombay gossip rags."

Betty stood quietly. The sun was setting behind a bank of cloud. "You're the kings of the world, you Asians," she said at last. "You're rich, you have all the power, you have all the money. We need you to help us, Jackie. We don't want you to fight each other."

"Politics," Jackie mumbled, surprised. "It's . . . it's just life." He paused. "Betty, listen to old Jackie. They don't like actresses with politics in Bombay. It's not like Tulsa Oklahoma. You have to be discreet."

She watched him slowly, her eyes wide. "You never said you'd take me to Bombay, Jackie."

"It could happen," Jackie muttered.

"I'd like to go there," she said. "It's the center of the world." She gripped her arms and shivered. "It's getting cold. I need my sweater."

The actors had arrived, in a motor-driven tricycle cab. The Japanese began dressing them in stage armor. Macduff began practicing kendo moves.

Jackie walked to join Mr. Baisho. "May I call on your phone, please?"

"I'm sorry?" Baisho said.

Jackie mimed the action. "Bombay," he said. He wrote the number on a page in his notebook, handed it over.

"Ah," Baisho said, nodding. "*Wakarimashita.*" He dialed a number, spoke briefly in Japanese, waited, handed Jackie the phone.

There was a rapid flurry of digital bleeping. Jackie, switching to Hindi, fought his way through a screen of secretaries. "Goldie," he said at last.

"Jackieji. I've been asking for you."

"Yes, I heard." Jackie paused. "Have you seen the films?"

Goldie Vachchani grunted, with a sharp digital echo. "The first two. Getting your footing over in Blighty, yaar? Nothing so special."

"Yes?" Jackie said.

"The third one. The one with the half-breed girl and the Moon and the soundtrack."

"Yes, Goldie."

Goldie's voice was slow and gloating. "That one, Jackie. That one is special, yaar. It's a smasheroo, Jackie. An ultrahit! Bloody champagne and flower garlands here, Jackie boy. It's big. Mega."

"You liked the Moon, eh," Jackie said, stunned.

"Love the Moon. Love all that nonsense."

"I did hear about your brother's government appointment. Congratulations."

Goldie chuckled. "Bloody hell, Jackie. You're the fourth fellow today to make that silly mistake. That Vachchani fellow in aeronautics, he's not my brother. My brother's a bloody contractor; he builds bloody houses, Jackie. This other Vachchani, he's some scientist egghead fellow. That Moon stuff is stupid crazy, it will never happen." He laughed, then dropped his voice. "The fourth one is shit, Jackie. Women's weepies are a drug on the bloody market this season, you rascal. Send me something funny next time. A bloody dance comedy."

"Will do," Jackie said.

"This girl Betty," Goldie said. "She likes to work?"

"Yes."

"She's a party girl, too?"

"You might say so."

"I want to meet this Betty. You send her here on the very next train. No, an aeroplane, hang the cost. And that soundtrack man too. My kids love that damned ugly music. If the kids love it, there's money in it."

"I need them both, Goldie. For my next feature. Got them under contract, yaar."

Goldie paused. Jackie waited him out.

"You got a little tax trouble, Jackie? I'm going to see to fixing that silly business, yaar. See to that straightaway. Personally."

Jackie let out a breath. "They're as good as on the way, Goldieji."

"You got it then. You're a funny fellow, Jackie." There was a digital clatter as the phone went dead.

The studio lights of the Japanese crew flashed on, framing Jackie in the graveyard in a phosphorescent glare. "Bloody hell!" Jackie shouted, flinging the phone away into the air and clapping his hands. "Party, my crew! Big party tonight for every bloody soul, and the bill is on Jackie Amar!" He whooped aloud. "If you're not drunk and dancing tonight, then you're no friend of mine! My God, everybody! My God, but life is good."

DANCING ON AIR

Nancy Kress

▼

Born in Buffalo, New York, Nancy Kress now lives in Brockport, New York. She began selling her elegant and incisive stories in the mid-seventies, and has since become a frequent contributor to *Asimov's Science Fiction, The Magazine of Fantasy & Science Fiction, Omni*, and elsewhere. Her books include the novels *The Prince of Morning Bells, The Golden Grove, The White Pipes, An Alien Light*, and *Brain Rose*, and the collection *Trinity and Other Stories*. Her most recent books are the novel version of her Hugo- and Nebula-winning story, *Beggars in Spain*, and a new collection, *The Aliens of Earth*, and a sequel to *Beggars in Spain*, entitled *Beggars and Choosers*, will be out soon. She has also won a Nebula Award for her story "Out of All Them Bright Stars." She has had stories in our Second, Third, Sixth, Seventh, Eighth, Ninth, and Tenth Annual Collections.

In the compelling and powerful novella that follows, she gives us a look at the surprising future of one of the oldest of all the performing arts—and embroils us as well in a complex and suspenseful web of mystery, intrigue, passion, betrayal, and murder.

> *"When a man has been guilty of a mistake, either in ordering his own affairs, or in directing those of State, or in commanding an army, do we not always say, So-and-so has made a false step in this affair? And can making a false step derive from anything but lack of skill in dancing?"*
>
> *—Molière*

Sometimes I understand the words. Sometimes I do not understand the words.

Eric brings me to the exercise yard. A man and a woman stand there. The man is tall. The woman is short. She has long black fur on her head. She smells angry.

Eric says, "This is Angel. Angel, this is John Cole and Caroline Olson."

"Hello," I say.

"I'm supposed to understand that growl?" the woman says. "Might as well be Russian!"

"Caroline," the man says, "you promised. . . ."

"I know what I promised." She walks away. She smells very angry. I don't understand. My word was *hello*. *Hello* is one of the easy words.

The man says, "Hello, Angel." He smiles. I sniff his shoes and bark. He smells friendly. I smell two cats and a hot dog and street tar and a car. I feel happy. I like cars.

The woman comes back. "If we have to do this, then let's just do it, for Chrissake. Let's sign the papers and get out of this hole."

John Cole says, "The lawyers are all waiting in Eric's office."

Eric's office smells of many people. I go to my place beside the door. I lie down. Maybe later somebody takes me in the car.

A woman looks at many papers and talks. "A contract between Biomod Canine Protection Agency, herein referred to as the party of the first part, and the New York City Ballet, herein referred to as the party of the second part, in fulfillment of the requirements of Columbia Insurance Company, herein referred to as the party of the third part, as those requirements are set forth in Policy 438-69, Section 17, respecting prima ballerina Caroline Olson. The party of the first part shall furnish genetically modified canine protection to Caroline Olson under, and not limited to, the following conditions . . ."

The words are hard.

I think words I can understand.

My name is Angel. I am a dog. I protect. Eric tells me to protect. No people can touch the one I protect except safe people. I love people I protect. I sleep now.

"Angel," Eric says from his chair, "wake up now. You must protect."

I wake up. Eric walks to me. He sits next to me. He puts his voice in my ear.

"This is Caroline. You must protect Caroline. No one must hurt Caroline. No one must touch Caroline except safe people. Angel—*protect Caroline.*"

I smell Caroline. I am very happy. I protect Caroline.

"Jesus H. Christ," Caroline says. She walks away.

I love Caroline.

We go in the car. We go very far. Many people. Many smells. John drives the car. John is safe. He may touch Caroline. John stops the car. We get out. There are many tall buildings and many cars.

"You sure you're going to be okay?" John Cole says.

"You've protected your investment, haven't you?" Caroline snarls. John drives away.

A man stands by the door. The man says, "Evening, Miss Olson."

"Evening, Sam. This is my new guard dog. The company insists I have one, after . . . what's been happening. They say the insurance company is paranoid. Yeah, sure. I need a dog like I need a knee injury."

"Yes, ma'am. Doberman, isn't he? He looks like a gooooood ol' dog. Hey, big fella, what's your name?"

"Angel," I say.

The man jumps and makes a noise. Caroline laughs.

"Bioenhanced. Great for my privacy, right? Rover, Sam is safe. Do you hear me? Sam is *safe*."

I say, "My name is Angel."

Caroline says, "Sam, you can relax. Really. He only attacks on command, or if I scream, or if he hasn't been told a person is safe and that person touches me."

"Yes, ma'am." Sam smells afraid. He looks at me hard. I bark and my tail moves.

Caroline says, "Come on, Fido. Your spy career is about to begin."

I say, "My name is Angel."

"Right," Caroline says.

We go into the building. We go in the elevator. I say, "Sam has a cat. I smell Sam's cat."

"Who the fuck cares," Caroline says.

I am a dog.

I must love Caroline.

2

Two days after the second ballerina was murdered, Michael Chow, senior editor of *New York Now* and my boss, called me into his office. I already knew what he wanted, and I already knew I didn't want to do it. He knew that, too. We both knew it wouldn't make any difference.

"You're the logical reporter, Susan," Michael said. He sat behind the desk, always a bad sign. When he thought I'd want an assignment, he leaned casually against the front of the desk. Its top was cluttered with print-outs; with disposable research cartridges, some with their screens alight; with pictures of Michael's six children. *Six.* They all looked like Michael: straight black hair and a smooth face like a peeled egg. At the apex of the mess sat a hardcopy of the *Times* 3:00 P.M. on-line lead: AUTOPSY DISCOVERS BIOENHANCERS IN CITY BALLET DANCER. "You have an in. Even Anton Privitera will talk to you."

"Not about this. He already gave his press conference. Such as it was."

"So? You can get to him as a parent and leverage from there."

My daughter Deborah was a student in the School of American Ballet, the juvenile province of Anton Privitera's kingdom. For thirty years he had ruled the New York City Ballet like an anointed tyrant. Sometimes it seemed he could even levy taxes and raise armies, so exalted was his reputation in the dance world, and so good was his business manager John Cole at raising funds and enlisting corporate patrons. Dancers had flocked to the City Ballet from Europe, from Asia, from South America, from the serious ballet schools in the patrolled zones of America's dying cities. Until bioenhancers, the New York City Ballet had been the undisputed grail of the international dance world.

Now, of course, that was changing.

Privitera was dynamic with the press as long as we were content with what he wished us to know. He wasn't going to want to discuss the murder of two dancers, one of them his own.

A month ago Nicole Heyer, a principal dancer with the American Ballet Theater, had been found strangled in Central Park. Three days ago the body of Jennifer Lang had been found in her modest apartment. Heyer had been a bioenhanced dancer who had come to the ABT from the Stuttgart Ballet. Lang, a minor soloist with the City Ballet, had of course been natural. Or so everybody thought until the autopsy. The entire company had been bioscanned only three weeks ago, Artistic Director Privitera had told the press, but apparently these particular viroenhancers were so new and so different that they hadn't even shown up on the scan.

I wondered how to make Michael understand the depth of my dislike for all this.

"Don't cover the usual police stuff," Michael said, "nor the scientific stuff on bioenhancement. Concentrate on the human angle you do so well. What's the effect of these murders on the other dancers? Has it affected their dancing? Does Privitera seem more confirmed in his company policy now, or has this shaken him enough to consider a change? What's he doing to protect his dancers? How do the parents feel about the youngsters in the ballet school? Are they withdrawing them until the killer is caught?"

I said, "You don't have any sensitivity at all, do you, Michael?"

He said quietly, "Your girl's seventeen, Susan. If you couldn't get her to leave dancing before, you're not going to get her to leave now. Will you do the story?"

I looked again at the scattered pictures of Michael's children. His oldest was at Harvard Law. His second son was a happily married househusband, raising three kids. His third child, a daughter, was doing six-to-ten in Rocky Mountain Maximum Security State Prison for armed robbery. There was no figuring it out. I said, "I'll do the story."

"Good," he said, not looking at me. "Just hold down the metaphors, Susan. You're still too given to metaphors."

"*New York Now* could use a few metaphors. A feature magazine isn't supposed to be a TV holo bite."

"A feature magazine isn't art, either," Michael retorted. "Let's all keep that in mind."

"You're in luck," I said. "As it happens, I'm not a great lover of art."

I couldn't decide whether to tell Deborah I had agreed to write about ballet. She would hate my writing about her world under threat.

Which was a reason both for and against.

September heat and long, cool shadows fought it out over the wide plaza of Lincoln Center. The fountain splashed, surrounded by tourists and students and strollers and derelicts. I thought Lincoln Center was ugly, shoe-box architecture stuck around a charmless expanse of stone unredeemed by a little splashing water. Michael said I only felt that way because I hated New York. If Lincoln Center had been built in Kentucky, he said, I would have admired it.

I had remembered to get the electronic password from Deborah. Since the first murder, the New York State Theater changed it weekly. Late afternoons was heavy rehearsal time; the company was using the stage as well as the new studios. I heard the Spanish bolero from the second act of *Coppelia*. Deborah had been trying to learn it for weeks. The role of Swanilda, the girl who pretends to be a doll, had first made the brilliant Caroline Olson a superstar.

Privitera's office was a jumble of dance programs, costume swatches, and computers. He made me wait for him for twenty minutes. I sat and thought about what I knew about bioenhanced dancers, besides the fact that there weren't supposed to have been any at City Ballet.

There were several kinds of bioenhancement. All of them were experimental, all of them were illegal in the United States, all of them were constantly in flux as new discoveries were made and rushed onto the European, South American, and Japanese markets. It was a new science, chaotic and contradictory, like physics at the start of the last century, or cancer cures at the start of this one. No bioenhancements had been developed specifically for ballet dancers, who were an insignificant portion of the population. But European dancers submitted to experimental versions, as did American dancers who could travel to Berlin or Copenhagen or Rio for the very expensive privilege of injecting their bodies with tiny, unproven biological "machines."

Some nanomachines carried programming that searched out deviations in the body and repaired them to match surrounding tissue. This speeded the healing of some injuries some of the time, or only erratically, or not at all, depending on whom you believed. Jennifer Lang had been receiving these treatments, trying desperately to lessen the injury rate that went hand-in-hand with ballet. The nanomachines were highly experimental, and nobody was sure what long-term effect they might have, reproducing themselves in the human body, interacting with human DNA.

Bone builders were both simpler and more dangerous. They were altered viruses, reprogrammed to change the shape or density of bones. Most of the experimental work had been done on old women with advanced osteoporosis. Some grew denser bones after treatment. The rest didn't. In ballet, the legs are required to rotate 180 degrees in the hip sockets—the famous "turn out" that had destroyed so many dancers' hips and knees. If bones could be altered to swivel 180 degrees *naturally* in their sockets, turn out would cause far less strain and disintegration. Extension could also be higher, making easier the spectacular *arabesques* and *grand battement* kicks.

If the bones of the foot were reshaped, foot injuries could be lessened in the unnatural act of dancing on toe.

Bioenhanced leg muscles could be stronger, for higher jumps, greater speed, more stamina.

Anything that helped metabolic efficiency or lung capacity could help a dancer sustain movements. They could also help her keep down her weight without anorexia, the secret vice of the ballet world.

Dancers in Europe began to experiment with bioenhancement. First cautiously, clandestinely. Then scandalously. Now openly, as a mark of pride. A dancer with the Royal Ballet or the Bolshoi or the Nederlands Dans Theater who didn't have his or her body enhanced was considered undevoted to movement. A dancer at the New York City Ballet who did have his or her body enhanced was considered undevoted to art.

Privitera swept into his office without apology for being late. "Ah, there you are. What can I do for you?" His accent was very light, but still the musical tones of his native Tuscany were there. It gave his words a deceptive intimacy.

"I've come about my daughter, Deborah Anders. She's in the D level at SAB. She's the one who—"

"Yes, yes, yes, I know who she is. I know all my dancers, even the very young ones. Of course. But shouldn't you be talking with Madame Alois? She is the director of our School."

"But you make all the important decisions," I said, trying to smile winningly.

Privitera sat on a wing chair. He must have been in his seventies, yet he moved like a young man: straight strong back, light movements. The famous bright blue eyes met mine shrewdly. His vitality and physical presence on stage had made him a legendary dancer; now he was simply a legend. Whatever he decided the New York City Ballet should be, it became. I didn't like him. The absolute power bothered me—even though it was merely power over an art form seen by only a fraction of the people who watched soccer or football.

"I have three questions about Deborah, Mr. Privitera. First—and I'm sure you hear this all the time—can you give me some idea of her chances as a professional dancer? She'll have to apply to college this fall, if she's going to go, and although what she really wants is to dance professionally, if that's not going to happen then we need to think about other—"

"Yes, yes," Privitera said, swatting away this question like the irrelevancy he considered it to be. "But dance is never a second choice, Ms. Anders."

"Matthews," I said. "Susan Matthews. Anders is Deborah's name."

"If Deborah has it in her to be a dancer, that's what she will be. If not—" He shrugged. People who were not dancers ceased to exist for Anton Privitera.

"That's what I want to know. Does she have it in her to be a professional dancer? Her teachers say she has good musicality and rhythm, but . . ."

My hands gripped together so tightly the skin was gray.

"Perhaps. Perhaps. You must leave it to me to judge when the time comes."

"But that's what I'm saying," I said, as agreeably as I could. "The time *has* come. College—"

"You cannot hurry art. If Deborah is meant to be a dancer she will become one. Leave it to me, dear."

Dear. It was what he called all his dancers. I saw that it had just slipped out. *Leave it to me, dear. I know best.* How often did he say that in class, in rehearsal, during a choreography session, before a performance?

The muted strains of *Coppelia* drifted through the walls. I said, "Then let me ask my second question. As a parent, I'm naturally concerned about Deborah's safety since these awful murders. What steps has City Ballet taken to ensure the safety of the students and dancers?"

The intense eyes contracted to blue shards. But I could see the moment he decided the question was within a parent's right to ask. "The police do not think there is danger to the students. This . . . madman, this *bestia*, apparently attacks only full-fledged dancers, soloists and principals who have tried to reach art through medicine and not through dancing. No dancer in my company or my school is bioenhanced. My dancers believe as I do: You can achieve art only through talent and work, through opening yourself to the dance, not through mechanical aids. What they do at the ABT—that is *not art*! Besides," he added, with an abrupt descent to the practical, "students cannot afford bioenhancing operations."

Idealism enforced by realism—I saw the combination that kept the City Ballet a success, despite the technically superior performances of bioenhanced dancers. I could almost hear dancers and patrons alike: "*The only* real *ballet.*" "*Dance that preserves the necessary illusion that the performers' bodies and the audience's are fundamentally the same.*" "*My dear, he's simply the most wonderful man, saving the precious traditions that made dance great in the first place. We've pledged twenty thousand dollars—*"

I decided to push. "But Jennifer Lang apparently found a way to afford illegal bioenhancements that—"

"That has nothing to do with your Deborah," Privitera said, standing in one fluid movement. His blue eyes were arctic. "Now if you will excuse me, many things call me."

"But you haven't said what you *are* doing for the students' safety," I said, not rising from my chair, trying to sound as if my only interest were parental. "Please, I need to know. Deborah . . ."

He barely repressed a sigh. "We have increased security, Ms. Anders. Electronic surveillance both at SAB and Lincoln Center has been added to, with specifics that I cannot discuss. We have hired additional escorts for those students performing small professional roles who must leave Lincoln Center after ten at night. We have created new emphasis on teaching our young dancers the importance, the complete *necessity*, of training their bodies for dance, not relying on drugs and operations that can only offer tawdry imitations of the genuine experience of art."

I doubted City Ballet had actually done all that: it had only been three days since Jennifer Lang's murder. But Privitera's rhetoric helped me ask my last questions.

"Have any other parents withdrawn their sons and daughters from SAB? For that matter, have any of your dancers altered their performance schedules? How has the company as a whole been affected?"

Privitera looked at me with utter scorn. "If a dancer—even a student dancer—leaves me because some *bestia* is killing performers who do what I have insisted my dancers *not* do—such a so-called dancer should leave. There is no place for such a dancer in my school or my company. Don't you understand, Ms. Anders—this is the *New York City Ballet*."

He left. Through the open door the music was clear: still the Spanish dance from *Coppelia*. The girl who turned herself into a beautiful doll.

Michael was right. I was definitely too given to metaphors.

As I walked down the hall, it occurred to me that Privitera hadn't mentioned increased bioscanning. Surely that would make the most sense—discover which dancers were attaining their high jumps and strong *developpés* through bioenhancement, and then eliminate those dancers from the purity of the company? Before some *bestia* did it first.

Deborah, I knew, was taking an extra class in Studio 3. I shouldn't go. If I went, we would only fight again. I pushed open the door to Studio 3.

I sat on a hard small chair with the ballet mothers waiting for the class to end. I knew better than to talk to any of them. They all wanted their daughters to succeed in ballet.

Barre warm-ups were over. The warm air smelled of rosin on wood. Dancers worked in the center of the floor, sweat dripping off their twirling and leaping bodies. *Bourées, pirouettes, entrechats.* "Non, non!" the teacher called, a retired French dancer whom I had never seen smile. "When you jump, your arms must help. They must pull you through from left to right. Like this."

Deborah did the step wrong. "Non, non!" the teacher called. "Like this!"

Deborah still did it wrong. She grimaced. I felt my stomach tighten.

Deborah tried again. It was still wrong. The teacher gestured toward the back of the room. Deborah walked to the barre and practiced the step alone while the rest of the class went on leaping. *Plié, relevé*, then . . . I didn't know the names of the rest of these steps. Whatever they were, she was still doing them wrong. Deborah tried over and over again, her face clenched. I couldn't watch.

When Deborah was fourteen, she ran away from home in St. Louis to her father's hovel in New York, the same father she had not seen since she was three. She wanted to dance for Anton Privitera, she said. I demanded that Pers, whom I had divorced for desertion, send her back. He refused. Deborah moved into his rat-trap on West 110th, way outside Manhattan's patrolled zone. The lack of police protection didn't deter her, the filthy toilet down the hall didn't deter her, the nine-year-old who was shot dealing sunshine on the stoop next door didn't deter her. When I flew to New York, she cried but refused to go home. She wanted to dance for Anton Privitera.

You can't physically wrestle a fourteen-year-old onto a plane. You can argue, and scream, and threaten, and plead, and cry, but you cannot physically move her. Not without a court order. I filed for breach of custody.

Pers did the most effective thing you can do in the New York judicial system: nothing. Since Pers was an indigent periodically on public assistance, the court appointed a public defender for him. The public defender had 154 cases. He asked for three continuances in a row. The judge had a docket full six months ahead. In less than a year and a half Deborah would be sixteen, legally entitled to leave home. She auditioned for Privitera, and the School of American Ballet accepted her.

Another kid was shot, this one on the subway just before Pers's stop. She was twelve. A boy was knifed, a young mother was raped, houses were torched. Pers's lawyer resigned. Another was appointed, who immediately filed for a continuance.

I quit my job with *St. Louis On-Line* and moved to New York. I left behind a new promotion, a house I loved, and a man I had just started to care about. I found work on Michael's magazine, for half the prestige and two-thirds the salary, in a city twice as expensive and three times as dangerous. I took a two-room apartment on West Seventy-fifth, shabby but decent, just inside the patrolled zone. From my living room window I could see the shimmer of the electronic fence marking the zone. The shimmer bent to exclude all of Central Park north of Seventieth. I bought a gun.

After a few tense weeks, Deborah moved in with me. We lived with piles of toe shoes and surgical tape, with leotards and tights drying on a line strung across the living room, with *Dance* magazine in tattered third-hand copies that would go on to be somebody else's fourth-hand copies, with bunions and inflamed tendons and pulled ligaments. We lived with Deborah's guilt and my anger. At night I lay awake on the pull-out sofa, staring at the ceiling, remembering the day Deborah had started kindergarten and I had opened a college fund for her. She refused now to consider college. She wanted to dance for Anton Privitera.

Privitera had not yet invited her to join the company. She had just turned seventeen. This was her last year with the School. If she weren't invited into the corps de ballet this year, she could forget about dancing for the New York City Ballet.

I sat with the ballet mothers and watched. Deborah's extension was not as high as some of the other girls', her strength not always enough to sustain a slow, difficult move.

So glamorous! the ballet mothers screeched. So beautiful! So wonderful for a girl to know so young what she wants to do with her life! The ballet mothers apparently never saw the constant injuries, the fatigue, the competition that made every friend a deadly rival, the narrowing down of a young world until there is only one definition of success: Do I get to dance for Privitera? Everything else is failure. Life and death, determined at seventeen. "I don't know what I'll do if Jeannie isn't asked to join the company," Jeannie's mother told me. "It would be like we both died. Maybe we would."

"You're so unfair, Mom!" Deborah shouted at me periodically in the tiny, jammed apartment. "You never see the good side of dancing! You're so against me!"

Is it so unfair to hope that your child will be forced out of a life that can only break her body and her heart? A life whose future will belong only to those willing to become human test tubes for inhuman biological experiments?

Nicole Heyer, the dead ABT dancer, had apparently come to the United States from Germany because she could not compete with the dazzlingly bioenhanced dancers in her own country. Jennifer Lang, an ordinary girl from an ordinary Houston family, had lacked the money for major experimentation. To finance her bioenhancements in European labs, she had rented herself out as a glamorous and expensive call girl. Fuck a ballerina! That was how her killer had gotten into her apartment.

In her corner of Studio 3, Deborah finally got the sequence of steps straight, although I could see she was wobbly. She rejoined the class. The room had become as steamy as a Turkish bath. Students ran and leapt the whole length of the hall, corner to corner, in groups of six. "*Grand jeté* in third *arabesque*," Madame called. "Non, non, more extension, Lisa. Victoria, more quick—*vite! vite!* One, two . . . next group."

Deborah ran, jumped, and crashed to the ground.

I stood. Jeannie's mother put a hand on my arm. "You can't go to her," she said matter-of-factly. "You'll interfere with her discipline."

Madame ran gnarled hands over Deborah's ankle. "Lisa, help her to the side. Ninette, go tell the office to send the doctor. Alors, next group, *grand jeté* in third *arabesque*. . . ."

I shook off Jeannie's mother's hand and walked slowly to where Deborah sat, her face twisted in pain.

"It's nothing, Mom."

"Don't move it until the doctor gets here."

"I said it's nothing!"

It was a sprain. The doctor taped it and said Deborah shouldn't dance for a week.

At home she limped to her room. An hour later I found her at the barre.

"Deborah! You heard what the doctor said!"

Her eyes were luminous with tears: Odette as the dying swan, Giselle in the mad scene. "I have to, Mom! You don't understand! They're casting *Nutcracker* in two weeks! I have to be there, dancing!"

"Deborah—"

"I can dance through the injury! Leave me alone!"

Deborah had never yet been cast in Privitera's *Nutcracker*. I watched her transfer her weight gingerly to the injured ankle, wince, and *plié*. She wouldn't meet my eyes in the mirror.

Slowly I closed the door.

That night we had tickets to see *Coppelia*. Caroline Olson skimmed across the stage, barely seeming to touch ground. Her *grand jetés* brought gasps from the sophisticated New York ballet audience. In the final act, when Swanilda danced a tender *pas de deux* with her lover Franz, I could see heads motionless all over the theater, lips slightly parted, barely breathing. Franz turned her slowly in a liquid *arabesque*, her leg impossibly high, followed by *pirouettes*. Swanilda melted from one pose to another, her long silken legs forming a perfect line with her body, flesh made light and strong and elegant as the music itself.

Beside me, I felt Deborah's despair.

3

Caroline jumps. She jumps with her hind legs out straight, one in front and one in back. She runs in circles and jumps again. Dmitri catches her.

"No, no," Mr. Privitera says. "Not like that. *Promenade en couronne,*

ue effacé. Now the lift. Dimitri, you are handling her like a
ke this.''

_icks up Caroline. My ears raise. But Mr. Privitera is safe.
____touch Caroline. Dmitri can touch Caroline. Carlos can touch
Caroline.

Dmitri says, ''It's the damn *dog*. How am I supposed to learn the part with
him staring at me, ready to tear me limb from limb? How the hell am I supposed
to concentrate?''

John Cole sits next to me. John says, ''Dmitri, there's no chance Angel will
attack you. His biochip is state-of-the-art programming. I told you. If you're in
his 'safe' directory, you'd have to actually attack Caroline yourself before Angel
would act, unless Caroline told him otherwise. There's no real danger to break
your concentration.''

Dmitri says, ''And what if I drop her accidentally? How do I know that won't
look like an attack to that dog?''

Caroline sits down. She looks at John. She looks at Dmitri. She does not look
at me. She smiles.

John says, ''A drop is not an attack. Unless Caroline screams—and we all
know she never does, no matter what the injury—there's no danger. Believe
me.''

''I don't,'' Dmitri says.

Everybody stands quiet.

Mr. Privitera says, ''Caroline, dear, let me drop you. Stand up. Ready—
lift.''

Caroline smells surprised. She stands. Mr. Privitera picks up Caroline. She
jumps a little. He picks her up over his head. She falls down hard. My ears raise.
Caroline does not scream. She is not hurt. Mr. Privitera is safe. Caroline said
Mr. Privitera is safe.

''See?'' Mr. Privitera says. He breathes hard. ''No danger. Positions, please.
Promenade en couronne, attitude, arabesque effacé, lift.''

Dmitri picks up Caroline. The music gets loud. John says in my ear, ''Angel—
did Caroline go away from her house last night?''

''Yes,'' I say.

''Where did Caroline go?''

''Left four blocks, right one block. Caroline gave money.''

''The bakery,'' John says. ''Did she go away to any more places, or did she
go home?''

''Caroline goes home last night.''

''Did anyone come to Caroline's house last night?''

''No people come to Caroline's house last night.''

''Thank you,'' John says. He pats me. I feel happy.

Caroline looks at us. A woman ties a long cloth on Caroline's waist. The
woman gives Caroline a piece of wood. Yesterday I ask John what the wood is.
Yesterday John says it is a fan. The music starts, faster. Caroline does not jump.
Yesterday Caroline jumps with the fan.

"Caroline?" Mr. Privitera says. "Start here, dear."

Caroline jumps. She still looks at John. He looks at me.

Some woman here smells of yogurt and a bitch collie in heat.

Caroline opens the bedroom door. She comes out. She wears jeans on her hind legs. She wears a hat on her head. It covers all her fur. She walks to the door. She says to me, "Stay, you old fleabag. You hear me? Stay!"

I walk to the door.

"Christ." Caroline opens the door a little way. She pushes her body through the door. She closes the door. I push through the door hard with her.

"I said stay!" Caroline opens the door again. She pushes me. I do not go inside. Caroline goes inside. I follow Caroline.

"Take two," Caroline says. She opens the door. She walks away. She goes back. She closes the door. She opens the door. She closes the door. She turns around. She goes through the door and closes it hard. She is very fast. I am inside alone.

"Gotcha, Fido!" Caroline says through the door.

I howl. I throw myself against the door. I bark and howl. The light goes on in my head. I howl and howl.

Soon Caroline comes through the door. A man holds her arm. He smells of iron. He talks to a box.

"Subject elected to return to her apartment, sir, rather than have me accompany her to her destination. We're in here now."

Caroline grabs the box. "John, you shit, how *dare* you! You had the dog bio-wired! That's an invasion of privacy, I'll sue your ass off, I'll quit the company, I'll—"

"Caroline," John's voice says. I look. There is no John smell. John is not here. Only John's voice is here. "You have no legal grounds. This man is allowed to accompany you, according to the protection contract you signed. *You* signed it, my dear. As for quitting the City Ballet . . . that's up to you. But while you dance for us, Angel goes where you do. If he gets too excited over not seeing you, the biosignal triggers. Just where were you going that you didn't want Angel with you?"

"To turn tricks on street corners!" Caroline yells. "And I bet he has a homing device embedded in him, too, doesn't he?"

She smells very angry. She is angry at me. I lie on the floor. I put my paws on my head. It is not happy here.

The man says, "Departing the apartment now, sir." He leaves. He takes the small box.

Caroline sits on the floor. Her back is against the door. She looks at me. My paws are on my head. Caroline smells angry.

Nothing happens.

A little later Caroline says, "I guess it's you and me, then. They set it up that way. I'm stuck with you."

I do not move my paws. She still smells angry.

"All right, let's try another approach. Disarm the enemy from within. Psycho-logical sabotage. You don't have any idea what I'm talking about, do you? What did they give you, a five-year-old's IQ? Angel . . .''

I look at Caroline. She says my right name.

". . . tell me about Sam's cat."

"What?"

"Sam's cat. You said that first day you came home with me that you smelled a cat on Sam, the day doorman. Do you still smell it? Can you tell what kind of cat it is?"

I am confused. Caroline says nice words. Caroline smells angry. Her back is too straight. Her fur is wrong.

"Is it a male cat or a female cat? Can you tell that?"

"A female cat," I say. I remember the cat smell. My muscles itch.

"Did you want to chase it?"

"I must never chase cats. I must protect Caroline."

Caroline's smell changes. She leans close to my ear.

"But did you *want* to chase it, Angel? Did you want to get to behave like a dog?"

"I want to protect Caroline."

"Hoo boy. They did a job on *you*, didn't they, boy?"

The words are too hard. Caroline still smells a little angry. I do not understand.

"It's nothing compared to what they're doing in South America and Europe," she says. Her body shakes.

"Are you hurt?" I say.

Caroline puts a hand on my back. The hand is very soft. She says no words.

I am happy. Caroline talks to me. She tells me about dancing. Caroline is a dancer. She jumps and runs in circles. She stands high on her hind legs. People come in cars to watch her. The people are happy when Caroline dances.

We walk outside. I protect Caroline. We go many places. Caroline gives me cake and hot dogs. There are many smells. Sometimes Caroline and I follow the smells. We see many dogs and many cats. The man with the small box comes with us sometimes. John says the man is safe.

"What if I tell Angel you're not 'safe'?" Caroline says to the man. He follows us on a long walk. "What if I order him to tear you limb from limb?" She smells angry again.

"You don't have programming override capacity. The biochip augmenting his bioenhancement is very specific, Ms. Olson. I'm hardwired in."

"I'll bet," Caroline says. "Did anybody ask Angel if he wants this life?"

The man smiles.

We go to Lincoln Center every day. Caroline dances there. She dances in the day. She dances at night. More people watch at night.

John asks me where Caroline and I go. Every day I tell him.

Nobody tries to touch Caroline. I protect her.

"I can't do it," Caroline tells a man on the street corner. The man stands very close to Caroline. I growl soft. "For God's sake, Stan, don't touch me. The dog. And I'm probably being watched."

"Do they care *that* much?"

"I could blow the whistle on the whole unofficial charade," Caroline says. She smells tired. "No matter what Privitera's delusions are. But then we'd lose our chance, wouldn't we?"

"Thanks for the time," the man says, loud. He smiles. He walks away.

Later John says, "Who did Caroline talk to?"

"A man," I say. "He wants the time."

Later Caroline says, "Angel, we're going tonight to see my mother."

4

Demonstrators dyed the fountain at Lincoln Center blood red.

They marched around the gruesome jets of water, shouting and resisting arrest. I sprinted across the plaza, trying to get there to see which side they were on before the police carted all of them away. Even from this distance I could tell they weren't dancers, not with those thick bodies. The electronic placards dissolved from HOW MANY MUST DIE FROM DENYING EVOLUTION! to FREE MEDICAL RESEARCH FROM GOVERNMENT STRAIGHTJACKETS! to MY BODY BELONGS TO ME! Pro-human bioenhancement, then. A holograph projector, which a cop was shutting down, spewed out a ten-foot high holo of Jane and June Welsh, Siamese twins who had been successfully separated only after German scientists had bioenhanced their bodies to force alterations in major organs. The holo loop showed the attached twins dragging each other around, followed by the successfully separated twins waving gaily. The cop did something and Jane and June disappeared.

"They died," I said to a demonstrator, a slim boy wearing a FREE MY BODY! button. "Ultimately, neither of their hearts could stand the stress of bioenhancement."

He glared at me. "That was their risk to take, wasn't it?"

"Their combined IQ didn't equal your weight. How could they evaluate risk?"

"This is a *revolution*, lady. In any revolution you have casualties that—" A cop grabbed his arm. The boy took a wild swing at him and the cop pressed his nerve gun to the boy's neck. He dropped peacefully, smiling.

Abruptly more people gathered, some of them wilier than the boy. Demonstrators stood with their hands on their heads, singing slogans. Media robocams zoomed in from the sky; the live crews would be here in minutes. A group of counter-demonstrators formed across the plaza, in front of the Met. I backed away slowly, hands on my head, not singing—and stopped abruptly halfway across the chaotic plaza.

An old woman in a powerchair was watching the demonstration with the most intense expression I had ever seen. It was as if she were watching a horrifying execution, judging it judiciously as art. Bodyguards flanked the chair. She wore an expensive, pale blue suit and large, perfectly matched pearls. Her wrinkled, cold face was completely familiar. This was how Caroline Olson would look in forty years, if she refused all cosmetic treatment.

She caught me watching her. Her expression didn't change. It passed over me as if I didn't exist.

I took the chance. "Ms. Olson?"

She didn't deny the name. "Yes?"

"I'm a reporter with *New York Now*, doing an article on the New York City Ballet. I'd like to ask you a few questions about your daughter Caroline, if that's all right."

"I never give interviews."

"Yes, ma'am. Just a few informal questions—you must be so proud of Caroline. But are you worried about her safety in light of the recent so-called ballerina murders?"

She shocked me. She smiled. "No, not at all."

"You're *not*?"

She gazed at the break-up of the demonstration. "Do you know the work on dancers' bodies they're doing in Berlin?"

"No, I—"

"Then you have no business interviewing anyone on the subject." She watched the last of the demonstrators being dragged away by the cops. "The New York City Ballet is finished. The future of the art lies with bioenhancement."

I must have looked like a fish, staring at her with my mouth working. "But Caroline is the prima ballerina, she's only twenty-six—"

"Caroline had a good run. For a dancer." She made a signal, an imperious movement of her hand, and one of the bodyguards turned her chair and wheeled it away.

I trotted after it. "But, Ms. Olson, are you saying you think your daughter and her whole company *should* be replaced by bioenhanced dancers because they can achieve higher lifts, fewer injuries, more spectacular turn out—"

"I never give interviews," she said, and the other bodyguard moved between us.

I gazed after her. She had spoken about Caroline as if her daughter were an obsolete Buick. It took me a moment to remember to pull out a notebook and tell it what she had said.

Someone dumped something into the fountain. Immediately the red disappeared and the water spouted clear. A bioenhanced dog trotted over and lapped at the water, the dog's owner patiently holding the leash while his pink-furred, huge-eyed poodle drank its fill.

After an hour at a library terminal at *New York Now*, I knew that Anna Olson was a major contributor to the American Ballet Theater but not to the New York City Ballet, where her daughter had chosen to dance. Caroline's father was dead. He had left his widow an East Side mansion, three Renoirs, and a fortune invested in Peruvian sugar, Japanese weather-control equipment, and German pharmaceuticals. According to *Ballet News*, mother and daughter were estranged. To find out more than that, I'd need professional help.

Michael didn't want to do it. "There's no money for that kind of research, Susan. Not to even mention the ethics involved."

"Oh, come on, Michael. It's no worse than using criminal informers for any other story."

"This isn't your old newspaper job, Susie. We're a feature magazine, remember? We don't use informants, and we don't do investigative reporting." He leaned against his desk, his peeled-egg face troubled.

"The magazine doesn't have to do any investigating at all. Just give me the number. I know you know it. If I'd been doing the job I should have for the last two years instead of sulking because I hate New York, I'd know it, too. Just the number, Michael. That's all. Neither you nor the magazine will even be mentioned."

He ran his hand through his hair. For the first time, I noticed that it was thinning. "All right. But, Susan—don't get obsessed. For your own sake." He looked at the picture of his daughter doing time in Rock Mountain.

I called the Robin Hood and arranged to see him. He was young—they all are—maybe as young as twenty, operating out of a dingy apartment in Tribeca. I couldn't judge his equipment: beyond basic literacy, computers are as alien to me as dancers. Like dancers, they concentrate on one aspect of the world, dismissing the rest.

The Robin Hood furnished the usual proofs that he could tap into private databanks, that he could access government records, and that his translation programs could handle international airline d-bases. He promised a two-day turnaround. The price was astronomical by my standards, although probably negligible by his. I transferred the credits from my savings account, emptying it.

I said, "You do know that the original Robin Hood transferred goods for free?"

He said, not missing a beat, "The original Robin Hood didn't have to pay for a Seidman-Nuwer encrypter."

I really hadn't expected him to know who the original Robin Hood was.

When I got home, Deborah had fallen asleep across her bed, still dressed in practice clothes. The toes of her tights were bloody. A new pair of toe shoes was shoved between the bedroom door and the door jamb; she softened the stiff boxes by slamming the door on them. There were three E-mail messages for her from SAB, but I erased them all. I covered her, closed her door, and let her sleep.

I met with the Robin Hood two days later. He handed me a sheaf of hardcopy. "The City Ballet injury records show two injuries for Caroline Olson in the last four years, which is as far back as the files are kept. One shin splint, one pulled ligament. Of course, if she had other injuries and saw a private doctor, that wouldn't show up on their records, but if she did see one it wasn't anybody on the City Ballet Recommended Physician List. I checked that."

"Two injuries? In four *years*?"

"That's what the record shows. These here are four-year records of City Ballet bioscans. All negative. Nobody shows any bioenhancement, not even Jennifer Lang. These are the City Ballet attendance figures over ten years, broken down by subscription and single-event tickets."

I was startled; the drop in attendance over the last two years was more dramatic than the press had ever indicated.

"This one is Mrs. Anna Olson's tax return for last year. All that income—all of it—is from investments and interests, and none of it is tied up in trusts or entails. She controls it all, and she can waste the whole thing if she wants to. You asked about unusual liquidation of stock in the last ten years: There wasn't any. There's no trust fund for Caroline Olson. This is Caroline's tax return— only her salary with City Ballet, plus guest appearance fees. Hefty, but nothing like what the old lady controls.

"This last is the air flight stuff you wanted: No flights on major commercial airlines out of the country for Caroline in the last six years, except when the City Ballet did its three international tours, and then Caroline flew pretty much with everybody else in the group. Of course if she did go to Rio or Copenhagen or Berlin, she could have gone by chartered plane or private jet. My guess is private jet. Those aren't required to file passenger lists."

It wasn't what I'd hoped to find. Or rather, it was half of what I'd hoped. No dancer is injured that seldom. It just doesn't happen. I pictured Caroline Olson's amazing extension, her breathtaking leaps; she reached almost the height expected of male superstars. And her crippled horror of a mother had huge amounts of money. *"Caroline had a good run."*

I would bet my few remaining dollars that Caroline Olson was bioenhanced, no matter what her bioscans said. Jennifer Lang's had been negative, too. Apparently the DNA hackers were staying one step ahead of the DNA security checkers. Although it was odd that the records didn't show a single dancer trying to get away with bioenhancement, not even once, even in the face of Privitera's fervency. There are always some people who value their own career advancement over the received faith.

But I had assumed that Caroline would have needed to leave the country. Bioenhancement labs are large, full of sensitive and costly and nonportable equipment and dozens of technicians. Not easy to hide. Police investigators had traced both Jennifer Lang and Nicole Heyer to Danish labs. I didn't think one could exist illegally in New York.

Maybe I was wrong.

The Robin Hood watched me keenly. In the morning light from the window he looked no older than Deborah. He had thick brown hair, nice shoulders. I wondered if he had a life outside his lab. So many of them didn't.

"Thanks," I said.

"Susan—"

"What?"

He hesitated. "I don't know what you're after with this data. But I've worked with friends of Michael's before. If you're thinking about trying to leverage anything to do with human bioenhancement . . .''

"Yeah?"

"Don't." He looked intently at his console. "That's out of both our leagues. Magazine reporters are very small against the kind of high-stakes shit those guys are into."

"Thanks for the advice," I said. And then, on impulse, "Would you by any chance like a home-cooked meal? I have a daughter about your age, seventeen, she's a dancer. . . .''

He stared at me in disbelief. He shook his head. "You're a *client*, Susan. And anyway, I'm twenty-six. And I'm married." He shook his head again. "And if you don't know enough not to ask a Robin Hood to dinner, you *really* don't know enough to mess around with bioenhancement. That stuff's life or death."

Life or death. Enough for a bioenhancement corporation to murder two dancers?

But I rejected that idea. It was always too easy to label the corporations the automatic bad guys. That was the stuff of cheap holovids. Most corporate types I knew just tried to keep ahead of the IRS.

I said, "Most life-and-death stuff originates at home."

I could feel him shaking his head as I left, but I didn't turn around.

5

Caroline and I ride in a taxi. It is late at night. We ride across the park. Then we ride more. Caroline says words to a gate. A man opens the gate to a very big house. He smells surprised. He wears pajamas. "Miss Caroline!"

"Hello, Seacomb. Is my mother in?"

"She's asleep, of course. If there's an emergency—"

"No emergency. But my apartment pipes sprung a leak and I'll be spending the night here. This is my dog, Angel. Angel, Seacomb is safe."

"Of course, miss," Seacomb says. He smells very unhappy. "It's just—"

"Just that you have orders not to let me use this house?"

"No, miss," the man says. "My orders are to let you use the house as you choose. Only—"

"Of course they are," Caroline says. "My mother wants me to grovel back here. She's been planning for that. Well, here I am. Only she's taken a sleeping pill and is out cold until morning, right?"

"Yes, miss," the man says. He smells very unhappy. There are no cats or dogs in this place, but there are mice. The mice droppings smell interesting.

"I'll sleep in the downstairs study. And, oh, Seacomb, I'm expecting guests. Please disable the electric gate. They'll use the back entrance, and I'll let them in myself. You needn't take any trouble about it."

"It's no trouble to—"

"I said I'll let them in myself."

"Yes, miss," Seacomb says. He smells very very unhappy.

He leaves. Caroline and I go down stairs. Caroline drinks. She gives me water. I smell a mouse in a cupboard. My ears raise. There are interesting things here.

"Well, Angel, here we are at my mother's house. Do you remember your mother, boy?"

"No," I say. I am confused. The words are a little hard.

"There are some people coming for a party. Some dancers. Kristine Meyers is coming. You remember Kristine Meyers?"

"Yes," I say. Kristine Meyers dances with Caroline. They run in circles and jump high. Caroline jumps higher.

"We're going to talk about dancing, Angel. This is a prettier house than mine to talk about dancing. This is a good house for a party, which is what we're going to have. My mother lets me use her house for parties. Remember that, boy."

Later Caroline opens the door. Some people stand there. We go into the basement. Kristine Meyers is there. She smells frightened. Some men are with her. They carry papers. They talk a long time.

"Here, Angel, have a pretzel," a man says. "It's a party."

Some people dance to a radio. Kristine smells angry and confused. Her fur stands up. Caroline says words to her. The words are hard. The words are long. I have a pretzel. Nobody touches Caroline.

We are there all night. Kristine cries.

"Her boyfriend is gone," Caroline says to me.

In early morning we go home. We go in a taxi. Somebody is sick in the taxi yesterday. It smells bad. Caroline sleeps. I sleep. Caroline does not go to class.

In the afternoon we go to Lincoln Center. Kristine is there. She sleeps on a couch in the lounge. Caroline dances with Dmitri.

John Cole bends close to my ear. "You went out with Caroline all last night."

"Yes," I say.

"Where did you go?"

"We go to Caroline's mother's house. We go to a party. Caroline's mother lets Caroline use her house for parties."

"Who was at this party?"

"Dancers. Kristine is at the party. Kristine is safe."

John looks at Kristine. She still sleeps on the couch.

"Who else was at the party? What did they do?"

I remember hard. "Dancers are at the party. We eat pretzels. We talk about dancing. People dance to the radio. Nobody touches Caroline. There is music."

John's body relaxes. "Good," he says. "Okay."

"I like pretzels," I say. But John does not give me a pretzel today.

Caroline and I walk in the park. There are many good smells. Caroline sits under a tree. The long fur on her head falls down. She pats my head. She gives me a cookie.

"It's easy for you, isn't it, Angel?" Caroline says.

I say, "The words are hard."

"You like being a dog? A bioenhanced servant dog?"

"The words are hard."

"Are you happy, Angel?"

"I am happy. I love Caroline."

She pats my head again. The sun is warm. The smells are good. I close my eyes.

"I love to dance," Caroline says. "And I hate that I love it."

I open my eyes. Caroline smells unhappy.

"Goddamn it, I love it anyway. I do. Even though it wasn't my choice. You didn't choose what you are, either, did you, Angel? They goddamn made you what they needed you to be. Yet you love it. And for you there's no account due."

The words are too hard. I put my nose into Caroline's front legs. She puts her front legs around me. She holds me tight.

"It's not *fair*," Caroline whispers into my fur.

Caroline does not hold me yesterday. She holds me today. I am happy. But Caroline smells unhappy.

Where is my happy if Caroline smells unhappy?

I do not understand.

6

Deborah didn't get cast in *Nutcracker*. An SAB teacher told her she might want to consider auditioning for one of the regional companies rather than City Ballet—a death sentence, from her point of view. She told me this quietly, without histrionics, sitting cross-legged on the floor sewing ribbons onto a pair of toe shoes. Not wanting to say the wrong thing, I said nothing, contenting myself with touching her hair, coiled at the nape of her neck into the ballerina bun. Two days later she told me she was dropping out of high school.

"I need the time to dance," she said. "You just don't understand, Mom."

The worst thing I could do was let her make me into the enemy. "I do understand, honey. But there will be lots of time to dance after you finish school. And if you don't—"

"Finishing is a year away! I can't afford the time. I have to take more classes, work harder, get asked into the company. *This year*. I'm sorry, Mom, but I just can't waste my time on all that useless junk in school."

I locked my hands firmly on my lap. "Well, let's look at this reasonably. Suppose after all you do get asked to join the company—"

"I *will* be asked! I'll work so hard they'll have to ask me!"

"All right. Then you dance with them until, say, you're thirty-five. At thirty-five you have over half your life left. You saw what happened to Carla Cameri and Maura Jones." Carla's hip had disintegrated; Maura's Achilles tendon had forced her into retirement at thirty-two. Both of them worked in a clothing store, for pitifully small salaries. Dancers didn't get pensions unless they'd been with the same company for ten years, a rarity in the volatile world of artistic directors with absolute power, who often fired dancers because they were remaking a company into a different "look."

I pressed my point. "What will you do at thirty or thirty-five with your body debilitated and without even a high school education?"

"I'll teach. I'll coach. I'll go back to school. Oh, Mom, how do I know? That's decades away! I have to think about what I need to do for my career now!"

No mother love is luminous enough to make a seventeen-year-old see herself at thirty-five.

I said, "No, Deborah. You can't quit school. I'd have to sign for you, and I won't."

"Daddy already did."

We looked at each other. It was too late; she'd already made me into the enemy. Because she needed one.

She said, in a sudden burst of passion, "You don't understand! You never felt about your job the way I feel about ballet! You never loved anything enough to give up everything else for it!" She rushed to her room and slammed the door. I put my head in my hands.

After a while, I started to laugh. I couldn't help it. *Never loved anything enough to give up everything else for it.*

Right.

Pers wasn't available to yell at. I phoned six times. I left messages on E-mail, even though I had no idea whether he had a terminal. I made the trip out of the protected zone to his apartment. The area was worse than I remembered: glass, broken machinery, shit, drug paraphernalia. The cab driver was clearly eager to leave, but I made him wait while I questioned a kid who came out of Pers's building. The boy, about eight, had a long pus-encrusted cut down one cheek.

"Do you know when Pers Anders usually comes home? He lives in 2C."

The kids stared at me, expressionless. The cab driver leaned out and said, "One more minute and I'm leaving, lady."

I pulled out a twenty-dollar bill and held it close to me. "When does Pers Anders usually come home?"

"He moved."

"Moved?"

"Left his stuff. He say he go someplace better than this shithole. I hear him say it. Don't you try to prong me, lady. You give me that money."

"Do you know the address?"

He greeted this with the scorn it deserved. I gave him the money.

Deborah left school and started spending all day and much of the night at Lincoln Center. Finally I walked over to SAB and caught her just before a partnering class. She had twisted a bright scarf around her waist, over her leotard, and her sweaty hair curled in tendrils where it had escaped her bun.

"Deborah, why didn't you tell me your father had moved?"

She looked wary, wiping her face with a towel to gain time. "I didn't think you'd care. You hate him."

"As long as you still visit him, I need to know where he is."

She considered this. Finally she gave me the address. It was a good one, in the new luxury condos where the old main library had been.

"How can Pers afford *that*?"

"He didn't say. Maybe he's got a job. Mom, I have class."

"Pers is allergic to jobs."

"Mom, Mr. Privitera is teaching this class *himself*!"

I didn't stay to watch class. On the way out, I passed Privitera, humming to himself on his way to elate or cast down his temple virgins.

The police had released no new information on the ballerina murders.

I turned in the article on the New York City Ballet. It seemed to me neither good nor bad; everything important about the subject didn't fit the magazine's focus. There weren't too many metaphors. Michael read it without comment. I worked on an article about computerized gambling, and another about holographic TV. I voted in the presidential election. I bought Christmas presents.

But every free minute, all autumn and early winter, I spent at the magazine library terminals, reading about human bioenhancement, trying to guess what Caroline Olson was having done to herself. What might someday lie in Deborah's future, if she were as big a fool then as she was being now.

"Don't get obsessed," Michael had said.

The literature was hard to interpret. I wasn't trained in biology, and as far as I could see, the cutting-edge research was chaotic, with various discoveries being reported one month, contradicted the next. All the experiments were carried out in other countries, which meant they were reported in other languages, and I didn't know how far to trust the biases of the translators. Most of them seemed to be other scientists in the same field. This whole field seemed to me like a canoe rushing toward the falls: nobody in charge, both oars gone, control impossible.

I read about splendid, "revolutionary" advances in biological nanotechnology that always seemed under development, or not quite practical yet, or hotly disputed by people practicing other kinds of revolutionary advances. I read about genesplicing retroviruses and setting them loose in human organs to accomplish potentially wonderful things. Elimination of disease. Perfect metabolic functioning. Immortality. The studies were always concerned with one small, esoteric facet of scientific work, but the "Conclusions" sections were often grandiose, speculating wildly.

I even picked up hints of experimental work on altering genetic makeup *in vitro*, instead of trying to reshape adult bodies. Some scientists seemed to think this might actually be easier to accomplish. But nowhere in the world was it legal to experiment on an embryo not destined for abortion, an embryo that would go on to become a human being stuck with the results of arbitrary and untested messing around with his basic cellular blueprints. Babies were not tinker toys—or dogs. The Copenhagen Accord, signed twenty-seven years ago by most technologically civilized countries, had seen to that. The articles on genetic modification *in vitro* were carefully speculative.

But then so was nearly everything else I read. The proof was walking around in inaccessible foreign hospitals, or living in inaccessible foreign cities—the anonymity of the experimental subjects seemed to be a given, which also made me wonder how many of them were experimental casualties. And if so, of what kind.

Michael wasn't going to want any article built on this tentative speculation. Lawsuits would loom. But I was beyond caring what Michael wanted.

I learned that the Fifth International Conference on Human Bioenhancement was going to be held in Paris in late April. After paying the Robin Hood, I had no money left for a trip to Paris. Michael would have to pay for it. I would have to give him a reason.

One night in January I did a stupid thing. I went alone to Lincoln Center and waited by the stage door of the New York State Theater. Caroline Olson came out at 11:30, dressed in jeans and parka, accompanied only by a huge black Doberman on the most nominal of leashes. They walked south on Broadway, to an all-night restaurant. I sat myself at the next table.

For the past few months, her reviews had not been good. "A puzzling and disappointing degeneration," said *The New Yorker*. "Technical sloppiness not associated with either Olson or Privitera," said *Dance Magazine*. "This girl is in trouble, and Anton Privitera had better find out what kind of trouble and move to correct it," said the *Times On-Line*.

Caroline ate abstractedly, feeding bits to the dog, oblivious to the frowns of a fastidious waiter who was undoubtedly an out-of-work actor. Up close, the illusion of power and beauty I remembered from *Coppelia* evaporated. She looked like just another mildly pretty, self-absorbed, overly thin young woman. Except for the dog, the waiter/actor didn't give her a second glance.

"We go now?" the dog said.

I choked on my sandwich. Caroline glanced at me absently. "Soon, Angel."

She went on eating. I left, waited for her, and followed her home. She and the dog lived on Central Park South, a luxury building where the late-night electronic surveillance system greeted them both by name.

I took a cab home. Deborah had never mentioned that the City Ballet prima ballerina was protected by a bioenhanced Doberman. She knew I'd written the story about the ballerina murders. Anton Privitera hadn't mentioned it, either, in his press conference about dancer safety. I wondered why not. While I was parceling out wonder, I devoted some to the question of City Ballet's infrequent, superficial, and always-positive bioscans. Shouldn't a company devoted to the religion of "natural art" be more zealous about ferreting out heretics?

Unless, of course, somebody didn't really want to know.

Privitera? But that was hard to reconcile with his blazing, intolerant sincerity.

It occurred to me that I had never seen an admittedly bioenhanced dancer perform. Until tonight, I'd gone to finished performances rarely and only with Deborah, who of course scorned such perverts and believed that they had nothing to teach her.

She was out when I got back to our apartment. Each week, it seemed, she was gone more. I fell asleep, waiting for her to come home.

7

Snow falls. It is cold. Caroline and I walk to Lincoln Center. A man takes Caroline's purse. He runs. Caroline says "Shit!" Then she says, "Angel? Go stop him!" She drops my leash.

I run and jump on the man. He screams. I do not hurt him. Caroline says *stop him*. She does not say *attack him*. So I stand on the man's chest and growl and nip at his foreleg. He brings out a knife. Then I bite him. He drops the knife and screams again. The police come.

"Holy shit," Caroline says to me. "You really do that. You really do."

"I protect Caroline," I say.

Caroline talks to police. Caroline talks to reporters. I get a steak to eat.

I am happy.

The snow goes away. The snow is there many many days, but it goes away. We visit Caroline's mother's house for two more parties in the basement. It gets warm in the park. Ducks live in the water again. Flowers grow. Caroline says not to dig up flowers.

I lie backstage. Caroline dances on stage. John and Mr. Privitera stand beside me. They smell unhappy. John's shoes smell of tar and food and leaves and cats and other good things. I sniff John's shoes.

"She looks exhausted," John says. "She's giving it everything she's got, but it's just not there, Anton."

Mr. Privitera says no words. He watches Caroline dance.

"William Scholes attacked again in the *Times*. He said that watching her had become painful—'like watching a reed grown stiff and brittle.' "

"I will talk to her again," Mr. Privitera says.

"Scholes called the performance 'a travesty,' " John says.

Caroline comes backstage. She limps. She wipes her face with a towel. She smells afraid.

"Dear, I'd like to see you," Mr. Privitera says.

We go to Caroline's dressing room. Caroline sits down. She trembles. Her body smells sick. I growl. Caroline puts a hand on my head.

Mr. Privitera says, "First of all, dear, I have good news for all of us. The police have caught that unspeakable murderer who killed Jennifer Lang and the ABT dancer."

Caroline sits up a little straighter. Her smell changes. "They did! How?"

"They caught him breaking into the Plaza Hotel room where Marie D'Arbois is staying while she guests with ABT."

"Is Marie—"

"She's fine. She wasn't alone, she had a lover or something with her. The madman just got careless. The police are holding back the details. Marie, of course, is another of those bioenhanced dancers. I don't know if you ever saw her dance.''

''I did,'' Caroline says. ''I thought she was wonderful.''

Caroline and Mr. Privitera look hard at each other. They smell ready to attack. But they do not attack. I am confused. Mr. Privitera is safe. He may touch Caroline.

Mr. Privitera says, ''We must all be grateful to the police. Now there's something else I need to discuss with you, dear.''

Caroline closes her hand on my fur. She says, ''Yes?''

''I want you to take a good long rest, dear. You know your dancing has deteriorated. You tell me you're not doing drugs or working sketchily, and I believe you. Sometimes it helps a dancer to take a rest from performing. Take class, eat right, get strong. In the fall we'll see.''

''You're telling me you're cutting me from the summer season at Saratoga.''

''Yes, dear.''

Caroline is quiet. Then she says, ''There's nothing wrong with me. My timing has just been a little off, that's all.''

''Then take the summer to work on your timing. And everything else.''

Mr. Privitera and Caroline look hard at each other again. Caroline's hand still pulls my fur. It hurts a little. I do not move.

Mr. Privitera leans close to Caroline. ''Listen, dear. *Jewels* was one of your best roles. But *tonight* . . . and not just *Jewels*. You wobbled and wavered through *Starscape*. Your Nikiya in the 'Shades' section of *La Bayadère* was . . . embarrassing. There is no other word. You danced as if you had never learned the steps. And you couldn't even complete the *Don Quixote pas de deux* at the gala.''

''I fell! Dancers get injured all the time! My injury rate compared to—''

''You've missed rehearsals and even performances,'' Mr. Privitera says. He stands up. ''I'm sorry, dear. Take the summer. Rest. Work. In the fall, we'll see.''

Caroline says, ''What about the last two weeks of the season?''

Mr. Privitera says, ''I'm sorry, dear.''

He walks to the door. He puts his hand on the door. He says, ''Oh, at least you won't have to be burdened with that dog anymore. Now that the madman's been caught, I'll have John notify the protection agency to come pick it up.''

Caroline raises her head. Her fur all stands up. She smells angry. Soon she runs out the door. Mr. Privitera is gone. She runs to the offices. ''John! John, you bastard!''

The office hall is dark. The doors do not open. John is not here.

Caroline runs up steps to the offices. She falls. She falls down some of the steps and hits the wall. She lies on the floor. She holds her hind foot and smells hurt.

''Angel,'' she says. ''Go get somebody to help me.''

I go to the lounge. One dancer is there. She says, ''Oh! I'm sorry, I didn't know that anybody—Angel?''

''Caroline is hurt,'' I say. ''Come. Come fast.''

She comes. Caroline says, "Who are you? No, wait—Deborah, right? From the corps?"

"No, I'm not . . . I haven't been invited to join the corps yet. I'm a student at SAB. I'm just here a lot. . . . Are you hurt? Can you stand?"

"Help me up," Caroline says. "Angel, Deborah is safe."

Deborah tries to pick up Caroline. Caroline makes a little noise. She cannot stand. Deborah gets John. He picks up Caroline.

"It's nothing," she says. "No doctor. Just get me a cab . . . dammit, John, don't fuss, it's nothing!" She looks at John hard. "You want to take Angel away from me."

John smells surprised. He says, "Who told you that?"

"His Majesty himself. But now you've decided whatever you thought I was doing so privately doesn't matter any more, is that right?"

"It's a mistake. Of course you can keep the dog. Anton doesn't understand," John says. He smells angry.

"No, I'll just bet he doesn't," Caroline says. "You might have picked a kinder way to tell me I'm through at City Ballet."

"You're not through, Caroline," John says. Now he smells bad. His words are not right. He smells like the man who takes Caroline's purse.

"Right," Caroline says. She sits in the cab.

Deborah steps back. She smells surprised.

"I'm keeping the dog," Caroline says. "So we're in agreement, aren't we, John? Come on, Angel. Let's go home."

We go to class. Caroline cannot dance. She tries and then stops. She sits in a corner. Mr. Privitera sits in another corner. Caroline watches Deborah. The dancers raise one hind leg. They spin and jump.

Madame holds up her hand. The music stops. "Deborah, let us see that again, *s'il vous plaît*. Alone."

The other dancers move away. They look at each other. They smell surprised. The music starts again and Deborah raises one hind leg very high. She spins and jumps.

Mr. Privitera says, "Let me see the bolero from *Coppelia*. Madame says you know it."

"Y-yes," Deborah says. She dances alone.

"Very nice, dear," Mr. Privitera says. "You are much improved."

The other dancers look at each other again.

Everybody dances.

Caroline watches Deborah hard.

8

Deborah's face looked like every Christmas morning in the entire world. She grabbed both my hands. "They invited me to join the company!"

My suitcase lay open on the bed, surrounded by discarded clothes I wasn't taking to the bioenhancement conference in Paris. My daughter picked up a pile of spidersilk blouses and hurled them into the air. In the soft April air from the open window the filmy, artificial material drifted and danced. "I can't believe it! They asked me to join the company! I'm *in*!"

She whirled around the tiny room, rising on toe in her street shoes, laughing and exclaiming. My silence went unnoticed. Deborah did an *arabesque* to the bedpost; then plopped herself down on my best dress. "Don't you want to know what happened, Mom?"

"What happened, Deborah?"

"Well, Mr. Privitera came to watch class, and Madame asked me to repeat the variation alone. God, I thought I'd die. Then *Mr. Privitera*—not Madame— asked me to do the bolero from *Coppelia*. For an awful minute I couldn't remember a single step. Then I did, and he said it was very nice! He said I was much improved!"

Accolades from the king. But even in my numbness I could see there was something she wasn't telling me.

"I thought you told me the company doesn't choose any new dancers this close to the end of the season?"

She sobered immediately. "Not usually. But Caroline Olson was fired. She missed rehearsals and performances, and she wasn't even taking the trouble to prepare her roles. Her reviews have been awful."

"I saw them," I said.

Deborah looked at me sharply. "Ego, I guess. Caroline's always been sort of a bitch. So apparently they're not letting her go to Saratoga, because Tina Patrochov and a guest artist are dividing her roles, and Mr. Privitera told Jill Kerrigan to learn Tina's solo from *Sleeping Beauty*. So that left a place in the corps de ballet, and they chose me!"

I had had enough time to bring myself to say it.

"Congratulations, sweetheart."

"When does your plane for Paris leave?"

This non-sequitur—if it was that—turned me back to my packing. "Seven tonight."

"And you'll be gone ten days. You'll have a great time in Paris. Maybe the next time the company goes on tour, I'll go with them!"

She whirled out of the room.

I sat at the end of the bed, holding onto the bedpost. When Deborah was three, she'd wanted to ride on a camel. Somehow it had become an obsession. She talked about camels in daycare, at dinnertime, at bedtime. She drew pictures of camels, misshapen things with one huge hump. Camels were in short supply in St. Louis. Ignore it, everyone said, kids forget these things, she'll get over it. Deborah never forgot. She didn't get over it. Pers had just left us, and I was consumed with the anxiety of a single parent. Finally I paid a friend to tie a large wad of hay under a blanket on his very old, very swaybacked horse. A Peruvian camel, I told my three-year-old. A very special kind. You can have a ride.

"That's not a camel," Deborah had said, with nostril-lifted disdain. "That's a heffalunt!"

I read last week in *World* that the animal-biotech scientists have built a camel with the flexible trunk of an elephant. The trunk can lift up to forty-five pounds. It is expected to be a useful beast of burden in the Sahara.

I finished packing for Paris.

Paris in April was an unending gray drizzle. The book and software stalls along the Seine kept up their electronic weather shields, giving them the hazy, streaming-gutter look of abandoned outhouses. The gargoyles on Notre Dame looked insubstantial in the rain, irrelevant in the face of camels with trunks. The French, as usual, conspired to make Americans—especially Americans who speak only rudimentary French—feel crass and barbaric. My clothes were wrong. My desire for a large breakfast was wrong. The Fifth International Conference on Human Bioenhancement had lost my press credentials.

The conference was held in one of the huge new hotels in Neuilly, near the EuroDisney Gene Zoo. I couldn't decide if this was an attempt to provide entertainment or irony. Three hundred scientists and doctors, a hundred press, and at least that many industrial representatives, plus groupies, thronged the hotel. The scientists presented papers; the industrial reps, mostly from biotech or pharmaceutical firms, presented "infoforums." The moment I walked in, carrying provisional credentials, I felt the tension, a peculiar kind of tension instantly recognizable to reporters. Something big was going on. Big and unpleasant.

From the press talk in the bar I learned that the presentation to not miss was Thursday night by Dr. Gerard Taillebois of the Pasteur Research Institute, in conjunction with Dr. Greta Erbland of Steckel und Osterhoff. This pairing of a major research facility with a commercial biotech firm was common in Europe. Sometimes the addition of a hospital made it a triumvirate. A hand-written addendum on the program showed that the presentation had been moved from the Napoleon Room to the Grand Ballroom. I checked out the room; it was approximately the size of an airplane hangar. Hotel employees were setting up acres of chairs.

I asked a garçon to point out Dr. Taillebois to me. He was a tall, bald man in his sixties or seventies who looked like he hadn't slept or eaten in days.

Wednesday night I went to the Paris Opéra Ballet. The wet pavement in front of the Opéra House gleamed like black patent leather. Patrons dripped jewels and fur. This gala was why Michael had funded my trip; my first ballet article for *New York Now* had proved popular, despite its vapidity. Or maybe because of it. Tonight the famous French company was dancing an eclectic program, with guest artists from the Royal Ballet and the Kirov. Michael wanted five thousand words on the oldest ballet company in the world.

I watched bioenhanced British dancers perform the wedding *pas de deux* from *Sleeping Beauty*, with its famous fishdives; Danish soloists in twentieth-century dances by George Balanchine; French ballerinas in contemporary works by their brilliant choreographer Louis Dufrot. All of them were breathtaking. In the new ballets, especially choreographed for these bioenhanced bodies, the dancers executed sustained movements no natural body would have been capable of making at all, at a speed that never looked machinelike. Instead the dancers were flashes of light: lasers, optic signals, nerve impulses surging across the stage and triggering pleasure centers in the brains of the delighted audience.

I gaped at one *pas de trois* in which the male dancer lifted two women at once, holding them aloft in swallow lifts over his head, one on each palm, then turning them slowly for a full ninety seconds. It wasn't a bench-pressing stunt. It was the culmination of a yearning, lyrical dance, as tender as any in the great nineteenth century ballets. The female dancers were lowered slowly to the floor, and they both flowed through a *fouette of adage* as if they hadn't any bones.

Not one dancer had been replaced in the evening's program due to injury. I tried to remember the last time I'd seen a performance of the New York City Ballet without a last-minute substitution.

During intermission, profoundly depressed, I bought a glass of wine in the lobby. The eddying crowd receded for a moment, and I was face to face with Anna Olson, seated regally in her powerchair and flanked by her bodyguards. Holding tight to her hand was a little girl of five or six, dressed in a pink party dress and pink tights, with wide blue eyes, black hair, and a long slim neck. She might have been Caroline Olson twenty years ago.

"Ms. Olson," I said.

She looked at me coldly, without recognition.

"I'm Susan Matthews. We met at the private reception for Anton Privitera at Georgette Allen's," I lied.

"Yes?" she said, but her eyes raked me. My dress wasn't the sort that turned up at the private fundraisers of New York billionaires. I didn't give her a chance to cut me.

"This must be your—" granddaughter? Caroline, an only child, had never interrupted her dancing career for pregnancy. Niece? Grandniece? "—your ward."

"Je m'appelle Marguerite," the child said eagerly. "Nous regardons le ballet."

"Do you study ballet, Marguerite?"

"Mais oui!" she said scornfully, but Anna Olson made a sign and the bodyguards deftly cut me off from both of them. By maneuvering around the edge of the hall, I caught a last, distant glimpse of Marguerite. She waited patiently in line to go back to her seat. Her small feet in pink ballet slippers turned out in a perfect fifth position.

Thursday afternoon I drove into Paris to rent an electronic translator for the presentation by Taillebois and Erbland. The translators furnished by the conference were long since claimed. People who had rented them for the opening talks simply hung onto them, afraid to miss anything. The Taillebois/Erbland presentation would include written handouts in French, English, German, Spanish, Russian, and Japanese, but not until the session was over. I was afraid to miss anything, either.

I couldn't find an electronic translator with a brand name I trusted. I settled for a human named Jean-Paul, from a highly recommended commercial agency. He was about four feet ten, with sad brown eyes and a face wrinkled into fantastic crevasses. He told me he had translated for Charles DeGaulle during the crisis in Algeria. I believed him. He looked older than God.

We drove back to Neuilly in the rain. I said, "Jean-Paul, do you like ballet?"

"Non," he said immediately. "It is too slippery an art for me."

"Slippery?"

"Nothing is real. Girls are spirits of the dead, or joyous peasants, or other silly things. Have you ever seen any real peasants, Mademoiselle? They are not joyous. And girls lighter than air land on stage with a thump!" He illustrated by smacking the dashboard with his palm. "Men die of love for those women. Nobody dies for love. They die for money, or hate, but not love. Non."

"But isn't all art no more than illusion?"

He shrugged. "Not all illusion is worth creating. Not silly illusions. Dancers wobbling on tippy toes . . . non, non."

I said carefully, "French dancers can be openly bioenhanced. Not like in the United States. To some of us, that gives the art a whole new excitement. Technical, if not artistic."

Jean-Paul shrugged again. "Anybody can be bioenhanced, if they have the money. Bioenhancement, by itself it does not impress me. My grandson is bioenhanced."

"What does he do?"

Jean-Paul twisted his body toward me in the seat of the car. "He is a soccer player! One of the best in the world! If you followed the sport you would know his name. Claude Despreaux. Soccer—now *there* is illusion worth creating!"

His tone was exactly Anton Privitera's, talking about ballet.

Thursday evening, just before the presentation, I finally caught Deborah at home. Her face on the phonevid was drawn and strained. "What's wrong?"

"Nothing, Mom. How's Paris?"

"Wet. Deborah, you're not telling me the truth."

"Everything's fine! I just . . . just had a complicated rehearsal today."

The corps de ballet does not usually demand complicated rehearsals. The function of the corps is to move gracefully behind the soloists and principal dancers; it's seldom allowed to do anything that will distract from their virtuosity. I said carefully, "Are you injured?"

"No, of course not. Look, I have to go."

"Deborah . . ."

"They're waiting for me!" The screen went blank.

Who was waiting for her?

When I called back, there was no answer.

I went to the Grand Ballroom. Jean-Paul had been holding both our seats, lousy ones, since noon. An hour later, the presentation still had not started.

The audience fidgeted, tense and muttering. Finally a woman dressed in a severe suit entered. She spoke German. Jean-Paul translated into my ear.

"Good evening. I am Katya Waggenschauser. I have an announcement before
we begin. I regret to inform you that Dr. Taillebois will not appear. Dr. Taillebois
. . . He. . . ." Abruptly she ran off the stage.

The muttering rose to an astonished roar.

A man walked on stage. The crowd quieted immediately. Jean-Paul translated
from the French, "I am Dr. Valois of the Pasteur Institute. Shortly Dr. Erbland
will begin the presentation. But I regret to inform you that Dr. Taillebois will
not appear. There has been an unfortunate accident. Dr. Taillebois is dead."

The murmuring rose, fell again. I heard reporters whispering into camphones
in six languages.

"In a few minutes Dr. Erbland will make her and Dr. Taillebois's presentation.
Please be patient just a few moments longer."

Eventually someone introduced Dr. Erbland, a long and fulsome introduction,
and she walked onto the stage. A thin, tall woman in her sixties, she looked
shaken and pale. She opened by speaking about how various kinds of bioenhancement differed from each other in intent, procedure, and biological mechanism.
Most bioenhancements were introduced into an adult body that had already
finished growing. A few, usually aimed at correcting hereditary problems, were
carried out on infants. Those procedures were somewhat closer to the kinds of
genetic re-engineering—it was not referred to merely as "bioenhancement"—
that produced new strains of animals. And as with animals, science had long
known that it was possible to manipulate pre-embryonic human genes in the
same way, *in vitro*.

The audience grew completely quiet.

In vitro work, Dr. Erbland said, offered by its nature fewer guides and guaran-
tees. There were many coded redundancies in genetic information, and that made
it difficult to determine long-term happenings. The human genome map, the
basis of all embryonic re-engineering, had been complete for forty years, but
"complete" was not the same as "understood." The body had many genetic
behaviors that researchers were only just beginning to understand. No one could
have expected that when embryonic re-engineering first began, as a highly experimental undertaking, that genetic identity would be so stubborn.

Stubborn? I didn't know what she meant. Apparently, neither did anybody
else in the audience. People scarcely breathed.

This experimental nature of embryonic manipulation in humans did not, of
course, stop experimentation, Dr. Erbland continued. Before such experimentation was declared illegal by the Copenhagen Accord, many laboratories around
the world had advanced science with the cooperation of voluntary subjects.
Completely voluntary, she said. She said it three times.

I wondered how an embryo volunteered.

These voluntary subjects had been re-engineered using variants of the same
techniques that produced *in vitro* bioenhancements in other mammals. Her company, in conjunction with the Pasteur Research Institute, had been pioneers in
the new techniques. For over thirty years.

Thirty years. My search of the literature had found nothing going back that far. At least not in the journals available on the standard scientific nets. If such "re-engineered" embryos had been allowed to fully gestate, and had survived, they were just barely within the cut-off date for legal existence. Were we talking about embryos or people here?

Dr. Erbland made a curious gesture: raising both arms from the elbow, then letting them fall. It looked almost like a plea. Was she making a public confession of breaking international law? Why would she do that?

Over such a long time, Dr. Erbland continued, the human genetic identity, encoded in "jumping genes" in many unsuspected redundant ways, reasserted itself. This was the subject of her and Dr. Taillebois's work. Unfortunately, the effect on the organism—completely unanticipated by anyone—could be biologically devastating. This first graphic showed basal DNA changes in a re-engineered embryo created twenty-five years ago. The subject, a male, was—

A holograph projected a complicated, three-dimensional genemap. The scientists in the audience leaned forward intently. The non-scientists looked at each other.

As the presentation progressed, anchored in graphs and formulas and genemap holos, it became clear even to me what Dr. Erbland was actually saying.

European geneticists had been experimenting on embryos as long as thirty years ago, and never stopped. They'd allowed some of those embryos to become people. Against international law, and without knowing the long-term effects. And now the long-term effects, like old bills, were coming due, and those people's bodies were destroying themselves at the genetic level.

We had engineered a bioenhanced cancer to replace the natural one we had conquered.

It was a few moments before I noticed that Jean-Paul had stopped translating. He sat like stone, his wrinkled face lengthened in sorrow.

The audience forgot this was a scientific conference. "How many people have been re-engineered at an embryonic level?" someone shouted in English. "Total number worldwide!"

Someone else shouted, "*¿Todos van a morir?*"

"*Les lois internationales—*"

"*Der sagt—*"

Dr. Erbland broke into a long, passionate speech, clearly not part of the prepared presentation. I caught the word "sagt" several times: *law*. I remembered that Dr. Erbland worked for a commercial biotech firm wholly owned by a pharmaceutical company.

The same company in which Anna Olson owned a fortune in stock.

Jean-Paul said quietly, "My grandson. Claude. He was one of those embryos. They told us it was safe. . . ."

I looked at the old man, slumped forward, and I couldn't find any sympathy for him. That appalled me. A cherished grandson. . . . But they had *agreed*, Claude's parents, to play Russian roulette with a child's life. In order to produce a superior soccer player. *"Soccer—now there is an illusion worth creating."*

I remembered Anna Olson at the demonstration by the Lincoln Center fountain: *"Caroline had a good run. For a dancer."* Caroline Olson, Deborah said, had been fired because she missed rehearsals and performances. The *Times* had called her last performance "a travesty." Because her body was eating itself at a genetic level, undetectable by the City Ballet bioscans that assumed you could compare new DNA patterns to the body's original, which no procedure completely erased. But for Caroline, the original itself had carried the hidden blueprint for destruction. For twenty-six years.

The ultimate ballet mother had made Caroline into what Anna Olson *needed* her to be. For as long as Caroline might last.

And then I remembered little Marguerite, standing with her perfect turn out in fifth position.

I stood and pushed my way to the exit. I had to get out of that room. Nobody else left. Dr. Erbland, rattled and afraid, tried to answer questions shouted in six languages. I shoved past a woman who was punching her neighbor. Gendarmes appeared as if conjured from the floorboards. Maybe that would be next.

The hardcopies of Dr. Taillebois's original presentation were stacked neatly on tables in the lobby. I took one in English. As I went out the door, I heard a gendarme say clearly to somebody, *"Oui, il s'a suicidé, Dr. Taillebois."*

I didn't want to stay an hour longer in Paris. I packed at the hotel and changed my ticket at Orly. On the plane home I made myself read the Taillebois/Erbland paper. Most of it was incomprehensible to me; what I understood was obscene. I kept seeing Marguerite in her pink ballet slippers, Caroline staggering on stage. If my lack of sympathy for Taillebois and Erbland was a lack in me, then so be it.

For the first time since Deborah had entered the School of American Ballet, and despite the dazzling performances at the Paris Opéra, I found myself respecting Anton Privitera.

When I landed at Kennedy, at almost midnight, there was a message from the electronic gate keeper, "Call this number immediately. Urgent and crucial." I didn't recognize the number.

Deborah. An accident. I raced to the nearest public phone. But it wasn't a hospital; it was an attorney's office.

"Ms. Susan Matthews? Hold, please."

A man's face came on the screen. "This is James Beecher, Ms. Matthews. I'm attorney for Pers Anders. He's being held without bail, pending trial. He left a message for you, most urgent. The message is—"

"Trial? On what charges?" But I think I already knew. The well-cut suit on the lawyer. The move to an expensive neighborhood. Pers was working for somebody, and there weren't very many things he knew how to do.

"The charges are dealing in narcotics. First-degree felony. The message is—"

"Sunshine, right? No, that wouldn't have been expensive enough for Pers," I said bitterly. "Designer viruses? Pleasure center beanos?"

"The message is, 'Don't look in the caverns of the moon.' That's all." The screen went blank.

I stared at it anyway. When Deborah was tiny, in the brief period a million years ago when Pers and I were still together and raising her, she had a game she loved. She'd hide a favorite toy somewhere and call out, 'Don't look in the closet! Don't look under the bed! Don't look in the sock drawer!' The toy was always wherever she said not to look. The caverns of the moon was what she called her bedroom, but that was much later, long after Pers had deserted us both but before she tracked him down in New York. I didn't know that he even knew about it.

Don't look in the caverns of the moon.

I took a helo right to the Central Park landing stage, charging it to the magazine. The last five blocks I ran, past the automated stores that never sleep and the night people who had just gotten up. Deborah wasn't home; she didn't expect me back from Paris until tomorrow. I tore apart her bedroom, and in an old dance bag I found it, flattened between the mattress and box spring. No practiced criminal, my Deborah.

The powder was pinkish, with no particular odor. There was a lot of it. I had no idea what it was; probably it had a unique name to go with a unique formula matched to some brain function. What kind of father would use his own daughter as a courier for this designer-gene abyss? Would the cops have already been here if I'd come home a day later? An hour later?

I flushed it all down the toilet, including the dance bag, which I first cut into tiny pieces. Then I searched the rest of the apartment, and then I searched it again. There were no more drugs. There was no money.

She wasn't running stuff for Pers for free. Not Deborah. She had spent the money somewhere.

"They asked me to join the company! He said it was very nice! He said I was much improved!"

I made myself sit and think. It was one o'clock in the morning. Lincoln Center would be locked and dark. She might be at a restaurant with other dancers; she might be staying the night with a friend. I called other SAB students. Each answered sleepily. Deborah wasn't there. Ninette told me that after the evening performance Deborah had said she was going home.

"Well, yes, Ms. Matthews, she did seem a little tense," Ninette said, stifling a yawn, her long hair tousled on the shoulders of her nightgown. "But it was only her second night in actual performance, so I thought . . ." The young voice trailed off. I wasn't going to be told whatever this girl thought. Clearly I was an interfering mother.

You bet I was.

I waited another hour. Deborah didn't come home. I called a cab and went to Caroline Olson's apartment on Central Park South.

It had to be Caroline. She must have known she herself was bioenhanced, and I had seen her dance before her downfall: the complete abandon to ballet, the joy. Maybe she thought that helping other dancers to illegal bioenhancement was a favor to them, a benefit. She might be making a distinction—the same one Dr. Erbland had made—between the ultimately destructive re-engineering done to her *in vitro* and the bioenhancements done to European dancers. Or maybe she didn't connect her own sudden deterioration with how her mother had genetically consecrated her to ballet.

Or maybe she did. Maybe she knew that her meteoric success was what was now killing her. Maybe she was so sick and so enraged that she *wanted* to destroy other dancers along with her. If she couldn't dance out her full career, then neither would they.

Or maybe she thought it was worth it. A short life but a brilliant one. Anything for art. Most dancers ended up crippling their bodies anyway, although more slowly. The great Suzanne Farrell had ended up with a plastic hip, her pelvis destroyed by constant turnout. Mikhail Baryshnikov ruined his knees. Miranda Mains was unable to walk by the time she was 28. Maybe Caroline Olson thought no sacrifice was too great for ballet, even a life.

But not my Deborah's.

I buzzed the security system of Caroline's apartment for five solid minutes. There was no answer. Finally the system said politely, "Your party does not answer. Further buzzing may constitute legal harassment. You should leave now."

I got back in the cab, chewing on my thumb. I felt that kind of desperation you think you can't live through; it consumes your belly, chokes your breath. The driver waited indifferently. *Where?* God, in New York they could be anywhere.

Anywhere nobody would think to look for illegal medical operations. Anywhere safe, and protected, and easily accessible by dancers, without suspicion.

I gave the driver Anna Olson's address, remembered from the tax return pirated by the Robin Hood. Then I transferred the gun from my purse to my pocket.

I think I wasn't quite sane.

9

Caroline and I ride in a taxi. I like taxis. I put my head out the window. The taxi has many smells. We stop at Deborah's house. Caroline and I go get Deborah.

"I've changed my mind," Deborah says. Her door is open only a little. She stands behind the door. "I'm not going."

"Yes, you are," Caroline says.

Deborah says, "You're not my mother!"

Caroline changes her smell. She has a cane to walk. She leans on her cane. Her voice gets soft. "No, I'm not your mother. And I'm not going to push you like a mother. Believe me, Deborah, I know what that's like. But as a senior dancer, I'm going to ask you to come with me. I'm willing to beg you to come. It's that important. Not just to you, but to me."

Deborah looks at the floor.

"Don't be embarrassed. Just understand that I mean it. I'll beg, I'll grovel. But first I'm asking, as a senior member of the company."

Deborah looks up. She smells angry. "Why do you care? It's *my* life!"

"Yes. Yours and Privitera's." Caroline closes her eyes. "You owe him something, too. No, don't consider that. Just come because I'm asking you."

Deborah still smells angry. But she comes.

We ride in the taxi to Caroline's mother's house. I say, "Is there a party tonight?"

Deborah laughs. It sounds funny. Caroline says, "Yes, Angel. Another party. With music and dancers and talking. And you can have some pretzels."

"I like pretzels," I say. "Does Deborah like pretzels?"

"No," Deborah says, and now she smells scared.

We go in the back way. Caroline has a key. People come to the basement. Someone starts music. "Not so loud!" a man says.

"No, it's all right," Caroline says. "My mother's still in Europe and the staff is on vacation while she's gone. We have the place to ourselves."

A woman brings me a pretzel. People talk. Caroline and Deborah and two men talk in the corner. I don't hear the words. The words at parties are very hard. I watch Caroline, and eat pretzels, and watch two people dance to the radio.

"Christ," the man dancer says, "is this fake revelry really necessary?"

"Yes," the woman says. She looks at me. "Caroline says yes."

In the corner, two men show Deborah some papers. Caroline sits with them. Deborah starts to cry.

I watch Caroline. Deborah may touch Caroline. The two men may touch Caroline. But Caroline says parties are happy. No people smell happy. I do not understand.

The buzzer rings.

Nobody moves. People look at each other. Caroline says, "Is the gate still open? Let it go. It's probably kids. There's nobody home but us."

The buzzer rings and rings. Then it stops. Caroline talks to Deborah. The door opens at the top of the stairs.

A man with Caroline takes a bottle from his pockets very fast. He puts the papers on the floor and pours the bottle on it. The papers disappear. "All right, everybody, this is a party," he says.

Steps run down the stairs. A voice calls, "Wait! You can't go down there! Young woman! You can't go down there!" The voice is angry. It is Caroline's mother.

I walk to Caroline. She smells surprised.

A woman comes into the basement. She holds a gun. My ears raise. I stand next to Caroline.

"Nobody move," the woman says. Deborah says, "Mom!"

Caroline looks at the woman, then at Deborah, then at the woman. She walks with her cane to the woman.

"Stay right there," the woman says. She smells angry and scared. I move with Caroline.

"Christ, you sound like a bad holovid," Caroline says. "You're Deborah's mother? What the hell do you think you're doing here?"

From the top of the stairs Caroline's mother calls, "Caroline! What is the meaning of this?"

The woman says very fast, "Deborah, you're making a terrible mistake. Bioenhancement may help your dancing for a while, but it could also kill you. The conference on genetics in Paris—they presented scientific proof that one kind of bioenhancement kills, and if they're just finding that out now about enhancements done twenty-five years ago—then who knows what kind of insane risk you're running with these other kinds? Don't take my word for it, it's on-line this morning. Pers was arrested, damn him, and I found your drug stash just before the police did. That's how you're paying for this, isn't it? Debbie—how could you be such a damn *fool*?"

"Wait a minute," Caroline says. She leans on her cane. "You thought we brought Deborah here *to bioenhance her*?" Caroline starts to laugh. She puts her hand on her face. "Oh my God!"

Caroline's mother calls from the top of the stairs, "I'm phoning the police."

Caroline says, very fast, "Go bring her down here, James. You'll have to lift her out of her chair and carry her. Keith, get her chair." The two men run up the stairs.

Caroline is shaking. I stand beside her. I growl. The woman still has the gun. She points the gun at Caroline. I wait for Caroline to tell me *Attack*.

The woman says, "Don't try to deny it. You'd do anything for ballet, wouldn't you? All of you. You're *sick*—but you're not murdering my daughter!"

Caroline's face changes. Her smell changes. I feel her hand on my head. Her hand shakes. Her body shakes. I smell anger bigger than other angers. I wait for *Attack*.

Deborah says, "You're all wrong, Mom! Just like you always are! Does this look like a bioenhancement lab? *Does it?* These people aren't enhancing me—they're trying to talk me *out* of it! These two guys are doctors and they're trying to 'deprogram' me—just like *you* tried to program me all my life! You never wanted me to dance, you always tried to make me into this cute little college-bound student that *you* needed me to be. Never what *I* needed!"

The men carry Caroline's mother and Caroline's mother's chair down the steps. They put Caroline's mother in the chair. Caroline's mother also smells angry. But Caroline smells more angry than anybody.

Caroline says, "Sound familiar, Mother dear? What Deborah's saying? What did *you* learn at the genetic conference? What I've been telling you for months, right? Your gift to dance is dying. Because you wanted a prima ballerina at *any* price. Even if *I'm* the one to pay it."

Caroline's mother says, "You love dance. You wanted it as much as I did. You were a star."

"I never got to find out if I would have been one anyway! That isn't so inconceivable, is it? And then I might have still been dancing! But instead I was . . . *made*. Molded, sewed, carpentered. Into what *you* needed me to be!"

Deborah's mother lowers her gun. Her eyes are big. Caroline's mother says, "You were a star. You had a good run. Without me, you might have been *nothing*. Worthless."

A man says, very soft, "Jesus H. Christ."

Caroline is shaking hard. I am afraid she will fall again. Her hand is on her cane. The cane shakes. Her other hand is on me.

Caroline says, "You cold, self-centered-bitch—"

A little girl runs down the stairs.

The little girl says, "Tante Anna! Tante Anna! Où êtes-vous?" She stops at the bottom of the steps. She smells afraid. "Qui sont tout ces gens?"

Caroline looks at the little girl. The little girl has no shoes. She has long black fur on her head. Her hind feet go out like Caroline's feet when Caroline dances. The toes look strange. I don't understand the little girl's feet.

Caroline says again, "You cold, self-centered bitch." Her voice is soft now. She stops shaking. "When did you have her made? Five years ago? Six? A new model with improved features? Who will decay all the sooner?"

Caroline's mother says, "You are a hysterical fool."

Caroline says, "Angel—*attack*! Now!"

I attack Caroline's mother. I knock over the chair. I bite her foreleg. Someone screams, "Caroline! For God's sake! Caroline!" I bite Caroline's mother's head. I must protect Caroline. This person hurts Caroline. I must protect Caroline.

A gun fires and I hurt and hurt and hurt—

I love Caroline.

10

The town of Saratoga, where the American Ballet Theater is dancing its summer season, is itself a brightly colored stage. Visitors throng the racetrack, the brand-new Electronics Museum, the historical battle sites. In 1777, right here, Benedict Arnold and his half-trained revolutionaries stopped British forces under General John Burgoyne. It was the first great victory of freedom over the old order.

Until this year, the New York City Ballet danced here every summer. But the Performing Arts Center chose not to renew the City Ballet contract. In New York, too, City Ballet attendance is half of what it was only a few years ago.

The Saratoga pavilion is open to the countryside. Ballet lovers fill the seats, spread blankets up the sloping lawn, watch dancers accompanied not only by Tchaikovsky or Chopin but also by crickets and robins. In Saratoga, the ballet smells of freshly mown grass. The classic "white ballets"—*Swan Lake, Les Sylphides*—are remembered green. Small girls whose first taste of dance is at Saratoga will dream, for the rest of their lives, of toe shoes skimming over wildflowers.

I take my seat, in the back of the regular seating, as the small orchestra finishes tuning up. The conductor enters to the usual thunderous applause, even though nobody here knows his name and very few care. They have come to see the dancers.

Debussy floats out over the countryside. *Afternoon of a Faun*: slow, melting. On the nearly bare stage, furnished only with barre and mirrors, a male dancer in practice clothes wakes up, stretches, warms up his muscles in a series of slow, languorous moves.

A girl appears in the mirror, which isn't really a mirror but an empty place in the backdrop. A void. She, too, stretches, poses, *pliés*. Both dancers watch the mirrors. They are so absorbed in their own reflections that they only gradually become aware of each other's presence. Even then, they exist for each other only as foils, presences to dance to. In the end the girl will step back through the mirror. There is the feeling that for the boy, she may not really have existed at all, except as a dream.

It is Deborah's first lead in a one-act ballet. Her extension is high, her turn out perfect, her movements sure and strong and sustained, filled with the joy of dancing. I can barely stand to look at her. This is her reward, her grail, for continuing her bioenhancement. She isn't dancing for Anton Privitera, but she is dancing. A year and a half of bioenhancement, bought legally now in Copenhagen and paid for by selling her story to an eager press, has given her the physical possibilities to match her musicality, and her rhythm, and her drive.

The faun finally touches the girl, turning her slowly *en attitude*. Deborah smiles. This is her afternoon. She's willing to pay whatever price the night demands, even though science has no idea yet what, for her kind of treatments, it might be.

Privitera must have known that some of his dancers were bioenhanced. The completely inadequate bioscans at City Ballet, the phenomenally low injury rate of his prima ballerina—Privitera *must* have known. Or maybe his staff let him remain in official ignorance, keeping from him any knowledge of heresy in the ranks. There was a rumor that Privitera's business manager, John Cole, even tried to keep Caroline from "deprogramming" dancers who wanted bioenhancement. The rumor about Cole was never substantiated. But in the last year, City Ballet has been struggling to survive. Too many patrons have withdrawn their favor. The mystique of natural art, like other mystiques, didn't last forever. It had a good run.

"If you could have chosen, and that was the *only* way you could have had the career, would you have chosen the embryonic engineering anyway?" was the sole thing Deborah asked Caroline in jail, through bullet-proof plastic glass and electronic speaking systems, under the hard eyes of matrons. Caroline, awaiting trial for second-degree murder, didn't seem to mind Deborah's brusqueness, her self-absorption. Caroline was silent a long time, her gaunt face lengthened from the girlish roundness I remembered. Then she said to Deborah, "No."

"*I* would," Deborah said.

Caroline only looked at her.

They're here, Caroline and her dog. Somewhere up on the grass, Caroline in a powerchair, Angel hobbling on the three legs my bullet left him. Caroline was acquitted by reason of temporary insanity. They didn't let Angel stay with her during the trial. Nor did they let him testify, which would have been abnormal but not impossible. Five-year-olds can testify under some circumstances, and Angel has the biochip-and-reengineered intelligence of a five-year-old. Maybe it wouldn't have been so abnormal. Or maybe all of us, not just Anton Privitera, will have to change our definition of abnormal.

Five-year-olds know a lot. It was Marguerite who cried out, "Vous avez assassiné ma tante Anna!'' She knew whom I was aiming at, even if the police did not. But Marguerite couldn't know how much I loathed the old woman who had made her daughter into what her mother needed her to be—just as I, out of love, had tried to do to mine.

On stage, Deborah *pirouettes*. Maybe her types of bioenhancement will be all right, despite the growing body of doubts collected by Caroline's doctor allies. When the first cures for cancer were developed from reengineered retroviruses, dying and desperate patients demanded they be administered without long, drawn-out FDA testing. Some of those patients died even sooner, possibly from the cures. Some lived to be ninety. The edge of anything is a lottery, and protection doesn't help—not against change, or madmen, or errors of judgment. *I protect Caroline*, Angel kept saying after I shot him, yelping in pain between sentences. *I protect Caroline*.

Deborah flows into a *retiré*, one leg bent at the knee, and rises *on point*. Her face glows. Her partner lifts her above his head and turns her slowly, her feet perfectly arched in their toe shoes, dancing on air.

A VISIT TO THE FARSIDE

Don Webb

▼

Don Webb is a small-press veteran whose exuberantly unclassifiable fiction has appeared in more than sixty magazines in the United States, Great Britain, France, Norway, and India. Since the middle of the eighties, he has been a frequent contributor to *Asimov's Science Fiction* (his first sale there, "Jesse Revenged," is still spoken of admiringly by connoisseurs of the gonzo, and may well be one of the weirdest "Wild West" stories ever written), and his stories have also been included in *Interzone, Amazing, New Pathways, Fantasy Tales, When the Music's Over*, and elsewhere. He is the author of the very strange "collection" called *Uncle Ovid's Exercise Book*, and of two recent chapbook collections, *The Bestseller and Other Tales* and *The Seventh Day and After*, and he is currently working on a novel. He lives with his wife Rosemary in Austin, Texas.

In the eccentric little story that follows, he takes us to a human-colonized Moon, a familiar venue for science fiction stories . . . but no setting is safely familiar once Webb gets his hands on it, as you shall see.

Sasha hated checkpoints.

Any Soviet citizen could enter the American ghetto, but her father had access to the central computer. Information belonged to the state as surely as the means of production belonged to the workers—so what her father did was technically a crime.

A tiny probe removed an infinitesimally small piece of dermis from her left index finger. Enzymes would quickly coax the DNA away from the rest. They would further slice the DNA into small manageable strands—GGACTTA, for example. The negatively charged strands would swim through a conducting agarose trying to reach the positive terminal. The strands would leave their patterns on filter paper, and the DNA print would be checked by the central computer. Such jobs were low priority. It would be twenty, maybe twenty-five, minutes before the central computer told Director Illych Borodin Maservich that his daughter was in the subbasement of the Patrice Lumumba Moon Base.

By that time she would have accomplished her mission. She would've told Todd she was never going to see him again.

The American sector stank with their ethnic cooking, marijuana, and tobacco. Everyone looked at Sasha as she made her way through the labyrinth of storefronts, brothels, and gambling dens. Correction: Everyone looked at Director Maservich's daughter. There had been rumors. . . .

There were eyes everywhere. Eyes. Sasha was shorter than the Americans. Like all Soviet citizens, she followed a careful exercise program and took calcium supplements. She didn't have long, brittle, American bones. *She* could walk on the Earth anytime. In fact, she had, twice. With her dark hair and cobalt eyes, she was every Russian farmboy's dream.

Todd Morlan worked at the Tail o' the Pup, a preposterous American establishment. The Tail was a ten-meter-long "hot dog" painted in appropriate browns, reds, and yellows. The service counter—exactly 1.75 meters from the floor— roughly bisected the wienie. The Tail served hot dogs, hamburgers, malts, shakes, beer, coffee, kosher pickles, hot soft pretzels, and hashish candy. All synthetic, of course. Todd was laying a wienie into an open bun, and Sasha fell in love again.

Todd was red-haired, dark-skinned, and 2.1 meters tall. All in all, a typical American, except for his virginal skull. Todd's mother had kept it that way. She had ambitions for Todd.

The customer had left, and those enormous brown eyes were staring at her.

"Can I help you, love?"

"I. I. I want to talk to you."

"You *are* talking to me," he said. He began to pour synthetic potato mash into fry molds. He could be so difficult at times.

"I need to talk to you seriously."

"Hey, Pop. Can you watch the counter for a minute?"

Todd's fat father came bounding out from behind the protein synthesizers. He was proud his son was nailing a Russian chick. He'd been some sort of official at the American Farside base decades ago. He grunted his assent, which was about as articulate as he got these days. A tiny cassette was attached to his bald head. Todd put his hands on the counter and vaulted over. He gave Sasha a little hug which completely exorcised her purpose in being there. Maybe she should just feed what she had to say to a servo and send it down here.

"Come along, love. We'll go someplace *secure* to talk."

A joke. No place was beyond her father's ears. They went deeper into Little America until they came to a tiny freight elevator. Hands plucked at her tunic. Buy this. Buy that. Smoke a genuine hookah pipe. Try genuine Southwest chili. Spot the lady. Snatches of music: rock-'n'-roll, country-'n'-western, electronic jazz. Each kiosk had its own sound—each loud and hideous and from a different period of America's frozen past. The elevator was a relief even though it was small and dimly lit. Sasha was surprised when Todd pushed the DOWN button. She had thought this was the lowest level. Perhaps it was true. Perhaps Americans did hold occult secrets. What was that old chemistry slogan? *Vista Interiora Terrae Recitficando Invenies Occultum Lapidem. Go to the interior of the Earth to find and refine the hidden stone.*

The door opened on the blackness of an air-filled basalt tunnel. Todd took a light from his blue jeans pocket and hung it around his neck.

The first thing Sasha saw were illegal sides of beef in bubbling clone tanks. The steaks must garner a fantastic price on the black market—not American boodle, real Soviet rubles. Then were tanks for cannabis, then tobacco, then hydroponically grown tomatoes. Todd smiled at her. He was putting her love to a test. Either she could report this contraband now or join him in the ranks of criminal.

This wasn't fair.

"Don't they need light?" Sasha asked, pointing at the plants.

"Of course," said Todd. "But they shut off for several seconds when the elevator comes down. We don't want to reveal all our secrets at once."

"But the elevator's there in plain sight. Anyone could find it."

"Could you?"

She thought of the sights and smells of Little America.

Too much data, she decided.

"No."

"Besides, haven't you studied Revised Economics? The State requires the 'lubrication' that a black market provides. It hedges the bets for Five Year Planners."

They stepped out of the elevator. Lights flickered on in the plant tanks.

Todd asked, "So what did you need to talk about?"

Nothing. Nothing now.

"I just wanted to see you. I need you."

"That's my girl."

Todd led her down the basalt tunnel.

"How many people know about this?"

"That's a dangerous question. Most of the Americans, I guess. Some of the higher-placed bureaucrats must have realized that the contraband they buy must come from somewhere. All of the American kids. This area functions as a Lovers' Lane."

"Lovers' Lane?"

Todd began to demonstrate.

One word could describe both Comrade Director Maservich and Mrs. Sally Morlan: ambitious.

Maservich was stuck in the smallest of the Moon bases. Patrice Lumumba lay four hundred kilometers west of the landing site of Luna 19. It barely made what the capitalists would've called a profit—mining, ceramics manufacturing, special atmosphere pharmaceuticals.

Eventually it would be closed down, but before then he would be directing another base. Maybe Tsiolkovsky Base, pride of the Soviet Moon.

When the air supply at Farside had gone critical and the Congress of the plugged-in land was unwilling to do anything, the Supreme Soviet ordered him to take in the refugees as a "humanitarian" gesture. Thirty Earth years ago. He knew he would've been promoted if it hadn't been for the Americans. They were a contaminant. They had ruined his career. They and Comrade Risolski's theory of "economic lubrication." He wanted to flood the lower levels with disinfectant.

He sat in his chair watching home movies. He didn't notice the warning flag on his terminal. His father had been placed—the ambassador to the People's Republic of Mongolia. There he is now, putting his son in a yak-pulled troika, drinking bitter buttered tea, sledding the snows of Ulan Bator. That was the life, and it would be Director Maservich's life again.

Todd's mother, Sally Morlan, was determined that Todd would leave the American ghetto and join Soviet life. There was no hope for Todd's father. He didn't understand. He thought Little America would be around forever. She saw the printout on the wall. Someday Soviet pity would vanish and the Americans would be deported to the earth, where the gravity would kill most of them. She kept a black capsule hidden on her person for such an eventuality.

At first she welcomed the liaison between Todd and Alexandra Maservich. But she came to realize that Maservich would never allow a marriage. That Todd was just some sort of fling for Alexandra. Broaden her small world. Make her a woman of the cosmos.

Here's a sample conversation between Todd and his mother (as recorded by a chuka-bug two standard days before he and Sasha ran off):

Sally: I heard you were topside yesterday. Betty saw you—

Todd: Your friend the maid? The social climber?

Sally: Betty saw you speaking English. Up there. How many times have I told you to speak Russian? We didn't spend all that boodle to get you tutored in Russian for nothing.

Todd: I was talking—if you must know—to a fellow American.

Sally: Never speak to them. Who was it?

Todd: I don't see why you're interested, but it was Greg Peterson.

Sally: The servo mechanic?

(Silence. Presumably Todd makes an affirmative gesture.)

Sally: Well, what were you talking about?

Todd: There's a rumor that the base is going to be closed down. "Desirable" Americans will be divided among the four remaining Soviet bases. "Undesirables" will be deported by auto-rocket to Denver.

Sally: When?

Todd: You know these rumors. Soon. Always soon.

Sally: You need to stop seeing that girl.

Todd: I figure I'm an "undesirable" anyway, so why should I stop anything? My ticker will be bursting soon enough.

Sally: You're perfectly desirable. Smart. Not a tapehead.

Todd: They would rather have tapeheads. Addicts are easier to control. Besides, the Great Russians have never been too keen on mulattoes.

Sally: There's an Official Policy—

Todd: Yeah, there's an Official Policy—

(This goes on in the course of a regular son-mother argument for quite some time.)

Sally slipped a new cassette in. Her ebony features relaxed. She has become a Cleopatra whom all powerful men love.

The basalt tunnel was lit by the plant tanks and the humans' afterglow. All concepts of time and responsibility have been dissolved by the feeling of joy. Sasha decides this is a real state, by its ability to replace all other states no matter how long they have been part of her routine.

"Todd, tell me a story."

The relationship between sex and storytelling is a very old one, going all the way back to Scheherazade and the Sultan. And what better place for a story than a tunnel beneath the surface of the Moon?

"This is something that really happened a long time ago. When they were salvaging Farside Station. This Russian girl"—he hugged Sasha—"and this American guy went with their folks to salvage. Well, the salvage teams were real busy so these two went off in a crawler. They were, you know, in love. So they went into a small crater beyond the sight line from Farside. They were just about to get to it, when they got a message from the circumlunar satellite that a cargo 'bot—you know, one of the big four-armed types—had gone berserk and that everyone should leave Farside. Well, the girl wanted to leave right then, but the guy argued that they were safe where they were. Well, they argued for a while, and the guy saw that he wasn't getting anywhere—so he kicked the crawler into Emergency Full and shot out of the crater toward the base. The girl said she thought she heard the crawler hit something, but the guy was so ticked off he didn't say anything. When they got to base and beyond the airlock and everything, they got out of the crawler. And there, hooked on the girl's door, was the torn-off arm of a cargo 'bot."

Sasha immediately disbelieved the story—not because of the improbable behavior of the robot—but because she wanted theirs to be the first love of an American and a Soviet.

"That can't be so."

"It is too so. I heard it from my dad."

"If it was so, everybody would know about it."

"The kids probably didn't tell anyone because they didn't want to get in trouble."

"Then how come your dad knew about it?"

"Because he was in charge of Farside salvage. He knew where all the vehicles went. At least the American vehicles."

"Well," said Sasha triumphantly, "there aren't any more American vehicles, so we can't go check for severed robotic arms."

"There are too American vehicles."

Oops! He wasn't supposed to say that. That he was telling what he shouldn't was all over his face. Sasha saw that there were secrets beyond this—a whole maze of American secrets darker than space.

Todd decided to continue; he would tell all, he would tell her the biggest Secret. No, he would show it. It was time for his escape. So he continued talking, trying hard to sound as though he had never stopped to think. "There *are* American vehicles. We can go see the very crawler."

"You've seen it?"

"No. But I know where it's at."

"Take me."

She thought she was returning the testing challenge of love.

Todd touched the light around his neck, bringing it to full intensity. They walked down the tunnel slowly. Todd looked for something.

There was a fissure in the basalt—a lighter finger of breccia had intruded. Todd ran his beam along the length of the breccia. He passed the light from top to bottom three times. Almost silently a section of the tunnel wall slid away revealing a descending staircase.

All Sasha could think of was Dante: *Abandon all hope ye who enter here.*

All Todd could think of was Romeo and Juliet, except he would rewrite it. He would let the star-crossed lovers escape to a world free from their families.

Todd went first. Sasha followed. Then the doorway closed. The air was very stale here. Except for Todd's medallion, no light shone. They descended at least twelve meters when the darkness of an artificial grotto opened before them. Todd's light revealed three vehicles: two American crawlers and an out-of-date Soviet mining rig.

He said, "See?"

"So they're crawlers. That doesn't mean there are severed robotic arms. Let's go look."

"It's the further one, I think."

"*Korosho.*"

Sasha led the way. There wasn't any arm. There were scratches, but anything might cause scratches. Sasha slowly shook her head; she decided that once again Todd was suffering from the American disease of irrationality.

Todd said, "Well, that was thirty years ago. They probably removed the arm. It was in the way or something."

"Todd, your dad was just having you on."

"Dad wouldn't lie to me."

"Oh it's just folklore. Everyone knows Americans—"

She'd said it. He finished it.

"Everyone knows Americans are liars."

"It's not a big deal, Todd."

"Sure it's a big deal. You're thinking of marrying me and you think I'm a liar. You think that basically I can't be trusted, nor can my people be trusted. Look around you. Do you see how much I trust you? I brought you here. Here! I could be killed for bringing you here, and all you have to offer is tired Soviet platitudes."

"I'm sorry, Todd, I really am. It's just a saying, it's not what I feel here."

She put his hand over her heart.

Todd's voice became very intimate. "I could show you something. Something really big. Something that would change your mind about Americans."

"Show me."

"We'll have to take a crawler out."

"Where?"

"To Farside Base."

Todd opened the doors of the crawler. The lithium batteries still held their charge. He powered it up, disconnecting the navigational to the circumlunar satellite, which would have told the planetary computer their location. Orange indicator lights revealed that the crawler didn't have a good atmosphere seal. They would have to wear suits.

Sasha hated the old-style American suits. Damp and clinging yellow latex, they simply made you feel nasty. Todd toggled a switch, and a section of the grotto wall swung open. They rolled forward into an airlock. The air didn't leave the crawler right away, but continued to hiss for several seconds beyond the lock. Wasteful American extravagance. They drove through a long, dark, basalt tunnel, finally emerging into a small cave in a crater floor. The Russian base lay two klicks behind them in the lunar highlands.

Todd activated a scoop on the front of the crawler which picked regolite—crater dust—and deposited it behind them, obscuring tracks which otherwise would last as long as the Moon itself. The Earth was behind them, to the east. It would sink slowly behind the horizon as the crawler rolled forward at a somewhat less than thrilling thirty-five kilometers an hour. It would take two hours to reach Farside station, but Sasha didn't care. This was an adventure. She had to be realistic with herself—Todd would be on a rocket back to Earth, and she couldn't sustain her girlish dreams much longer. She wondered how long it would take her father to find her.

Through their suits they could hear the dull gravel roar of the scoop; their radios were on, albeit at minimum power, but neither spoke until the crawler had left the crater rim.

Sasha asked, "Why do Americans need secret vehicles?"

"We like to keep an ace in the hole. Congress may open up Farside again. The program could start up anytime."

"You wouldn't need secret vehicles for that. Besides what can you do with two crawlers and a miner?"

"So folks could get away if your dad ever went crazy."

"There's nowhere to go."

"There's a place to go. Not all the Americans know about it. My mom doesn't even know about it. But Farside had a very special project going—the Sarfatti Project. Sarfatti began looking for what determines Planck's constant. He wanted to find the root of all reality. He found it in an old SETI transcription."

"The U.S. program that listened for extraterrestrial communication?"

"Yeah, for years they hid this long code from the Andromeda Galaxy. Eventually they released it to Sarfatti. It's called the *Yellow Text* of Thanos Kon. Really it was called by a long and boring code sequence, but someone cooked up a fanciful name for it."

Sasha knew then that Todd was a hopeless romantic, that he would waste his life on irrational quests. In short, that her tall, bronze love was typically American. But as the Earth dropped out of sight, it was a time for love and fancy, so she played along.

"What was revealed in the *Yellow Text* of Thanos Kon?"

"Hey, I'm being serious."

"*Korosho.* What was Sarfatti working on?"

"Sarfatti found out that will and intent came before the forming of Planck's constant. That there was a way for an individual consciousness to play in an endlessly creative fashion without ever settling on a universe line to move through."

They were in a smooth, hilly area now. Occasionally a bump would send the cruiser flying for a few meters. When they reached the tracks the salvage vehicles had left thirty years ago, Tom shut off the scoop to conserve batteries. He went on with his fairy tale.

"Of course, that would be a meaningless existence. If you thought of something, you'd *be* it. There would cease to be a self and just an all. But Sarfatti went further. He found that you could create—through will alone—a different universe line to live in."

"In other words, you could click your ruby slippers three times and say, 'There's no place like home!' and you'd go there."

"Not necessarily. You couldn't control all the factors. It was more like, 'Be careful what you wish for; you might get it.' "

"You really think that all this you're telling me is real, don't you?"

In the harsh light of the lunar day, they could see one of the wings of Farside. Farside had been partially sublunar. Americans had always dug in. Originally it had been planned as a half-buried pentagon, but it had expanded in all directions as the radically pro-space Congress of the thirties had poured money into the Moon like there was no tomorrow. These strangely angled wings shot in all directions, suggesting an alien architecture fitted to this hostile world. Several holes appeared in the gleaming surface of the base—opened by micrometeors over the decades. Todd pulled the crawler up to a jagged hole, probably made by the salvage crews to pull out some valuable piece of equipment.

They turned on their suit lights as they stepped inside. Todd led the way down the long corridor toward the original pentagon. Sasha was impressed by the size and the waste. In its day, Farside had been the largest of the bases in operation on the Moon. With typical American expansiveness, it was just beyond view of the Earth. By claiming this view of the fabulous formless darkness, Americans had felt closer to the unknown which is space. It was a long walk to the central pentagon. Todd examined some controls, touched a switch, and the lights flickered on.

"The salvage crews left a small reactor going, so that if they ever needed to visit the base again they would have ample power."

Just as they reached the central pentagon, they felt a vibration. In the corridor to the left, something big was moving. Sasha didn't believe it. It was a cargo 'bot. A big, three-armed cargo 'bot. Todd began to laugh.

She grabbed him.

He hugged her and said, "It's all a joke. Look."

He touched three wall controls quickly and the 'bot stopped. He continued, "It scares off people from the real secret—that's what folklore was invented to do in the first place."

Todd led them through the pentagon. Every cubicle had either been cleaned out by the salvage teams, or had everything smashed by the 'bot. They crunched through piles of crushed boards, spaghetti wires, destroyed bits of wooden furniture brought from Earth as status symbols, lunar mineral displays, silicon data storage crystals, robotic parts. Everywhere were the heavy wheel tracks of the three-armed 'bot. Todd went into one room, seemingly no different from the rest. He stood in front of a closet door, and said, "Here is the Farside Secret."

He opened the door, which somewhat anticlimatically revealed only a closet. Then he pulled Sasha toward him and slammed the door behind him. It's not a big thing to descend in an elevator in the Moon's reduced gravity, but Sasha found the brief descent shocking enough.

The closet did not then open onto the magician's cave that she had been half suspecting. It was a small, densely packed lab, with some more or less familiar-looking high-energy physics equipment. She was waiting for Todd to uncover this hoax as he had the 'bot above. Already she was thinking of this experience as a story to tell her grandchildren, whom as she pictured them were clearly not Todd's descendants after all. She would play on a little while longer. She wanted to be able to tell the story of how she was young and foolish and brave.

"This is it," Todd said. "Sarfatti's dream machine buried in an abandoned base that looks away from Earth. This is the escape route for the desperate. It's our escape route."

"What?"

"You know as well as I do that I'll be jailed for this, if I go back. So you've got to choose whether to follow me into another world and we live—perhaps—happily ever after, or stay here and be trapped into a lifetime of endless five-year plans."

"You can't make me decide this. You have no right."

"You decided it when you followed me into the tunnels under Little America. We've been gone—what is it?—four hours now. The Central Computer no doubt told your dad that you had entered the American ghetto at least three hours ago. Even now agents are swarming through Little America. If we stay I'll be a dead Romeo, with a literally broken heart in the gravity of Denver. You'll be a good career space agent living an emotional life as barren as the rocks you'll see every day through your viewports. Choose romance."

At that moment the battle between romance and reason was decided. She would go with Todd, or at least let him try his technomagic. She had to swallow hard before she could speak.

"I'll go," she said.

Todd activated a terminal and typed in a password, which she noticed was "Rotwang." A few indicator lights came on. Nothing dramatic.

"We have to stand here." He indicated a roughly circular area, which perhaps looked a little scorched or discolored.

Sasha wondered if she was going to die. She held onto his arm very tightly.

She had expected a long, mathematical description of the worlds they were going to bring into being. Todd said very simply, "I want a universe line similar to this where Soviet space doesn't beat out the American program."

As he spoke, the words appeared on the terminal. For a couple of minutes nothing happened, and Sasha was mad at the solemnity of this gag he was trying to pull. How could he offer something so important and it just be a joke? She was about to break free and slap him when the dizziness hit.

It seemed as though they were moving in every possible direction at once, including turning inside out. It was neither a long nor a short time, because they were in a place where time was not. Something there—something native to that timeless void—was both perplexed by their choice and amused by it. There was something like laughter—if Sasha believed in devils, she would have characterized it as a devil's laugh. Except that whatever it was, in whatever place they were, had neither sound nor substance.

It was hard to tell how long they had been staring at the lunar landscape in front of them. There was no clear moment of transition from eternity into time. It took several seconds for their minds to start again, and for them to realize what had happened.

They were the same—same dirty suits and stale air—but Farside Base was gone. Farside was gone. The crawler was gone. The footprints and tracks were gone. They were in the base of a very deep crater, corresponding to the depths of the Farside lab. Todd turned his radio up to maximum gain, but there was only the meaningless hiss of cosmic rays.

No Americans. No Russians. No machine to try for another wish.

After a long silence, he would suggest that maybe they should walk back to Patrice Lumumba base. After a longer silence, she would agree.

They had come to another world, but not one they would have understood. They came to a world where Communism had fallen, and America had turned its back on space. No competition for the fabled ores of the asteroids, no pride in setting up bases to stare from the far side of the Moon. Even if they had had enough air to walk all the klicks back to see the Moon, no one knew how to build a rocket to get to the Moon. Their signals would have been wasted on a disbelieving drug manufacturing plant at an L-5 point.

They walked until they dropped, but they found their love as they dropped, and fell in an embrace. Thus they met the end of Romeo and Juliet, despite Todd's attempt to break free from myth.

Three hundred years later, when the true Space Age began, their well-preserved corpses would be a source of plays and novels, and they would live on always as one of the great mysteries of that age.

—for Allen Varney

ALIEN BOOTLEGGER

Rebecca Ore

▼

Rebecca Ore made her first sale to *Amazing* in 1986. Although she would make several more sales to *Amazing* over the next few years, as well as sales to *Asimov's Science Fiction* and elsewhere, she has made her biggest impact on the science fiction world to date with her novels, and especially with the intricate and intelligent depiction of alien life forms that characterizes her well-known "Alien" trilogy, *Becoming Alien, Being Alien*, and *Human to Human*. Her other novels include *Declaration Rules* and the well-received *The Illegal Rebirth of Billy the Kid*. Her most recent books are her first collection, *Alien Bootlegger and Other Stories*, and a fantasy novel, *Slow Funeral*.

Ore lives in Critiz, Virginia, in the same kind of Appalachian country she describes so lovingly and with such a keen eye for regional cultural differences in much of her fiction—as in the sly and fast-paced novella that follows, the richly comic and ultimately quite profound story of an entrepreneur muscling in on new territory who has a bit of an *edge* on the competition. . . .

.

1

Lilly Nelson at the Hardware Store

When I first saw the alien was the first warm day after a terrible winter of layoffs. Years like these, men stare at the seed packs, the catalogues for fertilizer spreaders, and wonder if they've got enough land for a distiller's corn crop. Or would the mills hire back soon enough as to make farming superfluous? Rocky Mount was full that day of men speculating about turning back to what their ancestors did back when southwestern Virginia was the frontier. Sort of like what didn't starve out the great-grandparents won't starve out us. But few had kept their tractors. No one had draft animals. The ancestors had hated farming like crazy, and the descendants really wanted the factories to start hiring again. But meantime, let's get some equipment clerk to distract us or go out and gossip about the alien.

My own business wasn't off—none of my Driving Under the Influence clients had written me a bad check yet—but I'd still gone to the hardware store, even knowing how crowded it would be. I needed my own distraction. Fibroids waited in my uterus for a sonogram on Tuesday, so today I hefted plastic mesh bags full of spring bulbs, comparing the lies on the package flap to the real flowers I'd seen the last summer I'd planted them.

Just my luck, I'd have to have surgery. Odd, I'd never wanted children, and it would have been absurd to have a child to take care of when I was forty-three and had my aunt Berenice to worry about, but to have it come to this. Then while I was drinking a Dr Pepper for the caffeine to soothe my addiction headache and waiting for a clerk to sell me some dahlias, the alien walked in and I was finally distracted.

Nobody wanted to acted like a gawking hick. We watched each other to time one quick stare apiece, aiming our eyes when nobody else was looking. The hardware store itself looked weird after I looked away. The alien jolted my eyes into seeing more detail than I'd ever noticed before—dead flies on a fly strip, the little bumps in the plastic weave under my fingers, a cracked front tooth in the clerk's face as he came around the counter.

"Welding equipment," the alien said as a nervous man in a business suit tugged on one of his long bony arms. "Stainless steel welding equipment, stainless-steel pipe, stainless sheets, stainless-steel milk tank."

The clerk looked at me. I nodded, meaning *okay, deal with that first.*

As the clerk came to him, the alien adjusted the flow on an acetylene torch. He looked like a man crossed with a praying mantis, something a farmer watched for crop-damaging tendencies. In the chitinous head, the eyes looked more jelly-like than decent, though I suspect my own eyes in that head would look just as bad. Actually, the eyes were more or less like human eyes; it was the ears that were faceted like stereo speakers. Big enough. Little indentations inside the facets. I bet it could tell you precisely where a noise was coming from.

So here the alien is, one of the ones about which we've been reading all the reassurances the government chose to give us, I thought. One was hiking the Japanese central mountain crest trail. That was the one the media went crazy over, but others were living in Africa working on tilapia and other food-fish recombinant DNA projects and weaving handicrafts or in Europe taking sailing lessons or studying automotive mechanics. They'd all arrived in a faster-than-light ship and said they were tourists. Yeah, sure, but they had that FTL ship and we didn't.

"Lilly, told you I been seeing saucers since 1990 down in Wytheville off I-77 junction," a bootlegger's driver said to me quietly. I looked at the man and wondered if he was driving for one of the DeSpain cousins now. Berenice was always curious about the DeSpains, as though they were a natural phenomenon, not criminals at all. She accused me of resenting criminals who made more money than I did.

"Look at its ears," I said, meaning *let's not talk until it's out of the building at least.*

He considered them and looked back at me with tighter lips.

I shrugged and visualized the fibroids down inside me, flattened sea cucumbers squirming around. Maybe the alien would bring us better medicine? He bought his equipment and said, "Pickup truck with diplomatic plates."

"Bring it around to the side," the clerk said, trying to sound normal, almost making it.

After the alien left, the bootlegger's driver said, "What is he planning to weld stainless for?"

We all knew one of the options—still-making, no lead salts in stainless-steel boys' product, and the metal was cheaper than copper. Or maybe he was setting up a dairy? "Maybe he's a romantic." I paused. "You ever consider working for Coors?" I said before walking back to the office. I knew his answer before he could have replied—driving legal was a boring-ass job; driving illegal was an adventure.

Tomorrow was Legal Aid, so I wanted to get the partnership papers filed on the Witherspoon Craft Factory before five. I dreaded Legal Aid. When times were bad, the men screamed at their wives and children, and the women wanted divorces. If he beats you, I'd always say, I'll help you, but just for yelling at you, come on, honey, you can't support kids on seven dollars an hour. Better to dust off the old copper pot and get a gristmill, clean the coil, fill a propane tank, and cook some local color in the basement that tax evaders and tourists pay good money for.

When we heard the aliens were just tourists, the first joke everyone in Franklin County seemed to have heard or simultaneously invented was if having one around was going to drive up real estate taxes again.

When I got into the office, the answering machine was blinking. My aunt Berenice spoke off the disc: "I remembered hearing where Patty Hearst was hiding, but I think it was just some fire-mouthing. Even then, I was getting too old for simple rhetoric. Bring me something . . . I forget now . . . when you come home. And, Lilly, your message makes you sound impossibly country."

It wasn't that she was that senile, Berenice was simply righteously paranoid from a long radical life. I made a note to pick up some single scotch malt from Bobby. He was making fine liquor for now. An independent, but maybe everyone would leave him alone because he made such classic liquor. And he had hospital bills to pay. Pre-existing condition in his child.

Then I wondered why I wasn't more excited about the alien. Maybe because I had so much to worry about myself, like who was going to take care of Berenice when I went under the knife?

I filled the partnership papers at the courthouse and drove by Bobby's to pick up the single malt. When I pulled up at his house, he was sitting on the porch, twitching a straw in his hand.

"Bobby," I said. He had to know what I was here for.

"Yo, Luce. I had a visitor today."

"Um," meaning *are you going to be a client of mine anytime soon?*

"One of the DeSpains."

"You been aging it for five years—"

He interrupted, "More."

"So didn't you just slip it to friends like I suggested? It's not like you do it for a living."

"I do need the money. But I wanted to make really good liquor. Seemed less desperate that way."

"It's fine liquor," I said.

"It was fine liquor," Bobby said. "DeSpain isn't going to make me his man."

"Well, Bobby," I said, watching the straw still rolling between his hands, "be careful." What could I tell him? Dennis DeSpain wasn't the roughest cousin, and nothing in the liquor business was as rough as the drug business. "You don't have any liquor now?" Bobby shook his head, the straw pausing a second. Now I had to stop by the ABC store before I went home. Daddy always said legal liquor had artificial dyes and synthetic odors in it.

When I got up to go, Bobby said, "I guess my wife will have to start waiting tables over at the Lake. I'm just lucky I'm on first shift. In the dye house." We both knew why the dye house never laid anyone off—the heat drove close to a hundred percent turnovers there.

"When I was younger," I said as I got my car keys back out of my purse, "I was going to reform the world. Then, Franklin County. Now . . ."

"Yeah, now," Bobby said.

"Well, I won't have you as a client, then."

He jerked his shoulders. "I don't know what I thought I was doing."

"Liquor-making the old way is a fine craft."

"Oh, shut the fuck up, Lilly. I thought if I did it fine, it wouldn't be so desperate. Man with bad debts turns to making liquor."

So, bad times and no simple solutions. I sighed and got in the car, then remembered the alien buying stainless-steel welding equipment, his fingers longer than a man's but fiddling with the valve with the same bent-head attention as a skilled human.

I drove back to the ABC store. The alien was leaning against the wall of the ABC store, eating Fig Newtons. At his feet was an ABC store brown bag full of what looked like sampler bottles. The man with him looked even more nervous than the two of them in the hardware store, furtive like. When the alien opened his mouth to bite, I saw his teeth were either crusted with tartar or very weird. They were also rounded, like a child draws teeth, not squared. He stopped to watch me go in. When I came out with the legal malt whiskey, I nodded to him.

"Lawyer," he said. "Ex-radical. Wanted to meet you, but not so much by accident that you'd be suspicious." I went zero to the bone. The voice seemed synthetic, the intonation off even though the accent was utter broadcast journalism.

"He's very interested in Franklin County," his human guide said. "And liquor." Poor guy sounded like he knew precisely why the alien had bought all the stainless-steel welding equipment and the liquor samples.

"Really?" I said, not quite asking, remembering quite well the year when most of the distillers went to stainless steel—thank God, no more of the car-radiator stills that killed drinkers.

The man said, "I'm Henry Allen, with the State Department. He's Turkemaw of Svarti, a guest of our government."

"And a vegetarian," I said, having recovered enough to pass by them and get back in my car. A farmer would try Sevrin dust or even an illegal brew of DDT if he saw the alien in a stand of corn.

I don't know why I think farmer—I've never farmed day one in my life and I lived in New York for years. Berenice complains I sound like I'm trying to pass for redneck, but the sound's inside my head, too. Back at home, a chill intensifying with the dark, Berenice and a young black woman were sitting on the porch talking. They didn't have the porch light on, so I knew they'd been sitting there awhile, Berenice in the swing, the black woman stiff on the teak bench, both so absorbed in each other they were oblivious to the cold and dark. I tried to remember her name . . . Mary . . . no, Marie, a chemical engineering student who'd grow up to be one of those black women who'd gone to college and become plant chemical control officers, rather ferocious about their rise up. Berenice loved anyone who had ears to listen and hadn't heard all her stories yet.

As I got out of the car, I felt a bit ashamed of myself for thinking that. She'd told me enough about Marie that I should have realized Berenice listened to her, too.

When Berenice said, "And the Howe women I knew from Boston said that Emily Dickinson was a senator's daughter and that she tried like a motherfucker to get published," the girl threw her head back and laughed. Laughed without holding back, genuinely fond of my aunt, genuinely amused, so I thought better of her.

Marie said, "They didn't teach me that at Tech."

"No, professors all want to believe they're more than schoolteachers, but they don't know what real poets are like." Berenice could be fierce about this. One of her husbands or lovers wrote poetry books that sold in the forties of thousands. "Always remember you're more than a chemical engineering student, Marie. Everyone is always more than the labels other people want to put on them."

"Of course I'm more than a chemical engineer," Marie said, tightening the dignity muscles again. I reminded myself of what I'd been like at eighteen and felt more compassionate to us all.

"Terrella—" Berenice began. I remembered hearing about Terrella, the black woman bootlegger in the forties who killed a man.

"Terrella," Marie said. "That kind of kin threatens me."

I set the bottle down by Berenice. She sniffed and opened it, sniffed again. "Argh, fake esters. What happened to Bobby's?"

"DeSpain."

Marie stiffened. Yeah, I remembered too late that I'd named a lover she'd just broken with. Berenice had heard quite a bit about it, as Berenice, when she was in her best mind, could get people to talk. I'd hear more later. Berenice said, "Lilly, get three glasses."

"I don't want to talk about Terrella," Marie said again. As I got the little glasses we used for straight liquor, I wondered if two denials made a positive. Terrella wore long black skirts way into the fifties, with a pistol and a knife hidden in the folds. Her hair had grown into dreadlocks before we ever knew the style was a style and had a name. She left $25,000 and a house to her daughter when she died, which was remarkable for a black woman in those days, however she got the money. Berenice admired people who could work around the system and not lose, even when they were criminals. To Berenice, one should never resign oneself to any status other people thought appropriate.

"So you're kin to Terrella," I said, putting all the glasses on the table that went with the bench and pouring us each about an inch of the Scotch.

"I'm even kin to Hugous, the man who runs The Door 18."

"Smart man," Berenice said. "Terrella was smart, too."

"She was a hoodlum," Marie said. "Hugous—"

"Hugous puts money aside, no matter how he makes it," Berenice said. "That's always useful in a capitalist state. Considering that sloppy capitalism's all we have to work with." Berenice freed her long gray hair to dangle radical-hippie style and grinned at me. So she'd always been looser and more tolerant than I. I had enough rigidity to get a law degree so that I could support her. Retirement homes, even ones better than she could have afforded, terrified her.

Not that we weren't more two of a kind than anyone else in the county, but I always wanted to organize the poor while she thought the poor ought to kick liberal ass as well as boss ass.

"I saw the alien today after I made the appointment for the sonogram," I said.

"Fibroids. Mother had them," Berenice said. "They thought they were cancer and sent her womb to Wake Forest."

"Jesus, Berenice," Marie said. "That's like hearing Dennis talk about jail rape."

So, I wondered, what was the context? Did Dennis rape or get raped? Berenice picked up her scotch and drank it all down in one swallow, the crepey skin jerking on her scrawny neck, the long gray hair flying. "Well, Marie, you like your life?"

"It's fine," the girls said tonelessly. "I like Montgomery County better than here."

Meaning gossip in Rocky Mount about Dennis DeSpain was a problem, I thought, and none of the Tech students knew yet that she had outlaw kin. I looked at Berenice. Marie got up to go, her hypercorrect suit wrinkled anyway around her rump. I watched as she got in her little Honda.

"Berenice, I saw the alien buying welding equipment."

Berenice said in a conspiratorial whisper, "Marie can weld, too."

"DeSpain won't like that."

"Dennis taught Marie about bootlegging. She left him because he tempted her."

"Tempted her? I mean, it isn't like half of Rocky Mount didn't see them having breakfast and smelling of come last fall."

"Tempted her to become a bootlegger. I suspect it's become like any other supervisory job to Dennis and he needs to have someone new see him as glamorous and dangerous."

"Jesus, I thought he was about half in the Klan, certainly able to fuck blacks, but not able to admit they've got brains as good as a white boy's."

"Marie's definitely smarter than most white boys." Berenice looked for the clip she'd pulled out of her hair and tucked all her hair in the clip behind her neck again. "She's specializing in alcohols and esters. State's going to legalize liquor-making one of these days to get some of the taxes."

"Why would a Tech student want to make liquor?" I said, angry that she'd risk a college degree for something that trivial. Not so trivial, perhaps, if one was Bobby sweating in a polyester dye house for two dollars an hour over minimum wage, but for a chemical engineering student—stupid.

"I didn't say she was making liquor now," Berenice said. She looked down at her hands, then rubbed a large brown patch between her index finger knuckle and her thumb. "First sign I had I was getting old were wrinkles going up and down my fingers on the palm side. Nobody ever warned me about them. I like Marie, but the youth doesn't rub off, does it?"

"Berenice, there's an alien in Franklin County."

"So the government put it here. We never have any real say, do we? Alien? No different than a foreigner in most folks' minds." *Foreigner* means from outside our home county. The Welsh brought the concept with them, which is only fitting, as *welsh* means foreigner in Anglo-Saxon. Berenice continued, "You think Marie's sad, don't you? Like self-cultural genocide? Maybe she'd be happier if she were more like Terrella?"

"Cultural genocide is a stupid term. It trivializes things like really murdered people."

"Well, then I'll just say she's awful divided against herself then."

"Are we supposed to judge blacks?"

"It's racist not to," Berenice said, and I realized she'd been teasing me. Berenice could be such a yo-yo, but she'd ceased to take herself seriously without giving up what had been good about her ideals. Taking her in, I had to watch her mind wobble, but right now Berenice seemed fine, not bitterly ironic, not lapsing into the past because the present jammed in short-term memory, three-minute chunks throwing each past three minutes into oblivion. "Lilly, you're sure you're going to have to have surgery?" She asked sharply as though needing surgery were my fault.

If I did have cancer, Berenice would be extremely pissed. She'd have to go to a nursing home. The jittery insistance I tolerated for the delight she was on good days would get drugged out of her. I nodded, then said yes because she wasn't looking at me directly.

Berenice poured herself another whiskey, drained it, and said, "I've lived fully, interestingly. I'd rather lose my present than my past. At least senility won't suck that away. Did I tell you about the time I hitchhiked down to Big Sur and met Henry Miller?"

Not that she hadn't had senile moments already, I thought in pity. Then I realized I had not heard about Henry Miller and said, "Tell me."

DeSpain in Tailwater

DeSpain cast out with his Orvis rod, the Hardy Princess reel waiting for a big brown trout to inhale his Martin's Crook rigged behind the gold-plated spinner. He was missing Marie, wanted her back and wanted to kill her, but he'd do a sixteen-inch-plus trout instead.

Or break the law and kill a little one. But DeSpain had principles. He broke the law only for serious money. One of his nephews who'd gone to Johns Hopkins said that DeSpain was trying to work sympathetic magic with the law.

The Smith River fell with the sun as the Danville and Martinsville offices and factories turned out their lights. *All but poachers out of the water in half an hour.* DeSpain remembered what the guide told him about tying on a stonefly nymph, but he hated strike indicators and fishing something he couldn't see upstream.

Intending this to be the last cast of the day, DeSpain pulled up the sink tip and cast the big wet fly and the spinner across the river, shooting out line, then reeling it in. Then he saw the alien standing in bare legs in the cold Smith River, casting with the guide, coming along the opposite bank. DeSpain realized that the alien was two feet longer in the legs than the guide, who was up to his hips in the river, closer to the bank than the alien.

DeSpain yelled, "I knew the Smith was famous nationally, but this is ridiculous."

The alien said, "DeSpain. Liquor distributor. Still maker."

The Smith wasn't chilly enough to suit DeSpain right then, and his waders were much too warm. He'd heard the alien was rude. Correct—rude or very alien. DeSpain remembered gossip about the alien and said, "Turkemaw, Svarti resident extraterrestrial, mate went back home after two weeks here." He felt better.

"Dennis, you fishing a stonefly nymph?" the guide asked.

DeSpain pretended not to hear and left his line in the water, no orange foam strike indicator on the leader, obviously either real cocky about his skill with upwater nymphs or not fishing one.

The alien pushed a button on a small box hanging like a locket around his neck. The box laughed.

DeSpain remembered hearing last week from one of his drivers that the alien had bought stainless-steel welding rods and that its farm had corn acreage. Everyone wondered if so conspicuous a creature was going to be so very more flagrantly making liquor. Or maybe the creature was making spaceships in its basement? "Be careful," he said to both of them. After they waded on, DeSpain caught the spinner and fly in his hand, then switched to the stonefly nymph.

A trout took it. As he played it, then reeled it in, it came jaws out of the water, eyeballs rolled to see the hook in its mouth. He netted it, then measured it: fifteen inches three-quarters. *We can fix that,* DeSpain thought as he broke the fish's spine and stretched. *Bingo, sixteen and one-tenth. The hell I work sympathetic magic with the law.*

Satisfied with the dead trout, DeSpain left the river, his eidetic memory reviewing his investments, both legal and illegal. *I have to be so mean with the illegal ones.* Fourteen trucks out with piggyback stills, $200,000 in a Uzbek metallurgical firm, $50,000 in Central Asian cotton mills, and maybe $500,000 in various inventories, legal and illegal.

His brain began to run more detail, like a self-programming and overeager computer. No spreadsheets, he thought as he began to wonder again if he'd bought into the global equivalent of just another Franklin County. He had first wondered if the Armenians were cheating him, but then he considered he was damn apt at bullying other men into working for him. Let other people run their butts off when the law came to blow a still.

The true reality of the world wasn't Tokyo's glitter, DeSpain had long since decided after one trip to Tokyo, but the harsh little deals driven in places like Rocky Mount and Uralsk. Tokyo and New York could evaporate and the small traders would still be off making deals, machine oil under their nails, doing the world's real business.

But that nigger bitch got away from him like no man had ever been able to. Goddamn great body and smart, too. He had a lust like a pain for women like her and his wife, Orris. Yeah, Orris, she wanted him to have only simple women on the side.

He pulled the rod apart and wound down the line to keep the two sections together and the fly hook in the keeper. The trunk security chimed as he opened it. He pushed the code buttons and put the rod and vest in it before he stripped off his waders and boots and put them in a bag, then laid the trout carefully on ice, making sure it stayed stretched out.

Remembering that he paid $400 to get a ten percent casting improvement over the cheaper generic rod, DeSpain thought, *Wouldn't do that in business, but . . .*

"If you just want to kill trout, may I suggest a spinning rod," the clerk had said in tones that condemned meat fishing and people too cheap or insensitive to the nuances of a $400 rod.

Liquor. A man needs the illegal to bankroll him for the legal. "It's not romantic with me," he said out loud, thinking about the folklorist who'd come from Ferrum to tape his father about his grandfather's suicide after the feds broke his ring in the thirties.

DeSpain felt a touch of guilt that he was sending bootleg money out of the country, but no more than when he yanked an extra fraction of an inch out of a Smith River brown so that it would go over sixteen inches. He turned the key in the Volvo's ignition and drove home.

His wife came out when she heard the garage door open. When she wore her red silk dress like she was, she expected to go out to eat. Her hair was blowing, but instead of reaching to smooth it, she folded her arms across her breasts. DeSpain pulled on into the garage and turned off the electric eye. "Orris," DeSpain said in the garage, "what did you fix for dinner?"

"Steven's at Mother's. You owe me, Dennis. The bitch is a college student. You've even taken her out for breakfast."

"Why does that make it different? She's just another one of my dancing girlfriends. I'm tired."

"I can drive myself to Roanoke if you're that tired. I know what it means when a man wants to talk to a woman in the morning. And you were telling her about still workings. At breakfast."

DeSpain knew if he stayed home Orris would harangue his ass off about that bitch Marie. When a particular black woman was seducing him out of moonshine technology and college tuition, then he should have known Orris would see the woman as a real rival. "Okay, let's go. You don't have to drive." He wouldn't tell her that Marie had left him.

"To the Japanese place."

The Japanese place made Dennis nervous. Orris had picked up more about Japan than he had. "I need to log some items on the bulletin board." He watched Orris carefully for a loosening of those arms before he went inside. He got his Toshiba out of the safe, unfolded it, and plugged in the phone line. His bat file brought up all his bulletin boards: Posse Commitatus, the Junk Market, Technology Today, and Loose Trade. He pushed for the Loose Trade bulletin board and scanned through the messages. All his messages were coded:

TO RICHARD CROOK: BOONE MILLS LOST HUBCAP, FOUND, NO PROBLEM. GOT GAS AT THE USUAL. SPINNER.

TO MR. MAX: COLLEAGUES REALLY APPRECIATED THE LOBSTER. WOULD LIKE TO ORDER DOZEN MORE CHICKEN-SIZED.

TO RICHARD CROOK: HOPE CAN BUY ANOTHER FIVE LAMB'S FLEECES, WASHABLE TANNED.

TO BUD G. R. HARESEAR: NEED SOME SENSE OF PROGRESS REPORT.

One of his trucks had almost been busted at the Cave Spring I-81 exit Exxon station. Three of his suppliers needed deliveries. DeSpain made code notes and purged the messages. Then he noticed that the alien was asking in plain text if anyone wanted to sell it an old tractor. *Why is he on* this *bulletin board*? DeSpain swore he'd bring in the feds if the alien was going to be able to distill openly when people had to be discreet about it. *Fool, the feds brought the alien here to begin with.*

After DeSpain exited Loose Trade, he took his accounting disks out of his safe. He needed to ship out twenty-seven gallons to the small bars and then collect on some of the larger accounts. Follett's salary came due again. DeSpain paid his men full rate when they were in jail and half rate when they were on probation and not working a full schedule, but Follett would be off probation next week. Damn Follett, DeSpain thought, he just sits there when he's raided. Most of his still men had never been busted. He wrote a check on his hardware store account.

An image of the researcher listening to his grandmother came to mind, all romantic-ass about the business, and believing the guff that no one ever died at a still raid, that both sides of the game had an understanding. Yeah, and the mountain counties averaged a murder a week in the twenties and thirties.

His grandfather wouldn't have hanged himself over a game.

Orris came in and said, as though she hadn't been bitching at him minutes earlier, "I hope your foreign investments do well."

DeSpain rubbed his eyes and said, "I've got to go back over there in September."

"I'd like to go with you this time."

"Babe, it's just like Detroit over there. Really."

"If you went to Detroit for a month, I'd want to come along."

He wasn't sure if she were implying anything further, so he decided to just stomp change the subject. "You think I should wear a suit?" Wrong, that sounded hick asking his more sophisticated wife what to wear in the larger sense. DeSpain learned how to dress at Emory & Henry before they threw him out for getting arrested.

She said, "It's not Sunday."

"Man who looks like he was just in the river they know is rich enough not to care what a waiter thinks. Mud equals real estate."

Orris said, "Not on a nigger or a neck, mud doesn't."

DeSpain wondered if she thought her red dress would look like polyester if he didn't dress to match. He said, "I'll change," and she stepped her skinny body out on her high heels without indicating whether she was pleased or not. *Orris, an iris root.* DeSpain had looked it up once and wondered who in her family knew such an arcane thing.

He folded his computer and put all his records and it back in the safe, then found a blue suit to wear with a string tie. String ties made Orris nervous.

On the drive to Roanoke, she said, "Don't do that to me again."

"What, with a college student?" Dennis realized she knew the affair was over, but did she know the how and why?

"Right, Dennis."

"And if I did it with some poor-ass good old girl, I'd probably be fucking your family."

"So crude, but then what was I to expect, marrying a bootlegger."

"Not that I'm not employing half your cousins. The bitch left me, if that's any damn consolation."

She laughed, then said, "One of my friends said at least recently you'd been more considerate."

Stomp change again. "Did I tell you I saw the alien when I was fishing?"

"Dennis, you are so obvious when you don't want to talk about something. I heard he was rich."

"I suppose. He had a guide with him."

"And I've heard he's rude. Is he?"

"He told me to my face I was a still maker and a liquor investor."

"Maybe he's just alien, doesn't know not to think out loud. At least he didn't tell you about he knew about Marie."

"Gee, Orris, you can find the good side of anyone, can't you?"

"Not everyone," Orris said. They pulled up to the restaurant and walked in. "I need sashimi tonight," she said as if eating raw fish took guts.

Marie

Sometimes I play black and tough, but not at Tech. It'd be too easy to slide from a Dennis DeSpain to a drunk rich frat boy who knows his daddy's lawyer will get him off if he leaves a woman to strangle in ropes, or to a cracker trucker with a knife.

I hate my colorful ancestors, the liquor queens, the Jesus priestesses. Times were I suspected they just renamed a Dahomey god Jesus so they could keep on writhing to him.

But here I was, home for the weekend in a brick house in a compound that reminded me unpleasantly of anthropology class, the whole lineage spread kraal-style from broke-down trailers to $100,000 brick ranch houses with $20,000 in landscaping.

We were at least in one of the nice houses; Momma was waiting for me. "You broke with DeSpain like I told you. I'm satisfied."

"Yes, ma'am."

"I saw what you were taking at Tech when your grades came. We're not paying for you to learn bootlegging."

"Chemical engineering, Mamma."

She sat down on the piano bench and closed her eyes. I sat down on one of the red velvet armchairs and leaned my head back against the antimacassar. "I know they can use you at DuPont or in a dye house. Find a place that will pay you to take a master's in business. Daddy's been knowing a white boy all his life that's now doing that."

I wondered if we'd moved away from the trailer kin what my life would have been like. I could have grown up in Charlotte, North Carolina—black, white, and mulatto all doing airy things like architecture and graphics design. Momma saw the look on my face and said, "Do you think you collected all the white blood in the family?"

"No, Mamma."

"You white granddaddies better than that DeSpain."

Lapsing out of proper English again, Mamma? I rolled my eyes at her and said, "I need be studying." Yeah, yeah, I know Black English grammar has its own formal structure and I was hashing it.

"You need the computer?"

"Maybe I shouldn't have come home for the weekend. It's so depressing around here."

"You are an example to your kin."

I thought about Grannie crocheting billions of antimacassars like giant mutant snowflakes, rabidly industrious while her sisters slid by on their asses. "Do you think they really appreciate it?"

Momma asked, half interested and half to abruptly change the subject, "Is there really an alien down near Endicott?"

"He was walking around Rocky Mount, trying to pass for a good old boy. Yeah, let me get on the computer." Momma grew up associating computers with school as they didn't have node numbers and nets and gossip by the megabyte when she was coming along. I could access all sorts of trash while she thought I was studying.

Orris had left me a message on Loose Trade: DENNIS'S DANCING GIRLFRIEND: SORRY, BETTER LUCK/CHOICE NEXT TIME. I felt my tongue begin to throb; I'd pushed against my teeth so hard.

But before I sniped back at her, I noticed messages about the alien: ALIEN IS A BASTARD. HEARD WHEN PEOPLE CLAIM THEY WERE KIDNAPPED BY HIM, HE SAYS HE DOESN'T REMEMBER THEM IN A WAY THAT MAKES EVEN CRAZY PEOPLE FEEL REAL TRIVIAL.

I wondered if he had really kidnapped people, if his people had.

Another message about the alien: HE'S OFF BACK ABOUT A MILE AND A HALF FROM THE HARDTOP. WON'T LET THE HIGHWAY DEPARTMENT SELL HIM THE SURFACE TREATMENT EITHER.

I left a message to Dennis: MRS. DESPAIN CALLED. TERRELLA IF YOU WANT TO THINK OF ME THAT WAY. I knew he wanted me to be more like her than I could ever wish to be.

Then the alien came on the board in real time: PLEASE, I HOPE TO DO BUSINESS HERE. MY WIFE LEFT ME. I WISH ONLY TO LIVE QUIETLY. YOUR RESIDENT ALIEN.

Someone quickly typed back: ARE YOU FOR REAL?

I DON'T REMEMBER KIDNAPPING ANYONE FROM THIS COUNTY.

I wondered why an alien would be doing business on a semi-honest bulletin board and remembered Lilly saw him buying welding equipment. I typed, THIS BULLETIN BOARD ISN'T AS SECURE AS THE SYSTEMS OPERATOR MAY HAVE TOLD YOU WHEN YOU SIGNED ON.

The alien replied: IF I NEEDED SECURITY, I WOULDN'T BE ON THIS PLANET.

2

Lilly: As Alien as It Gets

The next Saturday, as I helped Berenice with her bath, I told her how startled I'd been when the alien told me my name and occupation.

"Lilly, you afraid of the alien?" she asked me, sitting in the tub covered with bubbles. I turned on the sprayer and began rinsing her hair.

"I was startled."

"Do you hate being startled at your age? I hate limping."

"Well, if you'd let me help you with the bath yesterday, you . . ." Nope, I needed to help her in and out of the tub all the time.

Berenice bent forward and pulled the drain lever down. "The alien wants to see you. He called here."

"Why?"

"He's on that bulletin board everyone uses for selling liquor."

"Everyone doesn't use it for selling liquor."

"DeSpain's on it. Bobby's on it." She leaned on me as she stood up, all baggy skin over what seemed to have been fairly decent muscles. I rinsed her free of soap and wrapped a towel around her. "I said I was your aunt and that I'd like to talk to him even if you couldn't come. I faxed him my Freedom of Information file."

"Does he have a name?"

"He's calling himself Turk. Can we go over this afternoon? He said it would be acceptable. You don't have any appointments."

I shrugged and walked her into her bedroom. She sat down on the bed to dry off while I got together her panties, bra, slacks, socks, and top. L.L. Bean shipped just this week the thirtieth or so pair of a shoe she'd been wearing for over five decades. She watched me pull the paper out of the toes. "I don't wear them out often these days," she said as she wiggled into the slacks and top. I put the socks on her feet, smoothing them, then slipped the shoes on, tying the knots tightly so the laces wouldn't come undone and trip her. "So I've lived to see an alien in Franklin County."

And Berenice was going to make the most of it even if he wasn't the sort of client I wanted. I held her elbow as we walked to the car.

"Why did you fax him your Freedom of Information file?" I asked while the car ran diagnostics on the pollution control devices.

"Well, I thought an alien who came to Franklin County might be weird." She didn't want to see him unless he found the file unobjectionable.

I don't tell people about my past, but Berenice lets anyone she meets know what a bit part player she was in the events of '68. And I'm being cynical because bit player is all I've been, too. But Berenice refuses to admit that anyone has more than a bit part. I said, "I hope Turk was impressed."

The car diagnostics showed that the catalytic converter would need to be replaced soon. Thanks to the reprogramming I'd done to prolong the active-with-warning phase, that probably meant the converter was gone completely by now, as I'd been getting a REPLACE SOON reading for about four months now.

"There is a reason to keep the car burning clean."

"I guess, Berenice," I said as I pulled out of our driveway, "but I've got to replace the air conditioner at the office first."

"Your lungs aren't as fragile as mine."

"Don't play Earth Firster with me this afternoon, okay."

"No, that's not appropriate, considering who we're going to see."

I asked, "And where does this Turk live?"

"Shooting Creek section. Patrick and Franklin. On the line. He's renting from Delacort heirs."

I could visualize the place, three miles of mud roads, oil pan gashing rocks, then the house, some three-story family place slowly twisting to the ground, riddled with powderpost beetles. The grandchildren would own and neglect it and rent it to summer people. Or aliens, why not? Maybe the Turk liked leaking roofs?

We drove down to Ferrum and took the road toward Shooting Creek. The road was exactly as I'd imagined it, but the house looked like several military freight helicopters had to have dropped it in last week. It was a replica of a ranch house. No, just because an alien lived there didn't mean it wasn't actually a ranch house.

Berenice looked a long while, then said, "I wonder if he got the design from TV real estate channels."

The alien came up to us, his machine laughing for him. "Ladies, lawyer, radical social worker. Berenice's file fascinates."

"Where did you get the house?" I asked.

Turk said, "Restored it."

Berenice looked slightly disappointed. I tried to remember what I could about the Delacourt family, but they were as mixed a bunch as anyone in the area, from jewel thieves to corporate executives.

We followed Turk around to the kitchen entrance. The backyard looked freshly bulldozed, raw soil faintly hazed with grass seedlings. I heard an exhaust fan running and couldn't make out where the sound was, exactly. Exhaust fans in strange places trigger my sniffing reflex—but no mash odor here, or alcohol smell either.

Turk moved a few magazines—one in some alien script that could have been just another Earth language—and we sat down.

"Do you want to meet people or do you prefer to be left alone?" I asked.

His ear facets glinted as he shifted his head. "Some people," he answered. His tongue flicked out, bristled at the tip. Like a lory, I thought, a nectar-feeding parrot. He asked, "Would you like a drink?" That was the most complete sentence I'd heard him speak.

"Yes," Berenice said quickly.

The alien made the kitchen look bizarre. His hands made the brushed nickel sink fixtures look like spacecraft gizmos that would regulate fuel mixes or the temperature of water, just as he was doing here, filling a glass teakettle that looked like laboratory equipment. The light mix—I thought—he's got weird-spectrum tubes in the fixtures. Then my mind redid some parameters and the kitchen looked like a kitchen with an alien in it, setting a glass teakettle on a burner. Berenice tightened the muscles around her mouth. She didn't consider tea a drink.

"Why did you come to Franklin County?" I asked.

"I heard about Franklin County from time-aged analogues," Turk said as he reached up in his cupboard for glasses and a teacup. Berenice watched the teacup as though hoping it wasn't for her. "But isn't here Franklin County?" He stuck his hand back into the cupboard and came back with a bottled and bonded vodka. Berenice smiled, but sat down when her legs began to quiver.

The Turk poured vodka, then tonic into two glasses for us, then put some dried green leaves in a strainer, balanced the strainer over his own cup, and filled it from the teakettle. He narrowed his eyes, but his face seemed bizarre even with that expression. I realized he'd made it with eyelids alone, without shifting a face muscle. His face skin was too rigid for muscle gestures to penetrate.

I moved to take the drink the Turk offered me and realized I was stiff. He came closer to Berenice with hers, recognizing her feebleness, perhaps.

It was alcohol but not vodka. Berenice said, "I understand you're on Loose Trade."

An iridescent flush washed over the Turk's face. He lifted his strainer and put it in the sink. The herb he'd used in his brew wasn't tea, but wasn't anything I knew to be illegal. He added white grains, about a quarter cup, of what was either sugar or salt. A sugar or a salt, I reminded myself, or protein crystals, not necessarily dextrose or sodium chloride.

I smelled my drink again and caught an echo of that herb smell as though he'd put a sprig of the herb in the liquor bottle.

Berenice said, "Can you drink alcohol yourself?"

"No." The alien put his tongue down close to his tea and rolled it into a tube. He dangled the fringed end in the tea for a few seconds before drawing the tea up. His eyes widened as if the tea startled him. Definitely a drug, I thought.

Berenice sipped her drink, but she kept her face carefully in neutral. She said, "You know this isn't vodka?"

"Yes," the alien said. "I would like to put Lilly on retainer." He spoke as though he'd memorized the phrase.

"I'm not a bootlegger lawyer," I said.

"Don't be so stuffy," Berenice said. "They're social outlaws."

"They all become mill owners in the end."

The alien said, "I will never become a mill owner in the end."

I stopped mentally cursing all the liquor makers and investors and looked more closely at the alien. "What is your civic standing here?"

"Resident alien," he said. "I am legally human."

"What kind of retainer?" I said, thinking about replacing the old air conditioner with one more compatible with the ozone layer.

"Ten thousand for the year. I can pay you now." He went to one of the cabinets and began laying hands on it, then pushing it. The door opened as if it were quite dense. Turk pulled out a contract and then counted out ten stacks of bills, Crestar bank wrappers still on them.

I asked, "Do you expect to get busted?"

He looked at me, flushed rainbow again, then said, "I plan to have fun."

I hated him for a second. "It's not a game for the people around here. People get killed."

"Killed is an option. Bored, not."

"Glad you feel that way. You're risking it." I looked over his contract. I'd have to defend him in any criminal or civil suit during the year of retainer for my usual fee less twenty-five percent. I sighed and signed it, then said, "You really need a checking account."

Berenice said, "Or DeSpain's broker."

Turk said, "I had most invested in a money market."

I wondered how long the aliens had been dealing with the government, and what these aliens were to a ACLU part-time radical lawyer like me. "Why me?"

The alien studied me three seconds, then said, "You're odd."

"I don't know why I'm agreeing to this."

Berenice said, "Because you get bored in Rocky Mount, too."

Turk blinked slowly at me, then nodded as if translating blinks to nods with his cross-species semiotic dictionary. I blinked at him and he triggered his laugh machine. I thought I'd gotten too old for illegal thrills, but then Berenice proved that was impossible for those of my lineage.

Bobby Wasn't Working

MR. B. CORN WON'T DO IT, DeSpain read on the computer screen. *Damn Bobby, I'm going to get the boys to beat him.*

He went in to the bathroom and saw Orris washing her feet, rubbing them under the running tap in the tub. It reminded him of broke mountain people living in waterless shacks, hauling jugs of water up from neighbors. Her mother had grown up like that, washing bony dirty feet with water from milk cartons, in a thirty-dollar-a-month house wired for enough electricity to take care of the stove and the rented TV. Seeing Orris washing her feet made DeSpain's stomach lurch. "You need a bath, Orris, take a whole one."

"I just got my feet dirty when I was working in the garden." She looked up at him with her pale eyes. He suspected she washed her feet this way to tell him that he was only a bit further from the shacks than she.

"Bobby won't work for me."

"You do what you need to," Orris said. She got out of the way of the toilet so he could piss, which he always needed to do when he got angry. Her dress rode up her thighs as she toweled her feet dry.

"I'm glad you understand that."

"Why does washing my feet bother you so?"

"It reminds me of welfare bitches too broke to have tubs."

"I was doing it in one of our *three* tubs. You do what you need to do, Dennis, and I trust the tubs won't evaporate."

DeSpain thought, *don't keep leaving Steve with your mother to let him pick up hick ways, too,* but said, "I really won't trust the money until I've got a good income coming from something safe."

"Safe? Then maybe I do need to keep in practice for water conservation if you think we might end up back having to haul it from a well." Orris smiled and went out of the bathroom in her bare feet, heels chapped as though shoes were new to her.

DeSpain had kin, distant kin, living on roads so rough Social Service made visits in four-wheel-drive vehicles. "Safe. Like a marina on the lake. The Russian stuff isn't safe enough."

Orris, from her bedroom, said, "You'd be bored shitless smiling at rich foreigners and gassing their idiot two-bedroom yachts in a lake too small for an overnight cruise."

"You want one of those yachts."

"Not here. Maybe in Russia, on the Black Sea." He could tell from her voice that she was smiling.

"I guess I should call the nephews and cousins."

"Is he making liquor behind your back, Dennis?"

"He won't make it. I thought it would be great for the lake people—good liquor, fine made, aged. Run them some bull about our Scottish heritage and

Bobby's old family equipment passed on for twelve generations. Look, I already do the same thing as gassing tourists' boats.''

"If he quit . . . I don't know, Dennis. I know you can't afford to get soft-headed.''

"You want to go with the boys and lay in a few licks, too?''

"Might take you up on that, Dennis.''

The notion of Orris in jeans and a pillowcase hood beating a man appalled Dennis. She was strong enough, he knew. He said, "Let us men take care of it.''

"Okay, Dennis, but I'll go if you need me. Maybe if I beat up his wife . . .''

"Well, I appreciate that, Orris.'' Dennis went back in his room, turned off the computer, and put the 9-millimeter Beretta Orris gave him for Christmas in his briefcase. Pausing in front of the dresser, he stared at his collection of car keys and decided to take the pickup he'd gotten at the government auction. Let them take it and resell it again. He wondered if they could seize the Volvo, just because it might have come from liquor money. He pulled off his white shirt and pulled on a Japanese T-shirt he'd picked up in the Urals. Then dark glasses with the enhancer circuit in case he got caught by the dark. He grimaced at himself and added a Ford Motor Company baseball cap. Maybe some chewing tobacco? he wondered.

Orris's reflection appeared in the dresser mirror. "Wear that cap in Uralsk where nobody knows what it means,'' she said, "not here.''

"We both hoed up our roots, haven't we?''

"It's tacky, considering what you're going out to do. Or are you stalling?''

He threw the cap on the bed and left, feeling pretty obvious in the truck that had been auctioned after seizures four times now.

His nephews and cousins were at one of their houses with a pool, barbecuing a split pig over half an oil drum full of charcoal, drinking beer and swimming naked while their women sat around in bathing suits looking embarrassed. "Ken,'' DeSpain said to the cousin whose house it was, "I need a little help with Bobby.'' Ken had built forty houses on the lake, run drugs, and retired at thirty-four after investing in detox centers. DeSpain's broker said detox centers could lose you money if the Feds stopped the Medicaid subsidy.

Ken pulled himself out of the pool and said, "Is he undercutting you?''

"No, he just not working. Your brothers want to help me?''

"Gee, Dennis, we've got this pig on.'' Ken padded over to the oil drum and brushed on a mix of vinegar and red pepper, then turned the crank of the spit. He'd geared the crank so one man could roll a whole pig. "You want us to deal with it without you. Say while you're off on a lunch boat cruising the lake?''

"I'm going, too. Be nice.''

"Thanks, Dennis, but I don't think so. You ought to get out of that stupid-ass liquor business anyhow.''

"Feds don't bother a man these days.''

"Feds don't bother much since when their budgets got cut. You just do what they're not specializing in busting.''

DeSpain felt like he'd gobbled down half a pound of hot pork already. "We don't have to go tonight, but I don't like someone sneaking out on me."

"You plan to beat on him, too?" Ken used a long fork to twist off some barbecue. He held the fork out to DeSpain, who pinched the meat away and tasted it. "Done?" Ken asked.

"Done," DeSpain said.

"You know, we put my daughter in that Montessori school, but I made Helen go out and work to pay for it."

"Maybe I should put Steve in it, too."

"Don't know. Helen plans to have Ann go to law school, medical school, something a woman can make money on around here. Stevie, I don't know if he needs more than public school."

"Stevie will get all he needs," DeSpain said.

Ken said, "We starting to sound like women in the mommy wars. Get naked. Swim."

"I'm ready to talk to Bobby tonight." DeSpain noticed two teenaged nephews pulled up to the poolside, arms folded across the rim. "You boys want to go?"

"Beat someone up?" The one who spoke looked at the other.

DeSpain couldn't even remember their names. The family was drifting apart. But maybe tonight that was just was well. "Can we use one of the other cars?"

Ken said, "Nope. We can't afford to lose any of them."

The boys toweled off and pulled on jeans and cutoff T-shirts. DeSpain grimaced. Six-packs in hand, they climbed up into the truck bed.

As DeSpain drove the truck toward Bobby's, he looked up at the rearview mirror and saw the bigger nephew poke the littler one in the ribs below the shirt. They both laughed and the little one threw up a leg as the truck turned.

Nobody's a professional anymore, DeSpain thought. He thought about taking them back to Ken's, but kept going and pulled up to Bobby's house.

Bobby came up to the door with a shotgun in his hand. "Leave me alone, DeSpain."

"Bobby, all I want is to protect you, find you good sales." DeSpain stayed in the cab of the truck.

"I won't make liquor for you."

The two nephews in the back of the truck stood up. The bigger one smiled. DeSpain looked back at them, then at Bobby and said, "I didn't come here to beat on you. But I do have a market for what you're making and can help you out with any cash-flow problems."

The bigger nephew said, "We didn't bring guns this time."

"Damn and a half," the little one said, "why didn't I bring my old AK-47? We'll have to remember that next time."

"Think a little plastique in the basement might help his attitude, Dennis," the bigger one said.

Dennis opened his briefcase and slid his hand inside, felt the Beretta, then sighed. "Bobby, I don't know what you're trying to do to me."

"I've got three shells in this, DeSpain. I can kill all of you."

"Well, tonight, I guess you could, Bobby. If that's what you want to do. But I don't think it would be lawful, seeing as how I'm sitting in my truck and the boys aren't armed. You do something like that and you'll have both law and the DeSpains against you."

The boys in the back made DeSpain more nervous than Bobby himself, but they had sense enough to shut up. The little one popped open another beer. Bobby did swing the gun up slightly, DeSpain noticed. He also noticed that Bobby was trembling. When the shotgun went down again, DeSpain looked around the yard and saw a car motor dangling from a hoist, a car sitting on blocks, leads from a diagnostic computer running out one window. "Cash-flow problems?" DeSpain suggested.

"Damn you, Dennis DeSpain," Bobby said.

"You don't want to kill anyone, Bobby," DeSpain said. He eased the safety off on the Beretta. Sometimes a man would shoot you when you said such a thing just to prove you wrong. Bobby's wife came out then and he gave her the shotgun and spoke to her too softly for DeSpain to make out.

The little cousin whistled. Bobby's wife looked back as if she wanted to give the gun back to her husband, but finally went into the house.

"I hope you didn't ask her to call the sheriff, Bobby. We're here to work this out like businessmen."

"Dennis, I don't want to make liquor."

"Well, you did make the liquor and you were looking for customers. I'm not asking you to make white liquor. That aged barley malt of yours would be real good to have around Smith Mountain Lake. Hey, Bobby, let me loan you something to get that car back together. No, let me give you something." DeSpain arched his back to get at his wallet and pulled out four hundred dollars. He stuck his arm out of the cab and said, "Won't that help?"

"You know that it would." Bobby wouldn't come take it.

Then, in the house, Bobby's sick baby cried. Bobby closed his eyes one long moment and came up and took the money. "It takes years to age. I dumped all I made, all that was aging."

"Don't worry, Bobby. We're both young men, you especially. I've got someone working accelerating the aging process. I've thought about counterfeiting bottled-in-bond liquors, to diversify, so to speak."

"Can I quit when I get out from under?" Bobby asked.

Oh, Bobby, you'll never get out from under, DeSpain thought, but he said, "Sure, Bobby. The main thing was, I didn't want you calling attention to the business. Amateurs often aren't discreet enough, and if anyone gets real obvious, then the state's going to come in serious in the county."

"You made it sound like I was competing with you and you were going to beat my butt if I didn't work for you regardless."

"Well, yeah, I'd be less than honest if I said I welcomed competition, but the real concern was for the business as a whole. And you were hardly serious competition, just making fine liquor I happen to have a personal fondness for."

Bobby looked like he knew he was being lied to, but he'd settle since DeSpain fed him lies that let him keep some face. DeSpain watched him, amazed that someone could think to get into liquor-making with a face so connected to his thoughts. They both settled into an agreeable silence.

"Aw, shit, Dennis, you not going to need us to beat him up?" the bigger nephew finally said.

"Not tonight," Dennis said. "Bobby here understands my concerns. I'll take you for a treat." He drove them up to Roanoke, where he called Maudie from a phone booth to see if the girl the bigger nephew liked was available.

She was. Dennis got back in the truck and drove them to the little house behind the brick fence up near Hollins—very clean women, Miss Maudie had.

"Hi, Dennis, what can I do for you?" Maudie asked as she got them beyond the door. She was a skinny woman with long thick dark-blond hair, gray in it, who wore gold bangles from wristbone to elbow on her left arm to be used as brass knuckles in a fight.

"I'll just listen to music. The boys want to have fun." Patsy, the girl his nephew thought was so neat, came out with a girl DeSpain hadn't seen before. She was a deep mountain girl, or an imitation of one, barefoot and in gingham shorts and tube top for the tourists, DeSpain thought. He grimaced at Maudie, who took his arm and led him to the parlor where a couple of high-school-looking boys sat drinking and listening to jazz piano played by a half-black, half-Chinese girl. She wore a thin blue negligee but was playing her piano so earnestly it wasn't sexy.

"She's a student at Hollins," Maudie said as she slid a iced whiskey into Dennis's hand. "She's from Mississippi."

"Aren't they all college girls?"

"Want to talk?"

Dennis sipped his drink, listening to the nephews babbling about how they'd just whipped the shit out of one of his competitors and didn't even get bloody. "No, I'm tired. Will you be needing supplies, now that I'm here?"

"Send me in more apple brandy, if you can get some. I'm tired, too. Some of these girls are absolute cunts."

"I'll let you know how the Russian deals go."

"That apartment house you told me to buy is doing reasonable, but it's too much like this to be what I'd like to do."

"What would you like to do?"

Maudie shrugged like whatever it was she was way too old and wise to try. "You know how it is, Dennis. We have to work out our own retirement plans."

The half-breed girl paused in her playing, stared at the keyboard as if pushing the keys with brain waves, then put her hands back and began playing something classical that reminded Dennis of a time he and Orris had been to the Roanoke Symphony with Orris's college roommate. He'd felt considerably uncomfortable then, but was somewhat relieved now that he could recognize the music as classical, that a half-breed whore wasn't impossibly different from him. Dennis asked Maudie, "Do you ever feel like you were leading a whole bunch of different lives, here, the other investments?"

"Aren't we all?"

The half-breed girl stared at Dennis then, playing on as if her fingers knew the keyboard better than her eyes. She sighed and looked as if she was going to cry.

"Does she fuck, too?" Dennis asked.

"She's having a bad night. Let's see about someone else."

"No, I'll come back for her."

"The alien tried last night."

"Damn. He's on one of my bulletin boards, too. Just one of them in this area, isn't there?"

"Yes."

"If he's making liquor here, I'm gonna collide with the bastard."

"Here here, or here on Earth?"

"Franklin County, Patrick, wherever the hell he's living now."

"Didn't say. Seemed sleazy, but I don't know how his kind's supposed to be."

"And he wanted to fuck her?" The half-breed girl's fingers jerked discords on the keyboard and her shoulders rounded. Dennis felt sorry for her; then for an instant he wondered what Orris would say if he fucked a Hollins girl, even one in a whorehouse. "Tell the boys I didn't buy them all night," Dennis said to Maudie. He went up to the girl and put a twenty on top of the piano, then went outside to stand by his truck until the boys finished.

3

Marie Sees Something Unusual

After my spring semester exams, I took what I learned from Tech and from Dennis DeSpain and set up a mechanically cooled still. One advantage of being a black woman engineering student is that you can get your hands on such wonderful things as a twelve-volt hydro heat pump and no one suspects you'll be making liquor with it. Run it with a transformer or solar and your electric bill won't jump like it would running equipment with regular house current. State ABC officers and the local narcs cruise Appalachian power bills looking for bills that are just too big.

The only house I could rent cheap enough was an old Giles County A-frame made of weird stiff foam-over-metal ribs, an early Tech architectural school folly. When I rented it, there was a big hole where a tree'd come down on it, so I had to patch it with new foam. Earlier owners and renters had done the same, so the house was mottled grays, browns, and creams, and lumpy inside and out along the corrugated foam ribs. Whatever, I liked it because it didn't look like a still house.

When I brought in the heat pump, I put it on the floor and sat in the gloom half ironic about the thrill. Me, bootlegging.

Actually, my body missed Dennis's body. So I was reverting to Terrella with her big skirts, her dreadlocks, and her pistol because I really wanted to call Dennis up and say, "It's okay. I don't really need you all the time."

Brain, tell the body no, I thought as I ran the heat exchanger coils into the basement water tank and then used a plumber's bit on my drill to bring them upstairs to the bedroom.

Reasonable enough to heat people with wood, but I'd cook my mash over precisely controlled electric heat.

Down under the house on the other side from the water tank, the mash, in five-gallon drums, fermented buried in compost, rigged to a meter that told me the sugar was now done. I'd used a wheat malt, since I remembered a white man friend of my grandfather's saying wheat made the best liquor he'd run. Sprout it just a little, dry it, grind it coarse, wet it down and add molasses and yeast, then some chicken shit. I left out the chicken shit, added nitrates and some urea instead. The mash was ready.

The still was upstairs in the bedroom, where a steady run of electricity wouldn't be suspicious. I took the heat pump and the transformer upstairs.

About halfway upstairs, I felt utterly foolish, but so? All I'd get if I was busted would be a suspended sentence. Tech wouldn't kick me out.

I opened the door to my still room and began building a marine plywood box for the cooler and coil. The wires from the coil thermocouple controlled the fan motor. I sat back on my heels wondering if I should insulate the box, then decided it was better to disperse the heat, even with the cooking element being also thermostatically controlled. The jigsaw cut the vents for the cold air and the exhaust; then I soldered the box and fitted it around the worm.

For the cooking thermostats, I'd taken old fishtank heaters and broken the override high points, then recalibrated them so I could keep the mash around 205. The cooking pot was insulated at the sides. I went downstairs for five gallons of mash.

Rather than lift a five-gallon wooden barrel, I drained the mash into a plastic water carrier. *Don't breathe it*, I'd heard all my life. It was more vomit-provoking than peyote. I needed an activated carbon filter face mask. Shit, I might have to make some money on liquor to pay for all this stuff, I thought as I lugged the mash upstairs. The mash gurgled into the pot like rotten oatmeal and I capped it quickly and began cooking.

The first couple of tablespoons I threw away. That's poisonous low-temperature fusels and esters. Then I began running the distillate into glass bottles, not quite having the equipment for another doubling still. I probed through my valved probe hole—temperature at the cap holding steady at 190, so I shouldn't be getting too much water boiling off, mostly alcohol.

Next, I'd automate, so I wouldn't have to be on site. I kept my eye on the distillate stream, and when it slowed down slightly, I ran the rest off and threw it away. Just save the middles.

As I waited for the cooker to cool, I fantasized rigging an automated still, computer-controlled, just like one of DeSpain's better operators had, hogs getting the spent mash augered up to them.

I love work with electronics and machines. I forget I'm black and a woman, which is very restful some days.

I lifted the top and went back to town to pick up a Spraypro respirator. The clerk looked at me funny and I realized I smelled of alcohol and mash. My hair'd frizzed half a foot beyond my head. Bad as picking up a man's odor from sex, I thought as I blushed. The clerk smiled and handed me the respirator. "Honey, I'd recommend a full-face airline respirator myself. What you got ain't good against mash fumes," he said and handed me an extra box of gas filter canisters.

"Thanks," I said. I hate being called honey. Colorwise, molasses would be more appropriate. Now, was he going to call a distributor and report me? Fool, I told myself, you didn't show him ID.

Back at the house, I put the liquor I'd stilled off in the refrigerator and began packing the mash up in a plastic heat-seal bag, snorting through the respirator the whole time. Then I hauled the cooking vessel into the bathroom and scrubbed it out before putting the first run through. First wine, the old people called the first run.

I used an old iron to heat-seal the mash bag. I should have rigged a centrifuge to whirl out the remaining liquor. Next time, I thought as I lugged the bag downstairs, I'd find out how to process the spent mash in an ecologically correct way. Freeze-dry it and get some pigs to eat it.

The alcohol, when I doubled it, tested out at 190 proof. It tasted like straight grain alcohol, which was, after all, what it was. I wondered what chemicals made scotch scotch and not vodka. DeSpain once asked me if I could counterfeit aged liquors. I swirled the liquor in its glass jar, watching the fine fine bubbles bead up. Surely it could be done. But this batch I poured in a small oak cask that I'd charred inside with a propane torch. I took the cask to the basement and put it in the compost bin.

Leaving the house with the bagged mash in a plastic trash can to dump in someone's field, I thought that distilling could get to be rather boring if that's all one did. Obviously, Dennis had sense enough to hire poor boys to tend still for him.

As I dumped the mash in a pig pasture, I considered I might sell the liquor at The Door 18, a juke joint near Fairystone Park made with a real hotel door in front. Hugous, a third cousin some removed, ran it and sold liquor and marijuana to his friends. A big, even more distant kinsman played jazz bass there on weekends. I knew of the place through trailer cousins who'd taken me there a couple of times before Mamma heard about it. Back in my dorm room, I changed into something red velveteen.

It's a long drive and I took a disk of some white guy reading a piece for next year's English as I go. The guy narrating finds someone floating in a swimming pool over a woman name Daisy when I turn off 57 to the road leading to the place. Couple miles further, there's a big dirt parking lot and two Dobermans wandering around looking for white people to bite. I sort of nod to them and push through The Door 18 and see Hugous sitting wiping glasses and smiling. The big cousin is booming out jazz chords to a hymn playing tinny from a little Taiwanese tape deck.

"Hi, Hugous, you know Albert?"

"Been knowing him since he was a baby."

"I'm his second cousin once removed. We all live on Tiggman Adams Boulevard."

"One them Crowley people."

"Yeah. You might have heard of Tirrella."

"Midwife. She catched my daddy."

I wondered how long I ought to reckon kin with Luther, but decided to get down to business, slant-wise. "You have something a woman could drink."

The cousin playing with the bass stopped. Hugous shrugged and said, "Woman shouldn't, but a woman could." He fetched a bottle from under the counter and poured me a tiny shot.

It wasn't just liquor. The alcohol wheeled the other chemicals into the blood-stream faster. I felt buzzy and the dust motes seemed to be stars. Deep laugh, then bass chords. I managed to say, "I bet it's a hit."

Hugous nodded. We stared at each other, then I had a vision—Dennis DeSpain riding a still barrel, guiding it through the stars by the coil. Then back to The Door 18. Then a vision: a long pink car with women in it squealing. Then I saw Hugous had moved. "How long does it last?" The ocean swept me away to a steel gull-winged car where an Arab-looking man sat counting money. He looked like the photo Dennis had shown me of his partner.

"Oh, tiny time."

"I was going to ask you if I could sell you some liquor." I waited for another vision, but the special effects seemed to be over.

"No more illegal than untaxed liquor, this stuff. Quick change stuff."

I asked, "Can I have a sample? Maybe I can duplicate it?"

"Sure and a half." Hugous put some in a grapefruit juice bottle. "It been to Tech already, though. Nice, not so much effect you got to have it, mellow, not going to attract lots of attention. Some folks confuse it with having a daydream, like the drug wasn't putting in more than they could do themselves musing."

The alcohol part wasn't missing either. I felt very nice now. "Well, if you need any straight liquor, then I could help you. Where did you get this?"

"Alien up in Franklin County. He cra-zy." Hugous's nephew hit a low bass chord on *crazy* and boinged the strings as though he and Hugous'd rehearsed hitting the emphasis. Or else the drug wasn't completely metabolized out.

"Stupid. Everyone can identify him."

"Maybe he got kin working for him," the nephew said.

Hugous said, not really asking, "Maybe he worse to cross than the law. Uglier than the law."

"Maybe it's like if a dog could take up stilling," I said. "Like he isn't human."

"Or they don't have no idea an alien do the unlawful like us," Hugous's nephew said. I was about to tell him I wasn't an us when I caught sight of myself in my velveteen dress in the bar mirror.

DeSpain, you turned me into this velveteen fool.

* * *

I was starting to move my stuff out to the A-frame when Berenice called me at the dorm. "Marie, what are you doing for the summer?"

Stilling, I thought but didn't say. "I rented a house off in Giles. I have to be out of the dorm by next week."

"I don't want to make this sound like I was looking for a maid, but Lilly's going in to have a hysterectomy. Marie, I don't want to have to go to a nursing home, not even for a month."

If it had been Lilly, I'd have taken offense, but Berenice sounded desperate, which is pitiful in a seventy-six-year-old radical woman. Did I really want to get into stilling? Berenice couldn't wait out my pause and said, "We can help pay next year's tuition."

"I've got a full scholarship."

"Can't you get out of the house in Giles County?"

"Not easy. I'd lose my deposit." And I'd have to move this illegal equipment.

"We can pay for it."

"Let me think about it." Shit, why not? I wouldn't have to distill to pay the summer rent then, or go back to Momma's surrounded by all those various kin, some who wanted me to be starchy like them, the others waiting for me to fall. "Would you want me to clean?"

"No, really, I can manage that. Just help with the groceries, carrying them, not buying them. I've got a power vacuum system in the walls."

"*Je ne suis pas une* maid."

"Of course not. *Vous être* companion. Lilly told me it wasn't cancer. Do you think she's lying? If she still wants me to go to the Institute, then I'm going to be paranoid."

I felt like I'd just tottered back from the edge of a cliff, a criminal career, Dennis DeSpain's black mistress and business partner. "Why would Lilly lie to you about that?" I could keep the house in Giles and sneak off from time to time when Berenice visited old radical friends.

"I just realized she could die before me. It isn't likely, but she could. To spite me. I want her around to rub my feet when I'm dying."

"Oh, Berenice."

"And you'll have to go back to school in the fall."

"Yes, regardless of whatever else happens."

"Good for young people to be tough. You're not headed for the grave, so what concern of yours is it?"

Momma doesn't want me to ever work as a maid, I thought. "I could get paralyzed by a car and then you and Lilly would both have to take care of me."

Berenice laughed. I might as well have something more legal to do this summer. And Berenice and Lilly would discourage me from going back to DeSpain and making liquor both. I said, "I think you're being a bit fussy, Berenice." My belly was going, *DeSpain, DeSpain*.

"Sorry. Will you help us out?" She sounded much younger then, more like a regular person instead of whizzy Berenice.

"Sure. And you tell me I'm being a fool if I start talking to Dennis DeSpain again."

"Well, we don't want you to do that. Lilly's representing the alien."

"He'll need her soon," I said.

"Explain."

"I shouldn't have said that," I said, remembering their paranoia that their phones were tapped.

"I agree with you, twice," Berenice said.

"I'll bring my stuff over now if you've got a spare room."

"Then it's a done deal." Berenice sounded so relieved. We hung up.

I went downstairs with my computer and saw Dennis waiting by my car. He didn't look angry, so I hoped he hadn't found out about my own still.

"Marie."

"Dennis, I'm going to be taking care of Berenice Nelson while Lilly's in the hospital having surgery."

"Orris thought we were getting too serious. That's when I realized how much I . . ." Dennis couldn't quite say *wanted*, but he knew *lusted* would be a bit too crude. Seeing him cooled me off a little. I guess. "Would Berenice . . . yeah, she'd mind, wouldn't she? How come you're doing maid's work for her?"

"Companion, not maid. Because otherwise I have to stay at home with all my loser relatives."

"Not all of them are losers, Marie."

"No, but the ones who aren't tell me how stupid it is to have an affair with a cracker bootlegger. No offense, Dennis."

"Orris was threatened because you're at Tech."

"Like if I'd been at New River or cleaning up rooms, Orris would have approved? Jesus, Dennis, how can even a bootlegger stand to be married to such a bitch?"

He twitched his face muscles and froze them. I feared I'd protested too much or that he'd caught some vocal cord corrosion from my breathing in over mash. "Orris made herself into a lady."

Well, I *was* just insulting his wife. "I'm honored that she considers me a threat, but, Dennis, I quit you. Not the other way around."

"I thought of you when I saw a Chinese Negro Hollins student."

"Go after her then, Dennis."

"She was a whore."

"Dennis, if it takes slutting to get rid of you, I'll take out a license."

"You're not like that."

"Not before I met you, I wasn't. I'm still an honors chemical engineering student. I'm not sleazing around with a poly sci degree just to say I'm not a mill hand."

"You think you're better than us?"

"I will be."

"Christ, Marie. I want to see you again." Then he said, "Lilly's that alien's lawyer, isn't she?" Dennis is so sneaky. Maybe he had my phone tapped to see where I'd be next?

"I don't know."

"When she going in for surgery, Marie?" He started to come closer, but moved back when I stiffened.

"I don't know that, either."

"Well, I can ask around. Probably call her office. Have someone else call. She refused to represent me."

"Well, she has better sense than some people."

"Marie, I just want to talk to you." He ought to have known *talking to* in Black English meant *seeing*, meant *going out with*, all those euphemisms. He smiled slightly as if he'd realized what he'd have said if he'd been talking Black.

"Dennis, what you thinking about that alien?"

"I been seeing sign of its dealing on Loose Trade. And someone got Hugous's account away from me."

"You been following him?"

He shuddered ever so slightly. "I dunno."

I didn't want to provoke Dennis by asking if he feared the alien.

DeSpain Identifies a Trade Rival at Least Once

DeSpain decided the alien seemed to be in the liquor business without anyone's permission—no legal license, even if a man could get one in Southwest Virginia, no agreements with the present illegal distributors. But the only thing wrong was that the alien seemed too open about what he was doing. DeSpain sat in front of his computer for an hour as Loose Trade deals popped on and off the screen. He wondered what arcane connections this alien could have.

Orris came in and leaned her breasts against his back. The nipples felt accusing. "How's Steve doing in school?" DeSpain asked.

"I have no idea. You signed his report card last week. I told you I wanted to see it." Her voice rumbled through his body.

"I've got a rival. He hired that Lilly Nelson woman to represent him."

"I've heard that she never represents liquor makers."

"He's that fucking alien. I guess minority something or other played a part, manipulated her sympathies. How is he getting away with it? Who is he paying off?"

"Is he really that much of a threat?"

"Somebody's taken half my nigger accounts."

Orris pulled her breasts out of his back so her voice wasn't vibrating through his spine and ribs but hit him straight in the ears. "You don't need a female black to be helping. What about bringing in a male?"

"I've got to find out what I'm up against." DeSpain sat thinking in front of the keyboard, then exited the system and said, "I'll go pay him a visit. No threats, just sniff around a little."

"Take me out to lunch first."

They drove to the Shogun, where Orris ordered miso soup and a cold noodle dish. DeSpain stared at the octopus legs with their organic suction cups and said, "I'll order in a minute."

Orris said, "Europeans think Americans work too much." She and the Japanese chef always slightly mocked every other living being who wasn't Japanese or Orris.

The Japanese chef giggled. DeSpain felt his face turn red. Orris whispered, "Ask him what Japanese eat for lunch."

DeSpain knew what he felt about the businessmen who ordered various sushi cuts set up on plastic slabs, talking about Citicorp, Mitsubishi, and the Orvis catalogue center. "Knowing you, it's miso soup and noodles."

"Precisely."

"Well, bad enough dealing with them all so superior in Tokyo. Now they moving to Roanoke." DeSpain heard the old accent grip his voice and saw the business guys at the table wince. Well, if they were so stupid as to eat sushi for lunch when real Japanese ate miso soup and noodles, DeSpain wasn't going to cringe.

"You couldn't deal with an Osaka bean tractor factory. What makes you think you can cut an alien out of your territory?"

"Shit, Orris. If I'd known you were in this mood, I'd have brung you an Elastrator and you could snag my balls with the rubber rings." DeSpain scowled at the businessmen too dumb to know what to order from a Japanese for lunch.

The chef muttered, "Europeans think Americans work too hard. Europeans must not work at all."

DeSpain said to Orris, "You made his day." He ordered miso soup himself and ate it even if it did seem made from fermented leaves and slightly rotten soybeans. He asked the chef, "Is it hot in Japan?"

"Not all over," the chef said.

When they finished eating, DeSpain said, "Orris, would you want to go with me to see the alien?"

Orris looked as if she wanted to remind him that on their wedding day he'd promised to handle all the illegalities without bothering her. Then she sighed and said, "Why not? If I'm with you, it's just a social call, right."

"Right."

"What about Steve?"

Dennis said, "Go call your mother and see if she can pick him up at the bus stop."

DeSpain waited. Orris came back from the phone booth and nodded. He helped her in the car and asked, "Scenic route or 220?"

"Let's just get there okay. I don't want to be too late coming home or Mother will worry."

They took 220 to Rocky Mount and picked up 40. Orris said, "I sometimes wish we lived in Roanoke."

"Man once told me Roanoke had the worse vice for a city that size he'd ever seen."

Orris laughed. "I'm not being hypocritical," DeSpain said. "Liquor's not like drugs. People can afford liquor without stealing."

"I said when I married you that I understood what you did. Are you getting too soft, perhaps?"

Shit on Orris when she had these Elastrator moods. They passed out of the rest of Rocky Mount in silence. Then, as they passed Ferrum College and began the mountain part of the ride, Orris said, "I have a tremendous nostalgia for the present."

"What do you mean by that?" DeSpain said, sure that Orris had deliberately made a confusing statement.

"Whatever happens at the alien's house will be the future. I love everything in my life up to that moment."

"Even me?"

"I do love you, Dennis. You make my life dramatic, but you're not so brutal that you make me nervous. Even if that reduces your efficiency."

"You think this alien's going to gobble us up."

A semi was laboring up the road, having ignored the warnings back in Woolwine. Orris watched it, Dennis watched it, both wondering if it would collapse on them and make all Orris's fears of the alien moot. It tottered on the turn but didn't fall.

"I saw one once crush a Volkswagen on Route 8," Orris said. "Mother beat me for coming home late. I had to go back and cut across to 58. We'd gone to the beach music festival and we were going to take the parkway home."

"You want to go to the beach music festival? It's next week."

"I really am worried about what we're going to be doing in the next hour."

"And you still remember your mamma whipping you for coming home late, even worry about it at twenty-seven years old. God, Orris, she won't whip Steve because we're late."

"This alien, I hear that he spies on us. He memorizes what people do."

"He knew what I did."

"Did you tell me that?"

"I can't remember."

They shut up again. Dennis looked over at Orris and saw her lips move as if she was worrying them with her teeth, without letting the teeth show. Discreetly scared.

Another truck passed them, on straight enough road that they didn't have to worry. Then Dennis saw a glimpse of faceted ears under a baseball cap, the alien driving a deluxe Oldsmobile van. "That's him," he said to Orris. "In the cruiser van." He found a driveway and turned around.

Orris said, "Maybe the trucks are his, too. It's a bit unusual to see two tractor-trailer rigs trying to make it up Route 40 in the same hour."

"Well, at least he didn't know we were coming," Dennis said, noting the license plate on the cruiser: TURK. It reminded him that he had to fly over to Uralsk the first of July.

The Oldsmobile pulled over. Dennis pulled over behind him. The alien came out of the car and handed Dennis house keys and said, "You can wait for me at my house." His English was better than it had been when DeSpain was fishing on the Smith.

Orris took the alien's house keys from Dennis and said, "Thanks."

Dennis wondered if she'd gone nuts. He asked the alien, "You want us to wait for you at your house. Why?"

"You were looking for me, weren't you?"

"Yes." Dennis wondered for a second how the alien knew, then remembered that he'd turned around to follow the Oldsmobile.

"We should talk, you and I," the alien said. "And you must know where my house is if you were driving this way."

"People gossip," Orris said to the alien as he turned to go back to the Oldsmobile cruiser. The alien shrugged his shoulders before he got back in the car.

DeSpain started his car again. For an instant he thought about following the alien, now disappearing around a curve. *Those were his trucks. He's really operating at scale.* "What do you think?" he said to Orris.

"It's your business. Is it better to be friendly at first or hostile?"

"I don't know in this case. He's traveling awful conspicuous." He turned toward Patrick County. Orris looked at the alien's house keys. DeSpain glanced over briefly and saw a cylinder key and two computer card keys on the chain.

Yes, those were his trucks, DeSpain thought as they pulled in the dirt road full of double tire tracks just beyond the Patrick County line that would wind back into Franklin. "I know someone's in on this," he said.

"Do you bribe law enforcement officers?" Orris asked almost as if it had never occurred to her.

"You're supposed to be discreet." DeSpain tried to sort out the tracks—at least two tractor-trailer rigs, the cruiser, and one motorcycle. "This is crazy."

"Unless he has alien weapons." Orris said that as if she'd discarded the thought really, but just wanted to mention it in case.

The Volvo motor cut dead, the car rolling uphill on its own momentum as though the timing belt broke. But it wasn't the kind of car that broke its timing belt. DeSpain threw on the brakes to keep from rolling backward and tried the lights—no electrical system. "You know, if he'd been human," DeSpain said to Orris, "I wouldn't have been so stupid as to take his goddamn keys."

Orris said, "We'll have to wait for him now."

"If he's got a phone, I'm calling a tow truck. Of course he'd got a phone line out."

"Maybe it's dedicated to computers?"

"Orris, I'll get someone to get me a tow truck. I think a motorcycle went in and not out."

Orris sighed and opened the car door. "Shouldn't we push it off the road?"

"Shit." DeSpain saw that he could roll the Volvo backwards downhill. Once he did that, he tried to start it again. It started. Something a few yards away killed electrical systems. He was glad he didn't have a pacemaker. "We can mail him his keys."

Just then they heard the motorcycle in the distance. Its sound shifted, dopplering in on them. They saw the helmeted motorcyclist dressed in unstudded leathers, a skid scuff along one arm. He stopped, went to a tree, then said, "You can bring the car through now.'' The voice was broadcast outside the helmet, which was too opaque to see though. The face screen looked newer than the rest of the helmet, which seemed to have been abraded in the same accident that scarred the leather jacket.

DeSpain followed the motorcyclist back to the house, stopping twice when the man got off and fiddled with various trees. The motorcyclist asked, ''Do you have the keys? Turk locked me out.''

Before DeSpain could decided whether to admit he did, Orris said, ''Yes.''

The motorcyclist took off his helmet. He had short dark hair and a perfect nose with a matching jawline that DeSpain had priced once at a plastic surgeon's at $25,000. DeSpain wondered what was this clown. He said to the man, ''I'm Dennis DeSpain. Turk is the alien, right?'' When the man nodded, he kept on, ''He sent out a load of liquor.''

''We're not sure what to make of this, Mr. DeSpain, but then you're a liquor distributor, too, aren't you?''

''I don't know a man who's proved it in nine years. We've got a hardware store in town, health-food store by the lake, motel, overseas investments.''

''Mr. DeSpain, neither the Department of Defense nor the State Department cares about Franklin County illegalities except that an alien is here, modeling his behavior after you people, giving keys to his house to local moonshiners.''

''I'm not a moonshiner,'' DeSpain said. He always associated the terms *moonshine* and *moonshiner* with people from Greensboro who wanted to play folkloristic. ''I wanted to meet the alien.''

''Why? Don't explain. I know why.''

''And why haven't you federal people done anything?''

Orris said, ''Why don't we go inside? I'm Orris DeSpain. And what shall we call you?''

''Henry Allen,'' the man said. Orris gave the keys to DeSpain, who found the hole for the round key and the slots for the two cards. Allen said, ''Put the two cards in first, then turn the key. Otherwise, you release the Dobermans.''

DeSpain put the cards in carefully, then turned the key. He listened for dogs before he opened the door. ''Do you know he's hired a lawyer?''

''We need to know more about Turk and his relationships to the other aliens before we do anything.''

''He must know what he'd doing is illegal, so why don't you bust him?'' DeSpain looked around the entranceway and saw nothing alien about it—chrome chandelier, flocked white wallpaper, terrazzo tile.

''This way's the living room,'' Allen said.

They went to the left through an archway. The men sat down on suede chairs, leaving the couch to Orris. She took off one shoe and dragged her nylon-covered toes through the deep pile. DeSpain knew she could feel if the carpet was wool or synthetic, even through her stockings.

''I think he thought I'd go home after we finished talking,'' Allen said. ''So he locked me out. But he knows what I'm doing.''

Orris said, ''Maybe he has our house bugged? And he didn't want you to meet us.''

"Orris," DeSpain said, thinking she'd gone a bit paranoid with that.

"He could easily," Allen said.

"And you letting him bug U.S. citizens?"

"We're trying to see what's going on. We . . ." The man stopped talking as if realizing that the alien could be listening in now.

A wheeled robot turtle came in and triangulated each of them with its servomotor neck. Allen said, "If you remember anything after it sprays us, call State."

DeSpain had only a vague recollection of it later. He and Orris were driving home when the radio programs told them that five hours had elapsed.

Orris looked at her watch and said, "Mother will be furious."

4

The Game of the Name

I *hate it when I can't remember*, DeSpain thought as he shaved himself in the morning. Vague images of a wheeled turtle named Henry Allen floated through his mind. He decided he'd gotten drunk with a human cohort of the alien's. Nothing had been resolved. The alien never came back.

Orris watched him from the bathroom door. She looked haggard without the polish makeup gave her.

"I'm going to see Hugous at The Door 18. He's buying from the alien."

"Dennis, I think our memories were tampered with. Maybe you should let this one alone."

"Orris, maybe that alien is just checking out the territory before whole bunches of alien bootleggers come in."

"And maybe his kind is going to push us out of the business. You've got other investments."

"Orris, now you want me to quit." DeSpain wondered if Marie would have dared him on and decided that she would have. He finished shaving and combed his hair, then put on a suit to show respect to Hugous.

Orris didn't volunteer to come this time. She found the Volvo keys for him and looked down and to the side as she dangled the keys out to him on her straight-out arm and index finger, as rigid as an admonishing statue.

Be that way, DeSpain thought. Her mother had yelled at them when they picked up Steve, tucking him in the backseat of the Volvo still half asleep.

Hugous was out on a tractor plowing corn land behind The Door 18. DeSpain wondered how, even with income from The Door, the man could afford a balloon-tired air-conditioned cab item like the yellow machine now folding the ends of its giant harrows and turning in the field. The harrows unfolded and the steel spikes bounced against the clay, then impaled the clods.

DeSpain went through the hanging open old hotel door and sat down at the bar, watching the dust motes in the sun coming in through the back window. He figured this'd get some communication from Hugous faster than going out to the field and yelling through the machine noise.

A small camera over the bar swiveled. DeSpain crouched, uneasy. Turtles with mobile steel necks. He reached over the bar and brought out a bottle and glass. Let's see what the alien's making, he thought. He poured a taste in a glass and drank.

Scuffed leather . . . call the State Department and ask for Henry Allen . . . motorcycles . . . stalled engines.

Damn stuff is drugged. And I was drugged with something the opposite earlier. We didn't get blind drunk.

Hugous came in with just the sweat he'd built up walking away from the air-conditioned tractor cab. He said, "DeSpain. You go on now after you pay me for my liquor."

DeSpain had never heard the man sound so full of menace. He had to call the State Department, ask for Henry Allen before this alien's man did something worse to his memory. "How much I owe you?"

Hugous's chest rumbled something too nasty to be a chuckle. "About five hundred dollars from all the time you cheat me," he said, "but five dollars will cover what you just drank."

DeSpain pulled out a twenty and looked up at the camera. It nodded at him, but then he saw the remote controller in the black man's fist. Hugous nodded, too.

Why doesn't someone stop the alien? What the alien could do to a man's memory was a national security threat. He wasn't just a business rival; he had tricks beyond human nature. DeSpain went to a public phone at a country store out Route 57 near Philpott and used his phone credit card to call the State Department. "I'm looking for a man named Henry Allen," he said to the first human-sounding interactive voice that picked up after the touch-tone connection messages had played.

Another voice, male, replied, "Henry Allen is on vacation."

"I saw him in Franklin County." DeSpain wondered if the alien sent out a bug from The Door 18 to follow him, but continued, "He was observing the alien."

"My information is that he's on vacation. Could you leave a number where he can call you back?"

DeSpain left the number of the motel he co-owned with a third cousin down near the Henry County line, a man who often took messages for him. Then he said, "Look, the alien is selling drugs disguised in bootleg liquor. I think you ought to look into it. He has another drug that destroys more than short-term memory."

"Alcohol does that," the man said.

"It isn't alcohol," DeSpain said. "I seriously advise someone to look into it. Someone else. Henry's too cozy with the alien."

"Mr. DeSpain, our voice-print records show that you served a month of a two-year suspended sentence for liquor distribution when you were nineteen. And your driver's license was suspended. What are you trying to pull?"

"Okay, okay, I used to sell liquor. The alien is doing it now and he's mixed drugs in it. Memory-flash drugs."

"Mr. DeSpain, I advise you to mind your own business."

I am, DeSpain thought. "Henry asked me to call him at the State Department if I got any memories back. I'm doing precisely that now."

"Henry Allen is on vacation."

DeSpain hung up and wondered if Henry Allen would be reprimanded for speaking to a felon. Then he wondered if that bitch Marie knew enough biochemistry to make an antidote to the alien's drugs.

He thought about calling her, remembered how nasty Marie's mother was. Instead, he called up the Virginia Alcohol Beverage Control Board—this is how people at the stills went from being independent to employees of distributors in the first place.

"ABC," the voice answered.

"I'd like to report a still." DeSpain hoped the ABC office didn't have a voice analyzer. "The alien who's living below Ferrum."

"You want to give a name?"

"No."

"Sounds dubious to me. Why should this alien be making liquor?"

"Send one of your people to The Door 18 on Route 666 in Patrick County." DeSpain heard a helicopter flying over, toward the phone booth. He hung up the phone. The helicopter swung around overhead. He pulled out his Beretta and wished he'd thought to bring a gas mask. The gun felt hot in his hand. DeSpain hoped he wasn't being bombarded with microwaves.

The phone rang. *Should I shoot or answer it?*

He picked up the phone and breathed into it, just to let whoever know someone was listening. "DeSpain? This is Henry Allen."

"Are you in the helicopter?"

"I can hear it. I'm sorry, DeSpain."

DeSpain stepped outside, checked the helicopter's belly for police insignia, and raised his gun, fired, missed the gas tanks. The helicopter swung out of range and hovered.

Allen yelled into the phone. DeSpain went to pick up the receiver and said, "Fortunately, the helicopter didn't seem to have an effective drug delivery system on board. So what can you do for me?"

"I need help evaluating the situation."

"Your alien's drugging the liquor supplies. Is that your helicopter out there? State Department? CIA?"

"Go in the grocery and wait."

DeSpain wondered if the clerks had called the deputies already, but crouched down and ran to the store. A young man behind the cash register had a twelve-gauge pointing at DeSpain's belly. DeSpain smiled and tried to put his automatic up. Outside, the helicopter had grappled his car's front bumper and was half dragging, half lifting it away.

"Dennis DeSpain, who are you messing with these days?" the man with the twelve-gauge said.

DeSpain remembered the man now: as a teenager, he'd driven liquor to Roanoke for DeSpain when his daddy was in jail. DeSpain finally got his automatic back in its holster. "Jack, sorry, Jack. I don't know who's out there, but it's not ABC or local law."

"Aliens abducted a couple from around here," one of the other men in the store said. "They used a helicopter just like that." The machine he pointed to had finally wenched DeSpain's Volvo under its belly and was flying away.

DeSpain wondered if all the hillbilly paranoia about aliens was accurate, a real war was going on while most Americans watched television. The helicopter came back and landed outside the phone booth. The alien, wearing body armor and a helmet, got out and spoke into the phone.

"Son of a bitch," DeSpain said. "I'm going to call the fucking State Department back and tell them they lied."

One of the guys said. "Government always lies. DeSpain, you especially ought to know that."

The alien moved slowly toward the store. Half the guys in the store pulled out boot knives or handguns. A Yankee woman began screaming when the man next to her pulled an Uzi out of his attaché case. DeSpain nodded to the man with the Uzi, Jones, a competitor who occasionally tried to set up shop around the 122 bridge. Jones said to the woman, who'd shut it down to gasping, "You go outside and make peace, you think guns so bad."

The woman was going toward the door when the phone rang. The store manager swung his twelve-gauge around across his shoulder and answered the phone, "Kirtland General Store." He handed the phone to DeSpain and said, "Guy named Allen."

DeSpain said into the phone, "The son of a bitch stole my car, he tinkered with my memory, he's coming in now."

Allen said, "Tell him he needs to talk to Droymaruse."

DeSpain said, "Tell him to talk to Droymaruse? Who the fuck is Droymaruse, and what the fuck good will that do?"

"It's another one of his people," Allen said.

At the same time, the woman said, "I'll give him the message." She was pretty brave for a pacifist, DeSpain thought as she went to the door, opened it, and said, "You need to talk to Droymaruse."

The alien stopped and turned around. DeSpain asked Allen, "What the fuck was that all about?"

"Droymaruse claims he doesn't know what he's doing, either."

The helicopter blades began turning. DeSpain wondered whether he could drive his car away, if he dared. He said to the world at large, "I need a beer."

Allen's voice from the receiver seemed remote. He seemed to be saying, "I'll come pick you up." DeSpain wondered if they'd all been drugged anyway. He couldn't remember feeling this buzzed since the night the ABC and state drug people snagged his car. Almost like the helicopter had done today, but it had been a big road hook adapted from gear used to land planes on carriers. Popped up out of the highway and bang-go. They'd torn his car to large metal shreds looking for cocaine even after they found the liquor.

"Here's your beer. We won't charge you for the army," the manager said.

He fitted his shotgun back under the counter, then took DeSpain's money. "You've got to drink it off premises," he said when DeSpain popped the top.

"Oh, give me a fucking break," DeSpain said. The other customers stared him down, so DeSpain decided to go out front anyway. He wrapped the can in a brown paper bag and walked through the parking lot to the weeds near a power line, drained the can in two breaths.

Allen came up on his stupid motorcycle. "I don't think your car is drivable. Can you ride on the back of this?"

DeSpain decided to chance it. "But let me drive," he said, aware of his competition watching from inside.

"You have to wear the helmet, then. I don't have a spare." Allen handed the helmet to DeSpain, who grunted as he forced the thing on. Allen's braincase was a tad too little.

DeSpain gunned the engine and felt Allen's fingers tighten around his waist, then tap—*be careful with my machine.* Sumbitch pantywaist cookie pusher, DeSpain thought, twisting his wrist and stomping on the pedals to get the Honda moving. He headed up toward Franklin County waiting for a helicopter to pounce, but made it home okay.

Orris and Steve came out when they heard the unfamiliar machine. DeSpain wanted to curse them out for not being more careful, but instead introduced Henry Allen: "Mr. Allen is with the State Department. He's helping figure out the alien."

"Glad to meet you. I'm Orris DeSpain and this is our son, Steve. Would you like to come in?"

"Your husband and I need to talk. Thanks."

"Tea or coffee?" Orris asked. "I've got fruit compote or a cheesecake."

"Coffee, that's enough," Allen said.

Orris nodded and went to the kitchen. The men sat down, DeSpain and Henry on the couch. DeSpain looked at his son and said, "You know you're not supposed to go outside if you don't recognize the car."

"Sorry," Steve said.

"We're going to be in the basement talking after we have our coffee."

"Is this man investigating you? Kids at school say you're a bootlegger."

Allen's lip on one side went back, so fast that if DeSpain wasn't looking at him, he would have missed the expression. Allen said, "We're asking your daddy's advice on how to deal with someone who's making drugged liquor."

Damn, DeSpain thought, you have the dialect almost right, Mr. Diplomatic Corps, except that I never wanted my son to know where half the money comes from. Steve looked at his father and sighed like a little old man. He said, "It's okay, Daddy, the teacher says liquor-making should be legal, without taxes."

DeSpain said, "Steve, we're not talking about me. Why don't you go find your mother?"

"But, Daddy, we've been talking about this in school."

"Go. I'll tell you about moonshine later."

Steve went out, his feet dragging his sock toes under.

Allen said, "I thought a moonshine area would be more rugged."

"Never could grow corn on a 45-degree slope," DeSpain said. "Also, how you going to get enough sugar in? In the old days, we used about a ton a week. Took trains to deliver."

"Now there's not much market for moonshine, I suppose," Allen said, "other than the blind pigs."

"As long the price doubles from federal tax, you gonna have a market for it," DeSpain said. "But I've personally gotten out of it."

Allen looked like he was going to contradict DeSpain, but instead asked, "Do you know the alien has a lawyer on retainer? Lilly Nelson."

DeSpain said, "She'd never take human liquor makers as clients unless they were black and she thought they were innocent."

Orris brought in the coffee. Steve, with a little smile on his face, carried in the cups and saucers. Mr. Allen stood, but DeSpain didn't. Orris served them quietly and then said to Steve, "Let's leave the men alone, sweetheart. Dennis, he was in the hall, listening."

"Daddy's talking to a federal man."

Allen said, "I'm not here to bust moonshiners. I'm here to find out what the alien is doing and why."

"Steve, the alien wrecked my memory Wednesday and then tried to attack me today. He isn't one of us just because he makes liquor."

Orris was smiling as if thinking *since when does a new liquor distributor not have to hack a place for himself*? She said, "Steve, now, or we can't go swimming before the pool closes."

"Oh, goody, a bribe. I want to know what's going on."

DeSpain said, "Don't act like such a jerk in front of company."

"Okay, but we can swim all night at my uncle's."

Orris said, "Those people are a bit rough."

Allen said, "Look, if you don't listen to your parents, I'm going to have to swat you."

"Daddy won't let you."

"Come on, Steve, go with your mother, now. Orris, call back before you leave, okay?"

After Orris and Steve had left, Allen said, "Droymaruse will keep Turkemaw busy for a few hours. I don't believe they're all tourists, but that's what they claim. Somebody's got to be crew. At least, Droymaruse."

DeSpain needed to check his bulletin boards. Pending deals from Roanoke to the Urals needed his attention soon. His real business could slump while the government used him to fight the alien. Maybe he could make a deal with the alien himself. Lilly Nelson did. Sentimentality for minorities quite overcame her prejudice against distillers. DeSpain said, "Since Reagan, the feds have been out of the still-busting business. Why are you here?"

"We've got information enough to say the business continues, which did surprise me when I was assigned to Turkemaw, but we're more concerned that his people get a good impression of us."

"Like Americans in Russia who were real rollovers. You know how much I had to be fighting that."

"Yes, we're beginning to understand Turkemaw might be probing us in some way, with plausible deniability by the others. It seems a shame to start interplanetary relations on a paranoid basis, though."

"Knew a paranoid once. He had great ideas if you could put them together. I used him for a while in security," DeSpain said. He remembered how the man didn't work out in the end, rather spectacularly, but DeSpain himself had a good working knowledge of plausible deniability.

"I get your meaning," Allen said. "Maybe there were kidnappings."

"Especially of folks who wander about of a night." DeSpain decided he'd drift dialect toward the folksy, keep Allen slightly to way off guard, depending on how bigoted he was. "Folks coming back from something they shouldn't outta gone to might like to be kidnapped." Nope, that comment was a little too perceptive. "So what do you want to do? I ain't had no experience with stereo-speaker-eared creatures."

"Give it a break, DeSpain. I also know you went to Emory and Henry."

"God, you're smarter than I thought you was. Man, you must have gone to Harvard."

"Princeton."

"Even better."

"We know Turk's lawyer is going in for surgery in a few days. She'll be pretty inactive for a month. If he put a lawyer on retainer, he must feel vulnerable in a way we haven't spotted yet."

"He's making illegal liquor. He's drugging people."

"State doesn't get involved in disputes between businessmen, even illegal businessmen. That's Department of Justice."

"I resent you implying that I'm in illegal businesses." DeSpain didn't want any competitors, human or alien, to hear what he needed to say. "Let's go out back. Bring your coffee if you want. Orris has a wonderful garden." Any more talk along these lines needed to be done in the trailer, DeSpain decided. DeSpain swept his trailers for bugs and replaced them every so often, renovated them enough to pick up some profit. Broken-down trailers cluttered the landscape so badly DeSpain could get all he wanted for the hauling. Allen refilled his coffee cup and followed DeSpain out the back door.

This month's trailer sat on concrete blocks about five feet from the ground. A stack of old mill machinery packing boxes made the stairs. Allen climbed up the boxes to the trailer looking as if he would rather have crawled but the coffee cup got in his way; then he carefully put his weight onto the trailer floor. DeSpain watched the State Department man look around at the rubber soundproofing, then explained, "I rehab trailers from time to time. Soundproof so the neighbors don't complain about late-hour drilling and sawing."

"I'd have thought you would have your secure room away from home. Don't most people in your business try to keep the family out of it?"

"Orris would worry if I had a place out." Maybe Allen was a new-style federal revenuer, DeSpain thought, running a fancy variant sting operation with this alien. "So what do you want me to do for you, and how much protection will I get? I take it you don't want him gunned down."

"No. We'll protect you, but not for that." Allen put his coffee cup down. "We want to know why he's making liquor. Just like we want to know why one's breeding fish in Africa."

DeSpain smiled slightly, sure the man came stocked with too many stories of bib-overalled pickup truck drivers with semiautomatics in the gun racks. "How did the alien get his attention focused on me?"

"You threaten to inform on independent still men who wouldn't work for you."

"No, not me personally, but it has been done that way." DeSpain wondered if Bobby had gone to talking. "Look, why don't you tell the other aliens what Turkemaw is doing? And if they don't stop him, then you know who is doing what here."

"We don't know that their motivations are human. We won't know why."

"God, you need better spies. Shit, Turk knows us by name and occupation."

Henry Allen sighed. "I had no idea why he was so curious."

"You got him everyone's name, face, occupation?"

"Just eccentrics."

"How am I eccentric?"

"You're a trout-fishing moonshiner. I thought that was pretty funny. Like a radical lawyer living in Rocky Mount."

"So you set me up for him?" DeSpain wondered if people playing by their human rules would be able to deal with aliens. "How much do you know about them?"

"They have space travel and we don't. They know where we live and we don't know where they live. State and Defense consider both those things to be critical."

"Maybe we ought to belly-crawl to 'um and cut a deal.'

"Or get some of them to come here and educate us. Americans and Europeans did that for the Japanese."

"Allen, you've got to be able to tell me more than you're telling me. Yes, the man—alien—is taking over some of the local distillers' accounts, and yes, in the past we'd work over trade competitors in various ways. Mostly psychological, like threatening to turn them in to the law. But it was a decent business. Distillers I know never poisoned their buyers with lead salts. Shit, man, one distiller even tested for poisons."

"I notice you're not saying that was you."

"How do I know Turk isn't working for the feds in a tax grab?"

"I can offer you immunity if you testify against him, should we go that route. We need someone who understands the business and who can get close to him."

"Considering he drugged my memory out when I had my wife with me coming for a social visit, I don't think he exactly trusts me."

"You can find someone for us."

Bobby would be perfect, DeSpain thought. "I might be able to help you, but it's going to take some looking. I really don't have the connections I used to. Honest."

Henry Allen looked around the trailer, moving his head up and down, not just his eyes. He grinned when he saw DeSpain got his point. Yeah, nobody innocent would have a trailer rigged like this. DeSpain decided to get rid of this trailer and use his alternate secure room until this anti-alien deal had gone down.

5

Bobby Considers a Proposition Only a Trifle More Appealing

What DeSpain really wanted to do was to take Orris and the boy to the coast, take a charter out to the Gulf Stream; and kill a marlin. If only he were really rich, out of the mountains, with a accent nobody could trace, he could . . .

Do what? He had to tell Bobby to get close to the alien. But that might be dangerous if Bobby was so pissed about being bullied into work that he'd side with the alien.

"Orris, I'm going out."

"When will you be back?" she asked, her hands full of flowers she was arranging in an iron Japanese vase.

"By midnight. I'm taking the truck."

He drove to Bobby's after calling a garage to rescue his Volvo. Suit in a truck sure looks weird, he thought as he looked down at himself.

Bobby and his wife were sitting on the front porch snuggling their children, a little skinny girl against Bobby and the ailing baby boy sprawled in his wife's lap. Bobby said to his wife, "Think you better get the chaps inside." The little girl looked at DeSpain and ran. Bobby's wife lifted the boy up against her shoulder and stood up. She looked from Bobby to DeSpain, one hand cupped behind the boy's head.

DeSpain came up the porch steps and opened the door for her. He could barely hear her thank-you.

After she was inside, Bobby said, "So what brings you here, Mr. DeSpain?"

"I'm thinking that if you can help me out a little, then I might be willing to see you set up as an independent."

"You want me to go with your nephews and beat on somebody?"

"Bobby, just find me out some information."

"I'm not real good at being sneaky, Mr. DeSpain."

"Well, if you can do this for me, I'll see to it that you don't have to be devious anymore. Get close to the alien, offer him your liquor."

"That's not all."

"Well, I've got to consider what I want to know after you get close to him." DeSpain needed to know how much the alien intended to expand his operation. Maybe this wasn't a fuss, but if it was, and if the local law wouldn't cooperate at all, he could use Bobby to deliver a bomb.

"Shit, DeSpain, you wouldn't ask much."

"Are you afraid of the alien?"

"Sheriff talked about his helicopter and your car over the radio. Claim was, the alien's grapple brake cut loose and you just happened to be snagged. Dennis, maybe you're picking on something you ought not."

DeSpain's belly tightened, but he thought he was keeping his voice right when he said, "State Department is behind us checking."

Bobby said, "Put that way, I'll call on the space guy."

DeSpain said, "If he isn't in the phone book, then I can arrange for you to leave him E-mail." He got up, not quite sure that Bobby wouldn't side with the alien himself, but if it looked like it was going that way, he'd bring in his cousins again.

"Will you really leave me alone if I tell you about the alien?"

"Surely."

"Gonna look bad for you if you can't protect your own."

DeSpain didn't think of Bobby as his own.

When the Lawyer's Away

I asked in the recovery room if my operation was over, asked enough times that about the fifth time I was apologizing for asking. After I got that clear and was upstairs, I didn't feel like talking. Nurses came in offering painkillers. One was so nervous when I refused, I took the shot anyway. Stainless-steel staples ran every quarter inch from just below my navel to a finger span above the pubic bone.

I napped for a while, then woke up to see Marie sitting by my bed. She squirmed with all she had to tell me.

"Am I okay?" I asked. I had an oxygen gizmo poked into both nostrils and an intravenous needle holding my wrist rigid.

"It looked like a big gizzard," she told me, "only round."

"The doctor normally shows the organs only to the family." I've heard that only Southern doctors come out with the organs.

"But what I'm really here about is Bobby. He came by to see Berenice this morning. He's scared. DeSpain . . ."

"Uh. What about the biopsy?"

"I know you're not feeling quite up to working now, but Bobby wonders what it would take to get a court order to keep DeSpain from bothering him."

"What does DeSpain . . ." *Why did I come back here to practice,* I thought, *when I could have shared a practice in Charlottesville?* People would have let me recover in peace then. "Was my biopsy okay?"

"I don't know. They'd tell you first."

"Marie, I like you a lot and all but—"

"Well, maybe it can wait for a couple of days. DeSpain wants Bobby to check out the alien for him. Spy for him."

"I should be out in another three days. Tell them all to wait."

"Five days. The day of surgery counts as day zero."

I was too tired to suggest anything. Marie put a piece of ice in my mouth, then more, spooning ice into my mouth as if it were oatmeal. I threw up. Marie buzzed in a nurse to take care of the pan.

Argh. I don't know if I recovered faster from the worry or not, but after Marie left, I got up to use the toilet. The nurse rolled the IV with one hand and held me up with the other.

"Have you heard anything about the alien?" I asked.

She shook her head, but with nurses, one never can be sure whether the sign is for *no* or *you're not ready to get involved in that yet, honey.*

I slept after she gave me the pain shot, then woke up about four hours later, not particularly in pain, but really awake when the night nurse came in to take my blood pressure, temperature, and pulse.

"Need anything?" she asked.

I mumbled no and closed my eyes. I'd call my alien client tomorrow and advise him to stop doing anything that could get him arrested until I got better.

In the morning, I watched the IV needle keep coming and coming out of my hand as the nurse pulled. "That's why they taped you so good," she said as she covered the hole. As I reached for the phone to call Turk, I felt a dull ache at my wrist bones from the four-inch needle.

Turk's voice reminded me of how weak I still was. "This is your lawyer, Lilly Nelson. Don't mess with Bobby Vipperman. DeSpain's trying to get him to inform on you, but he doesn't want to do it."

"Thank you for the information," the alien said and hung up. I suddenly remembered the first time I'd seen him, how alien he seemed then. Over the phone, I forgot those stereo speaker ears.

Humans Getting Together

Bobby ignored me. Bobby was what we call a dumb-ass naive racist, so prevalent in Southwest Virginia they made DeSpain look good to me. "Berenice, that alien was right behind me, even when I was going ninety. I heard he knows everything in the county. I don't guess anyone could tell me how he came to know DeSpain wanted me to investigate him."

I asked, "Where were you?"

"I was driving around below Ferrum, thinking about spying on him, Marie. Berenice, maybe I should stand up for my own kind and help DeSpain deal with him."

Berenice said, "I'll get you some tea. Sit with Marie while I set up." Bobby sat off from me on the porch while Berenice made iced tea.

"You been seeing DeSpain, Marie?" he finally asked, raising his chin from where he'd been keeping it tucked.

"I'm not talking to DeSpain anymore," I said, flushing. "I told Lilly that DeSpain asked you to spy on Turk. I felt bad about disturbing her."

"But that Turk thing is her client. And you're keeping house for them." He sounded like that was the one thing about me made sense.

"I'm helping a friend, not working as a maid."

"I guess."

"Bobby, whatever all bad you want to say about Dennis, he talked to me like I was just another person."

He looked startled. "I'm just not used to talking to college people I didn't grow up with."

Maybe that was it, not racism at all, I wondered. But then Bobby looked away and tightened his face muscles. Maybe he didn't like to be talked down to by Dennis's ex-mistress, but I wasn't in the mood to credit him with a good motive.

Berenice came out with the iced tea. I went back for glasses and she filled them. Bobby almost said something to me, maybe telling me to help the poor old white lady, but he looked back at Berenice.

"All I ever wanted was to work honest," he said.

"All I ever wanted was to work smart and honest," I said.

"Marie, don't bait him."

Poor bastard looked so grateful at Berenice. I sat back and sipped my iced tea. Bobby said, "She's a bigot toward rednecks." My iced tea flew up my nose.

Berenice said, "You both know that Turk is making illegal liquor and drugs, both. Liquor is one thing, but drugs another."

"And we're all humans together," Bobby said.

"Maybe Dennis is playing Turk's role in the Urals?" Berenice said. "Getting ganged up on by the locals or cheating them. It isn't quite clear."

"What we gonna do now, in this country?"

I said, "Lilly warned Turk that Dennis wants you to get information on him."

Bobby set his glass down and stood up and paced. "Oh, Lordy, why'd she do that."

We women both looked at each other as if we'd realized that lawyer's messages that were sensible to a human might work different on alien brains. Berenice said, "I think maybe I ought to go see the alien."

"Lilly's due back day after tomorrow," I said.

"I'll go see him before then," Berenice said. She still had her driver's license, but I knew Lilly tried to keep her from driving. Said enough retired people clogged the roads.

"You . . . can you go with her?" Bobby said.

"He's selling liquor at The Door 18, so he might not mind a black woman much," I said.

Berenice said, "I've been rather bored lately for a woman who used to break bank windows."

"Why'd you do that?" Bobby asked.

"Banks represented imperial powers in the world," Berenice replied, her eyes defocusing as she recalled when she was young, blond, and an absolute stone radical. I had kin like that on Staten Island. We left them there even when Granddad was selling lots on our road to maybe common-law wives. Berenice said, "I've got to call Turk for a convenient time."

I rather hoped we couldn't go until after Lilly got back, but Berenice came back out to the porch before we finished our tea and said, "We can come right over now."

Bobby looked grateful. He finished his tea in two big swallows, then took off out of there.

I didn't feel really well, rather nauseated, but Berenice just grinned and handed me the keys to the old miniature Cadillac.

The car was rigged with electronic gadgets from a cellular phone to a radar detector to an old Toshiba laptop computer, everything absolutely dusty. I slid in and wiped the steering wheel off with the second tissue that popped out of the box. Berenice opened the laptop and pushed its jack into the cigarette lighter hole. "The batteries are dead," she said.

"What about the car batteries?" I asked.

"I've been recharging them every month. Some days I get in and just let it run in neutral. Pretty sad, huh."

"Bad for the air to idle a car," I said. Then I realized she must have driven the car here from the last place she'd been really free, not the old aunt needing a niece to take care of her.

"Had the tires changed last year. The old ones rotted through."

"Maybe we should wait until Lilly gets back?"

"She won't be fit for a deal like this for six weeks. And I'm so old, I won't scare him like a younger human."

So I turned the ignition, hoping that it wouldn't start. *This was worse than being a velveteen fool for a white bootlegger*, I thought as the engine cranked and ran with just a few spits at first. We reversed, then went down the driveway.

"Damn fine car. Small for a Caddy, though," Berenice said. She fished out a cable and seemed to be setting up a cellular phone connection to the laptop. I stopped watching when we drove through Rocky Mount, then looked at the rearview mirror to see if we were being followed. Berenice began pecking keys on the laptop. "Aha," she said, "Turk's having trouble expanding."

"That means he's going to be real testy?"

"The humans don't cooperate with him as much as they did when he first set up operations. I was more concerned with the human behavior than his."

"His we going to be looking at soon."

"Marie, he hasn't killed anyone, even when provoked."

"So far," I said.

"Marie, if you're going to be an old lady about this, I should have left you at home." She typed stiffly. I glanced at her fingers and saw how swollen the knuckles were. She paused in the keying in and said, "I hate being an old lady myself."

"What are you doing?"

"Checking Dennis's business volume," she said. "Bobby gave me some clues. I'm in through an aquarium store that handles illicit Asian arrowanas."

"Don't data hackers have to have fast reflexes?" I asked.

"No. An old lady who's methodical. Patient. Did I ever tell you . . . no, now's not the time. In another case, there was this German who marched through most of the open data on Tymnet. Methodical, yeah, like a Methodist." I wondered if her brain had overloaded. She looked up and rubbed her eyes with her middle fingers, hands flat against her face. "I did think the Legion of Doom was terrible."

"Sorry, but I don't know what you're talking about."

"I was older then than Lilly is now." She hit two keys and pulled out the computer-to-phone cord. "Turk could home in on the signal from the phone."

"But he doesn't kill humans," I said.

"Just mucks with their memory, but age is doing that to me already."

"Not today."

"Adrenaline. I remember everything about protest marches. I even remember how testy you were with Bobby just minutes ago."

I wondered if any of the Vietnamese I knew would think she did them any favors, but didn't say more, just followed her directions into Patrick County, then back into Franklin on the dirt road that led to Turks. When I saw the place, I kinda asked, "An alien in a ranch house?"

"He makes it look real alien," Berenice said.

The alien came out dressed in railroader's overalls, not farmer's: that is, the blue and white pinstriped ones, not the solid denim. No shirt, just naked leather skin. One of my aunts used to tell about a Philadelphia man back in the late seventies who'd come to homestead the hills dressed in such things. Turk made pinstripe overalls look more preposterous than I could imagine they could look even on doofus white hippie boy. Then, if you looked again, they looked sinister under that alien head, with only the eyes to look human. I wondered if the faceted ear domes were brittle.

"Hi, Turk," Berenice was saying.

"Ah." He paused, sniffed the air, and finished with "Berenice, my lawyer's aunt. And"—another sniff from the wiggling slots—"the woman who visited The Door 18."

I'd heard he was half about omniscient, but he wasn't, then, old people and blacks he hadn't gotten files on. "Yes," I said, not wanting to explain that I was Dennis DeSpain's ex-lover and thanking Hugous for not mentioning my name. I remembered one of my great-grandmothers telling me how we always could use white bigotry, let them think us dumb, and sneak around back of the attitude. "I'm Berenice's nurse, Mary." I'd respond to Mary like it was my real name.

Berenice looked over at me curiously, then grinned. Turk waved a bare arm at us, motioning us in. The leather seemed stretchy, not wrinkled over the joints like human skin. He asked, "Does anyone know you're here?"

"Lilly," Berenice said, "and a couple of people in town."

Bare and sterile, the hall smelled of disinfectant, but Turk kept leading us into the kitchen, which smelled of alcohol and fruit. It was crammed full of dehydrators, moldy pots, retorts, scraps of stainless steel; the counters were cut up and burned in places. Turk looked at the mess and said, "Nobody comes to visit."

Berenice walked around the room, sniffing almost like Turk, her old nostrils in her long nose wobblingly flexible. She said, "I've come to talk about Bobby."

The alien froze. Then he said, "Can I get you something to drink?"

I shook my head. Berenice said, "Thank you. Water, no ice." She watched the water come out of the tap. "DeSpain attempted to blackmail Bobby into spying on you. Bobby came to us. He doesn't want to get involved."

"He came to you only after I caught him attempting to invade my property," Turk said.

I wanted to say something, but that might spoil my humble maid act. Berenice said, "Don't do anything. Let Lilly work it out when she's better."

"Bobby and Dennis DeSpain are illegal problems for me to have. Not a lawyer's responsibility. Perhaps Lilly could help me with the State Department, as that is a legal problem I have."

Berenice looked like she wondered if her memory was still hyped. "State Department?"

"A man named Henry Allen."

"What do you want Lilly to do?"

"Get an injunction to stop him. I will take care of my illegal business rivals."

I hated myself for wanting to warn Dennis, but my hind brain threw me a flash of his little white-bread throat sweating, breath and blood bobbing through it. I'd never been just another one of his black mistresses.

"Don't do anything until Lilly gets back. You might not understand as much of human law and custom as you think."

"The State Department knows I'm making illegal liquors, but it does nothing."

"Human custom," Berenice said, "isn't particularly codified anywhere."

"I have human custom for my liquor," Turk said.

I said, "I think we'd better go."

Berenice suddenly looked old and forgetful again. I was about to ask if she knew where she was when she nodded.

As we drove home, she said, "Damn, sometimes," but didn't say more. Her eyes grew vague and trembled in her head. She opened the laptop, but just looked at it as if she'd known once what it could do.

"Took a lot out of you?"

She sighed.

After we got out of the car back at the house, she said, "I'd like to know more about their customs."

"Berenice, there's only so much you can do."

"I think if one thing happens, I can very well do another."

"What?"

"Marie, sometimes you have to defend your own, but who is my own?"

Sounded to me like the old cranial blood vessels were constricting. We went inside and saw the message light blinking on the answering machine.

It was Bobby. "Berenice, I can't let an old lady deal with all this."

I said, "What the fuck does he mean?"

Berenice said, "I hope he doesn't mean he's going to try to help DeSpain regardless."

The next message was from Lilly. "I called, but you aren't in. Turk called and asked if I could get an injunction against the State Department. He said it should be a civil liberties issue. Do you have any idea of what he's talking about?"

Berenice said, "Marie, wouldn't it be nice to have more tea?" She sounded like she was trying not to be the kind of woman supported all through her teenaged years by my great-aunts. A suggestion this was, not an order.

"I'd kinda prefer limeade myself," I said. "I've got some in the freezer."

Berenice said, "Sounds great to me."

"Aren't you going to call Lilly back?"

She reached for the phone as I went to the kitchen to make limeade. When I got back with the pitcher, she said, "We women are just going to sit. That's what Lilly suggested."

I poured her a glass first. "Berenice, that's best."

"I don't think it's best," she said, but I could see that her ankles were swelling.

"Want me to take off your shoes?"

She grimaced, but when I had her shoes off, she reached down stiffly and massaged her ankles. "Go talk to Dennis."

"I—"

"I don't mean you should offer your body in exchange for Bobby. Tell him to leave the alien alone."

"He wouldn't listen to me. It would hurt his gonads if his wife would put him on the phone."

"Chicks to the front," she said. I realized, after a moment of utter doubt as to her sanity, that the phrase came from radical times before women's lib.

"So far Turk hasn't hurt anyone."

"It doesn't look to me like he tried to leave people unbruised."

6

The Semi-Accidental Mess

Bobby was sweating as he told DeSpain what had happened to him, but DeSpain compared it to losing his Volvo to the alien's helicopter and to Henry Allen's memory lapses. After Bobby wound down, DeSpain said, "You must have done something stupid." Bobby looked guiltier than he should. "Tell him you're defecting from me. Just go right up and join him. Don't just nose around on his roads."

"He knows I'm working for you."

"I suspect he does, Bobby." DeSpain hid his anger, easy to do with such a sap. "How do you think he found out about it?"

"I asked Lilly and Berenice to help me."

"Lilly works for the Turk. You ought not have done that, using women. It's real easy, Bobby." DeSpain wasn't sure he cared now what happened to Bobby. "Just go up to the Turk and tell him you want to work for the most aggressive boss."

"Dennis. Mr. DeSpain."

"When I was twelve, I used to sneak out to where the revenuers lived and run a thing so their trunk lights would drain the batteries. I could fix them without ever touching the engine compartment or opening a car door."

"When I was that age, I was milking cows for Daddy."

"You would have been." DeSpain had brought a piece of rebar he'd filed almost through and patched with black wax. He broke the rebar across his knee.

Bobby said, "The old hippie woman was going to see the Turk. With the maid, you know the one you used to—"

"If an aged student agitator and a nigger bitch can see the Turk, then I don't see why you can't talk to him. I meant for you to do something straightforward, not sneak around his operation sites. Of course that made him suspicious."

Bobby's eyes flew sideways like he just thought of something, a lie or maybe a truth he didn't want to tell. The men sat so still that DeSpain heard Bobby's wife inside talking to her babies. Make the boy feel guilty, DeSpain decided, and he said, "You making it dangerous for Lilly and Berenice, dragging them into it."

Bobby didn't answer, but nodded slightly.

DeSpain said, "Bobby, I'll talk to you next week, then." He stood up and brushed off the back of his suit, then made sure he'd scattered the fake rebar wax crumbs. As he went back to his truck, he thought that he could play this several ways.

When he got back home, Henry Allen had posted him a note on Loose Trade. CONSIDER THAT THE SIXTEEN-INCH LIMIT ON THE SMITH HAS BEEN CHANGED JUST FOR YOU.

Other Loose Trade subscribers had left electronic giggles. DeSpain wondered for a second if Allen was mocking him, then decided to read the message as a license to kill the Turk.

He wasn't sure he could. Might be that the Turk would kill him, and maybe that was what the government wanted. And he wasn't sure that Allen's message had official standing. What was it about deniability? He almost typed *can't be just for me*, then backed up a few days to see what action there'd been earlier. He noticed a complaint from Luck Aquatics for messages they hadn't made and wondered why the hacker hadn't erased the charges. Some ecology freaks, he decided. Ecology, taxes—got so a man couldn't run an airconditioner without a federal permit.

Then he wondered if the message was from the real Henry Allen of if the Turk was luring him into an ambush. He reached for his phone and called the State Department. "Hi, I'm Dennis DeSpain in Franklin County and I want to talk to Henry Allen. I've talked to him before."

"Please hold." DeSpain waited, then the voice came back. "Mr. DeSpain, Henry Allen says you should proceed with caution. He wishes you well on your fishing trip."

"Is self-defense okay?"

Pause for music. "If it legally passes for self-defense."

"Before, I couldn't even defend myself?"

"I'm not privy to interpretations," the voice said. DeSpain hung up, pulled out his microfiche collection, and began going over old court cases beginning with Sidna Allen's trial in the Hillsboro Courthouse shootout. Yeah, DeSpain thought, if I'm understanding all this correctly, before the State Department decided not to protect the Turk, if I'd shot him, even in self-defense with him shooting at me first, I'd have pulled time like old Sidna for killing an officer of the court, even when the officers drew first.

Well, now DeSpain could defend himself against the Turk. He wasn't altogether thrilled.

Lilly's Attempted Convalescence

The doctor read me the biopsy report. Even though they hadn't found cancer in what they cut out, and even though the ovaries looked good for another five years, I ought to keep coming back every year for checkups, and, no they didn't get as high as my gallbladder, so I couldn't know what to expect there.

Berenice looked confused when I told her; not one of her better days, I thought. Marie, who'd brought her, said, "So, Berenice, you won't have to go to the nursing home any time soon."

Berenice smiled brightly and said, "Marie's been real good to me." Marie looked a trifle annoyed.

I sensed something, but didn't feel well enough to get into whatever hassle they'd had between them. I said, "Let's get me home. The hospital got their staples back."

I spent a day recovering in my own bed before I got a call from Turk regarding the State Department man, Henry Allen. I was lying down with a pillow against the incision, the phone on speaker mode. "I want to know if you can do anything to keep Henry Allen from encouraging Dennis DeSpain from trying to kill me."

"Can you prove it?"

"He left a message for DeSpain on Loose Trade, saying that the limit on trout sizes was canceled just for him."

I wondered if I could break my retainer contract due to Turk's being a Loose Trade subscriber. "Turk, you don't know what that trash means."

"DeSpain called the State Department for a clarification."

"Look, as your lawyer, I advise you that distilling liquor, much less adding drugs to it, is illegal. DeSpain keeps a low enough profile that while everyone knows what he does, nobody has ever proved he financed a raided still. And I wouldn't take Dennis as a client unless the court assigned me. Dennis can't sue you, you can't sue the State Department. Really, seriously, why ever you're making liquor, stop."

"I think this is an American Civil Liberties action, restraint of trade."

"It's tax evasion."

"It is the forcing of grain and fruit harvesters to sell decomposable products rather than add value by manipulation and set price by aging."

"Why don't you just . . ." I was about to tell him to give it away, but that wasn't his point. "Make Dennis an offer. Tell him you'll help him. After all, you think the law, not the business, is wrong."

"Is that legal advice?"

"No, it isn't legal advice. It's personal advice."

"DeSpain is hunting me. Can I kill his dogs if they attack me?"

I wondered what was going on here. "Please stay out of trouble for a couple of weeks until I've recovered from the surgery. Or perhaps you'd like to find another lawyer while I'm laid up?" Please.

"Do the human laws governing self-defense apply to me?"

"Turk, I'll get you an opinion on that." I guessed I ought to do that now. "I'll get back to you." I wished I could have told him no, but he could sue me for malpractice if he survived an attack.

Is this interplanetary protocol or just commonwealth rules? I wondered as I dialed Withold's office. "Can I speak to Withold?" I said to the secretary. "I need his opinion on a client's options."

"Commonwealth's attorney Withold Brunner."

"Withold, this is Lilly. I'm that alien Turk's lawyer. I just want to clarify a few things. Is Turk going to be legally treated as a human being under the laws of the commonwealth, or is there some sort of diplomatic immunity I should be aware of? Or how would he be treated if he acted against a human in self-defense?"

"Lilly, legally, he's human, subject to state and federal laws. State wanted us to be tolerant at first, but they've pulled out now. Didn't know you were representing bootleggers now."

"Thanks. I was intrigued by the alienness." I called Turk back and told him that he could defend himself. Never take another client on retainer this side of a corporation, I decided.

That afternoon Bobby Vipperman came by. Marie let him in and didn't offer anything to him. I lay on the couch half asleep, the surgery line feeling tense.

"Sorry to bother you, ma'am."

"What do you want, Bobby?"

"Just to talk."

"About what, Bobby."

He sighed like he was about to sing. Some of his people were singers in the poverty-stricken days when people needed aesthetic anesthesia against weather so coldly hostile it froze piss in bedside slop jars. Life then was so mean that boils quickly ran to blood poisoning and killed you at sixty. I took a closer look at him and saw that he'd pulled himself into a posture out of that old culture. That's why I'd thought of high lonesome singing. He was making himself into a little artwork fit for a ballad. I said, "I'm tired, Bobby. Can you stay where DeSpain can't find you for a few days until I can get a body mike for you? If he threatens you again and we've got a record of it—"

"It's all right," he said.

"Bobby, Turk can legally defend himself." God, if DeSpain didn't have him by the balls, I didn't know what was. I'd seen men who went to war or riot, then when war and riot ended, became demolition divers, drag racers, all to prove an image of masculinity women over twenty never were impressed with. I didn't understand this emotionally, no more than men understood women's haute couture combat dressing.

I almost asked Bobby to sing one of the old high lonesome songs to me, but by thirty I'd gone beyond where nostalgia crosses into sentimentality.

And I had to get sleep or I'd bitch out my aunt next stupid thing she remembered about the sixties. "Do as I say, Bobby." The other side of this was animal business, a subalpha sucking up to the dog who beat him.

He didn't answer me, just gave me a look like *what can a man expect from a pacifist liberal pinko woman?* and went on his way.

I began to wonder if I'd feel guilty over what seemed to be about to happen. No, I decided, testosterone rules.

Behind the house, I heard the Cadillac start. "Marie?"

Nobody but me was home. I went into my own bedroom and fell asleep against what I feared was going on. A pillow against my belly pushed my stitches back.

Collected Artifacts

"Marie, don't follow him directly there," Berenice told me. "Take 640 up to the parkway."

I said, "Have you noticed how redneck Lilly gets when she's tired?"

"She spent only seventeen years away, split into bits," Berenice said. "And all the mountain shit—it's like brain fungus. You think you've gotten completely modern when bam, you're listening to a string band play a ballad that you're about to reenact in real life. Is it that way for you and the blues culture sometimes?"

"I fucking hate it."

"Yeah, and I bet you've got at least one lowdown dress. Turn here, go up on the parkway and sneak down."

"You don't sound like a big-city radical woman now."

"Yeah."

"Bobby's hopeless. What are you planning to do, Berenice?"

"I want to see what happens."

I ran up 640 as fast as I could without rounding a curve at fifty-five and smashing some slow old boy. "I'm a chemical engineering student at Tech," I said.

"Meaning," Berenice said, "that all this—and DeSpain, too—is hopelessly out of context?"

I felt like three hundred years of rust was moving in on my stainless-steel lab equipment. "I've got to remember why I hate Hugous and The Door 18."

"Don't have to hate them."

"He's buying liquor from this Turk."

Berenice shut up then. I wondered a second if I wasn't on the wrong side, but drove on. Sometimes sides don't matter as much as being loyal.

No, Tech student, I told myself, that's an attitude that'll yank all your accomplishments right out from under you. "What's important, Berenice, being right or being loyal?"

"Sometimes you don't have the least fucking idea," she said. "I remember cops charging a late-night march on East 79th Street, seeing the fire-mouths, the ones who talked heavy trashing, lose it, seeing the Puerto Rican garage attendants grinning and waving. We cowered among Mercedes and Porsches while the garage guys closed the doors. Odd. We amused them, more than anything else, but those Puerto Ricans save our asses from a beating.''

"Meaning?"

"Panic is disgraceful. I remember thinking that I'd rather get clubbed than to panic.''

God, she was losing it. I hoped she'd know what she was doing when we got to the Turk's. Was I obeying her because she was a white woman, as dotty as she was? Had the bastards gotten that far into me?

The Turk was waiting for us at the house. He'd folded Bobby over one arm and his pinstripe overalls were bloody.

I stopped the car. Berenice said, "Reverse slowly."

I looked at her. Her face was immobile, her breathing shallow. Then I began backing. Something stalled the car out and the Turk came up and draped Bobby across the hood. "Good-bye," he told us. Berenice didn't look at him.

I started the car again, fearing that I'd flooded it. I couldn't look at Bobby laying across the hood, so I backed all the way out into Patrick County.

When we reached hardtop, Berenice and I lifted Bobby's body. It stretched. "He's got no spine," Berenice said. I pulled his shirt aside and saw the incision sewn back up. My heart lurched. *At least the alien has to cut to get at them*, I thought. We lugged Bobby's taffy body into the trunk and drove to call the Franklin County sheriff.

"The alien said it was self-defense," the sheriff said. "He has tapes to prove it, he says."

Faked? An alien who could stall your car out, we'd never know, I thought. We waited by the store for the ambulance.

"Berenice, we should have stopped him."

She shook her head, but I couldn't figure precisely what she meant.

When we got back to Lilly's house, the high wailing time had come. Bobby's wife, Sylvia, had her nails raking her face, screams coming out against Lilly and DeSpain. Her children in the car bawled to see their momma so upset, out of control.

She came at me with "his nigger bitch lover."

Berenice took her hands before she got me. I said, "I didn't put DeSpain up to anything."

"You cunt and a half." She might have been outraged, but not enough to be fighting an old woman. Berenice kept holding Sylvia's hands.

Dennis drove up then with Orris in a new car, a Saab. We nodded to each other and she smiled slightly, like *is he worth it to fight over*? Sylvia turned away from Berenice and screamed at Dennis, "You killed him, you coward bastard."

"I didn't tell him to attack the Turk," Dennis said. "Still, I'll take care of you."

Orris looked at Sylvia, then back at me, then straight ahead over the Saab's sloping hood. She reached over and cut the lights off while Dennis kept talking, "Bobby was a good man. He wanted to defend us against the alien."

"You bastard, you and your overeducated hillbilly wife and your nigger bitch and you killed him."

"Sylvia, I didn't want it to happen this way."

I looked back at Orris. She mouthed something at me. I jerked my head *what* and she said, "You'll find out."

Dennis stopped trying to soothe Sylvia and looked at Orris, who shrugged. She said, "Sylvia, we will take care of you. Why don't you call your minister and go home? Your children are scared to see you like this."

Sylvia looked at her children, who shrank back as if she were a stranger. "Oh, babies, I'm sorry your momma was so nasty-mouthed, but these people killed your daddy."

Berenice said, "I'm so sorry, Sylvia." She hugged Sylvia once, then stepped back. Lilly stared at DeSpain.

"Dennis," I said, "you ought go." And flinched to hear myself drop the infinitive marker *to* in front of Miss Orris.

"He going," Orris said. I didn't know if she was mocking me or dropping from stress into her own first tongue. We looked at each other again. I felt like we women had made a conspiracy against Dennis, but for doing what I wasn't sure.

Lilly said, "Sylvia, I can't drive yet, but I can ride with you to the emergency room. If you don't mind, Marie will take your car and the children back home."

Dennis started his car and was out of there. Sylvia said, "Can she sit with them until I get home?" She hadn't asked me, but I nodded. She looked exhausted now, face soppy with tears, wrinkles etching in heavier, a mill woman married to another mill hand. Half the income now, she'd drop down into welfare unless Dennis did take care of her. Racism was Sylvia's secret defense against knowing where in the social heap she was. I could play maid one night.

"Thanks, Marie," Lilly said, meaning more than Sylvia could understand.

The kids cried on the way home. I bathed them and rocked them. The sickly baby sucked on my arm as if he thought his mother had died and I could be recruited for the role if he tried hard enough.

Lilly and Sylvia pulled up after I got them to sleep. Sylvia looked drugged. Lilly said, "We've arranged for a forensic autopsy anyway. And we've been talking to the funeral home and her minister."

You're the Turk's lawyer, I thought.

Sylvia said, "Are my babies okay?"

"They're asleep," I said. "Please don't wake them."

"I want to see them."

She went in and put her hand on the boy's chest to see if he still breathed. We led her off to her own bed when she stumbled. "He's been sick," she said as Lilly and I undressed her.

"Do you want either of us to stay?" Lilly asked.

"I'm fine," Sylvia said. "My sister will be over in the morning. She's on third shift."

I wished we'd get out of here—the poverty made me feel guilty for being a college student, for having a school teacher mother. We went back to the living room with the framed photos of kin, weddings, and babies. Sylvia put her hands to her face and twitched her head. Lilly and I left.

"I guess she'll be all right," I said. "Dennis can't afford not to take care of her."

Lilly said, "Dennis will for a while. When people forget, he'll quit."

"How are you doing?"

"I'm going to sleep for the next twenty-four hours."

"You shouldn't let people bother you while you're like this."

"I told them to wait, didn't I?"

We drove home. Lilly winced as she got out of the car, bracing her hands against the doorframe. She reached for her surgical scar, but pulled her hands away as if remembering she couldn't touch it. I helped her with her shower to make sure she didn't fall, then gave her a pain pill and a sleeping pill. "Enough. You've got to get better first."

She pushed a pillow against her belly and said, "Should I let them all kill each other?"

"None of those trash are worth getting sick over. Go to sleep." I pulled the sheet over her.

As Lilly turned to her side and adjusted the pillow against her incision, I looked out her back bedroom window and stopped myself from exclaiming out loud, *Oh, shit.* The old compact Cadillac was gone. *You can't deal with this, Lilly,* I thought as I looked back at her in bed, eyes blinking in the dark, not quite asleep.

I went downstairs to call the sheriff, thinking about Bobby's body folded over his arm. No spine. I wondered if the Turk collected spines as trophies. Well, I thought, maybe Berenice was old enough to die. Old radical like her, she'd probably get a kick out of it and die biting and head-butting, too.

I said to the dispatcher, "Berenice Nelson, Lilly Nelson's aunt, is out driving in a 1986 compact Cadillac. She's too old to be doing this."

"Does she have a valid driver's license?"

"Yes, she has her license but—"

"Has she been declared incompetent?"

"No. How long does she have to be missing before you do anything?"

"Twenty-four hours, unless her mental state was clouded or confused the last time you saw her."

"Well, actually, she threatened to deal with the alien, so doesn't that qualify as confused?"

Don't Take the Spine, That's Alien

DeSpain knew that he had to avenge Bobby's death if he was going to get his black accounts back. He put on the bulletproof vest with the false muscle lines, found the infrared goggles, then called his cousins. His cousins said they were busy, so he drove the truck into Rocky Mount and picked up a couple of guys at Jeb's Old War Parlor. "It'll be a good fight," DeSpain said. "I'll pay you five hundred each."

One man smiled and asked, "Where are your cousins?" But the others weren't listening. Three of them, two logging crew workers with less than twenty fingers between them, and a loudmouth fool DeSpain planned to put on point, nodded. They followed DeSpain out and climbed in back of the truck. "Any of you have a bike?" he asked them. Get them in first, he thought, then come in behind and shoot the fucker.

The mouthy one did, a huge overdone Harley. DeSpain said, "That's all right. I've got something lighter back at the house." They detoured back to pick up the moped the law made Dennis use after his liquor-running bust.

That would do. If the motor shorted out, DeSpain could pedal it. He gunned the truck to keep the guys in back from laughing and headed through the night toward the Turk's.

The guys in back yelled at each other and into the wind. DeSpain didn't care what they said. He was rather glad now that he wasn't using cousins. His left foot tapped against the bottom strip around the doorframe, then went to the clutch for the turn off 40. He'd thought about going around on the mountainside, but no, pass the sheep farm, then turn, turn again.

DeSpain stopped the truck. "Here, you take it down to the house," he told the fat mouthy one. "I'll follow right behind you. Road's rough. If the truck stalls out, then we'll have to walk in."

"We're going after the alien," one of the other men said softly.

"Damn straight," DeSpain said. "He killed Bobby Vipperman. Yanked out his spine."

"Bobby was no fighter," the fat mouthy man said.

Just like you, DeSpain thought, but he said, "Bobby was a bit soft or he'd"— no, can't say *or he'd have got himself out of the mill* because that's probably where kin of theirs worked—"have taken the Turk out."

"I see the Turk in town," the third man said softly. "He knows important people. State Department man was with him."

"The State Department told me the Turk's fair game now." The men DeSpain had hired squeezed in the cab together. The older logger drove. DeSpain started the moped, swearing praise for lithium batteries. If I can't get this alien, he might as well take me, DeSpain thought. He touched his 9-millemeter Beretta in his shoulder holster and the knife against his back. His spine, too sympathetic with Bobby Vipperman's spine, seemed to twist under the knife.

The truck stalled. The fat man got out and, screaming, ran back through the dark. The radio suddenly cut on, induced into playing by the strong electric currents. Turk talked alien at them through the radio, obvious, terrible threats.

The two men still in the truck watched as DeSpain's moped stalled out. "Guess we get seven hundred fifty each," the younger logger said, scratching his nose with the stub of his index finger.

"Seems like it," DeSpain said. "You want more beer before we go in?"

"Not hardly," the man said, looking at the other man, who could have been his older brother. "You got two more pair of those night goggles? Are we beating or shooting?

"Defend yourselves however."

"Maybe we should talk a thousand," the older man said. "Seems like it's a bit more dangerous than poaching black walnut logs."

"Here," DeSpain said, fishing for his wallet, "I'll give you both three hundred each before, seven hundred after."

"Write us a note on it," the younger man said.

"The Turk knows we're here. We better get moving," DeSpain said.

"He'll wonder why we're sitting out here," the older man said, "and maybe come out of the house. Write us the note."

DeSpain wrote them a promise for seven hundred each after they talked to the Turk. Away from the house, that was where they ought to confront the alien. He thought, *next time, man or woman, alien or human, gets in my face, I'm going to kill 'em first offense.*

The two loggers let DeSpain pass them. He pedaled the moped up as far as he could go without actually seeing the house, then stopped and pulled down the night goggles. A ghost of infrared behind the trees. Too hot to get a good reading through these cheap goggles. He yelled, hoping those stereo speaker ears were keen enough to hear him, "Turk, we've got to talk."

"My lawyer's aunt warned me you were coming."

Shit on the old bat. "Don't believe what she told you. She's crazy."

"You and she are not in collaboration." The alien said it like he was reading voice stresses. DeSpain figured maybe stress analyzers came with the ears.

The two loggers stopped. "Come up to the house alone," the Turk called.

DeSpain whispered, "You won't get paid."

The older man said, "We've got enough."

"He'll kill you anyway," DeSpain said. "He can identify you through your voices."

"Don't believe Mr. DeSpain," the alien said.

"Hell, I'm one of you. He's alien. He's selling drugs. I just sell liquor."

"Dennis, this alien stops the truck, he tore out Bobby Vipperman's spine, he's buddies with Hugous at The Door 18, and you want all two of us to march on him?" The men stared at the gun in Dennis's hand.

He looked at it himself, then said, "Do what you want to. You'll have run off and left me."

They did. He thought about shooting them, but went on toward the Turk. Maybe we should work together, he thought, but I don't understand the motivations. Why here? Why liquor? Why with the blacks first? He said, "I'm not coming in your house where you can drug me."

"Fine. We'll come out with lights, action, cameras. I'll even have a human witness."

Berenice, Marie's friend, bitches both. DeSpain sweated under his bulletproof vest. The damn thing seemed glued to him by now, heavier than before, loaded with quarts of sweat. He put the Beretta in his front waistband, pointed to the left. Neither his spine nor his legs wanted him to walk forward, but he could force his body forward by thinking about how everyone would pick him apart if he couldn't deal with this alien. He wondered if news that an alien pushed him off his home territory would get back to Uralsk. The Armenians were being difficult enough as was. Forward, get a look at the guy through the goggles if he's hotter than 75 degrees at the surface.

If he sees infrared, DeSpain realized, he'll know I've got a bulletproof vest on . . . damn, damn, damn.

"Mr. Dennis DeSpain, who served time for running liquor while drunk," the Turk said, as if identifying Dennis for all time with his previous lowest moment.

"Turk, who the State Department no longer protects," DeSpain said, watching the heat patch resolve into two figures, one Berenice, tiny, uniformly warm across the body, the other the Turk, large, with cold blotches over the head and torso. *I bet I could see him if I took the goggles off.*

"I can't see," Berenice said. "What are you doing?"

Bastard's lights flared infrared. DeSpain clawed the goggles away from his eyes, blinded from glare. He threw himself toward the bushes he'd seen before, pulled his gun, and tried to hear sounds, fire at sounds.

But speakers cut on, electric guitars being mutilated by band saws, microphones being run through hammer mills. "Mary and Jesus Chain," he thought someone shouted. A chitinous foot pinned his gun hand. He tried to kick, but the damn thing had such reflexes. The Turk had him by a leg. The foot against his hand squeezed its toes until he dropped the gun. Then the alien lifted DeSpain, still blinded, and tied his legs together. Another heave and he was dangling head down on what had to have been a hook. DeSpain wondered why the alien didn't just hook him through his Achilles tendons. Maybe Bobby's tendons hadn't held?

Then he heard a whuffled gunshot, a crack, and a second shot that went splat. The terrible sound stopped and he was just dangling blind there, wondering if the shots had been inside the electronic equipment or out. After a second DeSpain said, "I can't see."

"Figured you couldn't." It was Berenice. "I couldn't for an instant myself even though I'd closed my eyes. He didn't figure an old lady'd get him. The back of his neck cracked like a lobster."

"You warned him I was coming."

"Shit, Dennis, if I cut you loose, can you fall okay? If it was me up there, I'd break a hip coming down."

"Cut me loose."

"First, the Turk knew you'd come before I even told him. I told him so he'd let me get at his back." DeSpain fell onto the alien's body, which half grabbed at him. He scuttled away and tried to blink away the green blobs still blinding him. Berenice kept talking. "I couldn't know whether I could get through the skull and I didn't know where he had vital organs, so I went for his neck. One shot to crack him, the second to get the neuroconnectors."

DeSpain said, "Do you know where there's a phone in the house?"

"I'll drive you home. I don't want to explain the gun I used. Plastic. I used to have friends like that, smuggle them onto airplanes."

"I could say Henry Allen gave it to me."

"Dennis, I'll tell everyone you saved me. Let you keep your balls on with the other distributors and I won't have to explain this gun."

Marie Cleans Up

I got there too late to do anything, passed the alien dead next to a hook with cut ropes. Berenice and Dennis were walking up the steps to the front door, both looking tired and sweaty.

"I killed him," Dennis said. "In self-defense." Berenice got the door open; maybe the alien had been so sure of himself that it wasn't locked. We went in the house and saw Bobby's spine, cleaned white, curved like a fish over the mantel. Berenice said, "It looks rather handsome." Dennis shuddered. I thought it jangled between weirdly beautiful and grotesque—conceptual overload and exhaustion running my visual centers like the spine was an optical illusion.

Berenice found the phone and called the sheriff's department. I took the phone from her and told the dispatcher, "You shits couldn't investigate right away, could you?"

When the deputies arrived, they told Berenice to wipe the prints off the gun and help them destroy the tapes that were still rolling out in the yard where Turk had his meat hook. Dennis looked more guilty than I'd ever seen him.

"You mean you didn't save her. She saved you?"

"Damn tapes." I loved him then as hard as ever, nakedly happy to be alive, embarrassed for being saved by an old lady.

One of the deputies asked, "Where in the hell did she get a plastic pistol?"

The sheriff himself arrived in his business suit and after listening to a few people said to Berenice, "If you weren't as old as you are, we'd arrest you. Marie, take her home." They stripped Dennis of his bulletproof vest and his knife, and cuffed him.

"Take him straight to the hospital and call Dr. Tucker," Berenice said. "The lights blinded him. If you don't take care of him, he'll sue."

She never gets the keys again, I decided as I drove the Cadillac home. Berenice slumped over halfway home, asleep and drooling, looking a mess in early morning sun.

7

Aftermath for the Lawyer

Neither Marie nor Berenice woke me up when they got back. The first I heard about the second killing was at ten-thirty when Orris DeSpain called me to ask about filing separation papers.

"Marie was there again," she said, "and your aunt. Berenice killed Turk while Dennis dangled helpless. They brought out Bobby's spine and took it to the funeral home for burial."

But I'd told them all to wait. "What are you talking about?" I said. Why didn't they let me know what was going on? "Berenice?"

"Berenice. The alien turned his back on her and she killed him with a plastic explosives gun." Orris sounded as though she'd always known Berenice was dangerous.

I'd ask Marie. Berenice would lie. "Okay, Orris, but why are you filing separation papers?"

"I'm going for a law degree at George Washington University. It makes more sense than shooting Dennis or Marie. What is this, some ballad with me as the villainess against the Nut Brown Maid?"

"Get another lawyer, Orris. I really don't want to hear about it." I figured she'd just called me to see what I'd known about the situation.

I got furious. Then my incision started throbbing, so I just lay back in bed, carefully bent so to relieve tension on that.

Berenice came in then and said, "I think we should tell you that your client Turkemaw is dead."

"Orris DeSpain told me. Damn you, I told all of you to wait."

Berenice sat down in a chair by my bed and looked at her hands, turning them this way and that. "If I'da been younger, I'da been in trouble. What if Turk's people don't understand? I could have been risking the planet."

"Wasn't it self-defense?"

"I killed him to save that Dennis DeSpain. Shit, was Dennis any better? Used the plastic gun. Never knew where that gun came from other than someone stole it. Never knew why I kept it, either."

I said, "Don't forget what he did to Bobby."

She said, "I'm confused about Bobby. Isn't he dead?"

Two days later, when I was trying to sleep in the afternoon, still using a pillow to hold the stitches in, a couple more aliens and a State Department man came by.

The other aliens were more alien than Turk. How, I wasn't sure, but as soon as I saw the other aliens, I knew Turk had been pushing his own limits the way he pushed Dennis DeSpain's. He hadn't been born or bred to be human, but he was crazy enough to fake it. These new aliens wore sashes and wristbands, not blue coveralls, and looked neater than Turk had looked. And they didn't look a bit like tourists.

"Was there a reason to kill Turkemaw?" the State Department guy asked. He wasn't the one I'd seen with Turk earlier.

Berenice said, "I'm sorry, but he was killing humans."

One of the aliens said, "We wondered," so flatly I decided they had rather globally wondered and sent us Turk to see how we'd react. A test. These aliens would never explain how the test worked. No right way, no wrong way, no blame.

"Is Dennis free then?" I asked.

"Your local law is holding him for the gun he couldn't use." The alien sounded vaguely confused, but then nobody arrested Berenice for her much-more-illegal gun, that CIA special that someone, probably a European leftist studying war in the Middle East, had stolen thirty years earlier, a talisman gun that had drifted around radical circles until Berenice stopped it when she returned to Rocky Mount.

The State Department man asked Berenice, "Do you remember who gave you that gun?"

"An old lady my age remember something like that?" Her eyes went vague, unfocused, then flickered toward me. Yes, I thought, absolutely, but nobody pushed for an answer. Both the State Department guy and the aliens stood for a few seconds looking at Berenice as though she were a monument, then left without saying good-bye.

After the door closed, Berenice said, "I'm sorry all this came at the time it did. I feel most guilty that I did enjoy it. Just a little, you understand. I hadn't been out like that in a long damn time."

I wished I wasn't getting the impression she'd done the right thing. And I pitied Turk, even if he were the alien equivalent of Dennis DeSpain. Someone trickier than he let him come. "Just don't get into more trouble until mid-August." I decided I'd have to take care of Bobby's kids—I'd been half responsible for him getting killed.

"I didn't mean to get you upset. And I didn't save Bobby, did I? All I got out of it was some more memories." She stopped as if checking that at least those memories moved from short-term to long-term memory. "I didn't think I could get more memories at my age. But poor Bobby."

Neither of us saved Bobby, old aunt. The warranty on my body has expired, even if the biopsy was negative, and here we are, later in life than we imagined when we were younger. In your radical days, did you ever expect to be so old? I thought I'd skip middle age myself, but no.

Yes, I was glad she showed Rocky Mount a bit of the old young Berenice who'd run radical in the streets.

Orris filed her separation papers with commonwealth's attorney Withold Brunner representing her. Everyone thought that bitchy of her, but she didn't betray any of Dennis's illegal business. But then Dennis rolled over when he heard who her lawyer was.

As Orris said she was going to do, she went to Georgetown University, but instead of returning to Rocky Mount or Roanoke as a lawyer, she became a State Department officer. When she was back once, trolling for gossip about Dennis and Marie, she said, "Henry Allen inspired me to do it."

"He seemed rather doofus to me," I said.

"Precisely. I knew I could do a better job."

Some time in the next year I sold the miniature Cadillac to make sure Berenice never again went adventuring and came home after signing the papers to incredible guilt. With the sale of her car or the death she'd caused or just aging in general, she never again was as clear or vigorous as the night she killed the alien. Sylvia, Bobby's widow, helped me with her. I felt odd, no possible children of my own, but with a sudden family that I had to support. I began taking bootleggers as clients.

Marie had married Dennis when the divorce was final. He told all his buddies he did it to strengthen his alliances with his black dealers. Rumor in the rougher bars and jukes had it Berenice had been about to shoot him next when Marie saved him. My bootlegger clients kept me informed as to various twists of the county's oral traditions.

When Marie got her chemical engineering degree a few years later, she applied for a legal distilling license for fuel-grade alcohol. They hired me to help them. We took it out in Marie's name because of Dennis's record.

Dennis saved Marie from becoming the officious techie I had imagined as her future when I first met her. Her white husband seemed to have made her wicked enough to be tolerant of human foibles—Berenice's senility, her outlaw cousins. With DeSpain with her, even trout fishing probably seemed erotic and slimy fun dirty. Whatever, years after Marie got her chemical engineering degree and her legal liquor license, you could suspect she still kept a shake-baby dress or two. I hoped she didn't think keeping a space for her outlaw side was a failing. I saw it as a sign of grace.

But poor Dennis. By the time he was forty, he was strictly legal.

We all met around Berenice's grave sometime after he'd turned forty-three. Marie wore a light purple velveteen dress that I knew wasn't disrespectful of the mourners of this particular dead.

Marie said, "Berenice said this color would make a white woman look yellow green. She said I ought to wear it a lot."

I said, "She refused to believe that you'd turn out to be just another dye-house chemist."

Marie looked at Dennis and said, "Is it so different?"

Dennis said, "We're doing better than that, Marie." He seemed embarrassed. He said, "Lilly, I'm sorry."

I knew he meant for Bobby, and just nodded. But then don't we middle-class Southerners always fail the rednecks who trust us? When Bobby was in high school, he asked his daddy's supervisor about getting in a support group for the college-bound. The supervisor earlier had said to the social worker organizing the group, "You damn fool, you're stealing my best future workers." And the supervisor told Bobby he'd be happier avoiding high-class anxieties and the college-bound support group was just a scam to give the social worker a job.

Funny, how I'd forgotten that until now.

The aliens neither invaded nor gave us FTL drive diagrams. Not while I was alive, at least.

Last time we heard about Orris, she was the American cultural attaché to Angola. *Time* magazine printed a photo of her driving a Land-Rover out of the embassy gates with the president's daughter. She was laughing.

DEATH ON THE NILE

Connie Willis

▼

Connie Willis lives in Greeley, Colorado, with her family. She first attracted attention as a writer in the late seventies with a number of outstanding stories for the now-defunct magazine *Galileo*, and she went on to establish herself as one of the most popular and critically acclaimed writers of the 1980s. In 1982, she won two Nebula Awards, one for her superb novelette "Fire Watch," and one for her poignant short story "A Letter from the Clearys"; a few months later, "Fire Watch" went on to win her a Hugo Award as well. In 1989, her powerful novella "The Last of the Winnebagos" won both the Nebula and the Hugo, and she won another Nebula in 1990 for her novelette "At the Rialto." Last year, her landmark novel *Doomsday Book* won both the Nebula Award and the Hugo Award, *as* did her short story "Even the Queen"—making her one of the most honored writers in the history of science fiction, and, as far as I know, the only person ever to win *two* Nebulas and *two* Hugos in the same year. Her other books include *Water Witch* and *Light Raid*, written in collaboration with Cynthia Felice, *Fire Watch*, a collection of short fiction, and the outstanding *Lincoln's Dreams*, her first solo novel. Her most recent book is a major collection, *Impossible Things*, and a new novella, "Uncharted Territory." She has had stories in our First, Second, Fourth, Sixth, Seventh, Eighth, Ninth, and Tenth Annual Collections.

In the wry but ultimately moving story that follows, she describes, with typical panache, one woman's dream vacation to Egypt—a trip that soon leads her on a quest for self-discovery far more profound and bizarre than anything she could ever have bargained for. . . .

Chapter 1: Preparing for Your Trip—What to Take

" 'To the ancient Egyptians,' " Zoe reads, " 'Death was a separate country to the west—' " The plane lurches. " '—the west to which the deceased person journeyed.' "

We are on the plane to Egypt. The flight is so rough the flight attendants have strapped themselves into the nearest empty seats, looking scared, and the rest of us have subsided into a nervous window-watching silence. Except Zoe, across the aisle, who is reading aloud from a travel guide.

This one is Somebody or Other's *Egypt Made Easy*. In the seat pocket in front of her are Fodor's *Cairo* and Cooke's *Touring Guide to Egypt's Antiquities*, and

153

there are half a dozen others in her luggage. Not to mention Frommer's *Greece on $35 a Day* and the Savvy Traveler's *Guide to Austria* and the three or four hundred other guidebooks she's already read out loud to us on this trip. I toy briefly with the idea that it's their combined weight that's causing the plane to yaw and careen and will shortly send us plummeting to our deaths.

" 'Food, furniture, and weapons were placed in the tomb,' " Zoe reads, " 'as provi—' " The plane pitches sideways. " '—sions for the journey.' "

The plane lurches again, so violently Zoe nearly drops the book, but she doesn't miss a beat. " 'When King Tutankhamun's tomb was opened,' " she reads, " 'it contained trunks full of clothing, jars of wine, a golden boat, and a pair of sandals for walking in the sands of the afterworld.' "

My husband Neil leans over me to look out the window, but there is nothing to see. The sky is clear and cloudless, and below us there aren't even any waves on the water.

" 'In the afterworld the deceased was judged by Anubis, a god with the head of a jackal,' " Zoe reads, " 'and his soul was weighed on a pair of golden scales.' "

I am the only one listening to her. Lissa, on the aisle, is whispering to Neil, her hand almost touching his on the armrest. Across the aisle, next to Zoe and *Egypt Made Easy*, Zoe's husband is asleep and Lissa's husband is staring out the other window and trying to keep his drink from spilling.

"Are you doing all right?" Neil asks Lissa solicitously.

"It'll be exciting going with two other couples," Neil said when he came up with the idea of our all going to Europe together. "Lissa and her husband are lots of fun, and Zoe knows everything. It'll be like having our own tour guide."

It is. Zoe herds us from country to country, reciting historical facts and exchange rates. In the Louvre, a French tourist asked her where the Mona Lisa was. She was thrilled. "He thought we were a tour group!" she said. "Imagine that!"

Imagine that.

" 'Before being judged, the deceased recited his confession,' " Zoe reads, " 'a list of sins he had not committed, such as, I have not snared the birds of the gods, I have not told lies, I have not committed adultery.' "

Neil pats Lissa's hand and leans over to me. "Can you trade places with Lissa?" Neil whispers to me.

I already have, I think. "We're not supposed to," I say, pointing at the lights above the seats. "The seat belt sign is on."

He looks at her anxiously. "She's feeling nauseated."

So am I, I want to say, but I am afraid that's what this trip is all about, to get me to say something. "Okay," I say, and unbuckle my seat belt and change places with her. While she is crawling over Neil, the plane pitches again, and she half-falls into his arms. He steadies her. Their eyes lock.

" 'I have not taken another's belongings,' " Zoe reads. " 'I have not murdered another.' "

I can't take any more of this. I reach for my bag, which is still under the window seat, and pull out my paperback of Agatha Christie's *Death On the Nile*. I bought it in Athens.

"About like death anywhere," Zoe's husband said when I got back to our hotel in Athens with it.

"What?" I said.

"Your book," he said, pointing at the paperback and smiling as if he'd made a joke. "The title. I'd imagine death on the Nile is the same as death anywhere."

"Which is what?" I asked.

"The Egyptians believed death was very similar to life," Zoe cut in. She had bought *Egypt Made Easy* at the same bookstore. "To the ancient Egyptians the afterworld was a place much like the world they inhabited. It was presided over by Anubis, who judged the deceased and determined their fates. Our concepts of heaven and hell and of the Day of Judgment are nothing more than modern refinements of Egyptians ideas," she said, and began reading out loud from *Egypt Made Easy*, which pretty much put an end to our conversation, and I still don't know what Zoe's husband thought death would be like, on the Nile or elsewhere.

I open *Death on the Nile* and try to read, thinking maybe Hercule Poirot knows, but the flight is too bumpy. I feel almost immediately queasy, and after half a page and three more lurches I put it in the seat pocket, close my eyes and toy with the idea of murdering another. It's a perfect Agatha Christie setting. She always has a few people in a country house or on an island. In *Death on the Nile* they were on a Nile steamer, but the plane is even better. The only other people on it are the flight attendants and a Japanese tour group who apparently do not speak English or they would be clustered around Zoe, asking directions to the Sphinx.

The turbulence lessens a little, and I open my eyes and reach for my book again. Lissa has it.

She's holding it open, but she isn't reading it. She is watching me, waiting for me to notice, waiting for me to say something. Neil looks nervous.

"You were done with this, weren't you?" she says, smiling. "You weren't reading it."

Everyone has a motive for murder in an Agatha Christie. And Lissa's husband has been drinking steadily since Paris, and Zoe's husband never gets to finish a sentence. The police might think he had snapped suddenly. Or that it was Zoe he had tried to kill and shot Lissa by mistake. And there is no Hercule Poirot on board to tell them who really committed the murder, to solve the mystery and explain all the strange happenings.

The plane pitches suddenly, so hard Zoe drops her guidebook, and we plunge a good five thousand feet before it recovers. The guidebook has slid forward several rows, and Zoe tries to reach for it with her foot, fails, and looks up at the seat belt sign as if she expects it to go off so she can get out of her seat to retrieve it.

Not after that drop, I think, but the seat belt sign pings almost immediately and goes off.

Lissa's husband instantly calls for the flight attendant and demands another drink, but they have already gone scurrying back to the rear of the plane, still looking pale and scared, as if they expected the turbulence to start up again before they make it. Zoe's husband wakes up at the noise and then goes back to sleep. Zoe retrieves *Egypt Made Easy* from the floor, reads a few more riveting facts from it, then puts it face down on the seat and goes back to the rear of the plane.

I lean across Neil and look out the window, wondering what's happened, but I can't see anything. We are flying through a flat whiteness.

Lissa is rubbing her head. "I cracked my head on the window," she says to Neil. "Is it bleeding?"

He leans over her solicitously to see.

I unsnap my seat belt and start to the back of the plane, but both bathrooms are occupied, and Zoe is perched on the arm of an aisle seat, enlightening the Japanese tour group. "The currency is in Egyptian pounds," she says. "There are one hundred piasters in a pound." I sit back down.

Neil is gently massaging Lissa's temple. "Is that better?" he asks.

I reach across the aisle for Zoe's guidebook. "Must-See Attractions," the chapter is headed, and the first one on the list is the Pyramids.

"Giza, Pyramids of. West bank of Nile, 9 mi. (15 km.) SW of Cairo. Accessible by taxi, bus, rental car. Admission L.E.3. Comments: You can't skip the Pyramids, but be prepared to be disappointed. They don't look at all like you expect, the traffic's terrible, and the view's completely ruined by the hordes of tourists, refreshment stands, and souvenir vendors. Open daily."

I wonder how Zoe stands this stuff. I turn the page to Attraction Number Two. It's King Tut's tomb, and whoever wrote the guidebook wasn't thrilled with it either. "Tutankhamun, Tomb of. Valley of the Kings, Luxor, 400 mi. (668 km.) south of Cairo. Three unimpressive rooms. Inferior wall paintings."

There is a map, showing a long, straight corridor (labeled Corridor) and the three unimpressive rooms opening one onto the other in a row—Anteroom, Burial Chamber, Hall of Judgment.

I close the book and put it back on Zoe's seat. Zoe's husband is still asleep. Lissa's is peering back over his seat. "Where'd the flight attendants go?" he asks. "I want another drink."

"Are you sure it's not bleeding? I can feel a bump," Lissa says to Neil, rubbing her head. "Do you think I have a concussion?"

"No," Neil says, turning her face toward his. "Your pupils aren't dilated." He gazes deeply into her eyes.

"Stewardness!" Lissa's husband shouts. "What do you have to do to get a drink around here?"

Zoe comes back, elated. "They thought I was a professional guide," she says, sitting down and fastening her seatbelt. "They asked if they could join our tour." She opens the guidebook. " 'The afterworld was full of monsters and demigods in the form of crocodiles and baboons and snakes. These monsters could destroy the deceased before he reached the Hall of Judgment.' "

Neil touches my hand. "Do you have any aspirin?" he asks. "Lissa's head hurts."

I fish in my bag for it, and Neil gets up and goes back to get her a glass of water.

"Neil's so thoughtful," Lissa says, watching me, her eyes bright.

" 'To protect against these monsters and demigods, the deceased was given *The Book of the Dead*,' " Zoe reads. " 'More properly translated as *The Book of What is in the Afterworld, The Book of the Dead* was a collection of directions for the journey and magic spells to protect the deceased.' "

I think about how I am going to get through the rest of the trip without magic spells to protect me. Six days in Egypt and then three in Israel, and there is still the trip home on a plane like this and nothing to do for fifteen hours but watch Lissa and Neil and listen to Zoe.

I consider cheerier possibilities. "What if we're not going to Cairo?" I say. "What if we're dead?"

Zoe looks up from her guidebook, irritated.

"There've been a lot of terrorist bombings lately, and this is the Middle East," I go on. "What if that last air pocket was really a bomb? What if it blew us apart, and right now we're drifting down over the Aegean Sea in little pieces?"

"Mediterranean," Zoe says. "We've already flown over Crete."

"How do you know that?" I ask. "Look out the window." I point out Lissa's window at the white flatness beyond. "You can't see the water. We could be anywhere. Or nowhere."

Neil comes back with the water. He hands it and my aspirin to Lissa.

"They check the planes for bombs, don't they?" Lissa asks him. "Don't they use metal detectors and things?"

"I saw this movie once," I say, "where the people were all dead, only they didn't know it. They were on a ship, and they thought they were going to America. There was so much fog they couldn't see the water."

Lissa looks anxiously out the window.

"It looked just like a real ship, but little by little they began to notice little things that weren't quite right. There were hardly any people on board, and no crew at all."

"Stewardess!" Lissa's husband calls, leaning over Zoe into the aisle. "I need another ouzo."

His shouting wakes Zoe's husband up. He blinks at Zoe, confused that she is not reading from her guidebook. "What's going on?" he asks.

"We're all dead," I say. "We were killed by Arab terrorists. We think we're going to Cairo but we're really going to heaven. Or hell."

Lissa, looking out the window, says, "There's so much fog I can't see the wing." She looks frightenedly at Neil. "What if something's happened to the wing?"

"We're just going through a cloud," Neil says. "We're probably beginning our descent into Cairo."

"The sky was perfectly clear," I say, "and then all of a sudden we were in the fog. The people on the ship noticed the fog, too. They noticed there weren't any running lights. And they couldn't find the crew." I smile at Lissa. "Have you noticed how the turbulence stopped all of a sudden? Right after we hit that air pocket. And why—"

A flight attendant comes out of the cockpit and down the aisle to us, carrying a drink. Everyone looks relieved, and Zoe opens her guidebook and begins thumbing through it, looking for fascinating facts.

"Did someone here want an ouzo?" the flight attendant asks.

"Here," Lissa's husband says, reaching for it.

"How long before we get to Cairo?" I say.

She starts toward the back of the plane without answering. I unbuckle my seat belt and follow her. "When will we get to Cairo?" I ask her.

She turns, smiling, but she is still pale and scared-looking. "Did you want another drink, ma'am? Ouzo? Coffee?"

"Why did the turbulence stop?" I say. "How long till we get to Cairo?"

"You need to take your seat," she says, pointing to the seat belt sign. "We're beginning our descent. We'll be at our destination in another twenty minutes." She bends over the Japanese tour group and tells them to bring their seat backs to an upright position.

"What destination? Our descent to where? We aren't beginning any descent. The seat belt sign is still off," I say, and it bings on.

I go back to my seat. Zoe's husband is already asleep again. Zoe is reading out loud from *Egypt Made Easy*. "The visitor should take precautions before traveling in Egypt. A map is essential, and a flashlight is needed for many of the sites."

Lissa has gotten her bag out from under the seat. She puts my *Death on the Nile* in it and gets out her sunglasses. I look past her and out the window at the white flatness where the wing should be. We should be able to see the lights on the wing even in the fog. That's what they're there for, so you can see the plane in the fog. The people on the ship didn't realize they were dead at first. It was only when they started noticing little things that weren't quite right that they began to wonder.

"A guide is recommended," Zoe reads.

I have meant to frighten Lissa, but I have only managed to frighten myself. We are beginning our descent, that's all, I tell myself, and flying through a cloud. And that must be right.

Because here we are in Cairo.

Chapter Two: Arriving at the Airport

"So this is Cairo?" Zoe's husband says, looking around. The plane has stopped at the end of the runway and deplaned us onto the asphalt by means of a metal stairway.

The terminal is off to the east, a low building with palm trees around it, and the Japanese tour group sets off toward it immediately, shouldering their carry-on bags and camera cases.

We do not have any carry-ons. Since we always have to wait at the baggage claim for Zoe's guidebooks anyway, we check our carry-ons, too. Every time we do it, I am convinced they will go to Tokyo or disappear altogether, but now I'm glad we don't have to lug them all the way to the terminal. It looks like it is miles away, and the Japanese are already slowing.

Zoe is reading the guidebook. The rest of us stand around her, looking impatient. Lissa has caught the heel of her sandal in one of the metal steps coming down and is leaning against Neil.

"Did you twist it?" Neil asks anxiously.

The flight attendants clatter down the steps with their navy-blue overnight cases. They still look nervous. At the bottom of the stairs they unfold wheeled metal carriers and strap the overnight cases to them and set off for the terminal. After a few steps they stop, and one of them takes off her jacket and drapes it over the wheeled carrier, and they start off again, walking rapidly in their high heels.

It is not as hot as I expected, even though the distant terminal shimmers in the heated air rising from the asphalt. There is no sign of the clouds we flew through, just a thin white haze which disperses the sun's light into an even glare. We are all squinting. Lissa lets go of Neil's arm for a second to get her sunglasses out of her bag.

"What do they drink around here?" Lissa's husband asks, squinting over Zoe's shoulder at the guidebook. "I want a drink."

"The local drink is zibib," Zoe says. "It's like ouzo." She looks up from the guidebook. "I think we should go see the Pyramids."

The professional tour guide strikes again. "Don't you think we'd better take care of first things first?" I say. "Like customs? And picking up our luggage?"

"And finding a drink of . . . what did you call it? Zibab?" Lissa's husband says.

"No," Zoe says. "I think we should do the Pyramids first. It'll take an hour to do the baggage claim and customs, and we can't take our luggage with us to the Pyramids. We'll have to go to the hotel, and by that time everyone will be out there. I think we should go right now." She gestures at the terminal. "We can run out and see them and be back before the Japanese tour group's even through customs."

She turns and starts walking in the opposite direction from the terminal, and the others straggle obediently after her.

I look back at the terminal. The flight attendants have passed the Japanese tour group and are nearly to the palm trees.

"You're going the wrong way," I say to Zoe. "We've got to go to the terminal to get a taxi."

Zoe stops. "A taxi?" she says. "What for? They aren't far. We can walk it in fifteen minutes."

"Fifteen minutes?" I say. "Giza's nine miles west of Cairo. You have to cross the Nile to get there."

"Don't be silly," she says, "they're right there," and points in the direction she was walking, and there, beyond the asphalt in an expanse of sand, so close they do not shimmer at all, are the Pyramids.

Chapter Three: Getting Around

It takes us longer than fifteen minutes. The Pyramids are farther away than they look, and the sand is deep and hard to walk in. We have to stop every few feet so Lissa can empty out her sandals, leaning against Neil.

"We should have taken a taxi," Zoe's husband says, but there are no roads, and no sign of the refreshment stands and souvenir vendors the guidebook complained about, only the unbroken expanse of deep sand and the white, even sky, and in the distance the three yellow pyramids, standing in a row.

" 'The tallest of the three is the Pyramid of Cheops, built in 2690 B.C.,' " Zoe says, reading as she walks. " 'It took thirty years to complete.' "

"You have to take a taxi to get to the Pyramids," I say. "There's a lot of traffic."

"It was built on the west bank of the Nile, which the ancient Egyptians believed was the land of the dead."

There is a flicker of movement ahead, between the pyramids, and I stop and shade my eyes against the glare to look at it, hoping it is a souvenir vendor, but I can't see anything.

We start walking again.

It flickers again, and this time I catch sight of it running, hunched over, its hands nearly touching the ground. It disappears behind the middle pyramid.

"I saw something," I say, catching up to Zoe. "Some kind of animal. It looked like a baboon."

Zoe leafs through the guidebook and then says, "Monkeys. They're found frequently near Giza. They beg for food from the tourists."

"There aren't any tourists," I say.

"I know," Zoe says happily. "I told you we'd avoid the rush."

"You have to go through customs, even in Egypt," I say. "You can't just leave the airport."

" 'The pyramid on the left is Kheophren,' " Zoe says, "built in 2650 B.C.' "

"In the movie, they wouldn't believe they were dead even when somebody told them," I say. "Giza is *nine* miles from Cairo."

"What are you talking about?" Neil says. Lissa has stopped again and is leaning against him, standing on one foot and shaking her sandal out. "That mystery of Lissa's, *Death on the Nile?*"

"This was a *movie*," I say. "They were on this ship, and they were all dead."

"We saw that movie, didn't we, Zoe?" Zoe's husband says. "Mia Farrow was in it, and Bette Davis. And the detective guy, what was his name—"

"Hercule Poirot," Zoe says. "Played by Peter Ustinov. 'The Pyramids are open daily from 8 A.M. to 5 P.M. Evenings there is a *Son et Lumière* show with colored floodlights and a narration in English and Japanese.' "

"There were all sorts of clues," I say, "but they just ignored them."

"I don't like Agatha Christie," Lissa says. "Murder and trying to find out who killed who. I'm never able to figure out what's going on. All those people on the train together.''

"You're thinking of *Murder on the Orient Express*,'' Neil says. "I saw that.''

"Is that the one where they got killed off one by one?'' Lissa's husband says.

"I saw that one,'' Zoe's husband says. "They got what they deserved, as far as I'm concerned, going off on their own like that when they knew they should keep together.''

"Giza is nine miles west of Cairo,'' I say. "You have to take a taxi to get there. There is all this traffic.''

"Peter Ustinov was in that one, too, wasn't he?'' Neil says. "The one with the train?''

"No,'' Zoe's husband says. "It was the other one. What's his name—''

"Albert Finney,'' Zoe says.

Chapter Four: Places of Interest

The Pyramids are closed. Fifty yards (45.7 m.) from the base of Cheops there is a chain barring our way. A metal sign hangs from it that says "Closed'' in English and Japanese.

"Prepare to be disappointed,'' I say.

"I thought you said they were open daily,'' Lissa says, knocking sand out of her sandals.

"It must be a holiday,'' Zoe says, leafing through her guidebook. "Here it is. 'Egyptian holidays.' '' She begins reading. " 'Antiquities sites are closed during Ramadan, the Muslim month of fasting in March. On Fridays the sites are closed from eleven to one P.M.' ''

It is not March, or Friday, and even if it were, it is after one P.M. The shadow of Cheops stretches well past where we stand. I look up, trying to see the sun where it must be behind the pyramid, and catch a flicker of movement, high up. It is too large to be a monkey.

"Well, what do we do now?'' Zoe's husband says.

"We could go see the Sphinx,'' Zoe muses, looking through the guidebook. "Or we could wait for the *Son et Lumière* show.''

"No,'' I say, thinking of being out here in the dark.

"How do you know that won't be closed, too?'' Lissa asks.

Zoe consults the book. "There are two shows daily, seven-thirty and nine P.M.''

"That's what you said about the Pyramids,'' Lissa says. "*I* think we should go back to the airport and get our luggage. I want to get my other shoes.''

"*I* think we should go back to the hotel,'' Lissa's husband says, "and have a long, cool drink.''

"We'll go to Tutankhamun's tomb,'' Zoe says. " 'It's open every day, including holidays.' '' She looks up expectantly.

"King Tut's tomb?'' I say. "In the Valley of the Kings?''

"Yes,'' she says, and starts to read. "It was found intact in 1922 by Howard Carter. It contained—''

All the belongings necessary for the deceased's journey to the afterworld, I think. Sandals and clothes and *Egypt Made Easy*.

"I'd rather have a drink," Lissa's husband says.

"And a nap," Zoe's husband says. "You go on, and we'll meet you at the hotel."

"I don't think you should go off on your own," I say. "I think we should keep together."

"It will be crowded if we wait," Zoe says. "I'm going now. Are you coming, Lissa?"

Lissa looks appealingly up at Neil. "I don't think I'd better walk that far. My ankle's starting to hurt again."

Neil looks helplessly at Zoe. "I guess we'd better pass."

"What about you?" Zoe's husband says to me. "Are you going with Zoe or do you want to come with us?"

"In Athens, you said death was the same everywhere," I say to him, "and I said, 'Which is what?' and then Zoe interrupted us and you never did answer me. What were you going to say?"

"I've forgotten," he says, looking at Zoe as if he hopes she will interrupt us again, but she is intent on the guidebook.

"You said, 'Death is the same everywhere,' " I persist, "and I said, 'Which is what?' What did you think death would be like?"

"I don't know . . . unexpected, I guess. And probably pretty damn unpleasant." He laughs nervously. "If we're going to the hotel, we'd better get started. Who else is coming?"

I toy with the idea of going with them, of sitting safely in the hotel bar with ceiling fans and palms, drinking zibib while we wait. That's what the people on the ship did. And in spite of Lissa, I want to stay with Neil.

I look at the expanse of sand back toward the east. There is no sign of Cairo from here, or of the terminal, and far off there is a flicker of movement, like something running.

I shake my head. "I want to see King Tut's tomb." I go over to Neil. "I think we should go with Zoe," I say, and put my hand on his arm. "After all, she's our guide."

Neil looks helplessly at Lissa and then back at me. "I don't know. . . ."

"The three of you can go back to the hotel," I say to Lissa, gesturing to include the other men, "and Zoe and Neil and I can meet you there after we've been to the tomb."

Neil moves away from Lissa. "Why can't you and Zoe just go?" he whispers at me.

"I think we should keep together," I say. "It would be so easy to get separated."

"How come you're so stuck on going with Zoe anyway?" Neil says. "I thought you said you hated being led around by the nose all the time."

I want to say, Because she has the book, but Lissa has come over and is watching us, her eyes bright behind her sunglasses. "I've always wanted to see the inside of a tomb," I say.

"King Tut?" Lissa says. "Is that the one with the treasure, the necklaces and the gold coffin and stuff?" She puts her hand on Neil's arm. "I've always wanted to see that."

"Okay," Neil says, relieved. "I guess we'll go with you, Zoe."

Zoe looks expectantly at her husband.

"Not me," he says. "We'll meet you in the bar."

"We'll order drinks for you," Lissa's husband says. He waves goodbye, and they set off as if they know where they are going, even though Zoe hasn't told them the name of the hotel.

" 'The Valley of the Kings is located in the hills west of Luxor,' " Zoe says and starts off across the sand the way she did at the airport. We follow her.

I wait until Lissa gets a shoeful of sand and she and Neil fall behind while she empties it.

"Zoe," I say quietly. "There's something wrong."

"Umm," she says, looking up something in the guidebook's index.

"The Valley of the Kings is four hundred miles south of Cairo," I say. "You can't walk there from the Pyramids."

She finds the page. "Of course not. We have to take a boat."

She points, and I see we have reached a stand of reeds, and beyond it is the Nile.

Nosing out from the rushes is a boat, and I am afraid it will be made of gold, but it is only one of the Nile cruisers. And I am so relieved that the Valley of the Kings is not within walking distance that I do not recognize the boat until we have climbed on board and are standing on the canopied deck next to the wooden paddlewheel. It is the steamer from *Death on the Nile*.

Chapter 5: Cruises, Day Trips, and Guided Tours

Lissa is sick on the boat. Neil offers to take her below, and I expect her to say yes, but she shakes her head. "My ankle hurts," she says, and sinks down in one of the deck chairs. Neil kneels by her feet and examines a bruise no bigger than a piaster.

"Is it swollen?" she asks anxiously. There is no sign of swelling, but Neil eases her sandal off and takes her foot tenderly, caressingly, in both hands. Lissa closes her eyes and leans back against the deck chair, sighing.

I toy with the idea that Lissa's husband couldn't take any more of this either, and that he murdered us all and then killed himself.

"Here we are on a ship," I say, "like the dead people in that movie."

"It's not a ship, it's a steamboat," Zoe says. " 'The Nile steamer is the most pleasant way to travel in Egypt and one of the least expensive. Costs range from $180 to $360 per person for a four-day cruise.' "

Or maybe it was Zoe's husband, finally determined to shut Zoe up so he could finish a conversation, and then he had to murder the rest of us one after the other to keep from being caught.

"We're all alone on the ship," I say, "just like they were."

"How far is it to the Valley of the Kings?" Lissa asks.

" 'Three-and-a-half miles (5 km.) west of Luxor,' " Zoe says, reading. " 'Luxor is four hundred miles south of Cairo.' "

"If it's that far, I might as well read my book," Lissa says, pushing her sunglasses up on top of her head. "Neil, hand me my bag."

He fishes *Death on the Nile* out of her bag, and hands it to her, and she flips through it for a moment, like Zoe looking for exchange rates, and then begins to read.

"The wife did it," I say. "She found out her husband was being unfaithful."

Lissa glares at me. "I already knew that," she says carelessly. "I saw the movie," but after another half-page she lays the open book face-down on the empty deck chair next to her.

"I can't read," she says to Neil. "The sun's too bright." She squints up at the sky, which is still hidden by its gauzelike haze.

" 'The Valley of the Kings is the site of the tombs of sixty-four pharoahs,' " Zoe says. " 'Of these, the most famous is Tutankhamun's.' "

I go over to the railing and watch the Pyramids recede, slipping slowly out of sight behind the rushes that line the shore. They look flat, like yellow triangles stuck up in the sand, and I remember how in Paris Zoe's husband wouldn't believe the *Mona Lisa* was the real thing. "It's a fake," he insisted before Zoe interrupted. "The real one's much larger."

And the guidebook said, Prepare to be disappointed, and the Valley of the Kings is four hundred miles from the Pyramids like it's supposed to be, and Middle Eastern airports are notorious for their lack of security. That's how all those bombs get on planes in the first place, because they don't make people go through customs. I shouldn't watch so many movies.

" 'Among its treasures, Tutankhamun's tomb contained a golden boat, by which the soul would travel to the world of the dead,' " Zoe says.

I lean over the railing and look into the water. It is not muddy, like I thought it would be, but a clear waveless blue, and in its depths the sun is shining brightly.

" 'The boat was carved with passages from the *Book of the Dead*,' " Zoe reads, " 'to protect the deceased from monsters and demigods who might try to destroy him before he reached the Hall of Judgment.' "

There is something in the water. Not a ripple, not even enough of a movement to shudder the image of the sun, but I know there is something there.

" 'Spells were also written on papyruses buried with the body,' " Zoe says.

It is long and dark, like a crocodile. I lean over farther, gripping the rail, trying to see into the transparent water, and catch a glint of scales. It is swimming straight toward the boat.

" 'These spells took the form of commands,' " Zoe reads. " 'Get back, you evil one! Stay away! I adjure you in the name of Anubis and Osiris.' "

The water glitters, hesitating.

" 'Do not come against me,' " Zoe says. " 'My spells protect me. I know the way.' "

The thing in the water turns and swims away. The boat follows it, nosing slowly in toward the shore.

"There it is," Zoe says, pointing past the reeds at a distant row of cliffs. "The Valley of the Kings."

"I suppose this'll be closed, too," Lissa says, letting Neil help her off the boat.

"Tombs are never closed," I say, and look north, across the sand, at the distant Pyramids.

Chapter 6: Accommodations

The Valley of the Kings is not closed. The tombs stretch along a sandstone cliff, black openings in the yellow rock, and there are no chains across the stone steps that lead down to them. At the south end of the valley a Japanese tour group is going into the last one.

"Why aren't the tombs marked?" Lissa asks. "Which one is King Tut's?" and Zoe leads us to the north end of the valley, where the cliff dwindles into a low wall. Beyond it, across the sand, I can see the Pyramids, sharp against the sky.

Zoe stops at the very edge of a slanting hole dug into the base of the rocks. There are steps leading down into it. "Tutankhamun's tomb was found when a workman accidentally uncovered the top step," she says.

Lissa looks down into the stairwell. All but the top two steps are in shadow, and it is too dark to see the bottom. "Are there snakes?" she asks.

"No," Zoe, who knows everything, says. "Tutankhamun's tomb is the smallest of the pharoah's tombs in the Valley." She fumbles in her bag for her flashlight. "The tomb consists of three rooms—an antechamber, the burial chamber containing Tutankhamun's coffin, and the Hall of Judgment."

There is a slither of movement in the darkness below us, like a slow uncoiling, and Lissa steps back from the edge. "Which room is the stuff in?"

"Stuff?" Zoe says uncertainly, still fumbling for her flashlight. She opens her guidebook. "Stuff?" she says again, and flips to the back of it, as if she is going to look "stuff" up in the index.

"*Stuff,*" Lissa says, and there is an edge of fear in her voice. "All the furniture and vases and stuff they take with them. You said the Egyptians buried their belongings with them."

"King Tut's treasure," Neil says helpfully.

"Oh, the *treasure,*" Zoe says, relieved. "The belongings buried with Tutankhamun for his journey into the afterworld. They're not here. They're in Cairo in the museum."

"In Cairo?" Lissa says. "They're in Cairo? Then what are we doing here?"

"We're dead," I say. "Arab terrorists blew up our plane and killed us all."

"I *came* all the way out here because I wanted to see the treasure," Lissa says.

"The coffin is here," Zoe says placatingly, "and there are wall paintings in the antechamber," but Lissa has already led Neil away from the steps, talking earnestly to him.

"The wall paintings depict the stages in the judgment of the soul, the weighing of the soul, the recital of the deceased's confession," Zoe says.

The deceased's confession. I have not taken that which belongs to another. I have not caused any pain. I have not committed adultery.

Lissa and Neil come back, Lissa leaning heavily on Neil's arm. "I think we'll pass on this tomb thing," Neil says apologetically. "We want to get to the museum before it closes. Lissa had her heart set on seeing the treasure."

" 'The Egyptian Museum is open from 9 A.M. to 4 P.M. daily, 9 to 11:15 A.M. and 1:30 to 4 P.M. Fridays,' " Zoe says, reading from the guidebook. " 'Admission is three Egyptian pounds.' "

"It's already four o'clock," I say, looking at my watch. "It will be closed before you get there." I look up.

Neil and Lissa have already started back, not toward the boat but across the sand in the direction of the Pyramids. The light behind the Pyramids is beginning to fade, the sky going from white to gray-blue.

"Wait," I say, and run across the sand to catch up with them. "Why don't you wait and we'll all go back together? It won't take us very long to see the tomb. You heard Zoe, there's nothing inside."

They both look at me.

"I think we should stay together," I finish lamely.

Lissa looks up alertly, and I realize she thinks I am talking about divorce, that I have finally said what she has been waiting for.

"I think we should all keep together," I say hastily. "This is Egypt. There are all sorts of dangers, crocodiles and snakes and . . . it won't take us very long to see the tomb. You heard Zoe, there's nothing inside."

"We'd better not," Neil says, looking at me. "Lissa's ankle is starting to swell. I'd better get some ice on it."

I look down at her ankle. Where the bruise was there are two little puncture marks, close together, like a snake bite, and around them the ankle is starting to swell.

"I don't think Lissa's up to the Hall of Judgment," he says, still looking at me.

"You could wait at the top of the steps," I say. "You wouldn't have to go in."

Lissa takes hold of his arm, as if anxious to go, but he hesitates. "Those people on the ship," he says to me. "What happened to them?"

"I was just trying to frighten you," I say. "I'm sure there's a logical explanation. It's too bad Hercule Poirot isn't here—he'd be able to explain everything. The Pyramids were probably closed for some Muslim holiday Zoe didn't know about, and that's why we didn't have to go through customs either, because it was a holiday."

"What happened to the people on the ship?" Neil says again.

"They got judged," I say, "but it wasn't nearly as bad as they'd thought." They were all afraid of what was going to happen, even the clergyman, who hadn't committed any sins, but the judge turned out to be somebody he knew. A bishop. He wore a white suit, and he was very kind, and most of them came out fine."

"Most of them," Neil says.

"Let's *go*," Lissa says, pulling on his arm.

"The people on the ship," Neil says, ignoring her. "Had any of them committed some horrible sin?"

"My ankle hurts," Lissa says. "Come *on*."

"I have to go," Neil says, almost reluctantly. "Why don't you come with us?"

I glance at Lissa, expecting her to be looking daggers at Neil, but she is watching me with bright, lidless eyes.

"Yes. Come with us," she says, and waits for my answer.

I lied to Lissa about the ending of *Death on the Nile*. It was the wife they killed. I toy with the idea that they have committed some horrible sin, that I am lying in my hotel room in Athens, my temple black with blood and powder burns. I would be the only one here then, and Lissa and Neil would be demigods disguised to look like them. Or monsters.

"I'd better not," I say, and back away from them.

"Let's go then," Lissa says to Neil, and they start off across the sand. Lissa is limping badly, and before they have gone very far, Neil stops and takes off his shoes.

The sky behind the Pyramids is purple-blue, and the Pyramids stand out flat and black against it.

"Come on," Zoe calls from the top of the steps. She is holding the flashlight and looking at the guidebook. "I want to see the Weighing of the Soul."

Chapter 7: Off the Beaten Track

Zoe is already halfway down the steps when I get back, shining her flashlight on the door below her. "When the tomb was discovered, the door was plastered over and stamped with the seals bearing the cartouche of Tutankhamun," she says.

"It'll be dark soon," I call down to her. "Maybe we should go back to the hotel with Lissa and Neil." I look back across the desert, but they are already out of sight.

Zoe is gone, too. When I look back down the steps, there is nothing but darkness. "Zoe!" I shout and run down the sand-drifted steps after her. "Wait!"

The door to the tomb is open, and I can see the light from her flashlight bobbing on rock walls and ceiling far down a narrow corridor.

"Zoe!" I shout, and start after her. The floor is uneven, and I trip and put my hand on the wall to steady myself. "Come back! You have the book!"

The light flashes on a section of carved-out wall, far ahead, and then vanishes, as if she has turned a corner.

"Wait for me!" I shout and stop because I cannot see my hand in front of my face.

There is no answering light, no answering voice, no sound at all. I stand very still, one hand still on the wall, listening for footsteps, for quiet padding, for the sound of slithering, but I can't hear anything, not even my own heart beating.

"Zoe," I call out, "I'm going to wait for you outside," and turn around, holding onto the wall so I don't get disoriented in the dark, and go back the way I came.

The corridor seems longer than it did coming in, and I toy with the idea that it will go on forever in the dark, or that the door will be locked, the opening plastered over and the ancient seals affixed, but there is a line of light under the door, and it opens easily when I push on it.

I am at the top of a stone staircase leading down into a long wide hall. On either side the hall is lined with stone pillars, and between the pillars I can see that the walls are painted with scenes in sienna and yellow and bright blue.

It must be the anteroom because Zoe said its walls were painted with scenes from the soul's journey into death, and there is Anubis weighing the soul, and, beyond it, a baboon devouring something, and, opposite where I am standing on the stairs, a painting of a boat crossing the blue Nile. It is made of gold, and in it four souls squat in a line, their kohl-outlined eyes looking ahead at the shore. Beside them, in the transparent water, Sebek, the crocodile demigod, swims.

I start down the steps. There is a doorway at the far end of the hall, and if this is the anteroom, then the door must lead to the burial chamber.

Zoe said the tomb consists of only three rooms, and I saw the map myself on the plane, the steps and straight corridor and then the unimpressive rooms leading one into another, anteroom and burial chamber and Hall of Judgment, one after another.

So this is the anteroom, even if it is larger than it was on the map, and Zoe has obviously gone ahead to the burial chamber and is standing by Tutankhamun's coffin, reading aloud from the travel guide. When I come in, she will look up and say, " 'The quartzite sarcophagus is carved with passages from *The Book of the Dead.*' "

I have come halfway down the stairs, and from here I can see the painting of the weighing of the soul. Anubis, with his jackal's head, standing on one side of the yellow scales, and the deceased on the other, reading his confession from a papyrus.

I go down two more steps, till I am even with the scales, and sit down.

Surely Zoe won't be long—there's nothing in the burial chamber except the coffin—and even if she has gone on ahead to the Hall of Judgment, she'll have to come back this way. There's only one entrance to the tomb. And she can't get turned around because she has a flashlight. And the book. I clasp my hands around my knees and wait.

I think about the people on the ship, waiting for judgment. "It wasn't as bad as they thought," I'd told Neil, but now, sitting here on the steps, I remember that the bishop, smiling kindly in his white suit, gave them sentences appropriate to their sins. One of the women was sentenced to being alone forever.

The deceased in the painting looks frightened, standing by the scale, and I wonder what sentence Anubis will give him, what sins he has committed.

Maybe he has not committed any sins at all, like the clergyman, and is worried over nothing, or maybe he is merely frightened at finding himself in this strange place, alone. Was death what he expected?

"Death is the same everywhere," Zoe's husband said. "Unexpected." And nothing is the way you thought it would be. Look at the Mona Lisa. And Neil. The people on the ship had planned on something else altogether, pearly gates and angels and clouds, all the modern refinements. Prepare to be disappointed.

And what about the Egyptians, packing their clothes and wine and sandals for their trip. Was death, even on the Nile, what they expected? Or was it not the way it had been described in the travel guide at all? Did they keep thinking they were alive, in spite of all the clues?

The deceased clutches his papyrus and I wonder if he has committed some horrible sin. Adultery. Or murder. I wonder how he died.

The people on the ship were killed by a bomb, like we were. I try to remember the moment it went off—Zoe reading out loud and then the sudden shock of light and decompression, the travel guide blown out of Zoe's hands and Lissa falling through the blue air, but I can't. Maybe it didn't happen on the plane. Maybe the terrorists blew us up in the airport in Athens, while we were checking our luggage.

I toy with the idea that it wasn't a bomb at all, that I murdered Lissa, and then killed myself, like in *Death on the Nile*. Maybe I reached into my bag, not for my paperback but for the gun I bought in Athens, and shot Lissa while she was looking out the window. And Neil bent over her, solicitous, concerned, and I raised the gun again, and Zoe's husband tried to wrestle it out of my hand, and the shot went wide and hit the gas tank on the wing.

I am still frightening myself. If I'd murdered Lissa, I would remember it, and even Athens, notorious for its lack of security, wouldn't have let me on board a plane with a gun. And you could hardly commit some horrible crime without remembering it, could you?

The people on the ship didn't remember dying, even when someone told them, but that was because the ship was so much like a real one, the railings and the water and the deck. And because of the bomb. People never remember being blown up. It's the concussion or something, it knocks the memory out of you. But I would surely have remembered murdering someone. Or being murdered.

I sit on the steps a long time, watching for the splash of Zoe's flashlight in the doorway. Outside it will be dark, time for the *Son et Lumière* show at the pyramids.

It seems darker in here, too. I have to squint to see Anubis and the yellow scales and the deceased, awaiting judgment. The papyrus he is holding is covered with long, bordered columns of hieroglyphics and I hope they are magic spells to protect him and not a list of all the sins he has committed.

I have not murdered another, I think. I have not committed adultery. But there are other sins.

It will be dark soon, and I do not have a flashlight. I stand up. "Zoe!" I call, and go down the stairs and between the pillars. They are carved with animals—cobras and baboons and crocodiles.

"It's getting dark," I call, and my voice echoes hollowly among the pillars. "They'll be wondering what happened to us."

The last pair of pillars is carved with a bird, its sandstone wings outstretched. A bird of the gods. Or a plane.

"Zoe?" I say, and stoop to go through the low door. "Are you in here?"

Chapter Eight: Special Events

Zoe isn't in the burial chamber. It is much smaller than the anteroom, and there are no paintings on the rough walls or above the door that leads to the Hall of Judgment. The ceiling is scarcely higher than the door, and I have to hunch down to keep from scraping my head against it.

It is darker in here than in the anteroom, but even in the dimness I can see that Zoe isn't here. Neither is Tutankhamun's sarcophagus, carved with *The Book of the Dead*. There is nothing in the room at all, except for a pile of suitcases in the corner by the door to the Hall of Judgment.

It is our luggage. I recognize my battered Samsonite and the carry-on bags of the Japanese tour group. The flight attendants' navy-blue overnight cases are in front of the pile, strapped like victims to their wheeled carriers.

On top of my suitcase is a book, and I think, "It's the travel guide," even though I know Zoe would never have left it behind, and I hurry over to pick it up.

It is not *Egypt Made Easy*. It is my *Death on the Nile*, lying open and face-down the way Lissa left it on the boat, but I pick it up anyway and open it to the last pages, searching for the place where Hercule Poirot explains all the strange things that have been happening, where he solves the mystery.

I cannot find it. I thumb back through the book, looking for a map. There is always a map in Agatha Christie, showing who had what state-room on the ship, showing the stairways and the doors and the unimpressive rooms leading one into another, but I cannot find that either. The pages are covered with long unreadable columns of hieroglyphics.

I close the book. "There's no point in waiting for Zoe," I say, looking past the luggage at the door to the next room. It is lower than the one I came through, and dark beyond. "She's obviously gone on to the Hall of Judgment."

I walk over to the door, holding the book against my chest. There are stone steps leading down. I can see the top one in the dim light from the burial chamber. It is steep and very narrow.

I toy briefly with the idea that it will not be so bad after all, that I am dreading it like the clergyman, and it will turn out to be not judgment but someone I know, a smiling bishop in a white suit, and mercy is not a modern refinement after all.

"I have not murdered another," I say, and my voice does not echo. "I have not committed adultery."

I take hold of the doorjamb with one hand so I won't fall on the stairs. With the other I hold the book against me. "Get back, you evil ones," I say. "Stay away. I adjure you in the name of Osiris and Poirot. My spells protect me. I know the way."

I begin my descent.

FRIENDSHIP BRIDGE

Brian W. Aldiss

▼

One of the true giants of the field, Brian W. Aldiss has been publishing science fiction for more than thirty years, and has more than two dozen books to his credit. His classic "Hothouse" series (assembled into the novel *The Long Afternoon of Earth*) won a Hugo Award in 1962. "The Saliva Tree" won a Nebula Award in 1965, and his novel *Starship* won the Prix Jules Verne in 1977. He took another Hugo Award in 1987 for his critical study of science fiction, *Trillion Year Spree*, written with David Wingrove. His other books include the acclaimed Helliconia trilogy—*Helliconia Spring, Helliconia Summer, Helliconia Winter*—*The Malacia Tapestry, An Island Called Moreau, Frankenstein Unbound*, and *Cryptozoic!*. His latest books include the collections *Seasons In Flight* and *A Tupolev Too Far*, the novels *Dracula Unbound* and *Remembrance Day*, and a memoir, *Bury My Heart at W. H. Smith's*. Upcoming is a new novel, *Somewhere East of Life*, and a collection of poems, *Home Life with Cats*. His story "FOAM," to which "Friendship Bridge" is a sequel of sorts (and both of these are related to his upcoming novel), was in our Ninth Annual Collection. He lives with his family in Oxford, England.

In the sly and darkly witty story that follows, Aldiss takes us to a distant and war-torn country in company with a man on a quest to find himself, quite literally—or all the pieces of him that are *left*, anyway. . . .

Someone he did not know was with him. They passed a place where light bulbs were made. He accepted all this. And this square was named after an enemy he could not recall. Everything was wooden.

He—or it was someone like him—was climbing wooden stairs. Laughter from an upper room. When he got there, after enormous effort, a madman with his hair alight was waiting to cut his head off. To remove it slice by slice.

And he seemed to want to have it done to him.

The noise was awful, as of cracking bone . . .

1. The Speech

The sound of firing in the Prospekt Svobody roused Burnell. He sat on the side of his bed, shaking, trying to compose himself. When the shots ceased, and the sound of running feet, he got up and went over to the window. Outside lay the avenue, lined with acacias, bathed in the acidic light of another Central Asian day. He could see no bodies. Perhaps the army had been celebrating an imagined victory.

Burnell spent some while soaking his face and regarding it disapprovingly in the mirror. Then he washed, rebandaged his leg and turned out his suitcase looking for a clean shirt. His dirty one he threw over a chair in distaste. He struggled into the ill-fitting suit which a Shi'ite tailor had run up for him. Before leaving the room he locked his suitcase.

The elevators of the Hotel Ashkhabad had ceased working, possibly during the war with Uzbekistan. The war with Uzbekistan could be blamed for many discomforts. A notice on the elevator gates said: PLEASE DESCEND TOMORROW. Burnell took the unswept staircase down to the foyer. A number of men in shaggy hats, some of them with light machine-guns hitched over their shoulders, stood about smoking. There was this to be said for Burnell's locally made suit; he appeared less foreign in it, and less an object of suspicion.

Since the dining room of the hotel did not open before two P.M., Burnell went out into the street to his favourite café. Heat was already beginning to bite and the smog to thicken. He liked the tree-lined streets about the centre of the city; he had been in worse places.

The Koreans had established a fast-food restaurant called Tony's. Entering, Burnell found himself a seat by the window, where he ordered coffee and yoghurt. By local standards, Tony's was both clean and elegant. At eight in the morning, it was already full of customers, all male, who appeared to have settled in comfortably for the day. The yoghurt was excellent.

Unsmiling but polite, the Koreans moved among the tables. Joseph Stalin had exiled their grandfathers here in the 1950s.

Sympathy with countries trying to live down their abysmal past and come to terms with an uncertain present was part of Burnell's survival kit in troubled parts of the world. He nevertheless disliked appointments that were not kept and contacts who never turned up. He prepared himself now, as he crunched a sweet, hard biscuit with his coffee, to meet one such contact three days later than arranged.

Through the throng, a broad-built man with a powerful face was bearing down on Burnell. Abed Assaad drew up a chair from another table and seated himself opposite Burnell.

Roy Burnell was slenderly built, in his early forties; he felt himself fragile against this mountainous man, whose head sat like a boulder on his frame. He smiled and greeted Burnell, enquiring after his wound.

"Which wound?" Burnell asked.

Assaad said, "The leg, isn't it, no?"

"I thought you meant . . . Never mind." Hastily, Burnell brought from his breast-pocket the crumpled business card he had found awaiting him in his pigeonhole in the hotel. He smoothed it.

It read:

Dr. Abed Assaad
Curator-in-Chief
Archaeological Intensities Museum
1 Khiva Street
Ashkhabad
Turkmenistan Soviet Union

Seeing it, Assaad said, "Is my old card. You see a misprint there, unfortunately. Also this nation naturally does not longer belong to the Soviet Union
since the days of Boris Yeltsin."

Burnell nodded. He added, compressing his lips, that his arrangements for
this visit to Ashkhabad had been made in Frankfurt. It was understood that Dr.
Assaad or a deputy would meet him at Ashkhabad airport. No one had come.
Nor had his hotel been booked, as promised.

Burnell had had to make his own arrangements, with some rather unofficial
assistance from Murray-Johnson at the British Consulate. He had been in the
city for three days, frustrated at every turn when it came to meeting qualified
people. His work was almost done and only now had Dr Assaad appeared.

Dr. Assaad nodded his head as he listened to Burnell's complaints, comment-
ing only that the city was full of tourists, each with various demands. As he did
so, he retrieved his card and tucked it into the breast pocket of his grey jacket.

"You received my letter, Dr. Assaad?"

By way of answer, Assaad summoned a waiter and ordered two glasses of
wine. He also suggested cake, but Burnell refused.

"Cake is good when not stale. But maybe too sweet for your British taste,
possibly? I am sorry not to meet at the aeroport. Frankfurt is one place and
Ashkhabad another. What cities have you seen?"

Burnell said that Murray-Johnson and a Unesco representative had driven him
to Mary, with its five walled cities, but his parent body, World Cultural Heritage,
had already registered the site.

With a non-committal shrug, Assaad said, "I know Mr. Murray-Johnson,
naturally. Maybe he understands the problems of a new nation like Turkmenistan,
maybe not. Possibly not. Since we have democracy, there are problems at all
levels with bureaucracy. Is difficulty with organizations, you understand? New
times, new problems."

"I understand the same people are in power under President Diyanizov since
the coup as were before."

Assaad swept this statement away with a broad gesture. He hunched himself
over the table, so that his powerful chest made a considerable approach towards
Burnell. In a low voice, he said, "Careful what names you mention. Get to know
the immense changes which—what is it?—yes, convulse Central Asia. Get to
know me better, Mr. Burnell. You will find a good man in a sea of imbeciles,
unhappily. Don't take offence. New avenues are difficult to open. Much has
been closed down since the war. I tell you, confidentially. The Archaeological
Antiquities Museum is closed down. Even worst, is now a school for sons of

mullahs, you understand? I have no job, though I do it still, as I can. Otherwise, I have to trade to support myself and my wife, indefinitely . . .''

He slumped back in his chair and smiled as if he was the happiest man in the world. When the waiter brought two small glasses of thin yellow liquid, he drained his glass at once. Burnell took his more slowly.

"Maybe too much sweet for the British taste, understandably?"

"So who looks after the local antiquities now? Isn't there a government department any longer?"

"Of course, of course. It pulls things down, not up. We can get no money from World Bank for reconstruction. Of course nothing from Moscow. Maybe we walk in the park where we can speak? Is not too hot for you?"

"Not too hot for British taste, no," said Burnell with a smile.

Assaad smiled and winked as he handed a wad of folding money to the waiter. "I like humour. There's quite a lot, eh?"

Pushing through the swing-doors into the avenue, they found the dry heat awaiting them. Assaad said in a hurried voice, "You mention the president's name in there, so you make me nervous. Listeners may consider we plot."

The park had been a pleasant place, abutting an immense building which was once the local KGB headquarters. A burnt-out gun-carrier stood among splintered trees, a reminder of the recent coup. Small boys played on it, shooting each other in friendly fashion.

Old men, bent and solitary, walked among birches. Their woollen clothes were grey with age. Their hands were clasped behind their backs.

"People listen in cafés," said Assaad, matching his stride to Burnell's. "Not many men speak English here, but they are suspicious, unavoidably. All nations in Central Asia search a new cultural identity, rightly. It makes them suspicious."

"Your English is good."

As they passed a melon-seller, Assaad frowned at the man as if he embodied all the country's vices.

"I am among the savages, Mr. Burnell, frankly. It's a refreshment to hear your English spoken as only an Englishman can. Killing is the local occupation. Turkmeni tribes are peaceful nice people, but when the money and jobs run out, then kill, kill . . . Ten thousand men were killed here last February in the riots. Still there's shooting. We have no justice. Criminality on every level—tribal rivalries, once suppressed. Propaganda from the government. The water's bad. Medicine short. Epidemics rising. And I can nowhere find *The Hand of Ethelberta*."

"Sorry? Who's Ethelberta?"

Assaad looked pained. He halted and scrutinized Burnell's face. "You naturally know *The Hand of Ethelberta*? By your great novelist Thomas Hardy. It is the one of his best novels, understandably. Here, no such item can be found. Publishers in London and Paris are far distant. Not to be discovered in all the stalls of the grand bazaar. Maybe the mullahs pronounce it blasphemous. Do you say *The Hand of Ethelberta* is blasphemous? For over three years I have searched it."

"You read much English literature, Dr. Assaad?"

He threw up his hands, as if wishing not to delve deeper into the miseries of life. "Well, it's the case that we all have hidden agendas in our lives. You also, I believe, Mr. Burnell?" He gave a sideways glance at Burnell.

Burnell was not as yet willing to confide in his new acquaintance. He was due to meet Murray-Johnson again, and could check on Assaad's credentials. His answer was evasive.

After a brief silence, Assaad said with a sigh, "Anyhow, I must assist you if I can do it. That's the point. That's my wish, intensely, to make you welcome in this city. Life is not simple here for foreigners.

"You write from Frankfurt that in the name of Culture you must visit the old mosque, 6 kilometers from here, the mosque of Mustapha Pasha. Is of great historic interest, very very beautiful. The dome of azure rises on parapets. In the front is a porch, supported by six slender marble columns. And on top of the porch, very unusually, is four small cupolas. The mosque is well built of worked sandstone, a rarity hereabouts, and of bricks in double rows. The date is from end fifteenth century and is famous in architecture.

"I shall drive you to see it in my brother's car, since he owes me a favour."

The offer had come too late. Burnell had hired a taxi and driven out to the mosque the previous day. Hence his annoyance with Dr. Assaad. He had found the mosque much decayed and hideously restored. The old mihrab, from which the Koran was read, proved to be a shoddy new construction. Most of the original interior tilework of the mosque was missing. Nothing remained that his parent organization, World Cultural Heritage, would wish to record. He said as much to Assaad, adding, "It's not worth a prayer, never mind a visit."

"Ah, your English humour! 'Not worth a prayer, never mind a visit . . .' 'Not worth a prayer . . .' Very very good. Anyhow, I agree, it's an ugly structure, entirely. It was built by a Jew."

Burnell, always alert for anti-Semitism, bridled at this and rattled off a lecture about the enlightened Rabbi Moshe Gourits, who, to celebrate his cordial relationship with his Muslim neighbors, had financed the building of the mosque in 1491.

Bringing learning to bear, Assaad asserted, "The Jew built in 1498, excuse me, by the Christian calendar. A bad year. Torquemada died and Savonarola was burnt."

"The matter with the mosque," Burnell said, "is not that it was built by a Jew, but that it has been restored by Communists."

Assaad gave him a melancholy look. "I am a Syrian by birth, although many year pass since I see my native land. Forgive my simplicity. Jews and Syrians . . ." He drew a finger across his throat and hung out his tongue. Then he treated Burnell to a smile of wide and untrustworthy charm.

Feeling he had been unjust, feeling, as he so often did on his travels, that he would never understand other people, Burnell said, "It is hot. Excuse me. Possibly there is some other memorable structure I should inspect which is not in the Frankfurt files?"

Assaad winked again, and held aloft a celebratory finger, perhaps as a token that he had won over this stiff and difficult Englishman. 'Tomorrow I come early to your hotel in my brother's car and I take you to inspect the Friendship Bridge.

"It's as you would say it, 'Worth a prayer, never mind a visit.' "

Burnell had procured a vintage postcard of the railway station. On it he wrote a few lines to his ex-wife in California, posting it before Dr Assaad arrived in an old Volkswagen Golf.

The nightmares had visited him again during a sleepless night. His leg pained him and he felt feverish.

Would Stephanie tear up the card, supposing it ever arrived in Los Angeles? Ashkhabad was further from Moscow than Moscow was from London. Even in the new twenty-first-century world, it remained a remote place, one hardly considered by the outside world until the disintegration of the Soviet Union in the 1990s. What would Los Angeles make of it? These cards he sent her from the distant places to which his profession took him had once been mute pleas to Stephanie to think of him, possibly even to love him again. Hope, much like the view of Ashkhabad railway station, had faded with the years. Now his cards were little more than boasts, pathetic even to himself. Dearest Stephanie, Ashkhabad is a pleasant modern city, situated on the world's longest irrigation canal. Look, I'm here, and enjoying myself. Moderately.

But there was another reason for his being somewhere east of the Caspian, apart from his quest for buildings which World Cultural Heritage might consider worth recording and preserving.

This he explained to Dr. Assaad as they drove in the oven of the car away from the hotel.

Burnell's life had been disrupted, like a plate dropped on a tile floor. He was still trying to put the pieces together.

Roy Edward Burnell was a specialist in ecclesiastical architecture, just commencing commissioned work in Frankfurt, headquarters of the largely Germanic EC. He had stumbled into the Antonescu Clinic in Budapest. The Clinic had pillaged his memories, only parts of which he had been able to regain. Some of his most private moments had been sold round the world on the black market to the false-memory addicts of Nostovision.

"I need your help, Dr. Assaad," he said. "You see, I believe a fragment of my memory which I vitally need is here—here in Ashkhabad. I have been led to believe that President Diyanizov has it."

He started to explain how he had managed to buy back stretches of his memory in Budapest. The parts, if retrieved, could be reinserted in his brain. But Dr. Assaad was not listening. He sounded his horn to drive pedestrians from the middle of the crowded street. The roadway was choked with vehicles, all hooting.

"It was in Budapest . . . A small nameless square off Fo Street," Burnell found himself saying. "Next to the Ministry of Light Industry. And to think I went there voluntarily . . . A new form of mental vandalism . . ." He pressed a hand to his face, close to where emptiness had its throne.

"Hang up a moment," said Assaad. Then more angrily, "Curses!" He stopped the car abruptly. People were jostling past the vehicle, swarming ahead to where a posse of armed police controlled a barricade.

"*Merde*," said Assaad. "I should have drove the other way. Now we're stuck, obviously. In the main square, the President's chief general, General Makhkamov, will address the people today. I forgot it . . . We cannot escape. It would look hostile. We leave the car and go to listen to Makhkamov."

"Is it safe?"

"For us or for the car? Come. Men must listen to lies occasionally. It's duty." After parking his brother's car under a tree, Assaad removed the spark plugs from the engine and locked all the doors.

A crowd was gathering outside the main mosque. Looking about, Burnell saw a handful of veiled women, standing close together in the shade of a tree. All the rest were men and boys, mostly wearing suits, with keffiyehs slung round their heads.

Women! The element of Muslim society which Burnell found most dispiriting was their seclusion. When women were to be seen, most went shrouded in *chadors* from head to foot. He missed their presence in shops, in restaurants, on the street. He had visited a brothel but felt more compassion than lust for the girls imprisoned there. The lean hags of Tartary held little appeal.

Yesterday, a woman driving a car had waved a greeting to him. He had been too surprised to return the wave. Later he realized she must have been on the staff of a European embassy. He still carried an impression of her smile, her hair blowing free, her naked wrist, unbraceleted.

"You see," Assaad said into Burnell's ear, "President Diyanizov stands for the development of Turkmenistan as a modern secular state after the Turkish pattern. This General Makhkamov supports him. Both men are of the same tribe. But the mullahs wish to follow Iran into a fundamentalist Islamic pattern, which will mean a closed society and many difficulties for us Unbelievers. So the General Makhkamov may say something interesting. We may learn which way the struggle goes, hopefully."

He added, "One problem is, here we are closer to Iran than Turkey. And more close still to nowhere . . ."

The sun shone. In the main, the crowd stood silent. Burnell could see no foreigners apart from himself. On the outskirts of the gathering stood a more rural kind of man, dark of visage, turbaned, some with dogs and small hairy goats on strings. Beyond them, lining the square, were tanks with their guns pointing inwards. All waited with a patience Burnell tried hard to feel in himself.

A band played distantly, its notes bleached in the fierce sunlight.

General Makhkamov was a sturdy man, small of stature, with dark piercing eyes which searched the crowd before he ascended a podium to speak. He was in uniform, shaven, moustached, with a row of medals on his chest and a military strut. Burnell had seen such men before; in his experience they did not last long. But there was an unending supply of them.

Assaad translated some of Makhkamov's speech into Burnell's right ear.

" 'Those of you who fought in the war against a cruel enemy, you will be rewarded. Those cowards who stayed at home will get nothing when the time comes . . . Our brave heroes, all those who took up arms, all those prepared to die for our nation, all those who stood fast against an evil foe and trod the path of Allah and legality, all those who bathed themselves in the gore of the invader—they all shall come to high office . . . We shall see it happen . . . We shall become a great nation in world affairs, guarding our independence under a just God . . . Your scars, your medals, your courage, your loyalty, shall gain you power. And we shall be ruled by brave and honourable men . . .' ''

Assaad turned away in disgust when the speech and prayers were over. He remarked to Burnell as they got back into the car, ''Oh, to live in a country where cowards are allowed to rule . . .''

''People always rant like that after a war. Nothing ever gets done. So what are the indications? Which will prevail? The secular state or the Islamic one?''

Flinging the car violently into gear, Assaad backed through the dispersing crowd, hooting continually. ''Muddles, Mr. Burnell. Nothing clear. You see, it's not just the religious question. Also are tribes competing—Ersaris, Yomuds, Goklans, two sort of Tekkes . . . Not bad people, pretty easy-going, unlike my own countrymen, I'm afraid to say it. What are you to do?''

He shrugged his ample shoulders, smiled, shouted a curse at a cyclist he had just missed.

''You don't plan to go back to Syria or to the West?''

''The West I hate, honestly. Not her books but her ambitions. Is the cause of many troubles. Russia always makes mistakes in looking to the West, in envy or in admiration. But I hate Russia more and more. And Turkmenistan most.'' He laughed, removed his hands from the wheel to exclaim, ''All men here believe Genghis Khan's blood runs still in their veins. What a life, is it! And my wife is Goklan tribe, wishing never to eat the bread of a different nation . . . Syria I don't like. Do you like your own country, the country of Thomas Hardy?''

''Yes, I suppose so. It's much changed.''

They were moving through suburbs now. Pleasant trees grew here and there, mitigating the utilitarian aspect of the streets.

''Then why you are come to such a place as this?''

''As I was trying to explain, I believe President Diyanizov has a vital fragment of my memory. I want it restored to me. Can you secure me an audience with him? Frankfurt was unhelpful in that respect.''

''What you want back your memory for? It makes only trouble. You see this fine little General Makhkamov, who never met a live enemy on the battlefield, he stirs up memory in his people. They hold thousand-year-old grudges against the people in the north. Isn't that mad, I'd say! Memory is the curse of nations. Best to be free of all memory.''

''So you can't help?''

''Maybe tomorrow. Be in no hurry. Old Goklan saying is, 'Sit on your horse and see the grass grow . . .' Today we visit the bridge.''

Sweating in the heat, Burnell, who hated asking favours, pursued the question. ''Dr. Assaad, this fragment of my memory—well, I've been informed by a dealer that it was sold to President Diyanizov. One of a very limited number of prints. If I could get hold of it, I could have it reinserted. It's one of a crucial period of my life. Without it—I can't explain. I'm a prey to nightmares. I never feel complete.''

The thin traffic ahead was slowing. They were approaching a crossroads. A motorcyclist roared up and down the road, signalling vehicles to stop. Assaad muttered to himself and wound down his window. Imitating the action, Burnell thrust his head into the heat, tasting the bitter tang of unburnt diesel. A tank was manoeuvring into position ahead in a haze of exhaust, establishing a roadblock. Armed guards unbaled razor wire across the road, directed by an officer, while a guardpost with the national flag was being set up.

Two soldiers were moving away pedestrians. A woman shouted harshly at them, gesticulating while her child screamed. Cars backed and revved down a side road, directed by a policeman holding an incongruous pink parasol.

"What's up?" Burnell asked, thinking even as he did so that the question was foolish. Assaad did not answer. He switched off his engine and sat waiting while an officer on a motorbike approached the car. The officer thrust his face through the window, looked about suspiciously and demanded their papers. Burnell and Assaad handed them over, the latter conversing in a mild way, his face full of smiles.

The officer scrutinized Burnell's EC passport and WCH credentials, returning them with a few courteous-sounding remarks.

"He says you are not to look so worried," Assaad translated. "As a foreign visitor from the West, you are welcome here, and will not be harmed. He wishes to announce he follows English football."

More conversation passed between Assaad and the officer until Assaad was ordered to turn the car round and head back to town. The officer gave them a salute and a smile as they moved off, before turning to the next vehicle to arrive.

"I happen to know where he lives," Assaad remarked, "and once sold his brother some carpets at a good price, financially. We cannot leave the city today. It seems that after we left the main square, Academy Square, some naughty fellow shot at the General Makhkamov whom we listened to. Now they seek this naughty fellow, and have closed the city . . . It's just a game these people play.

"So, it's tomorrow we must visit the Friendship Bridge."

2. The Bullet

Robert Murray-Johnson was a red-haired man with a square jaw and an air of good humour. Burnell had already discovered that this good humour concealed an agreeable vein of misanthropy, which found ample to feed on in the Turkmeni capital to which Murray-Johnson had been posted.

He collected Burnell from the Hotel Ashkhabad just as night was falling and the intense heat of the day promising to abate. The back of his small car was loaded with tennis racquets and sports gear.

"You're sure you want to do this, Roy?" Without pausing for an answer, he went on, "Your friend Dr. Assaad came to see me as soon as he dropped you this morning. He knows his way round the city okay, poor bugger. His survival depends on it. We do him a favour, stretch a point now and then. After all, Syria is rather popular in Britain just now, can't think why. Seems Britain's popular in Syria too—again, can't think why.''

"They read Thomas Hardy.''

As he steered into the heavy evening traffic, past the camel-coloured Russian tour buses lined up outside the hotel, Murray-Johnson explained that it was impossible for any foreigner, apart from heads of state, to have audience with the President. Certainly, no matter as personal as a stolen memory could be broached, even through intermediaries.

However, Dr. Assaad knew someone who owed him a favour who kept a Nostovision shop in the back streets of Ashkhabad. NV had been banned in most of Central Asia because of its high pornographic content; but, as with most things—said Murray-Johnson with a sly smile—there was a way round that. Assaad had arranged that they could look the stock over.

Chinese-built trams rattled along the centre of the avenue as they eased their way down the long Ulitza Engleska. Murray-Johnson cheerfully put a gloss on the street name by explaining to Burnell that the British Army had defeated the Red Army near Ashkhabad in 1918, and occupied the area. As they passed a busy market, where the fruit stalls outside its portals were illuminated by small kerosene lamps, the street grew more drab.

"About here," Murray-Johnson muttered. "Dog's Piss Alley . . .''

He turned down a side street, to pull up next to a ramshackle *chaykhana* from which loud music boomed. The day had turned as purple as a bruise. Assuring Burnell he had been here many times before, he led the way down an alley beside the teahouse, and banged on the door of a large building constructed of breeze blocks. Fruit bats poured from an enormous quercus tree overshadowing the building. The door was promptly unlocked from inside and Burnell and Murray-Johnson were admitted.

A beefy man standing inside held out his hand. Murray-Johnson passed over some cash.

They had entered a large store. Racks filled with diverse goods formed narrow aisles. Murray-Johnson moved down the aisles without hesitation. In a glass-fronted office on the far side sat a small wizened man with oriental features, introduced to Burnell as Mr. Khan.

Mr. Khan put aside a cigarette, coughed, and led them to the Nostovision department. NV bullets were piled everywhere, each in its plastic pack. Large signs above the racks indicated categories: MURDER, LOVE, SEX, ADVENTURE, CHILDHOOD, and so on. All the stock was second- and third-hand.

Here were stored true memories, some legitimately obtained—for many people were ready to sell exceptional parts of their life memories to NV studios—and some stolen, as Burnell's had been in Budapest. These thousands of memories represented fragments of real lives—happy, sad, crazy. Memories of mad people had enjoyed a vogue in the West a year earlier.

Khan shuffled among his wares in silk slippers, pointing vaguely here and there, explaining in broken German. While the legitimate bullets were labelled correctly, stolen memories were deliberately mislabelled, as a provision against prosecution. Seeing Burnell's expression of despair, Khan winked, raised a knowing finger and took him to a side table.

Following Murray-Johnson's instructions, the storekeeper had set aside six NV bullets sorted from his stock. All their plastic cases bore the legend "*Fabriqué en San Marino.*" This, Khan assured them, meant the bullets originated in an illegal studio in Budapest. It was the studio's way of covering its tracks.

"Do you buy these from the President when he's finished with them?" Burnell asked.

Half-closing his rheumy eyes, Khan gave him a sidelong glance and said, "Mein herr, I am a poor trader, ask no more. *Die Welt zerfällt in Tatsachen.* But there are no facts here, illusions only."

"What's he on about?" Murray-Johnson asked.

"Believe it or not, I think he's quoting Wittgenstein: 'The world divides into facts' . . . Let's have a look at these bullets."

He sorted through the cases, conscious that hope was making his heart beat faster. Their titles suggested an arbitrary knowledge of the English language: "Not in the Tree Ran any Lake," "In the Hat Warfare a Sky Tooth Jumper," "Animals Sequestered with a Green," and others, equally oblique.

Four of the familiar Nostovision receivers stood against one wall. Burnell seated himself in one of the chairs and adjusted the plastic helmet over his head before switching on. He inserted one of the bullets into the system unit and touched a couple of keys.

His eyes closed. Almost at once, he lost a clear perception of his surroundings—an instance of how quickly short-term memory decayed. Peculiar lassitude overcame him. In what felt like the fibre of his being, electric current was stimulating the amacrine cells of his brain. Next second, the synaptic transfer was made: the memory data stored in the bullet flooded his cortex with mnemons.

The interior of the hut was dim. Its details had not registered. The floor—he could see that clearly enough—was bare earth. An animal of some kind was there. A bed of a sort with a blanket on filled one side of the room. A barefoot woman crouched by the bed. Some details were sharp: the big blue flowers on her dress, crawling round the outline of a buttock, ascending across the broad back to the neck. She wept into her large hands, spatulate fingers pressed to forehead.

Burnell too was making noises, sobs part-stifled. He moved nearer to the woman, putting a gnarled hand on her shoulder. Hand and shoulder smudged into dimness, lost by the distortions of a tear.

He looked down as she did at a child lying on the blanket. He knew it had died of a variety of ills, mainly pneumonia, brought on by near-starvation. It was a boy. The boy's lips were drawn back, revealing pale gums in a horrifying grimace. Burnell reached out and closed the mouth and eyes. The woman rose, beginning to shriek, beating her head with clenched fists in her pain.

Feeling his own weakness, Burnell stooped, tenderly lifting the dead child. Probably he was the father of the weeping woman; probably she was the mother of the boy. He had other people in his mind, dark, concerned, slow-moving.

Slow-moving himself, he carried the boy from the shack. The woman remained behind, standing against a wall. Again the blue flowers on the dress, drooping.

The world outside was dung-coloured. He felt the sun at zenith weighing on his shoulders, a familiar burden. Other people arrived, walking as if in a fog. They spoke an incomprehensible language—yet Burnell understood it. They shared his grief. All suffered alike. A sense of community was strong.

He settled himself under a tree, easing himself down against its slender trunk, still clutching the dead child. The boy was as light as a toy in his arms. Cross-legged in the shade, he also wept. Old men squatted by him, prodding grey fingers abstractedly in the dust.

Burnell said to them, "We have not long before we follow him."

A leaf fell from the branches above. It floated down to the forehead of the dead boy. All the world was lost in concentration on the leaf. It settled green on the puzzled black forehead. It turned yellow, altering its living shape as it did so. Within minutes, heat withered it and turned it brown. It became nothing, and blew away on the lightest breeze. The boy's cheek too had already begun to wither . . .

"It's not mine, it's not mine!" He was speaking the foreign tongue as he switched off. Though Khan and Murray-Johnson came into view, and the warehouse, his sense of bereavement remained. He removed the cap and had to walk about. Khan, used to such reactions in his memory-store, grinned and proffered a cigarette, which Burnell accepted. Murray-Johnson, in one of the other chairs, was smiling, eyes closed.

Pacing up and down, puffing inexpertly, Burnell could imagine the old man— the old man he had briefly been—going to the nearest city to sell his memories to an NV agent for almost nothing, to gain a few pence for the funeral of his grandson. Then he would be free of all memory, and presumably would no longer grieve.

He might, however, suffer a sense of loss similar to that which Burnell felt, having been robbed of some of his memories of life with Stephanie.

It was all he could do to force himself back to the apparatus and to try another bullet labelled "*Fabriqué en San Marino.*" Fortunately, the next bolts of memory were less harrowing. A trip in a powerboat over a great reef, with a huge party on a small island. A frivolous life in a Patagonian town, lived by a woman who ran a successful milliner's. An apartment in a bleak township where snow always lay thick, with drunken fights and an excursion to hunt reindeer. An uneventful week in a small dusty village, where a married couple lived in fear of their mentally deficient son . . .

All these invasions were as real to Burnell as his own life. He escaped from each of them exhausted, awed by the rigours of human existence, entranced by the people he had been. Their joys, their sorrows, became fairly quickly eradicated, since no transference was made in the NV projector from the short-term to the long-term memory. Already the poor old man with his dead grandson was beginning to sink from mind, though a fading leaf of sadness remained.

"Shirts in a Cupboard" opened in an outdoor setting. He was aware of this new mnemonic person as little more than a pair of boots and a pair of hands, one of which clutched a sickle. Heat made the hands and arms glisten. He saw that the hands were those of a youth. He felt himself to be young and lusty. The sickle swung and swung, almost without cease. It was early summer. He was cutting down cow parsley and goosegrass.

Burnell worked his way along steadily, from right to left, avoiding a camellia which had finished flowering. Every now and then, he caught glimpses of a garden, a smoothly mown lawn. Tantalizingly, he saw a woman walking beside an ornamental pond, tall and dark. But he bent his back and continued with the work.

It was finished. Burnell wiped the sickle on his jeans and laid it on an oak bench. He entered a house, ascending a narrow stair to the bathroom. By contrast with the sunshine, the interior was dark. Pictures framed and glazed on the walls yielded not their true subjects but reflections of distant doors and windows.

In the bathroom, Burnell pulled off his shirt and washed his face and torso, drying them on a blue towel. He caught a mere glimpse of himself in the mirror above the basin. Fair, sharp-featured, possibly early twenties . . .

Leaving the sweaty shirt on the floor, he trod over it and went across to find a clean one in the airing cupboard. He pulled the door open.

Inside the cupboard, newly laundered clothes were in immaculate array. Ironed sheets were stored on a high shelf, together with duvet covers. Burnell's shirts were hanging in orderly fashion. He saw a pile of his clean handkerchiefs, his socks rolled into balls. Her dresses were there too, crisp, creaseless.

Without a further glance, Burnell reached forward towards the shirts and—

—without a pause was running down the right wing with the ball at his feet. Green field, brown blur of crowd in stadium. The Italian mid-fielder Raniero charging towards him. The roar of the spectators went unnoticed in his heightened state. Burnell swerved at the last moment, tapping the ball round to the left of his opponent's boots, instantly recapturing it. Ahead lay the goalmouth and—

He squeezed the on/off bulb in his fist. The memory died. He was gasping with shock. Bootleg memory bullets so often contained no credits, no fade-ins or editorial matter; they simply switched from one fragment of one person's memory to another, unrelated. In a composite bullet, snatches of various memories were frequently incorporated, as here, perhaps lopped from longer sequences.

Leaning back with his eyes closed, Burnell let his pulse rate sink to a more normal level. Damn the footballer! He concentrated on the airing-cupboard episode with a pained solicitude. The main question was, had he stumbled on a fragment of his own memory or not? The answer was less simple than it appeared.

While suspecting it might be a true Burnell memory, he recognized a strong desire that it should be. It was baffling not to be sure. But memory—he recalled the old saying—"played strange tricks" . . .

A trivial hour in a summer afternoon . . . the passage of twenty years . . . youth's happy habit of inattention . . .

In the early days of their association, Stephanie and he had bought a large derelict country mansion, assisted by money from his father. It had been done for its challenge; also in part to try to please his father as well as Stephanie. They had worked on the restoration of house and garden. He had not thought of that period of his life for years. But was it *that* house and garden in the bullet? Why had he felt no immediate stab of recognition?

Well . . . weeds were weeds, wherever found. He had managed no clear look at the woman by the fish pool, being unable to see anything the memorizer did not see. And the rear of the house, the stairs, the landing . . . they were common to thousands of houses, with only minor variations. Again, the memorizer was taking no particular notice of his surroundings, being familiar with them. Detail had been scanty . . .

It was on the airing cupboard that Burnell concentrated his thought. The memorizer had looked into the cupboard merely to find a clean shirt, taking for granted its orderliness.

What now impressed Burnell was precisely that orderliness. He saw in it a clue to his separation from his wife.

Suppose he had just seen himself, almost been himself, as he was twenty and more years ago . . . Then the woman by the fish pool had been Stephanie, Stephanie when young, Stephanie when they were first in love, when they had high hopes of each other, when magic still played about their relationship . . .

It followed that the airing cupboard was in Stephanie's domain.

That small room, large enough to walk into, was almost a secret compartment in the old house; yes, Stephanie's domain, kept for the most part in darkness. She controlled it, she stocked it with the clothes she had washed and ironed. Not a sock there but knew her caring touch . . .

Murray-Johnson was shaking his shoulder. "Wake up, old cocker."

Reluctantly, Burnell removed his helmet and got out of the chair. While Murray-Johnson enthused about an absolutely disgusting memory he had lived through, Burnell bought the airing-cupboard memory from Mr. Khan for an extortionate price.

On the way back to the hotel in Murray-Johnson's car, he puzzled over the question of whether he had actually stumbled across a fragment of his own memory—in which case, back in Frankfurt, he could have an expert reinsert it in his long-term memory; it would be life reclaimed. But he had to be sure. The ascetic side of his nature was repelled by the idea of having false memories inserted, though many people thought nothing of doing so, in order to look back on lives they had never lived.

Thanking Murray-Johnson profusely for a helpful evening, Burnell refused the offer of a drink and retired to his hotel room to consider matters.

These days, he lived out of his suitcase. Samsonite was his home. He had forgotten to lock the suitcase when in the room at midday. Clothes, both laundered and dirty, lay about the room. His books and papers had been left strewn here and there. A half-eaten melon attracted flies on the windowsill. His alarm clock lay face-down beside the bed. He perceived newly the disorder. So this was the kind of man he was, or had become . . .

And perhaps the clue to the break between him and Stephanie lay within that airing cupboard, along those sweet-smelling ledges. The orderliness of her mind was demonstrated, for those who cared to look and understand, in that snug little hot closet of hers, where all was stowed neatly away, cared for, made pristine, tended. Tended . . . Had *he* not tended things? Had he failed to tend their relationship? Had he not been *tender*? His mind too much on his career? Had he not been appreciative enough of her qualities, simply because they did not match with his?

"Oh, Stephanie . . ." The airing cupboard served as a revelation. And yet . . . he could still in no way be certain that it was his house, their cupboard, her care . . .

Once again he found himself up against the brick wall of the question: how does a man manage to get through his life? How can he learn to swim through the sea of circumstance which confronts him?

He stood in the middle of his untidy room—motionless, but in a storm of conflicting thought which found no exterior expression.

The phone rang. He went to it with relief. Dr. Assaad spoke, reminding him of their appointment the following noon.

"Did you have luck with my friend Mr. Khan?" he asked.

Burnell looked down at the bullet in his hand. "Mr. Khan was very helpful," he said.

3. The Storm

Noon, under a leaden sky and a temperature of 95 degrees. Even with the air-conditioning working, it was hot in the car of Dr. Assaad's brother.

"Is not too many kilometres to the Friendship Bridge," Assaad said, as Burnell mopped under his collar.

They reached the roundabout where on the previous day the roadblock had been in operation. Today, the site was deserted. The road ahead lay empty. A beggar woman sat under a tree, a small child crawling on hands and knees beside her. Before them lay open country.

The asphalt soon gave out and they were travelling over a dirt road. The straggling outskirts of the city disappeared in an amber smog behind. A wind was rising, stirring the dust. Mountains lay distantly ahead, their crusty ridges no more than a blue outline against the hazy blue of the sky, as if they delineated a country without material substance.

Dr. Assaad whistled cheerfully. "Land of Hope and Glory." Burnell shrank from joining in.

The River Garakhs was fast, icy and grey. For a short distance, the Garakhs marked a division between two distinct worlds: Turkmenistan and Iran. This was where, for over half of the previous century, the great world of the Soviet Union had expired and the more enduring world of Islam had commenced.

Here, God and Marx had surrendered in the face of the mountains and mosques of Muhammad.

The true national frontier, running for miles in either direction, was formed by the Kopet Dagh Mountains. Their monotonous flanks loomed on the far side of the river, extending as far as the eye could see, eroded, practically treeless. An Iranian settlement of mud-coloured huts had grown up on the far banks of the Garakhs. A road led from the settlement into the range. Nothing moved except dust. The Iranian sky to the south was leaden.

On the northern side of the river, Turkmenistan presented no more enlivening a spectacle. The land, lying almost at sea level, was a salt desert. Habitation had ceased as soon as they had left the capital, apart from a few yurts here and there, by which Akhal-teke horses were tethered. The desolate expanses were punctuated at one point by oil wells. Assaad remarked that the Japanese were prospecting.

Later, they passed a party of ragged horsemen galloping at full speed beside a railway line. Later still, a few miles from their destination, Burnell watched a group of people walking with some camels and a mule—an archaic frieze soon left behind in the dust. The dust was a problem, whipped up by an increasing wind.

The road from Ashkhabad, potholes and all, petered out at the river.

"In the spring, after rain, the wild tulips are blooming here, everywhere," Dr. Assaad said. "The landscape is colourful." He stopped the car and sat with his great body leaning forwards, drumming his fingers on the wheel and peering out at the intermittent dust clouds. "I remember it so."

Burnell sighed.

"It'll be all right," Assaad said, motioning with his head for Burnell to get out.

The two men walked towards the bridge. It was unfinished—scarcely begun.

The Friendship Bridge at the Garakhs resembled a failed animal of some earlier epoch. It stuck its snout a short way over the flood, as if blindly to quiz the Iranian shore. It had been designed much as a child's bridge is constructed from wooden blocks. One stump of pillar stood on the near bank. A second stump stood in the swirling torrent. Over the stumps had been laid, in giant concrete sections, intimations of road, a kind of archetypal road, no more than 10 yards long, crumbling already.

This truncated lump of masonry was left with its far end hanging over the water and its near end jutting some feet above the land, dislocated from the road below.

Burnell walked beneath it, hands in pockets, gazing up at reinforcing rods trailing worm-like from the body of concrete. He was bitterly angry. To a man whose book, *Architrave and Archetype*, had been accepted as a standard work, this abortive hulk was an insult—certainly nothing worth two hours' travel over bumpy roads.

"Let's get back to town," he said. "I have important things to do. I must return to Frankfurt."

"Yes, yes, instantly," said Dr. Assaad, conjuring up one of the adverbs of which he seemed fond. "But first we must climb on the bridge. Then you will understand, surely."

He led the way. Burnell felt obliged to follow as the big man heaved himself up a ladder set against the near pillar.

With agility, it was possible to swing up, grasp a girder and pull oneself on to the flat part of the bridge. Clouds of dust met them. Lizards scuttled into hiding. The wound in Burnell's leg ached in the heat.

They stood together, the Syrian and the Englishman, high above the ground. Burnell shielded his eyes with a hand. "Look, hadn't we better get back?"

The sun had assumed the aspect of a withered orange. It cast a bronze gloom over the land.

Assaad said, "I know you have things on your mind, Mr. Burnell. We all have them. Once past youth, all men have things on mind. Women likewise, probably." He walked along to the edge of the concrete structure, to gaze down into the water, letting wind and dust whip against his suit.

"This bridge is called the Friendship Bridge for obvious reasons. The Turkmeni say for a joke it is called Friendship Bridge because, like friendship, it should never have been started and will never finish . . . Huh. Not too much humorous for British taste, eh?"

Burnell said, "I've lost my sense of humour. Sorry."

"The first stone was laid by the late President of Turkmenistan. He was a devout Muslim, an ayatollah. But the war swept him out of power, happily. He died of some disease soon after. As people do. With the onslaught of war, President Diyanizov ordered work here all to stop. Of course it will never be resumed. We no longer wish to be so friendly with Iran since their last revolution. Some recall an old Goklani saying, 'Iranian ponies have only three and a half legs.' "

Some of this was lost in the wind. Burnell turned his back to the gale and said, speaking formally, "Dr. Assaad, a storm's brewing. Best to get back to Ashkhabad."

Assaad's large face was already powdered with dust.

He shook his head sadly, disappointed by Burnell's lack of perception. Turning his back on the river, he frowned at Burnell. As if preparing to make a speech, he clutched his lapels.

"This place is what you should remember to carry back to England with you. In its fashion, it is even a victory for the West! Yes, a monument for the magnetic attraction of the West, felt even in this country where not a copy of *The Hand of Ethelberta* is to be had for money or love." He gave a sardonic smile, tight-lipped, and stared down at the pattern of wooden planking embedded in fossil imprint in the concrete blocks at his feet. "Many men wished to embrace Islam when Soviet Union collapsed, but the pull of the West was even stronger. Happily, some men wish not to grovel to Mecca five times every day . . ."

A battery of winds sprang up. Light gravels were scooped from the river bank and dashed into their faces. The men were blown across the bridge. Assaad dragged Burnell down beside him. They crouched for shelter under the low parapet. The wind roared as it rushed overhead, suddenly making its intentions clear.

"When it is stopped, we go back to the car," Assaad said, his face close to Burnell's. "These storms last no long time. Do not worry."

"It was madness to come out here."

Assaad laughed. "And maybe we were both mad to leave our own countries, probably . . . To escape memories or to find them . . . *Che sera, sera*, isn't that what the Italians say? You travel but you have no cosmopolitan spirit, Mr. Burnell. You must appreciate what has befallen here. You should regard Friendship Bridge as a memorial to a crucial moment in history.

"When Soviet Union collapsed, was a great day for all the world. Also for Turkmeni peoples. They had been long suppressed. The place was bankrupt. Then the frontiers were open, suddenly. Never before open except in the lives of very old people. Freedom—that word we all like to hear!

"A great procession of ordinary people came from Ashkhabad. My wife was among them. They came along the road we have taken, to this point, to look across at Iran, a free country. Before, all the whole frontier was patrolled and people could be shot who came near here."

From his crouched position, resting his elbows on the concrete, Assaad imitated the action of someone firing a rifle.

"And across the other side of this river, Iranians appeared! They cheered to this side, this side cheered to them. Can you imagine? On that day, were two thousand Turkmeni here, maybe two hundred Irani there. After all, there are same families on both sides of the frontier, divided only by that monster Stalin.

"That particular day, was icy rain in the air—not this nice warm sand. But some of the Ashkhabad youths, they strip off their clothes and swim across the river at this point. One young boy age thirteen, he drown. Otherwise, is great rejoicing. The people embrace, each to each, warmly. It was an occasion of many tears and kisses, Mr. Burnell, many tears and kisses. My wife stood here. She waved to her older sister across the river."

He fell silent, letting the sand scour their ears.

"One Iranian has a loud-shouter? Yes, loud-hailer. He calls out news. He calls names, telephone numbers, radio wavelengths. Names of lost relations are called across this river. Many people wept. Weeping because lives are broken. You can imagine. All spoken is—what do you call it?—reconciling words, privately. No words of politics, no words of religion. Only poor people stood here. No great ones."

As Assaad paused, Burnell thought, Oh yes, he has ties of love to this land he affects to hate . . .

Assaad continued. "The people congregated on both sides of the river till the sun was set. The date was the thirteenth of Azar by the Muslim calendar.

"The brave boys swam back here again. Some had gifts such as worry beads and sweetmeats. The newspapers in Ashkhabad described that day as a day of seething emotions. There were demands that a bridge should be built, so that Muslim should be united with Muslim. A bridge of friendship.

"Under the old ayatollah president, the construction of the bridge was begun. Then it was discovered that the Iranians did not build a road to the bridge on their side, cunningly. Instead, they waged another war with Iraq, their other neighbour. And both sides began to worry about illegal border crossings. Remember, Turkmenistan was then being attacked by the Afghanistan guerrillas.

"The rest I have already told. This bridge makes me very happy—naturally, because it's not complete. The bridges should be built not to the south, to Islam, but to the West, to Hungary and Germany and France and England—where change is not a criminal act."

As he rambled on, Assaad's voice was at times dominated by the wind, which now seemed to consist as much of sand as air. Burnell found his thoughts wandering.

In his work, he was accustomed to monuments that endured, beautiful structures whose very endurance inspired reverence. Although he had no religious faith, he venerated the buildings it was his duty to catalogue.

Because there was melancholy as well as honour in the task, Edward Gibbon's *Decline and Fall of the Roman Empire* had long been his favourite reading. Able to recite whole passages of the old unbeliever by heart, particularly when slightly drunk, Burnell recalled now, crouching against the concrete, Gibbon's reflections on transience. "The art of man is able to construct," Gibbon had said, "monuments far more permanent than the narrow span of his own existence: yet these monuments, like himself, are perishable and frail; and in the boundless annals of time his life and his labours must equally be measured as a fleeting moment."

And if that labour should be to stock, without fuss, an airing cupboard with fresh sweet clothes . . . It was important, surely, to remember that monument to past love. Even if not his . . .

He saw his own life as no more than a wormcast in a vast tract of history. And his family? His grandfather had lived through the dissolution, peaceful on the whole, as on the whole the disintegrating institution had been, of the British Empire. His father had lived through the collapse of the Communist empire. He was himself passing his life in the years following those momentous events, during the expansionist phase of the EC superstate.

The Turkmeni were seeking some kind of political stability which so far eluded them. No models of stable modern government in their past existed from which they might gain strength; there were only memories of horrendous oppression, massive abuses of morality (and agriculture) and, more distantly, the legend of that Golden Horde which had once thrown a shadow of terror over all Christendom. In fact, the Friendship Bridge represented an attempt of hope, a hand stretched towards an imagined outer world.

He sensed something of the complexity of emotions Dr Assaad felt. His wife's sister must remain on the other side of the torrent. That was part of a historical necessity. Burnell's anger against the Syrian faded. Despite the discomfort of the sandstorm, he was glad to be here, where no Englishman, as far as he knew, had ventured. Perhaps Assaad was wrong and he did have a cosmopolitan spirit . . .

And how had he come here? Certainly, he had managed to obtain no introduction to President Diyanizov from the authorities in Frankfurt or London. Fearful of the paid assassin, Diyanizov saw no visitors. Had he ever really hoped that he might retrieve that vital missing period of his memory? Or had he found it, without realizing as much?

Burnell had drifted because he was, essentially, a drifter. Despite the best of educations, he had refused to join the family's merchant bank. He had dedicated himself to . . . Well, dedication was hardly a word he cared to apply to himself.

His father was now confined to a motorized chair. An old embittered man who trundled slowly about his estate. Soon he would inevitably pass away. The estate would be broken up. And the avenue of lime trees planted by his grandfather . . . Already Burnell could feel immense regret latent in him, awaiting the release of his father's death.

His father had liked, had loved, Stephanie. Of course Burnell had no more chance of getting her back than there was of standing and demanding, successfully, that the sandstorm cease.

But there was that vital scene to be retrieved, to be reinstated in memory. He needed better evidence than a cupboard full of shirts he failed to recognize. Oh, Stephanie, how did our relationship go so badly wrong? You were the most precious thing in my life. Had there been someone more precious to you than I? If only I knew, if only I could remember . . .

But would things then be different? Could he rectify a past fault? Could that broken bridge ever be reconstructed to cross the chilly river of separation?

Tears filled his eyes, to be instantly dried by the heat.

He felt his own identity fading into the abrasive world about him. Never was it more clear to him why, and how fatally, he clung to the memorials of the past. And the time would come, not today, perhaps not tomorrow, when he would join the dead, and the broken estates, when he would succumb to the same processes of mutability which had transformed the bridge from design to ruin. Yes, the time would come.

Well, it was no great matter . . .

The sand was gathering about the two figures, who crouched as if imploring Allah for his mercy. It lay thickly drifted under the parapet.

Roy Burnell yielded up his thoughts to let the sand take over. He heard it howling through Turkmenistan, through the universe, covering everything, the living and the dead.

INTO THE MIRANDA RIFT

G. David Nordley

▼

Here's a suspenseful science fiction adventure of exploration in the grand manner and on a grand scale, full of strange dangers and even stranger wonders, and demonstrating that if you can't get around a problem, and you can't get over it, and you can't get under it, sometimes the only choice you have is to go right on ahead *through* it. . . .

New writer G. David Nordley is a retired Air Force officer and physicist who has become a frequent contributor to *Analog* in the last couple of years, winning that magazine's Analytical Laboratory readers poll last year for his story "Poles Apart." He has also sold stories to *Asimov's Science Fiction, Tomorrow, Mindsparks, F&SF,* and elsewhere. He lives in Sunnyvale, California.

I

This starts after we had already walked, crawled, and clawed our way fifty-three zig-zagging kilometers into the Great Miranda Rift, and had already penetrated seventeen kilometers below the mean surface. It starts because the mother of all Mirandaquakes just shut the door behind us and the chances of this being rescued are somewhat better than mine; I need to do more than just take notes for a future article. It starts because I have faith in human stubbornness, even in a hopeless endeavor; and I think the rescuers will come, eventually. I am Wojciech Bubka and this is my journal.

Miranda, satellite of Uranus, is a cosmic metaphor about those things in creation that come together without really fitting, like the second try at marriage, ethnic integration laws, or a poet trying to be a science reporter. It was blasted apart by something a billion years ago and the parts drifted back together, more or less. There are gaps. Rifts. Empty places for things to work their way in that are not supposed to be there; things that don't belong to something of whole cloth.

Like so many great discoveries, the existence of the rifts was obvious after the fact, but our geologist, Nikhil Ray, had to endure a decade of derision, several rejected papers, a divorce from a wife unwilling to share academic ridicule, and public humiliation in the pop science media—before the geology establishment finally conceded that what the seismological network on Miranda's surface had found had, indeed, confirmed his work.

Nikhil had simply observed that although Miranda appears to be made of the same stuff as everything else in the Uranian system, the other moons are just under twice as dense as water while Miranda is only one and a third times as dense. More ice and less rock below was one possibility. The other possibility, which Nikhil had patiently pointed out, was that there could be less of *everything*; a scattering of voids or bubbles beneath.

So, with the goat-to-hero logic we all love, when seismological results clearly showed that Miranda was laced with substantial amounts of nothing, Nikhil became a minor Solar System celebrity, with a permanent chair at Coriolis, and a beautiful, high-strung, young renaissance woman as a trophy wife.

But, by that time, I fear there were substantial empty places in Nikhil, too.

Like Miranda, this wasn't clear from his urbane and vital surface when we met. He was tall for a Bengali, a lack of sun had left his skin with only a tint of bronze, and he had a sharp face that hinted at an Arab or a Briton in his ancestry; likely both. He moved with a sort of quick, decisive energy that nicely balanced the tolerant good-fellow manners of an academic aristocrat in the imperial tradition. If he now distrusted people in general, if he kept them all at a pleasantly formal distance, if he harbored a secret contempt for his species, well, this had not been apparent to Catherine Ray, M.D., who had married him after his academic rehabilitation.

I think she later found the emptiness within him and part of her had recoiled, while the other, controlling, part found no objective reason to leave a relationship that let her flit around the top levels of Solar System academia. Perhaps that explained why she chose to go on a fortnight of exploration with someone she seemed to detest; oh, the stories she would tell. Perhaps that explained her cynicism. Perhaps not.

We entered the great rift three days of an age ago, at the border of the huge chevron formation: the rift where two dissimilar geologic structures meet, held together by Miranda's gentle gravity and little else. Below the cratered, dust-choked surface, the great rift was a network of voids between pressure ridges; rough wood, slap-glued together by a lazy carpenter on a Saturday night. It could, Nikhil thinks, go through the entire moon. There were other joints, other rifts, other networks of empty places—but this was the big one.

Ah, yes, those substantial amounts of nothing. As a poet, I was fascinated by contradiction and I found a certain attraction to exploring vast areas of hidden emptiness under shells of any kind.

I fill voids, so to speak. I was an explicit rebel in a determinedly impressionist literary world of artful obscurity which fails to generate recognition or to make poets feel like they are doing anything more meaningful than the intellectual equivalent of masturbation—and pays them accordingly. The metaphor of Miranda intrigued me; an epic lay there beneath the dust and ice. Wonders to behold there must be in the biggest underground system of caverns in the known

Universe. The articles, interviews, and talk shows played out in my mind. All I had to do was get there.

I had a good idea of how to do that. Her name was Miranda Lotati. Four years ago, the spelunking daughter of the guy in charge of "Solar System Astrographic's" project board had been a literature student of mine at Coriolis University. When I heard of the discovery of Nikhil's mysterious caverns, it was a trivial matter to renew the acquaintance, this time without the impediments of faculty ethics. By this time she had an impressive list of caves, mountains, and other strange places to her credit, courtesy of her father's money and connections, I had thought.

She had seemed a rough-edged, prickly woman in my class, and her essays were dry condensed dullness, never more than the required length, but which covered the points involved well enough that honesty had forced me to pass her.

Now, armed with news of the moon Miranda's newly discovered caverns, I decided her name was clearly her destiny. I wasn't surprised when an inquiry had revealed no current relationship. So, I determined to create one and bend it toward my purposes. Somewhat to my surprise, it worked. Worked to the point where it wasn't entirely clear whether she was following my agenda, or I, hers.

Randi, as I got to know her, was something like a black hole; of what goes in, nothing comes out. Things somehow accrete to her orbit and bend to her will without any noticeable verbal effort on her part. She can spend a whole evening without saying anything more than "uh-huh." Did you like the Bach? Nice place you have. Are you comfortable? Do you want more? Did you like it? Do you want to do it again tomorrow?

"Uh-huh."

"Say, if you go into Miranda someone should do more than take pictures, don't you think? I've thrown a few words around in my time, perchance I could lend my services to chronicle the expedition? What do you think?"

"Uh-huh."

My contract with her was unspoken, and was thus on her terms. There was no escape. But we are complementary. I became her salesman. I talked her father into funding Nikhil, and talked Nikhil into accepting support from one of his erstwhile enemies. Randi organized the people and things that started coming her way into an expedition.

Randi was inarticulate, not crazy. She went about her wild things in a highly disciplined way. When she used words, she made lists: "Batteries, CO_2 Recyclers, Picks, Robot, Ropes, Spare tightsuits, Tissue, Vacuum tents, Medical supplies, Waste bags, etc."

Such things came to her through grants, donations, her father's name, friends from previous expeditions, and luck. She worked very hard at getting these things together. Sometimes I felt I fit down there in "etc.," somewhere between the t and the c, and counted myself lucky. If she had only listed "back door," perhaps we would have had one.

As I wrote she was lying beside me in our vacuum tent, exhausted with worry. I was tired, too.

* * *

We wasted a day, sitting on our sausage-shaped equipment pallets, talking, and convincing ourselves to move on.

Nikhil explained our predicament: Randi's namesake quivers as it bobs up and down in its not quite perfect orbit, as inclined to be different as she. Stresses accumulate over ages, build up inside and release, careless of the consequences. We had discovered, he said, that Miranda is still shrinking through the gradual collapse of its caverns during such quakes. Also, because the gravity is so low, it might take years for a series of quakes and aftershocks to play itself out. The quake danger wouldn't subside until long after we escaped, or died.

We had to make sure the front door was closed. It was—slammed shut. The wide gallery we traversed to arrive at this cavern is now a seam, a disjoint. A scar and a change of color remain to demarcate the forcible fusion of two previously separate layers of clathrate.

Sam jammed all four arms into the wall, anchored them with piton fingers, pressed part of its composite belly right against the new seam, and pinged until it had an image of the obstructed passage. "The closure goes back at least a kilometer," it announced.

The fiber optic line we have been trailing for the last three days no longer reached the surface either. Sam removed the useless line from the comm set and held it against the business end of its laser radar. "The break's about fifteen kilometers from here," it reported.

"How do you know that?" I asked.

"Partial mirror." Randi explained on Sam's behalf. "Internal reflection."

Fifteen kilometers, I reflected. Not that we really could have dug through even one kilometer, but we'd done some pretending. Now the pretense ceased, and we faced reality.

I had little fear of sudden death, and in space exploration, the rare death is usually sudden. My attitude toward the risks of our expedition was that if I succeeded, the rewards would be great, and if I got killed, it wouldn't matter. I should have thought more about the possibility of enduring a long, drawn-out process of having life slowly and painfully drain away from me, buried in a clathrate tomb.

The group was silent for a long time. For my part, I was reviewing ways to painlessly end my life before the Universe did it for me without concern for my suffering.

Then Nikhil's voice filled the void. "Friends, we knew the risks. If it's any consolation, that was the biggest quake recorded since instruments were put on this moon. By a factor of ten. That kind of adjustment," he waved his arms at obvious evidences of faults in the cavern around us, "should have been over with a hundred million years ago. Wretched luck, I'm afraid."

"Perhaps it will open up again?" his wife asked, her light features creased with concern behind the invisible faceplate of her helmet.

Nikhil missed the irony in her voice and answered his wife's question with an irony of his own. "Perhaps it will. In another hundred million years." He actually smiled.

Randi spoke softly; "Twenty days. CO_2 catalyst runs out in twenty days. We have two weeks of food at regular rations, but we can stretch that to a month or more. We have about a month of water each, depending on how severely we ration it. We can always get more by chipping ice and running it through our waste reprocessors. But without the catalyst, we can't clean air."

"And we can't stop breathing," Cathy added.

"Cathy," I asked, "I suppose it is traditional for poets to think this way, so I'll ask the question. Is there any way to, well, end this gracefully, if and when we have to?"

"Several," she replied with a shrug. "I can knock you out first, with anesthetic. Then kill you."

"How?" I ask.

"Does it matter?"

"To a poet, yes."

She nodded, and smiled. "Then, Wojciech, I shall put a piton through your heart, lest you rise again and in doing so devalue your manuscripts which by then will be selling for millions." Cathy's rare smiles have teeth in them.

"My dear," Nikhil said, our helmet transceivers faithfully reproducing the condescension in his tone, "your bedside manner is showing."

"My dear," Cathy murmured, "what would you know about anything to do with a bed?"

Snipe and countersnipe. Perhaps such repartee held their marriage together, like gluons hold a meson together until it annihilates itself.

Sam returned from the "front door." "We can't go back that way, and our rescuers can't come that way in twenty days with existing drilling equipment. I suggest we go somewhere else." A robot has the option of being logical at times like this.

"Quite right. If we wait here," Nikhil offered, "Miranda may remove the option of slow death, assisted or otherwise. Aftershocks are likely."

"Aftershocks, cave-in, suffocation," Randi listed the possibilities, "or other exits."

Nikhil shrugged and pointed to the opposite side of the cavern. "Shall we?"

"I'll follow you to hell, darling," Cathy answered.

Randi and I exchanged a glance which said; thank the lucky stars for *you*.

"Maps, such as they are," Randi began. "Rations, sleep schedule, leadership, and so on. Make decisions now, while we can think." At this she looked Nikhil straight in the eye, "While we care."

"Very well then," Nikhil responded with a shrug. "Sam is a bit uncreative when confronted with the unknown, Cathy and Wojciech have different areas of expertise, so perhaps Randi and I should take turns leading the pitches. I propose that we don't slight ourselves on the evening meal, but make do with minimal snacks at other times—"

"My darling idiot, we need protein energy for the work," Cathy interrupted. "We will have a good breakfast, even at the expense of dinner."

"Perhaps we could compromise on lunch," I offered.

"Travel distance, energy level, sustained alertness."

"On the other hand," I corrected, "moderation in all things. . . ."

By the time we finally got going, we were approaching the start of the next sleep period, and Randi had effectively decided everything. We went single file behind the alternating pitch leaders. I towed one pallet. Cathy towed the other, and Sam brought up the rear.

There was a short passage from our cavern to the next one, more narrow than previous ones.

"I think . . . I detect signs of wind erosion," Nikhil sent from the lead, wonder in his voice.

"Wind?" I said, surprised. What wind could there be on Miranda?

"The collisions which reformed the moon must have released plenty of gas for a short time. It had to get out somehow. Note the striations as you come through."

They were there, I noted as I came through, as if someone had sandblasted the passage walls. Miranda had breathed, once upon a time.

"I think," he continued, "that there may be an equilibrium between the gas in Miranda's caverns and the gas torus outside the ring system. Miranda's gravity is hardly adequate to compress that very much. But a system of caverns acting as a cold trap and a rough diffusion barrier . . . hmm, maybe."

"How much gas?" I wondered.

He shook his head. "Hard to tell that from up here, isn't it?"

We pushed half an hour past our agreed-to stop time to find a monolithic shelter that might prove safe from aftershocks. This passage was just wide enough to inflate our one meter sleeping tubes end to end. We ate dinner in the one Randi and I used. It was a spare, crowded, smelly, silent meal. Even Nikhil seemed depressed. I thought, as we replaced our helmets to pump down to let the Rays go back to their tent, that it was the last one we would eat together in such circumstances. The ins and outs of vacuum tents took up too much time and energy.

We repressurized and I savored the simple pleasure of watching Randi remove her tightsuit and bathe with a damp wipe in the end of the tent. She motioned for me to turn while she used the facility built into the end of our pallet, and so I unrolled my notescreen, slipped on its headband, and turned my attention to this journal, a process of clearly subvocalizing each word that I want on the screen.

Later she touched my arm indicating that I was next, kissed me lightly and went to bed between the elastic sheets, falling asleep instantly.

My turn.

Day four was spent gliding through a series of large, nearly horizontal caverns. Miranda, it turns out, *is* still breathing. A ghost breath to be sure, undetectable except with such sensitive instruments as Sam contains. But there appears to be a pressure differential; gas still flows through these caverns out to the surface. Sam can find the next passage by monitoring the molecular flow.

We pulled ourselves along with our hands, progressing like a weighted diver in an underwater cave; an analogy most accurate when one moves so slowly that lack of drag is unremarkable.

As we glided along I forgot my doom, and looked at the marbled ice around me with wonder. Randi glided in front of me and I could mentally remove her dusty coveralls and imagine her hard, lithe, body moving in its skin-hugging shipsuit. I could imagine her muscles bunch and relax in her weight-lifter's arms, imagine the firm definition of her neck and forearms. A poet herself, I thought, who could barely talk, but who had written an epic in the language of her body and its movement.

Sam notified us that it was time for another sounding and a lead change. In the next kilometer, the passage narrowed, and we found ourselves forcing our bodies through cracks that were hardly large enough to fit our bones through.

My body was becoming bruised from such tight contortions, but I wasn't afraid my tightsuit would tear; the fabric is slick and nearly invulnerable. On our first day, Randi scared the hell out of me by taking a hard-frozen, knife-edged sliver of rock and trying to commit hari-kiri with it, stabbing herself with so much force that the rock broke. She laughed at my reaction and told me that I needed to have confidence in my equipment.

She still has the bruise, dark among the lighter, older blemishes on her hard-used body. I kiss it when we make love and she says "Uh-huh. Told you so." Randi climbed Gilbert Montes in the Mercurian antarctic with her father and brother carrying a full vacuum kit when she was thirteen. She suffered a stress fracture in her ulna and didn't tell anyone until after they reached the summit.

The crack widened and, to our relief, gave onto another cavern, and that to another narrow passage. Randi took the lead, Nikhil followed, then me, then Cathy, then Sam.

Sam made me think of a cubist crab, or maybe a small, handleless lawn mower, on insect legs instead of wheels. Articulate and witty with a full range of simulated emotion and canned humor dialog stored in its memory, Sam was our expert on what had been. But it had difficulty interpreting things it hadn't seen before, or imagining what it had never seen, and so it usually followed us.

By day's end we had covered twenty-eight kilometers and were another eighteen kilometers closer to the center. That appeared to be where the road went, though Nikhil said we were more likely to be on a chord passing fifty kilometers or so above the center, where it seems that two major blocks came together a billion years ago.

This, I told myself, is a fool's journey, with no real chance of success. But how much better, how much more human, to fight destiny than to wait and die.

We ate as couples that night, each in our own tents.

II

On day five, we became stuck.

Randi woke me that morning exploring my body, fitting various parts of herself around me as the elastic sheets kept us pressed together. Somehow, an intimate dream I'd been having had segued into reality, and I felt only a momentary surprise at her intrusion.

"You have some new bruises," I told her after I opened my eyes. Hers remained closed.

"Morning," she murmured and wrapped herself around me again. Time slowed as I spun into her implacable, devouring wholeness.

But of course time would not stop. Our helmets beeped simultaneously with Sam's wake-up call, fortunately too late to prevent another part of me from becoming part of Randi. Sam reminded us, that, given our fantasy of escaping from Miranda's caverns, we had some time to make up.

Randi popped out of the sheets and spun around airborne in a graceful athletic move, and slowly fell to her own cot in front of me, exuberantly naked, stretching like a sensual cat, staring right into my enslaved eyes.

"Female display instinct—harmless, healthy, feels good."

Harmless? I grinned and reminded her: "But it's time to spelunk."

"Roger that," she laughed, grabbed her tightsuit from the ball of clothes in the end of the tent, and started rolling it on. They go on like a pair of pantyhose, except that they are slick on the inside and adjust easily to your form. To her form. I followed suit, and we quickly depressurized and packed.

It took Sam an hour to find the cavern inlet vent, and it was just a crack, barely big enough for us to squeeze into. We spent an hour convincing ourselves there was no other opportunity, then we wriggled forward through this crack like so many ants, kits and our coveralls pushed ahead of us, bodies fitting any way we could make them fit.

I doubt we made a hundred yards an hour. Our situation felt hopeless at this rate, but Sam assured us of more caverns ahead.

Perhaps it would have been better if Nikhil had been on lead. Larger than Randi and less inclined to disregard discomfort, he would have gone slower and chipped more clathrate, which, as it turned out, would have been faster.

Anyway, as I inched myself forward, my mind preoccupied with the enigma of Randi, Miranda groaned—at least that's what it sounded like in my helmet, pressed hard against the narrow roof of the crack our passage has become. I felt something. Did the pressure against my ribs increase? I fought panic, concentrating on the people around me and their lights shining past the few open cracks between the passage and their bodies.

"I can't move." That was Cathy. "And I'm getting cold."

Our tightsuits were top of the line "Explorers," twenty layers of smart fiber weave sandwiched with an elastic macromolecular binder. Despite their thinness the suits are great insulators, and Miranda's surrounding vacuum is even better.

Usually, conductive losses to the cryogenic ice around us are restricted to the portions of hand or boot that happen to be in contact with the surface and getting *rid* of our body heat is the main concern. Thus, the smart fiber layers of our suits are usually charcoal to jet black. But if almost a square meter of you is pressed hard against a cryogenic solid, even the best million atom layer the Astrographic Society can buy meets its match, and the problem is worse, locally.

The old expression, "colder than a witches tit" might give you some idea of Cathy's predicament.

"I can't do much," I answered, "I'm almost stuck myself. Hang in there."

"Sam," Cathy gasped, her voice a battleground of panic and self control, "wedge yourself edge up in the crack. Keep it from narrowing any more."

"That's not going to work, Cathy," it replied. "I would be fractured and destroyed without affecting anything."

"Remember your laws!" Cathy shrieked. "You have to obey me. Now do it, before this crushes my ribs! Nikhil, make the robot obey me!"

"Cathy, dear," Nikhil asks, "I sympathize with your discomfort, but could you hold off for a bit? Let us think about this."

"I'll be frozen solid in minutes and you want to think. Damnit, Nikhil, it hurts. Expend the robot and save me. I'm your doctor."

"Cathy," Sam says, "We will try to save you, but we have gone only a hundred kilometers since the quake, and there may be a thousand to go. If we encounter such difficulties every hundred kilometers, there may be on the order of ten of them yet to come. And you only have one robot to expend, as you put it. Sacrificing me now places the others in an obviously increased risk. Nothing is moving now, so thinking does not entail any immediate increased risk."

"Damn your logic. I'm getting frostbite. Get me out of here!"

Embarrassed silence slammed down after this outburst, no one even breathing for what seemed like a minute. Then Cathy started sobbing in short panicky gasps, which at least let the rest of us know she was still alive.

Randi broke the silence. "Can the rest of you move forward?"

"Yes," Nikhil answers, "a little."

"Same here," I add.

"Sam," Randi ordered. "Telop bug. Rope."

"I have these things."

"Uh-huh. Have your telop bug bring the rope up to me, around Cathy. When I've got it, put a clamp on it just behind Cathy's feet."

"Yes, Randi," Sam acknowledged its orders. "But why?" It also requested more information.

"So Cathy's feet can . . . grab—uh—get a foothold on it." Randi's voice showed her frustrations with speech, but no panic. "Can you model that? Make an image? See what will happen?"

"I can model Cathy standing on a clamp on the rope, then rotate horizontal like she is, then put the passage around her. . . . I've got it!" Sam exclaimed. "The telop's on its way."

"Please hurry," Cathy sobs, sounding somewhat more in control now.

I felt the little crablike telop scuttling along through the cracks between my flesh and the rock. The line started to snake by me, a millimeter Fullerene fiber bundle that could support a dinosaur in Earth gravity, a line of ants marching on my skin. I shivered just as the suit temperature warning flashed red in my visor display. The telop's feet clicked on my helmet as it went by. I waited for what seemed hours that way.

"Grab the line." Randi commanded and we obeyed. "Feet set, Cathy?"

"I can't . . . can't feel the clamp."

"OK. I'll take up some of the, the slack . . . OK now, Cathy?"

"It's there. Oh, God I hope this works."

"Right," Randi answered. "Everyone. Grab. Heave."

I set my toe claws and gave it my best effort forward. Nothing seemed to move much.

"Damn!" Randi grunted.

"Use the robot, I'm freezing," Cathy sobbed.

"Dear," Nikhil muttered, "she *is* using the robot. She's just not *being* one."

I started to get cold myself. My toes were dug in, but I couldn't bend my knees, so everything was with the calves. If I could just get my upper legs into it, I thought. If I just had a place to stand. Of course, that was it.

"Randi," I asked, "If Cathy grabbed the rope with her hands, stood on Sam and used all of her legs? Wouldn't that make a difference?"

Her response was instantaneous. "Uh-huh. Sam, can you, uh, move up under Cathy's feet and, uh, anchor yourself."

"Do you mean under, or behind so that she can push her feet against me?"

"I meant behind, Sam. Uh," Randi struggled with words again, "uh, rotate model so feet are down to see what I see, er, imagine."

"Yes . . . I can model that. Yes, I can do that, but Cathy's knees cannot bend much."

"Roger, Sam. A little might be enough. OK, Cathy, understand?"

"Y-Yes, Randi." Seconds of scraping, silence, then "OK I've got my feet on Sam."

"Then let's try. Pull on three. One, two, three."

We all slid forward a bit this time, but not much. Still it was much more progress then we'd made in the last half hour.

"Try again." I feel her take up the slack. "One, two, three."

That time it felt like a cork coming out of the bottle.

Over the next hour, we struggled forward on our bellies for maybe another 110 meters. Then Randi chipped away a final obstruction and gasped.

Haggard and exhausted as I am, my command of the language is inadequate to my feelings as I emerged from the narrow passage, a horizontal chimney actually, onto the sloping, gravelly ledge of the first great cavern. Involuntarily, I groaned; the transition from claustrophobia to agoraphobia was just too abrupt. Suddenly, there was this immense space with walls that faded into a stygian blackness that swallowed the rays of our lights without so much as a glimmer in return.

My helmet display flashed red numbers which told me how far I would fall, some six hundred meters; how long I would fall, just over two minutes, and how fast I would hit, almost ten meters per second; a velocity that would be terminal for reasons not involving air resistance. Think of an Olympic hundred meter champion running full tilt into a brick wall. I backed away from the edge too quickly and lost my footing in Miranda's centigee gravity.

In slow frustration, I bounced; I couldn't get my clawed boots down to the surface, nor reach anything with my hands. Stay calm, I told myself, I could push myself back toward the cavern wall on the next bounce. I waited until I started to float down again and tried to reach the ledge floor with my arm, but my bounce had carried me out as well as down.

A look at the edge showed me that my trajectory would take me over it before I could touch it. There was nothing I could do to save myself—my reaction pistol was in a pallet. Visions of Wile E. Coyote scrambling in air trying to get back to the edge of a cliff went through my mind, and I involuntarily tried to swim through the vacuum—not fair, at least the coyote had air to work with.

The helmet numbers went red again as I floated over the edge. Too desperate now to be embarrassed, I found my voice and a sort of guttural groan emerged. I took another breath, but before I could croak again, Cathy grabbed my arm and clipped a line to my belt. She gave my hand a silent squeeze as, anchored firmly to a piton, I pressed my back against the wall of the cavern to get as far as I could from the edge of the ledge. I shook. Too much, too much.

I canceled any judgment I'd made about Cathy. Judge us by how far, not how, we went.

Sam told us the cavern was twenty-seven kilometers long and slanted severely downhill. Our ledge topped a six-hundred-meter precipice that actually curved back under us. We gingerly made our camp on the ledge, gratefully retreated to our piton-secured tents, and ate a double ration silently, unable to keep our minds off the vast inner space which lay just beyond the thin walls of our artificial sanity.

Sleep will be welcome.

Day six. The inner blackness of sleep had absorbed my thoughts the way the cavern absorbed our strobes, and I woke aware of no dreams. After a warm, blousy, semiconscious minute, the cold reality of my predicament came back to me and I shivered. It had taken a full day to complete the last ten kilometers, including five hours of exhausted unconsciousness beneath the elastic sheets. We would have to make much better time than that.

That morning, Randi managed to look frightened and determined at the same time. No display behavior this morning—we dressed efficiently, packed our pallet and turned on the recompressors minutes after waking. Breakfast was ration crackers through our helmet locks.

I stowed the tent in the pallet and turned to find Randi standing silent at the edge. She held the Fullerene line dispenser in one hand, the line end in the other, snapped the line tight between them, and nodded. We had, I remembered, fifty kilometers of Fullerene line.

"Randi, you're not considering . . ."

She turned and smiled at me the way a spider smiles to a fly. Oh, yes she was.

"Preposterous!" was all Nikhil could say when Randi explained what she had in mind. Cathy, docile and embarrassed after yesterday's trauma, made only a small, incoherent, frightened giggle.

And so we prepared to perform one of the longest bungee jumps in history in an effort to wipe out the entire length of the passage in, as it were, one fell swoop. Nikhil drilled a hole through a piece of the cavern wall that looked sufficiently monolithic and anchored the line dispenser to that. Sam, who was equipped with its own propulsion, would belay until we were safe, then follow us.

Randi stretched a short line segment between two pitons and showed us how to use it to brace ourselves against the wall in Miranda's less-than-a-milligee gravity. We held our flylike position easily and coiled our legs like springs.

"Reaction pistols?" Randi asked.

"Check." Nikhil responded.

"Feet secure?"

Three "Checks" answered.

"Line secure."

Sam said "Check."

Randi cleared her throat. "On three now. One, two, *three*."

We jumped out and down, in the general direction of Miranda's center. After a brief moment of irrational fear, we collected ourselves and contemplated the wonders of relativity as we sat in free fall while the "roof" of the cavern flashed by. It was a strange experience; if I shut my eyes, I felt just like I would feel floating outside a space station. But I opened my eyes and my light revealed the jagged wall of the cavern whipping by a few dozen meters away. It was, I noted, getting closer.

Judiciously taking up the slack in our common line, Nikhil, who was an expert at this, used the reaction pistol to increase our velocity and steer us slightly away from the roof. A forest of ice intrusions, curved like elephant tusks by eons of shifting milligravity, passed by us too close for my comfort as the minuscule gravity and the gentle tugs of the reaction pistol brought us back to the center of the cavern.

We drifted. Weight came as a shock: our feet were yanked behind us and blood rushed to our heads as the slack vanished and the line started to stretch. Randi, despite spinning upside down, kept her radar pointed "down." We must have spent twenty seconds like that, with the pull on our feet getting stronger with every meter farther down. Then, with surprising quickness the cavern wall stopped rushing past us. Randi said "Now!" and released the line, leaving us floating dead in space only a kilometer or so from the cavern floor.

I expended a strobe flash to get a big picture of the cavern wall floating next to us. It looks like we are in an amethyst geode; jumbles of sharp crystals everywhere and a violet hue.

"Magnificent." Cathy said with a forced edge in her voice. Trying to make contact with us, to start to put things back on a more normal footing after yesterday, I thought.

"Time to keep our eyes down, I should think," Nikhil reminded her, and the rest of us. "Wouldn't want to screw up again, would we?"

There was no rejoinder from Cathy so I glanced over at her. Her visor was turned toward the crystal forest and apparently frozen in space. A puff from my reaction pistol brought me over to her and my hand on her arm got her attention. She nodded. The crystals were huge, and I wondered at that, too.

I checked my helmet display—its inertial reference function told me I was fifty kilometers below the surface and the acceleration due to Miranda's feeble gravity was down to seven centimeters per second squared, so when we touched down to the rugged terrain a kilometer below in just under three minutes . . . we'd hit it at 11 meters per second. I thought again of that Olympic hundred-meter dash champion running full tilt into a brick wall.

"Randi, I think we're too high." I tried to keep my voice even. This was the sort of thing we left to Sam, but he wasn't with us just now.

As if in answer, she shot a lined piton into the wall next to us, which was starting to drift by at an alarming rate.

"Swing into the wall feet first, stop, fall again," she said.

"Feet toward the wall!" Nikhil echoed as the tension started to take hold, giving us a misleading sense of down. The line gradually pulled taut and started to swing us toward the wall. Then it let go, leaving us on an oblique trajectory headed right toward the forest of crystals. Piton guns are neat, but no substitute for a hammer.

"No problems," Nikhil says. "We dumped a couple of meters per second. I'll try this time."

He shot as Randi reeled her line in.

Eventually we swung into the wall. Cathy seemed rigid and terrified, but bent her legs properly and shielded her face with her arms as the huge crystals rushed to meet us.

They shattered into dust at our touch, hardly even crunching as our boots went through them to the wall.

"What the. . . ." I blurted, having expected something more firm.

"Deposition, not extrusion?" Randi offered, the questioning end of her response clearly intended for Nikhil.

"Quite so. Low gravity hoarfrost. Hardly anything to them, was there?"

"You, you knew, didn't you?" Cathy accused, her breath ragged.

"Suspected," Nikhil answered without a trace of feeling in his voice, "but I braced just like the rest of you. Not really certain then, was I?"

"Hello everyone, see you at the bottom," Sam's voice called out, breaking the tension. Three of us strobed and spotted the robot free falling past us.

The wall on which we landed curved gently to the lower end of the cavern, so we covered the remaining distance in hundred-meter leaps, shattering crystals with each giant step, taking some sort of vandalistic delight in the necessity of destroying so much beauty. We caught up to Sam laughing.

"This way," it pointed with one of its limbs at a solid wall, "there is another big cavern, going more or less our way. It seems to be sloped about one for one instead of near vertical."

Our helmet displays reproduced its seismologically derived model which was full of noise and faded in the distance, but clearly showed the slant down.

After a couple of false leads we found a large-enough crack leading into the new gallery. Cathy shuddered as she squeezed herself in.

That cavern was a mere three kilometers deep—we could see the other end.

We shot a piton gun down there, and cheered when it held; using the line to keep us centered, we were able to cross the cavern in ten minutes.

Cathy dislodged a largish boulder as she landed, and it made brittle, tinkling, ice noises as it rolled through some frost crystals.

"Hey," I said when the significance of that got through to me. "I heard that!"

"We have an atmosphere, mostly methane and nitrogen. It's about ten millibars and nearly a hundred Kelvins," Sam answered my implied question. Top-of-the-line robot, Sam.

It occurred to me then that, should we all die, Sam might still make it out. Almost certainly would make it out. So someone will read this journal.

The next cavern went down as well and after that was another. We kept going well past our planned stopping time, almost in a daze. Our hammers made echoes now, eerie high-pitched echoes that rattled around in the caverns like a steelie marble dropped on a metal plate.

We made camp only 170 kilometers above Miranda's center, eighty-five below the surface. Nikhil told us that if the rift continued like this, along a chord line bypassing the center itself, we were more than one-third of the way through, well ahead of schedule.

Randi came over to me as I hammered in the piton for a tent line and put a hand on my arm.

"Psyche tension; Cathy and Nikhil, danger there."

"Yeah. Not much to do about it, is there?"

"Maybe there is. Sleep with Cathy tonight. Get them away from each other. Respite."

I looked at Randi, she was serious. They say tidal forces that near a black hole can be fatal.

"Boys in one tent, girls in the other?"

"No. I can't give Cathy what she needs."

"What makes you think I can?"

"Care about her. Make her feel like a person."

Honestly, I was not that much happier with Cathy's behavior than Nikhil's. Though I thought I understood what she was going through and made intellectual allowances, I guess I saw her as being more of an external situation than a person to care about. What Randi was asking wouldn't come easy. Then, too, there was the other side of this strange currency.

"And you? With Nikhil?"

"Skipped a week of classes at Stanford once. Went to a Nevada brothel. Curious. Wanted to know if I could do that, if I needed to, to live. Lasted four days. Good lay, no personality." She tapped the pocket of my coveralls where my personal electronics lived, recording everything for my article. "You can use that if we get out. Secrets are a headache." She shrugged. "Dad can handle it."

"Randi . . ." I realized that, somehow, it fit. Randi seems to be in a perpetual rebellion against comfort and normalcy, always pushing limits, taking risks, seeking to prove she could experience and endure anything. But unlike some mousy data tech who composes sex thrillers on the side, Randi has no verbal outlet. To express herself, she has to live it.

"Randi, I can see that something has to be done for Nikhil and Cathy, but this seems extreme."

"Just once. Hope." She smiled and nestled herself against me. "Just be nice. Don't worry about yourself. Let her lead. Maybe just hugs and kisses, or listening. But whatever, give. Just one night, OK? So they don't kill themselves. And us."

It took me a minute or so to digest this idea. Another thought occurred to me. Randi and I were single—not even a standard cohab file—but Nikhil and Cathy. . . . "Just how are you going to suggest this to them?" I asked.

Randi shook her head and looked terrified. "Not me!"

I don't think I'm going to be able to finish the journal entry tonight.

III

Day seven. Last night was an anticlimax. Nikhil thought the switch was jolly good fun, in fact he seemed relieved. But Cathy . . . once her nervousness had run its course, she simply melted into my arms like a child and sobbed. I lay there holding her as she talked.

Born to a wealthy Martian merchant family, she'd been an intellectual rebel, and had locked horns with the authoritarian pastoral movement there which eventually gave rise to the New Reformation. When she was fifteen, she got kicked out of school for bragging about sleeping with a boy. She hadn't, but: "I resented anyone telling me I couldn't so much that I told everyone that we did."

Her parents, caught between their customers and their daughter, got out of the situation by shipping her off to the IPA space academy at Venus L1. She met Nikhil there as an instructor in an introductory paleontology class.

She got her MD at twenty-two and plunged into archeoimmunology research. A conference on fossil disease traces linked her up with Nikhil again, who had been ducking the controversy about Miranda's internal structure by using p-bar scans to critique claims of panspermia evidence in Triton sample cores. His outcast status was an attraction for her. They dated.

When he became an instant celebrity, she threw caution to the wind and accepted his proposal. But, she found, Nikhil kept sensual things hidden deep, and there was a cold, artificial hollowness where his sense of fun should be. Cathy said they had their first erudite word fight over her monokini on their honeymoon, and they had been "Virginia Woolfing" it ever since.

"Damn dried-up stuffed-shirted bastard's good at it," she muttered as she wrapped herself around me that night. "It stinks in here, you know?" Then she fell asleep with tears in her eyes. She was desirable, cuddly, and beyond the stretch of my conscience.

That morning, when our eyes met and searched each other, I wondered if she had any expectations, and if, in the spirit of friendship, I should offer myself. But I decided not to risk being wrong, and she did nothing but smile. Except, possibly for that brief look, we were simply friends.

Randi didn't say anything about her night in Nikhil's tent; I didn't expect her to. She gave me a very warm and long hug after she talked to Cathy. We were all very kind to each other as we broke camp and began casting ourselves along a trail of great caverns with the strides of milligee giants.

Cathy passed out the last of our calcium retention pills that morning. In a week or so we would start to suffer some of the classic low gravity symptoms of bone loss and weakness. It didn't worry us greatly—that was reversible, if we survived.

At day's end, I was not physically exhausted, but my mind is becoming numb with crystal wonders. Where are these crystals coming from? Or rather where had they come from; Sam and Nikhil concurred that the existing gas flow, through surprising in its strength, is nowhere near enough to deposit these crystal forests in the few hundred million years since Miranda's remaking.

We were 150 kilometers deep now and Nikhil said these rocks must withstand internal pressures of more than ninety atmospheres to hold the caverns open. Not surprisingly, the large caverns didn't come as often now, and when they did, the walls were silicate rather than clathrate; rock slabs instead of dirty ice. I thought I heard them groan at a higher pitch last night.

"It's after midnight, universal time," Cathy announced. She seemed recovered from her near panic earlier, and ready to play her doctor role again. But there seemed something brittle in her voice. "I think we should get some sleep now." She said this as we pushed our baggage through yet another narrow crack between the Rift galleries Sam kept finding with his sonar, so Randi and I had a chuckle at the impossibility of complying with the suggestion just then. But she had a point. We had come one-half of the way through Miranda in five of our twenty days—well ahead of schedule.

Nikhil, on lead, missed her humor and said: "Yes, dear, that sounds like a very good idea to me. Next gallery, perhaps."

"You humans will be more efficient if you're not tired," Sam pointed out in a jocular tone that did credit to its medical support programmers. But I thought its feigned robot chauvinism probably did not sit well with Cathy.

"We," I answered, "don't have a milligram of antihydrogen in our hearts to feed us."

"Your envy of my superior traits is itself an admirable trait, for it recognized—"

"Shiva!" Nikhil shouted from the head of our column.

"What is it?" Three voices asked, almost in unison.

"Huge. A huge cavern. I . . . you'll have to see it yourselves."

As we joined him, we found he had emerged on another ledge looking over another cavern. It didn't seem to be a particularly large one to start—our lights carried to the other side—just another crystal cathedral. Then I looked down— and saw stars. Fortunately, my experience in "Randi's Room" kept my reaction in check. I did grab the nearest piton line rather quickly, though.

"Try turning off your strobes," Nikhil suggested as we stuck our heads over the ledge again.

The stars vanished, we turned the strobes on again, and the stars came back. The human eye is not supposed to be able to detect time intervals so small, so perhaps it was my imagination. But it seemed as though the "stars" below came on just after the strobe flashed.

"Ninety kilometers," Sam said.

"Ninety kilometers!?" Nikhil blustered in disbelief, his composure still shaken. "How is this possible? Clathrate should not withstand such pressure."

Randi anchored herself, dug into the supply pallet I'd been towing, and came up with a geologist's pick. She took a swing at the ledge to which the gentle three and a half centimeters per second local gravity had settled us and a sharp plink made its way to my ears, presumably through my boots.

"Nickel iron?" Nikhil asked.

"Uh-huh. Think so," Randi answered. "Fractured, from here down."

"Maybe this is what broke Miranda up in the first place," Cathy offered.

"Pure supposition," Nikhil demurred. "Friends, we must move on."

"I know. Take samples, analyze later." Randi said. "Got to move."

"Across or down?" I asked. This wasn't a trivial question. Our plan was to follow the main rift, which, presumably, continued on the other side. But down was an unobstructed ninety kilometer run leading to the very core of the moon. I thought of Jules Verne.

"We need to get out of this moon in less than two weeks," Nikhil reminded us. "We can always come back."

"Central gas reservoir, chimneys, connected." Randi grunted.

After a nonplussed minute, I understood. If we went down the chimney, our path would leave the chord for the center. The Rift is along the chord; Sam could see it in his rangings. But, not being a gas vent, it wouldn't be well enough connected to travel. We had to find another back door.

"Oh, of course," Nikhil said. "All roads lead to Rome, which also means they all go *from* Rome. The outgassing, the wind from the core, is what connected these caverns and eroded the passages enough to let us pass through. She means our best chance is to find another chimney, and the best place to do that is at the core, isn't it."

"Uh-huh," Randi answered.

No one said anything; in the silence I swore I could hear dripping, and beneath that a sort of dull throbbing that was probably my pulse. At any rate, the pure dead silence of the upper caverns was gone. I risked another peek down over the edge. What was down there?

"We have a problem," Cathy informed us. "Poison gas. The nitrogen pressure is up to a twentieth of a bar, and that's more than there was on old Mars. It's enough to carry dangerous amounts of aromatics—not just methane, but stuff like cyanogen. I don't know if anyone else has noticed it, but this junk is starting to condense on some of our gear and stink up our tents. It might get worse near the core, and I can't think of any good way to decontaminate."

"Uh, rockets," Randi broke the silence. "Sam's rockets. Our reaction pistols. Try it first."

So we did. We figured out how far to stand from the jets, how long to stand in them—enough to vaporize anything on the surface of our coveralls and equipment, but not long enough to damage it—and how many times we could do it. Sam had enough fuel for 120 full decontaminations—more than we'd ever live to use. Cathy volunteered to be the test article, got herself blasted, then entered a tent and emerged saying it smelled just fine.

We decided to go for the core.

This close to the center of Miranda, gravitational acceleration was down to just over five centimeters per second squared, about one three-hundredth of Earth normal. Five milligees. Release an object in front of you, look away while you count one thousand one, and look back again: it will have fallen maybe the width of a couple of fingers, just floating. So you ignore it, go about other things and look back after ten minutes. It's gone. It has fallen ten kilometers and is moving three times as fast as a human can run; over thirty meters per second. That's if it hasn't hit anyone or anything yet. Low gravity, they drill you over and over again, can be dangerous.

That's in a vacuum, but we weren't in a vacuum any more. Even with the pallet gear apportioned, we each weighed less than ten newtons—about the weight of a liter of vodka back in Poland, I thought, longingly—and we each had the surface area of a small kite; we'd be lucky to maintain three meters per second in a fall at the start, and at the bottom, we'd end up drifting like snowflakes.

For some reason, I thought of butterflies.

"Could we make wings for ourselves?" I asked.

"Really, wings?" Nikhil's voice dripped with skepticism.

"Wings!" Cathy gushed, excited.

"Sheets, tent braces, tape, line. Could do." Randi offered.

"We are going to be very, very, sorry about this," Nikhil warned.

Four hours later, looking like something out of a Batman nightmare, we were ready.

Randi went first. She pushed herself away from the precipice with seeming unconcern and gradually began to drift downward. Biting my lip and shaking a bit, I followed. Then, came a stoic Nikhil and a quiet Cathy.

Ten minutes after jumping, I felt a tenuous slipstream and found I could glide after a fashion—or at least control my attitude. After some experimentation, Randi found that a motion something like the butterfly stroke in swimming seemed to propel her forward.

Half an hour down, and we found we could manage the airspeed of a walk with about the same amount of effort. Soon we were really gliding, and could actually gain altitude if we wanted.

After drifting down for another hour we came to the source of the dripping sound I had heard the night before. Some liquid had condensed on the sides of the chimney and formed drops the size of bowling balls. These eventually separated to fall a kilometer or so into a pool that had filled in a crack in the side of the chimney. The Mirandan equivalent of a waterfall looked like a time lapse splash video full of crowns and blobs, but it was at macroscale and in real time.

"Mostly ethane," Sam told us. Denser and more streamlined than we were, the robot maintained pace and traveled from side to side with an occasional blast from a posterior rocket: a "roam fart" it called it. If I ever get out of this, I will have to speak to its software engineers.

"Wojciech, come look at this!" Cathy yelled from the far side of the chimney. I sculled over, as did Randi and Nikhil.

"This had better be important," Nikhil remarked, reminding us of time. I needed one, having been mesmerized by drops that took minutes to fall and ponds that seemed to oscillate perpetually.

Cathy floated just off the wall, her position maintained with a sweep of her wings every three or four seconds. As we joined her, she pointed to a bare spot on the wall with her foot. Sticking out near the middle of it was a dirty white "T" with loopholes in each wing.

"It's a piton. It must be."

What she left unsaid was the fact that it certainly wasn't one of ours.

"Sam, can you tell how old it is?"

"It is younger than the wall. But that, however, looks to be part of the original surface of one of Miranda's parent objects. Do you see the craters?"

Now that he pointed it out, I did. There were several, very normal minicraters of the sort you find tiling the fractal surface of any airless moon, except two hundred kilometers of rock and clathrate lay between these craters and space. I had the same displaced, eerie feeling I'd had when, as a child, I had explored the top of the crags on the north rim of the Grand Canyon of the Colorado on Earth, over two thousand meters above sea level—and found seashells frozen in the rock.

"The piton," Sam added, "is younger than the hoar crystals, because the area was first cleared."

Something clicked in place for me then. The crystals surrounding the bare spot were all about a meter long. "Look at the length of the nearby crystals," I said, excited with my discovery. "Whatever cleared the immediate area must have cleared away any nearby crystal seeds, too. But just next to the cleared area it must have just pushed them down and left a base from which the crystals could regenerate. So the height of the crystals just outside the cleared area is the growth since then."

"But what do you think that growth rate is?" Nikhil asked. "We can't tell, except that it is clearly slow now. I regret to say this, because I am as interested as anyone else, but we must move on. Sam has recorded everything. If we regain the surface, other expeditions can study this. If we do not, then it does not matter. So, shall we?"

Without waiting for assent from the others, Nikhil rotated his head down and started taking purposeful wingstrokes toward the center of Miranda.

"Damn him," Cathy hissed and flew to the piton and, abandoning one wing sleeve, grabbed the alien artifact. So anchored, she put her feet against the wall it protruded from, grasped it with both hands, and pulled. Not surprisingly, the piton refused to move.

"Other expeditions. We'll come back." Randi told her.

Cathy gasped as she gave up the effort, and let herself drift down and away from the wall. We drifted with her until she started flying again. We made no effort to catch up to Nikhil, who by this time was a kilometer ahead of us.

The air, we could call it that now, was becoming mistier, foggier. Nikhil, though he still registered in my helmet display, was hidden from view. Sam's radar, sonar, filters, and greater spectral range made this a minor inconvenience for him, and he continued to flit from side to side of this great vertical cavern, gathering samples. When we could no longer see the walls, we gathered in the center. Incredibly, despite the pressure of the core on either side, the chimney widened.

"This stuff is lethal," Cathy remarked. "Everyone make sure to maintain positive pressure, but not too much to spring a leak; oxygen might burn in this. If this chimney were on Earth, the environmental patrol would demolish it."

A quick check revealed my suit was doing OK, but the pressure makeup flow was enough that I would think twice about being near anything resembling a flame. Our suits were designed, and programmed, for vacuum, not chemical warfare; we were taking them well beyond their envelope.

"Chimney needs a name." Randi said. "Uh-huh. Job for a poet, I think."

That was my cue. But the best thing I could come up with on the spot was "Nikhil's Smokestack." This was partly to honor the discoverer and partly a gentle dig at his grumpiness about exploring it. Cathy laughed, at least.

Having nothing else to look at, I asked Sam for a three-dimensional model of the chimney, which it obligingly displayed on my helmet optics. A three-dimensional cut-away model of Miranda reflected off my transparent face plate, appearing to float several meters in front of me. Our cavern was almost precisely aligned with Miranda's north pole, and seemed to be where two great, curved, hundred-kilometer chunks had come together. Imagine two thick wooden spoons, open ends facing.

These slabs were hard stuff, like nickel-iron and silicate asteroids. Theories abound as to how that could be; radioactivity and tidal stress might have heated even small bodies enough to become differentiated; gravitational chaos in the young solar system must have ejected many main belt asteroids and some might well have made it to the Uranian gravitational well; or perhaps the impact that had set Uranus to spinning on its side had released a little planetesimal core material into its moon system.

My body was on autopilot, stroking my wings every ten seconds or so to keep pace with Randi while I day-dreamed and played astrogeologist, so I didn't notice the air start to clear. The mist-cloud seemed to have divided itself to cover two sides of the chimney, leaving the center relatively free. Then they thinned and through gaps, I could see what looked to be a river running . . . beside? above? below?

"Randi, I think I can see a river."

"Roger, Wojciech."

"But how can that be? How does it stay there? . . ."

"Tides."

"Yes," Nikhil added. "The chimney is almost three kilometers wide now. One side is closer to Uranus than Miranda's center of mass and moving at less than circular orbital velocity for its distance from Uranus. Things there try to fall inward as if from the apoapsis, the greatest distance, of a smaller orbit. The other side is farther away than the center and moving at greater than orbital velocity. Things there try to move outward.

"The mass of Miranda now surrounds us like a gravitational equipotential shell, essentially canceling itself out, so all that is left is this tidal force. It isn't much—a few milligees, but enough to define up and down for fluids. In some ways, this is beginning to resemble the surface of Titan, though it's a bit warmer and the air pressure is nowhere near as high."

"Is that water below us?" Cathy asked.

"No," Sam answered. "The temperature is only two hundred kelvins, some seventy degrees below the freezing point of water. Water ice is still a hard rock here."

At the bottom, or end, of Nikhil's Smokestack was a three-kilometer rock, which had its own microscopic gravity field. The center of Miranda, we figured, was some 230 meters below us. Close enough so that we were effectively weightless. We let Sam strobe the scene for us, then set up our tents. Decontamination was a bit nervy, but most of the bad stuff was settled on either side of the tidal divide, and the air here was almost all cold dry nitrogen.

Nonetheless, set-up took until midnight, and we all turned in immediately.

It had been a very long day.

Nikhil and Cathy forgot last night that, while they were in a vacuum tent, the tent was no longer in a hard vacuum. Much of what we heard was thankfully faint and muffled but what came through in the wee small hours of the morning of day eight clearly included things like:

". . . ungrateful, arrogant pig . . ."

". . . have the self-discipline of a chimp in heat . . ."

". . . so cold and unfeeling that . . ."

". . . brainless diversions while our lives are in the balance . . ."

Randi opened her eyes and looked at me, almost in terror, then threw herself around me and clung. It might seem a wonder that this steely woman who could spit in the face of nature's worst would go into convulsions at the sound of someone else's marriage falling apart, but Randi's early childhood had been filled with parental bickering. There had been a divorce, and I gathered a messy one from a six-year-old's point of view, but she had never told me much more than that.

I coughed, loud as I could, and soon the sound of angry voices was replaced by the roar of distant ethane rapids.

Randi murmured something.

"Huh?" Was she going to suggest another respite?

"Could we be married? Us?"

It was her first mention of the subject. I'd developed my relationship with her with the very specific intention of creating and reporting this expedition, and had never, never, hinted to her I had any other designs on her person or fortune. I'd been pretty sure that the understanding was mutual.

"Uh, Randi. Look, I'm not sure we should think like that. Starving poets trying to fake it as journalists don't fit well in your social circle. Besides, that," I tossed my head in the direction of the other tent, "*that* doesn't seem to put me in the mood for such arrangements. Why—"

"Why is: you don't do that." Randi interrupted me. This was startling; she never interrupted, except in emergencies—she was the most nonverbal person I knew.

OK, I thought. This was an emergency of sorts. I kissed her on the forehead, then stifled a laugh. What a strange wife for a poet she would be! She sat there fighting with herself, struggling to put something in words.

"*Why* . . . is sex, working together, adventure, memories of this, not being afraid, not *fighting*."

My parents had had their usual share of discussions and debates, but raised voices had been very rare. The Ray's loud argument had, apparently, opened some old wounds for Randi. I held her and gave her what comfort I could. Finally, curiosity got the better of me.

"Your parents fought?"

"Dad wouldn't go to parties. Didn't like social stuff. Didn't like mom's friends. His money." Randi looked me in the eye with an expression somewhere between anger and pleading.

"So. She had him shot. Hired someone."

I'd never heard anything like that, and anything that happened to papa Gaylord Lotati would have been big news. "Huh?"

"Someone Mom knew knew someone. The punk wasn't up to it. Nonfatal chest wound. Private doctor. Private detective. Real private. A settlement. Uncontested divorce.

"I was six. All I knew then was dad was sick in the hospital for a week. Later mom just didn't come home from one of her trips. A moving van showed up and moved . . . moved some stuff. One of the movers played catch with me. Another van came and moved dad and me to a smaller house.

"And there was no more yelling, never, and no more mom. So you know now. When you hold me, that kind of goes away. I feel secure, and I want that feeling, forever."

What in a freezing hydrocarbon hell does one say to that? I just rocked her gently and stared at the wall of the tent, as if it could give me an answer. "Look, I care about you, I really do," I finally told her. "But I need to find my own 'whys.' Otherwise, the relationship would be too dependent." I grinned at her. "We should be more like Pluto and Charon, not like Uranus and Miranda."

"Who gets to be Pluto and who gets to be Charon?" she asked, impishly, eyes sparkling through embryonic tears, as she began devouring me. One does not escape from a black hole, and once I fell beneath her event horizon and we merged into a singularity, the question of who was Pluto and who was Charon, to the rest of the universe, mattered not. Nor did whatever noise we made.

We reentered the real Universe late for our next round of back-door searching; Cathy and Nikhil were almost finished packing their pallet when we emerged from our deflated tent. We stared at each other in mutual embarrassment. Nikhil put his hand on his wife's shoulder.

"Sorry. Bit of tension is all, we'll be all right." He waved at Miranda around us. "Now, shall we have another go at it?"

"Any ideas of where to look?" I asked.

"Ethane outlet?" Randi inquired.

Yes, I thought, those rivers had to go somewhere. I had, however, hoped to avoid swimming in them.

"There is," Sam announced, "a large cavern on the other side of this sidero-philic nodule."

"This what?" Cathy started.

"This bloody three-kilometer nickel iron rock you're standing on," Nikhil snapped before Sam could answer, then he caught himself and lamely added: "dear."

She nodded curtly.

Randi took a couple of experimental swings at the nodule, more, I thought, in frustration than from doubting Sam. "No holes in this. Best check edges," She suggested. We all agreed.

After five hours of searching, it was clear that the only ways out were the ethane rivers.

"Forgive me if I now regret giving in on the rift route," Nikhil had to say. Cathy was in reach, so I gave her hand a pat. She shrugged.

We had a right-left choice, a coin flip. Each side of the tidal divide had it's own ethane river and each river disappeared. Sam sounded and sounded around the ethane lakes at the end of Nikhil's Smokestack. The inner one, on the side toward Uranus, appeared to open into a cavern five kilometers on the other side of "Cathy's Rock," as we called the central nodule. The other one appeared to go seven kilometers before reaching a significant opening, but that opening appeared to lead in the direction of the rift. No one even thought to question Nikhil this time.

Now that the route was decided, we had to face the question of how to traverse it.

"Simple," Cathy declared. "Sam carries the line through, then we all get in a tent and he pulls us through."

"Unfortunately, I cannot withstand ethane immersion for that period of time." Sam said. "And you will need my power source, if nothing else, to complete the journey."

"Cathy," Randi asked. "Ethane exposure, uh, how bad?"

"You don't want to breathe much of it—it will sear your lungs."

"Positive pressure."

"Some could still filter in through your tightsuit pores."

She was right. If moisture and gas from your skin could slowly work its way out of a tightsuit, then ethane could probably work its way in.

Randi nodded. "Block tightsuit pores?"

A loud "What?" escaped me when I realized what she was considering. Tightsuits worked because they let the skin exhale: sweat and gasses could slowly diffuse through the porous, swollen, fabric. Stopping that process could be very uncomfortable—if not fatal. But Cathy Ray, M.D., didn't seem to be in a panic about it. Apparently, it was something one could survive for a while.

"Big molecules. Got any, Cathy?"

"I have some burn and abrasion coating, semi-smart fibers. The brand name is Exoderm; what about it, Sam?"

"Exoderm coating will not go through tightsuit pores. But it has pores of its own, like the tightsuits, and may allow some ethane to work its way in after a while. A few thousand molecules a second per square meter."

Randi shrugged. "And a tightsuit with pores blocked will cut that way down. Too little to worry about."

"I'm going with you," I announced, surprising myself.

Randi shook her head. "You try the outer passage if I don't make it. Get the gook, Cathy."

Cathy opened up one of the pallets and produced a spray dispenser. I started unpacking a vacuum tent.

"This is going to be a little difficult to do in a tent," Cathy mused.

"Wimps. Is it ready?" Randi asked.

Cathy nodded and gave an experimental squirt to her arm. For a moment, the arm looked like it was covered with cotton candy, but the fluff quickly collapsed to a flat shiny patch. Cathy pulled the patch off and examined it. "It's working just fine, all I need is some bare skin and a place to work."

Randi answered by hyperventilating, then before anyone could stop her, she dumped pressure, fluidly removed her helmet, deactivated her shipsuit seals and floated naked before us.

Cathy, to her credit, didn't let shock stop her. "Breath out, not in, no matter how much you want," she told Randi, and quickly started spraying Randi's back while Randi was still stepping out of the boots. In less than a minute, Randi was covered with the creamy gray stuff. Calmly and efficiently, Randi rolled her tightsuit back on over the goo, resealed, checked, and rehelmeted. It was all done in less than three minutes. Nikhil was speechless and I wasn't much better.

"You OK?" I asked, though the answer seemed obvious.

Randi shrugged. "One-tenth atmosphere, ninety below, no wind, no moisture, no convection, air stings a bit. Bracing. No problem—goo handles stings. Can hold breath five minutes."

"You . . . you'd best get on with it, now," Cathy said, struggling to maintain a professional tone in her voice. "Your skin will have as much trouble breathing out as the ethane has getting in."

Randi nodded. "Line dispenser. Clips. Piton gun."

I got my act together and dug these things out of the same pallet where Cathy had kept the Exoderm. Randi snapped the free end of the line to her belt, took it off, double-checked the clip, and snapped it back on again.

"Three tugs, OK? Wait five minutes for you to collect yourselves, then I start hauling. OK?"

We nodded. Then she reached for my helmet and held it next to hers.

"I'll do it. If not, don't embarrass me, huh?"

I squeezed her hand in an extremely inadequate farewell, then she released her boot clamps, grabbed her reaction pistol, and rocketed off to the shore of the ethane lake fifteen hundred meters away.

There was, I thought, no reason why one couldn't weave a fiber-optic comm line into the test line, and use it for communications as well as for hauling, climbing, and bungee jumping. But ours weren't built that way, and we lost radio with Randi shortly after she plunged into the lake. The line kept snaking out, but, I reminded myself, that could just be her body being carried by the current. I wondered whether that had been a line attached to the alien piton we'd found above, and how long it had hung there.

Assuming success, we prepared everything for the under-ethane trip. Tents were unshipped, and pallets resealed. I broke out another line reel and looped its end through a pitoned pulley on Cathy's Rock; just in case someone did come back this way.

"I doubt that will be needed," Nikhil remarked, "but we'll be thankful if it is. You're becoming quite proficient, Mr. Bubka."

"Thanks."

I kept staring at the dispenser, fighting back the irrational desire to reel her back.

Cathy grabbed the packed pallets and moved them nearer to the shore, where the changed orientation of the milligee fields left her standing at right angles to Nikhil and myself. She chose to sit there and stare at the lake where Randi had vanished.

I stayed and puttered with my pulleys.

Nikhil came up to me. "I don't think of myself as being Bengali, you know," he said out of the blue. "I was ten when my parents were kicked out of Calcutta. Politics, I understand, though the details have never been too clear to me. At any rate, I schooled in Australia and Cambridge, then earned my doctorate at Jovis Tholus."

I knew all this, but to make conversation, responded. "J.T.U. is New Reformationist, isn't it."

"It's officially non-sectarian, state supported, you know. The council may lean that way, but the influence is diffuse. Besides, there is no such thing as New Reformationist geology, unless you're excavating the Face of Mars." Nikhil waved his hand in a gesture of dismissive toleration. "So you see, I've lived in both worlds; the cool, disciplined, thoughtful British academic world, and the eclectic, compulsive, superstitious Bengali hothouse."

No question of which one he preferred. I thought, however, to find a chink in his armor. "You are an Aristotelian then?"

"I won't object to the description, but I won't be bound by it."

"Then the golden mean must have some attraction for you, the avoidance of extremes."

"Quite."

"OK, Nikhil. Consider then, that within rational safeguards, that the spontaneity may be useful. A safety valve for evolutionary imperatives. A shortcut to communication and ideas. Creativity, art. A motivation for good acts; compassion, empathy."

"Perhaps." He gave me a wintry smile. "I am not a robot. I have these things . . ." disgust was evident in the way he said 'things,' ". . . within me as much as anyone else. But I strive to hold back unplanned action, to listen to and analyze these biochemical rumblings before responding. And I *prefer* myself that way."

"Does Cathy?"

I regretted that as soon as I said it, but Nikhil just shook his helmeted head.

"Cathy doesn't understand the alternative. I grew up where life was cheap, and pain, commonplace. I saw things in Dum Dum, horrifying things . . . but things that nevertheless have a certain fascination for me." The expression in his unblinking brown eyes was contradictory and hard to read—perhaps a frightened but curious seven-year-old peered at me from beneath layers of adult sophistication. But did those layers protect him from us, or us from him? What had Randi's night with him been like?

"Well," he continued, "Cathy will never experience that sort of thing as long as I keep a grip on myself. She means too much to me, I owe her too much." He shook his head. "If she just would not ask for what I dare not give. . . . Between us, fellow?"

I'm not sure how I should have answered that, but just then Sam told us the line had stopped reeling out, I nodded briskly to him and we glided "down" to the ethane river shore to wait for the three sharp tugs that would signal us to follow.

They didn't come. We pulled on the line. It was slack. So we waited again, not wanting to face the implications of that. I updated my journal, trying not to think about the present.

IV

It was almost the end of the schedule day when I finally told Cathy to get ready to put the Exoderm on me. There was no debate; we'd probably waited longer than we should have. "Don't embarrass me," Randi had said. Grimly, I determined to put off my grief, and not embarrass her. The fate, I recalled, of many lost expeditions was to peter out, one by one. Damn, I would miss her.

The plan had been to take the other outlet, but we silently disregarded that: I would go the same way, just in case there was any chance of a rescue. I needed that little bit of hope, to keep going.

By the laws of Murphy, I was, of course, standing stark freezing naked in ethane-laced nitrogen half covered with spray gook and holding my breath when the original line went taut. Three times. Cathy and Nikhil had to help seal me back in. I was shaking so hard, almost fatally helpless with relief.

We had to scramble like hell to get Sam, Cathy, and Nikhil bagged in an uninflated tent. Since I was ready for immersion, and Randi had apparently survived said immersion, I would stay on the outside and clear us around obstacles. I was still double-checking seals as Randi started hauling. By some grace of the Universe, I had remembered to clip my pulley line to the final pallet, and it trailed us into the ethane lake.

It was cold, like skinny dipping in the Bering Sea. The ethane boiled next to my tightsuit and the space between it and my coveralls became filled with an insulating ethane froth. With that and the silvery white sheen of maximum insulation, my suit was able to hold its own at something like 290 kelvins. I shivered and deliberately tensed and relaxed every muscle I could think about, as we slipped through the ethane.

There wasn't much to see, the passage was wide, broadened perhaps by eons of flow. Strobes revealed a fog of bubbles around me, otherwise the darkness smothered everything.

The line drew us up? down? to the inside of the passage, out of the current. I grabbed the line and walked lightly against the tension of the pulling line as if I were rappelling on a low-gravity world. The tent with my companions and our pallets were thus spared bumping along the rough surface.

I asked for the time display, and my helmet told me we'd been under for an hour. We rounded a corner and entered a much narrower passage. I became so busy steering us around various projections that I forgot how cold I was. But I noted my skin starting to itch.

Then I caught a flash of light ahead. Did I imagine it?

No. In much less time than I thought, the flash repeated, showing a frothy hole in the liquid above us. Then we were at the boiling surface and Randi was waving at us as she pulled us to shore.

I flew out with a kick and a flap of my hands and was in her arms. A minute must have passed before I thought to release the rest of the expedition from their tent cum submarine.

"No solid ground at the end of the main branch. I came up in a boiling sea, full of froth and foam, couldn't see anything. Not even a roof. Had to come back and take the detour." She trembled. "I have to get in a tent quick."

But with all our decontamination procedures, there was no quick about it, and it was 0300 universal on day ten before we were finally back in our tubular cocoons. By that time, Randi was moaning, shivering and only half-conscious. The Exoderm came off as I peeled her tightsuit down and her skin was a bright angry red, except for her fingers and toes, which were an ugly yellow black. I linked up the minidoc and called Cathy, who programmed a general tissue regenerative, a stimulant, and directed that the tent's insulation factor be turned up.

By 0500, Randi was sleeping, breathing normally, and some of the redness had faded. Cathy called and offered to watch the minidoc so I could get some sleep.

The question I fell asleep with was, that with everyone's lives at stake, could I have pushed myself so far?

Day ten was a short one. We were all exhausted, we didn't get started until 1500.

Randi looked awful, especially her hands and feet, but pulled on her back-up tight suit without a complaint. My face must have told her what I was thinking because she shot me a defiant look.

"I'll do my pitch."

But Cathy was waiting for us and took her back into the tent, which repressurized. Nikhil and I shrugged and busied ourselves packing everything else. When the women reappeared, Cathy declared, very firmly, that Randi was to stay prone and inactive.

Randi disagreed. "I do my pitch . . . I, I, have to."

My turn. "Time to give someone else a chance, Randi. Me for instance. Besides, if you injure yourself further, you'd be a liability."

Randi shook her head. "Can't argue. Don't know how. I don't . . . don't want to be baggage."

"I'd hardly call it being baggage," Nikhil sniffed. "Enforced rest under medical orders. Now, if you're going to be a professional in your own right instead of Daddy's little indulgence, you'll chin up, follow medical orders, and stop wasting time."

"Nikhil dear," Cathy growled, "get your damn mouth out of my patient's psyche."

Nikhil was exactly right, I thought, but I wanted to slug him for saying it that way.

"Very well," Nikhil said, evenly ignoring the feeling in Cathy's voice, "I regret the personal reference, Randi, but the point stands. Please don't be difficult."

Lacking support from anyone else, Randi's position was hopeless. She suffered herself to be taped onto a litter improvised from the same tent braces, sheets, and tape we had used earlier to make her wings.

This done, Nikhil turned to me. "You mentioned leading a pitch?"

Fortunately, the route started out like a one-third-scale-version Nikhil's Smokestack. It wasn't a straight shot, but a series of vertical caverns, slightly offset. Sam rocketed ahead with a line, anchored himself, and reeled the rest of us up. The short passages between caverns were the typical wide low cracks and I managed them without great difficulty, though it came as a surprise to discover how much rock and ice one had to chip away to get through comfortably. It was hard work in a pressure suit, and my respect for Nikhil and Randi increased greatly.

At the end of the last cavern, the chimney bent north, gradually narrowing to a funnel. We could hear the wind blow by us. At the end was a large horizontal cavern, dry, but full of hoar crystals. The rift was clearly visible as a fissure on its ceiling. That was for tomorrow.

The ethane level was down enough for us to forego decontamination, and before we turned in we congratulated ourselves for traversing 60 percent of the rift in less than half our allotted time.

As we turned in, Randi said she had feeling in her fingers and toes again. Which meant she must have had no feeling in them when she was demanding to lead the pitch this afternoon.

She slept quietly, it was only midnight, and I was going to get my first good night's sleep in a long time.

Day eleven was thankfully over, we were all exhausted again, and bitterly disappointed.

The day started with a discovery that, under other circumstances, would have justified the entire expedition: the mummified remains of aliens, presumably those who had left the strange piton. There were two large bodies and one small, supine on the cavern floor, lain on top of what must have been their pressure suits. Did they run out of food, or air, and give up in that way? Or did they die of something else, and were laid out by compatriots we might find elsewhere?

They were six-limbed bipeds, taller than us and perhaps not as heavy in life, though this is hard to tell from a mummy. Their upper arms were much bigger and stronger than their lower ones and the head reminded me vaguely of a panda. They were not, to my memory, members of any of the five known spacefaring races, so, in any other circumstances, this would have been a momentous event. As it was, I think I was vaguely irritated at the complication they represented. Either my sense of wonder wasn't awake yet, or we'd left it behind, a few geode caverns back.

"How long?" Cathy asked Sam in a hushed voice. She, at least, was fascinated.

"If the present rate of dust deposition can be projected, about two hundred and thirty thousand years, with a sigma of ten thousand."

"Except for the pressure suits, they didn't leave any equipment," Nikhil observed. "I take that to mean that this cavern is *not* a dead end—as long as we do press on. You have your images, Sam? Good. Shall we?"

We turned to Nikhil, away from the corpses.

"The vent," he said, looking overhead, "is probably up there."

"The ceiling fissure is an easy jump for me," Sam offered. "I'll pull the rest of you up."

We got on our way, but the rift quit on us.

Once in the ceiling caves, we found there was no gas flowing that way, the way where Sam's seismological soundings, and our eyes, said the rift was. We chanced the passage anyway, but it quickly narrowed to a stomach-crawling ordeal. Three kilometers in, we found it solidly blocked and had to back our way out to return to the cavern. Another passage in the ceiling proved equally unpromising.

"Quakes," Nikhil said. "The rift must have closed here, oh, a hundred million years ago or so—from the dust." So, when dinosaurs ruled the Earth, Miranda had changed her maze, no doubt with the idea in mind of frustrating our eventual expedition.

Finally, Sam found the outlet airflow. It led back to the north.

"I hereby dub this the Cavern of Dead Ends," I proclaimed as we left, with what I hoped was humorous flourish.

Surprisingly, Nikhil, bless his heart, gave me one short "ha!"

Randi was not to be denied today, and took the first pitch out in relief of Nikhil. But she soon tired, according to Cathy, who was monitoring. I took over and pushed on.

The slopes were gentle, the path wide with little cutting to do, and we could make good time tugging ourselves along on the occasional projecting rock and gliding. We took an evening break in a tiny ten-meter bubble of a cavern and had our daily ration crackers, insisting that Randi have a double ration. No one started to make camp, a lack of action that signified group assent for another evening of climbing and gliding.

"We are," Sam said, showing us his map on our helmet displays, "going to pass very close to the upper end of Nikhil's Smokestack." No one said anything, but we knew that meant we were backtracking, losing ground.

There was a final horizontal cavern, and its airflow was toward the polar axis. We could pretty much figure out what that meant, but decided to put off the confirmation until the morning. I'd once read a classic ancient novel by someone named Vance about an imaginary place where an accepted means of suicide was to enter an endless maze and wander about, crossing your path over and over again until starvation did you in. There, you died by forgetting the way out. Here, we did not even know there *was* a way out.

The beginning of day twelve thus found us at the top of Nikhil's Smokestack again, on a lip of a ledge not much different than the one about a kilometer away where we had first seen it. We were very quiet, fully conscious of how much ground we had lost to the cruel calendar. We were now less than halfway through Miranda, with less than half our time left.

Sam circled the top of the Smokestack again, looking for outlets other than the one we had come through. There were none. Our only hope was to go back down.

"Do we," I asked, "try the inner river, or try the other branch of Randi's River and fight our way through the Boiling Sea?"

Nikhil, though he weighed less than four newtons, was stretched out on the ledge, resting. His radio voice came from a still form that reminded me in a macabre way of the deceased aliens back in the Cavern of Dead Ends.

"The Boiling Sea," he mused, "takes the main flow of the river, so it should have an outlet vent. It is obviously in a cavern, so it has a roof. Perhaps we could just shoot a piton up at it, blindly."

But I thought of Nikhil's Smokestack—a blind shot could go a long way in something like that.

"Sam could fly up to it," I offered. "If we protect it until we reach the Boiling Sea's surface, it could withstand the momentary exposure. Once at the ceiling, it could pull the rest of us up."

Cathy nodded and threw a rock down Nikhil's Smokestack, and we watched it vanish relatively quickly. Dense, I thought, less subject to drag. As it turned out, I wasn't the only one with that thought.

"Look what I have," Randi announced.

"What" was a large boulder, perhaps two meters across, and loose; Randi could rock it easily, though it must have had a mass of five or six tons. "Bet *it* doesn't fall like a snowflake," she said as she hammered a piton into it.

Even in the low gravity, it took two of us to lift it over the edge.

Two hours later, about a kilometer above Cathy's Rock, we jumped off into the drag of the slipstream and watched the boulder finish its fall. It crashed with a resounding thud, shattered into a thousand shards, most of which rebounded and got caught in the chimney walls. We soon reached local terminal velocity and floated like feathers in the dust back to the place we had first departed three days ago.

Cathy decided that Randi was in no shape for another immersion and didn't think I should risk it either. I did have a few red patches, though I'd spent nowhere near as much time in the ethane as Randi. We looked at Nikhil, who frowned.

Cathy shook her head. "My turn, I think." But her voice quavered. "I'm a strong swimmer and I don't think Nikhil's done it for years. You handle the spray, Wojciech. You don't have to cover every square centimeter, the fibers will fill in themselves, but make sure you get enough on me. At least fifteen seconds of continuous spray. Randi, I can't hold my breath as long as you. You'll have to help me get buttoned up again, fast."

When all was ready, she took several deep breaths, vented her helmet and stripped almost as quickly as Randi had. This, I thought as I sprayed her, was the same woman who panicked in a tight spot just over a week ago. The whole operation was over in a hundred seconds.

The pulley I'd left was still functional, but that would only get us to the branch in the passage that led to the Cavern of Dead Ends. From there on, Cathy would have to pull us.

It was not fun to be sealed in an opaque, uninflated tent and be bumped and dragged along for the better part of an hour with no control over anything. The return of my minuscule weight as Sam winched us up to the roof of the Boiling Sea cavern was a great relief.

Randi, Nikhil, and I crawled, grumbling but grateful, out of the tent onto the floor of the cave Sam had found a couple of hundred yards from the center of the domed roof of the cavern. The floor sloped, but not too badly, and with a milligee of gravity it scarcely mattered. I helped Nikhil with the tent braces and we soon had it ready to be pressurized. Sam recharged the pallet power supplies and Randi tacked a glowlamp to the wall. Cathy then excused herself to get the Exoderm out of her tightsuit while we set up the other tent.

Work done, we stretched and floated around our little room in silence.

I took a look out the cave entrance; all I could see of the cavern when I hit my strobe was a layer of white below and a forest of yellow and white stalactites, many of them hundreds of meters long, on the roof. The far side, which Sam's radar said was only a couple of kilometers away, was lost in mist.

Then I noticed other things. My tightsuit, for instance, didn't feel as tight as it should.

"What's the air pressure in here?"

"Half a bar," Sam responded. "I've adjusted your suits for minimum positive pressure. It's mostly nitrogen, methane, ethane, and ammonia vapor, with some other volatile organics. By the way, the Boiling Sea is mainly ammonia; we are up to 220 Kelvins here. The ethane flashes into vapor as it hits the ammonia—that's why all the boiling."

Miranda's gravity was insufficient to generate that kind of pressure, and I wondered what was going on.

"Wojciech," Randi whispered, as if she were afraid of waking something. "Look at the walls,"

"Huh?" The cave walls were dirty brown like cave walls anywhere—except Miranda. "Oh, no hoar crystals."

She rubbed her hand on the wall and showed me the brown gunk.

"I'd like to put this under a microscope. Sam?"

The robot came quickly and held the sample close to its lower set of eyes. I saw what it saw, projected on the inside of my helmet.

"This," it said, "has an apparent cellular structure, but little, if any structure within. Organic molecules and ammonia in a kind of gel."

As I watched, one of the cells developed a bifurcation. I was so fascinated, I didn't notice that Cathy had rejoined us. "They must absorb stuff directly from the air," she theorized. "The air is toxic, by the way, but not in low concentrations. Something seems to have filtered out the cyanogens and other really bad stuff. Maybe this."

"The back of the cave is full of them," Randi observed. "How are you?"

"My skin didn't get as raw as yours, but I have a few irritated areas. Physically, I'm drained. We're going to stop here tonight, I hope."

"This is one of the gas outlets of the Cavern of the Boiling Sea," Sam added. "It seems to be a good place to resume our journey. The passage is clear of obstructions as far as I can see, except for these growths, which are transparent to my radar."

"They impede the airflow," Nikhil observed, "which must contribute to the high pressure in here. I think they get the energy for their organization from the heat of condensation."

"Huh?" I wracked my memories of bonehead science.

"Wojciech, when a vapor condenses it undergoes a phase change. When ethane vapor turns back into ethane, it gives off as much heat as it took to boil it in the first place. That heat can make some of the chemical reactions this stuff needs go in the right direction."

"Are they alive?" I asked.

"Hard to say," Cathy responded. "But that's a semantic discussion. Are hoar crystals alive? There's a continuum of organization and behavior from rocks to people. Any line you draw is arbitrary and will go right through some gray areas."

"Hmpf," Nikhil snorted. "Some distinctions are more useful than others. This stuff breeds, I think. Let's take some samples, but we need to get some rest, too."

"Yes, dear." Cathy yawned in spite of herself.

In the tent, Randi and I shared our last regular meal; a reconstituted chicken and pasta dish we'd saved to celebrate something. The tent stank of bodies and hydrocarbons, but we were used to that by now, and the food tasted great despite the assault on our nostrils. From now on, meals would be crackers. But we were on our way out now, definitely. We had to be. Randi felt fully recovered now and smiled at me as she snuggled under her elastic sheet for a night's rest.

It must have been the energy we got from our first good meal in days. She woke me in the middle of our arbitrary night and gently coaxed me into her cot for lovemaking, more an act of defiance against our likely fate than an act of pleasure. I surprised myself by responding, and we caressed each other up a spiral of intensity which was perhaps fed by our fear as well.

There were the tidal forces near Randi's event horizon; she was not just strong for a woman, but strong in absolute terms; stronger than most men I have known including myself. I had to half-seriously warn her to not crack our low gravity–weakened ribs. This made her giggle and squeeze me so hard I couldn't breathe for a moment, which made her giggle again.

When we were done, she gestured to the tent roof with the middle finger of her right hand and laughed uncontrollably. I joined her in this as well, but I felt momentarily sad for Nikhil and Cathy.

It was another of those polite mornings, and we packed up and were on our way with record efficiency. We looked around for the vent and Sam pointed us right at the mass of brown at the rear of the cave.

"The gas goes into that, right through it," it said.

We called the stuff "cryofungus." It had grown out from either side of the large, erosion widened vertical crack that Sam found in the back of our cave until it met in the middle. However, the cryofungus colonies from either side didn't actually fuse there, but just pressed up against each other. So, with some effort, we found we could half push, half swim, our way along this seam.

We had pushed our way through five kilometers of "cryofungus" before a macabre thought occurred to me. The rubbery brown stuff absorbed organics through the skin of its cells. Did said organic stuff have to be gas? I asked Cathy.

"I did an experiment. I fed my sample a crumb of ration cracker."

"What happened?"

"The cracker sort of melted into the cryofungus. There are transport molecules all over the cell walls."

I thought a second. "Cathy, if we didn't have our suits on——"

"I'd think water would be a little hot for them, but then again water and ammonia are mutually soluble. If you want to worry, consider that your tightsuit is porous. It might," I could see her toothy smile in my mind, "help keep you moving."

"Nice, dear," Nikhil grumbled. "That gives a whole new meaning to this concept of wandering through the bowels of Miranda."

A round of hysterical laughter broke whatever tension remained between us, and resolved into a feeling of almost spiritual oneness among us. Perhaps you have to face death with someone to feel that—if so, so be it.

At the ten-kilometer point, the cryofungus started to loose its resiliency. At twelve, it started collapsing into brown dust, scarcely offering any more resistance than the hoar crystals. This floated along with the gas current as a sort of brown fog. I couldn't see, and had Sam move up beside me.

After three kilometers of using Sam as a seeing-eye dog, the dust finally drifted by us and the air cleared. It was late again, well past time to camp. We had been underground thirteen days, and had, by calculation, another eight left. According to Sam, we were still two hundred and fifteen kilometers below the surface. We decided to move on for another hour or two.

The passageway was tubular and fairly smooth, with almost zero traction. We shot pitons into the next curve ahead, and pulled ourselves along.

"Massive wind erosion," Nikhil remarked as he twisted the eye of a piton to release it. "A gale must have poured through here for megayears before the cryofungus choked it down."

Each strobe revealed an incredible gallery of twisted forms, loops, and carved rocks, many of which were eerily statuesque; saints and gargoyles. This led us into a slightly uphill kilometer-long cavern formed under two megalithic slabs, which had tilted against each other when, perhaps, the escaping gas had undermined them. After the rich hoarcrystal forest of the inbound path, this place was bare and dry. Sam covered the distance with a calculated jump carrying a line to the opposite end. We started pulling ourselves across. We'd climbed enough so that our weight was back to twenty newtons—minuscule, yes, but try pumping twenty newtons up and down for eighteen hours.

"I quit," Cathy said. "My arms won't do any more. Stop with me, or bury me here." She let go of the line, and floated slowly down to the floor.

It was silent here, no drippings, no whistling, reminiscent of the vacuum so far above. I tried to break the tension by naming the cavern. "This was clearly meant to be a tomb, anyway. The Egyptian Tomb, we can call it."

"Not funny, Wojciech," Nikhil snapped. "Sorry, old boy, a bit tired myself. Yes, we can make camp, but we may regret it later."

"Time to stop. We worked out the schedule for, for, maximum progress." Randi said. "Need to trust our judgment. Won't do any better by over-pushing ourselves now."

"Very well," Nikhil conceded, and dropped off as well. He reached Cathy and put his arm around her briefly, which I note because it was the first sign of physical affection I had seen between them. Randi and I dropped the pallets, and followed to the floor. We landed harder than we expected—milligee clouds judgment. Worse perhaps, because it combines a real up and down with the feeling that they don't matter.

We were very careful and civilized in making camp. But each of us was, in our minds, trying to reach an accommodation with the idea that, given what we had been through so far, the week we had left would not get us to the surface.

Before we went into our separate tents, we all held hands briefly. It was spontaneous, we hadn't done so before. But it seemed right, somehow, to tell each other that we could draw on each other that way.

V

That last was for day thirteen, this entry covers days fourteen and fifteen. Yes, my discipline in keeping the journal is slipping.

We'd come to think of Randi as a machine—almost as indestructible and determined as Sam, but last night, at the end of day fourteen that machine cried and shook.

Low rations and fatigue are affecting all of us now. We let Sam pull us through the occasional cavern, but it has mostly been wriggling through cracks with a human in the lead. We changed leads every time we hit a wide-enough place, but once that was six hours. That happened on Randi's lead. She didn't slack but when we finally reached a small cavern, she rolled to the side with her face to the wall as I went by. We heard nothing from her for the next four hours.

We ended up at the bottom of a big kidney-shaped cavern 160 kilometers below the surface; almost back to the depth of the upper end of Nikhil's Smokestack. We staggered through camp set-up, with Sam double-checking everything. We simply collapsed on top of the stretched sheets in our coveralls and slept for an hour or so, before our bodies demanded that we answer our needs. Washed, emptied, and a bit refreshed from the nap, Randi snuggled into my arms, then let herself go. Her body was a mass of bruises, old and new. So was mine.

"You're allowed a safety valve, you know," I told her. "When Cathy feels bad, she lets us know outright. Nikhil gets grumpy. I get silly and tell bad jokes. You don't have to keep up an act for us."

"Not for you, for, for me. Got to pretend I can do it, or I'll get left behind, with Mom."

I thought about this. A woman that would attempt to murder her husband to gain social position might have been capable of other things as well.

"Randi, what did that mean? Do you want to talk?"

She shook her head. "Can't explain."

I kissed her forehead. "I guess I've been lucky with my parents."

"Yeah. Nice people. Nice farm. No fighting. So why do you have to do this stuff?"

Why indeed? "To have a real adventure, to make a name for myself outside of obscure poetry outlets. Mom inherited the farm from her father, and that was better than living on state dividends in Poland, so they moved. They actually get to do something useful, tending the agricultural robots. But they're deathly afraid of losing it because real jobs are so scarce and a lot of very smart people are willing to do just about anything to get an Earth job. So they made themselves very, very nice. They never rock any boats. Guess I needed something more than nice.''

"But you're, uh, nice as they are.''

"Well trained, in spite of myself.'' Oh, yes, with all the protective responses a nonconformist learns after being squashed time and time again by very socially correct, outwardly gentle, and emotionally devastating means. "By the way, Randi, I hate that word.''

"Huh?''

"Nice.''

"But you use it.''

"Yeah, and I hate doing that, too. Look, are you as tired as I am?'' I was about to excuse myself to the questionable comforts of my dreams.

"No. Not yet. I'll do the work.''

"Really . . .''

"Maybe the last time, way we're going.'' We both knew she was right, but my body wasn't up to it, and we just clung to each other tightly, as if we could squeeze a little more life into ourselves. I don't remember falling asleep.

Day fifteen was a repeat, except that the long lead shift fell on Cathy. She slacked. For seven hours, she would stop until she got cold then move forward again until she got tired. Somehow we reached a place where I could take over.

What amazed me through all of that was how Nikhil handled it. There was no sniping, no phony cheeriness. He would simply ask if she was ready to move again when he started getting cold.

We ended the day well past midnight. For some reason, I was having trouble sleeping.

Today the vent finally led us to a chain of small caverns, much like the rift before we encountered the top of Nikhil's Smokestack. We let Sam tow us most of the way and had only two long crack crawls. The good news is our CO_2 catalyst use is down from our passivity, and we might get another day out of it.

The bad news is that Randi had to cut our rations back a bit. We hadn't been as careful in our counting as we should have been, thinking that because the CO_2 would get us first, we didn't have a problem in that area. Now we did. It was nobody's fault, and everyone's. We'd all had an extra cracker here and there. They add up.

We ended up exhausted as usual, in a five-hundred-meter gallery full of jumble. I called it "The Junk Yard.'' Sam couldn't find the outlet vent right away, but we made such good progress that we thought we had time to catch up on our sleep.

Day eighteen. We gained a total of fifteen kilometers in radius over the past two days. "The Junk Yard'' was a dead end, at least for anything the size of a human being. There was some evidence of gas diffusing upward through fractured clathrate, but it was already clear that it wasn't the main vent, which appeared to have been closed by a Miranda quake millions of years ago.

We had to go all the way back to a branch that Sam had missed while it was towing us through a medium-sized chimney. Logic and experience dictated that the outlet would be at the top of the chimney, and there was a hole there that led onward. To "The Junk Yard." Miranda rearranges such logic.

We spotted the real vent from the other side of the chimney as we rappelled back down.

"A human being," Cathy said when she saw the large vertical crack that was the real vent, "would have been curious enough to check that out. It's so deep."

"I don't know, dear," Nikhil said, meaning to defend Sam, I supposed, "with the press of time and all, I might not have turned aside, myself."

We were all dead silent at Nikhil's unintentional self-identification with a robot. Then Randi giggled and soon we were all laughing hysterically again. The real students of humor, I recall, say that laughter is not very far from tears. Then Nikhil, to our surprise, released his hold to put his arms around his wife again. And she responded. I reached out and caught them before they'd drifted down enough centimeters for their belt lines to go taut. So at the end of day seventeen, we had covered sixty kilometers of caverns and cracks, and come only fifteen or so nearer the surface.

By the end of day eighteen, we'd done an additional fifteen kilometers of exhausting crack crawling, found only one large cavern, and gave in to exhaustion, camping in a widening of the crack just barely big enough to inflate the tents.

What occurred today was not a fight. We didn't have enough energy for a fight.

We had just emerged into a ten-meter-long, ten-meter-wide, two-meter-high widening gallery in the crack we were crawling. Cathy was in the lead and had continued on through into the continuing passage when Nikhil gave in to pessimism.

"Cathy," he called, "stop. The passage ahead is getting too narrow, it's another bloody dead end. We should go back to the last large cavern and look for another vent."

Cathy was silent, but the line stopped. Randi, sounding irritated, said "No time," and moved to enter the passage after Cathy.

Nikhil yawned and snorted. "Sorry little lady. I'm the geologist and the senior member, and not to be too fine about it, but I'm in charge." Here he seemed to loose steam and get confused, muttering "You're right about no time—there's no time to argue."

No one said anything, but Randi held her position.

Nikhil whined. "I say we go back, an' this time, back we go."

My mind was fuzzy; we still had four, maybe five days. If we found the right chain of caverns, we could still make the surface. If we kept going like this, we weren't going to make it anyway. He might be right, I thought. But Randi wouldn't budge.

"No. Nikhil. You owe me one, Nikhil, for, for, two weeks ago. I'm collecting. Got to go forward now. Air flow, striations, Sam's soundings, and, and my money, damn it."

So much for my thoughts. I had to remember my status as part of Randi's accretion disk.

"Your *daddy's* money," Nikhil sniffed, then said loudly and with false jollity, "But never mind. Come on everyone, we'll put Randi on a stretcher again until she recovers . . . her senses." He started reaching for Randi: clumsy fumbling really. Randi turned and braced herself, boots clamped into the clathrate, arms free.

"Nikhil, back off," I warned. "You don't mean that."

"Ah appreciate your expertise with words, old chap." His voice was definitely slurred. "But these are mine and I mean them. I'm too tired to be questioned by amateurs anymore. Back we go. Come on back, Cathy. As for you . . ." He lunged for Randi again. At this point I realized he was out of his mind, and possibly why.

So did Randi, for at the last second instead of slapping him away and possibly hurting him, she simply jerked herself away from his grasping fingers.

And screeched loudly in pain.

"What?" I asked, brushing by the startled Nikhil to get to Randi's side.

"Damn ankle," she sobbed. "Forgot to release my boot grapples. Tired. Bones getting weak. Too much low g. Thing hurts."

"Broken?"

She nodded, tight lipped, more in control. But I could see the tears in her eyes. Except for painkiller, there was nothing I could do for her at the moment. But I thought there might be something to be done for Nikhil. Where was Cathy?

"Nikhil," I said as evenly as I could. "What's your O_2 partial?"

"I beg your pardon?" he drawled.

"Beg Randi's. I asked you what your O_2 partial is."

"I've been conserving a bit. You know, less O_2, less CO_2. Trying to stretch things out."

"What . . . is . . . it?"

"Point one. It should be fine. I've had a lot of altitude experience—"

"Please put it back up to point two for five minutes, and then we'll talk."

"Now just a minute, I resent the implication that—"

"Be reasonable Nikhil. Put it back up for a little, please. Humor me. Five minutes won't hurt."

"Oh perhaps not. There. Now just what is it you expect to happen?"

"Wait for a bit."

We waited, silently. Randi sniffed, trying to deal with her pain. I watched Nikhil's face slowly grow more and more troubled. Finally I asked:

"Are you back with us?"

He nodded silently. "I think so. My apologies, Randi."

"Got clumsy. Too strong for my own bones. Forget it. And you don't owe me, either. Dumb thing to say. It was my choice."

What was? Two weeks ago, in his tent?

"Very well." Nikhil replied with as much dignity as he could muster.

Who besides Randi could dismiss a broken ankle with "forget it." And who besides Nikhil would take her up on that? I shook my head.

Randi couldn't keep the pain out of her voice as she held out her right vacuum boot. "This needs some work. Tent site. Cathy." Nothing would show, of course, until it came off.

"Quite," Nikhil responded. "Well, you were right on the direction. Perhaps we should resume."

I waved him off for a moment and found a painkiller in the pallet for Randi, and she ingested it through her helmet lock, and gagged a bit.

"Still a little ethane here," she gave a little laugh. "Woke me up. I'll manage."

"Let me know." I was so near her event horizon now that everything I could see of the outside world was distorted and bent by her presence. Such were the last moments of my freedom, the last minutes and the last seconds that I could look on our relationship from the outside. My independent existence was stretched beyond the power of any force of nature to restore it. Our fate was to become a singularity.

It was a measure of my own hunger and fatigue that I half seriously considered exterminating Nikhil; coldly, as if contemplating a roach to be crushed. A piton gun would have done nicely. But, I thought, Cathy really ought to be in on the decision. She might want to keep him as a pet. Cathy, of course, was on the lead pitch. That meant she was really in charge, something Nikhil had forgotten.

"Cathy," I called, laying on the irony. "Randi has a broken ankle. Otherwise, we are ready to go again."

There was no answer, but radio didn't carry well in this material—too many bends in the path and something in the clathrate that just ate our frequencies like stealth paint. So I gave two pulls on our common line to signal OK, go.

The line was slack.

Cathy, anger with Nikhil possibly clouding her judgment, had enforced her positional authority in a way that was completely inarguable: by proceeding alone. At least I fervently hoped that was all that had happened. I pulled myself to where the passage resumed, and looked. No sign of anything.

"Sam, take the line back up to Cathy and tell her to wait up, we're coming."

Sam squeezed by me and scurried off. Shortly, his monitors in my helmet display blinked out; he was out of radio range as well.

Again, we waited for a tug on a line in a silence that shouted misery. Nikhil pretended to examine the wall, Randi stared ahead as if in a trance. I stared at her, wanting to touch her, but not seeming to have the energy to push myself over to her side of the little cave.

Both hope and dread increased with the waiting. The empty time could mean that Cathy had gone much farther than our past rate of progress had suggested, which would be very welcome news. But it could also mean that some disaster ahead had taken both her and Sam. In which case, we were dead as well. Or, like Randi's detour from the Boiling Sea, it could mean something we had neglected to imagine.

"Wojciech, Nikhil," Randi asked in her quiet, anticipatory, tone, "would you turn off your lamps?"

I looked at Nikhil, and he stared off into space, saying as much that he could not care less. But his light went out. I nodded and cut mine. The blackness was total at first, then as my pupils widened, I realized I could sense a gray-green contrast, a shadow. My shadow.

I turned around to the source of the glow. It was, of course, the crack behind me, through which Cathy and Sam had vanished. As my eyes adapted further, it became almost bright. It was white, just tinged with green. The shadows of rocks and ice intrusions made the crack look like the mouth of some beast about to devour us.

"Is there," I asked, "any reason why we should stay here?"

We left. The crack widened rapidly, and after an hour of rather mild crack-crawling, we were able to revert to our distance-eating hand-hauling routine. We covered ten kilometers almost straight up this way. With the sudden way of such things the crack turned into a tubular tunnel, artificial in its smoothness, and this in turn gave into a roughly teardropshaped, hundred-meter-diameter cavern with slick ice walls, and a bright circle at the top. I was about to use my piton gun when Randi tugged my arm and pointed out a ladder of double-looped pitons, set about two meters apart, leading up to the circle.

We were thus about to climb into Sphereheim when Cathy's line grew taut again.

That was, by the clock, the end of day nineteen. We were, it seemed, both too exhausted and too excited to sleep.

The cavern above was almost perfectly spherical, hence the name we gave it, and was almost fifteen kilometers in diameter. A spire ran along its vertical axis from the ceiling to the floor, littered like a Christmas tree with the kind of cantilevered platforms that seventy-five milligees permits.

By now, we had climbed to within forty kilometers of the surface, so this was all in a pretty good vacuum, but there were signs that things had not always been this way.

"Cathy?" Nikhil called, the first words he had spoken since the fight.

"Good grief, you're here already. We waited until we thought it was safe."

"We saw the light."

"It came on as soon as I got in here. Sam's been looking for other automatic systems, burglar protection, for instance."

"There," Sam interjected, "appear to be none. The power source is two stage—a uranium radionic long duration module, and something like a solid state fuel cell that works when it's warmed up. The latter appears to be able to produce almost a kilowatt."

"Good," I said, wondering if Sam's software could discern the contrary irritation in my voice. "Cathy, Randi has a broken ankle." Even in less than a hundredth of g, Randi wouldn't put any weight on it.

"Oh, no! We need to get a tent up right away. Sam, break off and come down here, I need you. And you!" She pointed at Nikhil. "This is a medical emergency now, and what I say goes. Do you have a problem with that?" The edge in Cathy's voice verged on hysteria.

Nikhil simply turned away without saying anything and began setting up the tent.

Randi reached for Cathy. "Cathy, Nikhil cut his oxygen too thin, trying to save CO_2 catalyst for all of us. He wasn't himself. Ankle hurts like hell, but that was my fault. I'd feel better if you weren't so, uh, hard on him. OK?"

Cathy stood quietly for a couple of seconds then muttered. "All right, all right. Give me a minute to collect things, and we'll get in the tent. I'll see what I can do. Wojciech?"

"Yes, Cathy?"

"As I guess everyone knows, I just blew it with my husband, and I can't fix things right now because I have to fix Randi's ankle. He's in a blue funk." She pulled the velcro tab up on one of her pockets, reached in and produced a small, thin, box. "Give him one of these and tell him I'm sorry."

I looked at her. She seemed on the brink of some kind of collapse, but was holding herself back by some supreme effort of will. Maybe that's what I looked like to her.

"Sorry, Wojciech," she whispered, "best I can do."

I gave her hand a squeeze. "We'll make it good enough, OK? Just hang in there, Doc."

She gave me a quick, tear-filled smile, then grabbed the minidoc and followed Randi into the tent, which inflated promptly.

Nikhil was sitting on the other pallet and I sat next to him. "Look, Nikhil, the way I see it, none of this stuff counts. All that counts is that the four of us get out of this moon alive."

He looked at me briefly, then resumed looking at the ground. "No, no. Wojciech, it counts. Do you understand living death? The kind where your body persists, but everything that you thought was you has been destroyed? My reputation . . . they'll say Nikhil Ray cracked under pressure. It got too tough for old Nikhil. Nikhil beats up on women. It's going to be bloody bad."

I remembered the box Cathy gave me, pulled it out and opened it. "Doctor's orders, Nikhil. She cares, she really does."

He gave me a ghastly grin and took a caplet envelope, unwrapped it and stuck it through his helmet lock. "Can't say as I approve of mind-altering drugs, but it wouldn't do to disappoint the doctor any more now, would it? I put her through medical school, did you know? She was eighteen when we met. Biology student studying evolution, and I was co-lecturing a paleontology section. Damn she was beautiful, and no one like that had ever . . ." he lifted his hands as if to gesture, then set them down again. "I broke my own rule about thinking first, and I have this to remind me, every day, of what happens when you do that."

"Look, Nikhil. She doesn't mean to hurt you." I tried to think of something to get him out of this, to put his mind on something else. "Say, we have a few minutes. Why don't we look around, it may be the only chance we get. Soon as Cathy's done with Randi, we'll need to get some sleep, then try to make it to the surface. We've forty kilometers to go, and only two days before our catalyst runs out.''

"My line, isn't that? Very well.'' He seemed to straighten a bit. "But it looks as if the visitors packed up pretty thoroughly when they left. Those platforms off the central column are just bare honeycomb. Of course, it would be a bit odd if they packed *everything* out.''

"Oh?''

"Field sites are usually an eclectic mess. All sorts of not-immediately-useful stuff gets strewn about. If the strewers don't expect the environmental police to stop by, it usually just gets left there by the hut site—the next explorer to come that way might find something useful.''

"I see. You think there might be a dump here, somewhere.''

"It seems they had a crypt. Why not a dump?''

What kind of alien technology might be useful to us, I didn't know. It would take a lot longer than the two days we had to figure out how to do anything with it. But the discussion had seemed to revive Nikhil a bit, so I humored him.

We found the junkyard. It was in a mound about a hundred meters from the tower base, covered with the same color dust as everything else. A squirt from my reaction pistol blew some of the dust away from the junk.

And it was just that. Discarded stuff. Broken building panels, a few boxes with electrical leads. What looked like a busted still. A small wheeled vehicle that I would have taken for a kid's tricycle, an elongated vacuum helmet with a cracked visor. Other things. I'd been rummaging for five minutes before I noticed that Nikhil hadn't gone past the still.

"Nikhil?''

"It is within the realm of possibility that I might redeem myself. Look at that.''

The most visible part was a big coil of what looked to be tubing. There were also things that looked like electric motors, and several chambers to hold distilled liquids.

"The tubing, Wojciech.''

"I don't understand.''

"If we breathe through it, at this temperature, the CO_2 in our breath should condense.''

"Oh! We could do without the CO_2 catalyst.'' Then I thought of the problem. "It wouldn't be very portable.''

"No, it wouldn't,'' Nikhil nodded slowly, judiciously. "But it doesn't have to be. Cathy and Randi can remain here while you, Sam, and I take the remaining catalyst and go for help.''

Did I hear him right? Then I thought it through. Randi was disabled, Cathy, by strength and temperament, was the least suited for the ordeal above us. It made sense, but Randi would . . . no, Randi would have to agree if it made sense. She was a pro.

"We'd better see if it works first.'' I said.

VI

An hour later, our still was working. Tape, spare connectors, the alien light source, and Sam's instant computational capabilities yielded something that could keep two relatively quiescent people alive. They'd have to heat it up to sublimate the condensed CO_2 every other hour, or the thing would clog, but it worked.

Randi's ankle was a less happy situation.

"Randi's resting now," Cathy told us when she finally emerged from the vacuum tent, exhausted. "It's a bad break, splintered. Her bones were weak from too much time in low gravity, I think. Anyway, the breaks extend into the calcaneus and her foot is much too swollen to get back into her vacuum boots. Had to put her in a rescue bag to get out of the tent." Cathy shot a look of contempt at her husband who stared down. "The swelling will take days to go down, and she should have much more nourishment than we have to give her."

"I . . ." Nikhil started, then, in a moment I shall remember forever, he looked confused. "I?" Then he simply went limp and fell, much like an autumn leaf in the gentle gravity of Miranda, to the cavern dust. We were both too surprised to catch him even though his fall took several seconds.

"No, no . . ." Cathy choked.

I knelt over Nikhil and straightened his limbs. I couldn't think of anything else to do.

"Stroke?" I asked Cathy.

She seemed to shake herself back into a professional mode. I heard her take a breath.

"Could be. His heart telemetry's fine. Or he may have just fainted. Let's get the other tent set up."

We did this only with Sam's help. We made errors in the set-up, errors which would have been fatal if Sam hadn't been there to notice and correct them. We were tired and had been eating too little food. It took an hour. We put Nikhil in the tent and Cathy was about to follow when she stopped me.

"The main med kit's in Randi's tent. I'll need it if I have to operate. She'll have gotten out of the rescue bag to sleep after I left. You'll have to wake her, get her back in the bag and depressure—"

I held up a hand. "I can figure it out, and if I can't, she can. Cathy, her foot's busted, not her head."

Cathy nodded and I could see a bit of a smile through her faceplate.

"Randi," I called, "Sorry to wake you, but we've got a problem."

"I heard. Comsets are dumb, guys. Can't tell if you talk *about* someone instead of *to* someone. Be right out with the med kit."

"Huh?" Cathy sounded shocked. "No, Randi don't try to put that boot on. Please don't."

"Too late," Randi answered. We watched the tension go out of the tent fabric as it depressurized. Randi emerged from the opening with the med kit and a sample bag. Cathy and I immediately looked at her right boot—it seemed perfectly normal, except that Randi had rigged some kind of brace with pitons and vacuum tape.

Then we looked at the sample bag. It contained a blue-green swollen travesty of a human foot, severed neatly just above the ankle, apparently with a surgical laser. I couldn't think of anything to do or say.

"Oh, no, Randi," Cathy cried and launched herself toward Randi. "I tried Randi, I tried."

"You didn't have time." The two women embraced. "Don't say anything," Randi finally said, "to him," she nodded at Nikhil's tent, "until we're all back and safe. Please, huh?"

Cathy stood frozen, then nodded slowly, took the sample bag and examined the foot end of the section. "Looks clean, anyway. At least let me take a look at the stump before you go, OK?"

Randi shook her head. "Bitch to unwrap. Cauterized with the surgical laser. Plastiflesh all over the stump. Sealed in plastic. Plenty of local. Don't feel anything. I did a good enough job, Cathy."

I finally found my voice. "Randi . . . why?"

"Nikhil's gone. Got to move. It's OK, Wojciech. They can regenerate. You and I got to get going."

"Me? Now?" I was surprised for a moment, then realized the need. Cathy had to stay with Nikhil. And I'd already seen too many situations where one person would have been stopped that we'd managed to work around with two. Also, our jury rigged CO_2 still's capacity was two people, max.

"No. Go as long as we can, then sleep. Eat everything we have left. Push for the surface. Only way."

Cathy nodded. She handed Randi's foot to me, almost absentmindedly, and went into the tent to attend to Nikhil. Randy laughed, took the foot from me, and threw it far out of sight toward Sphereheim's junk pile. In the low gravity, it probably got there.

I tried not to think about it as Randi and I packed, with Sam's help. Moving slowly and deliberately, we didn't make that many errors. What Randi had to draw on, I didn't know. I drew on her. In an hour, we were ready to go and said our farewells to Cathy.

She would have to wait there, perhaps alone if Nikhil did not recover, perhaps forever if we did not succeed. What would that be like, I wondered? Would some future explorers confuse her with the beings who had built the station in this cavern? Had we already done that with the corpses we found in the Cavern of Dead Ends?

I wished I had made love to Cathy that night we spent together. I felt I was leaving a relationship incomplete; a feeling, a sharing, uncommunicated. Here, even a last embrace would have been nice, but she was in her tent caring for her husband. Out of food, low on time, Randi and I had to go, and go now. In the dash to the surface, even minutes might be critical.

Tireless Sam scaled the alien tower, found the vent in the magnificent, crystal lined dome of the cavern roof, and dropped us a line. I was suspended among wonders, but so tired I almost fell asleep as Sam reeled us up. The experience was surreal and beyond description.

* * *

Of most of the next few days, I have little detailed memory. Sam dragged us through passages, chimneys, vents and caverns. Occasionally, it stopped at a problem that Randi would somehow rouse herself to solve.

On one occasion, we came to a wall a meter thick which had cracked enough to let gas pass through. Sam's acoustic radar showed a big cavern on the other side, so, somehow, we dug our way through. For all its talents, Sam was not built for wielding a pick. I leave this information to the designers of future cave exploration robots.

Randi and I swung at that wall in five-minute shifts for a three-hour eternity, before, in a fit of hysterical anaerobic energy, I was able to kick it through. We were too tired to celebrate—we just grabbed the line as Sam went by and tried to keep awake and living as it pulled us through another cave and another crack.

In one of a string of ordinary crystal caverns, we found another alien piton. Randi thought it might be a different design than the one we had found before, and had Sam pull it out and put it in a sample bag, which we stored on Sam— the most likely to survive.

I mentioned this because we were near death and knew it, but could still do things for the future. Everyone dies, I thought, so we all spend our lives for something. The only thing that matters at the end is: for what? In saving the piton, we were adding one more bit to the tally of "for what?"

This was almost certainly our last "night" in a tent. I think we both stunk, but I was too far gone to tell for sure. We'd gone for thirty-seven hours straight. Sam said we were within three kilometers of the surface, but the cavern trail lies parallel to this surface, and refused to ascend.

In theory, our catalyst was exhausted, but we continued to breathe.

Another quake trapped me.

Randi was in front of me. Somehow, she managed to squeeze aside and let Sam by to help. Sam chipped clathrate away from my helmet, which let me straighten my neck.

As this happened, there was another movement, a big slow one this time, and the groan of Miranda's tortured mantle was clearly audible as my helmet was pressed between the passage walls again. I could see the passage ahead of me close a little more with every sickening wave of ground movement, even as I could feel the pressure at my spot release a bit. But the passage ahead—if it closed with Randi on this side, we were dead.

"Go!" I told Randi. "It's up to you now." As if it hadn't always been so. I was pushed sideways and back again as another train of s-waves rolled through. Ice split with sharp retorts.

Sam turned sideways in the passage, pitting its thin composite against billions of tons of clathrate.

Randi vanished forward. "I love you," she said, "I'll make it."

"I know you will. Hey, we're married, OK?"

"Just like that?"

"By my authority as a man in a desperate position."

"OK. Married. Two kids. Deal?"

"Deal."

"I love you again."

Sam cracked under the pressure, various electronic innards spilling onto the passage floor. I couldn't see anything beyond him.

"Sam?" I asked. Useless question

"Randi?"

Nothing.

For some strange reason I felt no pressure on me now. Too worried for Randi, too exhausted to be interested in my own death, I dozed.

There was definitely CO_2 in my helmet when I woke again. It was pitch black—the suit had turned off my glowlamp to conserve an inconsequential watt or two. Groggy. I thought turning on my pack would help my breathing, vaguely thinking that the one percent weight on my lungs was a problem. To my surprise, I could actually turn.

In the utter dead black overhead, a star appeared. Very briefly, then I blinked and it vanished.

I continued to stare at this total darkness above me for minutes, not daring to believe I'd seen what I thought I'd seen, and then I saw another one. Yes, a real star.

I thought that could only mean that a crack to the surface had opened above me; incredibly narrow, or far above me, but open enough that now and then a star drifted by its opening. I was beyond climbing, but perhaps where photons could get in, photons could get out.

Shaking and miserable, I started transmitting.

"Uranus Control, Uranus Control, Wojciech Bubka here. I'm down at the bottom of a crack on Miranda. Help. Uranus Control, Uranus Control. . . ."

Something sprayed on my face, waking me again. Air, and mist as well.

I opened my eyes and saw that a tube had cemented itself to my faceplate and drilled a hole through it to admit some smaller tubes. One of these was trying to snake its way into my mouth. I opened to help it, and got something warm and sweet to swallow.

"Thanks," I croaked, around the tube.

"Don't mention it," a young female voice answered, sounding almost as relieved as I felt.

"My wife's in this passage, somewhere in the direction my head is pointed. Can you get one of these tubes to her?"

There was a hesitation. "Your wife."

"Miranda Lotati," I croaked. "She was with me. Trying to get to the surface. Went that way."

More hesitation.

"We'll try, Wojciech. God knows we'll try."

Within minutes, a tiny version of Sam fell on my chest and scuttled past Sam's wreckage down the compressed passage in her direction, trailing a line. The line seemed to run over me forever. I remember reading somewhere that while the journey to singularity is inevitable for someone passing into the event horizon of a black hole, as viewed from our Universe, the journey can take forever.

What most people remember about the rescue was the digger; that vast thing of pistons, beams, and steel claws that tore through the clathrate rift like an anteater looking for ants. What *they* saw, I assure you, was in no way as impressive, or scary, as being directly under the thing.

I was already in a hospital ship bed when they found Randi, eleven kilometers down a passage that had narrowed, narrowed, and narrowed.

At its end, she had broken her bones forcing herself through one more centimeter at a time. A cracked pelvis, both collarbones, two ribs, and her remaining ankle.

The last had done it, for when it collapsed she had no remaining way to force herself any farther through that crack of doom.

And so she had lain there, and, minute by minute, despite everything, willed herself to live as long as she could.

Despite everything, she did.

They got the first tubes into her through her hollow right boot and the plastiflesh seal of her stump, after the left foot had proved to be frozen solid. They didn't tell me at first—not until they had convinced themselves she was really alive.

When the rescuers reached Cathy and Nikhil, Cathy calmly guided the medic to her paralyzed husband, and as soon as she saw that he was in good professional hands, gave herself a sedative, and started screaming until she collapsed. She wasn't available for interviews for weeks.

But she's fine now, and laughs about it. She and Nikhil live in a large university dome on Triton and host our reunions in their house, which has no roof—they've arranged for the dome's rain to fall elsewhere.

Miranda, my wife, spent three years as a quadruple amputee, and went back into Miranda the moon that way, in a powered suit, to lead people back to the Cavern of Dead Ends. Today, it's easy to see where the bronze weathered flesh of her old limbs ends and the pink smoothness of her new ones start. But if you miss it, she'll point it out with a grin.

So, having been to hades and back, are the four of us best friends? For amusement, we all have more congenial companions. Nikhil is still a bit haughty, and he and Cathy still snipe at each other a little, but with smiles more often than not. I've come to conclude that, in some strange way, they need the stimulation that gives them, and a displacement for needs about which Nikhil will not speak.

Cathy and Randi still find little to talk about, giving us supposedly verbally challenged males a chance. Nikhil says I have absorbed enough geology lectures to pass doctorate exams; so maybe I will do that someday. He often lectures me toward that end, but my advance for our book was such that I won't have to do anything the rest of my life, except for the love of it. I'm not sure I love geology.

Often, on our visits, the four of us simply sit, say nothing, and do nothing but sip a little fruit of the local grape, which we all enjoy. We smile at each other and remember.

But don't let this studied difference of ours fool you. The four of us are bound with something that goes far beyond friendship, far beyond any slight conversation, far beyond my idiot critiques of our various eccentric personalities or of the hindsight mistakes of our passage through the Great Miranda Rift. These are the table crumbs from a feast of greatness, meant to sustain those who follow.

The sublime truth is that when I am with my wife, Nikhil, and Cathy, I feel elevated above what is merely human. *Then* I sit in the presence of these demigods who challenged, in mortal combat, the will of the Universe—and won.

The author would like to acknowledge the inspiration of Fritz Leiber (''A Pail of Air''), Hal Clement (Still River) and, of course, Jules Verne (A Journey to the Center of the Earth).

MWALIMU IN THE SQUARED CIRCLE

Mike Resnick

▼

Mike Resnick is one of the best-selling authors in science fiction, and one of the most prolific. His many novels include *The Dark Lady, Stalking the Unicorn, Paradise, Santiago, Ivory,* and *Soothsayer.* Of late, he has become almost as prolific as an anthologist, producing, as editor, *Inside the Funhouse: 17 SF stories about SF, Whatdunits, More Whatdunits,* and *Shaggy B.E.M. Stories,* a long string of anthologies coedited with Martin H. Greenberg that includes *Alternate Presidents, Alternate Kennedys, Alternate Warriors, Aladdin: Master of the Lamp,* and *Dinosaur Fantastic* (with several more Resnick/Greenberg anthologies on the way), as well as two anthologies coedited with Gardner Dozois, *Future Earths: Under African Skies* and *Future Earths: Under South American Skies.* He won the Hugo Award in 1989 for "Kirinyaga," one of the most controversial and talked-about stories in recent years. He won another Hugo Award in 1991 for another story in the Kirinyaga series, "The Manumouki." His most recent books (not counting anthologies) are the novels *Prophet, Lucifer Jones,* and *Purgatory,* and the collection *Will the Last Person to Leave the Planet Please Shut Off the Sun?,* and coming soon are new novels, *A Miracle of Rare Design* and *The Widowmaker in Springtime.* His stories have appeared in our Sixth, Seventh, and Ninth Annual Collections. He lives with his wife, Carol, and at least one (no doubt very tired) computer, in Cincinnati, Ohio.

Here he gives us all front-row seats at what surely must be the oddest boxing match in all history, one that has the life or death of millions and the fate of nations riding on it. . . .

> *While this effort was being made, Amin postured: "I challenge President Nyerere in the boxing ring to fight it out there rather than that soldiers lose their lives on the field of battle . . . Muhammad Ali would be an ideal referee for the bout."*
>
> —George Ivan Smith
> *Ghosts of Kampala* (1980)

> *As the Tanzanians began to counterattack, Amin suggested a crazy solution to the dispute. He declared that the matter should be settled*

239

*in the boxing ring. "I am keeping fit so that I can challenge President
Nyerere in the boxing ring and fight it out there, rather than having
the soldiers lose their lives on the field of battle." Amin added that
Muhammad Ali would be an ideal referee for the bout, and that he,
Amin, as the former Uganda heavyweight champ, would give the
small, white-haired Nyerere a sporting chance by fighting with one
arm tied behind his back, and his legs shackled with weights.*
—Dan Wooding and Ray Barnett
Uganda Holocaust (1980)

Nyerere looks up through the haze of blood masking his vision and sees the huge
man standing over him, laughing. He looks into the man's eyes and seems to
see the dark heart of Africa, savage and untamed.

He cannot remember quite what he is doing here. Nothing hurts, but as he
tries to move, nothing works, either. A black man in a white shirt, a man with
a familiar face, seems to be pushing the huge man away, maneuvering him into
a corner. Chuckling and posturing to people that Nyerere cannot see, the huge
man backs away, and now the man in the white shirt returns and begins shouting.

"Four!"

Nyerere blinks and tries to clear his head. Who is he, and why is he on his
back, half-naked, and who are these other two men?

"Five!"

"Stay down, Mwalimu!" yells a voice from behind him, and now it begins
to come back to him. *He* is Mwalimu.

"Six!"

He blinks again and sees the huge electronic clock above him. It is one minute
and fifty-eight seconds into the first round. He is Mwalimu, and if he doesn't get
up, his bankrupt country has lost the war.

"Seven!"

He cannot recall the last minute and fifty-eight seconds. In fact, he cannot
recall anything since he entered the ring. He can taste his blood, can feel it
running down over his eyes and cheeks, but he cannot remember how he came
to be bleeding, or laying on his back. It is a mystery.

"Eight!"

Finally his legs are working again, and he gathers them beneath him. He does
not know if they will bear his weight, but they must be doing so, for Muhammad
Ali—that is his name! Ali—is cleaning his gloves off and staring into his eyes.

"You should have stayed down," whispers Ali.

Nyerere grunts an answer. He is glad that the mouthpiece is impeding his
speech, for he has no idea what he is trying to say.

"I can stop it if you want," says Ali.

Nyerere grunts again, and Ali shrugs and stands aside as the huge man shuffles
across the ring toward him, still chuckling.

It began as a joke. Nobody ever took anything Amin said seriously, except for
his victims.

He had launched a surprise bombing raid in the north of Tanzania. No one knew why, for despite what they did in their own countries, despite what genocide they might commit, the one thing all African leaders had adhered to since Independence was the sanctity of national borders.

So Julius Nyerere, the Mwalimu, the Teacher, the President of Tanzania, had mobilized his forces and pushed Amin's army back into Uganda. Not a single African nation had offered military assistance; not a single Western nation had offered to underwrite so much as the cost of a bullet. Amin had expediently converted to Islam, and now Libya's crazed but opportunistic Quaddafi was pouring money and weapons into Uganda.

Still, Nyerere's soldiers, with their tattered uniforms and ancient rifles, were marching toward Kampala, and it seemed only a matter of time before Amin was overthrown and the war would be ended, and Milton Obote would be restored to the Presidency of Uganda. It was a moral crusade, and Nyerere was convinced that Amin's soldiers were throwing down their weapons and fleeing because they, too, know that Right was on Tanzania's side.

But while Right may have favored Nyerere, Time did not. He knew what the Western press and even the Tanzanian army did not know: that within three weeks, not only could his bankrupt nation no longer supply its men with weapons, it could not even afford to bring them back out of Uganda.

"I challenge President Nyerere in the boxing ring to fight it out there rather than that soldiers lose their lives on the field of battle. . . ."

The challenge made every newspaper in the western world, as columnist after columnist laughed over the image of the 330-pound Amin, former heavyweight champion of the Ugandan army, stepping into the ring to duke it out with the five-foot one-inch, 112-pound, 57-year-old Nyerere.

Only one man did not laugh: Mwalimu.

"You're crazy, you know that?"

Nyerere stares calmly at the tall, well-built man standing before his desk. It is a hot, humid day, typical of Dar es Salaam, and the man is already sweating profusely.

"I did not ask you here to judge my sanity," answers Nyerere. "But to tell me how to defeat him."

"It can't be done. You're spotting him two hundred pounds and twenty years. My job as referee is to keep him from out-and-out killing you."

"You frequently defeated men who were bigger and stronger than you," notes Nyerere gently. "And, in the latter portion of your career, younger than you as well."

"You float like a butterfly and sting like a bee," answers Ali. "But fifty-seven-year-old presidents don't float, and little bitty guys don't sting. I've been a boxer all my life. Have you ever fought anyone?"

"When I was younger," says Nyerere.

"How much younger?"

Nyerere thinks back to the sunlit day, some forty-eight years ago, when he pummeled his brother, though he can no longer remember the reason for it. In his mind's eye, both of them are small and thin and ill-nourished, and the beating amounted to two punches, delivered with barely enough force to stun a fly. The next week he acquired the gift of literacy, and he has never raised a hand in anger again. Words are far more powerful.

Nyerere sighs. "*Much* younger," he admits.

"Ain't no way," says Ali, and then repeats, "Ain't no way. This guy is not just a boxer, he's crazy, and crazy people don't feel no pain."

"How would *you* fight him?" asks Nyerere.

"Me?" says Ali. He starts jabbing the air with his left fist. "Stick and run, stick and run. Take him dancing til he drops. Man's got a lot of blubber on that frame." He holds his arms up before his face. "He catches up with me, I go into the rope-a-dope. I lean back, I take his punches on my forearms, I let him wear himself out." Suddenly he straightens up and turns back to Nyerere. "But it won't work for you. He'll break your arms if you try to protect yourself with them."

"He'll only have one arm free," Nyerere points out.

"That's all he'll need," answers Ali. "Your only shot is to keep moving, to tire him out." He frowns. "But . . ."

"But?"

"But I ain't never seen a fifty-seven-year-old man that could tire out a man in his thirties."

"Well," says Nyerere with an unhappy shrug, "I'll have to think of something."

"Think of letting your soldiers beat the shit out of *his* soldiers," says Ali.

"That is impossible."

"I thought they were winning," said Ali.

"In fourteen days they will be out of ammunition and gasoline," answers Nyerere. "They will be unable to defend themselves and unable to retreat."

"Then give them what they need."

Nyerere shakes his head. "You do not understand. My nation is bankrupt. There is no money to pay for ammunition."

"Hell, I'll loan it to you myself," says Ali. "This Amin is a crazy man. He's giving blacks all over the world a bad name."

"That is out of the question," says Nyerere.

"You think I ain't got it?" says Ali pugnaciously.

"I am sure you are a wealthy man, and that your offer is sincere," answers Nyerere. "But even if you gave us the money, by the time we converted it and purchased what we needed it would be too late. This is the only way to save my army."

"By letting a crazy man tear you apart?"

"By defeating him in the ring before he realizes that he can defeat my men in the field."

"I've seen a lot of things go down in the squared circle," says Ali, shaking his head in disbelief, "but this is the strangest."

*   *   *

"You cannot do this," says Maria when she finally finds out.

"It is done," answers Nyerere.

They are in their bedroom, and he is staring out at the reflection of the moon on the Indian Ocean. As the light dances on the water, he tries to forget the darkness to the west.

"You are not a prizefighter," she says. "You are Mwalimu. No one expects you to meet this madman. The press treats it as a joke."

"I would be happy to exchange doctoral theses with him, but he insists on exchanging blows," says Nyerere wryly.

"He is illiterate," said Maria. "And the people will not allow it. You are the man who brought us independence and who has led us ever since. The people look to you for wisdom, not pugilism."

"I have never sought to live any life but that of the intellect," he admits. "And what has it brought us? While Kenyatta and Mobutu and even Kaunda have stolen hundreds of millions of dollars, we are as poor now as the day we were wed." He shakes his head sadly. "I stand up to oppose Amin, and only Sir Seretse Khama of Botswana, secure in his British knighthood, stands with me." He pauses again, trying to sort it out. "Perhaps the old *mzee* of Kenya was right. Grab what you can while you can. Could our army be any more ill-equipped if I had funneled aid into a Swiss account? Could I be any worse off than now, as I prepare to face this madman in"—he cannot hide his distaste— "a boxing ring?"

"You must *not* face him," insists Maria.

"I must, or the army will perish."

"Do you think he will let the army live after he has beaten you?" she asks.

Nyerere has not thought that far ahead, and now a troubled frown crosses his face.

He had come to the office with such high hopes, such dreams and ambitions. Let Kenyatta play lackey to the capitalist West. Let Machal sell his country to the Russians. Tanzania would be different, a proving ground for African socialism.

It was a dry, barren country without much to offer. There were the great game parks, the Serengeti and the Ngorongoro Crater in the north, but four-fifths of the land was infested with the tsetse fly, there were no minerals beneath the surface, Nairobi was already the capital city of East Africa and no amount of modernization to Dar es Salaam could make it competitive. There was precious little grazing land and even less water. None of this fazed Nyerere; they were just more challenges to overcome, and he had no doubt that he could shape them to his vision.

But before industrialization, before prosperity, before anything else, came education. He had gone from the bush to the presidency in a single lifetime, had translated the entire body of Shakespeare's work into Swahili, had given form and structure to his country's constitution, and he knew that before everything came literacy. While his people lived in grass huts, other men had harnessed the atom, had reached the Moon, had obliterated hundreds of diseases, all because of the written word. And so while Kenyatta became the *Mzee*, the Wise Old Man, he himself became *Mwalimu*. Not the President, not the Leader, not the Chief of Chiefs, but the Teacher.

He would teach them to turn away from the dark heart and reach for the sunlight. He created the *ujamaa* villages, based on the Israeli kibbutzim, and issued the Arusha Declaration, and channeled more than half his country's aid money into the schools. His people's bellies might not be filled, their bodies might not be covered, but they could read, and everything would follow from that.

But what followed was drought, and famine, and disease, and more drought, and more famine, and more disease. He went abroad and described his vision and pleaded for money; what he got were ten thousand students who arrived overflowing with idealism but devoid of funds. They meant well and they worked hard, but they had to be fed, and housed, and medicated, and when they could not mold the country into his utopia in the space of a year or two, they departed.

And then came the madman, the final nail in Tanzania's financial coffin. Nyerere labeled him for what he was, and found himself conspicuously alone on the continent. African leaders simply didn't criticize one another, and suddenly it was the Mwalimu who was the pariah, not the bloodthirsty butcher of Uganda. The East African Union, a fragile thing at best, fell apart, and while Nyerere was trying to save it, Kenyatta, the true capitalist, appropriated all three countries' funds and began printing his own money. Tanzania, already near bankruptcy, was left with money that was not honored anywhere beyond its borders.

Still, he struggled to meet the challenge. If that was the way the *Mzee* wanted to play the game, that was fine with him. He closed the border to Kenya. If tourists wanted to see his game parks, they would have to stay in *his* country; there would be no more round trips from Nairobi. If Amin wanted to slaughter his people, so be it; he would cut off all diplomatic relations, and to hell with what his neighbors thought. Perhaps it was better this way; now, with no outside influence, he could concentrate entirely on creating his utopia. It would be a little more difficult, it would take a little longer, but in the end, the accomplishment would be that much more satisfying.

And then Amin's air force dropped its bombs on Tanzania.

The insanity of it.

Nyerere ducks a roundhouse right, Amin guffaws and winks to the crowd, Ali stands back and wishes he were somewhere else.

Nyerere's vision has cleared, but blood keeps running into his left eye. The fight is barely two minutes old, and already he is gasping for breath. He can feel every beat of his heart, as if a tiny man with a hammer and chisel is imprisoned inside his chest, trying to get out.

The weights attached to Amin's ankles should be slowing him down, but somehow Nyerere finds that he is cornered against the ropes. Amin fakes a punch, Nyerere ducks, then straightens up just in time to feel the full power of the madman's fist as it smashes into his face.

He is down on one knee again, fifty-seven years old and gasping for breath. Suddenly he realizes that no air is coming in, that he is suffocating, and he thinks his heart has stopped . . . but no, he can feel it, still pounding. Then he understands: his nose is broken, and he is trying to breathe through his mouth and the mouthpiece is preventing it. He spits the mouthpiece out, and is mildly surprised to see that it is not covered with blood.

"Three!"

Amin, who has been standing at the far side of the ring, approaches, laughing uproariously, and Ali stops the count and slowly escorts him back to the neutral corner.

The pen is mightier than the sword. The words come, unbidden, into Nyerere's mind, and he wants to laugh. A horrible, retching sound escapes his lips, a sound so alien that he cannot believe it came from him.

Ali slowly returns to him and resumes the count.

"Four!" Stay down, you old fool, Ali's eyes seem to say.

Nyerere grabs a rope and tries to pull himself up.

"Five!" I bought you all the time I could, say the eyes, but I can't protect you if you get up again.

Nyerere gathers himself for the most difficult physical effort of his life.

"Six!" You're as crazy as *he* is.

Nyerere stands up. He hopes Maria will be proud of him, but somehow he knows that she won't.

Amin, mugging to the crowd in a grotesque imitation of Ali, moves in for the kill.

When he was a young man, the president of his class at Uganda's Makerere University, already tabbed as a future leader by his teachers and his classmates, his fraternity entered a track meet, and he was chosen to run the four-hundred-meter race.

I am no athlete, he said; I am a student. I have exams to worry about, a scholarship to obtain. I have no time for such foolishness. But they entered his name anyway, and the race was the final event of the day, and just before it began his brothers came up to him and told him that if he did not beat at least one of his five rivals, his fraternity, which held a narrow lead after all the other events, would lose.

Then you will lose, said Nyerere with a shrug.

If we do, it will be your fault, they told him.

It is just a race, he said.

But it is important to *us*, they said.

So he allowed himself to be led to the starting line, and the pistol was fired, and all six young men began running, and he found himself trailing the field, and he remained in last place all the way around the track, and when he crossed the finish wire, he found that his brothers had turned away from him.

But it was only a game, he protested later. What difference does it make who is the faster? We are here to study laws and vectors and constitutions, not to run in circles.

It is not that you came in last, answered one of them, but that you represented us and you did not try.

It was many days before they spoke to him again. He took to running a mile every morning and every evening, and when the next track meet took place, he volunteered for the four-hundred-meter race again. He was beaten by almost thirty meters, but he came in fourth, and collapsed of exhaustion ten meters past the finish line, and the following morning he was re-elected president of his fraternity by acclamation.

There are forty-three seconds left in the first round, and his arms are too heavy to lift. Amin swings a roundhouse that he ducks, but it catches him on the shoulder and knocks him halfway across the ring. The shoulder goes numb, but it has bought him another ten seconds, for the madman cannot move fast with the weights on his ankles, probably could not move fast even without them. Besides, he is enjoying himself, joking with the crowd, talking to Ali, mugging for all the cameras at ringside.

Ali finds himself between the two men, takes an extra few seconds awkwardly extricating himself—Ali, who has never taken a false or awkward step in his life—and buys Nyerere almost five more seconds. Nyerere looks up at the clock and sees there is just under half a minute remaining.

Amin bellows and swings a blow that will crush his skull if it lands, but it doesn't, the huge Ugandan cannot balance properly with one hand tied behind his back, and he misses and almost falls through the ropes.

"Hit him now!" come the yells from Nyerere's corner.

"Kill him, Mwalimu!"

But Nyerere can barely catch his breath, can no longer lift his arms. He blinks to clear the blood from his eyes, then staggers to the far side of the ring. Maybe it will take Amin twelve or thirteen seconds to get up, spot him, reach him. If he goes down again then, he can be saved by the bell. He will have survived the round. He will have run the race.

Vectors. Angles. The square of the hypotenuse. It's all very intriguing, but it won't help him become a leader. He opts for law, for history, for philosophy.

How was he to know that in the long run they were the same?

He sits in his corner, his nostrils propped open, his cut man working on his eye. Ali comes over and peers intently at him.

"He knocks you down once more, I gotta call it off," he says.

Nyerere tries to answer through battered lips. It is unintelligible. Just as well; for all he knows, he was trying to say, "Please do."

Ali leans closer and lowers his voice.

"It's not just a sport, you know. It's a science, too."

Nyerere utters a questioning croak.

"You run, he's gonna catch you," continues Ali. "A ring ain't a big enough place to hide in."

Nyerere stares at him dully. What is the man trying to say?

"You gotta close with him, grab him. Don't give him room to swing. You do that, maybe I won't have to go to your funeral tomorrow."

Vectors, angles, philosophy, all the same when you're the Mwalimu and you're fighting for your life.

The lion, some four hundred pounds of tawny fury, pulls down the one-ton buffalo.

The hundred-pound hyena runs him off his kill.

The twenty-pound jackal winds up eating it.

And Nyerere clinches with the madman, hangs on for dear life, feels the heavy blows raining down on his back and shoulders, grabs tighter. Ali separates them, positions himself near Amin's right hand so that he can't release the roundhouse, and Nyerere grabs the giant again.

His head is finally clear. The fourth round is coming up, and he hasn't been down since the first. He still can't catch his breath, his legs will barely carry him to the center of the ring, and the blood is once again trickling into his eyes. He looks at the madman, who is screaming imprecations to his seconds, his chest and belly rising and falling.

Is Amin tiring? Does it matter? Nyerere still hasn't landed a single blow. Could even a hundred blows bring the Ugandan to his knees? He doubts it.

Perhaps he should have bet on the fight. The odds were thousands to one that he wouldn't make it this far. He could have supplied his army with the winnings, and died honorably.

It is not the same, he decides, as they rub his shoulders, grease his cheeks, apply ice to the swelling beneath his eye. He has survived the fourth round, has done his best, but it is not the same. He could finish fourth out of six in a foot race and be re-elected, but if he finishes second tonight, he will not have a country left to re-elect him. This is the real world, and surviving, it seems, is not as important as winning.

Ali tells him to hold on, his corner man tells him to retreat, the cut man tells him to protect his eye, but no one tells him how to *win*, and he realizes that he will have to find out on his own.

Goliath fell to a child. Even Achilles had his weakness. What must he do to bring the madman down?

He is crazy, this Amin. He revels in torture. He murders his wives. Rumor has it that he has even killed and eaten his infant son. How do you find weakness in a barbarian like that?

And suddenly, Nyerere realizes, you do it by realizing that he *is* a barbarian—ignorant, illiterate, superstitious.

There is no time now, but he will hold that thought, he will survive one more round of clinching and grabbing, of stifling closeness to the giant whose very presence he finds degrading.

Three more minutes of the sword, and then he will apply the pen.

He almost doesn't make it. Halfway through the round Amin shakes him off like a fly, then lands a right to the head as he tries to clinch again.

Consciousness begins to ebb from him, but by sheer force of will he refuses to relinquish it. He shakes his head, spits blood on the floor of the ring, and stands up once more. Amin lunges at him, and once again he wraps his small, spindly arms around the giant.

"A snake," he mumbles, barely able to make himself understood.

"A snake?" asks the cornerman.

"Draw it on my glove," he says, forcing the words out with an excruciating effort.

"Now?"

"Now," mutters Nyerere.

He comes out for the seventh round, his face a mask of raw, bleeding tissue. As Amin approaches him, he spits out his mouthpiece.

"As I strike, so strikes the snake," he whispers. "Protect your heart, madman." He repeats it in his native Zanake dialect, which the giant thinks is a curse.

Amin's eyes go wide with terror, and he hits the giant on the left breast.

It is the first punch he has thrown in the entire fight, and Amin drops to his knees, screaming.

"One!"

Amin looks down at his unblemished chest and pendulous belly, and seems surprised to find himself still alive and breathing.

"Two!"

Amin blinks once, then chuckles.

"Three!"

The giant gets to his feet, and approaches Nyerere.

"Try again," he says, loud enough for ringside to hear. "Your snake has no fangs."

He puts his hand on his hip, braces his legs, and waits.

Nyerere stares at him for an instant. So the pen is *not* mightier than the sword. Shakespeare might have told him so.

"I'm waiting!" bellows the giant, mugging once more for the crowd.

Nyerere realizes that it is over, that he will die in the ring this night, that he can no more save his army with his fists than with his depleted treasury. He has fought the good fight, has fought it longer than anyone thought he could. At least, before it is over, he will have one small satisfaction. He feints with his left shoulder, then puts all of his strength into one final effort, and delivers a right to the madman's groin.

The air rushes out of Amin's mouth with a *woosh!* and he doubles over, then drops to his knees.

Ali pushes Nyerere into a neutral corner, then instructs the judges to take away a point from him on their scorecards.

They can take away a point, Nyerere thinks, but they can't take away the fact that I met him on the field of battle, that I lasted more than six rounds, that the giant went down twice. Once before the pen, once before the sword.

And both were ineffective.

Even a Mwalimu can learn one last lesson, he decides, and it is that sometimes even vectors and philosophy aren't enough. We must find another way to conquer Africa's dark heart, the madness that pervades this troubled land. I have shown those who will follow me the first step; I have stood up to it, faced it without flinching. It will be up to someone else, a wiser Mwalimu than myself, to learn how to overcome it. I have done my best, I have given my all, I have made the first dent in its armor. Rationality cannot always triumph over madness, but it must stand up and be counted, as I have stood up. They cannot ask any more of me.

Finally at peace with himself, he prepares for the giant's final assault.

GUEST OF HONOR

Robert Reed

▼

Being the Guest of Honor at an important and high-powered function is usually a position to be desired, but, in the decadent world of ultrarich immortals portrayed in the poignant and haunting story that follows, it's an honor you might well be advised to avoid—if you *can*.

A relatively new writer, Robert Reed is a frequent contributor to *The Magazine of Fantasy & Science Fiction*, and he has also sold stories to *Asimov's Science Fiction, Universe, New Destinies, Tomorrow, Synergy*, and elsewhere. His books include the novels *The Lee Shore, The Hormone Jungle, Black Milk, The Remarkables*, and *Down the Bright Way*, and most recently a new novel, *Beyond the Veil of Stars*, has just been published. His stories have appeared in our Ninth and Tenth Annual Collections. He lives in Lincoln, Nebraska.

One of the robots offered to carry Pico for the last hundred meters, on its back or cradled in its padded arms; but she shook her head emphatically, telling it, "Thank you, no. I can make it myself." The ground was grassy and soft, lit by glowglobes and the grass-colored moon. It wasn't a difficult walk, even with her bad hip, and she wasn't an invalid. She could manage, she thought with an instinctive independence. And as if to show them, she struck out ahead of the half-dozen robots as they unloaded the big skimmer, stacking Pico's gifts in their long arms. She was halfway across the paddock before they caught her. By then she could hear the muddled voices and laughter coming from the hill-like tent straight ahead. By then she was breathing fast for reasons other than her pain. For fear, mostly. But it was a different flavor of fear than the kinds she knew. What was happening now was beyond her control, and inevitable . . . and it was that kind of certainty that made her stop after a few more steps, one hand rubbing at her hip for no reason except to delay her arrival. If only for a moment or two. . . .

"Are you all right?" asked one robot.

She was gazing up at the tent, dark and smooth and gently rounded. "I don't want to be here," she admitted. "That's all." Her life on board the *Kyber* had been spent with robots—they had outnumbered the human crew ten to one, then more—and she could always be ruthlessly honest with them. "This is madness. I want to leave again."

"Only, you can't," responded the ceramic creature. The voice was mild, unnervingly patient. "You have nothing to worry about."

"I know."

"The technology has been perfected since—"

"I know."

It stopped speaking, adjusting its hold on the colorful packages.

"That's not what I meant," she admitted. Then she breathed deeply, holding the breath for a moment and exhaling, saying, "All right. Let's go. Go."

The robot pivoted and strode toward the giant tent. The leading robots triggered the doorway, causing it to fold upward with a sudden rush of golden light flooding across the grass, Pico squinting and then blinking, walking faster now and allowing herself the occasional low moan.

"Ever wonder how it'll feel?" Tyson had asked her.

The tent had been pitched over a small pond, probably that very day, and in places the soft, thick grasses had been matted flat by people and their robots. So many people, she thought. Pico tried not to look at any faces. For a moment, she gazed at the pond, shallow and richly green, noticing the tamed waterfowl sprinkled over it and along its shoreline. Ducks and geese, she realized. And some small, crimson-headed cranes. Lifting her eyes, she noticed the large, omega-shaped table near the far wall. She couldn't count the place settings, but it seemed a fair assumption there were sixty-three of them. Plus a single round table and chair in the middle of the omega—*my table*—and she took another deep breath, looking higher, noticing floating glowglobes and several indigo swallows flying around them, presumably snatching up the insects that were drawn to the yellow-white light.

People were approaching. Since she had entered, in one patient rush, all sixty-three people had been climbing the slope while shouting, "Pico! Hello!" Their voices mixed together, forming a noisy, senseless paste. "Greetings!" they seemed to say. "Hello, hello!"

They were brightly dressed, flowing robes swishing and everyone wearing big-rimmed hats made to resemble titanic flowers. The people sharply contrasted with the gray-white shells of the robot servants. Those hats were a new fashion, Pico realized. One of the little changes made during these past decades . . . and finally she made herself look at the faces themselves, offering a forced smile and taking a step backward, her belly aching, but her hip healed. The burst of adrenaline hid the deep ache in her bones. Wrestling one of her hands into a wave, she told her audience, "Hello," with a near-whisper. Then she swallowed and said, "Greetings to you!" Was that her voice? She very nearly didn't recognize it.

A woman broke away from the others, almost running toward her. Her big, flowery hat began to work free, and she grabbed the fat, petalish brim and began to fan herself with one hand, the other hand touching Pico on the shoulder. The palm was damp and quite warm; the air suddenly stank of overly sweet perfumes. It was all Pico could manage not to cough. The woman—what was her name?— was asking, "Do you need to sit? We heard . . . about your accident. You poor girl. All the way fine, and then on the last world. Of all the luck!"

Her hip. The woman was jabbering about her sick hip.

Pico nodded and confessed, "Sitting would be nice, yes."

A dozen voices shouted commands. Robots broke into runs, racing one another around the pond to grab the chair beside the little table. The drama seemed to make people laugh. A nervous, self-conscious laugh. When the lead robot reached the chair and started back, there was applause. Another woman shouted, "Mine won! Mine won!" She threw her hat into the air and tried to follow it, leaping as high as possible.

Some man cursed her sharply, then giggled.

Another man forced his way ahead, emerging from the packed bodies in front of Pico. He was smiling in a strange fashion. Drunk or drugged . . . what was permissible these days? With a sloppy, earnest voice, he asked, "How'd it happen? The hip thing . . . how'd you do it?"

He should know. She had dutifully filed her reports throughout the mission, squirting them home. Hadn't he seen them? But then she noticed the watchful, excited faces—no exceptions—and someone seemed to read her thoughts, explaining, "We'd love to hear it *firsthand*. Tell, tell, tell!"

As if they needed to hear a word, she thought, suddenly feeling quite cold.

Her audience grew silent. The robot arrived with the promised chair, and she sat and stretched her bad leg out in front of her, working to focus her mind. It was touching, their silence . . . reverent and almost childlike . . . and she began by telling them how she had tried climbing Miriam Prime with two other crew members. Miriam Prime was the tallest volcano on a brutal super-Venusian world; it was brutal work because of the terrain and their massive lifesuits, cumbersome refrigeration units strapped to their backs, and the atmosphere thick as water. Scalding and acidic. Carbon dioxide and water made for a double greenhouse effect. . . And she shuddered, partly for dramatics and partly from the memory. Then she said, "Brutal," once again, shaking her head thoughtfully.

They had used hyperthreads to climb the steepest slopes and the cliffs. Normally hyperthreads were virtually unbreakable; but Miriam was not a normal world. She described the basalt cliff and the awful instant of the tragedy; the clarity of the scene startled her. She could feel the heat seeping into her suit, see the dense, dark air, and her arms and legs shook with exhaustion. She told sixty-three people how it felt to be suspended on an invisible thread, two friends and a winch somewhere above in the acidic fog. The winch had jammed without warning, she told; the worst bad luck made it jam where the thread was its weakest. This was near the mission's end, and all the equipment was tired. Several dozen alien worlds had been visited, many mapped for the first time, and every one of them examined up close. As planned.

"Everything has its limits," she told them, her voice having an ominous quality that she hadn't intended.

Even hyperthreads had limits. Pico was dangling, talking to her companions by radio; and just as the jam was cleared, a voice saying, "There . . . got it!", the thread parted. He didn't have any way to know it had parted. Pico was falling, gaining velocity, and the poor man was ignorantly telling her, "It's running strong. You'll be up in no time, no problem. . . ."

People muttered to themselves.

"Oh my," they said.

"Gosh."

"Shit."

Their excitement was obvious, perhaps even overdone. Pico almost laughed, thinking they were making fun of her storytelling . . . thinking, *What do they know about such things?* . . . Only, they were sincere, she realized a moment later. They were enraptured with the image of Pico's long fall, her spinning and lashing out with both hands, fighting to grab anything and slow her fall any way possible—

—and she struck a narrow shelf of eroded stone, the one leg shattered and telescoping down to a gruesome stump. Pico remembered the painless shock of the impact and that glorious instant free of all sensation. She was alive, and the realization had made her giddy. Joyous. Then the pain found her head—a great nauseating wave of pain—and she heard her distant friends shouting, "Pico? Are you there? Can you hear us? Oh Pico . . . *Pico?* Answer us!"

She had to remain absolutely motionless, sensing that any move would send her tumbling again. She answered in a whisper, telling her friends that she was alive, yes, and please, please hurry. But they had only a partial thread left, and it would take them more than half an hour to descend . . . and she spoke of her agony and the horror, her hip and leg screaming, and not just from the impact. It was worse than mere broken bone, the lifesuit's insulation damaged and the heat bleeding inward, slowly and thoroughly cooking her living flesh.

Pico paused, gazing out at the round-mouthed faces.

So many people and not a breath of sound; and she was having fun. She realized her pleasure almost too late, nearly missing it. Then she told them, "I nearly died," and shrugged her shoulders. "All the distances traveled, every imaginable adventure . . . and I nearly died on one of our last worlds, doing an ordinary climb. . . ."

Let them appreciate her luck, she decided. *Their luck.*

Then another woman lifted her purple flowery hat with both hands, pressing it flush against her own chest. "Of course you survived!" she proclaimed. "You wanted to come home, Pico! You couldn't stand the thought of *dying.*"

Pico nodded without comment, then said, "I was rescued. Obviously." She flexed the damaged leg, saying, "I never really healed," and she touched her hip with reverence, admitting, "We didn't have the resources on board the *Kyber.* This was the best our medical units could do."

Her mood shifted again, without warning. Suddenly she felt sad to tears, eyes dropping and her mouth clamped shut.

"We worried about you, Pico!"

"All the time, dear!"

". . . in our prayers . . . !"

Voices pulled upon each other, competing to be heard. The faces were smiling and thoroughly sincere. Handsome people, she was thinking. Clean and civilized and older than her by centuries. Some of them were more than a thousand years old.

Look at them! she told herself.

And now she felt fear. Pulling both legs toward her chest, she hugged herself, weeping hard enough to dampen her trouser legs; and her audience said, "But you made it, Pico! You came home! The wonders you've seen, the places you've actually touched . . . with those hands. . . . And we're so proud of you! So proud! You've proven your worth a thousand times, Pico! You're made of the very best stuff—!"

—which brought laughter, a great clattering roar of laughter, the joke obviously and apparently tireless.

Even after so long.

They were Pico; Pico was they.

Centuries ago, during the Blossoming, technologies had raced forward at an unprecedented rate. Starships like the *Kyber* and a functional immortality had allowed the first missions to the distant worlds, and there were some grand adventures. Yet adventure requires some element of danger; exploration has never been a safe enterprise. Despite precautions, there were casualties. People who had lived for centuries died suddenly, oftentimes in stupid accidents; and it was no wonder that after the first wave of missions came a long moratorium. No new starships were built, and no sensible person would have ridden inside even the safest vessel. Why risk yourself? Whatever the benefits, why taunt extinction when you have a choice.

Only recently had a solution been invented. Maybe it was prompted by the call of deep space, though Tyson used to claim, "It's the boredom on Earth that inspired them. That's why they came up with their elaborate scheme."

The near-immortals devised ways of making highly gifted, highly trained crews from themselves. With computers and genetic engineering, groups of people could pool their qualities and create compilation humans. Sixty-three individuals had each donated moneys and their own natures, and Pico was the result. She was a grand and sophisticated average of the group. Her face was a blending of every face; her body was a feminine approximation of their own varied bodies. In a few instances, the engineers had planted synthetic genes—for speed and strength, for example—and her brain had a subtly different architecture. Yet basically Pico was their offspring, a stewlike clone. The second of two clones, she knew. The first clone created had had subtle flaws, and he was painlessly destroyed just before birth.

Pico and Tyson and every other compilation person had been born at adult size. Because she was the second attempt, and behind schedule, Pico was thrown straight into her training. Unlike the other crew members, she had spent only a minimal time with her parents. Her sponsors. Whatever they were calling themselves. That and the long intervening years made it difficult to recognize faces and names. She found herself gazing out at them, believing they were strangers, their tireless smiles hinting at something predatory. The neat white teeth gleamed at her, and she wanted to shiver again, holding the knees closer to her mouth.

Someone suggested opening the lovely gifts.

A good idea. She agreed, and the robots brought down the stacks of boxes, placing them beside and behind her. The presents were a young tradition; when she was leaving Earth, the first compilation people were returning with little souvenirs of their travels. Pico had liked the gesture and had done the same. One after another, she started reading the names inscribed in her own flowing handwriting. Then each person stepped forward, thanking her for the treasure, then greedily unwrapping it, the papers flaring into bright colors as they were bent and twisted and torn, then tossed aside for the robots to collect.

She knew none of these people, and that was wrong. What she should have done, she realized, was go into the *Kyber*'s records and memorize names and faces. It would have been easy enough, and proper, and she felt guilty for never having made the effort.

It wasn't merely genetics that she shared with these people; she also embodied slivers of their personalities and basic tendencies. Inside Pico's sophisticated womb, the computers had blended together their shrugs and tongue clicks and the distinctive patterns of their speech. She had emerged as an approximation of every one of them; yet why didn't she feel a greater closeness? Why wasn't there a strong, tangible bond here?

Or was there something—only, she wasn't noticing it?

One early gift was a slab of mirrored rock. "From Tween V," she explained. "What it doesn't reflect, it absorbs and reemits later. I kept that particular piece in my own cabin, fixed to the outer wall—"

"Thank you, thank you," gushed the woman.

For an instant, Pico saw herself reflected on the rock. She looked much older than these people. Tired, she thought. Badly weathered. In the cramped starship, they hadn't the tools to revitalize aged flesh, nor had there been the need. Most of the voyage had been spent in cold-sleep. Their waking times, added together, barely exceeded forty years of biological activity.

"Look at this!" the woman shouted, turning and waving her prize at the others. "Isn't it lovely?"

"A shiny rock," teased one voice. "Perfect!"

Yet the woman refused to be anything but impressed. She clasped her prize to her chest and giggled, merging with the crowd and then vanishing.

They look like children, Pico told herself.

At least how she imagined children to appear . . . unworldly and spoiled, needing care and infinite patience. . . .

She read the next name, and a new woman emerged to collect her gift. "My, what a large box!" She tore at the paper, then the box's lid, then eased her hands into the dunnage of white foam. Pico remembered wrapping this gift—one of the only ones where she was positive of its contents—and she happily watched the smooth, elegant hands pulling free a greasy and knob-faced nut. Then Pico explained:

"It's from the Yult Tree on Proxima Centauri 2." The only member of the species on that strange little world. "If you wish, you can break its dormancy with liquid nitrogen. Then plant it in pure quartz sand, never anything else. Sand, and use red sunlight—"

"I know how to cultivate them," the woman snapped.

There was a sudden silence, uneasy and prolonged.

Finally Pico said, "Well . . . good. . . ."

"Everyone knows about Yult nuts," the woman explained. "They're practically giving them away at the greeneries now."

Someone spoke sharply, warning her to stop and think.

"I'm sorry," she responded. "If I sound ungrateful, I mean. I was just thinking, hoping . . . I don't know. Never mind."

A weak, almost inconsequential apology, and the woman paused to feel the grease between her fingertips.

The thing was, Pico thought, that she had relied on guesswork in selecting these gifts. She had decided to represent every alien world, and she felt proud of herself on the job accomplished. Yult Trees were common on Earth? But how could she know such a thing? And besides, why should it matter? She had brought the nut and everything else because she'd taken risks, and these people were obviously too ignorant and silly to appreciate what they were receiving.

Rage had replaced her fear.

Sometimes she heard people talking among themselves, trying to trade gifts. Gemstones and pieces of alien driftwood were being passed about like orphans. Yet nobody would release the specimens of odd life-forms from living worlds, transparent canisters holding bugs and birds and whatnot inside preserving fluids or hard vacuums. If only she had known what she couldn't have known, these silly brats. . . . And she found herself swallowing, holding her breath, and wanting to scream at all of them.

Pico was a compilation, yet she wasn't.

She hadn't lived one day as these people had lived their entire lives. She didn't know about comfort or changelessness, and with an attempt at empathy, she tried to imagine such an incredible existence.

Tyson used to tell her, "Shallowness is a luxury. Maybe the ultimate luxury." She hadn't understood him. Not really. "Only the rich can master true frivolity." Now those words echoed back at her, making her think of Tyson. That intense and angry man . . . the opposite of frivolity, the truth told.

And with that, her mood shifted again. Her skin tingled. She felt nothing for or against her audience. How could they help being what they were? How could anyone help their nature? And with that, she found herself reading another name on another unopened box. A little box, she saw. Probably another one of the unpopular gemstones, born deep inside an alien crust and thrown out by forces unimaginable. . . .

There was a silence, an odd stillness, and she repeated the name.

"Opera? Opera Ting?"

Was it her imagination, or was there a nervousness running through the audience? Just what was happening—?

"Excuse me?" said a voice from the back. "Pardon?"

People began moving aside, making room, and a figure emerged. A male, something about him noticeably different. He moved with a telltale lightness, with a spring to his gait. Smiling, he took the tiny package while saying, "Thank you," with great feeling. "For my father, thank you. I'm sure he would have enjoyed this moment. I only wish he could have been here, if only. . . ."

Father? Wasn't this Opera Ting?

Pico managed to nod, then she asked, "Where is he? I mean, is he busy somewhere?"

"Oh no. He died, I'm afraid." The man moved differently because he was different. He was young—even younger than I, Pico realized—and he shook his head, smiling in a serene way. Was he a clone? A biological child? What? "But on his behalf," said the man, "I wish to thank you. Whatever this gift is, *I* will treasure it. I promise you. I know you must have gone through hell to find it and bring it to me, and thank you so very much, Pico. Thank you, thank you. Thank you!"

Death.

An appropriate intruder in the evening's festivities, thought Pico. Some accident, some kind of tragedy . . . something had killed one of her sixty-three parents, and that thought pleased her. There was a pang of guilt woven into her pleasure, but not very much. It was comforting to know that even these people weren't perfectly insulated from death; it was a force that would grasp everyone, given time. Like it had taken Midge, she thought. And Uoo, she thought. *And Tyson.*

Seventeen compiled people had embarked on *Kyber*, representing almost a thousand near-immortals. Only nine had returned, including Pico. Eight friends were lost. . . . *Lost* was a better word than *death*, she decided. . . . And usually it happened in places worse than any Hell conceived by human beings.

After Opera—his name, she learned, was the same as his father's—the giving of the gifts settled into a routine. Maybe it was because of the young man's attitude. People seemed more polite, more self-contained. Someone had the presence to ask for another story. Anything she wished to tell. And Pico found herself thinking of a watery planet circling a distant red-dwarf sun, her voice saying, "Coldtear," and watching faces nod in unison. They recognized the name, and it was too late. It wasn't the story she would have preferred to tell, yet she couldn't seem to stop herself. Coldtear was on her mind.

Just tell parts, she warned herself.

What you can stand!

The world was terran-class and covered with a single ocean frozen on its surface and heated from below. By tides, in part. And by Coldtear's own nuclear decay. It had been Tyson's idea to build a submersible and dive to the ocean's remote floor. He used spare parts in *Kyber*'s machine shop—the largest room on board—then he'd taken his machine to the surface, setting it on the red-stained ice and using lasers and robot help to bore a wide hole and keep it clear.

Pico described the submersible, in brief, then mentioned that Tyson had asked her to accompany him. She didn't add that they'd been lovers now and again, nor that sometimes they had feuded. She'd keep those parts of the story to herself for as long as possible.

The submersible's interior was cramped and ascetic, and she tried to impress her audience with the pressures that would build on the hyperfiber hull. Many times the pressure found in Earth's oceans, she warned; and Tyson's goal was to set down on the floor, then don a lifesuit protected with a human-shaped force field, actually stepping outside and taking a brief walk.

"Because we need to leave behind footprints," he had argued. "Isn't that why we've come here? We can't just leave prints up on the ice. It moves and melts, wiping itself clean every thousand years or so."

"But isn't that the same below?" Pico had responded. "New muds rain down—slowly, granted—and quakes cause slides and avalanches."

"So we pick right. We find someplace where our marks will be quietly covered. Enshrouded. Made everlasting."

She had blinked, surprised that Tyson cared about such things.

"I've studied the currents," he explained, "and the terrain—"

"Are you serious?" Yet you couldn't feel certain about Tyson. He was a creature full of surprises. "All this trouble, and for what—?"

"Trust me, Pico. Trust me!"

Tyson had had an enormous laugh. His parents, sponsors, whatever—an entirely different group of people—had purposefully made him larger than the norm. They had selected genes for physical size, perhaps wanting Tyson to dominate the *Kyber*'s crew in at least that one fashion. If his own noise was to be believed, that was the only tinkering done to him. Otherwise, he was a pure compilation of his parents' traits, fiery and passionate to a fault. It was a little unclear to Pico what group of people could be so uniformly aggressive; yet Tyson had had his place in their tight-woven crew, and he had had his charms in addition to his size and the biting intelligence.

"Oh Pico," he cried out. "What's this about, coming here? If it's not about leaving traces of our passage . . . then *what*?"

"It's about going home again," she had answered.

"Then why do we leave the *Kyber*? Why not just orbit Coldtear and send down our robots to explore?"

"Because. . . ."

"Indeed! Because!" The giant head nodded, and he put a big hand on her shoulder. "I knew you'd see my point. I just needed to give you time, my friend."

She agreed to the deep dive, but not without misgivings.

And during their descent, listening to the ominous creaks and groans of the hull while lying flat on their backs, the misgivings began to reassert themselves.

It was Tyson's fault, and maybe his aim.

No, she thought. It was most definitely his aim.

At first, she thought it was some game, him asking, "Do you ever wonder how it will feel? We come home and are welcomed, and then our dear parents disassemble our brains and implant them—"

"Quiet," she interrupted. "We agreed. Everyone agreed. We aren't going to talk about it, all right?"

A pause, then he said, "Except, I know. How it feels, I mean."

She heard him, then she listened to him take a deep breath from the close, damp air; and finally she had strength enough to ask, "How can you know?"

When Tyson didn't answer, she rolled onto her side and saw the outline of his face. A handsome face, she thought. Strong and incapable of any doubts. This was the only taboo subject among the compilations—"How will it feel?"—and it was left to each of them to decide what they believed. Was it a fate or a reward? To be subdivided and implanted into the minds of dozens and dozens of near-immortals. . . .

It wasn't a difficult trick, medically speaking.

After all, each of their minds had been designed for this one specific goal. Memories and talent; passion and training. All of the qualities would be saved—diluted, but, in the same instant, gaining their own near-immortality. Death of a sort, but a kind of everlasting life, too.

That was the creed by which Pico had been born and raised.

The return home brings a great reward, and peace.

Pico's first memory was of her birth, spilling slippery-wet from the womb and coughing hard, a pair of doctoring robots bent over her, whispering to her, "Welcome, child. Welcome. You've been born from *them* to be joined with *them* when it is time. . . . We promise you . . . !"

Comforting noise, and mostly Pico had believed it.

But Tyson had to say, "I know how it feels, Pico," and she could make out his grin, his amusement patronizing. Endless.

"How?" she muttered. "How do you know—?"

"Because some of my parents . . . well, let's just say that I'm not their first time. Understand me?"

"They made another compilation?"

"One of the very first, yes. Which was incorporated into them before I was begun, and which was incorporated into me because there was a spare piece. A leftover chunk of the mind—"

"You're making this up, Tyson!"

Except, he wasn't, she sensed. Knew. Several times, on several early worlds, Tyson had seemed too knowledgeable about too much. Nobody could have prepared himself that well, she realized. She and the others had assumed that Tyson was intuitive in some useful way. Part of him was from another compilation? From someone like them? A fragment of the man had walked twice beside the gray dust sea of Pliicker, and it had twice climbed the giant ant mounds on Proxima Centauri 2. It was a revelation, unnerving and hard to accept; and just the memory of that instant made her tremble secretly, facing her audience, her tired blood turning to ice.

Pico told none of this to her audience.

Instead, they heard about the long descent and the glow of rare life-forms outside—a thin plankton consuming chemical energies as they found them—and, too, the growing creaks of the spherical hull.

They didn't hear how she asked, "So how does it feel? You've got a piece of compilation inside you . . . all right! Are you going to tell me what it's like?"

They didn't hear about her partner's long, deep laugh.

Nor could they imagine him saying, "Pico, my dear. You're such a passive, foolish creature. That's why I love you. So docile, so damned innocent—"

"Does it live inside you, Tyson?"

"It depends on what you consider life."

"Can you feel its presence? I mean, does it have a personality? An existence? Or have you swallowed it all up?"

"I don't think I'll tell." Then the laugh enlarged, and the man lifted his legs and kicked at the hyperfiber with his powerful muscles. She could hear, and feel, the solid impacts of his bootheels. She knew that Tyson's strength was nothing compared to the ocean's mass bearing down on them, their hull scarcely feeling the blows . . . yet some irrational part of her was terrified. She had to reach out, grasping one of his trouser legs and tugging hard, telling him:

"Don't! Stop that! Will you please . . . quit!?"

The tension shifted direction in an instant.

Tyson said, "I was lying," and then added, "About knowing. About having a compilation inside me." And he gave her a huge hug, laughing in a different way now. He nearly crushed her ribs and lungs. Then he spoke into one of her ears, offering more, whispering with the old charm, and she accepting his offer. They did it as well as possible, considering their circumstances and the endless groaning of their tiny vessel; and she remembered all of it while her voice, detached but thorough, described how they had landed on top of something rare. There was a distinct *crunch* of stone. They had made their touchdown on the slope of a recent volcano—an island on an endless plain of mud—and afterward they dressed in their lifesuits, triple-checked their force fields, then flooded the compartment and crawled into the frigid, pressurized water.

It was an eerie, almost indescribable experience to walk on that ocean floor. When language failed Pico, she tried to use silence and oblique gestures to capture the sense of endless time and the cold and darkness. Even when Tyson ignited the submersible's outer lights, making the nearby terrain bright as late afternoon, there was the palpable taste of endless dark just beyond. She told of feeling the pressure despite the force field shrouding her; she told of climbing after Tyson, scrambling up a rough slope of youngish rock to a summit where they discovered a hot-water spring that pumped heated, mineral-rich water up at them.

That might have been the garden spot of Coldtear. Surrounding the spring was a thick, almost gelatinous mass of gray-green bacteria, pulsating and fat by its own standards. She paused, seeing the scene all over again. Then she assured her parents, "It had a beauty. I mean it. An elegant, minimalist beauty."

Nobody spoke.

Then someone muttered, "I can hardly wait to remember it," and gave a weak laugh.

The audience became uncomfortable, tense and too quiet. People shot accusing looks at the offender, and Pico worked not to notice any of it. A bitterness was building in her guts, and she sat up straighter, rubbing at both hips.

Then a woman coughed for attention, waited, and then asked, "What happened next?"

Pico searched for her face.

"There was an accident, wasn't there? On Coldtear . . . ?"

I won't tell them, thought Pico. Not now. Not this way.

She said, "No, not then. Later." And maybe some of them knew better. Judging by the expressions, a few must have remembered the records. Tyson died on the first dive. It was recorded as being an equipment failure—Pico's lie—and she'd hold on to the lie as long as possible. It was a promise she'd made to herself and kept all these years.

Shutting her eyes, she saw Tyson's face smiling at her. Even through the thick faceplate and the shimmering glow of the force field, she could make out the mischievous expression, eyes glinting, the large mouth saying, "Go on back, Pico. In and up and a safe trip to you, pretty lady."

She had been too stunned to respond, gawking at him.

"Remember? I've still got to leave my footprints somewhere—"

"What are you planning?" she interrupted.

He laughed and asked, "Isn't it obvious? I'm going to make my mark on this world. It's dull and nearly dead, and I don't think anyone is ever going to return here. Certainly not to *here*. Which means I'll be pretty well left alone—"

"Your force field will drain your batteries," she argued stupidly. Of course he knew that salient fact. "If you stay here—!"

"I know, Pico. I know."

"But why—?"

"I lied before. About lying." The big face gave a disappointed look, then the old smile reemerged. "Poor, docile Pico. I knew you wouldn't take this well. You'd take it too much to heart . . . which I suppose is why I asked you along in the first place . . ." And he turned away, starting to walk through the bacterial mat with threads and chunks kicked loose, sailing into the warm current and obscuring him. It was a strange gray snow moving against gravity. Her last image of Tyson was of a hulking figure amid the living goo; and to this day, she had wondered if she could have wrestled him back to the submersible—an impossibility, of course—and how far could he have walked before his force field failed.

Down the opposite slope and onto the mud, no doubt.

She could imagine him walking fast, using his strength . . . fighting the deep, cold muds . . . Tyson plus that fragment of an earlier compilation—and who was driving whom? she asked herself. Again and again and again.

Sometimes she heard herself asking Tyson, "How does it feel having a sliver of another soul inside you?"

His ghost never answered, merely laughing with his booming voice.

She hated him for his suicide, and admired him; and sometimes she cursed him for taking her along with him and for the way he kept cropping up in her thoughts. . . . "Damn you, Tyson. Goddamn you, goddamn you . . . !"

No more presents remained.

One near-immortal asked, "Are we hungry?", and others replied, "Famished," in one voice, then breaking into laughter. The party moved toward the distant tables, a noisy mass of bodies surrounding Pico. Her hip had stiffened while sitting, but she worked hard to move normally, managing the downslope toward the pond and then the little wooden bridge spanning a rocky brook. The waterfowl made grumbling sounds, angered by the disturbances; Pico stopped and watched them, finally asking, "What kinds are those?" She meant the ducks.

"Just mallards," she heard. "Nothing fancy."

Yet, to her, they seemed like miraculous creatures, vivid plumage and the moving eyes, wings spreading as a reflex and their nervous motions lending them a sense of muscular power. A vibrancy.

Someone said, "You've seen many birds, I'm sure."

Of a sort, yes. . . .

"What were your favorites, Pico?"

They were starting uphill, quieter now, feet making a swishing sound in the grass; and Pico told them about the pterosaurs of Wilder, the man-sized bats on Little Quark, and the giant insects—a multitude of species—thriving in the thick, warm air of Tau Ceti I.

"Bugs," grumbled someone. "Uggh!"

"Now, now," another person responded.

Then a third joked, "I'm not looking forward to *that*. Who wants to trade memories?"

A joke, thought Pico, because memories weren't tradable properties. Minds were holographic—every piece held the basic picture of the whole—and these people each would receive a sliver of Pico's whole self. Somehow that made her smile, thinking how none of them would be spared. Every terror and every agony would be set inside each of them. In a diluted form, of course. The *Pico-ness* minimized. Made manageable. Yet it was something, wasn't it? It pleased her to think that a few of them might awaken in the night, bathed in sweat after dreaming of Tyson's death . . . just as she had dreamed of it time after time . . . her audience given more than they had anticipated, a dark little joke of her own. . . .

They reached the tables, Pico taking hers and sitting, feeling rather self-conscious as the others quietly assembled around her, each of them knowing where they belonged. She watched their faces. The excitement she had sensed from the beginning remained; only, it seemed magnified now. More colorful, more intense. Facing toward the inside of the omega, her hosts couldn't quit staring, forever smiling, scarcely able to eat once the robots brought them plates filled with steaming foods.

Fancy meals, Pico learned.

The robot setting her dinner before her explained, "The vegetables are from Triton, miss. A very special and much-prized strain. And the meat is from a wild hound killed just yesterday—"

"Really?"

"As part of the festivities, yes." The ceramic face, white and expressionless, stared down at her. "There have been hunting parties and games, among other diversions. Quite an assortment of activities, yes."

"For how long?" she asked. "These festivities . . . have they been going on for days?"

"A little longer than three months, miss."

She had no appetite; nonetheless, she lifted her utensils and made the proper motions, reminding herself that three months of continuous parties would be nothing to these people. Three months was a day to them, and what did they do with their time? So much of it, and such a constricted existence. What had Tyson once told her? The average citizen of Earth averages less than one off-world trip in eighty years, and the trends were toward less traveling. Spaceflight was safe only to a degree, and these people couldn't stand the idea of being meters away from a cold, raw vacuum.

"Cowards," Tyson had called them. "Gutted, deblooded cowards!"

Looking about, she saw the delicate twists of green leaves vanishing into grinning mouths, the chewing prolonged and indifferent. Except for Opera, that is. Opera saw her and smiled back in turn, his eyes different, something mocking about the tilt of his head and the curl of his mouth.

She found her eyes returning to Opera every little while, and she wasn't sure why. She felt no physical attraction for the man. His youth and attitudes made him different from the others, but how much different? Then she noticed his dinner—cultured potatoes with meaty hearts—and that made an impression on Pico. It was a standard food on board the *Kyber*. Opera was making a gesture, perhaps. Nobody else was eating that bland food, and she decided this was a show of solidarity. At least the man was trying, wasn't he? More than the others, he was. He was.

Dessert was cold and sweet and shot full of some odd liquor.

Pico watched the others drinking and talking among themselves. For the first time, she noticed how they seemed subdivided—discrete groups formed, and boundaries between each one. A dozen people here, seven back there, and sometimes individuals sitting alone—like Opera—chatting politely or appearing entirely friendless.

One lonesome woman rose to her feet and approached Pico, not smiling, and with a sharp voice, she declared, "Tomorrow, come morning . . . you'll live forever . . . !"

Conversations diminished, then quit entirely.

"Plugged in. Here." She was under the influence of some drug, the tip of her finger shaking and missing her own temple. "You fine lucky girl. . . . Yes, you are . . . !"

Some people laughed at the woman, suddenly and without shame.

The harsh sound made her turn and squint, and Pico watched her straightening her back. The woman was pretending to be above them and uninjured, her thin mouth squeezed shut and her nose tilting with mock pride. With a clear, soft voice, she said, "Fuck every one of you," and then laughed, turning toward Pico, acting as if they had just shared some glorious joke of their own.

"I would apologize for our behavior," said Opera, "but I can't. Not in good faith, I'm afraid."

Pico eyed the man. Dessert was finished; people stood about drinking, keeping the three-month-old party in motion. A few of them stripped naked and swam in the green pond. It was a raucous scene, tireless and full of happy scenes that never seemed convincingly joyous. Happy sounds by practice, rather. Centuries of practice, and the result was to make Pico feel sad and quite lonely.

"A silly, vain lot," Opera told her.

She said, "Perhaps," with a diplomatic tone, then saw several others approaching. At least they looked polite, she thought. Respectful. It was odd how a dose of respect glossed over so much. Particularly when the respect wasn't reciprocated, Pico feeling none toward them. . . .

A man asked to hear more stories. Please?

Pico shrugged her shoulders, then asked, "Of what?" Every request brought her a momentary sense of claustrophobia, her memories threatening to crush her. "Maybe you're interested in a specific world?"

Opera responded, saying, "Blueblue!"

Blueblue was a giant gaseous world circling a bluish sun. Her first thought was of Midge vanishing into the dark storm on its southern hemisphere, searching for the source of the carbon monoxide upflow that effectively gave breath to half the world. Most of Blueblue was calm in comparison. Thick winds; strong sunlight. Its largest organisms would dwarf most cities, their bodies balloonlike and their lives spent feeding on sunlight and hydrocarbons, utilizing carbon monoxide and other radicals in their patient metabolisms. Pico and the others had spent several months living on the living clouds, walking across them, taking samples and studying the assortment of parasites and symbionts that grew in their flesh.

She told about sunrise on Blueblue, remembering its colors and its astounding speed. Suddenly she found herself talking about a particular morning when the landing party was jostled out of sleep by an apparent quake. Their little huts had been strapped down and secured, but they found themselves tilting fast. Their cloud was colliding with a neighboring cloud—something they had never seen— and of course there was a rush to load their shuttle and leave. If it came to that.

"Normally, you see, the clouds avoid each other," Pico told her little audience. "At first, we thought the creatures were fighting, judging by their roaring and the hard shoving. They make sounds by forcing air through pores and throats and anuses. It was a strange show. Deafening. The collision point was maybe a third of a kilometer from camp, our whole world rolling over while the sun kept rising, its bright, hot light cutting through the organic haze—"

"Gorgeous," someone said.

A companion said, "Quiet!"

Then Opera touched Pico on the arm, saying, "Go on. Don't pay any attention to them."

The others glanced at Opera, hearing something in his voice, and their backs stiffening reflexively.

And then Pico was speaking again, finishing her story. Tyson was the first one of them to understand, who somehow made the right guess and began laughing, not saying a word. By then everyone was on board the shuttle, ready to fly; the tilting stopped suddenly, the air filling with countless little blue balloons. Each was the size of a toy balloon, she told. Their cloud was bleeding them from new pores, and the other cloud responded with a thick gray fog of butterflylike somethings. The somethings flew after the balloons, and Tyson laughed harder, his face contorted and the laugh finally shattering into a string of gasping coughs.

"Don't you see?" he asked the others. "Look! The clouds are enjoying a morning screw!"

Pico imitated Tyson's voice, regurgitating the words and enthusiasm. Then she was laughing for herself, scarcely noticing how the others giggled politely. No more. Only Opera was enjoying her story, again touching her arm and saying, "That's lovely. Perfect. God, precious . . . !"

The rest began to drift away, not quite excusing themselves.

What was wrong?

"Don't mind them," Opera cautioned. "They're members of some new chastity faith. Clarity through horniness, and all that." He laughed at them now. "They probably went to too many orgies, and this is how they're coping with their guilt. That's all."

Pico shut her eyes, remembering the scene on Blueblue for herself. She didn't want to relinquish it.

"Screwing clouds," Opera was saying. "That is lovely."

And she thought:

He sounds a little like Tyson. In places. In ways.

After a while, Pico admitted. "I can't remember your father's face. I'm sure I must have met him, but I don't—"

"You did meet him," Opera replied. "He left a recording of it in his journal— a brief meeting—and I made a point of studying everything about the mission and you. His journal entries; your reports. Actually, I'm the best-prepared person here today. Other than you, of course."

She said nothing, considering those words.

They were walking now, making their way down to the pond, and sometimes Pico noticed the hard glances of the others. Did they approve of Opera? Did it anger them, watching him monopolizing her time? Yet she didn't want to be with *them*, the truth told. Fuck them, she thought; and she smiled at her private profanity.

The pond was empty of swimmers now. There were just a few sleepless ducks and the roiled water. A lot of the celebrants had vanished, Pico realized. To where? She asked Opera, and he said:

"It's late. But then again, most people sleep ten or twelve hours every night."

"That much?"

He nodded. "Enhanced dreams are popular lately. And the oldest people sometimes exceed fifteen hours—"

"Always?"

He shrugged and offered a smile.

"What a waste!"

"Of time?" he countered.

Immortals can waste many things, she realized. But never time. And with that thought, she looked straight at her companion, asking him, "What happened to your father?"

"How did he die, you mean?"

A little nod. A respectful expression, she hoped. But curious.

Opera said, "He used an extremely toxic poison, self-induced." He gave a vague disapproving look directed at nobody. "A suicide at the end of a prolonged depression. He made certain that his mind was ruined before autodocs and his own robots could save him."

"I'm sorry."

"Yet I can't afford to feel sorry," he responded. "You see, I was born according to the terms of his will. I'm 99 percent his clone, the rest of my genes tailored according to his desires. If he hadn't murdered himself, I wouldn't exist. Nor would I have inherited his money." He shrugged, saying, "Parents," with a measured scorn. "They have such power over you, like it or not."

She didn't know how to respond.

"Listen to us. All of this death talk, and doesn't it seem out of place?" Opera said, "After all, we're here to celebrate your return home. Your successes. Your gifts. And you . . . you on the brink of being magnified many times over." He paused before saying, "By this time tomorrow, you'll reside inside all of us, making everyone richer as a consequence."

The young man had an odd way of phrasing his statements, the entire speech either earnest or satirical. She couldn't tell which. Or if there was a *which*. Maybe it was her ignorance with the audible clues, the unknown trappings of this culture. . . . Then something else occurred to her.

"What do you mean? 'Death talk. . . .' "

"Your friend Tyson died on Coldtear," he replied. "And didn't you lose another on Blueblue?"

"Midge. Yes."

He nodded gravely, glancing down at Pico's legs. "We can sit. I'm sorry; I should have noticed you were getting tired."

They sat side by side on the grass, watching the mallard ducks. Males and females had the same vivid green heads. Beautiful, she mentioned. Opera explained how females were once brown and quite drab, but people thought that was a shame, and voted to have the species altered, both sexes made equally resplendent. Pico nodded, only halfway listening. She couldn't get Tyson and her other dead friends out of her mind. Particularly Tyson. She had been angry with him for a long time, and even now her anger wasn't finished. Her confusion and general tiredness made it worse. Why had he done it? In life the man had had a way of dominating every meeting, every little gathering. He had been optimistic and fearless, the last sort of person to do such an awful thing. Suicide. The others had heard it was an accident—Pico had held to her lie—but she and they were in agreement about one fact. When Tyson died, at that precise instant, some essential heart of their mission had been lost.

Why? she wondered. Why?

Midge had flown into the storm on Blueblue, seeking adventure and important scientific answers; and her death was sad, yes, and everyone had missed her. But it wasn't like Tyson's death. It felt honorable, maybe even perfect. They had a duty to fulfill in the wilderness, and that duty was in their blood and their training. People spoke about Midge for years, acting as if she were still alive. As if she were still flying the shuttle into the storm's vortex.

But Tyson was different.

Maybe everyone knew the truth about his death. Sometimes it seemed that, in Pico's eyes, the crew could see what had really happened, and they'd hear it between her practiced lines. They weren't fooled.

Meanwhile, others died in the throes of life.

Uoo—a slender wisp of a compilation—was incinerated by a giant bolt of lightning on Miriam II, little left but ashes, and the rest of the party continuing its descent into the superheated Bottoms and the quiet Lead Sea.

Opaltu died in the mouth of a nameless predator. He had been another of Pico's lovers, a proud man and the best example of vanity that she had known— until today, she thought—and she and the others had laughed at the justice that befell Opaltu's killer. Unable to digest alien meats, the predator had sickened and died in a slow, agonizing fashion, vomiting up its insides as it staggered through the yellow jungle.

Boo was killed while working outside the *Kyber*, struck by a mote of interstellar debris.

Xon's lifesuit failed, suffocating her.

As did Kyties's suit, and that wasn't long ago. Just a year now, ship time, and she remembered a cascade of jokes and his endless good humor. The most decent person on board the *Kyber*.

Yet it was Tyson who dominated her memories of the dead. It was the man as well as his self-induced extinction, and the anger within her swelled all at once. Suddenly even simple breathing was work. Pico found herself sweating, then blinking away the salt in her eyes. Once, then again, she coughed into a fist; then finally she had the energy to ask, "Why did he do it?"

"Who? My father?"

"Depression is . . . should be . . . a curable ailment. We had drugs and therapies on board that could erase it."

"But it was more than depression. It was something that attacks the very old people. A kind of giant boredom, if you will."

She wasn't surprised. Nodding as if she'd expected that reply, she told him,

"I can understand that, considering your lives." Then she thought how Tyson hadn't been depressed or bored. How could he have been either?

Opera touched her bad leg, for just a moment. "You must wonder how it will be," he mentioned. "Tomorrow, I mean."

She shivered, aware of the fear returning. Closing her burning eyes, she saw Tyson's walk through the bacterial mat, the loose gray chunks spinning as the currents carried them, lending them a greater sort of life with the motion. . . . And she opened her eyes, Opera watching, saying something to her with his expression, and her unable to decipher any meanings.

"Maybe I should go to bed, too," she allowed.

The park under the tent was nearly empty now. Where had the others gone?

Opera said, "Of course," as if expecting it. He rose and offered his hand, and she surprised herself by taking the hand with both of hers. Then he said, "If you like, I can show you your quarters."

She nodded, saying nothing.

It was a long, painful walk, and Pico honestly considered asking for a robot's help. For anyone's. Even a cane would have been a blessing, her hip never having felt so bad. Earth's gravity and the general stress were making it worse, most likely. She told herself that at least it was a pleasant night, warm and calm and perfectly clear, and the soft ground beneath the grass seemed to be calling to her, inviting her to lie down and sleep in the open.

People were staying in a chain of old houses subdivided into apartments, luxurious yet small. Pico's apartment was on the ground floor, Opera happy to show her through the rooms. For an instant, she considered asking him to stay the night. Indeed, she sensed that he was delaying, hoping for some sort of invitation. But she heard herself saying, "Rest well, and thank you," and her companion smiled and left without comment, vanishing through the crystal front door and leaving her completely alone.

For a little while, she sat on her bed, doing nothing. Not even thinking, at least in any conscious fashion.

Then she realized something, no warning given; and aloud, in a voice almost too soft for even her to hear, she said, "He didn't know. Didn't have an idea, the shit." Tyson. She was thinking about the fiery man and his boast about being the second generation of star explorers. What if it was all true? His parents had injected a portion of a former Tyson into him, and he had already known the early worlds they had visited. He already knew the look of sunrises on the double desert world around Alpha Centauri A; he knew the smell of constant rot before they cracked their airlocks on Barnard's 2. But try as he might—

"—he couldn't remember how it feels to be disassembled." She spoke without sound. To herself. "That titanic and fearless creature, and he couldn't remember. Everything else, yes, but not that. And not knowing had to scare him. Nothing else did, but that terrified him. The only time in his life he was truly scared, and it took all his bluster to keep that secret—!"

Killing himself rather than face his fear.

Of course, she thought. Why not?

And he took Pico as his audience, knowing she'd be a good audience. Because they were lovers. Because he must have decided that he could convince her of his fearlessness one last time, leaving his legend secure. Immortal, in a sense.

That's what you were thinking . . .

. . . wasn't it?

And she shivered, holding both legs close to her mouth, and feeling the warm misery of her doomed hip.

She sat for a couple more hours, neither sleeping nor feeling the slightest need for sleep. Finally she rose and used the bathroom, and after a long, careful look through the windows, she ordered the door to open, and stepped outside, picking a reasonable direction and walking stiffly and quickly on the weakened leg.

Opera emerged from the shadows, startling her.

"If you want to escape," he whispered, "I can help. Let me help you, please."

The face was handsome in the moonlight, young in every fashion. He must have guessed her mood, she realized, and she didn't allow herself to become upset. Help was important, she reasoned. Even essential. She had to find her way across a vast and very strange alien world. "I want to get back into orbit," she told him, "and find another starship. We saw several. They looked almost ready to embark." Bigger than the *Kyber*, and obviously faster. No doubt designed to move even deeper into the endless wilderness.

"I'm not surprised," Opera told her. "And I understand."

She paused, staring at him before asking, "How did you guess?"

"Living forever inside our heads. . . . That's just a mess of metaphysical nonsense, isn't it? You know you'll die tomorrow. Bits of your brain will vanish inside us, made part of us, and not vice versa. I think it sounds like an awful way to die, certainly for someone like you—"

"Can you really help me?"

"This way," he told her. "Come on."

They walked for an age, crossing the paddock and finally reaching the wide tube where the skimmers shot past with a rush of air. Opera touched a simple control, then said, "It won't be long," and smiled at her. Just for a moment. "You know, I almost gave up on you. I thought I must have read you wrong. You didn't strike me as someone who'd go quietly to her death. . . ."

She had a vague, fleeting memory of the senior Opera. Gazing at the young face, she could recall a big, warm hand shaking her hand, and a similar voice saying, "It's very good to meet you, Pico. At last!"

"I bet one of the new starships will want you." The young Opera was telling her, "You're right. They're bigger ships, and they've got better facilities. Since they'll be gone even longer, they've been given the best possible medical equipment. That hip and your general body should respond to treatments—"

"I have experience," she whispered.

"Pardon me?"

"Experience." She nodded with conviction. "I can offer a crew plenty of valuable experience."

"They'd be idiots not to take you."

A skimmer slowed and stopped before them. Opera made the windows opaque—"So nobody can see you"—and punched in their destination, Pico making herself comfortable.

"Here we go," he chuckled, and they accelerated away.

There was an excitement to all of this, an adventure like every other. Pico realized that she was scared, but in a good, familiar way. Life and death. Both possibilities seemed balanced on a very narrow fulcrum, and she found herself smiling, rubbing her hip with a slow hand.

They were moving fast, following Opera's instructions.

"A circuitous route," he explained. "We want to make our whereabouts less obvious. All right?"

"Fine."

"Are you comfortable?"

"Yes," she allowed. "Basically."

Then she was thinking about the others—the other survivors from the *Kyber*—wondering how many of them were having second or third thoughts. The long journey home had been spent in cold-sleep, but there had been intervals when two or three of them were awakened to do normal maintenance. Not once did anyone even joke about taking the ship elsewhere. Nobody had asked, "Why do we have to go to Earth?" The obvious question had eluded them, and at the time, she had assumed it was because there were no doubters. Besides herself, that is. The rest believed this would be the natural conclusion to full and satisfied lives; they were returning home to a new life and an appreciative audience. How could any sane compilation think otherwise?

Yet she found herself wondering.

Why no jokes?

If they hadn't had doubts, wouldn't they have made jokes?

Eight others had survived the mission. Yet none were as close to Pico as she had been to Tyson. They had saved each other's proverbial skin many times, and she did feel a sudden deep empathy for them, remembering how they had boarded nine separate shuttles after kisses and hugs and a few careful tears, each of them struggling with the proper things to say. But what could anyone say at such a moment? Particularly when you believed that your companions were of one mind, and, in some fashion, happy. . . .

Pico said, "I wonder about the others," and intended to leave it at that. To say nothing more.

"The others?"

"From the *Kyber*. My friends." She paused and swallowed, then said softly, "Maybe I could contact them."

"No," he responded.

She jerked her head, watching Opera's profile.

"That would make it easy to catch you." His voice was quite sensible and measured. "Besides," he added, "can't they make up their own minds? Like you have?"

She nodded, thinking that was reasonable. Sure.

He waited a long moment, then said, "Perhaps you'd like to talk about something else?"

"Like what?"

He eyed Pico, then broke into a wide smile. "If I'm not going to inherit a slice of your mind, leave me another story. Tell . . . I don't know. Tell me about your favorite single place. Not a world, but some favorite patch of ground on any world. If you could be anywhere now, where would it be? And with whom?"

Pico felt the skimmer turning, following the tube. She didn't have to consider the question—her answer seemed obvious to her—but the pause was to collect herself, weighing how to begin and what to tell.

"In the mountains on Erindi 3," she said, "the air thins enough to be breathed safely, and it's really quite pretty. The scenery, I mean."

"I've seen holos of the place. It is lovely."

"Not just lovely." She was surprised by her authority, her self-assured voice telling him, "There's a strange sense of peace there. You don't get that from holos. Supposedly it's produced by the weather and the vegetation. . . . They make showers of negative ions, some say. . . . And it's the colors, too. A subtle interplay of shades and shadows. All very one-of-a-kind."

"Of course," he said carefully.

She shut her eyes, seeing the place with almost perfect clarity. A summer storm had swept overhead, charging the glorious atmosphere even further, leaving everyone in the party invigorated. She and Tyson, Midge, and several others had decided to swim in a deep-blue pool near their campsite. The terrain itself was rugged, black rocks erupting from the blue-green vegetation. The valley's little river poured into a gorge and the pool, and the people did the same. Tyson was first, naturally. He laughed and bounced in the icy water, screaming loud enough to make a flock of razor-bats take flight. This was only the third solar system they had visited, and they were still young in every sense. It seemed to them that every world would be this much fun.

She recalled—and described—diving feet first. She was last into the pool, having inherited a lot of caution from her parents. Tyson had teased her, calling her a coward and then worse, then showing where to aim. "Right here! It's deep here! Come on, coward! Take a chance!"

The water was startlingly cold, and there wasn't much of it beneath the shiny flowing surface. She struck and hit the packed sand below, and the impact made her groan, then shout. Tyson had lied, and she chased the bastard around the pool, screaming and finally clawing at his broad back until she'd driven him up the gorge walls, him laughing and once, losing strength with all the laughing, almost tumbling down on top of her.

She told Opera everything.

At first, it seemed like an accident. All her filters were off; she admitted everything without hesitation. Then she told herself that the man was saving her life and deserved the whole story. That's when she was describing the lovemaking between her and Tyson. That night. It was their first time, and maybe the best time. They did it on a bed of mosses, perched on the rim of the gorge, and she tried to paint a vivid word picture for her audience, including smells and the textures and the sight of the double moons overhead, colored a strange living pink and moving fast.

Their skimmer ride seemed to be taking a long time, she thought once she was finished. She mentioned this to Opera, and he nodded soberly. Otherwise, he made no comment.

I won't be disembodied tomorrow, she told herself.

Then she added, *Today, I mean today.*

She felt certain now. Secure. She was glad for this chance and for this dear new friend, and it was too bad she'd have to leave so quickly, escaping into the relative safety of space. Perhaps there were more people like Opera . . . people who would be kind to her, appreciating her circumstances and desires . . . supportive and interesting companions in their own right. . . .

And suddenly the skimmer was slowing, preparing to stop.

When Opera said, "Almost there," she felt completely at ease. Entirely calm. She shut her eyes and saw the raw, wild mountains on Erindi 3, storm clouds gathering and flashes of lightning piercing the howling winds. She summoned a different day, and saw Tyson standing against the storms, smiling, beckoning for her to climb up to him just as the first cold, fat raindrops smacked against her face.

The skimmer's hatch opened with a hiss.

Sunlight streamed inside, and she thought: *Dawn. By now, sure. . . .*

Opera rose and stepped outside, then held a hand out to Pico. She took it with both of hers and said, "Thank you," while rising, looking past him and seeing the paddock and the familiar faces, the green ground and the giant tent with its doorways opened now, various birds flying inside and out again . . . and Pico most surprised by how little she was surprised, Opera still holding her hands, and his flesh dry, the hand perfectly calm.

The autodocs stood waiting for orders.

This time, Pico had been carried from the skimmer, riding cradled in a robot's arms. She had taken just a few faltering steps before half-crumbling. Exhaustion was to blame. Not fear. At least it didn't feel like fear, she told herself. Everyone told her to take it easy, to enjoy her comfort; and now, finding herself flanked by autodocs, her exhaustion worsened. She thought she might die before the cutting began, too tired now to pump her own blood or fire her neurons or even breathe.

Opera was standing nearby, almost smiling, his pleasure serene and chilly and without regrets.

He hadn't said a word since they left the skimmer.

Several others told her to sit, offering her a padded seat with built-in channels to catch any flowing blood. Pico took an uneasy step toward the seat, then paused and straightened her back, saying, "I'm thirsty," softly, her words sounding thoroughly parched.

"Pardon?" they asked.

"I want to drink . . . some water, please . . . ?"

Faces turned, hunting for a cup and water.

It was Opera who said, "Will the pond do?" Then he came forward, extending an arm and telling everyone else, "It won't take long. Give us a moment, will you?"

Pico and Opera walked alone.

Last night's ducks were sleeping and lazily feeding. Pico looked at their metallic green heads, so lovely that she ached at seeing them, and she tried to miss nothing. She tried to concentrate so hard that time itself would compress, seconds turning to hours, and her life in that way prolonged.

Opera was speaking, asking her, "Do you want to hear why?"

She shook her head, not caring in the slightest.

"But you must be wondering why. I fool you into believing that I'm your ally, and I manipulate you—"

"Why?" she sputtered. "So tell me."

"Because," he allowed, "it helps the process. It helps your integration into us. I gave you a chance for doubts and helped you think you were fleeing, convinced you that you'd be free . . . and now you're angry and scared and intensely alive. It's that intensity that we want. It makes the neurological grafts take hold. It's a trick that we learned since the *Kyber* left Earth. Some compilations tried to escape, and when they were caught and finally incorporated along with their anger—"

"Except, I'm not angry," she lied, gazing at his self-satisfied grin.

"A nervous system in flux," he said. "I volunteered, by the way."

She thought of hitting him. Could she kill him somehow?

But instead, she turned and asked, "Why this way? Why not just let me slip away, then catch me at the spaceport?"

"You were going to drink," he reminded her. "Drink."

She knelt despite her hip's pain, knees sinking into the muddy bank and her lips pursing, taking in a long, warmish thread of muddy water, and then her face lifting, the water spilling across her chin and chest, and her mouth unable to close tight.

"Nothing angers," he said, "like the betrayal of someone you trust."

True enough, she thought. Suddenly she could see Tyson leaving her alone on the ocean floor, his private fears too much, and his answer being to kill himself while dressed up in apparent bravery. A kind of betrayal, wasn't that? To both of them, and it still hurt. . . .

"Are you still thirsty?" asked Opera.

"Yes," she whispered.

"Then drink. Go on."

She knelt again, taking a bulging mouthful and swirling it with her tongue. Yet she couldn't make herself swallow, and after a moment, it began leaking out from her lips and down her front again. Making a mess, she realized. Muddy, warm, ugly water, and she couldn't remember how it felt to be thirsty. Such a little thing, and ordinary, and she couldn't remember it.

"Come on, then," said Opera.

She looked at him.

He took her arm and began lifting her, a small, smiling voice saying, "You've done very well, Pico. You have. The truth is that everyone is very proud of you."

She was on her feet again and walking, not sure when she had begun moving her legs. She wanted to poison her thoughts with her hatred of these awful people, and for a little while, she could think of nothing else. She would make her mind bilious and cancerous, poisoning all of these bastards and finally destroying them. That's what she would do, she promised herself. Except, suddenly she was sitting on the padded chair, autodocs coming close with their bright, humming limbs; and there was so much stored in her mind—worlds and people, emotions heaped on emotions—and she didn't have the time she would need to poison herself.

Which proved something, she realized.

Sitting still now.

Sitting still and silent. At ease. Her front drenched and stained brown, but her open eyes calm and dry.

LOVE TOYS OF THE GODS

Pat Cadigan

▼

Here's a very funny look at one of the real stories *behind* those lurid headlines in tabloid newspapers that you scan while waiting in the checkout line in the supermarket—but *this* story Dares to Tell All . . . and then some! You may never be able to read the word "UFO" again without laughing. . . .

Pat Cadigan was born in Schenectady, New York, and now lives in Overland Park, Kansas. She made her first professional sale in 1980, and has subsequently come to be regarded as one of the best new writers in SF. She was the coeditor, along with husband Arnie Fenner, of *Shayol*, perhaps the best of the semiprozines of the late seventies; it was honored with a World Fantasy Award in the "Special Achievement, Non-Professional" category in 1981. She has also served as Chairman of the Nebula Award Jury and was a World Fantasy Award Judge. Her first novel, *Mindplayers*, was released in 1987 to excellent critical response, and her second novel, *Synners*, appeared in 1991 to even *better* response, as well as winning the prestigious Arthur C. Clarke Award. Her third novel, *Fools*, came out in 1992, and she is currently at work on a fourth, tentatively entitled *Parasites*. Her story "Pretty Boy Crossover" has recently appeared on several critics' lists as among the best science fiction stories of the 1980s; her story "Angel" was a finalist for the Hugo Award, the Nebula Award, *and* the World Fantasy Award (one of the few stories ever to earn that rather unusual distinction); and her collection *Patterns* has been hailed as one of the landmark collections of the decade. Her stories have appeared in our First, Second, Third, Fourth, Fifth, Sixth, Ninth, and Tenth Annual Collections. Her most recent book is a major new collection, *Dirty Work*.

The night Jimmy-Ray Carver got nailed by the alien, he ran five miles without stopping, all the way to Bill Sharkey's house, and busted in on our card game, screaming and yelling and carrying on like a sackful of crazed weasels. Good sex will do that to a person.

We all just sat and watched while Bill poured three fingers of Wild Turkey and tried to get the glass up to Jimmy-Ray's mouth without losing any, which was interesting enough that we all start laying bets as to whether Jimmy-Ray's gonna get outside of the Turkey or not and if he does, is he gonna puke it right up again on account of being over-excited and all. Shows you what kind of cards we were holding—talk about a cold deck.

Well, eventually Bill gets him sat down on the couch with the glass in his hand and Jimmy-Ray comes back to himself enough to know what he was holding and he starts sipping on it, calming down a lot although the hand holding the glass was shaking pretty hard still. So we all say fuck it and toss in the cards and Bart Vesey collects the pot because he bet that Jimmy-Ray was gonna keep the booze down, and we're all surprised and he ain't. Bart's always had a lot of faith in long shots.

"I'm standin' there in the little woods back of my house," Jimmy-Ray starts saying for about the millionth time, "and all of a sudden, there she is, right over my head and not a sound, swear to Christ not a sound, and then I can't move, I'm frozen there with my head up and then there's this bright light in my eyes and the next thing I know, it's like beam-me-up-Scotty—"

It wasn't like anything you couldn't have read in any supermarket tabloid, but we all sat and listened because Jimmy-Ray's one of us and he needed us to. Only Al Miller looked bored, but that's Al. If he was any more bored, they'd have him down to County Medical on a respirator.

"—what it was, but it's lookin' at me and I'm lookin' at it, I mean, I'm *tryin'* to look at it but that light's all funny and my eyes can't focus, and then I'm feelin' the *goddamnedest* thing, someone touching me—touching me"—Jimmy Ray looks around at all of us, scared-like—"touching me in my *head*."

Al Miller yawned right in his face but Jimmy-Ray's still freaking too much to pick up on this particular social cue. All Jimmy-Ray knows is, nobody threw a net over him yet so it's okay to go on.

"There's something lookin' through my head like somebody leafin' through a magazine and then it hits on what it was lookin' for all along, I guess and—" He stops to take a drink and he's gotta hold the glass with two hands. "Oh, Jesus, even I don't believe this, but it happened. I *know* it happened." He looks around at all of us again and Bill gives him a pat on the shoulder.

"You go on and say, Jimmy-Ray," Bill says. "You're among friends here."

"Yeah," Jimmy-Ray says, like he's not so goddam sure about *that*. "It was just like when I was down in the little woods. One moment I'm one place and the next moment I'm another and *wham!* like that, I'm in this thing that's like a cross between a hammock and a *trapeze*—"

I'm impressed. I sneak a look at Bart, who's kinda smilin' to himself while he's suckin' on a can of Rolling Rock.

"—and I'm all het up like I'm fifteen years old and I got a free ticket to the fanciest cathouse in the world—"

Het up. Only Jimmy-Ray would have used an expression like that. But that was Jimmy-Ray all over. If he'd been anybody else, he'd have just been calling himself plain old Jim. Grandmother raised him in church; what can you do?

"—I don't even know what it is and I don't even care, like I'm goin' for some kinda world record, look out, it's John Henry the steel-drivin' man—"

Bill makes him take some of the Turkey and winks at the rest of us.

"—and then, oh, Jesus, Jesus, no, I can't tell you this part," Jimmy-Ray pants.

"Now, now, I already told you, you are among friends." Bill pats his shoulder and looks to me. "Right, Fred?"

"Right," I say, and toast him with my own can of Rolling Rock, just because I feel like I should do something right then.

"Damn straight," adds Jack and Bart says, "You betcha," and Al goes, "Uh-huh," through another yawn.

"You don't *got* to tell what you don't want to," Bill goes on, "but if it'll make you feel better, spit it out and don't worry."

Jimmy-Ray's eyes look like a trapped animal's but what he's got to say is too big to hold inside. "It had me," he says hoarsely. "I mean, it had me." He lets his breath out in a rush, shaking his head and staring at the booze like he was gonna see something in it. "And it wasn't against my will, either." Now he looks around at all of us with his chin kinda lifted up, defiant, waiting for someone to call him something. "I said, 'Oh, you want to have me? You have me, go ahead and have me, any old thing you want.' And I guess I know what you-all think that makes me, and maybe I'd think it myself but, son of a bitch, I still don't know what it was, whether it was a woman or a man or both or neither or chocolate frozen yogurt. But I swear to you as I'm sittin' here, it was *the best*, the *goddam best* that I have ever been through. And fellas, I'm *scared*."

He finishes the Turkey and Bill pours him two more fingers. Jimmy-Ray gulps down half of it and I see Bill take the bottle off the end table and put it out of sight. First aid's one thing, but he's not letting Jimmy-Ray get tanked on the good stuff. If he wants to get hammered now, Bill will point him toward the Rolling Rock in the fridge.

"I'm scared because either I lost my mind and it didn't happen, or it did happen and now I'm a—I'm a—I'm a alien-fucker! Like all those people in them papers in the supermarket. And I don't know what it mighta done to me—aw, hell, what if it laid some eggs inside me and next week they come bustin' out like in that movie—"

Jimmy-Ray goes positively gray at the thought and Bill puts the bottle of Wild Turkey back on the end table. "Now don't go gettin' all hysterical again, JR," he says in a fatherly voice. "There's some things we all know and some things we'll never know, but I can assure you beyond the shadow of a doubt that you ain't in the family way."

Jimmy-Ray blinks at him.

"You ain't pregnant," Bill says patiently. "No eggs, no need to go worryin' that you're gonna belly-out or explode or anything."

"You believe me?" Jimmy-Ray goes bug-eyed again, which makes me think of how we used to think aliens was bug-eyed monsters but the only bug-eyes I ever seen are right here in front of me.

"Well, of *course* I believe you. We all do. Anybody here *not* believe Jimmy-Ray?"

Jimmy-Ray looks at all of us and we're all shaking our heads. "I believe you," Bart says, and I give him thumbs-up and Al gives him a good view of his tonsils with another yawn.

"See?" Bill says. "Told you you were among friends."

"Well," Jimmy-Ray says doubtfully. "Don't think it's like I don't appreciate it or nothin' but . . . *why*? Why do *you* all believe me when I can't hardly believe it myself?"

"Well why do you *think*?" Al says, yawning again. "Hell, do you *really* think you're the first person ever met up with a Unidentified Fuckin' Object?"

"Say *what*?" Jimmy-Ray turns to me, maybe because I'm sitting right next to him on the couch, or maybe because he's married to my second cousin, which makes us legal if distant family.

"Jimmy," I say, "we all believe you because we know you're tellin' the truth. We *know*. Okay?"

"You got to spell it out for him, Fred," Jack says, laughing a little. "We *all* been where you been tonight, guy. Welcome to the Alien-Fuckers Club, glad you could make it. I'd say that calls for a toast."

Bill gives him a look as he takes the Wild Turkey off the end table again. If Jack wants to toast, he can do it with his can; Bill ain't pouring him any of the Turkey, which is what we all know Jack's hoping. Bill starts to say something to Jimmy-Ray, but Jimmy-Ray's looking around at all of us like we've all sprouted two heads and there's horns on both of them.

"You're lyin'," he says, and I can see in those scared, trapped-animal eyes he knows we're not. "You're all lyin' because you think I'm crazy and in a minute, one of you's gonna go say he's gotta call his wife, but really, you'll be callin' County Medical to come throw a net over me, put me in a canvas jacket in the psycho ward—"

Even while he's saying it, I can tell he would prefer this to the other, and why he would is beyond me, but there you have it. "No such of a thing," Jack says, pointing a finger at him. "Come on, pull yourself together. Unless you're not plannin' to go home tonight."

Jimmy-Ray's eyes bugged out *again*. "Oh, sweet Jesus. How the hell am I gonna go home to Karen after this?"

"Well, that's something else we can tell you," Bill says, smiling. "Don't worry, it didn't spoil you for humans. I like women as much as *I* ever did. Maybe even more than I ever did. They ain't aliens, but it's all a matter of acceptin' everyone for what they are and not penalizin' 'em for not bein' what they ain't."

Jimmy-Ray's mouth has dropped open and I can't tell whether it's the alien stuff or Bill's preaching the gospel of tolerance that's got him so shocked. "Nah . . . nah . . . wait a minute here . . ." He looks at Bill and then me and then Jack. "It's a put-on," he says. "It's a joke. Y'all drugged my food and set me up."

"That'd be a neat trick," Bart says. "Tell me, how'd we get into your house and figure what you were eatin' tonight? How'd we get Karen to go along with it? And while we're at it, who'd we set you up with? I sure do want to meet her. Or I would if I hadn't met the alien first."

"Jesus," Jimmy-Ray says and his eyes get so big I'm sure they're gonna just roll right out on the carpet like marbles. "Jesus, you mean to tell me—you mean to *tell* me—"

"Seems like we just *did* tell you," Al says, too bored to live. "Now will you just for chrissakes pull it together here? We all got wild the first time and even the second time, and we had to take Bill's truck out and drive along behind Jack his third and fourth times because he was runnin' up and down the roads and we was afraid he'd get hit by a car. But we all got adjusted and you can, too, if you put your mind right."

"But—but what about your wives?" Jimmy-Ray says, not to Bill who lost Sara in a car wreck nine years ago, but to the rest of us.

"What *about* my wife?" Jack says, a little belligerent. "You want to say something about my wife, you better make it a compliment. And a tasteful one, too."

"How can you do this to them?" Jimmy-Ray says in a little hoarse voice, and then puts a hand to his head like he can't believe he's asking this.

"I'm not doing anything bad to *my* wife," Bart says.

"Nor me," adds Jack. "I love Irene and I respect her."

"But you just told me you're all goin' to this alien—and then you go home? To your wives?" Jimmy-Ray shook his head. "God, what if they *knew*?"

"Who said they don't?" says Al, too bored even to yawn now. "Come on, what do you think this is, 1955?"

"A wife isn't just a part of the furniture, you know," Jack says. "She's a whole person in her own right, and she's entitled to a life of her own besides what she shares with you."

I *almost* bust out laughing at the expression on Jimmy-Ray's face while he's hearing this stuff come out of Jack Foley, who looks like the kind of redneck who might proudly announce that he believes in beating his wife once a week whether she needs it or not. Which just goes to show you that looks don't tell you much.

"Listen here, Jimmy," I say, "we all been through some changes since the alien came." Jimmy-Ray gives me the fish-eye. "Uh, showed up, I mean. They ain't bad changes, either. I know that, even if they ain't the kind of changes your pastor would give his blessing to." I paused, thinking. "Well, actually, *your* pastor would. *Now.* Well, anyway, we're all different. And that's all of us I'm talkin' about, which includes wives."

Jimmy-Ray's blinking and his mouth is opening and closing and he doesn't know whether to shit or go blind. Then he turns green, shoves his glass at me, runs to the bathroom, and pukes like there's no tomorrow.

After a bit, Bill goes to see to him while Jack tells Bart he ought to turn the pot over to him because he'd bet Jimmy-Ray would puke and Bart's arguing that the puking time-limit has expired. Al's too bored to referee and I'm too tired. I go and call Joan and tell her I'll be a little late tonight. Somebody's got to take Jimmy-Ray home and I'm the only one going in that direction.

On the way to Jimmy-Ray's, I keep talking sense to him, quiet and calm, hoping he'll catch some of my mellow and smooth out. He still looks like he's seen a ghost or ten, but at least he's not freaking anymore. That's probably more the Turkey finally kicking in. By the time I leave him off in his front yard, he's bleary enough that I know he'll just go straight to bed and pass out. In the morning, maybe he'll just figure it was some kind of weird dream, which will let him cope okay for a while, until the alien picks him up again. After his second time, I figure, he'll straighten out, understand what a good thing it is we all got going here. Might take a third time, but Jimmy-Ray's young, not even thirty-five, and the younger you are, the faster you adjust.

And that just goes to show you how wrong a person can be. A little over a week later, I get a phone call from Bill right after supper. "Fred, you gotta get out here to my place. It's Jimmy-Ray."

"What happened?" I say. "Alien pick him up again already?"

"Nah. I don't wanna get into it on the phone. Just get your ass out here fast as you can."

I'd have been imagining all kinds of things except I didn't know what to think, so I just get my ass out to Bill's place and there's Jack and Bart and Al and it ain't poker night.

"That goddam Jimmy-Ray," Al is saying, almost showing a little life. "I say we call County Medical and have them send out the guys with the nets. What the fuck, who would argue?"

"What's he done?" I say, getting myself a can of Rolling Rock from the fridge.

"Oh, this is a good one," Bill says. "The little fucker went and talked, is what he done."

"Talked? To who?"

"To anybody and everybody he could get on the phone. He called every paper and TV and radio station in a five hundred mile radius and when they put him off, he called a bunch of those other papers, those fuckin' scandal rags that run all the stories about two-headed babies and guys that eat their own foot. They're comin' out to his place tomorrow to get the whole story and take pictures of the little woods behind his house."

I laugh like hell. "Well, so what? Jimmy-Ray gets his picture in a tabloid next to the story about the latest Elvis sighting. That should pretty much take care of him."

"Sure, it would," Jack says, all grim, "if the FBI weren't comin', too."

I think my chin hits the floor. "Jimmy-Ray called the FBI and they just said, 'Okay, Mr. Carver, we'll be right over'?"

"Not on the first call," Bill says, and lays it out for me. Jimmy-Ray called the FBI ten times a day every day for like three days until they sent a couple agents out. Apparently, that's how the FBI deals with cranks, all the people who call up and claim the KGB is controlling their thoughts with microwaves from space satellites and all that shit—they actually send out a couple of agents to talk to them and give them a story about how they checked on the microwaves and set up a machine to block them, nothing more to worry about, blah, blah, blah. It humors the cranks and gives the agents a chance to decide if they're harmless nutsoids or the kind of flakes who'd think they had to go assassinate the president on orders from space creatures.

So the FBI paid Jimmy-Ray a visit and somehow he got them out in the little woods and they found something—traces of the beam the alien used to pick him up, still sticking to some underbrush or something. Now *that* was a real stunner, because none of us ever saw anything in the way of traces or evidence, but Bart said he thought it was because Jimmy-Ray had spread so much poison around out there, trying to kill all the ticks. Jimmy-Ray was scared shitless he'd get Lyme Disease. The poison must have reacted to the beam somehow, and whatever the reaction was, it was strange enough that the FBI guys took samples back to their lab to get analyzed. Nobody knew exactly what the results were, but the FBI was coming back with a whole lab team.

Jimmy-Ray got back on the horn and called all over to tell everyone about that development, and there was going to be a regular media circus out at Jimmy-Ray's place in the morning.

"Yeah, but still, so what?" I says. "Whatever the FBI lab guys find still ain't gonna prove there was a UFO or a alien, just that Jimmy-Ray put a lotta poison in the little woods. You can't tell me the FBI believes it's anything *like* aliens—"

"Prob'ly they don't," Bill says, "but it's gonna be on the TV and the radio and in the papers and there's plenty others that *will* believe him. Like some of those people on the east coast, including that guy that wrote those books, What's-His-Name. And maybe he'll decide to pay Jimmy-Ray a visit, and Jimmy-Ray'll take him out in the little woods some night. Maybe it'll be exactly the right night. Or the wrong one, I should say. And the guy goes and tells his UFO pals, and then they come out here and Jimmy-Ray takes them out to the little woods. Are you startin' to get the picture?"

Am I ever. "Okay. So what do we do?"

Bill smiles. "Like the man said, I'm glad you asked that question."

Well, that would be the morning I have a dead battery. Finally get the truck started and I get out to Jimmy-Ray's half an hour later than I'd planned, and it's already pretty crazy out there. There's a bunch of reporters from regular papers as well as from those scandal rags and even a couple of TV crews, and the FBI's got them all corralled well back from the house, but then they had to call in some of the Highway Patrol for crowd control because just about everyone and their brother has shown up, too. Jimmy-Ray got serious telephone-itis after the FBI said they were gonna send out a lab team.

I push my way through the crowd and find Bill and the others right up front at the barricades the Hypos put up.

"No action yet," he says. "The lab team's later than you are."

"Couldn't be helped. I had a dead battery."

Bill kind of chuckles. "Not so loud. Everyone'll be saying aliens did it to keep you home."

I look over at the reporters and TV crews. "Anyone talked to them yet?"

Bill shakes his head and then points. Jimmy-Ray is coming out on the front porch with a couple of guys who are FBI for sure, along with the county sheriff, Ed Bailey, who's looking pretty serious. I hear cameras clicking away and there

are some videocameras going and people are calling out to Jimmy-Ray. Then
Karen comes out and she's obviously at a loss with this circus all over the place,
but what can she do?

Then the lab team shows up in a big van and they don't waste no time. Jimmy-
Ray and the FBI guys take them right out to the little woods. Bailey starts to tag
along but the FBI guys say something to him and he gets a sour look on his face.
Then he goes over to where the press is corralled.

"FBI says y'all might as well hold yer water, they gonna be out there awhile
takin' samples and lookin' around."

One reporter starts calling to Karen, saying he wants to interview her, and
then another one just starts shouting questions at her and she blushes and puts a
hand up to hide her face. Karen Carver's a quiet person, no shrinking violet but
not much for being the center of a lot of noisy attention, either, and this is
something completely beyond her, a real assault on her dignity.

Ten minutes later, the FBI lab team comes back around the house and they
look *real* put-out. Jimmy-Ray's running along behind the agents, talking real
fast, but they're not listening. One of the lab team is pushing a wheelbarrow full
of cans and bottles and he looks the maddest of all. Maybe it's because he got
stuck with the heavy work. While the rest of the lab team goes right to their van,
he stops right in front of all the reporters with his load.

"Just for your information," he says in a loud voice, and everyone shuts up
to listen, "we found this in the wooded area, very clumsily camouflaged under
some brush. Just a lot of insecticide and weed-killer and chemicals you can buy
in any hardware store, and it's all been splashed around with a liberal hand. Mr.
Carver's eagerness to provide evidence of an alien landing is a lot greater than
his concern for the health of his trees and the indigenous wildlife."

"Now, wait a *minute*," Jimmy-Ray says, "I don't know how all that got
there—"

The guy with the wheelbarrow rolls his eyes and goes on to the van with the
rest of the team and they just drive on out. Jimmy-Ray's running around trying
to get the FBI guys to stay but they're not having any more of him.

"I been set up!" Jimmy-Ray yells, and then he sees me and Bill and Bart and
Jack and Al. "There! There's my friends, they'll tell you!" He runs over to us
with this pleading look. "You got to back me up on this. You *got* to!"

"You're sure that's what you want, Jimmy-Ray?" Bill says.

The Hypos are removing the barricades now and everyone starts milling
around, waiting to see if there's going to be any more show. The press is starting
to pack it up.

"It's now or never," Jimmy-Ray says and looks at me. "Fred? You'll do it,
wontcha? You'll tell 'em I'm not fakin' this?"

I give a sigh and nod and Jimmy-Ray goes running over to the press yelling
he's got *corrobation*.

"That's '*corroboration*'!" Al calls after him, but he doesn't hear.

Bill gives me a little shove. "Well, go ahead. Get it over with."

The press doesn't seem too inclined to pay Jimmy-Ray much mind and I'm
not so sure they'll pay any attention to me, either, but I give it a try.

"Ladies and gentlemen of the press," I say, "Jimmy-Ray here is telling you the truth. He *has* been set up. Somebody set him up to look like a liar. I know for a fact that Jimmy-Ray has been visited by an alien."

A few of them stop and give me skeptical looks.

"I know, because I been visited, too. Just the way Jimmy-Ray has." I get a few laughs on that and then Bill is standing next to me. "It's a fact," he says. "I met the alien, too." He turns to the sheriff. "And so's Sheriff Bailey. Ain't that right, sheriff?"

"Dammit, Bill," says the sheriff, "if you wanna tell everybody about *your* private life, that's *your* affair, but why'd you have to go spill the beans on me for?"

Jimmy-Ray's mouth is so wide open it might get jammed that way. It occurs to me that's the only way I've seen him lately, and it ain't a good look for him.

"You might as well make a clean breast of it, Ed," Bart says to the sheriff. The press is definitely interested again. A couple of Jimmy-Ray's friends backing him up is one thing, but a sheriff is something else.

"Hey, what I do on my off hours ain't nobody's business but my own," Bailey says. "Just because I'm havin' sex with aliens doesn't mean I'm not in my cruiser ready to roll when somebody needs help. I take my beeper up to the saucer with me." The expressions on all those faces make me glad for Ed that he's retiring at the end of the month.

Jimmy-Ray looks like he's gonna bust something important. "I never told them it was *sex*!" he yells.

"Well, what did you hold out on 'em for?" yawns Al. "That's the best part. Otherwise, they'd just be a bunch of funny-lookin' tourists, even if they *are* from another galaxy."

"Did they say which galaxy?" one of the reporters calls out.

"Andromeda," Al says, boreder than shit. "Where else? It's the closest one, easy trip by space warp."

"Andromedans," says Bart and gives a sniff. "You can have 'em. I like the ones from our own galaxy better. They're all flat-headed, about yea high"—he puts his hand out at waist-level—"so I always got a place to put my beer."

"You don't like the ten-foot-tall ladies?" Jack says.

"I don't know as you can call 'em *ladies*," Bart says.

"Hey, they're *aliens*. Don't make no difference, you might as well call 'em ladies. They sure *look* like ladies. Great, big, beautiful ladies."

"I wasn't thinkin' of their looks," Bart says, so prim I almost bust out laughing. "I don't like my aliens that aggressive. Could spill the beer."

Then Bill jumps in talkin' about snake-people from Aldebaran and Jimmy-Ray about wets his pants. "It's not like that!" he yells. "It's *not* like that! It's something *beautiful* and *wonderful* and there's no snake-people, there's no flat-top beer-holders, there's—"

"Jimmy-Ray, I think you better come back in the house now and quiet down." Karen's there suddenly, pulling at his arm and kind of wincing at all the reporters.

"There's no ten-foot-tall ladies!" Jimmy-Ray screams, and everyone shuts up and looks at him.

"Well, maybe not for *you*," Jack says, after a long moment. "You got your preferences, I got mine. I don't know what you been foolin' around with, but the ten-foot-tall ladies kinda spoiled me for anything else." He turns back to the reporters who are sticking microphones and little tape recorders in his face. "See, they're big, but they got these little teeny-tiny—"

"Stop it!" Jimmy-Ray sobs, and breaks down crying. This is just too embarrassing for Karen, who lets go of him and moves away. I go over to her and pat her on the shoulder.

"It prob'ly won't last too much longer," I tell her.

She just rolls her eyes and a couple reporters break from the pack and come over. "What about you, Mrs. Carver? Did you know about these aliens?"

"You leave my wife alone!" Jimmy-Ray yells, and he runs over, but a chunky guy with a camera steps in front of him to get a picture of Karen.

"Well, of *course* I knew," she says, resigned that she's not gonna get away without having to do her part. "Jimmy-Ray and I don't keep secrets from each other. He knew when I had Elvis's babies, and he was completely understanding. He knew it was a childhood dream of mine, to be the mother of Elvis's children. It only took about six weeks—aliens are so much more advanced than we are—"

Jimmy-Ray has gone positively incoherent and he's either gonna bust a blood vessel in his head or start swinging. Bill and I drag him away kicking and screaming while Karen is still explaining how Elvis was really an alien and had to make like he died when he started to metamorphose into his new appearance, which was when he was getting fat and all.

We take Jimmy-Ray around the other side of the house and let him work it out. It's like watching a giant child have a temper tantrum and I really think he's gone over the brink and we'll never get him back. Maybe we should have just called County Medical in the first place, because it looks like that's where he's gonna end up after all.

But in about fifteen minutes, he's all blown out. He can't think of another bad thing to call me and Bill and everyone else except Karen, and it's just as well because he's starting to lose his voice anyway. Finally, he's just sitting on the ground with his fists on his knees and his face all red and breathing hard. Bill squats down and says, "Okay. Feel better?"

Jimmy-Ray looks at Bill and then at me. "Why?" he croaks. *"Why?"*

"Why?" Bill shakes his head. "Jimmy-Ray, are you *completely* stupid? Why in hell do you think?"

Jimmy-Ray just stares at him.

"You just make me *so mad* sometimes." Bill gets up. "Explain the facts of life to this chucklehead," he says to me. "He's married to *your* cousin."

"Second cousin," I say automatically, and kneel down next to Jimmy-Ray. "Look—you had a nice time that night, right? What kinda person kisses and tells? Did you used to do that in high school?"

"Get off it," Jimmy-Ray growls.

"Okay, right," I say, glancing at Bill, "it's not that. Suppose you got someone to believe you. Suppose you got a whole *bunch* of people to believe you, and they all came out here to wait for the alien and the alien picked them up. What do you think would happen?"

"I'd have corroboration," he says defiantly.

" 'Corroboration.' You'd also have crowds. They'd all tell their friends and their friends would tell more friends and pretty soon we'd have the whole damned country comin' here. Now you think on that for a minute. *The whole damned country.* People from New York City. Rock groups, and all their groupies. *Republicans.* Murderers on weekend furloughs. The goddam President and the whole Cabinet, too, and movie stars, not to mention the rest of California. *Geraldo.* How about *that*? You really want to share the alien with *Geraldo*? When your own *wife* goes there, too? What kinda person *are* you?"

Jimmy-Ray just keeps staring at me and I get up, brushing my pants off.

"We got a good thing here," Bill says, "and we *ain't* lettin' *anybody* spoil it. If Geraldo or anyone else wants an alien, let 'em go find one of their own. You got two choices: you pull yourself together and you go back and tell the reporters how you were proud Karen had Elvis's babies or any other crazy thing, the crazier the better. Got it? Or you're cut off. No more alien."

Now, that's the *only* lie we've actually told him because as far as we know, the alien doesn't actually talk to anyone and nobody seems to have any influence on it. It just shows up, beams you aboard, and has a good time with you. And that's not always sex, except for the alien, because it thinks of everything as sex all the time.

Anyway, we figure we got to throw the fear of God into Jimmy-Ray to make sure he behaves. And after a while, he comes around the house and tries a couple of lame stories about lizard-people that can lick their eyebrows. But all the reporters ignore him, maybe because they're all sure that lizard-people don't have eyebrows, or because it's too similar to Bill's snake-people. That's good enough, though, and after everybody leaves, we all go home, too.

Well, the story makes one scandal rag before it dies a natural death and life goes back to normal. Sometime after that, we hear Karen Carver's pregnant.

So that's nice, we all say, and think nothing else of it. But nine months later, we hear she delivers at County Medical and Jimmy-Ray just runs off and leaves her. Her being my second cousin and all, I go see her after she gets home, figuring she must be pretty upset.

"We had a terrible fight right in the delivery room," she tells me. "I just couldn't believe it, and neither could the doctor or any of the nurses. They had to make him leave. Then I got home with the baby and all his clothes and things were gone."

"That's awful," I say. "But some men are like that, Karen. Can't handle major responsibilities. Maybe he'll straighten out after a few weeks, though, and want to come back."

"I wouldn't take him," she says. "He's been a complete mope since that other business a while ago. I think it's just as well. I got plenty of help with the baby." She brightens up. "You want to see him?"

"Sure," I say, and she takes me into the baby's room.

Well, do I really have to tell you that then and there I see why Jimmy-Ray run off like he did? Karen nods at me. "You want to hold him?" And then without waiting for an answer, she picks him up and puts him right in my arms. "Don't worry, he won't break."

Having held three of my own and numerous others of relatives and friends, I ain't worried about that. I was just took by surprise for a minute there, because never have I seen a baby that looked *just like* Elvis. There are lots of real strong resemblances around here, of course, but no babies that were ever born *with* the sideburns. Not a single one.

CHAFF

Greg Egan

▼

Hot new Australian writer Greg Egan has been very impressive *and* very prolific in the early years of the nineties, seeming to turn up almost everywhere with high-quality stories. He is a frequent contributor to *Interzone* and *Asimov's Science Fiction*, and has made sales as well to *Pulphouse, Analog, Aurealis, Eidolon*, and elsewhere. Several of his stories have appeared in various "Best of the Year" series, including this one; in fact, he placed *two* stories in *both* our Eighth and Ninth Annual Collections—the first author ever to do that back-to-back in consecutive volumes—and placed another story in our Tenth Annual Collection. His first novel, *Quarantine*, appeared last year in England, to wide critical acclaim, and is due out shortly in the U.S.; and his second novel, *Permutation City*, is slated to appear in 1994. Coming up is a collection of his short fiction, and I think it's clear that Egan is well on his way to becoming one of the Big Names of the nineties.

Here he takes us to the steaming jungles of South America for an unsettling and hard-edged story that explores some of the same sort of territory as Conrad's *Heart of Darkness*—but then throws away the map and takes us into a whole new uncharted territory, one full of both promise and menace, for a glimpse of what may be the future of humanity. . . .

El Nido de Ladrones—the Nest of Thieves—occupies a roughly elliptical region, 50,000 square kilometres in the western Amazon Lowlands, straddling the border between Colombia and Peru. It's difficult to say exactly where the natural rain forest ends and the engineered species of El Nido take over, but the total biomass of the system must be close to a trillion tonnes. A trillion tonnes of structural material, osmotic pumps, solar energy collectors, cellular chemical factories, and biological computing and communications resources. All under the control of its designers.

The old maps and databases are obsolete; by manipulating the hydrology and soil chemistry, and influencing patterns of rainfall and erosion, the vegetation has reshaped the terrain completely: shifting the course of the Putumayo River, drowning old roads in swampland, raising secret causeways through the jungle. This biogenic geography remains in a state of flux, so that even the eye-witness

287

accounts of the rare defectors from El Nido soon lose their currency. Satellite images are meaningless; at every frequency, the forest canopy conceals, or deliberately falsifies, the spectral signature of whatever lies beneath.

Chemical toxins and defoliants are useless; the plants and their symbiotic bacteria can analyse most poisons, and reprogram their metabolisms to render them harmless—or transform them into food—faster than our agricultural warfare expert systems can invent new molecules. Biological weapons are seduced, subverted, domesticated; most of the genes from the last lethal plant virus we introduced were found three months later, incorporated into a benign vector for El Nido's elaborate communications network. The assassin had turned into a messenger boy. Any attempt to burn the vegetation is rapidly smothered by carbon dioxide—or more sophisticated fire retardants, if a self-oxidizing fuel is employed. Once we even pumped in a few tonnes of nutrient laced with powerful radioisotopes—locked up in compounds chemically indistinguishable from their natural counterparts. We tracked the results with gamma-ray imaging: El Nido separated out the isotope-laden molecules—probably on the basis of their diffusion rates across organic membranes—sequestered and diluted them, and then pumped them right back out again.

So when I heard that a Peruvian-born biochemist named Guillermo Largo had departed from Bethesda, Maryland, with some highly classified genetic tools— the fruits of his own research, but very much the property of his employers— and vanished into El Nido, I thought: At last, an excuse for the Big One. The Company had been advocating thermonuclear rehabilitation of El Nido for almost a decade. The Security Council would have rubber-stamped it. The governments with nominal authority over the region would have been delighted. Hundreds of El Nido's inhabitants were suspected of violating US law—and President Golino was aching for a chance to prove that she could play hard ball south of the border, whatever language she spoke in the privacy of her own home. She could have gone on prime time afterwards and told the nation that they should be proud of Operation Back to Nature, and that the 30,000 displaced farmers who'd taken refuge in El Nido from Colombia's undeclared civil war—and who had now been liberated forever from the oppression of Marxist terrorists and drug barons— would have saluted her courage and resolve.

I never discovered why that wasn't to be. Technical problems in ensuring that no embarrassing side-effects would show up down-river in the sacred Amazon itself, wiping out some telegenic endangered species before the end of the present administration? Concern that some Middle Eastern warlord might somehow construe the act as licence to use his own feeble, long-hoarded fission weapons on a troublesome minority, destabilizing the region in an undesirable manner? Fear of Japanese trade sanctions, now that the rabidly anti-nuclear Eco-Marketeers were back in power?

I wasn't shown the verdicts of the geopolitical computer models; I simply received my orders—coded into the flicker of my local K-Mart's fluorescent tubes, slipped in between the updates to the shelf price tags. Deciphered by an extra neural layer in my left retina, the words appeared blood red against the bland cheery colours of the supermarket aisle. I was to enter El Nido and retrieve Guillermo Largo. Alive.

Dressed like a local real-estate agent—right down to the gold-plated bracelet-phone, and the worst of all possible $300 haircuts—I visited Largo's abandoned home in Bethesda: a northern suburb of Washington, just over the border into Maryland. The apartment was modern and spacious, neatly furnished but not opulent—about what any good marketing software might have tried to sell him, on the basis of salary less alimony.

Largo had always been classified as *brilliant but unsound*—a potential security risk, but far too talented and productive to be wasted. He'd been under routine surveillance ever since the gloriously euphemistic Department of Energy had employed him, straight out of Harvard, back in 2005—clearly, too routine by far . . . but then, I could understand how 30 years with an unblemished record must have given rise to a degree of complacency. Largo had never attempted to disguise his politics—apart from exercising the kind of discretion that was more a matter of etiquette than subterfuge; no Che Guevara T-shirts when visiting Los Alamos—but he'd never really acted on his beliefs, either.

A mural had been jet-sprayed onto his living room wall in shades of near infrared (visible to most hip 14-year-old Washingtonians, if not to their parents). It was a copy of the infamous Lee Hing-cheung's *A Tiling of the Plane with Heroes of the New World Order*, a digital image which had spread across computer networks at the turn of the century. Early 90s political leaders, naked and interlocked—Escher meets the *Kama Sutra*—deposited steaming turds into each other's open and otherwise empty braincases—an effect borrowed from the works of the German satirist George Grosz. The Iraqi dictator was shown admiring his reflection in a hand mirror—the image an exact reproduction of a contemporary magazine cover in which the moustache had been retouched to render it suitably Hitleresque. The US President carried—horizontally, but poised ready to be tilted—an egg-timer full of the gaunt hostages whose release he'd delayed to clinch his predecessor's election victory. Everyone was shoe-horned in, somewhere—right down to the Australian Prime Minister, portrayed as a public louse, struggling (and failing) to fit its tiny jaws around the mighty presidential cock. I could imagine a few of the neo-McCarthyist troglodytes in the Senate going apoplectic, if anything so tedious as an inquiry into Largo's defection ever took place—but what should we have done? Refused to hire him if he owned so much as a *Guernica* tea-towel?

Largo had blanked every computer in the apartment before leaving, including the entertainment system—but I already knew his taste in music, having listened to a few hours of audio surveillance samples full of bad Korean Ska. No laudable revolutionary ethno-solidarity, no haunting Andean pipe music; a shame—I would have much preferred that. His bookshelves held several battered college-level biochemistry texts, presumably retained for sentimental reasons, and a few dozen musty literary classics and volumes of poetry, in English, Spanish and German. Hesse, Rilke, Vallejo, Conrad, Nietzsche. Nothing modern—and nothing printed after 2010. With a few words to the household manager, Largo had erased every digital work he'd ever owned, sweeping away the last quarter of a century of his personal archaeology.

I flipped through the surviving books, for what it was worth. There was a pencilled-in correction to the structure of guanine in one of the texts . . . and a section had been underlined in *Heart of Darkness*. The narrator, Marlow, was pondering the mysterious fact that the servants on the steamboat—members of a cannibal tribe, whose provisions of rotting hippo meat had been tossed overboard—hadn't yet rebelled and eaten him. After all:

> *No fear can stand up to hunger, no patience can wear it out, disgust*
> *simply does not exist where hunger is; and as to superstition, beliefs,*
> *and what you may call principles, they are less than chaff in a breeze.*

I couldn't argue with that—but I wondered why Largo had found the passage noteworthy. Perhaps it had struck a chord, back in the days when he'd been trying to rationalize taking his first research grants from the Pentagon? The ink was faded—and the volume itself had been printed in 2003. I would rather have had copies of his diary entries for the fortnight leading up to his disappearance—but his household computers hadn't been systematically tapped for almost 20 years.

I sat at the desk in his study, and stared at the blank screen of his work station. Largo had been born into a middle-class, nominally Catholic, very mildly leftist family in Lima, in 1980. His father, a journalist with *El Comercio*, had died from a cerebral blood clot in 2029. His 78-year-old mother still worked as an attorney for an international mining company—going through the motions of *habeas corpus* for the families of disappeared radicals in her spare time, a hobby her employers tolerated for the sake of cheap PR brownie points in the shareholder democracies. Guillermo had one elder brother, a retired surgeon, and one younger sister, a primary-school teacher, neither of them politically active.

Most of his education had taken place in Switzerland and the States; after his PhD, he'd held a succession of research posts in government institutes, the biotechnology industry, and academia—all with more or less the same real sponsors. Fifty-five, now, thrice divorced but still childless, he'd only ever returned to Lima for brief family visits.

After *three decades* working on the military applications of molecular genetics—unwittingly at first, but not for long—what could have triggered his sudden defection to El Nido? If he'd managed the cynical doublethink of reconciling defence research and pious liberal sentiments for so long, he must have got it down to a fine art. His latest psychological profile suggested as much: fierce pride in his scientific achievements balanced the self-loathing he felt when contemplating their ultimate purpose—with the conflict showing signs of decaying into comfortable indifference. A well-documented dynamic in the industry.

And he seemed to have acknowledged—deep in his heart, 30 years ago—that his "principles" were *less than chaff in a breeze.*

Perhaps he'd decided, belatedly, that if he was going to be a whore he might as well do it properly, and sell his skills to the highest bidder—even if that meant smuggling genetic weapons to a drugs cartel. I'd read his financial records, though: no tax fraud, no gambling debts, no evidence that he'd ever lived beyond his means. Betraying his employers, just as he'd betrayed his own youthful ideals to join them, might have seemed like an appropriately nihilistic gesture . . . but on a more pragmatic level, it was hard to imagine him finding the money, and the consequences, all that tempting. What could El Nido have offered him? A numbered satellite account, and a new identity in Paraguay? All the squalid pleasures of life on the fringes of the Third World plutocracy? He would have had everything to gain by living out his retirement in his adopted country, salving his conscience with one or two vitriolic essays on foreign policy in some unread left-wing netzine—and then finally convincing himself that any nation which granted him such unencumbered rights of free speech probably deserved everything he'd done to defend it.

Exactly what he *had* done to defend it, though—what tools he'd perfected, and stolen—I was not permitted to know.

As dusk fell, I locked the apartment and headed south down Wisconsin Avenue. Washington was coming alive, the streets already teeming with people looking for distraction from the heat. Nights in the cities were becoming hallucinatory. Teenagers sported bioluminescent symbionts, the veins in their temples, necks and pumped-up forearm muscles glowing electric blue, walking circulation diagrams who cultivated hypertension to improve the effect. Others used retinal symbionts to translate IR into visible light, their eyes flashing vampire red in the shadows.

And others, less visibly, had a skull full of White Knights.

Stem cells in the bone marrow infected with Mother—an engineered retrovirus—gave rise to something half-way between an embryonic neuron and a white blood cell. White Knights secreted the cytokines necessary to unlock the blood-brain barrier—and once through, cellular adhesion molecules guided them to their targets, where they could flood the site with a chosen neurotransmitter—or even form temporary quasi-synapses with genuine neurons. Users often had half a dozen or more sub-types in their bloodstream simultaneously, each one activated by a specific dietary additive: some cheap, harmless, and perfectly legitimate chemical not naturally present in the body. By ingesting the right mixture of innocuous artificial colourings, flavours and preservatives, they could modulate their neurochemistry in almost any fashion—until the White Knights died, as they were programmed to do, and a new dose of Mother was required.

Mother could be snorted, or taken intravenously . . . but the most efficient way to use it was to puncture a bone and inject it straight into the marrow—an excruciating, messy, dangerous business, even if the virus itself was uncontaminated and authentic. The good stuff came from El Nido. The bad stuff came from basement labs in California and Texas, where gene hackers tried to force cell cultures infected with Mother to reproduce a virus expressly designed to resist their efforts—and churned out batches of mutant strains ideal for inducing leukaemia, astrocytomas, Parkinson's disease, and assorted novel psychoses.

Crossing the sweltering dark city, watching the heedlessly joyful crowds, I felt a penetrating, dreamlike clarity come over me. Part of me was numb, leaden, blank—but part of me was electrified, all-seeing. I seemed to be able to stare into the hidden landscapes of the people around me, to see deeper than the luminous rivers of blood; to pierce them with my vision right to the bone.

Right to the marrow.

I drove to the edge of a park I'd visited once before, and waited. I was already dressed for the part. Young people strode by, grinning, some glancing at the silver 2025 Ford Narcissus and whistling appreciatively. A teenaged boy danced on the grass, alone, tirelessly—blissed out on Coca-Cola, and not even getting paid to fake it.

Before too long, a girl approached the car, blue veins flashing on her bare arms. She leant down to the window and looked in, inquiringly.

"What you got?" She was 16 or 17, slender, dark-eyed, coffee-coloured, with a faint Latino accent. She could have been my sister.

"Southern Rainbow." All twelve major genotypes of Mother, straight from El Nido, cut with nothing but glucose. Southern Rainbow—and a little fast food—could take you anywhere.

The girl eyed me sceptically, and stretched out her right hand, palm down. She wore a ring with a large multifaceted jewel, with a pit in the centre. I took a sachet from the glove compartment, shook it, tore it open, and tipped a few specks of powder into the pit. Then I leant over and moistened the sample with saliva, holding her cool fingers to steady her hand. Twelve faces of the "stone" began to glow immediately, each one in a different colour. The immunoelectric sensors in the pit, tiny capacitors coated with antibodies, were designed to recognize several sites on the protein coats of the different strains of Mother—particularly the ones the bootleggers had the most trouble getting right.

With good enough technology, though, those proteins didn't have to bear the slightest relationship to the RNA inside.

The girl seemed to be impressed; her face lit up with anticipation. We negotiated a price. Too low by far; she should have been suspicious.

I looked her in the eye before handing over the sachet.

I said, "What do you need this shit for? The world is the world. You have to take it as it is. Accept it as it is: savage and terrible. Be strong. Never lie to yourself. That's the only way to survive."

She smirked at my apparent hypocrisy, but she was too pleased with her luck to turn nasty. "I hear what you're saying. It's a bad planet out there." She forced the money into my hand, adding, with wide-eyed mock-sincerity, "And this is the last time I do Mother, I promise."

I gave her the lethal virus, and watched her walk away across the grass and vanish into the shadows.

The Colombian air force pilot who flew me down from Bogotá didn't seem too thrilled to be risking his life for a DEA bureaucrat. It was 700 kilometres to the border, and five different guerrilla organizations held territory along the way: not a lot of towns, but several hundred possible sites for rocket launchers.

"My great-grandfather," he said sourly, "died in fucking Korea fighting for General Douglas fucking MacArthur." I wasn't sure if that was meant to be a declaration of pride, or an intimation of an outstanding debt. Both, probably.

The helicopter was eerily silent, fitted out with phased sound absorbers, which looked like giant loudspeakers but swallowed most of the noise of the blades. The carbon-fibre fuselage was coated with an expensive network of chameleon polymers—although it might have been just as effective to paint the whole thing sky blue. An endothermic chemical mixture accumulated waste heat from the motor, and then discharged it through a parabolic radiator as a tightly focused skywards burst, every hour or so. The guerrillas had no access to satellite images, and no radar they dared use; I decided that we had less chance of dying than the average Bogotá commuter. Back in the capital, buses had been exploding without warning, two or three times a week.

Colombia was tearing itself apart; *La Violencia* of the 1950s, all over again. Although all of the spectacular terrorist sabotage was being carried out by organized guerrilla groups, most of the deaths so far had been caused by factions within the two mainstream political parties butchering each other's supporters, avenging a litany of past atrocities which stretched back for generations. The group who'd actually started the current wave of bloodshed had negligible support; *Ejército de Simón Bolívar* were lunatic right-wing extremists who wanted to "re-unite" with Panama, Venezuela and Ecuador—after two centuries of separation—and drag in Peru and Bolivia, to realize Bolívar's dream of *Gran Colombia*. By assassinating President Marín, though, they'd triggered a cascade of events which had nothing to do with their ludicrous cause. Strikes and protests, street battles, curfews, martial law. The repatriation of foreign capital by nervous investors, followed by hyperinflation, and the collapse of the local financial system. Then a spiral of opportunistic violence. Everyone, from the paramilitary death squads to the Maoist splinter groups, seemed to believe that their hour had finally come.

I hadn't seen so much as a bullet fired—but from the moment I'd entered the country, there'd been acid churning in my guts, and a heady, ceaseless adrenaline rush coursing through my veins. I felt wired, feverish . . . alive. Hypersensitive as a pregnant woman: I could smell blood, everywhere. When the hidden struggle for power which rules all human affairs finally breaks through to the surface, finally ruptures the skin, it's like witnessing some giant primordial creature rise up out of the ocean. Mesmerizing, and appalling. Nauseating—and exhilarating.

Coming face to face with the truth is always exhilarating.

From the air, there was no obvious sign that we'd arrived; for the last 200 kilometres, we'd been passing over rain forest—cleared in patches for plantations and mines, ranches and timber mills, shot through with rivers like metallic threads—but most of it resembling nothing so much as an endless expanse of broccoli. El Nido permitted natural vegetation to flourish all around it—and then imitated it . . . which made sampling at the edges an inefficient way to gather the true genetic stock for analysis. Deep penetration was difficult, though, even with purpose-built robots—dozens of which had been lost—so edge samples had to suffice, at least until a few more members of Congress could be photographed committing statutory rape and persuaded to vote for better funding. Most of the engineered plant tissues self-destructed in the absence of regular chemical and viral messages drifting out from the core, reassuring them that they were still *in situ*—so the main DEA research facility was on the outskirts of El Nido itself, a collection of pressurized buildings and experimental plots in a clearing blasted out of the jungle on the Colombian side of the border. The electrified fences weren't topped with razor wire; they turned 90 degrees into an electrified roof, completing a chainlink cage. The heliport was in the centre of the compound, where a cage within the cage could, temporarily, open itself to the sky.

Madelaine Smith, the research director, showed me around. In the open, we both wore hermetic biohazard suits—although if the modifications I'd received in Washington were working as promised, mine was redundant. El Nido's short-lived defensive viruses occasionally percolated out this far; they were never fatal, but they could be severely disabling to anyone who hadn't been inoculated. The forest's designers had walked a fine line between biological "self-defence" and unambiguously military applications. Guerrillas had always hidden in the engineered jungle—and raised funds by collaborating in the export of Mother—but El Nido's technology had never been explicitly directed toward the creation of lethal pathogens.

So far.

"Here, we're raising seedlings of what we hope will be a stable El Nido phenotype, something we call beta seventeen." They were unremarkable bushes with deep green foliage and dark red berries; Smith pointed to an array of camera-like instruments beside them. "Real-time infrared microspectroscopy. It can resolve a medium-sized RNA transcript, if there's a sharp surge in production in a sufficient number of cells, simultaneously. We match up the data from these with our gas chromatography records, which show the range of molecules drifting out from the core. If we can catch these plants in the act of sensing a cue from El Nido—and if their response involves switching on a gene and synthesizing a protein—we may be able to elucidate the mechanism, and eventually short-circuit it."

"You can't just . . . sequence all the DNA, and work it out from first principles?" I was meant to be passing as a newly-appointed administrator, dropping in at short notice to check for gold-plated paper clips—but it was hard to decide exactly how naive to sound.

Smith smiled politely. "El Nido DNA is guarded by enzymes which tear it apart at the slightest hint of cellular disruption. Right now, we'd have about as much of a chance of *sequencing it* as I'd have of . . . reading your mind by autopsy. And we still don't know how those enzymes work; we have a lot of catching up to do. When the drug cartels started investing in biotechnology, 40 years ago, *copy protection* was their first priority. And they lured the best people away from legitimate labs around the world—not just by paying more, but by offering more creative freedom, and more challenging goals. El Nido probably contains as many patentable inventions as the entire agrotechnology industry produced in the same period. And all of them a lot more exciting.''

Was that what had brought Largo here? *More challenging goals?* But El Nido was complete, the challenge was over; any further work was mere refinement. And at 55, surely he knew that his most creative years were long gone.

I said, ''I imagine the cartels got more than they bargained for; the technology transformed their business beyond recognition. All the old addictive substances became too easy to synthesize biologically—too cheap, too pure, and too readily available to be profitable. And addiction itself became bad business. The only thing that really sells now is novelty.''

Smith motioned with bulky arms towards the towering forest outside the cage—turning to face south-east, although it all looked the same. ''*El Nido* was more than they bargained for. All they really wanted was coca plants that did better at lower altitudes, and some gene-tailored vegetation to make it easier to camouflage their labs and plantations. They ended up with a small *de facto* nation full of gene hackers, anarchists, and refugees. The cartels are only in control of certain regions; half the original geneticists have split off and founded their own little jungle utopias. There are at least a dozen people who know how to program the plants—how to switch on new patterns of gene expression, how to tap into the communications networks—and with that, you can stake out your own territory.''

''Like having some secret, shamanistic power to command the spirits of the forest?''

''Exactly. Except for the fact that it actually works.''

I laughed. ''Do you know what cheers me up the most? Whatever else happens . . . the *real* Amazon, the *real* jungle, will swallow them all in the end. It's lasted—what? Two million years? *Their own little utopias!* In 50 years' time, or a hundred, it will be as if El Nido had never existed.''

Less than chaff in a breeze.

Smith didn't reply. In the silence, I could hear the monotonous click of beetles, from all directions. Bogotá, high on a plateau, had been almost chilly. Here, it was as sweltering as Washington itself.

I glanced at Smith; she said, ''You're right, of course.'' But she didn't sound convinced at all.

In the morning, over breakfast, I reassured Smith that I'd found everything to be in order. She smiled warily. I think she suspected that I wasn't what I claimed to be, but that didn't really matter. I'd listened carefully to the gossip of the scientists, technicians and soldiers; the name *Guillermo Largo* hadn't been mentioned once. If they didn't even know about Largo, they could hardly have guessed my real purpose.

It was just after nine when I departed. On the ground, sheets of light, delicate as auroral displays, sliced through the trees around the compound. When we emerged above the canopy, it was like stepping from a mist-shrouded dawn into the brilliance of noon.

The pilot, begrudgingly, took a detour over the centre of El Nido. "We're in Peruvian air space, now," he boasted. "You want to spark a diplomatic incident?" He seemed to find the possibility attractive.

"No. But fly lower."

"There's nothing to see. You can't even see the river."

"Lower." The broccoli grew larger, then suddenly snapped into focus; all that undifferentiated green turned into individual branches, solid and specific. It was curiously shocking, like looking at some dull familiar object through a microscope, and seeing its strange particularity revealed.

I reached over and broke the pilot's neck. He hissed through his teeth, surprised. A shudder passed through me, a mixture of fear and a twinge of remorse. The autopilot kicked in and kept us hovering; it took me two minutes to unstrap the man's body, drag him into the cargo hold, and take his seat.

I unscrewed the instrument panel and patched in a new chip. The digital log being beamed via satellite to an air force base to the north would show that we'd descended rapidly, out of control.

The truth wasn't much different. At a hundred metres, I hit a branch and snapped a blade on the front rotor; the computers compensated valiantly, modelling and remodelling the situation, trimming the active surfaces of the surviving blades—and no doubt doing fine for each five-second interval between bone-shaking impacts and further damage. The sound absorbers went berserk, slipping in and out of phase with the motors, blasting the jungle with pulses of intensified noise.

Fifty metres up, I went into a slow spin, weirdly smooth, showing me the thickening canopy as if in a leisurely cinematic pan. At 20 metres, free fall. Air bags inflated around me, blocking off the view. I closed my eyes, redundantly, and gritted my teeth. Fragments of prayers spun in my head—the detritus of childhood, afterimages burned into my brain, meaningless but unerasable. I thought: *If I die, the jungle will claim me. I am flesh, I am chaff. Nothing will remain to be judged.* By the time I recalled that this wasn't true jungle at all, I was no longer falling.

The airbags promptly deflated. I opened my eyes. There was water all around, flooded forest. A panel of the roof between the rotors blew off gently with a hiss like the dying pilot's last breath, and then drifted down like a slowly crashing kite, turning muddy silver, green and brown as it snatched at the colours around it.

The life raft had oars, provisions, flares—and a radio beacon. I cut the beacon loose and left it in the wreckage. I moved the pilot back into his seat, just as the water started flooding in to bury him.

Then I set off down the river.

El Nido had divided a once-navigable stretch of the Rio Putumayo into a bewildering maze. Sluggish channels of brown water snaked between freshly raised islands of soil, covered in palms and rubber plants, and the inundated banks where the oldest trees—chocolate-coloured hardwood species (predating the geneticists, but not necessarily unmodified)—soared above the undergrowth and out of sight.

The lymph nodes in my neck and groin pulsed with heat, savage but reassuring; my modified immune system was dealing with El Nido's viral onslaught by generating thousands of new killer T-cell clones *en masse*, rather than waiting for a cautious antigen-mediated response. A few weeks in this state, and the chances were that a self-directed clone would slip through the elimination process and burn me up with a novel autoimmune disease—but I didn't plan on staying that long.

Fish disturbed the murky water, rising up to snatch surface-dwelling insects or floating seed pods. In the distance, the thick coils of an anaconda slid from an overhanging branch and slipped languidly into the water. Between the rubber plants, hummingbirds hovered in the maws of violet orchids. So far as I knew, none of these creatures had been tampered with; they had gone on inhabiting the prosthetic forest as if nothing had changed.

I took a stick of chewing gum from my pocket, rich in cyclamates, and slowly roused one of my own sets of White Knights. The stink of heat and decaying vegetation seemed to fade, as certain olfactory pathways in my brain were numbed, and others sensitized—a kind of inner filter coming into play, enabling any signal from the newly acquired receptors in my nasal membranes to rise above all the other, distracting odours of the jungle.

Suddenly, I could smell the dead pilot on my hands and clothes, the lingering taint of his sweat and faeces—and the pheromones of spider monkeys in the branches around me, pungent and distinctive as urine. As a rehearsal, I followed the trail for 15 minutes, paddling the raft in the direction of the freshest scent, until I was finally rewarded with chirps of alarm and a glimpse of two skinny grey-brown shapes vanishing into the foliage ahead.

My own scent was camouflaged; symbionts in my sweat glands were digesting all the characteristic molecules. There were long-term side-effects from the bacteria, though, and the most recent intelligence suggested that El Nido's inhabitants didn't bother with them. There was a chance, of course, that Largo had been paranoid enough to bring his own.

I stared after the retreating monkeys, and wondered when I'd catch my first whiff of another living human. Even an illiterate peasant who'd fled the violence to the north would have valuable knowledge of the state of play between the factions in here, and some kind of crude mental map of the landscape.

The raft began to whistle gently, air escaping from one sealed compartment. I rolled into the water and submerged completely. A metre down, I couldn't see my own hands. I waited and listened, but all I could hear was the soft *plop* of fish breaking the surface. No rock could have holed the plastic of the raft; it had to have been a bullet.

I floated in the cool milky silence. The water would conceal my body heat, and I'd have no need to exhale for ten minutes. The question was whether to risk raising a wake by swimming away from the raft, or to wait it out.

Something brushed my cheek, sharp and thin. I ignored it. It happened again.

It didn't feel like a fish, or anything living. A third time, and I seized the object as it fluttered past. It was a piece of plastic a few centimetres wide. I felt around the rim; the edge was sharp in places, soft and yielding in others. Then the fragment broke in two in my hand.

I swam a few metres away, then surfaced cautiously. The life raft was decaying, the plastic peeling away into the water like skin in acid. The polymer was meant to be cross-linked beyond any chance of biodegradation—but obviously some strain of El Nido bacteria had found a way.

I floated on my back, breathing deeply to purge myself of carbon dioxide, contemplating the prospect of completing the mission on foot. The canopy above seemed to waver, as if in a heat haze, which made no sense. My limbs grew curiously warm and heavy. It occurred to me to wonder exactly what I might be smelling, if I hadn't shut down 90 per cent of my olfactory range. I thought: *If I'd bred bacteria able to digest a substance foreign to El Nido, what else would I want them to do when they chanced upon such a meal? Incapacitate whoever had brought it in? Broadcast news of the event with a biochemical signal?*

I could smell the sharp odours of half a dozen sweat-drenched people when they arrived, but all I could do was lie in the water and let them fish me out.

After we left the river, I was carried on a stretcher, blindfolded and bound. No one talked within earshot. I might have judged the pace we set by the rhythm of my bearers' footsteps, or guessed the direction in which we travelled by hints of sunlight on the side of my face . . . but in the waking dream induced by the bacterial toxins, the harder I struggled to interpret those cues, the more lost and confused I became.

At one point, when the party rested, someone squatted beside me—and waved a scanning device over my body? That guess was confirmed by the pinpricks of heat where the polymer transponders had been implanted. Passive devices—but their resonant echo in a satellite microwave burst would have been distinctive. The scanner found, and fried, them all.

Late in the afternoon, they removed the blindfold. Certain that I was totally disoriented? Certain that I'd never escape? Or maybe just to rub my face in El Nido's triumphant architecture.

The approach was a hidden path through swampland; I kept looking down to see my captors' boots not quite vanishing into the mud, while a dry, apparently secure stretch of high ground nearby was avoided.

Closer in, the dense thorned bushes blocking the way seemed to yield for us; the chewing gum had worn off enough for me to tell that we moved in a cloud of a sweet, ester-like compound. I couldn't see whether it was being sprayed into the air from a cylinder—or emitted bodily by a member of the party with symbionts in his skin, or lungs, or intestine.

The village emerged almost imperceptibly out of the impostor jungle. The ground—I could feel it—became, step by step, unnaturally firm and level. The arrangement of trees grew subtly ordered—defining no linear avenues, but increasingly *wrong* nonetheless. Then I started glimpsing "fortuitous" clearings to the left and right, containing "natural" wooden buildings, or shiny biopolymer sheds.

I was lowered to the ground outside one of the sheds. A man I hadn't seen before leaned over me, wiry and unshaven, holding up a gleaming hunting knife. He looked to me like the archetype of human as animal, human as predator, human as unself-conscious killer.

He said, "Friend, this is where we drain out all of your blood." He grinned and squatted down. I almost passed out from the stench of my own fear, as the glut overwhelmed the symbionts. He cut my hands free, adding, "And then put it all back in again." He slid one arm under me, around my ribs, raised me up from the stretcher, and carried me into the building.

Guillermo Largo said, "Forgive me if I don't shake your hand. I think we've almost cleaned you out, but I don't want to risk physical contact in case there's enough of a residue of the virus to make your own hyped-up immune system turn on you."

He was an unprepossessing, sad-eyed man; thin, short, slightly balding. I stepped up to the wooden bars between us and stretched my hand out towards him. "Make contact any time you like. I never carried a virus. Do you think I believe your *propaganda*?"

He shrugged, unconcerned. "It would have killed you, not me—although I'm sure it was meant for both of us. It may have been keyed to my genotype, but you carried far too much of it not to have been caught up in the response to my presence. That's history, though, not worth arguing about."

I didn't actually believe that he was lying; a virus to dispose of both of us made perfect sense. I even felt a begrudging respect for the Company, for the way I'd been used—there was a savage, unsentimental honesty to it—but it didn't seem politic to reveal that to Largo.

I said, "If you believe that I pose no risk to you now, though, why don't you come back with me? You're still considered valuable. One moment of weakness, one bad decision, doesn't have to mean the end of your career. Your employers are very pragmatic people; they won't want to punish you. They'll just need to watch you a little more closely in future. Their problem, not yours; you won't even notice the difference."

Largo didn't seem to be listening, but then he looked straight at me and smiled. "Do you know what Victor Hugo said about Colombia's first constitution? He said it was written for a country of angels. It only lasted 23 years—and on the next attempt, the politicians lowered their sights. Considerably." He turned away, and started pacing back and forth in front of the bars. Two Mestizo peasants with automatic weapons stood by the door, looking on impassively. Both incessantly chewed what looked to me like ordinary coca leaves; there was something almost reassuring about their loyalty to tradition.

My cell was clean and well furnished, right down to the kind of bioreactor toilet that was all the rage in Beverly Hills. My captors had treated me impeccably, so far, but I had a feeling that Largo was planning something unpleasant. Handing me over to the Mother barons? I still didn't know what deal he'd done, what he'd sold them in exchange for a piece of El Nido and a few dozen bodyguards. Let alone why he thought this was better than an apartment in Bethesda and a hundred grand a year.

I said, "What do you think you're going to do, if you stay here? Build your own *country for angels*? Grow your own bioengineered utopia?"

"Utopia?" Largo stopped pacing, and flashed his crooked smile again. "No. How can there ever be a *utopia*? There is no *right way to live*, which we've simply failed to stumble upon. There is no set of rules, there is no system, there is no formula. Why should there be? Short of the existence of a creator—and a perverse one, at that—why should there be some blueprint for perfection, just waiting to be discovered?"

I said, "You're right. In the end, all we can do is be true to our nature. See through the veneer of civilization and hypocritical morality, and accept the real forces which shape us."

Largo burst out laughing. I actually felt my face burn at his response—if only because I'd misread him, and failed to get him on side; not because he was laughing at the one thing I believed in.

He said, "Do you know what I was working on, back in the States?"

"No. Does it matter?" The less I knew, the better my chances of living.

Largo told me anyway. "I was looking for a way to render mature neurons *embryonic*. To switch them back into a less differentiated state, enabling them to behave the way they do in the foetal brain: migrating from site to site, forming new connections. Supposedly as a treatment for dementia and stroke . . . although the work was being funded by people who saw it as the first step towards viral weapons able to rewire parts of the brain. I doubt that the results could ever have been very sophisticated—no viruses for imposing political ideologies—but all kinds of disabling or docile behaviour might have been coded into a relatively small package."

"And you sold that to the cartels? So they can hold whole cities to ransom with it, next time one of their leaders is arrested? To save them the trouble of assassinating judges and politicians?"

Largo said mildly, "I sold it to the cartels, but not as a weapon. No infectious military version exists. Even the prototypes—which merely regress selected neurons, but make no programmed changes—are far too cumbersome and fragile to survive at large. And there are other technical problems. There's not much reproductive advantage for a virus in carrying out elaborate, highly specific modifications to its host's brain; unleashed on a real human population, mutants which simply ditched all of that irrelevant shit would soon predominate."

"Then . . . ?"

"I sold it to the cartels as *a product*. Or rather, I combined it with their own biggest seller, and handed over the finished hybrid. A new kind of Mother."

"Which does what?" He had me hooked, even if I was digging my own grave.

"Which turns a subset of the neurons in the brain into something like White Knights. Just as mobile, just as flexible. Far better at establishing tight new synapses, though, rather than just flooding the interneural space with a chosen substance. And not controlled by dietary additives; controlled by molecules they secrete themselves. Controlled by each other.''

That made no sense to me. "*Existing neurons* become mobile? Existing brain structures . . . melt? You've made a version of Mother which turns people's brains to mush—and you expect them to pay for that?''

"Not mush. Everything's part of a tight feedback loop: the firing of these altered neurons influences the range of molecules they secrete—which in turn, controls the rewiring of nearby synapses. Vital regulatory centres and motor neurons are left untouched, of course. And it takes a strong signal to shift the Grey Knights; they don't respond to every random whim. You need at least an hour or two without distractions before you can have a significant effect on any brain structure.

"It's not altogether different from the way ordinary neurons end up encoding learned behaviour and memories—only faster, more flexible . . . and much more widespread. There are parts of the brain which haven't changed in 100,000 years, which can be remodelled completely in half a day.''

He paused, and regarded me amiably. The sweat on the back of my neck went cold.

"You've used the virus—?''

"Of course. That's why I created it. For myself. That's why I came here in the first place.''

"For do-it-yourself neurosurgery? Why not just slip a screwdriver under one eyeball and poke it around until the urge went away?'' I felt physically sick. "At least . . . cocaine and heroin—and even White Knights—exploited *natural* receptors, *natural* pathways. You've taken a structure which evolution has honed over millions of years, and—''

Largo was greatly amused, but this time he refrained from laughing in my face. He said gently, "For most people, navigating their own psyche is like wandering in circles through a maze. That's what *evolution* has bequeathed us: a miserable, confusing prison. And the only thing crude drugs like cocaine or heroin or alcohol ever did was build short cuts to a few dead ends—or, like LSD, coat the walls of the maze with mirrors. And all that White Knights ever did was package the same effects differently.

"*Grey Knights* allow you to reshape the entire maze, at will. They don't confine you to some shrunken emotional repertoire; they empower you completely. They let you control *exactly who you are*.''

I had to struggle to put aside the overwhelming sense of revulsion I felt. Largo had decided to fuck himself in the head; that was his problem. A few users of Mother would do the same—but one more batch of poisonous shit to compete with all the garbage from the basement labs wasn't exactly a national tragedy.

Largo said affably, "I spent 30 years as someone I despised. I was too weak to change—but I never quite lost sight of what I wanted to become. I used to wonder if it would have been less contemptible, less hypocritical, to resign myself to the fact of my weakness, the fact of my corruption. But I never did.''

"And you think you've erased your old personality, as easily as you erased your computer files? What are you now, then? A saint? *An angel?*"

"No. But I'm exactly what I want to be. With Grey Knights, you can't really be anything else."

I felt giddy for a moment, light-headed with rage; I steadied myself against the bars of my cage.

I said, "So you've scrambled your brain, and you feel better. And you're going to live in this fake jungle for the rest of your life, collaborating with drug pushers, kidding yourself that you've achieved redemption?"

"The rest of my life? Perhaps. But I'll be watching the world. And hoping."

I almost choked. "Hoping for *what*? You think your habit will ever spread beyond a few brain-damaged junkies? You think Grey Knights are going to sweep across the planet and transform it beyond recognition? Or were you lying—is the virus really infectious, after all?"

"No. But it gives people what they want. They'll seek it out, once they understand that."

I gazed at him, pityingly. "What people *want* is food, sex and power. That will never change. Remember the passage you marked in *Heart of Darkness*? What do you think that *meant*? Deep down, we're just animals with a few simple drives. Everything else is *less than chaff in a breeze*."

Largo frowned, as if trying to recall the quote, then nodded slowly. He said, "Do you know how many different ways an ordinary human brain can be wired? Not an arbitrary neural network of the same size—but an actual, working *Homo sapiens* brain, shaped by real embryology and real experience? There are about ten-to-the-power-of-ten-million possibilities. A huge number: a lot of room for variation in personality and talents, a lot of space to encode the traces of different lives.

"But do you know what Grey Knights do to that number? They multiply it by the same again. They grant the part of us that was fixed, that was tied to 'human nature,' the chance to be as different from person to person as a lifetime's worth of memories.

"Of course Conrad was right. Every word of that passage was true—when it was written. But now it doesn't go far enough. Because now, all of human nature is *less than chaff in a breeze*. 'The horror,' the heart of darkness, is *less than chaff in a breeze*. All the 'eternal verities'—all the sad and beautiful insights of all the great writers from Sophocles to Shakespeare—are *less than chaff in a breeze*."

I lay awake on my bunk, listening to the cicadas and frogs, wondering what Largo would do with me. If he didn't see himself as capable of murder, he wouldn't kill me—if only to reinforce his delusions of self-mastery. Perhaps he'd just dump me outside the research station—where I could explain to Madelaine Smith how the Colombian air force pilot had come down with an El Nido virus in midair, and I'd valiantly tried to take control.

I thought back over the incident, trying to get my story straight. The pilot's body would never be recovered; the forensic details didn't have to add up.

I closed my eyes and saw myself breaking his neck. The same twinge of remorse passed over me. I brushed it aside irritably. So I'd killed him—and the girl, a few days earlier—and a dozen others before that. The Company had very nearly disposed of me. Because it was expedient—and because it was possible. That was the way of the world: power would always be used, nation would subjugate nation, the weak would always be slaughtered. Everything else was pious self-delusion. A hundred kilometres away, Colombia's warring factions were proving the truth of that, one more time.

But if Largo had infected me with his own special brand of Mother? And if everything he'd told me about it was true?

Grey Knights only moved if you willed them to move. All I had to do in order to remain unscathed was to choose that fate. To wish only to be exactly who I was: a killer who'd always understood that he was facing the deepest of truths. Embracing savagery and corruption because, in the end, there was no other way.

I kept seeing them before me: the pilot, the girl.

I had to feel nothing—and wish to feel nothing—and keep on making that choice, again and again.

Or everything I was would disintegrate like a house of sand, and blow away.

One of the guards belched in the darkness, then spat.

The night stretched out ahead of me, like a river which had lost its way.

GEORGIA ON MY MIND

Charles Sheffield

▼

One of the best contemporary "hard science" writers, British-born Charles Sheffield is a theoretical physicist who has worked on the American space program, and is currently chief scientist of the Earth Satellite Corporation. Sheffield is also the only person who has ever served as president of both the American Astronautical Society and the Science Fiction Writers of America. His books include the best-selling nonfiction title *Earthwatch*, the novels *Sight of Proteus, The Web Between the Worlds, Hidden Variables, My Brother's Keeper, Between the Strokes of Night, The Nimrod Hunt, Trader's World, Proteus Unbound, Summertide, Divergence, Transcendence, Cold as Ice*, and *Brother to Dragons* (which won the John W. Campbell Memorial Award), and the collections *Erasmus Magister* and *The McAndrew Chronicles*. His most recent books are a new novel, *The Mind Pool*, and two collections, *Dancing with Myself* and *One Man's Universe*. He is currently at work on a couple of novels. His stories have appeared in our Seventh and Eighth Annual Collections. He lives in Bethesda, Maryland.

Here he takes us along on a scientific treasure hunt with a pair of researchers who are trying to unravel a fascinating century-old scientific mystery, and who find much *more* than they bargained for. . . .

I first tangled with digital computers late in 1958. That may sound like the dark ages, but we considered ourselves infinitely more advanced than our predecessors of a decade earlier, when programming was done mostly by sticking plugs into plug-boards and a card-sequenced programmable calculator was held to be the height of sophistication.

Even so, 1958 was still early enough that the argument between analog and digital computers had not yet been settled, decisively, in favor of the digital. And the first computer that I programmed was, by anyone's standards, a brute.

It was called DEUCE, which stood for Digital Electronic Universal Computing Engine, and it was, reasonably enough to card players, the next thing after the ACE (for Automatic Computing Engine), developed by the National Physical Laboratory at Teddington. Unlike ACE, DEUCE was a commercial machine; and some idea of its possible shortcomings is provided by one of the designers' comments about ACE itself: "If we had known that it was going to be developed commercially, we would have finished it."

DEUCE was big enough to walk inside. The engineers would do that, tapping at suspect vacuum tubes with a screwdriver when the whole beast was proving balky. Which was often. Machine errors were as common a cause of trouble as programming errors; and programming errors were dreadfully frequent, because we were working at a level so close to basic machine logic that it is hard to imagine it today.

I was about to say that the computer had no compilers or assemblers, but that is not strictly true. There was a floating-point compiler known as ALPHA-CODE, but it ran a thousand times slower than a machine code program and no one with any self-respect ever used it. We programmed in absolute, to make the best possible use of the machine's 402 words of high-speed (mercury delay line) memory, and its 8,192 words of back-up (rotating drum) memory. Anything needing more than that had to use punched cards as intermediate storage, with the programmer standing by to shovel them from the output hopper back into the input hopper.

When I add that binary-to-decimal conversion routines were usually avoided because they wasted space, that all instructions were defined in binary, that programmers therefore had to be very familiar with the binary representation of numbers, that we did our own card punching with hand (not electric) punches, and that the machine itself, for some reason that still remains obscure to me, worked with binary numbers whose most significant digit was on the *right*, rather than on the left—so that 13, for example, became 1011, rather than the usual 1101—well, by this time the general flavor of DEUCE programming ought to be coming through.

Now, I mention these things not because they are interesting (to the few) or because they are dull (to the many) but to make the point that anyone programming DEUCE in those far-off days was an individual not to be taken lightly. We at least thought so, though I suspect that to high management we were all hare-brained children who did incomprehensible things, many of them in the middle of the night (when de-bug time was more easily to be had).

A few years later more computers became available, the diaspora inevitably took place, and we all went off to other interesting places. Some found their way to university professorships, some into commerce, and many to foreign parts. But we did tend to keep in touch, because those early days had generated a special feeling.

One of the most interesting characters was Bill Rigley. He was a tall, dashing, wavy-haired fellow who wore English tweeds and spoke with the open "a" sound that to most Americans indicates a Boston origin. But Bill was a New Zealander, who had seen at firsthand things, like the Great Barrier Reef, that the rest of us had barely heard of. He didn't talk much about his home and family, but he must have pined for them, because after a few years in Europe and America he went back to take a faculty position in the Department of Mathematics (and later the computer science department, when one was finally created) at the University of Auckland.

Auckland is on the north island, a bit less remote than the bleaker south island, but a long way from the East Coast of the United States, where I had put down my own roots. Even so, Bill and I kept in close contact, because our scientific interests were very similar. We saw each other every few years in Stanford, or London, or wherever else our paths intersected, and we knew each other at the deep level where few people touch. It was Bill who helped me to mourn when my wife, Eileen, died, and I in turn knew (but never talked about) the dark secret that had scarred Bill's own life. No matter how long we had been separated our conversations, when we met, picked up as though they had never left off.

Bill's interests were encyclopedic, and he had a special fondness for scientific history. So it was no surprise that when he went back to New Zealand he would wander around there, examining its contribution to world science. What was a surprise to me was a letter from him a few months ago, stating that in a farmhouse near Dunedin, towards the south end of the south island, he had come across some bits and pieces of Charles Babbage's Analytical Engine.

Even back in the late 1950s, we had known all about Babbage. There was at the time only one decent book about digital computers, Bowden's *Faster Than Thought*, but its first chapter talked all about that eccentric but formidable Englishman, with his hatred of street musicians and his low opinion of the Royal Society (existing only to hold dinners, he said, at which they gave each other medals). Despite these odd views, Babbage was still our patron saint. For starting in 1834 and continuing for the rest of his life, he tried—unsuccessfully—to build the world's first programmable digital computer. He understood the principles perfectly well, but he was thwarted because he had to work with mechanical parts. Can you imagine a computer built of cogs and toothed cylinders and gears and springs and levers?

Babbage could. And he might have triumphed even over the inadequacy of the available technology, but for one fatal problem: he kept thinking of improvements. As soon as a design was half assembled, he would want to tear it apart and start using the bits to build something better. At the time of Babbage's death in 1871, his wonderful Analytical Engine was still a dream. The bits and pieces were carted off to London's Kensington Science Museum, where they remain today.

Given our early exposure to Babbage, my reaction to Bill Rigley's letter was pure skepticism. It was understandable that Bill would *want* to find evidence of parts of the Analytical Engine somewhere on his home stamping-ground; but his claim to have done so was surely self-delusion.

I wrote back, suggesting this in as tactful a way as I could; and received in prompt reply not recantation, but the most extraordinary package of documents I had even seen in my life (I should say, to that point; there were stranger to come).

The first was a letter from Bill, explaining in his usual blunt way that the machinery he had found had survived on the south island of New Zealand because "we don't chuck good stuff away, the way you lot do." He also pointed out, through dozens of examples, that in the nineteenth century there was much more contact between Britain and its antipodes than I had ever dreamed. A visit to Australia and New Zealand was common among educated persons, a kind of expanded version of the European Grand Tour. Charles Darwin was of course a visitor, on the *Beagle*, but so also were scores of less well-known scientists, world travelers, and gentlemen of the leisured class. Two of Charles Babbage's own sons were there in the 1850s.

The second item in the package was a batch of photographs of the machinery that Bill had found. It looked to me like what it was, a bunch of toothed cylinders and gears and wheels. They certainly resembled parts of the Analytical Engine, or the earlier Difference Machine, although I could not see how they might fit together.

Neither the letter nor the photographs was persuasive. Rather the opposite. I started to write in my mind the letter that said as much, but I hesitated for one reason: many historians of science know a lot more history than science, and few are trained computer specialists. But Bill was the other way round, the computer expert who happened to be fascinated by scientific history. It would be awfully hard to fool him—unless he chose to fool himself.

So I had another difficult letter to write. But I was spared the trouble, for what I could not dismiss or misunderstand was the third item in the package. It was a copy of a programming manual, hand-written, for the Babbage Analytical Engine. It was dated July 7, 1854. Bill said that he had the original in his possession. He also told me that I was the only person who knew of his discovery, and he asked me to keep it to myself.

And here, to explain my astonishment, I have to dip again into computer history. Not merely to the late 1950s, where we started, but all the way to 1840. In that year an Italian mathematician, Luigi Federico Menabrea, heard Babbage talk in Turin about the new machine that he was building. After more explanations by letter from Babbage, Menabrea wrote a paper on the Analytical Engine, in French, which was published in 1842. And late that year Ada Lovelace (Lord Byron's daughter; Lady Augusta Ada Byron Lovelace, to give her complete name) translated Menabrea's memoir, and added her own lengthy notes. Those notes formed the world's first software manual; Ada Lovelace described how to program the Analytical Engine, including the tricky techniques of recursion, looping, and branching.

So, twelve years before 1854, a programming manual for the Analytical Engine existed; and one could argue that what Bill had found in New Zealand was no more than a copy of the one written in 1842 by Ada Lovelace.

But there were problems. The document that Bill sent me went far beyond the 1842 notes. It tackled the difficult topics of indirect addressing, relocatable programs and subroutines, and it offered a new language for programming the Analytical Engine—what amounted to a primitive assembler.

Ada Lovelace just might have entertained such advanced ideas, and written such a manual. It is possible that she had the talent, although all signs of her own mathematical notebooks have been lost. But she died in 1852, and there was no evidence in any of her surviving works that she ever blazed the astonishing trail defined in the document that I received from Bill. Furthermore, the manual bore on its first page the author's initials, L.D. Ada Lovelace for her published work had used her own initials, A.A.L.

I read the manual, over and over, particularly the final section. It contained a sample program, for the computation of the volume of an irregular solid by numerical integration—and it included a page of *output*, the printed results of the program.

At that point I recognized only three possibilities. First, that someone in the past few years had carefully planted a deliberate forgery down near Dunedin, and led Bill Rigley to ''discover'' it. Second, that Bill himself was involved in attempting an elaborate hoax, for reasons I could not fathom.

I had problems with both these explanations. Bill was perhaps the most cautious, thorough, and conservative researcher that I had ever met. He was painstaking to a fault, and he did not fool easily. He was also the last man in the world to think that devising a hoax could be in any way amusing.

Which left the third possibility. Someone in New Zealand had built a version of the Analytical Engine, made it work, and taken it well beyond the place where Charles Babbage had left off.

I call that the third possibility, but it seemed at the time much more like the third *impossibility*. No wonder that Bill had asked for secrecy. He didn't want to become the laughingstock of the computer historians.

Nor did I. I took a step that was unusual in my relationship with Bill: I picked up the phone and called him in New Zealand.

''Well, what do you think?'' he said, as soon as he recognized my voice on the line.

''I'm afraid to think at all. How much checking have you done?''

''I sent paper samples to five places, one in Japan, two in Europe and two in the United States. The dates they assign to the paper and the ink range from 1840 to 1875, with 1850 as the average. The machinery that I found had been protected by wrapping in sacking soaked in linseed oil. Dates for that ranged from 1830 to 1880.'' There was a pause at the other end of the line. ''There's more. Things I didn't have until two weeks ago.''

''Tell me.''

''I'd rather not. Not like this.'' There was another, longer silence. ''You *are* coming out, aren't you?''

''Why do you think I'm on the telephone? Where should I fly to?''

''Christchurch. South Island. We'll be going farther south, past Dunedin. Bring warm clothes. It's winter here.''

''I know. I'll call as soon as I have my arrival time.''

And that was the beginning.

The wavy mop of fair hair had turned to grey, and Bill Rigley now favored a pepper-and-salt beard which with his weather-beaten face turned him into an approximation of the Ancient Mariner. But nothing else had changed, except perhaps for the strange tension in his eyes.

We didn't shake hands when he met me at Christchurch airport, or exchange one word of conventional greeting. Bill just said, as soon as we were within speaking range, "If this wasn't happening to me, I'd insist it couldn't happen to anybody," and led me to his car.

Bill was South Island born, so the long drive from Christchurch to Dunedin was home territory to him. I, in that odd but pleasant daze that comes after long air travel—after you deplane, and before the jet lag hits you—stared out at the scenery from what I thought of as the driver's seat (they still drive on the left, like the British).

We were crossing the flat Canterbury Plains, on a straight road across a level and empty expanse of muddy fields. It was almost three months after harvest—wheat or barley, from the look of the stubble—and there was nothing much to see until at Timaru when we came to the coast road, with dull grey sea to the left and empty brown coastal plain on the right. I had visited South Island once before, but that had been a lightning trip, little more than a tour of Christchurch. Now for the first time I began to appreciate Bill's grumbling about "overcrowded" Auckland on the north island. We saw cars and people, but in terms of what I was used to it was a thin sprinkle of both. It was late afternoon, and as we drove farther south it became colder and began to rain. The sea faded from view behind a curtain of fog and drizzle.

We had been chatting about nothing from the time we climbed into the car. It was talk designed to avoid talking, and we both knew it. But at last Bill, after a few seconds in which the only sounds were the engine and the *whump-whump-whump* of windshield wipers, said: "I'm glad to have you here. There's been times in the past few weeks when I've seriously wondered if I was going off my head. What I want to do is this. Tomorrow morning, after you've had a good sleep, I'm going to show you *everything*, just as I found it. Most of it just *where* I found it. And then I want you to tell me what *you* think is going on."

I nodded "What's the population of New Zealand?"

Without turning my head, I saw Bill's quick glance. "Total? Four million, tops."

"And what was it in 1850?"

"That's a hell of a good question. I don't know if anyone can really tell you. I'd say, a couple of hundred thousand. But the vast majority of those were native Maori. I know where you're going, and I agree totally. There's no way that anyone could have built a version of the Analytical Engine in New Zealand in the middle of the last century. The manufacturing industry just didn't exist here. The final assembly could be done, but the sub-units would have to be built and shipped in big chunks from Europe."

"From Babbage?"

"Absolutely not. He was still alive in 1854. He didn't die until 1871, and if he had learned that a version of the Analytical Engine was being built *anywhere*, he'd have talked about it nonstop all over Europe."

"But if it wasn't Babbage—"

"Then who was it? I know. Be patient for a few more hours. Don't try to think it through until you've rested, and had a chance to see the whole thing for yourself."

He was right. I had been traveling nonstop around the clock, and my brain was going on strike. I pulled my overcoat collar up around my ears, and sagged lower in my seat. In the past few days I had absorbed as much information about Babbage and the Analytical Engine as my head could handle. Now I needed to let it sort itself out, along with what Bill was going to show me. Then we would see if I could come up with a more plausible explanation for what he had found.

As I drifted into half-consciousness, I flashed on to the biggest puzzle of all. Until that moment I had been telling myself, subconsciously, that Bill was just plain wrong. It was my way of avoiding the logical consequences of his being *right*. But suppose he *were* right. Then the biggest puzzle was not the appearance of an Analytical Engine, with its advanced programming tools, in New Zealand. It was the *disappearance* of those things, from the face of the Earth.

Where the devil had they gone?

Our destination was a farmhouse about fifteen miles south of Dunedin. I didn't see much of it when we arrived, because it was raining and pitch-black and I was three-quarters asleep. If I had any thoughts at all as I was shown to a small, narrow room and collapsed into bed, it was that in the morning, bright and early, Bill would show me everything and my perplexity would end.

It didn't work out that way. For one thing, I overslept and felt terrible when I got up. I had forgotten what a long, sleepless journey can do to your system. For the past five years I had done less and less traveling, and I was getting soft. For another thing, the rain had changed to sleet during the night and was driving down in freezing gusts. The wind was blowing briskly from the east, in off the sea. Bill and I sat at the battered wooden table in the farm kitchen, while Mrs. Trevelyan pushed bacon, eggs, homemade sausage, bread and hot sweet tea into me until I showed signs of life. She was a spry, red-cheeked lady in her middle sixties, and if she was surprised that Bill had finally brought someone else with him to explore Little House, she hid it well.

"Well, then," she said, when I was stuffed. "If you're stepping up the hill you'll be needing a mac. Jim put the one on when he went out, but we have plenty of spares."

Jim Trevelyan was apparently off somewhere tending the farm animals, and had been since dawn. Bill grinned sadistically at the look on my face. "You don't want a little rain to stop work, do you?"

I wanted to go back to bed. But I hadn't come ten thousand miles to lie around. The "step up the hill" to Little House turned out to be about half a mile, through squelching mud covered with a thin layer of sour turf.

"How did you ever find this place?" I asked Bill.

"By asking and looking. I've been into a thousand like this before, and found nothing."

We were approaching a solidly-built square house made out of mortared limestone blocks. It had a weathered look, but the slate roof and chimney were intact. To me it did not seem much smaller than the main farmhouse.

"It's not called 'Little House' because it's *small*," Bill explained. "It's Little House because that's where the little ones are supposed to live when they first marry. You're seeing a twentieth-century tragedy here. Jim and Annie Trevelyan are fourth-generation farmers. They have five children. Everyone went off to college, and not a one has come back to live in Little House and wait their turn to run the farm. Jim and Annie hang on at Big House, waiting and hoping.''

As we went inside, the heavy wooden door was snug-fitting and moved easily on oiled hinges.

''Jim Trevelyan keeps the place up, and I think they're glad to have me here to give it a lived-in feel,'' said Bill. ''I suspect that they both think I'm mad as a hatter, but they never say a word. Hold tight to this, while I get myself organized.''

He had been carrying a square box lantern. When he passed it to me I was astonished by the weight—and he had carried it for half a mile.

''Batteries, mostly,'' Bill explained. ''Little House has oil lamps, but of course there's no electricity. After a year or two wandering around out-of-the-way places I decided there was no point in driving two hundred miles to look at something if you can't see it when you get there. I can recharge this from the car if we have to.''

As Bill closed the door the sound of the wind dropped to nothing. We went through a washhouse to a kitchen furnished with solid wooden chairs, table, and dresser. The room was freezing cold, and I looked longingly at the scuttle of coal and the dry kindling standing by the fireplace.

''Go ahead,'' said Bill, ''while I sort us out here. Keep your coat on, though— you can sit and toast yourself later.''

He lit two big oil lamps that stood on the table, while I placed layers of rolled paper, sticks, and small pieces of coal in the grate. It was thirty years since I had built a coal fire, but it's not much of an art. In a couple of minutes I could stand up, keep one eye on the fire to make sure it was catching properly, and take a much better look at the room. There were no rugs, but over by the door leading through to the bedrooms was a long strip of coconut matting. Bill rolled it back, to reveal a square wooden trapdoor. He slipped his belt through the iron ring and lifted, grunting with effort until the trap finally came free and turned upward on brass hinges.

''Storage space,'' he said. ''Now we'll need the lantern. Turn it on, and pass it down to me.''

He lowered himself into the darkness, but not far. His chest and head still showed when he was standing on the lower surface. I switched on the electric lantern and handed it down to Bill.

''Just a second,'' I said. I went across to the fireplace, added half a dozen larger lumps of coal, then hurried back to the trapdoor. Bill had already disappeared when I lowered myself into the opening.

The storage space was no more than waist high, with a hard dirt floor. I followed the lantern light, to where a wooden section at the far end was raised a few inches off the ground on thick beams. On that raised floor stood three big tea chests. The lantern threw a steady, powerful light on them.

''I told you you'd see just what I saw,'' said Bill. ''These have all been out and examined, of course, but everything is very much the way it was when I found it. All right, hardware first.''

He carefully lifted the lid off the right-hand tea chest. It was half full of old sacks. Bill lifted one, unfolded it, and handed me the contents. I was holding a solid metal cylinder, lightly oiled and apparently made of brass. The digits from 0 through 9 ran around its upper part, and at the lower end was a cog wheel of slightly greater size.

I examined it carefully, taking my time. "It could be," I said. "It's certainly the way the pictures look."

I didn't need to tell him which pictures. He knew that I had thought of little but Charles Babbage and his Analytical Engines for the past few weeks, just as he had.

"I don't think it was made in England," said Bill. "I've been all over it with a lens, and I can't see a manufacturer's mark. My guess is that it was made in France."

"Any particular reason?"

"The numerals. Same style as some of the best French clock-makers—see, I've been working, too." He took the cylinder and wrapped it again, with infinite care, in the oiled sacking. I stared all around us, from the dirt floor to the dusty rafters. "This isn't the best place for valuable property."

"It's done all right for 140 years. I don't think you can say as much of most other places." There was something else, that Bill did not need to say. This was a perfect place for valuable property—so long as no one thought that it had any value.

"There's nowhere near enough pieces here to make an Analytical Engine, of course," he went on. "These must have just been spares. I've taken a few of them to Auckland. I don't have the original of the programming manual here, either. That's back in Auckland, too, locked up in a safe at the university. I brought a copy, if we need it."

"So did I." We grinned at each other. Underneath my calm I was almost too excited to speak, and I could tell that he felt the same. "Any clue as to who 'L.D.' might be, on the title page?"

"Not a glimmer." The lid was back on the first tea chest and Bill was removing the cover of the second. "But I've got another L.D. mystery for you. That's next."

He was wearing thin gloves and opening, very carefully, a folder of stained cardboard, tied with a ribbon like a legal brief. When it was untied he laid it on the lid of the third chest.

"I'd rather you didn't touch this at all," he said. "It may be pretty fragile. Let me know whenever you want to see the next sheet. And here's a lens."

They were drawings. One to a sheet, Indian ink on fine white paper, and done with a fine-nibbed pen. And they had nothing whatsoever to do with Charles Babbage, programming manuals, or Analytical Engines. What they did have, so small that first I had to peer, then use the lens, was a tiny, neat 'L.D.' at the upper right-hand corner of each sheet.

They were drawings of *animals*, the sort of multi-legged, random animals that you find scuttling around in tidal pools, or hidden away in rotting tree bark. Or rather, as I realized when I examined them more closely, the sheets in the folder were drawings of *one* animal, seen from top, bottom, and all sides.

"Well?" said Bill expectantly.

But I was back to my examination of the tiny artist's mark. "It's not the same, is it. That's a different 'L.D.' from the software manual."

"You're a lot sharper than I am," said Bill. "I had to look fifty times before I saw that. But I agree completely, the 'L' is different, and so is the 'D'. What about the animal?"

"I've never seen anything like it. Beautiful drawings, but I'm no zoologist. You ought to photograph these, and take them to your biology department."

"I did. You don't know Ray Weddle, but he's a top man. He says they have to be just drawings, made up things, because there's nothing like them, and there never has been." He was carefully retying the folder, and placing it back in the chest. "I've got photographs of these with me, too, but I wanted you to see the originals, exactly as I first saw them. We'll come back to these, but meanwhile: next exhibit."

He was into the third tea chest, removing more wrapped pieces of machinery, then a thick layer of straw, and now his hands were trembling. I hated to think how Bill must have sweated and agonized over this, before telling anyone. The urge to publish such a discovery had to be overwhelming; but the fear of being derided as part of the scientific lunatic fringe had to be just as strong.

If what he had produced so far was complex and mystifying, what came next was almost laughably simple—if it were genuine. Bill was lifting, with a good deal of effort, a bar, about six inches by two inches by three. It gleamed hypnotically in the light of the lantern.

"It is, you know," he said, in answer to my shocked expression. "Twenty-four carat gold, solid. There are thirteen more of them."

"But the Trevelyans, and the people who farmed here before that—"

"Never bothered to look. These were stowed at the bottom of a chest, underneath bits of the Analytical Engine and old sacks. I guess nobody ever got past the top layer until I came along." He smiled at me. "Tempted? If I were twenty years younger, I'd take the money and run."

"How much?"

"What's gold worth these days. US currency?"

"God knows. Maybe three hundred and fifty dollars an ounce?"

"You're the calculating boy wonder, not me. So you do the arithmetic. Fourteen bars, each one weighs twenty-five pounds—I'm using avoirdupois, not troy, even though it's gold."

"One point nine six million. Say two million dollars, in round numbers. How long has it been here?"

"Who knows? But since it was *under* the parts of the Analytical Engine, I'd say it's been there as long as the rest."

"And who owns it?"

"If you asked the government, I bet they'd say that they do. If you ask me, it's whoever found it. Me. And now maybe me and thee." He grinned, diabolical in the lantern light. "Ready for the next exhibit?"

I wasn't. "For somebody to bring a fortune in gold here, and just *leave* it. . . ."

Underneath his raincoat, Bill was wearing an old sports jacket and jeans. He owned, to my knowledge, three suits, none less than ten years old. His vices were beer, travel to museums, and about four cigars a year. I could not see him as the Two Million Dollar Man, and I didn't believe he could see himself that way. His next words confirmed it.

"So far as I'm concerned," he said, "this all belongs to the Trevelyans. But I'll have to explain to them that gold may be the least valuable thing here." He was back into the second tea chest, the one that held the drawings, and his hands were trembling again.

"These are what I *really* wanted you to see," he went on, in a husky voice. "I've not had the chance to have them dated yet, but my bet is that they're all genuine. You can touch them, but be gentle."

He was holding three slim volumes, as large as accounting ledgers. Each one was about twenty inches by ten, and bound in a shiny black material like thin sandpapery leather. I took the top one when he held it out, and opened it.

I saw neat tables of numbers, column after column of them. They were definitely not the product of any Analytical Engine, because they were hand-written and had occasional crossings-out and corrections.

I flipped on through the pages. Numbers. Nothing else, no notes, no signature. Dates on each page. They were all in October, 1855. The handwriting was that of the programming manual.

The second book had no dates at all. It was a series of exquisitely detailed machine drawings, with elaborately interlocking cogs and gears. There was writing, in the form of terse explanatory notes and dimensions, but it was in an unfamiliar hand.

"I'll save you the effort," said Bill as I reached for the lens. "These are definitely not by L.D. They are exact copies of some of Babbage's own plans for his calculating engines. I'll show you other reproductions if you like, back in Auckland, but you'll notice that these aren't *photographs*. I don't know what copying process was used. My bet is that all these things were placed here at the same time—whenever that was."

I wouldn't take Bill's word for it. After all, I had come to New Zealand to provide an independent check on his ideas. But five minutes were enough to make me agree, for the moment, with what he was saying.

"I'd like to take this and the other books up to the kitchen," I said, as I handed the second ledger back to him. "I want to have a really good look at them."

"Of course." Bill nodded. "That's exactly what I expected. I told the Trevelyans that we might be here in Little House for up to a week. We can cook for ourselves, or Annie says she'd be more than happy to expect us at mealtimes. I think she likes the company."

I wasn't sure of that. I'm not an elitist, but my own guess was that the conversation between Bill and me in the next few days was likely to be incomprehensible to Annie Trevelyan or almost anyone else.

I held out my hand for the third book. This was all handwritten, without a single drawing. It appeared to be a series of letters, running on one after the other, with the ledger turned sideways to provide a writing area ten inches across and twenty deep. There were no paragraphs within the letters. The writing was beautiful and uniform, by a different hand than had penned the numerical tables of the first book, and an exact half inch space separated the end of one letter from the beginning of the next.

The first was dated 12th October, 1850. It began:

> *My dear J.G., The native people continue to be as friendly and as kind in nature as one could wish, though they, alas, cling to their paganism. As our ability to understand them increases, we learn that their dispersion is far wider than we at first suspected. I formerly mentioned the northern islands, ranging from Taheete to Raratonga. However, it appears that there has been a southern spread of the Maori people also, to lands far from here. I wonder if they may extend their settlements all the way to the great Southern Continent, explored by James Cook and more recently by Captain Ross. I am myself contemplating a journey to a more southerly island, with native assistance. Truly, a whole life's work is awaiting us. We both feel that, despite the absence of well-loved friends such as yourself, Europe and finance is "a world well lost." Louisa has recovered completely from the ailment that so worried me two years ago, and I must believe that the main reason for that improvement is a strengthening of spirit. She has begun her scientific work again, more productively, I believe, than ever before. My own efforts in the biological sciences prove ever more fascinating. When you write again tell us, I beg you, not of the transitory social or political events of London, but of the progress of science. It is in this area that L. and I are most starved of new knowledge. With affection, and with the assurance that we think of you and talk of you constantly, L.D.*

The next letter was dated 14 December, 1850. Two months after the first. Was that time enough for a letter to reach England, and a reply to return? The initials at the end were again L.D.

I turned to the back of the volume. The final twenty pages or so were blank, and in the last few entries the beautiful regular handwriting had degenerated to a more hasty scribble. The latest date that I saw was October, 1855.

Bill was watching me intently. "Just the one book of letters?" I said.

He nodded. "But it doesn't mean they stopped. Only that we don't have them."

"If they didn't stop, why leave the last pages blank? Let's go back upstairs. With the books."

I wanted to read every letter, and examine every page. But if I tried to do it in the chilly crawl space beneath the kitchen, I would have pneumonia before I finished. Already I was beginning to shiver.

"First impressions?" asked Bill, as he set the three ledgers carefully on the table and went back to close the trapdoor and replace the coconut matting. "I know you haven't had a chance to read, but I can't wait to hear what you're thinking."

I pulled a couple of the chairs over close to the fireplace. The coal fire was blazing, and the chill was already off the air in the room.

"There are *two* L.D.'s," I said. "Husband and wife?"

"Agreed. Or maybe brother and sister."

"One of them—the woman—wrote the programming manual for the Analytical Engine. The other one, the man—if it is a man, and we can't be sure of that—did the animal drawings, and he wrote letters. He kept fair copies of what he sent off to Europe, in that third ledger. No sign of the replies, I suppose?"

"You've now seen everything that I've seen." Bill leaned forward and held chilled hands out to the fire. "I knew there were two, from the letters. But I didn't make the division of labor right away, the way you did. I bet you're right, though. Anything else?"

"Give me a chance. I need to *read*." I took the third book, the one of letters, from the table and returned with it to the fireside. "But they sound like missionaries."

"Missionaries and scientists. The old nineteenth-century mixture." Bill watched me reading for two minutes, then his urge to be up and doing something—or interrupt me with more questions—took over. His desire to talk was burning him up, while at the same time he didn't want to stop me from working.

"I'm going back to Big House," he said abruptly. "Shall I tell Annie we'll be there for a late lunch?"

I thought of the old farmhouse, generation after generation of life and children. Now there were just the two old folks, and the empty future. I nodded. "If I try to talk about this to them, make me stop."

"I will. If I can. And if I don't start doing it myself." He buttoned his raincoat, and paused in the doorway. "About the gold. I considered telling Jim and Annie when I first found it, because I'm sure that legally they have the best claim to it. But I'd hate their kids to come hurrying home for all the wrong reasons. I'd appreciate your advice on timing. I hate to play God."

"So you want me to. Tell me one thing. What reason could there be for somebody to come down here to South Island in the 1850s, *in secret*, and never tell a soul what they were doing? That's what we are assuming."

"I'm tempted to say, maybe they found pieces of an Analytical Engine, one that had been left untouched here for a century and a half. But that gets a shade too recursive for my taste. And they did say what they were doing. Read the letters."

And then he was gone, and I was sitting in front of the warm fire. I stewed comfortably in wet pants and shoes, and read. Soon the words and the heat carried me away 140 years into the past, working my way systematically through the book's entries.

Most of the letters concerned religious or business matters, and went to friends in England, France, and Ireland. Each person was identified only by initials. It became obvious that the female L.D. had kept her own active correspondence, not recorded in this ledger, and casual references to the spending of large sums of money made Bill's discovery of the gold bars much less surprising. The L.D.'s, whoever they were, had great wealth in Europe. They had not traveled to New Zealand because of financial problems back home.

But not all the correspondence was of mundane matters back in England. Scattered in among the normal chat to friends were the surprises, as sudden and as unpredictable as lightning from a clear sky. The first of them was a short note, dated January, 1851:

> *Dear J.G., L. has heard via A.v.H. that C.B. despairs of completing his grand design. In his own words, "There is no chance of the machine ever being executed during my own life and I am even doubtful of how to dispose of the drawings after its termination." This is a great tragedy, and L. is beside herself at the possible loss. Can we do anything about this? If it should happen to be no more than a matter of money. . . .*

And then, more than two years later, in April, 1853:

> *Dear J.G., Many thanks for the shipped materials, but apparently there was rough weather on the journey, and inadequate packing, and three of the cylinders arrived with one or more broken teeth. I am enclosing identification for these items. It is possible that repair can be done here, although our few skilled workmen are a far cry from the machinists of Bologna or Paris. However, you would do me a great favor if you could determine whether this shipment was in fact insured, as we requested. Yours etc. L.D.*

Cylinders, with toothed gear wheels. It was the first hint of the Analytical Engine, but certainly not the last. I could deduce, from other letters to J.G., that three or four earlier shipments had been made to New Zealand in 1852, although apparently these had all survived the journey in good condition.

In the interests of brevity, L.D. in copying the letters had made numerous abbreviations; w. did service for both "which" and "with," "for" was shortened to f. and so on. Most of the time it did not hinder comprehension at all, and reconstruction of the original was easy; but I cursed when people were reduced to initials. It was impossible to expand those back to discover their identity. A.v.H. was probably the great world traveler and writer, Alexander von Humboldt, whose fingerprint appears all across the natural science of Europe in the first half of the last century; and C.B. ought surely to be Charles Babbage. But who the devil was J.G.? Was it a man, or could it be a woman?

About a third of the way through the book, I learned that this was not just copies of letters sent to Europe. It probably began that way, but at some point L.D. started to use it also as a private diary. So by February, 1854, after a gap of almost four months, I came across this entry:

22 February. Home at last, and thanks be to God that L. did not accompany me, for the seas to the south are more fierce than I ever dreamed, although the natives on the crew make nothing of them. They laugh in the teeth of the gale, and leap from ship to dingy with impunity, in the highest sea. However, the prospect of a similar voyage during the winter months would deter the boldest soul, and defies my own imagination.

L. has made the most remarkable progress in her researches since my departure. She now believes that the design of the great engine is susceptible to considerable improvement, and that it could become capable of much more variation and power than ever A.L. suspected. The latter, dear lady, struggles to escape the grasp of her tyrannical mother, but scarce seems destined to succeed. At her request, L. keeps her silence, and allows no word of her own efforts to be fed back to England. Were this work to become known, however, I feel sure that many throughout Europe would be astounded by such an effort—so ambitious, so noble, and carried through, in its entirety, by a woman!

So the news of Ada Lovelace's tragic death, in 1852, had apparently not been received in New Zealand. I wondered, and read on:

Meanwhile, what of the success of my own efforts? It has been modest at best. We sailed to the island, named Rormaurma by the natives, which my charts show as Macwherry or Macquarie. It is a great spear of land, fifteen miles long but very narrow, and abundantly supplied with penguins and other seabirds. However, of the "cold-loving people" that the natives had described to me, if I have interpreted their language correctly, there was no sign, nor did we find any of the artifacts, which the natives insist these people are able to make for speech and for motion across the water. It is important that the reason for their veneration of these supposedly "superior men" be understood fully by me, before the way of our Lord can be explained to and accepted by the natives.

On my first time through the book I skimmed the second half of the letter. I was more interested in the "remarkable progress" that L.D. was reporting. It was only later that I went back and pondered that last paragraph for a long time.

The letters offered an irregular and infuriating series of snapshots of the work that Louisa was performing. Apparently she was busy with other things, too, and could only squeeze in research when conscience permitted. But by early 1855, L.D. was able to write, in a letter to the same unknown correspondent:

> *Dear J.G., It is finished, and it is working! And truth to tell, no one is more surprised than I. I imagine you now, shaking your head when you read those words, and I cannot deny what you told me, long ago, that our clever dear is the brains of the family—a thesis I will never again attempt to dispute.*

It is finished, and it is working! I was reading that first sentence again, with a shiver in my spine, when the door opened. I looked up in annoyance. Then I realized that the room was chilly, the fire was almost out, and when I glanced at my watch it was almost three o'clock.

It was Bill. "Done reading?" he asked, with an urgency that made me sure he would not like my answer.

"I've got about ten pages to go on the letters. But I haven't even glanced at the tables and the drawings." I stood up, stiffly, and used the tongs to add half a dozen pieces of coal to the fire. "If you want to talk now, I'm game."

The internal struggle was obvious on his face, but after a few seconds he shook his head. "No. It might point you down the same mental path that I took, without either of us trying to do that. We both know how natural it is for us to prompt one another. I'll wait. Let's go on down to Big House. Annie told me to come and get you, and by the time we get there she'll have tea on the table."

My stomach growled at the thought. "What about these?"

"Leave them just where they are. You can pick up where you left off, and everything's safe enough here." But I noticed that after Bill said that, he carefully pulled the fire-guard around the fender, so there was no possibility of stray sparks.

The weather outside had cleared, and the walk down the hill was just what I needed. We were at latitude 46 degrees south, it was close to the middle of winter, and already the Sun was sloping down to the hills in the west. The wind still blew, hard and cold. If I took a beeline south, there was no land between me and the "great Southern Continent" that L.D. had written about. Head east or west, and I would find only open water until I came to Chile and Argentina. No wonder the winds blew so strongly. They had an unbroken run around half the world to pick up speed.

Mrs. Trevelyan's "tea" was a farmer's tea, the main cooked meal of the day. Jim Trevelyan was already sitting, knife and fork in hand, when we arrived. He was a man in his early seventies, but thin, wiry, and alert. His only real sign of age was his deafness, which he handled by leaning forward with his hand cupped around his right ear, while he stared with an intense expression at any speaker.

The main course was squab pie, a thick crusted delicacy made with mutton, onions, apples and cloves. I found it absolutely delicious, and delighted Annie

Trevelyan by eating three helpings. Jim Trevelyan served us a homemade dark beer. He said little, but nodded his approval when Bill and I did as well with the drink as with the food.

After the third tankard I was drifting off into a pleasant dream state. I didn't feel like talking, and fortunately I didn't need to. I did my part by imitating Jim Trevelyan, listening to Annie as she told us about Big House and about her family, and nodding at the right places.

When the plates were cleared away she dragged out an old suitcase, full of photographs. She knew every person, and how each was related to each, across four generations. About halfway through the pile she stopped and glanced up self-consciously at me and Bill. "I must be boring you."

"Not a bit," I said. She wasn't, because her enthusiasm for the past was so great. In her own way she was as much a historian as Bill or me.

"Go on, please," added Bill. "It's really very interesting."

"All right." She blushed. "I get carried away, you know. But it's so good to have *youngsters* in the house again."

Bill caught my eye. Youngsters? Us? His grizzled beard, and my receding hairline. But Annie was moving on, backwards into the past. We went all the way to the time of the first Trevelyan, and the building of Big House itself. At the very bottom of the case sat two framed pictures.

"And now you've got me," Annie said, laughing. "I don't know a thing about these two, though they're probably the oldest thing here."

She passed them across the table for our inspection, giving one to each of us. Mine was a painting, not a photograph. It was of a plump man with a full beard and clear grey eyes. He held a church-warden pipe in one hand, and he patted the head of a dog with the other. There was no hint as to who he might be.

Bill had taken the other, and was still staring at it. I held out my hand. Finally, after a long pause, he passed it across.

It was another painting. The man was in half-profile, as though torn between looking at the painter and the woman. He was dark-haired, and wore a long, drooping moustache. She stood by his side, a bouquet of flowers in her hands and her chin slightly lifted in what could have been an expression of resolution or defiance. Her eyes gazed straight out of the picture, into me and through my heart. Across the bottom, just above the frame, were four words in black ink: "Luke and Louisa Derwent."

I could not speak. It was Bill who broke the silence. "How do you come to have these two, if they're not family?"

His voice was gruff and wavering, but Annie did not seem to notice.

"Didn't I ever tell you? The first Trevelyan built Big House, but there were others here before that. They lived in Little House—it was built first, years and years back, I'm not sure when. These pictures have to be from that family, near as I can tell."

Bill turned to glance at me. His mouth was hanging half-open, but at last he managed to close it and say, "Did you—I mean, are there *other* things? Things here, I mean, things that used to be in Little House."

Annie shook her head. "There used to be, but Grandad, Jim's dad, one day not long after we were married he did a big clear out. He didn't bother with the things you've been finding, because none of us ever used the crawl space under the kitchen. And I saved those two because I like pictures. But everything else went."

She must have seen Bill and me subside in our chairs, because she shook her head and said, "Now then, I've been talking my fool head off, and never given you any afters. It's apple pie and cheese."

As she rose from her place and went to the pantry, and Jim Trevelyan followed her out of the kitchen, Bill turned to me. "Can you believe it, I never thought to *ask*? I mean, I did ask Jim Trevelyan about things that used to be in Little House, and he said his father threw everything out but what's there now. But I left it at that. I never asked Annie."

"No harm done. We know now, don't we? Luke Derwent, he's the artist, and Louisa, she's the mathematician and engineer."

"And the *programmer*—a century before computer programming was supposed to exist." Bill stopped. We were not supposed to be discussing this until I had examined the rest of the materials. But we were saved from more talk by the return of Jim Trevelyan. He was holding a huge book, the size of a small suitcase, with a black embossed cover and brass-bound corners.

"I told you Dad chucked everything," he said. "And he did, near enough, threw it out or burned it. But he were a religious man, and he knew better than to destroy a Bible." He dropped it on the table, with a thump that shook the solid wood. "This comes from Little House. If you want to take a look at it, even take it on back there with you, you're very welcome."

I pulled the book across to me and unhooked the thick metal clasp that held it shut. I knew, from the way that some of the pages did not lie fully closed at their edges, that there must be inserts. The room went silent, as I nervously leafed through to find them.

The disappointment that followed left me as hollow as though I had eaten nothing all day. There were inserts, sure enough: dried wildflowers, gathered long, long ago, and pressed between the pages of the Bible. I examined every one, and riffled through the rest of the book to make sure nothing else lay between the pages. At last I took a deep breath and pushed the Bible away from me.

Bill reached out and pulled it in front of him. "There's one other possibility," he said. "If their family happened to be anything like mine. . . ."

He turned to the very last page of the Bible. The flyleaf was of thick, yellowed paper. On it, in faded multi-colored inks, a careful hand had traced the Derwent family tree.

Apple pie and cheese were forgotten, while Bill and I, with the willing assistance of Jim and Annie Trevelyan, examined every name of the generations shown, and made a more readable copy as we went.

At the time it finally seemed like more disappointment. Not one of us recognized a single name, except for those of Luke and Louisa Derwent, and those we already knew. The one fact added by the family tree was they were half-brother and sister, with a common father. There were no dates, and Luke and Louisa were the last generation shown.

Bill and I admitted that we were at a dead end. Annie served a belated dessert, and after it the two of us wrapped the two pictures in waterproof covers (though it was not raining) and headed back up the hill to Little House, promising Annie that we would certainly be back for breakfast.

We were walking in silence, until halfway up the hill Bill said suddenly, "I'm sorry. I saw it, too, the resemblance to Eileen. I knew it would hit you. But I couldn't do anything about it."

"It was the expression, more than anything," I said. "That tilt to the chin, and the look in her eyes. But it was just coincidence, they're not really alike. That sort of thing is bound to happen."

"Hard on you, though."

"I'm fine."

"Great." Bill's voice showed his relief. "I wasn't going to say anything, but I had to be sure you were all right."

"I'm fine."

Fine, except that no more than a month ago a well-meaning friend of many years had asked me, "Do you think of Eileen as the love of your life?"

And my heart had dropped through a hole in the middle of my chest, and lodged like a cold rock in the pit of my belly.

When we reached Little House I pleaded residual travel fatigue and went straight to bed. With so much of Jim Trevelyan's powerful home-brew inside me, my sleep should have been deep and dreamless. But the dead, once roused, do not lie still so easy.

Images of Eileen and the happy past rose before me, to mingle and merge with the Derwent picture. Even in sleep, I felt a terrible sadness. And the old impotence came back, telling me that I had been unable to change in any way the only event in my life that really mattered.

With my head still half a world away in a different time zone, I woke long before dawn. The fire, well damped by Bill before he went to bed, was still glowing under the ash, and a handful of firewood and more coal was all it needed to bring it back to full life.

Bill was still asleep when I turned on the two oil lamps, pulled the three books within easy reach, and settled down to read. I was determined to be in a position to talk to him by the time we went down to Big House for breakfast, but it was harder than I expected. Yesterday I had been overtired, now I had to go back and reread some of the letters before I was ready to press on.

I had been in the spring of 1855, with some sort of Analytical Engine finished and working. But now, when I was desperate to hear more details, Luke Derwent frustrated me. He vanished for four months from the ledger, and returned at last not to report on Louisa's doings, but brimming over with wonder at his own.

21 September, 1855. Glory to Almighty God, and let me pray that I never again have doubts. L. and I have wondered, so many times,

*about our decision to come here. We have never regretted it, but we
have asked if it was done for selfish reasons. Now, at last, it is clear
that we are fulfilling a higher purpose.*

*Yesterday I returned from my latest journey to Macquarie Island.
They were there! The "cold-loving people," just as my native friends
assured me. In truth, they find the weather of the island too warm in
all but the southern winter months of May to August, and were
almost ready to depart again when our ship made landfall. For they
are migrant visitors, and spend the bulk of the year in a more remote
location.*

*The natives term them "people," and I must do the same, for
although they do not hold the remotest outward aspect of humans,
they are without doubt intelligent. They are able to speak to the
natives, with the aid of a box that they carry from place to place.
They possess amazing tools, able to fabricate the necessities of life
with great speed. According to my native translators, although they
have their more permanent base elsewhere in this hemisphere, they
come originally from "far, far off." This to the Maori natives means
from far across the seas, although I am less sure of this conclusion.*

*And they have wonderful powers in medical matters. The Maori
natives swear that one of their own number, so close to death from
gangrenous wounds that death was no more than a day away, was
brought to full recovery within hours. Another woman was held,
frozen but alive, for a whole winter, until she could be treated and
restored to health by the wonderful medical treatment brought from
their permanent home by the "cold-loving people" (for whom in
truth it is now incumbent upon me to find a better name). I should
add that they are friendly, and readily humored me in my desire to
make detailed drawings of their form. They asked me through my
Maori interpreter to speak English, and assured me that upon my
next visit they would be able to talk to me in my own language.*

*All this is fascinating. But it pales to nothing beside the one
central question: Do these beings possess immortal souls? We are in
no position to make a final decision on such a matter, but L. and I
agree that in our actions we must assume that the answer is yes. For
if we are in a position to bring to Christ even one of these beings
who would otherwise have died unblessed, then it is our clear duty to
do so.*

It was a digression from the whole subject of the Analytical Engine, one so
odd that I sat and stared at the page for a long time. And the next entry, with its
great outburst of emotion, seemed to take me even farther afield.

*Dear J.G., I have the worst news in the world. How can I tell you
this—L.'s old disease is returned, and, alas, much worse than
before. She said nothing to me, but yesterday I discovered bright*

blood on her handkerchief, and such evidence she could not deny. At my insistence she has visited a physician, and the prognosis is desperate indeed. She is amazingly calm about the future, but I cannot remain so sanguine. Pray for her, my dear friend, as I pray constantly.

The letter was dated 25 September, just a few days after his return from his travels. Immediately following, as though Luke could not contain his thoughts, the diary ran on:

Louisa insists what I cannot believe: that her disease is no more than God's just punishment, paid for the sin of both of us. Her calm and courage are beyond belief. She is delighted that I remain well, and she seems resigned to the prospect of her death, as I can never be resigned. But what can I do? What? I cannot sit idly, and watch her slowly decline. Except that it will not be slow. Six months, no more.

His travels among the colony of the "cold-loving people" were forgotten. The Analytical Engine was of no interest to him. But that brief diary entry told me a great deal. I pulled out the picture of Luke and Louisa Derwent, and was staring at it when Bill emerged rumple-haired from the bedroom.

This time, I was the one desperate to talk. "I know! I know why they came all the way to New Zealand."

He stared, at me and at the picture I was holding. "How can you?"

"We ought to have seen it last night. Remember the family tree in the Bible? It showed they're half-brother and half-sister. And *this*." I held the painting out towards him.

He rubbed his eyes, and peered at it. "I saw. What about it?"

"Bill, it's a *wedding picture*. See the bouquet, and the ring on her finger? They couldn't possibly have married back in England, the scandal would have been too great. But here, where nobody knew them, they could make a fresh start and live as man and wife."

He was glancing across to the open ledger, and nodding. "Damn it, you're right. It explains everything. Their sin, he said. You got to that?"

"I was just there."

"Then you're almost at the end. Read the last few pages, then let's head down to Big House for breakfast. We can talk on the way."

He turned and disappeared back into the bedroom. I riffled through the ledger. As he said, I was close to the place where the entries gave way to blank pages.

There was just one more letter, to the same far-off friend. It was dated 6 October, 1855, and it was calm, even clinical.

Dear J.G., L. and I will in a few days be embarking upon a long journey to a distant island, where dwell a certain pagan native people; these are the Heteromorphs (to employ L.'s preferred term for them, since they are very different in appearance from other men, although apparently sharing our rational powers). To these beings we greatly wish to carry the blessings of Our Lord, Jesus Christ. It will be a dangerous voyage. Therefore, if you hear nothing from us within four years, please dispose of our estate according to my earlier instructions. I hope that this is not my last letter to you; however, should that prove to be the case, be assured that we talk of you constantly, and you are always in our thoughts. In the shared love of our savior, L.D.

It was followed by the scribbled personal notes.

I may be able to deceive Louisa, and the world, but I do not deceive myself. God forgive me, when I confess that the conversion of the Heteromorphs is not my main goal. For while the message of Christ might wait until they return to their winter base on Macquarie Island, other matters cannot wait. My poor Louisa. Six months, at most. Already she is weakening, and the hectic blush sits on her cheek. Next May would be too late. I must take Louisa now, and pray that the Maori report of powerful Heteromorph medical skills is not mere fable.

We will carry with us the word of Christ. Louisa is filled with confidence that this is enough for every purpose, while I, rank apostate, am possessed by doubts. Suppose that they remain, rejecting divine truth, a nation of traders? I know exactly what I want from them. But what do I have to offer in return?

Perhaps this is truly a miracle of God's bounty. For I can provide what no man has ever seen before, a marvel for this and every age: Louisa's great Engine, which, in insensate mechanic operation, appears to mimic the thought of rational, breathing beings. This, surely, must be of inestimable value and interest, to any beings, no matter how advanced.

Then came a final entry, the writing of a man in frantic haste.

Louisa has at last completed the transformations of the information that I received from the Heteromorphs. We finally have the precise destination, and leave tomorrow on the morning tide. We are amply provisioned, and our native crew is ready and far more confident than I. Like Rabelais, "Je m'en vais chercher un grand peut-être." God grant that I find it.

I go to seek a "great perhaps." I shivered, stood up and went through to the bedroom, where Bill was pulling on a sweater.

"The Analytical Engine. They took it with them when they left."

"I agree." His expression was a strange blend of satisfaction and frustration. "But now tell me this. *Where did they go?*"

"I can't answer that."

"We have to. Take a look at this." Bill headed past me to the kitchen, his arms still halfway into the sleeves. He picked up the folder of drawings that we had brought from the crawl space. "You've hardly glanced at these, but I've spent as much time on them as on the letters. Here."

He passed me a pen-and-ink drawing that showed one of the creatures seen from the front. There was an abundance of spindly legs—I counted fourteen, plus four thin, whiskery antennae—and what I took to be two pairs of eyes and delicate protruding eyestalks.

Those were the obvious features. What took the closer second look were the little pouches on each side of the body, not part of the animal and apparently strapped in position. Held in four of the legs was a straight object with numbers marked along its length.

"That's a scale bar," said Bill, when I touched a finger to it. "If it's accurate, and I've no reason to think Luke Derwent would have drawn it wrong, his 'Heteromorphs' were about three feet tall."

"And those side pouches are for tools."

"Tools, food, communications equipment—they could be anything. See, now, why I told you I thought for the past couple of weeks I was going mad? To have this hanging in front of me, and have no idea how to handle it."

"That place he mentioned. Macquarie Island?"

"Real enough. About seven hundred miles south and west of here. But I can promise you, there's nothing there relating to this. It's too small, it's been visited too often. Anything like the Heteromorphs would have been reported, over and over. And it's not where Derwent said he was going. He was heading somewhere else, to their more permanent base. Wherever that was." Bill's eyes were gleaming, and his mouth was quivering. He had been living with this for too long, and now he was walking the edge. "What are we going to *do?*"

"We're heading down to Big House, so Annie can feed us. And we're going to talk this through." I took his arm. "Come on."

The cold morning air cut into us as soon as we stepped outside the door. As I had hoped, it braced Bill and brought him down.

"Maybe we've gone as far as we can go," he said, in a quieter voice. "Maybe we ought to go public with everything, and just tell the world what we've found."

"We could. But it wouldn't work."

"Why not?"

"Because when you get right down to it, we haven't found *anything*. Bill, if it hadn't been you who sent me that letter and package of stuff, do you know what I would have said?"

"Yeah. Here's another damned kook."

"Or a fraud. I realized something else when I was reading those letters. If Jim and Annie Trevelyan had found everything in the crawl space, and shipped it to Christchurch, it would have been plausible. You can tell in a minute they know nothing about Babbage, or computers, or programming. But if you wanted two people who could have engineered a big fat hoax, you'd have to go a long way to find someone better qualified than the two of us. People would say, ah, they're computer nuts, and they're science history nuts, and they planned a fake to fool everybody.''

"But we didn't!''

"Who knows that, Bill, other than me and you? We have nothing to *show*. What do we do, stand up and say, oh, yes, there really was an Analytical Engine, but it was taken away to show to these aliens? And unfortunately we don't know where they are, either.''

Bill sighed. "Right on. We'd be better off saying it was stolen by fairies.''

We had reached Big House. When we went inside, Annie Trevelyan took one look at our faces and said, "Ay, you've had bad news then.'' And as we sat down at the table and she began to serve hot cakes and sausage, "Well, no matter what it is, remember this: you are both young, and you've got your health. Whatever it is, it's not the end of the world.''

It only seemed like it. But I think we both realized that Annie Trevelyan was smarter than both of us.

"I'll say it again,'' said Bill, after a moment or two. "What do we do now?''

"We have breakfast, and then we go back to Little House, and we go over *everything*, together. Maybe we're missing something.''

"Yeah. So far, it's a month of my life.'' But Bill was starting to dig in to a pile of beef sausage, and that was a good sign. He and I are both normally what Annie called "good eaters,'' and others, less kind, would call gluttons.

She fed us until we refused another morsel of food, then ushered us out. "Go and get on with it,'' she said cheerfully. "You'll sort it out. I know you will.''

It was good to have the confidence of at least one person in the world. Stuffed with food, we trudged back up the hill. I felt good, and optimistic. But I think that was because the materials were so new to me. Bill must have stared at them already until his eyes popped out.

Up at Little House once more, the real work started. We went over the letters and diary again, page by page, date by date, phrase by phrase. Nothing new there, although now that we had seen it once, we could see the evidence again and again of the brother-sister/husband-wife ambivalence.

The drawings came next. The Heteromorphs were so alien in appearance that we were often guessing as to the functions of organs or the small objects that on close inspection appeared to be slung around their bodies or held in one of the numerous claws, but at the end of our analysis we had seen nothing to change our opinions, or add to our knowledge.

We were left with one more item: the ledger of tables of numbers, written in the hand of Louisa Derwent. Bill opened it at random and we stared at the page in silence.

"It's dated October, 1855, like all the others,'' I said at last, "That's when they left.''

"Right. And Luke wrote 'Louisa has completed the necessary calculations.' ''

Bill was scowling down at a list of numbers, accusing it of failing to reveal to us its secrets. "Necessary for what?"

I leaned over his shoulder. There were twenty-odd entries in the table, each a two or three digit number. "Nothing obvious. But it's reasonable to assume that this has something to do with the journey, because of the date. What else would Louisa have been working on in the last few weeks?"

"It doesn't look anything like a navigation guide. But it could be intermediate results. Worksheets." Bill went back to the first page of the ledger, and the first table. "These could be distances to places they would reach on the way."

"They could. Or they could be times, or weights, or angles, or a hundred other things. Even if they are distances, we have no idea what *units* they are in. They could be miles, or nautical miles, or kilometers, or anything."

It sounds as though I was offering destructive criticism, but Bill knew better. Each of us had to play devil's advocate, cross-checking the other every step of the way, if we were to avoid sloppy thinking and unwarranted assumptions.

"I'll accept all that," he said calmly. "We may have to try and abandon a dozen hypotheses before we're done. But let's start making them, and see where they lead. There's one main assumption, though, that we'll *have* to make: these tables were somehow used by Luke and Louisa Derwent, to decide how to reach the Heteromorphs. Let's take it from there, and let's not lose sight of the only goal we have: We want to find the location of the Heteromorph base."

He didn't need to spell out to me the implications. If we could find the base, maybe the Analytical Engine would still be there. And I didn't need to spell out to him the other, overwhelming probability: chances were, the Derwents had perished on the journey, and their long-dead bodies lay somewhere on the ocean floor.

We began to work on the tables, proposing and rejecting interpretations for each one. The work was tedious, time-consuming, and full of blind alleys, but we did not consider giving up. From our point of view, progress of sorts was being made as long as we could think of and test new working assumptions. Real failure came only if we ran out of ideas.

We stopped for just two things: sleep, and meals at Big House. I think it was the walk up and down the hill, and the hours spent with Jim and Annie Trevelyan, that kept us relatively sane and balanced.

Five days fled by. We did not have a solution; the information in the ledger was not enough for that. But we finally, about noon on the sixth day, had a problem.

A *mathematical* problem. We had managed, with a frighteningly long list of assumptions and a great deal of work, to reduce our thoughts and calculations to a very unpleasant-looking nonlinear optimization. If it possessed a global maximum, and could be solved for that maximum, it might yield, at least in principle, the location on Earth whose probability of being a destination for the Derwents was maximized.

Lots of "ifs." But worse than that, having come this far neither Bill nor I could see a systematic approach to finding a solution. Trial-and-error, even with the fastest computer, would take the rest of our lives. We had been hoping that modern computing skills and vastly increased raw computational power could somehow compensate for all the extra information that Louisa Derwent had available to her and we were lacking. So far, the contest wasn't even close.

We finally admitted that, and sat in the kitchen staring at each other.

"Where's the nearest phone?" I asked.

"Dunedin, probably. Why?"

"We've gone as far as we can alone. Now we need expert help."

"I hate to agree with you." Bill stood up. "But I have to. We're out of our depth. We need the best numerical analyst we can find."

"That's who I'm going to call."

"But what will you tell him? What do we tell *anyone*?"

"Bits and pieces. As little as I can get away with." I was pulling on my coat, and picking up the results of our labors. "For the moment, they'll have to trust us."

"They'll have to be as crazy as we are," he said.

The good news was that the people we needed tended to be just that. Bill followed me out.

We didn't stop at Dunedin. We went all the way to Christchurch, where Bill could hitch a free ride on the university phone system.

We found a quiet room, and I called Stanford's computer science department. I had an old extension, but I reached the man I wanted after a couple of hops— I was a little surprised at that, because as a peripatetic and sociable bachelor he was as often as not in some other continent.

"Where are you?" Gene said, as soon as he knew who was on the line.

That may sound like an odd opening for a conversation with someone you have not spoken to for a year, but usually when one of us called the other, it meant that we were within dinner-eating distance. Then we would have a meal together, discuss life, death, and mathematics, and go our separate ways oddly comforted.

"I'm in Christchurch. Christchurch, New Zealand."

"Right." There was a barely perceptible pause at the other end of the line, then he said, "Well, you've got my attention. Are you all right?"

"I'm fine. But I need an algorithm."

I sketched out the nature of the problem, and after I was finished he said, "It sounds a bit like an under-determined version of the Traveling Salesman problem, where you have incomplete information about the nodes."

"That's pretty much what we decided. We know a number of distances, and we know that some of the locations and the endpoint have to be on land. Also, the land boundaries place other constraints on the paths that can be taken. Trouble is, we've no idea how to solve the whole thing."

"This is really great," Gene said—and meant it. I could almost hear him rubbing his hands at the prospect of a neat new problem. "The way you describe it, it's definitely non-polynomial unless you can provide more information. I don't know how to solve it, either, but I do have ideas. You have to give me *all* the details.''

"I was planning to. This was just to get you started thinking. I'll be on a midnight flight out of here, and I'll land at San Francisco about eight in the morning. I can be at your place by eleven-thirty. I'll have the written details.''

"That urgent?''

"It feels that way. Maybe you can talk me out of it over dinner.''

After I rang off, Bill Rigley gave me a worried shake of his head. "Are you sure you know what you're doing? You'll have to tell him quite a bit.''

"Less than you think. Gene will help, I promise.'' I had just realized what I *was* doing. I was cashing intellectual chips that I had been collecting for a quarter of a century.

"Come on,'' I said. "Let's go over everything one more time. Then I have to get out of here.''

The final division of labor had been an easy one to perform. Bill had to go back to Little House, and make absolutely sure that we had not missed one scrap of information that might help us. I must head for the United States, and try to crack our computational problem. Bill's preliminary estimate, of 2,000 hours on a Cray-YMP, was not encouraging.

I arrived in San Francisco one hour behind schedule, jet lagged to the gills. But I made up for lost time on the way to Palo Alto, and was sitting in the living room of Gene's house on Constanza by midday.

True to form, he had not waited for my arrival. He had already been in touch with half a dozen people scattered around the United States and Canada, to see if there was anything new and exciting in the problem area we were working. I gave him a restricted version of the story of Louisa Derwent and the vanished Analytical Engine, omitting all suggestion of aliens, and then showed him my copy of our analyses and the raw data from which we had drawn it. While he started work on that, I borrowed his telephone and wearily tackled the next phase.

Gene would give us an algorithm, I was sure of that, and it would be the best that today's numerical analysis could provide. But even with that best, I was convinced that we would face a most formidable computational problem.

I did not wait to learn just how formidable. Assuming that Bill and I were right, there would be other certainties. We would need a digital data base of the whole world, or at least the southern hemisphere, with the land/sea boundaries defined. This time my phone call gave a less satisfactory answer. The Defense Mapping Agency might have what I needed, but it was almost certainly not generally available. My friend (with a guarantee of anonymity) promised to do some digging, and either finagle me a loaner data set or point me to the best commercial sources.

I had one more call to make, to Marvin Minsky at the MIT Media Lab. I looked at the clock as I dialed. One forty-five. On the East Coast it was approaching quitting time for the day. Personally, I felt long past quitting time.

I was lucky again. He came to the phone sounding slightly surprised. We knew each other, but not all that well—not the way that I knew Bill, or Gene.

"Do you still have a good working relationship with Thinking Machines Corporation?" I asked.

"Yes." If a declarative word can also be a question, that was it.

"And Danny Hillis is still chief scientist, right?"

"He is."

"Good. Do you remember in Pasadena a few years ago you introduced us?"

"At the *Voyager Neptune* flyby. I remember it very well." Now his voice sounded more and more puzzled. No wonder. I was tired beyond belief, and struggling to stop my thoughts spinning off into non-sequiturs.

"I think I'm going to need a couple of hundred hours of time," I said, "on the fastest Connection Machine there is."

"You're talking to the wrong person."

"I may need some high priority access." I continued as though I had not heard him. "Do you have a few minutes while I tell you *why* I need it?"

"It's your nickel." Now the voice sounded a little bit skeptical, but I could tell he was intrigued.

"This has to be done in person. Maybe tomorrow morning?"

"Friday? Hold on a moment."

"Anywhere you like," I said, while a muttered conversation took place at the other end of the line. "It won't take long. Did you say tomorrow is *Friday*?"

I seemed to have lost a day somewhere. But that didn't matter. By tomorrow afternoon I would be ready and able to sleep for the whole weekend.

Everything had been rushing along, faster and faster, towards an inevitable conclusion. And at that point, just where Bill and I wanted the speed to be at a maximum, events slowed to a crawl.

In retrospect, the change of pace was only in our minds. By any normal standards, progress was spectacularly fast.

For example, Gene produced an algorithm in less than a week. He still wanted to do final polishing, especially to make it optimal for parallel processing, but there was no point in waiting before programming began. Bill had by this time flown in from New Zealand, and we were both up in Massachusetts. In ten days we had a working program and the geographic data base was on-line.

Our first Connection Machine run was performed that same evening. It was a success, if by "success" you mean that it did not bomb. But it failed to produce a well-defined maximum of any kind.

So then the tedious time began. The input parameters that we judged to be uncertain had to be run over their full permitted ranges, in every possible variation. Naturally, we had set up the program to perform that parametric variation automatically, and to proceed to the next case whenever the form of solution was not satisfactory. And just as naturally, we could hardly bear to leave the computer. We wanted to see the results of each run, to be there when—or if—the result we wanted finally popped out.

For four whole days, nothing emerged that was even encouraging. Any computed maxima were hopelessly broad and unacceptably poorly-defined. We went on haunting the machine room, disappearing only for naps and hurried meals. It resembled the time of our youth, when hands-on program debugging was the only sort known. In the late night hours I felt a strange confluence of computer generations. Here we were, working as we had worked many years ago, but now we were employing today's most advanced machine in a strange quest for its own earliest ancestor.

We must have been a terrible nuisance to the operators, as we brooded over input and fretted over output, but no one said an unkind word. They must have sensed, from vague rumors, or from the more direct evidence of our behavior, that something very important to us was involved in these computations. They encouraged us to eat and rest; and it seemed almost inevitable that when at last the result that Bill and I had been waiting for so long emerged from the electronic blizzard of activity within the Connection Machine, neither of us would be there to see it.

The call came at eight-thirty in the morning. We had left an hour earlier, and were eating a weary breakfast in the Royal Sonesta motel, not far from the installation.

"I have something I think you should see," said the hesitant voice of the shift operator. He had watched us sit dejected over a thousand outputs, and he was reluctant now to raise our hopes. "One of the runs shows a sharp peak. Really narrow and tight."

They had deduced what we were looking for. "We're on our way," said Bill. Breakfast was left half-eaten—a rare event for either of us—and in the car neither of us could think of anything to say.

The run results were everything that the operator had suggested. The two-dimensional probability density function was a set of beautiful concentric ellipses, surrounding a single land location. We could have checked coordinates with the geographic data base, but we were in too much of a hurry. Bill had lugged a Times atlas with him all the way from Auckland, and parked it in the computer room. Now he riffled through it, seeking the latitude and longitude defined by the run output.

"My God!" he said after a few seconds. "It's South Georgia."

After my first bizarre reaction—South Georgia! How could the Derwents have undertaken a journey to so preposterous a destination, in the southeastern United States?—I saw where Bill's finger lay.

South Georgia *Island*. I had hardly heard of it, but it was a lonely smear of land in the far south of the Atlantic Ocean.

Bill, of course, knew a good deal about the place. I have noticed this odd fact before, people who live *south* of the equator seem to know far more about the geography of their hemisphere than we do about ours. Bill's explanation, that there is a lot less southern land to know about, is true but not completely convincing.

It did not matter, however, because within forty-eight hours I too knew almost all there was to know about South Georgia. It was not very much. The Holy Grail that Bill and I had been seeking so hard was a desolate island, about a hundred miles long and twenty miles wide. The highest mountains were substantial, rising almost to ten thousand feet, and their fall to the sea was a dreadful chaos of rocks and glaciers. It would not be fair to say that the interior held nothing of interest, because no one had ever bothered to explore it.

South Georgia had enjoyed its brief moment of glory at the end of the last century, when it had been a base for Antarctic whalers, and even then only the coastal area had been inhabited. In 1916, Shackleton and a handful of his men made a desperate and successful crossing of the island's mountains, to obtain help for the rest of his stranded trans-Antarctic expedition. The next interior crossing was not until 1955, by a British survey team.

That is the end of South Georgia history. Whaling was the only industry. With its decline, the towns of Husvik and Grytviken dwindled and died. The island returned to its former role, as an outpost beyond civilization.

None of these facts was the reason, though, for Bill Rigley's shocked "My God!" when his finger came to rest on South Georgia. He was amazed by the *location*. The island lies in the Atlantic ocean, at 54 degrees south. It is six thousand miles away from New Zealand, or from the Heteromorph winter outpost on Macquarie Island.

And those are no ordinary six thousand miles, of mild winds and easy trade routes.

"Look at the choice Derwent had to make," said Bill. "Either he went *west*, south of Africa and the Cape of Good Hope. That's the long way, nine or ten thousand miles, and all the way against the prevailing winds. Or he could sail *east*. That way would be shorter, maybe six thousand miles, and mostly with the winds. But he would have to go across the South Pacific, and then through the Drake Passage between Cape Horn and the Antarctic Peninsula."

His words meant more to me after I had done some reading. The southern seas of the Roaring Forties cause no shivers today, but a hundred years ago they were a legend to all sailing men, a region of cruel storms, monstrous waves, and deadly winds. They were worst of all in the Drake Passage, but that wild easterly route had been Luke Derwent's choice. It was quicker, and he was a man for whom time was running out.

While I did my reading, Bill was making travel plans.

Were we going to South Georgia? Of course we were, although any rational process in my brain told me, more strongly than ever, that we would find nothing there. Luke and Louisa Derwent never reached the island. They had died, as so many others had died, in attempting that terrible southern passage below Cape Horn.

There was surely nothing to be found. We knew that. But still we drained our savings, and Bill completed our travel plans. We would fly to Buenos Aires, then on to the Falkland Islands. After that came the final eight hundred miles to South Georgia, by boat, carrying the tiny two-person survey aircraft whose final assembly must be done on the island itself.

Already we knew the terrain of South Georgia as well as anyone had ever known it. I had ordered a couple of SPOT satellite images of the island, good cloud-free pictures with ten meter resolution. I went over them again and again, marking anomalies that we wanted to investigate.

Bill did the same. But at that point, oddly enough, our individual agendas diverged. His objective was the Analytical Engine, which had dominated his life for the past few months. He had written out, in full, the sequence of events that led to his discoveries in New Zealand, and to our activities afterwards. He described the location and nature of all the materials at Little House. He sent copies of everything, dated, signed, and sealed, to the library of his own university, to the British Museum, to the Library of Congress, and to the Reed Collection of rare books and manuscripts in the Dunedin Public Library. The discovery of the Analytical Engine—or of any part of it—somewhere on South Georgia Island would validate and render undeniable everything in the written record.

And I? I wanted to find evidence of Louisa Derwent's Analytical Engine, and even more so of the Heteromorphs. But beyond that, my thoughts turned again and again to Luke Derwent, in his search for the "great perhaps."

He had told Louisa that their journey was undertaken to bring Christianity to the cold-loving people; but I knew better. Deep in his heart he had another, more selfish motive. He cared less about the conversion of the Heteromorphs than about access to their great medical powers. Why else would he carry with him, for trading purposes, Louisa's wondrous construct, the "marvel for this and every age"—a clanking mechanical computer, to beings who possessed machines small and powerful enough to serve as portable language translators.

I understood Luke Derwent completely, in those final days before he sailed east. The love of his life was dying, and he was desperate. Would he, for a chance to save her, have risked death on the wild southern ocean? Would he have sacrificed himself, his whole crew, and his own immortal soul, for the one-in-a-thousand chance of restoring her to health? Would *anyone* take such a risk?

I can answer that. Anyone would take the risk, and count himself blessed by the gods to be given the opportunity.

I want to find the Analytical Engine on South Georgia, and I want to find the Heteromorphs. But more than either of those, I want to find evidence that Luke Derwent *succeeded*, in his final, reckless gamble. I want him to have beaten the odds. I want to find Louisa Derwent, frozen but alive in the still glaciers of the island, awaiting her resurrection and restoration to health.

I have a chance to test the kindness of reality. For in just two days, Bill and I fly south and seek our evidence, our own "great perhaps." Then I will know.

But now, at the last moment, when we are all prepared, events have taken a more complex turn. And I am not sure if what is happening will help us, or hinder us.

Back in Christchurch, Bill had worried about what I would tell people when we looked for help in the States. I told him that I would say as little as we could get away with, and I kept my word. No one was given more than a small part of the whole story, and the main groups involved were separated by the width of the continent.

But we were dealing with some of the world's smartest people. And today, physical distance means nothing. People talk constantly across the computer nets. Somewhere, in the swirling depths of GEnie, or across the invisible web of an Ethernet, a critical connection was made. And then the inevitable crosstalk began.

Bill learned of this almost by accident, discussing with a travel agent the flights to Buenos Aires. Since then I have followed it systematically.

We are not the only people heading for South Georgia Island. I know of at least three other groups, and I will bet that there are more.

Half the MIT Artificial Intelligence lab seems to be flying south. So is a substantial fraction of the Stanford Computer Science Department, with additions from Lawrence Berkeley and Lawrence Livermore. And from southern California, predictably, comes an active group centered on Los Angeles. Niven, Pournelle, Forward, Benford and Brin cannot be reached. A number of JPL staff members are mysteriously missing. Certain other scientists and writers from all over the country do not return telephone calls.

What are they all doing? It is not difficult to guess. We are talking about individuals with endless curiosity, and lots of disposable income. Knowing their style, I would not be surprised if the *Queen Mary* were refurbished in her home at Long Beach, and headed south.

Except that they, like everyone else, will be in a hurry, and go by air. No one wants to miss the party. These are the people, remember, who did not hesitate to fly to Pasadena for the *Voyager* close flybys of the outer planets, or to Hawaii and Mexico to see a total solar eclipse. Can you imagine them missing a chance to be in on the discovery of the century, of any century? Not only to *observe* it, but maybe to become part of the discovery process itself. They will converge on South Georgia in their dozens—their scores—their hundreds, with their powerful laptop computers and GPS terminals and their private planes and advanced sensing equipment.

Logic must tell them, as it tells me, that we will find absolutely nothing. Luke and Louisa Derwent are a century dead, deep beneath the icy waters of the Drake Passage. With them, if the machine ever existed, lie the rusting remnants of Louisa's Analytical Engine. The Heteromorphs, if they were ever on South Georgia Island, are long gone.

I know all that. So does Bill. But win or lose, Bill and I are going. So are all the others.

And win or lose, I know one other thing. After we, and our converging, energetic, curious, ingenious, sympathetic horde, are finished, South Georgia will never be the same.

This is for Garry Tee—who is a professor of Computer Science at the University of Auckland;

—who is a mathematician, computer specialist, and historian of science;

—who discovered parts of Babbage's Difference Machine in Dunedin, New Zealand;

—who programmed the DEUCE computer in the late 1950s, and has been a colleague and friend since that time;

—who is no more Bill Rigley than I am the narrator of this story.

Charles Sheffield
December 31, 1991

CUSH

Neal Barrett, Jr.

▼

Born in San Antonio, Texas, Neal Barrett, Jr., grew up in Oklahoma City, Oklahoma, spent several years in Austin, hobnobbing with the likes of Lewis Shiner and Howard Waldrop, moved with his family to Fort Worth for a while, and, at last report, was back in Austin again. He made his first sale in 1959, and has been a full-time freelancer for the past twelve years. In the last half of the eighties, Barrett became one of *Asimov's Science Fiction*'s most popular writers, and gained wide critical acclaim for a string of pungent, funny, and unclassifiably *weird* stories he published there, such as "Ginny Sweethips' Flying Circus," "Perpetuity Blues," "Stairs," "Highbrow," "Trading Post," "Class of '61," as well as for other great stories such as "Diner," "Sallie C," and "Winter on the Belle Fourche," which were published in markets as diverse as *Omni, The Best of the West*, and *The New Frontier*. He has had stories in our Fourth, Sixth, and Tenth Annual Collections, as well *two* stories in our Fifth Annual Collection. His books include *Stress Pattern, Karma Corps*, the four-volume *Aldair* series, the critically acclaimed novel *Through Darkest America* and its sequel *Dawn's Uncertain Light*, and a *very* strange novel called *The Hereafter Gang*, which the *Washington Post* referred to as "the Great American Novel." His most recent books are the comic mafia novel *Pink Vodka Blues* (which was optioned for a big-budget Hollywood movie), a new mystery entitled *Dead Dog Blues*, and a collection of some of his shorter work, *Slightly Off Center*.

In the story that follows, an exceptional work even by Barrett's high standard, he treats us to the uproariously funny, profoundly sad, gritty, gentle, and deeply *weird* story of a *very* unusual boy . . . and what his coming-of-age could mean to us all.

The cars started coming in the early hot locust afternoon, turning off the highway and onto the powder-dry road, cars from towns with names like Six Mile and Santuck and Wedowee and Hawk, small-print names like Uchee and Landerville and Sprott, cars from big cities like Birmingham and Mobile and even out of state, all winding down the narrow choked-up road, leaving plumes of red dust for the other cars behind, down through the midsummer August afternoon into deep green shade under sweetgum and sycamore and pine.

The cars hesitated when they came to the bridge. The rust-iron, bolt-studded sides looked strong enough to hold the pyramids, but the surface of the bridge caused some alarm. The flat wooden timbers were weathered gray as stone, sagged and bent and bowed and warped every way but straight. Every time a car got across, the bridge gave a clatter-hollow death-rattle roll like God had made a center-lane strike. Reason said that the Buick up ahead had made it fine. Caution said this was a time to reflect on mortal life. One major funeral a day was quite enough. The best way to view these events was standing up.

Aunt Alma Cree didn't give two hoots about the bridge. She stopped in the middle of the span, killed the engine, and rolled the window down. There was nobody coming up behind. If they did, why they could wait. If they didn't want to wait, they could honk and stomp around, which wouldn't bother Alma Cree a bit. Alma had stood on the steps of Central High in Little Rock in '56, looking up at grim white soldiers tall as trees. Nine years later, she'd joined the march from Selma to Montgomery with Martin Luther King. Nothing much had disturbed her ever since. Not losing a husband who was only thirty-two. Not forty-three years teaching kids who were more concerned with street biology than reading *Moby Dick*.

She *sure* wasn't worried about a *bridge*. Least of all the one beneath her now. She knew this bridge like she knew her private parts. She knew that it was built around 1922 by a white man from Jackson who used to own the land. He didn't like to farm, but he liked to get away from his wife. Alma's grandfather bought the place cheap in '36, and the family had lived there ever since. The timber on the bridge had washed away seven times, but the iron had always held. The creek had claimed a John Deere tractor, a Chevy, and a '39 LaSalle. Alma knew all about the bridge.

She remembered how she and her sister Lucy used to sneak off from the house, climb up the railing, and lean out far enough to spit. They'd spit and then wait, wait for the red-fin minnows and silver baby perch to come to lunch. They never seemed to guess it wasn't something good to eat. Alma and Lucy would laugh until their sides nearly split, because spit fooled the fish every time. Didn't nobody have less sense, Mama said, than two stringy-legged nigger gals who couldn't hardly dry a dish. But Alma and Lucy didn't care. They might be dumb, but they didn't think spit was a fat green hopper or a fly.

Alma sat and smelled the rich hot scent of creek decay. She listened to the lazy day chirring in the trees, the only sound in the silent afternoon. The bottom lay heat-dazed and drugged, tangled in heavy brush and vine. The water down below was still and deep, the surface was congealed and poison green. If you spit in the water now it wouldn't sink. The minnows and the perch had disappeared. Farther up a ways, someone told Alma a year or two before, there was still good water, still cottonmouth heaven up there, and you could see a hundred turtles at a time, sleeping like green clots of moss on a log.

But not down here, Alma thought. Everything here is mostly dead. She remembered picking pinks and puttyroot beside the creek, lady fern and toadshade in the woods. Now all that was gone, and the field by the house was choked with catbrier and nettle, and honeylocust sharp with bristle-thorns. The homeplace itself had passed the urge to creak and sigh. Every plank and nail had settled in and sagged as far as it could go. The house had been built in a grove of tall pecans, thick-boled giants that had shaded fifty years of Sunday picnic afternoons. The house had outlived every tree, and now they were gone too. A few chinaberries grew around the back porch, but you can't hang a swing on a ratty little tree.

"One day, that house is going to fall," Alma said, in the quiet of the hot afternoon. One day it's going to see that the creek and the land are bone dry and Mr. Death has nearly picked the place clean. Driving up from the creek on the red-dust road, she could feel the ghosts everywhere about. Grandpas and uncles and cousins twice removed, and a whole multitude of great aunts. Papa and Mama long gone, and sister Lucy gone too. No one in the big hollow house except Lucy's girl Pru. Pru and the baby and Uncle John Fry, dead at a hundred and three. Dead and laid out in the parlor in a box.

Lord God, Alma thought, the whole family's come to this. A dead old man and crazy Pru, who's tried to swallow lye twice. John Ezekiel Fry and Pru, and a one-eyed patchwork child, conceived in mortal sin.

"And don't forget yourself," she said aloud. "*You* aren't any great prize, Alma Cree."

They couldn't all get in the parlor, but as many came in as they could, the rest trailing out in the hall and through the door and down the porch, crowding in a knot in the heat outside. The window to the parlor was raised up high, so everyone could hear the preacher's message fairly clear.

Immediate family to the front, is what Preacher Will said, so Alma had to sit in a straight-back chair by her crazy niece Pru. Pru to her left, a cousin named Edgar to her right, a man she had never laid eyes on in her life.

Where did they all come from? she thought, looking at the unfamiliar faces all about. Forty, maybe fifty people, driving in from everywhere, and not any three she could recall. Had she known them in the summer as a child, had they come to Thanksgiving some time? They were here, so they must be kin to Uncle Fry.

It was hot as an oven outside the house and in. Before the service got fully underway, a stout lady fainted in the hall. And, as a great ocean liner draws everything near it down into the unforgiving sea, Mrs. Andrea Simms of Mobile pulled several people with her out of sight. Outside, an asp dropped from a chinaberry tree down the collar of an insurance man from Tullahoma, Tennessee. Cries went out for baking soda, but Pru had little more than lye and peanut butter in the house, so the family had to flee.

Preacher Will extolled the virtues of John Ezekiel Fry, noting that he had lived a long life, which anyone there could plainly see. Will himself was eighty-three, and he was certain Uncle Fry had never been inside his church at any time. Still, you had to say *something*, so Will filled in with Bible verse to make the service last. He knew the entire Old Testament and the New, everything but Titus and part of Malachi, enough to talk on through the summer and the fall, and somewhere into June.

Alma felt inertia settling in. Her face was flushed with heat, and all her lower parts were paralyzed. Pru was swaying back and forth, humming a Michael Jackson tune. Cousin Edgar was dead or fast asleep. Not any of us going to last long, Alma thought, and Will isn't even into Psalms.

The Lord was listening in, or some northern saint who was mindful of the heat. At that very moment, the service came abruptly to a halt. A terrible cry swept through the house, ripped through every empty hall and dusty room, through every mousehole and weather crack, through every wall and floor. No one who heard the cry forgot. The sound was so lonely, so full of hurt and woe, so full of pain and sorrow and regret, a cry and a wail for all the grief and the misery the world had ever known, all the suffering and sin, all gathered in a single long lament.

Crazy Pru was up and on her feet, the moment the sound began, Crazy Pru with her eyes full of fright, with a mother's primal terror in her heart.

"Oh Lord God," she cried, "oh sweet Jesus, somethin's happened to my child! Somethin's wrong with little Cush!"

Pru tore through the crowd, fought to reach the hall, Aunt Alma right behind. The people gave way, parting as they came, then trailed right up the stairs, leaving Uncle John Ezekiel Fry all alone with a row of empty chairs, alone except for Leonard T. Pyne.

When Pru saw her child, she went berserk. She shrieked and pulled her hair, whirled in a jerky little dance, moaned and screamed and gagged, and collapsed in an overstuffed chair. Aunt Alma looked into the crib and thought her heart would surely stop. The child was bleeding from its single awful eye, bleeding from its mouth and from its nose, bleeding from its fingers and its toes, bleeding from its ears and from every tiny pore.

Alma didn't stop to think. She lifted up the child, this ugly little kicking screaming pinto-colored child with its possum arms and legs and its baked potato head, lifted up the child and shouted, "Get the *hell* out of my way, I'm coming through!"

Alma ran out of the room and down the hall, the child slick and wet and pulsing like a fancy shower spray. In the bathroom, she laid Cush quickly in the tub and turned the faucet on full. She splashed the child and slapped it, held it right beneath the rushing tap. The red washed away, but Alma didn't care about that. She prayed that the shock would trigger something vital inside and make the bleeding go away.

The child howled until Alma thought her ears would surely burst. It fought to get free from the water streaming down upon its head, it twisted like an eel in her hands, but she knew that she couldn't let it get away.

And then the bleeding stopped. Just like that. Cush stopped crying and the color in the tub went from red to pink to clear, and Alma lifted up the child, and someone handed her a towel.

"There now," Alma said, "you're going to be all right, you're going to be just fine."

She knew this was a lie. You couldn't look at this poor little thing with its one eye open, and one forever shut, and say everything'll be just fine. There wasn't anything fine about Cush. There wasn't now and there wouldn't ever be.

At the very same moment the child stopped bleeding upstairs, Uncle John Ezekiel Fry, dead at a hundred and three, farted in his coffin, shook, and gave a satisfying sigh. In the time it takes a fly to bat its wings, Fry remembered every single instant of his life, every word and past event, every second since May 24 in 1888, things that had touched him, and things that he didn't understand, things that he had paid no attention to at all. He remembered the Oklahoma Run and the Panic of '93. He remembered getting knifed when he was barely twenty-two. He remembered Max Planck. The Sherman Silver Purchase Act. Twenty-one-thousand, four-hundred-sixty-two catfish he'd eaten in his life. A truckload of Delaware Punch. Sixteen tank cars of whiskey and gin. Seven tons of pork. John Maynard Keynes. Teddy up San Juan Hill. Iwo Jima and Ypres. Tiger tanks and Spads. A golden-skinned whore named Caroline. Wilson got four hundred and thirty-five electoral votes, and Taft got only eight. The St. Louis Fair in 1904. Cornbread and beans. A girl in a red silk dress in Tupelo. Shooting a man in Mobile and stealing his silver watch. A lady in Atlanta under a lemon moon, wet from the river, diamond droplets on her skin, and coal-black moss between her thighs.

All this came to Uncle John Ezekiel Fry as he gripped the wooden sides of his box and sat up and blinked his eyes, sat and blinked his eyes and said, "*Whiskey-tit-February-cunt . . . Lindy sweet as blackberry pie . . .*"

There was no one in the room except Leonard T. Pyne. Walking hurt a lot, so he hadn't chased the crowd upstairs. He stared at John Fry, saw his hands on the box, saw a suit that looked empty inside, saw a face like an apple that's been rotting in the bin for some time. Saw tarball eyes that looked in instead of out, looked at things Leonard hoped to God he'd never see.

Leonard didn't faint and didn't scream. His hair didn't stand on end. He didn't do anything you'd think he ought to do, because he didn't for a minute believe a thing he saw. Dead men don't sit up and talk, he knew that. And if they don't, you wouldn't see them do it, so why make a fuss about that?

Leonard T. Pyne got up and walked out. He forgot he had knees near the size of basketballs. He forgot he couldn't walk without a crutch. He walked out and got into his car and drove away. He forgot he'd brought his wife Lucille. He drove back up the dirt road, across the bridge, and headed straight for New Orleans. He'd lived all his life south of Knoxville, Tennessee. He'd never gone to New Orleans, and couldn't think of any reason why he should.

When the folks came down from upstairs, Uncle John Ezekiel Fry was in the kitchen, pulling open cabinets and drawers, looking for a drink. Some people fell down and prayed. Some passed out, but that could have been the heat. People who'd come from out of state said it's just like Fry to pull a stunt like this, he never gave a shit about anyone else. The next time he died, they weren't about to make the trip.

Crazy Pru, when she gathered up her wits, when the baby looked fine, or as fine as a child like that could ever be, said God worked in wondrous ways, anyone could plainly see. What if she hadn't been broke, and they'd gone and had Uncle Fry embalmed instead of laid out in a box? He'd have been dead sure, and wouldn't have a chance of waking up and coming back.

The town undertaker, Marvin Doone, could feel Preacher Will's accusing eyes, and he couldn't think of anything to say. Will had felt sorry for the family, and slipped Doone the cash to do the body up right. Which Marvin Doone had *done*, sucking out all of Uncle Fry's insides, pumping fluids in and sewing everything up, dressing the remains in a black Sears suit, also courtesy of Will. There wasn't any question in Marvin Doone's mind that Fry had absolutely no vital parts, and how could he explain *that* to Will?

Preacher Will never spoke to Doone again.

Doone went home and drank half a quart of gin.

Uncle John Ezekiel Fry said, "*Nipple-pussy-Mississippi-rye*," or words to that effect, walked eight miles back to his own farm, where he ate a whole onion and fried himself some fish.

"Pru, you ought to sell this place and get you and the child into town," Alma said. "There isn't anything left here for you, there's not a reason in the world for you to stay."

"Place is all paid for," said Pru. "Place belongs to me."

They were sitting on the porch, watching the evening slide away, watching the dark crowd in along the creek, watching an owl dart low among the trees. Pru rocked the baby in her arms, and the baby looked content. It played with its little possum hands, it watched Aunt Alma with its black and sleepy eye.

"Paid for's one thing," Alma said. "Keeping up is something else. There's taxes on land, and somebody's got to pay for that. The place won't grow anything, the soil's dead. Near as I can tell, stinging nettle's not a cash crop."

Pru smiled and tickled the baby's chin, though Alma couldn't see that it had a chin at all.

"Me and Cush, we be just fine," Pru said. "We goin' to make it just fine."

Alma looked straight out in the dark. "Prudence, it's not my place to say it, but I will. Your mother was my sister and I guess I got the right. That is *not* a proper name for a child. I'm sorry, but it simply is not."

"Cush, that's my baby's name," Pru said.

"It's not right," Alma said.

Pru rocked back and forth, bare feet brushing light against the porch. "Noah woke," Pru said, "and he know his son Ham seen him naked in his tent. An' Noah say, 'I'm cursin' all your children, Ham, that's what I'm goin' to do. And lo, that's what he did. An' one of Ham's sons was called Cush.' "

"I don't care if he was or not," Alma said. "You want a Bible name, there's lots of names to choose, it doesn't have to be Cush."

Pru gave Alma a disconcerting look. The look said maybe-I'm-present-but-I-might-have-stepped-out.

"Lots of names, all right," Pru said, "but not too many got a *curse*. I figure Cush here, he oughta have a name with a curse."

Alma wasn't certain how she ought to answer that.

Alma found retirement a bore, just like she'd figured that she would. Her name was on the list for substitutes, but the calls that came were few and far between. She worked part-time for the Montgomery NAACP, taking calls and typing and doing what she could. She grubbed in the garden sometimes, and painted the outside of the house. She had thought for some time about a lavender house. The neighbors didn't take to this at all, but Alma didn't care. I might be into hot pink next year, she told Mrs. Sissy Hayes across the street. What do you think about *that*?

She hadn't been feeling too well since fall the year before. Getting tired too soon, and even taking afternoon naps. Something that she'd never done before. Painting the house wore her out, more than she cared to admit. I'm hardly even past sixty-five, she told herself. I'm a little worse for wear, but I'm not about to stop.

What she thought she ought to do was drop by Dr. Frank's and have a talk. Not a real appointment, just a talk. Stop by and talk about iron, maybe get a shot of B.

Dr. Frank gave her seventeen tests and said you'd better straighten out, Alma Cree. You're diabetic and you've got a bad heart. You're maybe into gout. I'm not sure your kidneys are the way they ought to be.

Alma drove home and made herself some tea. Then she sat down at the table and cried. She hadn't cried since Lucy passed away, and couldn't say when before that.

"Oh Jesus," Alma said aloud, the kitchen sun blurring through her tears. "I don't want to get old, and I sure don't want to die. But old's my first choice, I think you ought to know that."

Her body seemed to sense Alma knew she'd been betrayed. There were no more occasional aches and pains, no more little hints. The hurt came out in force with clear purpose and intent.

The pills and shots seemed to help, but not enough. Alma didn't like her new self. She'd never been sick and she didn't like being sick now. She had to quit the part-time job. Working in the garden hurt her knees. Standing up hurt her legs and sitting down hurt everything else. What I ought to do, Alma said, is take to drink. It seems to work for everyone else.

All this occurred after Uncle Fry's abortive skirt with death, and her trip down to the farm. In spite of her own new problems, Alma tried to keep in touch with Pru. She wrote now and then, but Pru never wrote back. Alma sent a little money when she could. Pru never said thanks, which didn't surprise Alma a bit. Pru's mother Lucy, rest her soul, had always been tight with a dollar, even when she wasn't dirt poor. Maybe cheap runs in Pru's blood, Alma thought. God knows everything *else* peculiar does. Lucy flat cheap, and her husband a mean-eyed drunk. No one knew who had fathered Pru's child, least of all Pru. Whoever he was, he couldn't account for Cush. Only God could take the blame for a child like Cush. Heredity was one thing, but that poor thing was something else. There weren't enough bad genes in Alabama to gang up and come out with a Cush.

Alma felt she had to see Pru. She was feeling some better, and Dr. Frank said the trip would do her good. She had meant to come before, but didn't feel up to the drive. In her letters to Pru, she had mentioned that she wasn't feeling well, and let it go at that. Not that Pru likely cared—Alma wouldn't know her niece was still alive if it wasn't for Preacher Will. Will wrote every six months, the same two lines that said Pru and the child were just fine. Alma doubted that. How could they be just fine? How were they eating, how were they getting by? It had been nearly—what? Lord, close to three years. That would make Cush about four. Who would have guessed the child would live as long as that?

As ever, Alma felt a tug from the past as she drove off the highway and onto the red dirt road. She was pleased and surprised to see the land looking fine, much better than it had the time before. The water at the creek was much higher, and running nearly clear. Wildflowers pushed up through the weeds and vines. As she watched the dark water, as she tried to peer down into the deep, a thin shaft of light made its way through the thick green branches up above, dropping silver coins in the shallows by the bank. Alma saw a sudden dart of color, quick crimson sparks against the citron-yellow light.

"Will you just look at that!" she said, and nearly laughed aloud. "Redfin minnows coming back. I'll bet you all still fool enough to eat spit!"

If her back wasn't giving her a fit, if she hadn't stiffened up from the drive, Alma would have hopped out and given spit a try. Instead, she drove through the trees and back out into the sun, up the last hill through the field and to the house.

For a moment, Alma thought that she'd gotten mixed up somehow and turned off on the wrong road. The catbrier and nettles were gone. The field was full of tall green corn. Closer to the house, the corn gave way to neat rows of cabbages, okra and tomatoes, squash and lima beans. The house was freshly painted white. All the windows had glossy black trim and new screens. A brick walk led up to the porch, and perched on the new gravel drive was a blue Ford pickup with oversize tires.

Alma felt a sudden sense of hopelessness and fear. Pru's gone, she thought. She's gone, and someone else is living here. She's gone, and there isn't any telling where that crazy girl went.

Alma parked behind the pickup truck. There wasn't any use in going in. Maybe someone would come out. She rolled the window down. A hot summer breeze dissolved the colder air at once. Alma thought about honking. Not a big honk, not something impolite, just a quick little tap. She waited just a moment, just a small moment more. Then something in the field caught her eye, and she turned and heard the rattle of the corn, looked and saw the green stalks part and saw the scarecrow jerk-step-jiggle down the rows, saw the denim overalls faded white hanging limp on the snap-dry arms, saw the brittle-stick legs, saw the mouse-nibble gray felt hat, stratified with prehistoric sweat, saw the face like a brown paper sack creased and folded thin as dust, saw the grease-spot eyes and the paper-rip mouth, saw this dizzy apparition held together now and then with bits of rag and cotton string.

"Why, Uncle John Ezekiel Fry," Alma said, "it's nice to find you looking so spry. Think the corn'll do good this year?"

"*Crowbar-Chattahoochee-suck*," said Uncle Fry. "*Cling peach-sourdough-crotch . . .*"

"Lord God," Alma said. She watched Uncle Fry walk back into the corn. Either Uncle John Fry or a gnat got in her eye, either John Ezekiel Fry or a phantom cloud of lint. If *he's* still here, Alma thought, then Pru's around, too, though something's going on that isn't right.

At that very moment, Alma heard the screendoor slam and saw Pru running barefoot down the steps—Pru, or someone who looked a whole lot like Pru, if Pru filled out and wasn't skinny as a rail, if she looked like Whitney what's-her-name. If she did her hair nice and bought a pretty pink dress and didn't look real goofy in the eyes. If all that occurred, and it seemed as if it had, then this was maybe Lucy's only daughter Prudence Jean.

"Aunt Alma, sakes alive," Pru said, "my, if this ain't a nice surprise!"

Before Aunt Alma could drag her aches and pains upright, Pru was at the car, laughing and grinning and hugging her to death.

"Say, you look fine," said Pru. "You look just as fine as you can be."

"I'm not fine at all, I've been sick," Alma said.

"Well, you sure look good to me," Pru said.

"It wouldn't hurt you much to write."

"Me and the alphabet never got along too good," said Pru. "But I sure think about you all the time."

Alma had her doubts about that. Pru led her up the brick walk across the porch and in the house. Once more, Alma felt alarmed, felt slightly out of synch, felt as if she'd found the wrong place, felt as if she might be out of state. A big unit hummed in the window and the air was icy cold. The wood floor was covered with a blue-flowered rug. There were pictures on the walls. A new lamp, a new couch, and new chairs.

"Pru," Alma said, "you want to tell me what's going on around here? I mean, everything sure looks nice, it looks fine. . . ."

"I bet you're hot," Pru said. "You just sit and I'll get some lemonade."

I'm not hot now, Alma thought. Isn't anybody hot, you got the air turned down to thirty-two. She could hear Pru humming down the hall. Probably got a brand new designer kitchen, too. A fridge and a stove colored everything but white.

Lord Jesus, the place painted up, a new truck and new screens and a house full of Sears! No wonder Preacher Will never said a whole lot.

Alma didn't want to think where the money came from, Pru looking slick as a fashion magazine, all her best parts pooching in or swelling out. What's a person going to think? A girl doesn't know her alphabet past *D*, she isn't working down at Merrill Lynch. What she's *working* is a Mobile dandy with a mouth full of coke-white teeth and a Cadillac to match.

It's not right, Alma thought. Looks like it pays pretty good, but it's not the thing a girl ought to do. That's what I'll say, I'll say, Pru, I know you've had a real bad time with Cush and all, but it's not the thing to do.

Pru brought the lemonade back, sat down and smiled like the ladies do in *Vogue* when they're selling good perfume.

"Aunt Alma," she said, "I bet you want to hear 'bout all this stuff I got around. I got an idea you maybe would."

Alma cleared her throat. "Well, if you feel like you *want* to tell me, Pru, that's fine."

"I sorta had good fortune come my way," Pru said. "I was workin' in the corn one day when my hoe hit somethin' hard. I dug it up and found a rusty tin can. Inside the can was a little leather sack. And inside *that*, praise God, was nine twenty-dollar gold coins lookin' fresh as they could be. I took 'em to the bank and Mr. Deek say, nine times twenty, Miz Pru, that's a hundred and eighty dollahs, but I'll give you two hundred on the spot. An' say I don't guess you will, Mr. Deek, I said I ain't near as touched as I maybe used to be. I said I seen a program 'bout coins on the public TV.

"So what I *did*, I took a bus down to Mobile an' found an ol' man cookin' fish. I say, can you read and write? He says he can, pretty good, and I say, buy me a book about coins and read me what it say. He does, and he reads up a spell and says, Lord Jesus, girl, these here coins is worth a lot. I says, tell me how much? He says, bein' mint condition like they is, 'round forty-two-thousand-ninety-three, seems to me. Well it took some doing, but I ended up gettin' forty-six. I give the man helped me a twenty dollar bill, and that left me forty-five, nine-hundred-eighty to the good. Now isn't that something? God sure been fine to me."

"Yes, He—well, He certainly has, Pru. I guess you've got to say that. . . ."

The truth is, Alma didn't know *what* to say. She was stunned by the news. All that money from an old tin can? Money lying out in that field for more than a hundred years? Papa and Mama living rag-dirt poor, and nobody ever found a nickel till Pru. Of course, Pru could use the money, that's a fact. But it wouldn't have hurt a thing if one or two of those coins had showed up about 1942.

Pru served Alma a real nice supper, and insisted she stay the night. Alma didn't argue a lot. The trip down had flat worn her out. Pru said she'd fixed up her grandma's room, and Alma didn't have to use the air.

All through the long hot brassy afternoon, while the sun tried to dig through the new weatherstripping and the freshly painted walls, Pru rattled on about the farm and Uncle Fry and how well the garden grew and this and that, talked about everything there was to talk about except Cush. Alma said maybe once or twice, how's Cush doing, and Pru said real quick Cush is doing fine. After that, Alma didn't ask. She tried to pay attention, and marvel at the Kenmore fridge and the noisy Cuisinart, but her mind was never far from the child. Pru seemed to know, seemed to feel the question there between them, felt it hanging in the air. And when she did, she hurried on to some brand new appliance colored fire-engine red or plastic green. And that was as far as Alma got about Cush.

Then, when the day was winding down, when the heat let up and Alma sat on the porch with a glass of iced tea, Pru came up behind her and touched Alma gently on the arm.

"I know you got to see him," Pru said. "I know that's what you gotta do."

Alma sat very still for a while, then she stood and looked at Pru. "The child's my kin," Alma said. "Just because he isn't whole doesn't mean I don't love him all the same."

Pru didn't say a thing. She took Alma's hand and led her down the front steps. The chinaberry trees had grown tall. Their limbs brushed the screened-in porch by the kitchen out back. The ground all around was worn flat, like it always used to be. Worn where the cistern had stood years before, worn on the path that led out behind the house. Alma could see the twisted ghosts of peach trees inside her head. She could see the smokehouse and the outhouse after that, the storm cellar off to the right, and Papa's chicken coop. And when she turned the far corner of the house, there was Cush, sitting in a new red wagon by the steps.

Alma felt herself sway, felt her legs give way, felt her heart might come to a stop. The creature in the wagon looked nothing like a child, nothing like anything that ought to be alive. The baked potato head seemed larger than before, the warped little body parched and seared, dried and shriveled to a wisp. The patchwork pattern of his skin was thick with suppurating sores, pimples and blisters, blots and stains and spots, postules and blotches, welts and bug bites, rashes and swellings and eruptions of every sort. Alma saw the possumlike hands were bent and twisted like a root, saw there wasn't any hair on Cush's head, saw Cush had somehow lost a leg, saw the child wore every conceivable deformity and flaw, every possible perversion of the flesh.

And then Pru sat down on the ground and said, "Cush, this here's your great-aunt Alma Cree. You was too young to recall, but you seen her once before. You want to try an' say hello, you want to try an' do that?"

Cush looked up at Alma with his black and milky eye, looked at Alma through his misery and pain, looked right at Alma Cree and smiled. The smile was something marvelous and terrible to see. One side of Cush's mouth stayed the same, while the other side cut a crooked path past his cheek and past his nose, cut a deep and awful fissure up his face. When you hiccup while you try to sign your name, when the line wanders up and off the page, this is how the smile looked to Alma Cree. Cush's lips parted and secreted something white, then Cush scratched and croaked and made a sound.

"*Haaalm' ah-ah . . . Haaalm' ah-ah,*" Cush said, and then the smile went away.

"*Alma,*" Pru said with pure delight, "that's *right*. See, Aunt Alma? Cush went and said your name!"

"That's real good, Cush," Alma said, "it sure is." She felt the sky whirl crazily about, felt the earth grind its teeth and come apart. She hoped to God she'd make it to the house.

*   *   *

"Pru, you can't take care of that child," Alma said. "You just can't do it by yourself. I know you've done all you could, but poor little Cush needs some help."

"I *got* help, Alma," said Pru, looking at her empty coffee cup. "Since I come into money, Cush has seen every kind of doctor there is. They give me all kinds of lotions, and ever' kind of pill they got. Ain't nothin' works at all, nothin' anyone can do."

"Pru," Alma said, "what happened to his *leg*?"

"Didn't anything happen," Pru said. "Jus' one day 'bout a year ago spring it dropped off. Cush give a little squeal an' I 'bout passed out, and that was all of that."

Tears welled in Pru's eyes. "Aunt Alma, I lay 'wake nights and I wonder just what's going on in God's head. I say, Pru, what's He thinking up there? What you figure He means to do? The farm's all shiny like Jesus reached down and touched the land. It hasn't ever been as fine before. The Lord's took the crazy from my head and got me looking real good, and give me everything there is. So how come He missed helpin' Cush, Aunt Alma? You want to tell me that? How come little Cush is somethin' Jesus flat forgot?"

"I don't know the Lord's ways," Alma said. "I wouldn't know how to answer that." Alma looked down at her hands. She couldn't look at Pru. "What I think I ought to say, what you ought to think about, is you've done about everything you can. There isn't much else you can do. You're young and you've got a life ahead, and there's places where Cush'd maybe be better off than he is . . ."

"*No!*"

The word came out as strong and solid as the hard red iron that held the bridge. "Cush is my child," Pru said. "I don't know why he's like he is, but he's mine. Alma, he isn't going anywhere but here."

Alma saw the will, saw the fierce determination in Pru, and knew at once there was nothing she could say, nothing that anyone could do.

"All right," she said, and tried her best to smile at Pru, "I guess that's the way it's got to be. . . ."

Cush liked the winter and the fall. In the summer and the spring, everything that creeped and flew and crawled did their best to seek him out. Fire ants and black ants and ants of every sort. Earwigs and stinkbugs and rusty centipedes. Sulphur butterflies made bouquets about his head to suck the sores around his eyes. Horseflies and deerflies bit his cheeks. Mosquitoes snarled about like Fokker D-IIIs, and black gnats clotted up his nose. Bees and yellow jackets stung his thighs. If a certain bug couldn't find Cush, Cush would somehow seek it out. With his single bent foot he'd push his wagon down the road. A scorpion would appear and whip its tail around fast and sting his toe.

His mother tried to keep him in the house. But Cush didn't like it inside. He liked to sit out and watch the trees. He liked to watch the hawks knifing high up in the sky. There were so many wonders to see. Every blade of grass, every new flower that pushed its way up through the soil, was a marvel to Cush's eye. He especially loved the creek. By the time he was five, he stayed there every day he could. He loved to watch the turtles poke their heads up and blink and look around. He loved to see the minnows dart about. There were more things that bit, more things around the creek that had a sting, but Cush was used to that.

Besides, staying indoors didn't help. Fresh paint and new doors and super-snug-tight screens couldn't keep the biters out. They knew Cush was there and they found a way in. Anywhere Cush might be, they wriggled in and found him out.

Cush didn't think about pain. Cush had hurt from the very first moment of his life. He didn't know there was anything else. It had never crossed his mind what *not* to hurt was like. A deaf child wonders what it might be like to hear, but he never gets it right.

Cush knew there was something different other persons felt, something that he sensed was maybe missing in his life. He didn't look like other people did, he knew that. Other people did things, and all he did was sit. Sit and look and think. Sit and get gnawed and stung and bit.

Once, in the late evening light, when Cush sat with his mother on the porch, the fan brought out from inside to try and keep the bugs at bay, Cush tried to sound a thought. That's how he looked at talk—sounding out a thought. He didn't try to sound a lot. Nothing seemed to come out right.

Still, on this night, he tried and tried hard. It was something that he knew he had to do. He worked his mouth up as best as he could and let it out.

After Pru ruled out strangulation or a stroke, she knew Cush was winding up to talk. "Hon, I'm not real sure what you're saying," Pru said, "you want to run through that again?"

Cush did. He tried again twice. Legs from old bugs, bits of vital parts, and something like liver-ripple tofu spewed out.

"Whuuuma faar?" Cush said. *"Mudd-whuum-spudoo?"*

Pru listened, and finally understood. When she did, she felt her heart would break in two. She nearly grabbed up Cush and held him tight. She hadn't tried that in three years, but she nearly did it then. "What am I *for*?" Cush had said. "Mother, what am I supposed to *do*?"

Oh Lord, thought Pru, how am I supposed to answer that? Sweet Jesus, put the right words inside my head. Pru waited, and nothing showed up that seemed divine.

"Why, isn't anything you *supposed* to do, Cush," Pru said. "God made the trees and the flowers and the sky, an' everything else there is to see. He made your Aunt Alma and he made you an' me. We're all God's children, Cush. I reckon that's about all we're supposed to be."

Cush thought about that. He thought for a very long time. He looked at his mother's words backward and forward, sideways and inside out. He still didn't know what he was for. He still didn't know what to do. Something, he was sure, but he couldn't think *what*. He was almost certain being one of God's flowers wasn't it.

The trip wore Alma to a nub. She took to her bed for three days, and slept through most of two. When she finally got up, she felt fine. Hungry, and weak in the knees, but just fine. All that driving, and seeing Cush and Pru, Alma thought, that's enough to do anybody in.

She thought about Pru and the farm. How nice Pru looked and how she didn't seem crazy anymore, and how the land and the creek were all coming back again. Everything was doing fine but Cush. Even Uncle Fry. It was like Pru said. All that good flowing in, and Cush not getting his share. It didn't seem right. It sure didn't seem fair.

Alma looked at the garden and decided it was far beyond repair. She dusted the house and threw the laundry in a sack. She went to the grocery store and back. Late in the afternoon, she got a notebook out and started writing things down. Not for any reason, just something she thought she ought to do. She wrote about the funeral and Uncle John Fry. She wrote about Pru and she wrote about Cush. She wrote about how the land had changed and how the creek was full of fish. Nothing that she wrote told her anything she didn't know before, but it seemed to help to get some things down.

Two weeks back from her trip, Alma got a call. Dotty Mae Kline, who'd taught school with Alma for thirty-two years, had retired the year after Alma did. She lived in Santa Barbara now, and said, Alma, why don't you come and stay awhile?

The idea took her by surprise. Alma thought of maybe fourteen reasons why she couldn't take a trip, then tossed them all aside. "Why not?" she said, and called to see when the next plane could fly her out.

Alma meant to stay a week and ended up staying four. She liked Santa Barbara a lot. It was great to be around Dotty Mae. They saw and did everything they could, and even came close to getting tipsy on California wine. Alma felt better than she'd ever felt before. Dotty Mae said that was the good Pacific air. But Alma knew air couldn't do a whole lot for diabetes, or a heart that now and then made a scary little flop.

When she got back home, Alma found a letter in her mailbox from Pru. The postmark was two weeks old. Alma left her bags in the hall, and opened Pru's letter at once. She saw the scrawly hand running up and down the page, and knew this was likely the only letter Pru had ever written in her life.

> *Dir Ant Alma,*
>
> *I bet yur supriz to here from me. The farm is luking fine. A agerkultr man is bout houndin me to deth. He says he don no how corn can git nin feet hi and cabig grow big as washtubs on a place like this. He says there isn no nutrunts in the soil I said I cant help that. Cush dropt a arm last week. Somethin like moss is startid growing on his hed. Otherwiz he doin fine. Uncl Fry is fine too.*
> *Luv Pru*
>
> *P.S. Friday last I wun 2 milun dollars from Ed McMahon. Alma heres a twenny dollar bill I got more than I can spend.*

"Lord God," Alma said, "all that money to a dumb nigger girl!"

She crushed the letter in her fist. She was overcome with anger, furious at

Pru. Things didn't *happen* like that, it wasn't right. All Pru had ever done was get herself knocked up. She hadn't done a full day's work in all her life!

Guilt rushed in to have its say, anger fighting shame, having it out inside her head. Alma was shaken. She couldn't imagine she'd said such a thing, but there it was. She'd tucked it away and out of sight, but it came right up awful quick, which meant it wasn't hiding out too deep.

The anger was there, and it wouldn't go away. Anger at Pru, who was everything she'd spent her life trying not to be. Mama and Papa and Lucy too. Never bringing college friends home because *their* folks were black doctors and CPAs, and she didn't want anyone to know that her family was dirt-poor Alabama overall and calico black, deep-South darkies who said "Yassuh" all the time, and fit the white picture of a nigger to a tee.

She remembered every coffee-chocolate-soot-gray-sable-black face that had passed through her class. Every face for forty-three years. Her soul had ached for every one, knowing the kind of world that she had to send them to. Praying that they'd end up where she was, instead of where she'd been, and all the time saying in her heart, "I'm glad I'm me and I'm not one of *them.*"

Alma sat on her couch in the growing afternoon. She looked at her luggage in the hall. She thought about smart-as-a-whip bright and funny Dotty Mae. She thought about Little Rock and Selma, and she thought about Pru.

"I'm still who I am," Alma said. "I might've let something else creep in, but I know that isn't *me.*" She sat and watched the day disappear, and she prayed that this was true.

In the morning, when she was rested from the trip, when the good days spent in California seemed to mingle with the pleasure and relief of coming back, when she could look at Pru's letter without old emotions crowding in, Alma got her notebook out and found a brand new page, and wondered what she ought to say.

Alma didn't care for things she couldn't understand. She liked to deal in facts. She liked things that had a nice beginning and an end. Dotty Mae Kline had taught Philosophy and Modern English Lit. Alma Cree had been content with Geometry and French.

She looked at Pru's letter. She looked at what she'd written down before. Everything good seemed to fasten on Pru. Everything had came to Cush. The farm was on drugs, on a mad horticultural high. Uncle Fry was apparently alive, and she didn't want to think about that. Alma tried to look for reason. She tried to find a pattern of events. She tried to make order out of things that shouldn't be. In the end, she simply set down the facts—though it went against her nature to call them that. She closed up her notebook and put it on the shelf. Completely out of sight. But not even close to out of mind.

Alma kept her quarterly appointment with Dr. Frank. Dr. Frank said, how are we doing, Alma? and Alma said we're doing just fine. Dr. Frank's nurse called back in a week. Dr. Frank wants to make a new appointment and redo some tests. What for? Alma said, and the nurse didn't care to answer that.

Alma hung up. She looked at the phone. She knew how she *felt*, she felt absolutely great. And she wasn't in California now, she was breathing plain Alabama air.

Alma knew what was wrong with the tests, she didn't have to think twice. Everything was fine inside, she didn't need a test to tell her that, and she'd never been more frightened in her life.

Pru woke up laughing and half scared to death. She sat up and looked around the room, making sure everything was fine, making sure everything was sitting where it should. Pru didn't like to dream. She had real good dreams now, everything coral rose and underwater green, nice colors floating all about, and a honey-sweet sax off somewhere to the right. Real good dreams, not the kind she'd had before. Not the kind with furry snakes and blue hogs with bad breath. Good's a lot better'n bad, thought Pru, but I could do without any dreams at *all*.

Pru's idea of what you ought to do at night was go to sleep and wake up. Dreams took you off somewhere that wasn't real, and Pru had come to cherish real a lot. Once you've been crazy, you don't much want to go back. It's sort of like making out with bears, once seems just about enough.

Pru drank a cup of coffee and started making oatmeal for Cush. Cush wouldn't likely touch it, but she felt she ought to try. The sun was an open steel furnace outside, and she turned all the units down to COLD. When the oatmeal was ready, she covered it with foil, found her car keys, and stepped out on the porch.

A light brown Honda was sitting in the drive. A white man was standing on the steps. Pru looked him up and down. He had blow-dry hair and a blue electric suit. He had rainwater eyes and white elevator shoes.

"What you want 'round here," Pru said. "What you doin' on my place?"

"I want to see the child," the man said.

"You ain't seein' any child," Pru said, "now git."

"God bless you," said the man.

"Same to you."

"I'll leave a few pamphlets if you like."

"What I'd *like* is you off my land now, an' you better do it quick."

The man turned and left.

"My boy isn't any freak," Pru shouted at his back. "I better not see your face again!"

She watched until the car disappeared. "Lord God," she said, and shook her head. They'd started showing up about June. She'd put a gate up, but they kept coming in. Black men in beards. White men in suits. Bald-headed men in yellow sheets. Foreign-looking men with white towels around their heads. Pru shooed them all out, but they wouldn't go away. I want to see the child, is what they said. The way they looked her in the eye flat gave Pru the creeps.

Pru stalked out to the truck. She looked for Uncle Fry. "You all goin' to leave my Cush alone," she said, mostly to herself. "I have to get me a 12-gauge and sit out on the road, you goin' to let my child be."

Uncle John Ezekiel Fry appeared, standing in the corn.

"Uncle Fry," Pru said, "you seen little Cush anywhere?"

"*Goat shit*," Uncle Fry said. "*Rat's ass-Atlanta, strawberry-pee . . .*"

"Thanks," said Pru, "you're sure a lot of help."

Pru knew where to find Cush. She left the pickup on the bridge, got her oatmeal, and started down the bank. You could leave that child in the house or on the porch. You could leave him on the steps out back. Whatever you did, Cush found his way to the bridge. The bridge was where he wanted most to be.

Pru squatted down and tried to see up in the dark, up past the last gray timbers of the bridge, up where the shadows met the web of ancient iron.

"You in there, Cush?" Pru said. "You tell me if you in there, child."

"*Mmmm-mupper-mud*," said Cush.

"That's good," said Pru. She couldn't see Cush, but she knew that he was there. Up in the cavern of the bank, up where the pale and twisted roots hid out from the hot and muggy day.

"I'm leavin' your oatmeal, hon," Pru said. "I'd like you to eat it if you can."

Cush wouldn't, she knew, he never did. The bowls were always where she left them, full of happy ants and flies.

Pru drove up to where the highway met the road to make sure the gate was shut. The man in the Honda was gone. No one else was snooping 'round, which didn't mean they wouldn't be back. I might ought to hire someone, Pru thought. I might send up Uncle Fry. Uncle Fry just standing there would likely keep 'em out.

Driving back across the creek to the house, Pru could see the farm sprawled out in lush array. She could feel the green power there, wild and unrestrained. The air was thick with the ripe and heady smell of summer growth. Every leaf and every blade, every seed and every pod seemed to quiver in the damp and steamy earth. Every fat green shoot pressed and tugged to reach the light, every blossom, every bud, fought to rip itself apart, fought to reach chromatic bliss.

Pru felt light-headed, slightly out of synch, like the time in Georgia when she'd found some good pot. The land seemed bathed in hazy mist. The corn and the house and the chinaberry trees were sharply etched in silver light. Everything was lemon, lavender, and pink, everything was fuzzy and obscure.

"Huh-unh," Pru said, "*no* way, I ain't havin' none of *that*."

She slammed on the brakes and ran quickly to the house. She moved through every single room and pulled all the curtains tight. She took a cold shower and changed her clothes twice. Then she went to the kitchen and made herself a drink.

Pru knew exactly where all the funny colors came from. They were leftover colors from her dream, and she didn't care for that. She didn't need pastel, she needed bright. She didn't need fuzzy, she needed flat solid and absolutely right. Primary colors are the key. Real is where it's at. Special effects don't improve your mental health.

Pru had watched a TV show that said you ought to learn to understand your dreams. Lord help us, she thought, who'd want to go and do *that*?

Pru fixed herself another drink. "I don't want to see funny colors," she said, "I don't want to know about a dream. I don't want to know 'bout *anything*, God, I don't already know *now*. . . ."

It surprised Cush to find out who he was. Sometimes, knowing made him glad. Sometimes, it frightened him a lot. One thing it did, though, was answer the questions he'd always had burning in his head. He knew what he was for. He knew for certain now what he had to do.

Cush didn't know *how* he knew, he just did. Mother didn't tell him and he didn't think it up by himself. Maybe he overheard the minnows in the creek. Minnows whisper secrets after dark. Maybe he heard it from the trees. Trees rumble on all the time. If you listen, you can learn a whole lot. If you listen real close, if you can stand to wait them out. A tree starts a word about April twenty-six, and drags it out till June.

Now I know, Cush thought. I know what it is I have to do. He felt he ought to be satisfied with that, he felt it ought to be enough. But Cush was only five. He hadn't had time to learn the end of one question is only the beginning of the next. He knew what he was for. He knew what it was he had to do. Now maybe someone would come and tell him *why* . . .

Cush heard the car stop on the bridge. The doors opened up and the people got out. Cush could see daylight through the planks. All the people wore white. The man and the woman and the boy, everybody spruced up, clean and shining white.

"Y'all stay here," the man said, "I'll drive up to the house."

"I'll read a verse and say a prayer," the woman said.

"Amen," said the little boy.

The man drove off. The woman sat down on a log. The little boy leaned on the railing and spat into the creek.

"Don't wander off," the woman said, "don't wander off real far."

The woman sat and read. The boy watched minnows in the creek. He heard a bird squawk somewhere in the trees. He saw a toad hop off behind a bush. Mother said toads were Satan's pets, but the boy thought toads were pretty neat. He walked off the bridge into the woods. He followed the toad down to the creek.

Stay away, Cush cried out in his head. *Stay away, little boy, don't be coming down here!*

The little boy couldn't hear Cush. The woman was heavy into John 13, and didn't know the little boy was gone. The boy saw the toad a foot away. Cush heard the cottonmouth sleeping in the brush. He heard it wake up and find the toad, heard it sense breakfast on the way.

Cush sat up with a start. Nerve ends nibbled by gnats began to quiver with alarm. Blood began to flow through contaminated pipes. He knew what was coming, what had to happen next.

Don't do it, snake, Cush shouted in his head. *Don't you bite that little boy!*

Snake didn't seem to hear, snake didn't seem to care.

Can't you see that boy's dressed up clean and white? Can't you see that's someone you shouldn't oughta bite?

Cush tried hard to push the words out of his head, tried hard to toss them out, tried to hurl them at the snake. Snake didn't answer. Snake was trying hard to figure where toad ended and little boy began.

Cush could scarcely breathe. He felt the ragged oscillation of his heart. *You want to bite something, bite me,* he thought as hard as he could. *Leave that little boy alone and bite me!*

Snake hesitated, snake came to a halt. It listened and it waited, it forgot about toad and little boy. It turned its viper will to something down below the bridge.

Something white as dead feet slid down a pale vine, something black and wet moved inside a tree. Green snakes, mean snakes, snakes with yellow stripes, king snakes, ring snakes, snakes of every sort began to ripple whip and slither through the bush, began to find their way to Cush. They coiled around his leg and bit his thigh. They wound around his neck and kissed his eye. Rat snakes, fat snakes, canebrake rattlers, and rusty copperheads. Coral snakes, hog snakes, snakes from out of state. Snakes with cool and plastic eyes smelling dry and stale and sweet. White-bellied cottonmouths old as Uncle Fry, some big as sewer pipes, some near as fat as tractor tires.

Snakes hissed and snapped and curled about until Cush was out of sight. Snakes cut and slashed and tried to find a place to bite. And when the fun was all done, when the snakes had managed all the harm they could, they crawled away to find a nap.

Cush lay swollen and distended like a giant Thanksgiving Day balloon, like a lacerated blimp, like a great enormous bloat. Eight brands of venom chilled his blood and couldn't even make a dent. Seventeen diseases, peculiar to the snake, battled the corruption that coursed through Cush every day, tried and gave it up and did their best to get away.

"Mom, guess what," little boy said on the bridge, "I found me a big green toad."

"Sweet Jesus," mother said, "don't touch your private parts until you wash. You do your thing'll fall right off!"

Mother turned to Psalms 91:3. A few minutes later, the car came back down the road. The man picked his family up fast. He'd faced Pru once and didn't care to try again.

Cush thought he heard the car drive away. He thought about the clean little boy. He thought about the nice white clothes. He wondered if his brand-new bites would bring the beetles and the gnats and the horseflies out in force.

It was nearly ten at night when Alma got the call from Preacher Will. Alma's heart nearly stopped. Oh Lord, she thought, it's Cush. Nothing short of death would get Will to use the phone. It's Pru, Will said, and you ought to come at once. What's wrong with Pru? Alma said, and Will rambled on about bad hygiene and mental fits.

Alma hung up. She was on the road at dawn, and at the gate at ten. There were cars parked up and down the highway, RVs and campers and several dozen tents. People stood about in the red dirt road. They sat and ate lunch beneath the trees. Uncle Fry stood guard and he wouldn't let them in.

"Uncle Fry," Alma said, "What exactly's going on? What are these people doing here, and what on earth is wrong with Pru?"

"*Oyster pie*," said Uncle Fry. "*Commanche-cock-Tallahassee-stew . . .*"

"Well, you're looking *real* fine," Alma said.

Uncle Fry unlocked the gate and let her in. Alma drove down the narrow dusty road toward the bridge. It hadn't been a year since she'd been to see Pru, but she was struck by the way the place had changed. It had flat been a wonder before, springing up new from a worn-out tangle of decay to a rich and fertile farm. She had marveled at the transformation then, but the land was even more resplendent now, more radiant and alive. The very air seemed to shine. Every leaf shimmered, every blade of grass was brilliant green. There were flowers that had certainly never grown here before. Birds that had never come near the place flashed among the trees.

Alma wondered how she'd write it down. That the worst farm in Alabama state was getting prettier every day? That scarcely said a thing. She wished she'd never started taking notes. All she had accomplished was to make herself more apprehensive, more uneasy than before. Putting things down made them seem like they were real. When you saw it on paper, it seemed as if the farm and little Cush and Uncle Fry, and Prudence Jean the millionaire, were just everyday events. And that simply wasn't so. Nothing was going on that made a lick of sense. Nothing that a reasonable person who was over sixty-five liked to think about at all.

"All right, I'm here," Alma said. "I want to know what's happening with Pru. I want to know what's going on. I want to know *why* those people are camping at the gate."

Preacher Will and Dr. Ben Shank were in the kitchen eating Velveeta Cheese and ginger snaps. Oatmeal cookies and deviled ham. There were Fritos and Cheetos, Milky Ways and Mounds, dips and chips of every sort. Every soft drink known to man. Junk food stock was very likely trading high.

"Folks say they want to see the child," said Preacher Will, popping up a Nehi Orange. "More of 'em coming ever' day."

Alma stared at Will. "They want to see Cush? What for?"

"There's blueberry pie on the stove," said Will.

"You make sure those people stay out," Alma said. "Lord God, no wonder poor Pru's in a snit! What's wrong with her, Ben, besides that?"

"Hard to say," said Dr. Shank, digging in a can of cold pears. "Pixilation of the brain. Disorders of the head. Severe aberrations of the mind. The girl's unsettled somewhat. Neurons slightly out of whack."

Alma had never much cared for Ben Shank. What could you say about a man who'd spent his whole adult life working on the tonsil transplant?

"Fine," Alma said, "you want to kind of sum it up? What's the matter with her, Ben?"

"Pru's daffy as a duck."

"I wouldn't leave Satan out of this," said Will.

"Maybe *you* wouldn't, *I* would," Alma said. "Where's Pru now?"

"Up in her room. Been there for three whole days, and she won't come out."

"That girl needs care," said Dr. Shank. "You ought to keep that in mind. I know a real good place."

"The arch fiend's always on the prowl," said Will, "don't you think he's not."

"What I think I better do is see Pru," Alma said.

Alma made her way through the parlor to the hall. Through cartons from K-Mart, Target, and Sears. Through tapes and cassettes, through a stack of CDs, past a tacky new lamp. Coming into money hadn't changed Pru's taste a whole lot.

Pru's room was nearly dark. The windows were covered up with blankets and sheets. The sparse bit of light that seeped in gave the room an odd undersea effect.

"Pru," Alma said, "you might want to talk me in. I don't care to fall and break a leg."

"I'm not crazy anymore," Pru said. "An' I don't care what that fool preacher says, I haven't got a demon in my foot."

"I know that," Alma said. She groped about and found a chair. "What you think's the matter with you, Pru? Why you sitting up here in the dark?"

Pru sat cross-legged in the middle of her bed. Alma couldn't see her face or read her eyes.

"If I'm sittin' in the dark, I can't *see*," Pru said. "I don't want to see a thing, Alma, seeing's what messes up my head."

"Pru, what is it you don't want to see," Alma said, almost afraid to ask. "You want to tell me that?"

"I ain't going to a looney house, Alma, that's a fact."

"Now, nobody's going to do that."

"I sit right here, I'll be fine. Long as I keep out the light."

"You don't like the light?"

"I flat can't take it no more," Pru said. "I can't stand anything *pink*. Everything's lavender or a wimpy shade of green. Everything's got a fuzzy glow. I'm sick to death of tangerine. I feel like I fell into a sack of them after-dinner mints. Lord, I'd give a dollar for a little piece of brown. I'd double that for something red."

Pru leaned forward on the bed. Alma reached out and found her hands. Her eyes were big and round and her hands were like ice.

"I'm scared, Aunt Alma," Pru said. "Corn don't come in baby blue. I never seen a apricot lettuce in my life. I *know* what's going on, I know that. Them Easter egg colors is leakin' through out of my dreams. They're comin' right in and I can't hold 'em back!''

Alma felt a chill, as if someone had pressed a cold Sprite against her back. She held onto Pru real tight.

"I haven't seen any blue corn," Alma said, "but I know what you're telling me, Pru. I want you to think on that, you understand? Hon, it isn't just *you*, it's not just something in your head. I could feel it driving in, like everything's humming in the ground. Like every growing thing on the place is just swelling up to bust.''

Alma gripped Pru's shoulder and looked right in her eyes. "You've got about the prettiest farm there is, but you and I know it isn't how it *ought* to be. It doesn't look right, Pru, and it isn't any wonder that you're having color problems in your head. Shoot, this place'd send Van Gogh around the bend.''

"Oh God, Aunt Alma, I'm scared," said Pru, "I'm scared as I can be!''

Tears trailed down Pru's cheeks and Alma took her in her arms.

"It's going to be fine," Alma said. "Don't you worry, it'll be just fine.''

"You ain't goin' to leave me here, are you?''

"Child, I am staying right here," Alma said, "I'm not going anywhere at all.''

Alma held her tight. She could feel Pru's tears, she could feel her body shake. I'm sure glad you're hugging real good, Alma thought, so you won't know that I'm scared, too.

Alma shooed Will and Dr. Shank out the door and started cleaning up the house. The kitchen took an hour and a half. She worked through geologic zones, through empty pizza cartons and turkey pot pies. Through Ritz Cracker boxes and frozen french fries. It might be that malnutrition was affecting Pru's head, Alma thought. A brain won't run in third gear on potato chips and Mounds.

She had the house in shape by late afternoon. Pru seemed better, but she wouldn't leave her room. Alma was alarmed to learn that Cush stayed at the creek all the time, that he wouldn't come back to the house at all.

"It isn't right," Alma said. "A little boy shouldn't live beneath a bridge.''

"Might be he shouldn't," Pru said, "but I reckon that he *is*.''

Alma fixed Pru supper, and took a plate up to the gate for Uncle Fry. If Uncle Fry had moved an inch since she'd left him there at ten, she couldn't tell. The cars were still there. People stood outside the gate and looked in. They didn't talk or move about. Some of the men had awful wigs. Some of the men were bald. Some of the men wore bib overalls. More than a few wore funny robes. They all gave Alma the creeps. What did they want with *Cush?* What did they think they'd *see?* As far as that goes, how did they even know that Cush was *there?*

"I don't want to think about that," Alma said, as she drove back toward the creek. "I've got enough on my mind with just Pru.''

* * *

Alma left the car on the road and took some oatmeal down to Cush. She walked through tall sweet grass down a path beside the bridge, down through a canopy of iridescent green. The moment she saw the creek, she stopped still. The sight overwhelmed her, it took her breath away. Thick strands of fern lined the stream on either side. Wild red roses climbed the trunk of every tree. Fish darted quicksilver-bright through water clear as air. Farther toward the bend, red flag and coralroot set the banks afire.

There was more, though, a great deal more than the eye could truly see. Standing on the bank in dusky shade, standing by the creek in citron light, Alma felt totally at peace, suspended in the quiet, inconceivably serene. The rest of the farm seemed far away, stirring in the steamy afternoon, caught up in purpose and intent, caught in a fever, in a frenzy of intoxicated growth.

The creek was apart from all that. It was finished and complete, in a pure and tranquil state. Alma felt certain nothing more could happen here that could possibly enhance this magic place. She felt she was seven, she felt she was ten, she felt her sister Lucy by her side. And as she stood there caught up in the spell, lost in the enchantment of the day, her eyes seemed to draw her to the bridge, to the shadows under old and rusted iron.

Alma held her breath. Something seemed to flicker there, vague and undefined, something like a dazzle or a haze. A pale shaft dancing for an instant through the quiet. Dust motes captured in an errant beam of light. It was there and it was gone and it wasn't gone at all.

"Hello, Aunt Alma," Cush said.

Alma stood perfectly still. She felt incredibly calm, she felt frightened and alarmed, she felt totally at ease.

"Are you there, Aunt Alma, are you there?"

"I'm right here, Cush," Alma said. "I'm glad to see you're talking some better than you could." His voice was a croak, like gravel in a can. "I've brought you some oatmeal, hon. You need to eat something hot and good."

"Tell mother that I'm doing just fine," Cush said. *"You tell her that for me."*

"Now, you ought to tell her that yourself," Alma said, "that's what you ought to do. Cush, you shouldn't be staying down here. You shouldn't be out beneath a bridge."

"I'm where I ought to be," Cush said.

"Now, why you say that?"

"This is where I got to stay, this is where I got to be."

"You already told me that. What I'd like to know is *why.*"

"This is where I am, Aunt Alma. Right here's where I got to be."

He may be different, Alma thought, but he's just as aggravating as any other child I've ever known.

"Now, Cush—" Alma said, and that's as far as Alma got. Words that might have been were never said. Alma was struck by a great rush of loneliness and joy, shaken to her soul by a wave of jubilation and regret, nearly swept away by chaos and accord.

As quickly as it came, the moment passed and let her go. Let her go but held her with the faint deep whisper of the earth. Held her with a hint of the sweet oscillation of the stars. She tried to remember the universal dance. Tried her best to hum the lost chord. There were things she had forgotten, there were things she almost knew. She hung on the restive edge of secrets nearly told, a breath away from mysteries revealed. She wondered if she'd died or if she'd just come to life. She wondered why they both looked just the same.

And when she found herself again, when her heart began to stir, she looked into the shadow of the bridge. She looked, and there was Cush. Cush, or a spiderweb caught against the sun; Cush, or a phantom spark of light.

"Cush, I know you're there," Alma said. "Cush, you *talk* to me, you hear?"

Alma stood and listened to the creek. She listened to a crow call far off in the trees. She listened and she waited in the hot electric summer afternoon. . . .

Pru wasn't any better and she wasn't any worse. Pastel shades were still clouding up her head. Mint seemed the color of the day. She said she felt she had a rush, and took three or four baths before dark. She soaked herself in European soap and rubbed Chinese lotions on her skin. Every hour and a half, she completely changed her clothes.

Alma couldn't take all the bathing and the changing and the scurrying about. It made her dizzy just to watch. She prowled through the kitchen, searching for anything that wasn't in a can or in a sack. Lord God, Alma thought, there's a garden outside that would bring Luther Burbank to tears, and Pru's got a corner on Spam.

She went outside and picked several ears of corn. She yanked up carrots big as Little League bats. She made a hot supper and a salad on the side, and took it up to Pru. Pru picked around a while and wrinkled up her nose.

"What kinda stuff is this?"

"Those are vegetables, Pru. You probably never saw one before. We grow 'em all the time on Mars."

"I ain't real hungry right now."

"Pretend you've got Fruit Loops and a Coke," Alma said. "I'll leave your plate here."

Alma went back downstairs and ate alone. She took a lot of time cleaning up. She did things she didn't have to do. She didn't want to think. She didn't want to think about Cush or what had happened at the bridge.

Nothing did any good at all. Cush was in her head and he wouldn't go away. "I don't even know what *happened* out there," Alma said. "I don't know if anything *did*."

Whatever it was, it had left her full of hope and disbelief, full of doubt and good cheer, full of bliss and awful dread. She felt she was nearly in tune, on the edge of perfect pitch. She felt she nearly had the beat. That's what he did, Alma thought. He gave me a peek somewhere and brought me back. Brought me back and never told me where I'd been.

Alma left the house and walked out onto the porch. The air was hot and still. Night was on the way, and the land and the sky were strangely green. It looked like Oz, right before the wizard came clean.

Oh Lord, Alma thought, looking out into the quickly fading light, I guess I knew. I knew and I didn't want to see. I wrote it all down and I thought that'd make it go away. The farm and the money and Uncle John Fry, nothing the way it ought to be. And all of that coming out of Cush. Coming from a child with awful skin and a baked potato head.

"Who *are* you, Cush," Alma called into the night. "Tell me who you are, tell me what you got to do!"

The cornfield shimmered with luminescent light. The air seemed electric, urgent and alive, she could feel it as it danced along her skin, she could feel the night press upon the land, she could feel the deep cadence of the earth.

"It's going to happen," Alma said, and felt a chill. "It's going to happen and it's going to happen here. *Who are you, Cush,*" she said again. *"Tell me what it is you've got to do. . . ."*

Alma tried to rest. She knew she wouldn't get away with that. Not in Pru's house, and not tonight. She dozed now and then. She made tea twice. The wind picked up and began to shake the house. It blew from the north, then shifted to the south. Tried the east and tried the west, and petered out.

A little after one, she fell asleep. At two, she woke up with a start. Pru was screaming like a cat. Alma wrapped her robe around herself and made her way back up the stairs.

"Don't turn on the light!" Pru shouted, when Alma opened up the door.

"Pru, I'm getting tired of trying to find you in the dark," Alma said. She felt her way around the walls. A glow from downstairs showed her Pru. She was huddled on the floor in the corner by the bed. She was shaking like a malted-milk machine: and her eyes were fever bright.

"Pru, what's the *matter* with you, child?" Alma sat down and held her tight.

"Oh God," Pru said, "my whole insides are full of fleas. It might be fire ants or bees, it's hard to tell. They're down in my fingers and my toes. They're crawling in my knees."

Alma felt Pru's head. "I'd say you're right close to a hundred and three. I'll find you an aspirin somewhere. I'll make a cup of tea."

"I've got some Raid beneath the sink, you might bring me some of that. Oh Jesus, Aunt Alma, I'm scared. I think something's wrong with Cush. I think he needs his mama bad. I think I better go and see."

"I don't think Cush needs a thing," Alma said, "I think Cush is doing fine. Pru, you better come downstairs and sleep with me. We'll keep off all the lights."

"Don't matter," said Pru. "Dark helps some, but it don't keep the pinks from sneakin' in. I can take them limes, I can tolerate the peach, but I can't put up with pink."

"I'll get a pill," Alma said, "you try and get some sleep."

Alma helped Pru back into bed and went out and closed the door. Lord God, she thought, I don't know what to do. You can't hardly reason with a person's got decorator colors in her head.

Alma's watch said a quarter after three. She didn't even try to go to bed. She sat in the kitchen and drank a cup of tea. She tried not to think about Cush. She tried not to think about Pru. Everything would work itself out. Everything would be just fine. She could hear Pru pacing about. Walking this way and that, humming a Ray Charles tune. Likely works good in the dark, Alma thought.

At exactly four o'clock, the lights began to flicker on and off. The wind came up again, this time blowing straight down. Alma knew high-school science by heart, and she'd never heard of *that*. Cups and dishes rattled on the shelves. The teapot slid across the sink. Cabinets and drawers popped open all at once. Peanut butter did a flip, and food from overseas hopped about.

Alma held onto the Kenmore stove. She knew that Sears made their stuff to last. In a moment, the rumbles and the shakes came abruptly to a halt. The wind disappeared, and Alma's ears began to pop. Something spattered on the window, something drummed upon the roof, and the rain began to fall. Alma ran into the parlor and peeked out through the blinds. Pink lightning sizzled through the corn. Every bush and every tree, every single blade of grass, was bathed in pale coronal light. Light danced up the steps and up the porch and in the house. It danced on the ceiling on the walls and on the floor. It crawled along the tables and the lamps.

Lord, Alma thought, this isn't going to set well with Pru. She listened, but she didn't hear a sound from upstairs. Pru wasn't singing anymore, but she wasn't up stomping or crying out.

The rain stopped as quickly as it came. Alma stepped out onto the porch. The very air was charged, rich and cool and clean. It made Alma dizzy just to breathe. The sky overhead was full of stars. The first hint of morning started glowing in the east, darts of color sharp as Northern Lights. And as the day began to grow, as the shadows disappeared, Alma saw them everywhere about, people standing in the road, people standing in the corn, people standing everywhere, and everyone looking past the field and through the woods, everyone looking toward the bridge.

Alma looked past the corn, past the people and the trees. Something pure and crystal bright struck her eyes, something splendid as a star, something radiant and white. Alma caught her breath. She looked at the light and she laughed and cried with joy. She felt she ought to sing. She felt goofy in the head, she felt lighter than a gnat. She felt as if someone had shot her up with bliss.

"It's going to happen," Alma said, "it's going to happen and it's going to happen here!"

Alma couldn't stay put. She couldn't just stand there with glory all about. She sprang off the porch and started running down the road. She hadn't run like that since she was ten. She ran down the road past the people, toward the bridge. The people sang and danced, the people swayed and clapped their hands. Alma passed Uncle John Ezekiel Fry. Uncle Fry grinned from ear to ear, and the light sparked off his tears.

"He's coming!" people shouted, "he's coming and he's just about here!"

"I can see him," someone said, "I can see him in the light!"

Alma was sure she heard bells, a deep sonorous toll that touched her soul and swept her clean. A noise like a thunderclap sounded overhead. Alma looked up, and the air was full of birds. Storks and cranes and gulls, hawks and terns and doves, eagles and herons, every kind of bird there was.

Alma laughed at the sky, Alma laughed at the bells, Alma laughed at the music in her head. It was Basin Street jazz, it was Mozart and Bach, it was old time Gregorian Rock.

Alma couldn't see the road and she couldn't see the bridge. She felt enveloped and absorbed. She felt like she was swimming in the light. It dazzled and it glittered and it sang. It hummed through her body like carbonated bees. It looked like the center of a star. It looked like a hundred billion fireflies in a jar.

"I *knew* you were something special, Cush," Alma cried. "I knew that, Cush, but I got to say I never guessed *who*!"

The light seemed to flare. It drowned her in rapture, an overdose of bliss. It was much too rich, too fine and too intense. It drove her back with joy, it drove her back with love. It lifted her and swept her off her feet. It swept her up the road and past the field and past the yard, and left her on the porch where she'd begun.

"Better not get too close," someone said, "better not get too near the light."

"That's my grand-nephew," Alma said, "you likely didn't know that. I guess I can do about anything I please."

Cush knew who he was. He knew what he was for. He knew what it was he had to do. And now, for the first time in his short and dreary life, in a life full of misery and pain, in a life filled with every dire affliction you could name, Cush knew the reason *why*. When he knew, when it came to him at last, Cush was overwhelmed with the wonder of the thing he had to do. It was awesome, it was fine, it was a marvel and a half, and Cush laughed aloud for the first time in his life.

And in that very instant, in the echo of his laugh, the spark that had smouldered in his soul, that had slept there in the dark, burst free in a rush of brilliant light. The light was the power, and Cush was the light, and Cush reached out and drew everything in. Everything wrong, everything that wasn't right. He drew in envy and avarice and doubt. He called in every plague and every blight. He called in every tumor, every misty cataract. He called in AIDS and bad breath. Ingrown toenails, anger and regret. The heartbreak of psoriasis, the pain of tooth decay. Migraines and chilblains, heartburn and cramps. Arthritic joints and hemorrhoids. Spasms and paralytic strokes. Hatred and sorrow and excess fat. Colic and prickly heat and gout.

Cush drew them all in, every sickness, every trouble, every curse, and every pain. Cush called them down and drew them into healing light, where they vanished just as if they'd never been.

"*I got it all sopped up, I did what I came to do,*" Cush cried, "*I got everything looking real fine!*"

Cush was the power, and Cush was the light. He was here and he was there, he was mostly everywhere. He could see Cincinnati, he could see Bangladesh. He could see Aunt Alma, see her rushing up the stairs. He could see his mother's room filled with swirls of pastel light. He could see her as she cried out with joy and surprise, see the wonder in her face, see the beauty in her smile as something blossomed inside her, blossomed for a blink and then appeared with silver eyes.

"Got it all ready for you, little sister," Cush called out from the light, *"Got it looking real fine, just as pretty as can be. I've done about all there is to do!"*

All the people standing in the road and in the field saw the light begin to quiver hum and shake, saw it rise up from the bridge, saw it rush into the early morning light.

"Hallelujah," said Uncle John Fry, standing in the tall green corn. "Hallelu-jah-Chattanooga-*bliss. . . ."*

ON THE COLLECTION OF HUMANS

Mark Rich

▼

Here's a mordant bit of advice for the Serious Collector, courtesy of new writer Mark Rich. . . .

Mark Rich is a small-press veteran who has just started to break into professional print, with sales this year to *Amazing, Analog, Expanse, Nova,* and *Full Spectrum 4*. His first book, *Lifting,* published by Wordcraft of Oregon, won the Leslie Cross Fiction Award from the Council of Wisconsin Writers. He lives in Stevens Point, Wisconsin.

Having received many queries regarding the collection of human beings, I think it appropriate to make some general points about the matter in a public forum.

Many new collectors and investigators are discovering what we have known for some time, viz., that a random or unguided collection of humans yields little useful information. Accepting certain parameters makes the collecting process more rewarding at all stages of study. Since many investigators share my belief that one issue above all needs resolution before we can proceed in other directions—the issue of why humanity has so thoroughly rejected its natural heritage—many likewise will take interest in the parameters I have set myself in my own pursuit of the question.

While physiologically humans are of a type and form a single breeding population, the investigator should not be deceived into believing that all individuals of the population are identical in what literature calls *mental-energetic characteristics*. The neurological component of the human operating system appears to allow significant variation in mental energies. In order to isolate the variant most useful for study, my colleagues and I make these suggestions:

First, collect from moving automobiles. While many collectors prefer to catch humans who are walking or running, automobile collections offer advantages far outweighing the slight difficulties involved. Mental-energetic characteristics can be detected more easily in the driving human than the walking human; moreover, walking humans are commonly unsuitable for our study. We have made a workable generalization that the smaller the vehicle, the less likely the human is to advance our understanding of human discord with nature. Humans walking, riding bicycles, and in smaller cars tend to exhibit less distance from nature to a statistically significant degree. Those on motorcycles also tend to depart from the human type we seek, sometimes in startling ways. The collector will obtain the best results from larger cars with high gloss, which usually contain humans of middle to high ranking in the normative social order. These humans yield exceptional results. In the landmark paper of Mardinak, Luskeccitet and the present writer, this human type yielded the entire set of data.

Second, do not collect from homes, which present too many hiding options for the human and make collecting overly time-consuming. In car collecting, we should note in comparison, the humans can sometimes be obtained by holding the car upside down and giving it a shake; if that fails, the collector need only remove the roof to obtain the human. We should also note that home-collecting has on the whole provided less consistent and satisfactory results, often due to damage to the specimens.

Third, if opportunity arises, collect from passenger planes. Experience has shown that humans removed from the front sections of such craft provide excellent results; as a bonus, the spaciousness of these fore areas, as opposed to the rear areas, make for easy collecting. Many collectors derive a great deal of enjoyment and satisfaction in catching airplanes. The relative scarcity of passenger aircraft, however, has meant that few researchers can rely exclusively on this source.

Some collectors raise the objection that many parts of the world do not reflect an adequately high ratio of automobiles to humans. Allow me to respond by noting that this very fact assures the relevance of car collecting. The borders of the areas of greatest human/nature discontinuity and the areas of highest automobile/human ratios draw nearly coterminous lines around the globe.

Allow me one further suggestion, which concerns the determination of subjects useful for study. I recommend such a determination process to be employed even after careful car collection.

While several good techniques have been suggested elsewhere, my co-workers and I have found the following to work well. First, we do not immediately remove the humans' clothing, following Empelbeam's suggestion that we can obtain better results from clothed individuals, at least with this particular type. However, we do remove either the pocket-wallets or side-purses of the subjects, an act which causes extreme disorientation in those subjects who are most useful for our study. Lusckeccitet has offered this explanation for the usefulness of this test: Humans ascend through the social-economic hierarchy by a totemistic practice which involves placing increasing amounts of *identity* or *worth* in the pocket-wallets or side-purse. The humans symbolically lodge these portions of their being in small wafers of plastic. While the "cards" serve several functions, including some transaction functions, humans use them most frequently in a social process called *identification*. The nervousness exhibited by humans from whom we take their "cards," indicates the degree of loss of *identity* or *worth* they suffer. Cogillinderva provides a telling example of this. Her study, soon to be published, shows that humans to whom we return identification wafers become calm; those to whom we give placebo wafers, however, become more distraught than even those to whom we never give back any wafers. We may even now hazard a generalization about determining specimen suitability: the more identity wafers or cards carried, the more suitable the human. The occasional individuals carrying no wafers usually prove entirely unsuitable; we recommend they be released or reserved for other studies.

While as a scientist I am pleased at the popularity of collecting humans, I can only repeat the request of others in my field that amateur researchers keep full collection data on all specimens. In this was they can help advance our understanding of this curious world.

THERE AND THEN

Steven Utley

▼

Steven Utley's fiction has appeared in *The Magazine of Fantasy & Science Fiction,
Universe, Galaxy, Amazing, Vertex, Stellar, Shayol*, and elsewhere. He was one of
the best-known new writers of the seventies, both for his solo work and for some
strong work in collaboration with fellow Texan Howard Waldrop, but fell silent at
the end of the decade and wasn't seen in print again for more than ten years. In the
last few years he's made a strong comeback, though, becoming a frequent contributor
to *Asimov's Science Fiction* magazine, as well as selling again to *The Magazine of
Fantasy & Science Fiction* and elsewhere. Utley is the coeditor, with Geo. W.
Proctor, of the anthology *Lone Star Universe*, the first—and possibly the only—
anthology of SF stories by Texans. His first collection will be coming up soon. He
lives in Austin, Texas.

In the stylish and perceptive story that follows, he takes us several hundred million
years back in time to the *very* remote past, back before dinosaurs were even a distant
glimmer in some scurrying little bottom-feeder's eyestalks, back to an embattled and
overworked scientific research station drifting in shallow prehistoric seas, for a
fascinating look at how *some* things never change, no matter what era it is. . . .

The wind had shifted, and the night was full of land smells, estuarine smells,
green slime, black mud, rotten eggs. The only sounds were ship and sea sounds;
occasionally, there was also a murmur of conversation in the shadow beneath
the eaves of the helicopter deck. Chamberlain's two assistants were back there
somewhere, tending equipment, their voices muffled as if by layers of flannel.
The moon had vanished into a vast, dense cloud bank. The fantail was so dark
that I could see little of Chamberlain except his glowing red eye and, intermittently, red-tinged highlights of his face and hands. He looked devilish in those
moments. He held the glowing eye sometimes between his fingers and sometimes
between his lips. Every so often, its glow would expire, and he'd fumble with
his pockets, there'd be a sputter of flame, the thick smells coming off the land
would momentarily mix with that of burning tobacco. I wondered again how he
had got his ancient and disagreeable vice past screening.

Chamberlain sat in his beat-up deck chair, surrounded by a mutant-toadstool growth of meteorological godknowswhat. I leaned against the rail. Hundreds of people lived and worked aboard, but late at night it was easy to get the feeling, and hard to get rid of it, that we were the only human beings in all the world. Actually, we represented a few tenths of a percent of present world population.

After a while, I said, "You should come."

"Too much work to do here."

"Oh, come on. We've both been cooped up here too long. We could both use some excitement."

"Hm." *Hm* was the sound Chamberlain made when he meant to laugh. "I hear they could use some excitement ashore, too. There's none of the tumult and squawk you just naturally associate with prehistoric times."

"You don't think a live sex act with trilobites will be exciting? Come on. A walk on the beach'll do you good."

"This the beach I smell? Ew."

"We'll be on a different beach. What you smell is blowing off the estuary. We'll be way around the coast from here."

"Still." The old deck chair squeaked unhappily as he shifted his weight. "I'm a meteorologist. Meteorologists aren't supposed to have to smell bad smells."

"Then don't smoke."

He called me a body-Nazi and ignited a new cigarette off the old. "Sure smells like the honey pot got kicked over."

"Gripe, gripe," I said. "You have it made. The weather never *does* anything here. The only forecast you ever make is, warm, east wind, possibility of showers. You sleep when you want, come out and play with your expensive toys when you want—"

"You've got no damn idea what my workload's like. Anybody has it made on this boat, it's you."

"—sit back and watch the sunset and drink till you nod off!"

He made a rumbling noise deep inside himself. "You know as well as I do that nothing enhances a sunset better'n a drink. And nothing enhances a drink better'n a nap." The glowing eye moved away from his face in the direction of his invisible assistants, Immelmanned, and went back to his face. When he spoke again, his voice was so quiet that I had to lean down into his nimbus of smoke to hear his words. "Those two wait till I'm asleep and then sneak away to fool around. If you know what I mean."

"How simply terribly shocking."

"It's true. Had my eye on 'em for a while." The eye brightened for a moment, fell away in his hand. "Definitely something going on between 'em."

"Well," I said, "what could be more romantic than holding hands under a prehistoric moon? Ooh woo, what a little moonlight can do."

"That from one of your damned old songs? Of course it is, got to be. I forgot, you're one of *them*. Listen, it's past the hand-holding stage with those two. They're up to the bucking-and-grunting stage."

I couldn't recall having seen either of Chamberlain's assistants in good light. Now, in my imagination, they appeared as shadows, rubbing against each other. I said, "Well, it's still most people's favorite way to pair-bond."

"Fat lot of good pair-bonding ever did *you*, Kev. None of your ex-wives has spoken to you in years."

"They've hardly been able to, under the circumstances."

"Anyway, you think I want a couple of disgruntled ex-lovers on my team?" He made a disgusted sound. "When they fall out, this boat won't be big enough for the two of 'em."

"Ship. This is a ship, not a boat."

"Ship, boat," he said dismissively.

"Rain, dew," I said, in the same tone. "If Captain Kelly ever hears you call his ship a boat, he'll keelhaul you, hang you from the yardarm, and make you walk the plank all in the same afternoon."

"He makes allowances for dotty scientists. Point is—"

"The point *is*, your young honeys are happy together right now. Maybe they'll stay happy together. There's always the possibility that things'll work out, you know."

"Hm. That what you told yourself along about the third time you got married?"

"Sure was."

"You are such a dog with women," he said, and extinguished his latest cigarette. A moment later, I heard a faint click in the darkness. "Want another drink?"

"Sure."

He gave me another capful of brandy from his flask. Officially, it was a long walk from the Paleozoic to the nearest liquor store. In fact, there was probably enough booze on board to float us the thousands of kilometers to Caledonian Land—proto-Greenland, Kalaallitt Nunaat-to-be. Old hands know that when a body needs a drink, only a drink will do. Pleasantly abuzz, I peered off into the darkness toward the shore. Its smells were palpable, but it wasn't even a glimmer in the night. The moon gave no sign of coming out of its cocoon of clouds. After a time, I realized that Chamberlain had fallen asleep. I left him snoring harshly in his deck chair, and his assistants to their alleged smooching, and went up to the helicopter deck.

The helicopters sat there like big metal sculptures of dragonflies lighted for Christmas. Mechanics tinkered with the motors while people wearing overalls loaded equipment and supplies. A shirtsleeved man stood by with the unmistakable air of a junior supervisor. He looked my way as I passed and seemed about to ask if I was authorized to be there, but then two of the mechanics said hello to me and I said hello back, and you could see the wheels turn behind the shirtsleeved man's face: maybe I wasn't a scruffy old stowaway, maybe I was somebody eccentric but important. I knew the mechanics and loaders but had no idea who he was. So many similar-looking people had arrived in the past few weeks that I didn't know who a tenth of them were.

The ship's engines throbbed suddenly as Captain Kelly got us under way. I put strangers out of my mind and strolled all the way forward and halfway back. Ours was in no way a lovely vessel. It had originally been designed and built during the Oughts to deliver Marines to beachheads and provide support with missiles and helicopter gunships. Not a lot had been done, or could have been done, to tone down its brooding militariness. The missile launchers were gone now, and the gun turret rebuilt to house one of the astronomy team's big telescopes, but the superstructure, helicopter deck, and boat bay had required no redesign. The forest of antennae, scanners, things, and stuff rising above the bridge looked formidably thorny. Except for human beings in helicopters, there wasn't an airborne creature on Earth, but still the dishes turned and cocked and listened, as intently as if swarms of kamikaze aircraft lurked over the horizon.

The task of renaming the vessel had fallen to a group of more or less prominent scientists, who duly voted to rechristen it *H. G. Wells*. Some nasty hustling little demagogue in Congress scotched that on the grounds of Wells's having been, besides a lousy stinking Brit—this, of course, was well after the end of the Special Relationship between the countries—a communist, or some closely related species of one-worlder. The story goes that, told to submit something "more patriotic and appropriate," most of the scientists next agreed that the vessel should be renamed after one or another of certain late-twentieth- and early-twenty-first-century presidents, because the ship, too, would move boldly into the past. "This kind of reckless sarcasm," a dissenter warned, "will backfire on us," and, sure enough, it did. Most of us since neglected to call the ship anything except "here" when we were aboard and "the ship" when we weren't. And we did keep a big framed portrait of Bertie Wells hanging in the rec room, over his alleged epitaph: Dammit, I told you so!

The brandy and the stroll conspired to fill me with a luxurious sense of peace and belonging. When my pocketphone buzzed, I murmured absently into the mouthpiece.

"Kevo," said Ruth Lott, "you're up."

Peace and belonging fled. Ruth had the mellifluous Georgia-accented voice I hated to hear. I said, "Ruth, all decent people are asleep at this hour."

"That's how I knew you'd be up."

"Okay, I'm up. I just hope you're calling about something really interesting, like maybe an out-of-clothes experience you personally have had."

The phone barely did her great sweet laugh justice. "I have a little job for you." She always had a little job for me. "Come see me, I'll tell you all about it."

I knew and she knew that she had me, but even a rabbit struggles in a lion's grip. I said, "It really is kind of late."

"Won't take but a minute." When I hesitated long enough to make her impatient, she said, "Oh, and before I forget—" her voice was as dulcet-toned as before, but I wasn't fooled "—note on your calendar, extension review next month."

"Now *that's* low!"

"Why, whatever do you mean?"

"It's blackmail!"

"No, actually, Kevo, it's extortion. Bye."

"Go ahead," I said into a suddenly dead phone, "hang up on me, see what it gets you."

Then, having no choice, I did as I was told.

Ruth was a Junoesque fiftyish woman with the world's sliest smile. She trained it on me when I appeared in her hatchway. She said, "Are those the best clothes you have?"

"I was—I *am* going ashore when we get to Number Four camp."

"Please see if you can't make yourself just a teensy bit more presentable. I want you to meet a party at the jump station in a little while."

"Since when am I the official greeter? You break your legs off above the knee?"

"These are media types, they make documentaries, videos, something. They're supposed to be very good." I gestured, *So?* and she added, "So you're all media types. You should get along."

"There's got to be someone else on this bucket who's—what am I supposed to do? It's not like these people will arrive in any condition to listen to me give a welcome speech."

"All you have to do is say hello, show them around when they're up to it, whatever. I'm making them your responsibility."

"But why *me?*"

"Because you are not snowed under with work, you bum. How often do you actually touch your wordboard?"

I gave her my most pained look. "Writing isn't just a matter of touching a wordboard. You'd know that if you'd ever had specialized training in the putting together of subjects and verbs so that they agree. The real work's mental."

"You're mental," and she laughed her laugh again. "How *is* the book coming along? Think you'll have it finished by the Mesozoic? Listen to me, and believe me when I tell you this, I'm doing you a favor. Once we're privatized—don't give me that look, we both know it's a done deal—once we're privatized, the new bosses will be looking very carefully at their assets and liabilities here. These include," and she ticked them off on her fingers, "one converted assault ship with some el strange-o scientists embarked, and some hired help, and you. You've been hanging on here for too long. It's time you had visible means of support. You need to be seen earning your keep. This little job won't take too much of a bite out of your life. Just till these newcomers get acclimated. Just make sure they have a good time."

"What, find them women, young boys?"

"I'm serious. Northemico's sponsoring them."

That impressed me. Northemico figured prominently in the push for privatization.

"Think of this," Ruth went on, "as sort of an opportunity to do what a writer's supposed to do, make all of this, this—" She gestured helplessly, unable to find a word that took in everything from ship's routine to the reality of our surroundings and circumstances. I supplied it.

"Stuff," I said.

"Right. Make all of this stuff make sense to them." She eyed my attire again. "It really will help if you try not to look so much like a beachcomber."

"I *am* a beachcomber."

"Kevo, I put up with you because you make me laugh." She leaned toward me confidentially. "Even Captain Kelly puts up with you. He thinks of you as our resident artistic type and has the weird idea that you're brilliant. God knows why. The new bosses, when they get here, aren't going to put up with you unless you seem to be of use around here. They'll probably institute a dress code, too. Now go on, get to the jump station," and she urged me on my way with the kind of little wave women use to dry their fingernail polish.

The tang of ozone in the jump station was as sharp as an icepick up the nose. I tried out looks and gestures of welcome on Cullum and Summers, the two techs on duty. Summers appeared to think I was pretty funny. Cullum appeared to think I thought I was pretty funny. They did the synchronization countdown. The medical team stood around the rail-enclosed sending-and-receiving platform and watched as its surface shimmered and grew bright.

First to arrive was a woman who was so shaken up by the experience that the medical team had to roll her away on a gurney. The man who followed her looked gray but insisted that he was okay, please take him topside. I couldn't talk him out of it. Cullum and Summers exchanged looks with me and quietly made a bet between themselves: I either would or would not get the fellow out of the jump station, through a short companionway, and onto the starboardside gangwalk before it was too late.

As it happened, I did, but just barely. The man made it the last couple of steps with both hands clapped over his mouth. He grabbed the rail, stood there uneasily for a moment, then leaned out over the dark sea, out into blackness, and retched at length. He didn't actually lose his lunch because he hadn't any lunch to lose. Only the first visitors to the Paleozoic hadn't known not to eat before making the jump. They had gone about suited as if for Mars—you weren't even supposed to breathe the air here, let alone cough up your socks. The past was supposed to be as brittle as a Ming vase—you didn't dare give it a cross look. It was years before people got comfortable with the idea that if the past was resilient enough to accommodate an 8500-ton ship, it could probably accommodate the everyday stupidity of the species embarked.

I stood behind and slightly to one side of the newcomer. When he turned from the rail, I handed him a bottle of spring water and said, "This'll help." He took it, rinsed, spat over the side. When he tried to hand the bottle back, I declined as if I were doing him a favor. He pulled a handkerchief from the breast pocket of his jacket and wiped his mouth. He was in his late twenties or early thirties and well-built. He would have had, ordinarily, what I call friendly good looks. At the moment, in the light of the safety lamp, he had the color of oatmeal.

"If you want," he said, "you can say you told me so."

"That is our motto here."

He gingerly felt around the lower edge of his ribcage. His hands fell abruptly to his sides when he saw me watching him.

"I should introduce myself," I said, and did.

"Rick King," he said. I was grateful that he didn't offer to shake hands.

"Can't those technicians do something to make it so you don't get rattled apart when you come through?"

"They've been working on it forever."

"You want more folks to come and visit you here, you're going to have to make the trip more pleasant." I didn't reply to that. The last thing I wanted was for more folks to come and visit me here. "They told me all those drugs I had to take would help."

"They did help. Without them, you'd be feeling *really* bad right about now."

"And this *smell*. Hits you right in the face."

"Uh huh. But we're moving away from it. Anyway, you get used to it."

He shook his head. "Can't imagine how."

"If you're up for it, a turn around the deck might be a good way to start."

I led him up a deck and forward. His color slightly improved after a couple of minutes, but heat and humidity were taking the last measure of starch out of him. I figured he was about ready to collapse, and I'd be able to hustle him off to quarters, then slip ashore before Ruth knew what was up.

"Except for the stink," King said, "I could be on a boat in the Caribbean or somewhere. With the stink, I guess I could be off the Texas coast. When I first heard about all this, I thought, wow, travel through time, see prehistoric monsters battling fang and claw, you bet!"

"Sorry, fang and claw haven't quite evolved yet."

"Well, so far, nothing's what I expected."

"Common observation." I had a niggling suspicion, founded on nothing more substantial than King's being some kind of film-maker, that all of his expectations had been shaped by the movies, that he had come prepared to see, besides primordial ferocity, jump-station technicians who were prematurely balding men dressed in white coats and carrying clipboards, not guys who could have been mistaken for air-conditioner repairmen and displayed much hairy butt-crack whenever they hunkered down to fix stuff. I wondered what King would make of the scientists ashore, who wore big khaki pants and canvas shoes that made them resemble ducks. Still, if he had to have crewcuts and creased slacks, there were always the naval reservists who attended to the actual running of the ship.

Suddenly, though not exactly unexpectedly, King made a sound like *ah-rurr* and pressed both hands against his abdomen. His expression was alarmed. "I think I better get to the restroom," he said.

"This way," I said, "to the head."

When he finished in there, I showed him where he was to bunk down. Someone had thoughtfully brought his gear from the jump station and stowed it for him. King took out an object the size of a wallet, unfolded it with the thoughtless ease of long practice, and slipped it over his close-cropped skull—a headheld camera. A thin cable ran from the jawpiece to batteries and recordpack in his pocket; the spikemike stuck out like half of a set of insect antennae. He looked my way, the headheld whirred faintly, and I pretended to become fascinated by the paint on the bulkhead. Headhelds disconcert me. I never know whether to make eye-contact with the wearer's natural eye or unnatural one.

"Be prepared is my motto," King said.

I looked at him in wonder. He was still a mess. I asked if he didn't really want to get some rest, and he said he was too excited. I sneaked a peek at my watch. The boat would be leaving soon, and I was bound and determined to be on it. I made my fateful decision and asked him, "Do you think you're up for a little boat ride and campout?"

"I'm up for anything."

I looked doubtful, and not just because I wanted to appear sincerely concerned about him. Then: "Okay, it's your funeral. I'll go get my things and meet you back here. We'll pop into sick bay to see how your friend's doing—" he had not once inquired about her in all this time "—and then we hit the beach."

"Great! D-day in the Devonian!"

Silurian, I thought as I turned away.

King's friend's name was Claire Duvall. Chance had treated him with kid gloves and smacked her upside the head: she had a mild concussion. King took the news well. I shouldn't have held that against him, because I was even more impatient than he to get to the boat bay, and with much better reason. Nevertheless, it rankled me.

The boat bay could have stood some redesign. The slap of waves against the hull reduced unamplified speech to so much mutter. You could ruin your voice working in this part of the ship. At night, you could ruin your eyes, too, and your shins if you weren't careful. Few lights showed. Captain Kelly, it was said, didn't like to excite the, understand, extremely limited imaginations of light-sensitive Paleozoic marine organisms. I could dimly see human figures working in and around a boat, and called down, "How soon till we leave?"

"Kev!" someone called back. "Come on if you're coming."

Someone else bawled out, "Will somebody up there please throw some goddamn light down here?" There ensued a bit of rude jawing back and forth, and then a shaft of stark white light suddenly spotlighted the ramp of the boat bay as if it were a stage. People froze like deer in traffic. I beheld the true object of my desire.

She looked like an ivory statuette from my vantage point. Up close and in good light, she had blue eyes and fair brown hair. She was wearing cut-offs and a T-shirt, and at any distance and in any light she had the best legs in the Paleozoic. Vicki Harris had been haunting my thoughts for some time. All at once, I had *seen* her, though I'd been looking at her for weeks, months, who knew how long? Sometimes it happens that way.

The light switched off. I remembered to breathe. King and I climbed down, and everybody found a place to sit amid the jumble of boxes in the boat. The motor coughed and gurgled as the pilot revved it. The sides of the bay loomed around us like immense black cliffs. As we eased out, the almost-full moon emerged from the purple clouds, suffusing the air with milky light. Above the rhythmic prum-pum of the motor and the hiss of water parting before the prow, King said, "My God," and then, "Wow!"

"No kidding," said someone behind me.

I looked around and found that I could just make out the faces of my companions. Cardwell and Jank were aft with Hirsch, the pilot; Vicki Harris sat amidships. All of them except Hirsch gazed upward. I'd have done so, too, but for the warm pleasure I got from gazing at Vicki Harris. She noticed me staring at her and cocked an index finger moonward to redirect my attention.

"Seen it," I said.

She flashed a grin. "Me too, but I never get over how it looks. It's like it's almost but not quite the same moon. Like the features I'm used to seeing don't exist yet."

"I asked Hill about that once. You know Sharon Hill? One of the astronomers. She told me it's the same moon, less some impact craters. The main difference is in rotational velocity or some such. We're seeing it sort of from behind and off to one side."

She directed a look past me. I heard a faint whirring and remembered King. I made introductions, and she reached around me to offer him a hand and said, "Mister King."

"Please," King said, "Rick," and held on to her a beat or two longer than I liked.

"Vick," she said.

"Vee for short," Jank said, behind her.

"Vee Vee," said Cardwell, "if you want to be really disarming."

"My delightful colleagues, Doctors Jankowski and Cardwell." Her tone of voice fell somewhere in the middle of affection, tolerance, and reproach. I'd learned from Jank—who'd affected not to find my sudden curiosity remarkable—that she hated her first name. I have few opinions about what parents should call their girl babies, though I know a trend when I see it: names ending with the letter *i* have become true artifacts; more and more young women are answering to monikers that end with *o*, Fujiko, Tamiko. Still, I had had a lovely, sweet girlfriend by the name of Vicki in high school and was ever afterward kindly predisposed toward anyone who bore it. Not, of course, that I didn't find Vicki Vick Vee Vee Harris entirely attractive in her own right.

"It's Cardwell's performing trilobites," I said, "whose antics we hope to see."

"I should get some great stuff," said King. He talked past me, to her. "I make documentaries and things." Talk about disarming. Documentaries and things.

She said, "Really?"

Vick and Rick, I suddenly thought, oh no.

Jank evidently thought it was a bit much, too, for he said, "*What* other things," and paused, and added, "Rick?"

"Commercials," King said, "infotainment, that kind of thing." I could tell that he was slightly taken aback.

"So which is it this time," Jank demanded, "documentary or commercial?"

"Documentary, of course."

"Of course. And when do you start?"

King lightly touched the headheld. "I already have. You don't have any objection to being on television, do you?"

Now Jank was taken aback.

"We've been on television," Cardwell said. "Not lately, though. Been a while since we had a documentary crew through here." He had the same interested attitude he'd had the time he showed me my first prehistoric shellfish. He could have been joining in two colleagues' discussion of trilobites.

By the way Jank shifted in his seat, I could tell that he was buckling down for business. He said to King, "You seem a little undercrewed."

"My partner was badly shaken up by the jump. But what you mean, of course, is, why aren't I hauling around a lot of help? No one does that any more unless they're making big Hollywood product."

Jank wouldn't let up. "What's your background?"

"Media arts, of course."

"Of course. Aren't there any real scientists who can do documentaries any more?"

"I took the famous crash course in rocks, bugs, and stones before I came." King laughed. "Whoa, Mister Overqualified, huh?"

"Yeah," said Jank, "thank goodness you're not just some facile slime-sucking adman."

Everyone lapsed into silence. Vick and I exchanged embarrassed smiles. The wind sweetened. Hirsch turned the boat and expertly took it in, bringing us to rest without so much as a bump alongside a natural stone jetty. We all scrambled ashore carrying something and were greeted by several of the semi-permanent residents of Number Four camp. The jetty dipped into the beach's sandy slope at the high-tide mark; the camp sat above. The moon was down and the sky was turning gray by the time we had the boat unloaded. I somehow found myself at Vick's side as we lugged the last of the cargo along the jetty. King and Cardwell were right behind us. Jank was already out of sight among the tents.

"Let's do breakfast," I said to Vick.

"Sounds good to me," and then, probably—I told myself—because she wanted to make up for Jank's rudeness, she said over her shoulder, "Join us, Mister King?"

"You bet." He obviously was happy that she'd asked but sorry that she hadn't called him Rick.

We entered the camp, and Vick veered off. "Meet you at the mess tent," she said to no one of us in particular. I didn't care for how King watched her walk away.

I had Cardwell and Jank's standing invitation to share their tentspace; a geologist named Crumhorn agreed to take King in, though it was on short notice. Cardwell and I delivered him to Crumhorn's tent and were about to move on when he said, "I don't believe I've actually sucked any slime since grade school. I'm just a film-maker, Kevin." When he spoke my name, I felt a sudden, irrational, tremendous urge to rub myself all over with hot sand or maybe ground glass. "If I said or did something to set Doctor Jankoski off—"

"Jankowski," I said.

"Oh, Jank," Cardwell said, "Jank's just," and shrugged as if that explained everything. He had the dimensions but not the temperament of a bear.

"Breakfast," I told King, "is in the big tent over yonder," and set off to get mine and left him to get his as he would.

Vick had saved two places at the table. I settled into one of them and happily stirred my coffee. We listened to Rubenstein, a cartographer, who, two days before, had completed a trek overland from Stinktown, Number Two camp, on the estuary. "Only sign of life we saw the whole time," he said, "was one of our own 'copters, headed inland."

Crumhorn dropped into a chair across from me and scooped up a piece of toast. I asked where his houseguest was, and he said, "Conked out. Just like that. Hi, how do you do, snork, zzz."

"I was wondering when it'd catch up with him. He jumped in a few hours ago, and he's been going like a chipmunk on an exercise wheel ever since."

"So," said De La Cerda, another geologist, "he's, what, a video producer or something?"

"Or something."

She shook her head. "These people just keep trickling in."

Rubenstein said, "You say that about everybody."

"I'm part-Indian," De La Cerda said, "and Indians know about people who keep trickling in. The Sioux had a word for white people, *wasichu*. It means, you can't get rid of them."

Rubenstein looked at her askance for a moment. Then: "You're not Sioux, you're *mestizo* or some goddamn something."

Hendryx, yet another geologist, said, "So *sue* her."

Amid the groans, Crumhorn observed that punning was a cry for help, and Westerman, the slight blonde botanist seated next to Hendryx, said, "I used to love this man. Now I'm for feeding him to the fishes."

Hendryx looked smug. "No fishes this time of the Paleozoic, right, Vick?"

"Just some armored ones that look like tadpoles wearing football padding."

"They always looked kind of art deco to me," said De La Cerda.

"Well," said Vick, "you have to go to Stinktown to find them, and then they're only about as big as your hand."

"Are they edible?" I said. One thing I did miss in the Silurian was catfish sandwiches.

Vick made a face. "They've got a taste sort of between salt and mud."

"Vick Harris," Rubenstein murmured over the rim of his coffee cup, "girl ichthyologist and gourmet." He sipped and grimaced. "Talk about salt and mud. So where're all the big exciting fish? Where's old Dinowhatsit? You know the one, ten meters long, armored head. Mouth like a big ugly pinking shears."

"Dunkleosteus, alias Dinicthys."

"Yeah, that's the one, where's old Dunkywhatsit?"

"Not even a glimmer in his great-great-granddaddy's eye, I'm afraid."

"So," De La Cerda said to me, "what about this video guy?"

"Northemico sent him to make a documentary about you folks."

Both De La Cerda and Rubenstein gave me the same sharp look, and Westerman said, flatly, "Northemico."

In spite of myself, I spread my fingers in the air and said, "He's just a filmmaker."

"You mean like you're just a writer, I'm just a botanist?" Westerman shook her head. "Nobody who's made the jump in the last month or so has been *just* anything. This film guy's just not as obscurely specialized as most of them."

"Wait a minute," Vick began, but Rubenstein cut her off.

"If he really *is* a film guy. Probably a spy."

"I don't think you're being fair," said Vick. "You can't go around automatically assuming someone's a spy just because—"

"Vick," said Rubenstein, "you gotta admit, Northemico and the rest of that pack've been slavering to get in here from day one. There's money waiting to be made here."

She appeared doubtful. "I don't see trilobites and seaweed as the basis for growth industries."

"Try oil." De La Cerda gave her a not-unkindly look. "Something's sure going on. On the ship—" she nodded vaguely in the direction of the sea "—we're suddenly cramped for space. Too many newcomers all at once. People I've never seen before are suddenly looking over my shoulder all the time. Suddenly it's harder to schedule use of a helicopter. Then it's just impossible, because they're all the time flying people and surveying equipment into the interior."

"And we all know," Westerman said, "that there's nothing *in* the interior to survey."

"Sure," said Hendryx, "not if you're a botanist!"

Westerman laughed along with him and then made a face at him. They must have been a riot in bed.

Crumhorn rested his elbows on the table and steepled his fingers. "No reason to think there's suddenly something mysterious or sinister going on," he said. "We've been surveying the interior ever since we got here."

"Think about what you just said," said De La Cerda. "*We've* been surveying. *We've* been doing this, that, every other thing. We, us, the members of this expedition. These other people belong to some whole other expedition. It's riding piggy-back on ours. Gradually, it's displacing ours."

"They want to know everything," Westerman said. "They don't want to tell you anything in return. Look, I don't mind answering questions about my work, I *like* talking about it. But these people ask all the wrong questions."

"What questions are those?" Hendryx demanded sharply.

"Tim," said Westerman. I looked at her in surprise. She was almost pleading with him. "We've talked about this."

"Bottom-line kind of questions," said De La Cerda. "Is there you-name-the-mineral here? Is there a lot of it? Things like that. And you can bet somebody's spent a lot of time calculating which natural resources might be safe to grab here and not have them missed four hundred million years from now."

Hendryx's wedge-like jaw jutted belligerently forward. "Nothing ever *was* missed, was it? So they can't have taken anything out. Or maybe they did, maybe you can take out whatever you want, because the past takes care of itself. It has so far."

Westerman folded her thin arms across her chest and gave him an angry look. "I can't believe I'm hearing this from you."

"You should get used to the idea that not everybody thinks exactly the way you do. From time to time, you might even try rethinking a position."

"Tim, you *know* if Northemico gets loose here, it'll make the Antarctic feeding frenzy look like a model of responsible conservation."

"That was different."

Several people demanded in chorus, "*How?*"

The beleaguered geologist glowered. "What *have* we missed from the Paleozoic? Maybe the stripmine scars are buried deep inside the earth. Maybe they've eroded completely away. Maybe they've been deformed beyond recognition and understanding."

"Lot of maybes," muttered Rubenstein.

"We know the landmasses are drawing together, and that the collision'll fold this whole region over on itself."

Everyone at the table was regarding Hendryx very seriously. Westerman said, "Are you saying anything people do here's okay as long as they hide the evidence under a mountain range?"

"Listen, the bills have to be paid, or we have to go home."

"This *is* home," De La Cerda said, "for some of us."

"You think so." Hendryx patted his lips with a napkin. "But you can't live here without supplies from the future, and the pipeline stays open only so long as somebody foots the bill to keep it open. If the government stops, then Northemico or somebody has to start, or that's all she wrote." He pushed his chair back, stood, surveyed the semicircle of mostly hostile faces before him. Vick hung back, and because she did, I hung back, too. "I want this expedition to continue as much as you do."

Westerman's mouth was set in a thin, straight line as she glared at his retreating back. An almost identical line creased her forehead. "I sometimes wonder," she said, "if good sex is worth all the aggravation."

After breakfast, Vick said she had to go with Cardwell to splash around in tide pools and collect specimens. I passed what passed for the cool part of the morning bringing whoever didn't have work to do up to date with the latest shipboard gossip and scurrilous rumor. It got definitely hottish toward midday, but then clouds scudded in at noon, dumped enough rain to cool things off reasonably, and, mission accomplished, scudded away. I took a long nap and was greatly improved for it. Rick King was up and around by late afternoon— days were shorter in the Silurian, and years consequently longer, by three dozen days—and looked rested, fit, and out of place in what I took to be the latest thing in twenty-first-century beachwear for men.

I had hoped simply to prowl the beach, poke at the occasional lump of cast-up sealife, and just enjoy being on land for a change. King, however, prevailed on me to steer him around and make such introductions as I didn't have to disturb anyone's work to make. Nearly everyone was polite, and De La Cerda, of all people, actually seemed charmed. Westerman couldn't keep suspicion out of her face, and King, to give him his due, received her chilly how-do-you-do and perfunctory handshake with admirable grace.

When we had run through the possible introductions, King studied the cliffs behind the camp. "What's up there?"

"More sand and rock."

"There a way up?"

I should have lied to him, but I didn't, so next I had to take him up the path to the top. He looked like Tarzan going up; I felt like Sisyphus. When we got up, he stood arms akimbo and gazed off at the low mountains in the distance while I sat on a rock and pretended that I wasn't panting for breath, that my heart wasn't rattling loosely in its mountings. It was getting into evening, and all of that bare jagged rock had begun to burn prettily.

Number Four camp was located on a stretch of coastline where erosion had cut away headlands to form slip-faulted cliffs. Detritus littered the narrow scalloped beach below. This was a rough bit of seafront, but wherever you made landfall, you found yourself on an inhospitable shore. The one-day North American west was a volcano range; one-day Appalachia was a chain of islands; between the two stretched an unbroken shallow sea. Just so one's sense of direction would be utterly skewed, the equator bisected this sea from the future site of San Diego to that of Iceland. Equatorial North America was geologically part of the great northern landmass, Laurasia, whose southern counterpart was Gondwanaland, comprising South America, Africa, India, Australia, Antarctica. In all the unsubmerged regions of the world there was very little soil, and what soil there was was thin, poor, and as vulnerable as life on land itself. Actual greenery existed only beside the waterways. It didn't measure up to the popular idea of a coal-forest, with fern trees, dragonflies as big as crows, salamanders as big as sofas. None of the flora was more than waist-high; most were much shorter. Carpeting the lowest and moistest patches of the immense badlands was *Cooksonia*, a rootless, leafless plant, no more, really, than a forked stem, towering a mighty five centimeters above the ground. The giant sequoias of the day were lycophytes, club mosses, growing to dizzying heights of one meter. They were comparatively sophisticated—stems with forked branches bearing clusters of small leaflets—but still fell short of what you'd call rank jungle growth. They didn't soften the land's serrate outline so much as make it look furry and itchy. Munching happily through all this green salad were millipedes, some of them big enough to provoke a shudder but all of them perfectly harmless. Munching happily through the millipedes were scorpions that looked and carried on as scorpions were always going to look and carry on. There were some book-gilled arthropods that rated the adjective "amphibious." There were no terrestrial vertebrates, excepting human beings. On the list of things yet to be were lungs, flowers, wings, thumbs, bark, milk, and penes. I was happier here than I'd ever been anywhere else.

King broke a long silence by saying, "This is good stuff." He patted the pocket containing the recordpack. "Long slow pan from the primordial ocean to the desert of barren rock and drifted sand." He fiddled with the headheld for another couple of seconds. "This world's one big still-life, though."

"Take it up with the folks who punched the hole in time. Maybe they can open up a more action-packed era for you. The Mesozoic, or World War Two."

"What do they do for excitement around here?"

I took my cue from his choice of pronouns. He excluded me from his subjects, to remind me, I supposed, that we were both media types, cousin- if not brother-professionals. I said, "That depends on who you talk to. For Cardwell, it's trilobites. For Westerman, it's club mosses."

"What is it for you?"

"Being here."

He brushed that away. "Being here isn't the be-all and end-all of your existence. You're a writer, writing a book."

I had come ostensibly to write a book about life on and around a research vessel embedded in mid-Paleozoic time. The book still wasn't finished, but, any more, it was beside the point. I had lost all sense of urgency about finishing it. I didn't need the money. I didn't need anything to do with writing a book, except as an excuse to stay.

I said, "I'm here because this is my home."

"Is it, now?" He shook his head. "*One day*, this place will be home. People won't just work and live here, they'll be born and die here. That's what makes a place home. Right now, this is summer camp. People come here, do the equivalent of making baskets and looking for arrowheads, and when the time comes, they go home."

"Hardly anyone goes ho—back. Not if they can help it. They just have to keep passing their extension reviews. It's less trouble to maintain us here than to replace us."

"Still—"

I slid off the rock. "It'll be dark soon. I'm not going to negotiate that path in the dark. Wouldn't advise you to try it, either."

I started down without waiting to see if he would follow. Later, in the mess tent, I saw him schmoozing with Hendryx and thought, Kindred spirits. Then I took it back. Hendryx was one of us. King, I swore, would never belong.

Everyone scattered into the dusk after supper, most of them claiming to have work that absolutely had to be done before Cardwell's show started. I changed to my least-ratty attire and went down to the high-tide mark ahead of everyone else to find the best seat. My chip player was in my pocket. I took it out and pressed the go button, and merely ancient music floated out over the prehistoric sea. It was "Stardust," recorded by Artie Shaw and His Orchestra in A.D. 1941. I stood swaying in time, enthralled as always by Billy Butterfield's incandescent trumpet, Jack Jenny's smoky trombone, Shaw's own soaring clarinet. Then, as I waited for the next track to begin, I heard somebody behind me and put my thumb on the stop button. Vick paused a short distance away. She said, "I heard music."

"Yes, you did," I said, and then, even more inanely, "I don't have earphones,

I hate earphones,'' and before I could stop myself, ''If God'd intended for us to listen to music on earphones. . . .'' Babbling.

Fortunately, I relaxed my finger on the button, and Shaw's rendition of ''I Surrender, Dear'' throbbed out of the player and enveloped us like a smoky blue cloud. I was gratified to note that she listened almost all the way through the track before she said anything.

''What *is* this music?''

''Jazz. Swing. Music.''

''It's,'' and she waited two whole seconds before finishing the sentence, ''lovely.'' She waited again, listened some more. ''Lovely and old.''

''Barely pre-World War Two,'' I said, trying not to sound defensive.

''God, my grandmother wasn't even born then.''

''Mine was a teenage girl in Indiana. She used to scrape up thirty-five cents somehow and go see Glenn Miller at the local theater. In those days, thirty-five cents was a lot of money for a teenage girl to scrape up.''

''This is Glenn Miller?''

''A contemporary. Artie Shaw.''

She looked like someone trying to decide if a name she'd never heard before meant anything to her. Then she admitted that it didn't.

''No need to apologize,'' I said. ''I'd be fairly astonished if you had heard of him. Pop music before Elvis Presley, before rock and roll, was like the Precambrian to members of my own generation.''

''I have heard of Elvis Presley.''

I decided from the way she said it that she probably didn't have him confused with some other, subsequent Elvis—Costello, Hitler, Christ, one of those. We listened to ''Moonglow,'' ''Begin the Beguine,'' and ''Summit Ridge Drive.'' The chip contained dozens of other tracks that I'd personally selected from Shaw's body of work, but I didn't want to be a mere tune jockey. I thumbed the stop button twice after ''Summit Ridge Drive'' to switch off the player.

''Certainly does grow on you,'' she said.

''Uh huh. I have Goodman and Ellington, too. Cab Calloway, Billie Holiday, dozens of—I think American pop music peaked sometime between nineteen thirty-five and nineteen fifty.'' I looked at her closely. ''I wrote a book about it once. Am I getting carried away here?''

She showed me a small gap between her thumb and forefinger. ''Only a little. I know people who'd make me listen to the whole Flucks catalogue.'' My utter ignorance of even a portion of the Flucks catalogue must have been obvious. ''Flucks does a lot of sub- and ultrasonic pieces. Some of them are said to make listeners lose, ah, muscular control.''

''Gosh, why couldn't Artie Shaw have recorded songs like that?''

She laughed. ''Well, I don't see the fun in it, either.''

Other people had been drifting down from the camp all this while. They made themselves comfortable, talked, drank, or simply stared out to sea and waited. Jank showed up with a bottle of brandy, and the three of us passed it around and heckled Cardwell to get the show started. The level of brandy in the bottle got lower and lower. Lulled by a murmur of waves and voices, I nodded off. When I awoke, with a start, the moon was out, the tide was in, and it had become as chilly on the beach as it ever got. Next to me, Jank was gently shaking Vick awake. Everyone else was heading back to camp.

"Rise up, Lazarus," Jank said, "and walk."

I said, incredulously, "I missed the show? You let me miss the show?"

"Wasn't any show." He nodded seaward, at Cardwell, who stood in the foam at the water's edge, a master of ceremonies whose star act had let him down. "Tomorrow night, maybe."

"Doesn't he know?"

"When they get here, they'll be here." Jank drew Vick to her feet, and I made a point of helping. "Tomorrow night, the night after—*some* night this week, anyway."

Between us, Vick nodded agreement, sleepily. "Moon's full. This is the season."

"How can even the trilobites know when it's time? There's only ever the one season."

"If it'll ease the pain of this disappointment," Vick said, "why not come snorkeling with us tomorrow?"

"Love to."

Jank and I saw her to her tent flap like gentlemen. I started softly whistling "Embraceable You" as we moved on, and then King bounced up out of the darkness and announced that he had wangled us invitations to a poker game in Rubenstein's tent. He was disheveled and dirty. His shoes looked to be a total write-off, and his beachwear wasn't in much better shape. I couldn't decide whether that ought to raise or lower him in my estimation—the one because he didn't care that he had ruined his expensive outfit, the other because I imagined he could afford not to care. He was thoroughly pleased with himself. Through the simple expedient of spending a night on a beach, he had begun to prove me wrong and become one of the guys. I had never been so disappointed with the people at Number Four camp.

"In all this time," Jank said, "I never knew I had to have an invitation to play poker with Rubenstein." He looked at me. "How about you?"

I was dead tired, but something made me answer, "Oh, why not?"

"Sure," said Jank, "why not?"

Rubenstein poured each of us a drink and dealt us in. The drink was heavenly, the cards were trash. I looked across the table at him and demanded, "These all you have?" He asked how many I wanted and peeled them off. I looked at them and thought, Worse and worse.

"Yow," said Jank. "No cards."

"Yow indeed," said De La Cerda. "You're much too happy with your hand."

"Aah, he's bluffing," I said. "Jank always bluffs."

De La Cerda threw her cards down. "He wants you to think he's bluffing. I fold." The rest of us played out the hand, to our regret. De La Cerda looked smug as Jank raked in chips. "Told you so."

The deal passed to Jank. As he shuffled, he said, without quite looking at King, "How'd you get this assignment?"

After a second, King realized that he was the person being addressed. "Applied for it, how else?"

"Applied to Northemico?"

"Yes." A pause. "Much as you applied to the government."

Jank snapped a card down on the table in front of King. "I applied through the University of Texas."

"Play cards," Rubenstein growled.

We played. Jank won the hand again. The deal passed to me. As I shuffled, King said to Jank, "You talk like you think the government's one thing and Northemico's another. Like they're separate, and one's good and one's not." He shrugged. "Or one's bad and one's worse."

Jank stared determinedly at his cards. "Aren't they? Separate, I mean."

"Public government, what you think of as *the* government—its job is just to keep the citizenry in line, make sure they don't make trouble for the *real* government. Real government is *private* government. Its job is helping rich people to become more so."

We stared at him, all but gaped, in fact. Jank finally said, "If that's so, why the whole big show of keeping the corporations out of the Paleozoic all this time?"

"Takes a while to agree on how to cut up a pie so that everybody's happy."

De La Cerda nodded slowly, as if agreeing against her will. "Like carving up old gangland cities. It's just good practice to keep your trouble away from your money."

Rubenstein said, "Does anybody here want to play *poker*, for chrissake?"

"Just a sec." King shut his fan of cards and closed his hands around it. He looked straight at Jank. "You've got some grudge against Northemico, so, because I'm here making a documentary for Northemico, you've got a grudge against me. Lots of people get made at the government. *I* get mad at it. Doesn't mean I'm mad at *you*, or anyone at this table, or anyone in this camp. I'm here to do my job, same as you."

"Remember the ad campaign," Jank said to nobody particularly, "when Antarctica finally got opened up?" I could tell from King's expression that he'd never imagined any connection between himself and Antarctica. "Yesterday's land of perpetual ice and snow, today's treasure chest of mineral wealth. My favorite was, What good is it to the penguins? Succinct. Punchy." He looked around at all our faces. "I'm willing to bet there's this bright entrepreneur somewhere who's seen pictures of the Silurian sea, how beautiful and serene it looks. He has a brainstorm. A luxury hotel in the prehistoric past! The Silurian Arms! Next thing you know, there's this whole big ad campaign pitched to assholes with money they don't know how to spend. The ads say crap like, Come back, come home, to a quiet and unspoiled world. Dine at Chez Paleozoic, gourmet cuisine from then to now."

King had sat back in his seat and folded his arms while Jank talked. Now he said, "You may have missed your true calling." He grinned to show that he really was trying to be a sport. "You'd have been an ace adman."

"No, I was born with a soul," and Jank grinned, too, like a carnivore. "About this luxury hotel. Hotels mean earth-moving equipment, mean draining all those smelly bayous. There'd have to be golf courses, too. Rich assholes can't live without golf. Golf courses mean landscaping Paleozoic Appalachia to resemble Palm Beach. There'd have to be colored people to work as caddies and grounds-keepers and do all the crap jobs, and poor neighborhoods for them to go home to at night. And golf courses mean effluent runoff, and particularly they mean grass, which as Westerman will tell you is a flowering plant, not due to appear until half past the Cenozoic. Someone decides club mosses are boring and a few palm trees wouldn't hurt. So-called sportsman won't get much of a kick out of little jawless fish, hey, this is prehistory, let's liven it up! Bio-concoct some big placoderms like Dunkleosteus, maybe even some plesiosaurs. Or just import bass. Earth history's going to get really twisted when all the little improvements take hold here."

King raised a shoulder in a half-shrug. "Sounds pretty farfetched to me. This is what's real. On the other side of the hole is an exhausted planet with nine billion people on it. On this side is a whole untouched planet."

"It's the *same* planet," Jank said. "Let Northemico go mine the moon instead, it's already dead."

"Too dead," said King, "and too far away. The Paleozoic's alive, and it's *here*. Are you going to sit there and tell me we should let our whole civilization run down so a few thousand folks here can go on admiring the place's natural splendors? Face facts. The thing's inevitable. When a thing's inevitable, the best you can do is accept it and try to find the good in it."

"Yeah." Jank pushed back his chair and got to his feet. "Just look where accepting the inevitable has got us so far."

I stood up, too. The buzz the first drink had given me was long gone; a second drink hadn't brought it back. Rubenstein, who had sat fuming with his cards fanned in his hand throughout Jank and King's set-to, cursed and flung down a full house.

Jank and I wove our way among the tents and down to the beach. I was past being ready for bed, but felt he needed me to stay with him. "Well," I said, "he's right about one thing. The Silurian Arms does sound pretty farfetched."

"Like twenty-first-century America would have to De La Cerda's damn Indians? *They* never expected to get overtaken by events, either. People never do, and yet they always are. All of us here are going to be overtaken by events any day now. Any moment. We can't outrun them, can't duck them."

"Then what do we do?"

"Then we face a choice between, I guess, becoming some sort of revolutionaries or goddamn acquiescing in another Antarctica. Put *that* in your book, Kev."

"I guess," I said, "we'll all just acquiesce. What else could we do, really?"

"Toss certain parties through the hole and then wreck the jump station."

I looked at him unhappily. We weren't just talking about golf courses in the Paleozoic now. "They'd just open up another hole."

"You don't just 'open up' another hole. You have to find one and then widen it. They could look for a long, long time. Even if they found one they could use, the odds against it being one that would bring them right back *here* are billions, trillions to one. Even if they didn't miss by much, they could miss by five or ten million years.''

"Which means," I said, "they don't play golf in the Silurian, they play it in the Ordovician or the Devonian.''

"At least they couldn't mess up the Silurian. You can't save everything, you save what you can.''

"Jank, the whole crew on the ship is Navy Reserve. They'd never throw in with mutineers. And you know that mutiny *is* what you're talking about.''

He was quiet for a moment. Then: "Yeah, hell, I know.''

"Plus, the ship's not self-sustaining, and what is there to *eat* here? Trilobites, seaweed, bony fish Vick says taste like salt and mud. At least at your luxury hotel we could get a decent meal, and a drink besides.''

He seemed unable to decide how much of what I said was serious and how much was meant to be funny. After a moment, he gave me a comradely punch on the arm and said, "Meet you on the jetty tomorrow A.M.'' He walked away, and I quickly lost sight of him in the gloom.

In the morning, it took a handful of aspirin to ease my aching head and three cups of burnt-tasting black coffee to get my eyes ungummed. The one other late-breakfaster was Rubenstein, who pointedly passed my table to sit at another one and hissed, by way of saying good morning, "A full house!''

I found Jank and Vick on the jetty, and King, too, all of them with masks and flippers in their hands. I hesitated when I saw King. He was an annoyance to Jank, but for me he was definitely shaping up as a rival. I was wearing faded cut-offs and suddenly became very conscious of the contrast provided by his sculpted thighs and calves and my scrawny knobby old-man's sticks. Vick, however, didn't recoil in horror when she looked at me, and I was further emboldened when she gave me a smile and a come-on shake of the head that a plaster saint couldn't have resisted. There is no way, I told myself, I'm *not* going into the water if King does.

Still, as Jank was getting me equipped, I said in an undertone, "What's he doing here?''

Jank shrugged helplessly. "He found out somehow and asked Vick if he could come along.''

"You want to drown him?''

"Maybe something will eat him.''

The four of us waded out until we had to swim, then swam out to where the water was six or seven meters deep. Sea and sky were warm, calm, and very clear. It was another perfect day in a ten-million-year summer.

The bottom reminded me of a *NatGeo* holo. Reef life only looks disorganized. Elsewhere in the world, coral polyps may already have been great, slow, patient architects, building barrier reefs the size of California; here, they were putting up lumpish, honeycombed bungalows. We passed over successive crescent-shaped zones dominated by gastropods, scalloped brachiopods, pink flower-like crinoids. In each zone, particular types of straight-shelled and slim tusk-shaped nautiloids jetted about above the bottom, looking like octopi in party hats. At their passing, particular types of elongate burrower disappeared under the sand with a minimum of fuss, and one or another variety of pillbug-shaped trilobite stopped grazing and dodged among the seaweed. The trilobites ranged from the fingernail- to the cracker-sized. There were prickly echinoderms, vase-shaped sponges, and limy stands of worm tubes. The first time I had ever seen any of these creatures, in clear, calf-deep water at low tide, with Cardwell standing beside me and pointing them out, I'd been disappointed. There's nothing *strange* about them, I'd thought, they're just these inoffensive little marine animals, going about their business. In spite of myself, I had, like King after me, expected more in the way of red-mawed ferocity, or of glandular imbalance, at the very least. None of these creatures was longer than my forearm. Most were smaller than my fingers.

This wasn't a scary sea by later standards. Most of the marine life that was equipped to bite hugged the bottom, where the food was, and, consequently, where the eating occurred. On dives, you stayed off the bottom and always scrupulously observed the rule against touching anything unfamiliar unless Jank or one of the other marine specialists handed it to you. We glided as huge, remote, and inaccessible as planets above the world of burrowers and scurriers. Only a few of the nautiloids seemed to notice, and all they did was track us as we passed overhead. Halfway through the Paleozoic Era, there was already that unnerving gleam of intelligence in cephalopod eyes. I glanced over my shoulder to see how my companions were doing and saw King watching, not the sea bottom, but Vick's. The headheld—I hadn't seen him without it since he donned it aboard the ship—made him look as if he were wearing an echinoderm for a cap.

Directly below us, the free-swimmers suddenly executed hard turns and rocketed away with their delicate pale tentacles fluttering behind. That spooked the more alert bottom-dwellers, and the nimbler of these made for cover among the corals. An instant later, something moved angularly across the feeding ground. It had many variously sized and shaped appendages sticking out from under its streamlined headpiece, which was adorned with two blister-like eyes as purposeful-looking as radar housings on fighter aircraft. One set of long appendages resembled nothing so much as vise-grips, another looked like sculls, and several short bristly pairs between the two were expressly for locomotion. The flattened body behind the head was divided into a dozen segments; the tail ended in an awl-like spike. The animal tore straight into a hapless trilobite. The vise-grips went to work, raising a swirl of mud and wreaking fearful havoc—the trilobite flew apart at the joints.

All of us remembered at the same moment that we occasionally had to bob up for air. We broke the surface together, and King spat out his mouthpiece and yelled, "What the hell *is* it?"

"Eurypterid!" Jank told him.

"Sea scorpion!" I put in.

We went back under. Below our waving flippers, the eurypterid swept bits of butchered trilobite under the front edge of its head. The victim's survivors had quit the area as fast as their zillions of tiny legs could carry them, or had wedged themselves into crevices in the coral. Only some cephalopods warily hovered close by, tasting blood.

The eurypterid ate as if it didn't have a care in the world. Maybe it really didn't. It was the biggest animal I had seen in all the time I'd sojourned here, and even I knew a thing or two about its tribe. Eurypterids—the term "sea scorpion" was misleading; the animals' closest relatives were horseshoe crabs— were the biggest arthropods of all time. The biggest ever found, *Pterygotus*, was two meters long, almost three with its main claws outstretched. The one before us measured only about half that, but we maintained our distance, and I personally would've preferred the view from a strong glass-bottomed boat.

The thing finished its repast and half-scuttered, half-swam into a dark space beneath a coral shelf. Jank signaled to King and me to stay where we were, and then he and Vick went down to where they could peer under the shelf. I was relieved when they kicked away and rose, and grateful, too. I was becoming fatigued. We swam until we could wade, then splashed toward the jetty. I noticed that I was going in faster than I had gone out, impelled, no doubt, by that silly fear some people have of getting a leg laid open by a flick of a marine monster's spiky tail. Unmindful of me, Jank and Vick were talking breathlessly of eurypterid body parts, the chelicerae and the telson, the prosoma this, the ophisthosoma that. King kept abreast of them, not so much listening to what they said as simply watching them say it. That damned headheld.

We flopped panting onto the rocks, and Jank grinned at me and said, "I spent a whole year at Stinktown trying to study big live eurypterids close-up. Came away with almost nothing to show for it except a scar this long." He held up his forefinger and thumb to show me how long.

"How do you mean," said King, "close-up?"

Jank's grin shrank to a smile, but he was too excited, he couldn't keep himself from answering, he'd have answered a blood enemy's questions about his specialty right then. "I tried nets and lobster pots. The varmints busted the lobster pots to pieces with their tails. I got this smallish one in a nylon net, almost a baby to the one we just saw, and had it half over the gunwale when it became annoyed and started taking the boat apart. It sideswiped me on its way back into the water."

"So, what, you just dived and looked at them?"

Jank shook his head. "Not at Stinktown. The water's too muddy. It would've been like diving in chocolate milk. With the possibility of blundering into a power saw thrown in."

"Well, I take it back," King said happily, "I really thought this place was empty," and he got up and strolled away.

"Empty," Jank breathed, "Jesus!" I tried to gauge Vick's reaction, but she was busy with her mask and flippers and didn't look up.

We were celebrities at suppertime. As happens with marine life that gets away, the eurypterid grew larger and more fearsome with each telling, until I capped matters by describing it as having been big enough to gut an orca and likening it to a lawn mower as it ripped through mats of hapless bottom-feeders. Spirits remained high as everyone collected on the beach afterward. Cardwell was having to put up with a lot of heckling and did so calmly, like Leonardo's man who knows the truth and doesn't have to shout. King kept circling him. Arty shot, I thought, and sort of happened upon Vick among the rocks at the base of the jetty. Before I could say a word to her, however, somebody on the beach shouted, "They're here!"

A foaming wave cast up a dozen glistening shoe-sized lumps almost at my feet. The next wave brought another dozen, and the one after that, scores, hundreds. I heard Cardwell give a whoop—it was more of a bellow, actually— and my first thought was that the sound would scare away the creatures we had gathered to watch. Then I remembered that eardrums, too, were on the list of the yet-to-be. Cardwell rose to his full height and spread his arms in welcome, and from around him came applause and a ragged chorus of male and female voices, "*Ta dah!*" and one lone smart-aleck's demand, "Yeah, but what's your *next* trick going to be?" Everybody stood up and began moving noisily back and forth along the tide line. Almost at once I found King tagging along with Vick and me, but for at least a little while I didn't care. It was *showtime*.

Within twenty minutes, there were thousands of trilobites on the beach, females with males in tow. The females half-buried themselves in wet sand and dumped their eggs while the males released sperm. It doesn't sound like anything you'd want to lose your head about, but trilobite males were as eager as males of any species—some females had three or four suitors tagging after them—and there were hazards such as never spiced up human procreation.

Sometimes a trilobite was overturned. It would kick a bit with its legs, then contract the muscles running along its back, roll itself into a ball, and let the next wave draw it into deeper water—where it was at considerable risk from cephalopods and other predators. The press of bodies behind pushed some overturned trilobites too far onto land for waves to pull them back. Vick picked up one of these and showed me the paired, jointed legs. King leaned in between us to capture the moment for posterity. Vick turned and lightly chucked the animal back into the water, and then several more after it. Otherwise, they'd have still been on the beach, dying, when the sun rose. King stayed with us and managed to stay with her in particular. I was thinking about chucking him into the water when he asked her, "Why do you throw them back in? What about natural selection and all that?"

"What about it?" she said. "It's getting on toward the Devonian Period. Trilobites are on their way out anyway."

"Then why . . . ?"

I stopped, picked up a stranded animal, made an underhand toss seaward. After a moment, King did the same. Vick looked pleased with both of us, which of course only half-pleased me. I wondered how to get him to go be in somebody else's face for a while. God sent somebody—who, I didn't see and didn't care— to snag him by the arm and direct his attention to an especially frenzied or imaginative expression of arthropod passion. I offered up a prayer of thanks, motioned Vick to come with me, offered up more thanks when she did. We strolled for a bit, saying nothing, then climbed onto the jetty. The chip player was in my pocket, loaded with a sampler program. We looked at the moon and the sea and listened first to a Tommy Dorsey rendition of "Moonlight in Vermont" and next to a "Moonglow" by one of Benny Goodman's combos. She sighed. What a little moonlight can do.

At length, she said, "Can you dance to this music?"

My heart raced. I had picked out these tracks myself, with serious kootchiness in mind. June moon spoon. I said, "Millions did."

"No, can *you* dance to it?"

"I do what people've always done. I fake it. If all you want to do is hold on to somebody and move in time with the music, it's easy." I opened my arms. After a moment, she came into them. "Okay, now put your left hand on my shoulder. I hold you lightly at the waist. Now put the edge of your right foot against the inside of my left foot, and the inside of your left foot against the outside of my right foot."

"This is already starting to get complicated," but she leaned away from me and looked down to position her feet. "Tab A into slot A. Tab B into slot B. Got it."

"Don't press your feet against mine so tightly. Maintain the contact lightly. Relax, stay loose."

She shifted on her feet and leaned back in against me. I was happier for that.

"Now just glide with me when I move," I said. "I'm going to lead with my right foot and follow with my left. We take one step this way." We took the step that way, stiffly, like automatons. "Then another. Then I angle off a bit and take one step back. I learned how to do this in junior high school. It's served me well for over fifty years."

I could have kicked myself for reminding her how old I was.

The jetty lay like a titan's vertebrae half-buried in the sand, pitted and uneven and altogether not an ideal surface for what we were about. Nevertheless, she began to get the hang of moving with me, began to loosen up, and I held her close and as tightly as I dared and got dizzy on her scent. After a minute or so of that, I said, "Song's almost over." It was "Sleepy Lagoon." "We're going to end with a dip."

"What's *aieep!*"

"See?"

She was laughing and lost track of her feet and almost fell. I steadied her and didn't give her a chance to slip out of my arms, or to think about doing it. I'd picked these tracks and known what I was about when I picked them. Billie Holiday started singing "You're My Thrill," a performance that could raise goose pimples on a corpse. Vick made a sound like *ooh*. Then came an instrumental version of "Where or When" by Duke Ellington and His Orchestra; Paul Gonsalves's vaporous saxophone enfolded us. Behind us, somebody said, "Yo. Fred and Ginger. Want a drink?"

It was Cardwell, feet planted wide, face beatific in the moonlight. He held up a silver flask and offered us the screw-on cup. It looked like a thimble among his thick fingers. We gave him a smart little bit of applause, and I said, "Bravo, Doctor Cardwell!"

Vick asked him, "Who're Fred and Ginger?"

"Don't mind him," I said, "he's living in the past."

Cardwell, who was almost my age, snorted like a happy bull. "We're *all* living in the past!"

We sat down on the end of the jetty and proceeded to get pretty silly together. She was between us, and at some point she slipped her arms around our necks and gave us a squeeze. We talked about trilobites and about nothing in particular, or didn't talk at all but listened to "Happiness is a Thing Called Joe" and "Blue Flame" by Woody Herman, "Body and Soul" by Benny Goodman, "Lover Man" by Holiday. We took turns dozing. It finally worked out, just at dawn, that Cardwell was dozing and Vick and I were watching the sea lighten and the night retreat to the west. She looked sleepy and content, past being drunk but still short of hungover. There was a small dab of mud on her neck. I brushed it away and said, "Doctor Harris."

She said, "Mister Barnett."

"How come both of us've been here as long as we have, and I've only recently realized what a swell person you are?"

A smile spread across her face. "You're slow."

Kiss her, moron, I told myself.

And at that very moment, King came scrambling up the side of the jetty like the evil monkey he was and dropped into a squat before us. I heard the headheld's faint whir and saw its eye seek Vick's face. I couldn't tell from her expression whether she, too, was conscious of having been interrupted at a crucial moment. "All I can say," he said, "is, wow!" Mister Articulate. Someone on the beach hallooed and called him to breakfast by name. Somehow, he was still one of the guys. It eluded me.

Not everyone had stayed up drinking for nights running, or was old, so not everyone at breakfast felt entirely as washed out as I did. I wanted to hang around, to head King off at the pass if the need arose, but started to nod and almost face-dived into my food. I bade Vick as gallant a farewell as I was able without being a total clown and hobbled achingly off to my cot. The snoring hillock on the next cot was Cardwell; he had almost the same beatific look on his face. Jank, in skivvies, sat in a camp chair and scratched his pectorals. He nodded at a scrap of paper on my cot. "That came in from Sparks a couple minutes ago."

I carefully sat down on the cot. "You wouldn't have any hair of the dog, would you?"

He looked around blearily. "Is it after noon yet?"

I looked at the writing on the paper. *Call me. Ruth.* "Later," I said, and became unconscious.

Which was a mistake, because by the time I regained consciousness, Ruth, who was not someone who liked to be kept waiting, had had time to put a fine vindictive edge on her plans for me. Another mistake was concluding my account of King's impromptu beach holiday by telling her that he seemed well on the way to carving out a secure niche for himself in the camp and I therefore ought to be relieved of all responsibility for him. She agreed. Then, in as sweet-Southern-sexy a voice as though she were telling me to go ahead, pick something out of the *Kama Sutra*, she added, "This will allow you to devote your time to your *other* guest, Ms. Duvall, when you get back to the ship tonight." I sputtered, protested, tried to argue. She wouldn't argue. "Just make sure you're with Hirsch when she comes back," she said, "bye, hon," and signed off.

I spent some time complaining to anybody who would listen, but hardly anybody could listen. Everyone had work to do. Toward sundown, however— by which time I was well past disbelief and outrage and clear to the sullen cranks—Jank showed up at the tent to watch me toss my meager gear into my threadbare seabag and listen to me damn Ruth. When I had exhausted her as a subject, I started in on King, whom I likened, in swift succession, to a burr under my saddle, a thorn in my side, and sand in my undershorts. Jank burst out laughing.

My surprise and pain at his unsympathetic reaction showed. He said, "Sorry. Don't mean to make light."

"Keep an eye on Mister Smarm while I'm off the beach, okay? Don't let him work his bolt too much." I closed the bag and looked around. "Are you all the send-off I'm getting?"

"It's not like you're going *back*, Kev."

"I don't suppose you know where Vick's got to."

"Off checking specimens with Cardwell, where else?"

We didn't shake hands. It wasn't as though I were going back. We separated outside the tent, and I walked disconsolately through the camp. There were voices in Rubenstein's tent: the poker game was gearing up. At the end of the jetty, I found Hirsch fiddling around in the boat. We exchanged nods, and I was about to get in when I heard my name called. I turned to see three people coming along the jetty, Vick and Cardwell dressed in hideous Hawaiian shirts—both his; there was sufficient material in the one Vick wore for five or six dresses in her size—and King tagging along, duded up as usual. He hung back as they approached the boat. Vick hugged me warmly, gave me a quick kiss on the corner of the mouth, and said, "Sorry we didn't get to see much of you today."

"Well, *you* have a day job."

"I just wanted to make sure you knew I had a wonderful time last night."

"Cardwell supplied the trilobites and the booze."

Cardwell sighed like an old steam engine and said, "I just catered. You guys danced." He handed me some old-fashioned letters, written on paper, sealed in envelopes with names and addresses inscribed on them in ink. "Didn't get these into the mail pouch in time."

"No problemo."

I stepped away, stepped down into the boat. King had got it all with the headheld. The boat pulled away from the jetty. Luminous in the golden light of evening, Vick and Cardwell waved to me, and I to them, and as far as I was concerned at that moment the only way the scene could have been improved— short, of course, of a last-minute reprieve for me and the simultaneous annihilation by lightning of Rick King—would have been for Cardwell to strum on a ukelele and Vick in a grass skirt to call out *aloha oe* while Bing Crosby crooned, Soon I'll be sailing. . . .

Back on the ship, I pointedly did not report immediately to Ruth. I unpacked, showered to sluice off beach grit and thwarted hopes, stretched out on my bunk, with an anthology of essays plugged into the machine so I wouldn't look just like some old bum taking a nap, and took a nap. I was awakened by the ship's getting under way and lay staring up at the major decorative touch in my little compartment.

It was a framed reproduction, given to me as a birthday present by my third wife shortly before she called me a bastard and threw the cat at my head, of a map of mid-Paleozoic North America as it had been reconstructed by Charles Schuchert and other early-twentieth-century, pre-plate-tectonics paleogeographers. They had, among other things, rather seriously underestimated the extent of continental inundation and postulated persistent borderlands separated by seaways. I'd always been drawn to the region labeled *Llanoria (Mexia)*, comprising what I regarded as home territory, northeastern Mexico, southern and southeastern Texas, Louisiana, bits of Oklahoma and Arkansas. Disappointingly, where Schuchert had postulated land, later, better-equipped geologists had found evidence only of muddy sea bottom. Yet I remained charmed by Llanoria and the other strangely shaped, exotically named land masses, *Laurentia (Canadia)*, *Cordillera (Cascadia)*, *Appalachia*, enclosing an inland sea studded with lesser lands, *Siouia, Wisconsin Isle, Adirondack Island*. I think the reason for the enduring appeal of this outmoded representation was that Schuchert and his colleagues must have approached their task not simply with the idea in mind of mapping a prehistoric continent according to the data available, but also with something like the pleasure Frank Baum and Edgar Rice Burroughs derived from filling in their maps of Oz and Barsoom.

I went to the mess and glumly ate. Then I sat thinking that I really ought to go see Ruth. *Then* I sat thinking that I really ought to go visit Chamberlain on the fantail, and wondered what I should say to him about Vick, and concluded that I didn't feel like being disapproved of by a solitary drunk who hadn't been involved with a woman since the Treaty of Ghent, who hadn't even been ashore in all the years he'd spent here. Then I went to see Ruth, who while waiting for me had thought up all sorts of little jobs for me to do.

The days dragged into a week. Claire Duvall got shakily back on her feet. I took her on brief tours, introduced her to various people, and disliked her a lot. She was attractive in her way, with eyes so blue they were almost violet and hair so black it was almost blue, like a comic-book character's, but I found her irritating company. All she could talk about was what a genius Rick was.

Ruth informed me that other newcomers, ''important ones''—suits, in short—

would soon be arriving, too, and maybe I should become the official greeter after all, since I was so good at it, and this was definitely the time to upgrade my wardrobe. I looked landward and burned with the torments of the damned. I couldn't even get a personal message to shore—Sparks regretfully informed me that radio traffic was at an all-time high, all day every day the air crackled with messages, either highly technical or else coded, from the interior. I was miserable enough to wonder if Ruth had somehow heard something about Vick and me, was keeping me on the ship and off the air out of spite, and more nonsense in that vein. The wasichu, those unsociable, obscurely specialized personnel who were taking over the expedition, continued to arrive and depart by helicopter, mysteriously, sinisterly. The suits didn't come and didn't come and didn't come.

On the afternoon of the eighth day, there was a knock, and Chamberlain appeared in the hatchway, flask in hand. He said, "I got tired of waiting for you to come visit me." He gave me a closer look. "You sulking alone in here, or you want someone to get you good and drunk and listen to your tale of woe."

"I'm in no mood to be made fun of."

"Oh, come on." He was looking around for a place to sit. I moved a box of book chips, and he plopped himself down with a grunt. "Can I smoke?"

"I wish you wouldn't."

He heaved a sigh that was almost a whimper, fidgeted, remembered the flask. "Want a drink?"

I took a long swallow and handed the flask back to him. "I drink too much."

"Right now, you look like you can't drink enough."

"I'm about six minutes from going on a killing spree."

"Hm." He took a drink, stowed the flask, put his hands on his knees. "Our tail *is* tied in a knot today."

"You wouldn't understand."

"Welty, Eudora Welty, said that, whatever wonderful things we may do, fly to the moon, whatever—travel through time—we're driven by a small range of feelings. She said all our motives can still be counted on our fingers."

"You got that out of one of my books!"

"It matter where I got it if it's true?"

I regarded him sullenly.

"Man your age shouldn't pout," he said. He waited, heaved another sigh, slapped his thighs. "Well, I'm not going to try and pry it out of you. I'm your *friend*, schmuck. You need to talk, *talk*, I'll listen. You may find you're blowing whatever it is all out of proportion."

"I don't *have* a sense of proportion right now. Sorry, but there're just some things that're bigger than I am."

"Have it your way. I'm going back where I can smoke. Come join me when you feel better. You don't want to sweat out the storm of the Silurian in this little box."

"What? Storm?"

Halfway through the hatchway, Chamberlain turned and gave me a big happy grin. "All signs meteorological point to a big 'un piling up in the east. They're evacuating the windward camps."

He almost didn't get through the hatchway before I did.

When the boat arrived with the contingent from Number Four camp, I spotted Vick at once. A moment later, I spotted King as well. He had shucked his fancy beachwear in favor of cut-offs and a T-shirt. He was sitting beside her in the boat. They were talking to each other. Whatever they were talking about, she looked as if she found it very interesting indeed. I told myself that it was only clinical interest, but even as I did, the sharp barb of jealousy sank into my aorta, as I saw, realized, that she was holding his hand, there was a sick awful sinking feeling in the pit of my stomach, I knew he had novelty going for him, and sculpted muscles, and youth, and he'd surely let only me see him sick and whiny, and I hardly counted. . . .

Everything looked so ordinary. Everyone was tired and dirty. No one paid any attention to the new lovers, regarded them strangely or enviously or hatefully or any way at all, not even Jank, who sat at the bow looking gloomily preoccupied. What really drove home the idea that, somehow, incredibly, she was *with* King was her looking up, seeing me, smiling, waving, calling out a friendly greeting. She was radiant with guiltless happiness. I moved my hand at my side, the best I could do by way of waving back. Suddenly desperate to escape from the boat bay, I turned to go, and there stood Claire Duvall, staring down at the two people among all the people in the boat, with an expression of disbelief on her face that was only beginning to yield to hurt and anger. She looked the way I felt. I brushed past her and stumbled numbly through the ship. Someone touched my arm and said, ''Hey, Kev, you okay?'' and I made a noise, slipped past, kept walking until I was in my cabin, shut in.

I sat down. I exhaled emphatically, as if that would take care of matters, let me go on with my day, my life. Of course it didn't. I promptly found myself trying to pinpoint in memory the instant when the spark must have leaped between them. I shook those thoughts out of my skull only so I could wonder if she let him wear the headheld when they had sex, and if this wasn't strictly a short-term pheromone-propelled kind of relationship anyway. It seemed to me that world-view had to matter even between the sheets, but then I thought of Westerman and Hendryx's relationship, which had endured for years, and even prospered at times, in the face of major differences of opinion on every subject imaginable. I'd made so bold as to ask them about that, one time when we were sitting around ruining our livers, and received for an answer giggles from her and a dreamy grin from him. Pheromones.

I decided I needed some music and stuck Coleman Hawkins into the player. ''I'm Through With Love,'' ''What Is There to Say?'' I could have gone with Cab Calloway or Fats Waller, who would've worked hard to cheer me up; at least I didn't choose Holiday and ''Good Morning, Heartache.'' For all the difference it made. I went right on foundering in my tarpit of self-pity. I'd always loved women and the company of women. I'd had girlfriends since I was in third grade, lovers since I was in my mid-teens, a lifetime of love's ups and downs, ins and outs. Yet I couldn't believe how awful I felt *now*. I felt every bit as awful now as when I'd been a high-school sophomore and Judy Biesemeyer had broken my heart. Nothing had a right, I told myself, to hurt me as much in my sixties as it had at fifteen, and yet why, I asked myself, would I ever have thought that it *wouldn't*? To which I could only answer, duh, dunno, just stupid, I guess. And at last it struck me, I hadn't just been passed over, I wasn't just stupid, I was *ridiculous* was what I was, a lover boy trapped in a flabby, loose-skinned, wrinkling, balding, shrinking, crumbling body, and the best I could hope for was that she hadn't noticed how ridiculous I was, that she had thought of me the whole time merely as a sweet old gent, not as—

I glared at my antique map of Llanoria, land that never was, and decided what I really needed was a drink. I stood up and sat right back down again. The deck was tilted. Then it was level. Then it was tilted again, but in the opposite direction. I stuck my head into the companionway and yelled at the first person I saw, "The ship's pitching!"

"Storm," he said, as if replying to a child, and unhurriedly went on about his business.

On the fantail, Chamberlain was sitting in his deck chair and peering out to sea while his assistants busied themselves among the gadgets. I could hear people yelling at one another up on the helicopter deck as they lashed down aircraft. The ship raced with the sea and before a cool, moisture-heavy wind. Far astern, spanning the horizon, seeming to reach clear into the ionosphere, were sheer cliffs of dark gray cloud.

"Sweet Jesus," I said, "where did *that* come from?"

"If that's not a number twelve on the Beaufort scale, I'll eat my barometer." Chamberlain spared me a glance along his shoulder. "You look worse now than you did before."

I barely heard him. I couldn't take my eyes off the clouds. Then my pocketphone buzzed, and the bane of my existence said, "Kevo, get down to the jump-station. Those vee-eye-pees are definitely on the way. You've got just enough time to change into some decent clothes."

"They're coming *now*?" I was holding on to the rail with one hand and needed two. "There's a big storm on the way, too."

"How're they supposed to know what they're jumping into? Twenty minutes, dear heart."

I screeched into the speaker and tossed the pocketphone overboard. Then I said, "Oh, hell, I shouldn't've done that. Some rockhound'll find it."

Chamberlain said, "We won't leave a trace."

"Can I have a drink? I'm having a bad day. First—and now suits jumping in."

He handed me the flask. "Cheer up. You're probably going to be treated to the sight of very self-important people puking like cats."

"Some treat."

He took a pack of cigarettes from his shirt pocket, shook out one of the nasty things, braced himself against the rail with his back to the wind to light up. "Hurry on back here when you can. You don't want to miss this, it's going to be quite a blow. We can't outrun it, despite what the Navy may let on. May not even be able to ride it out on the lee shore."

I said, "You'd be a much happier person if you'd get yourself a girlfriend," but the truth was, he looked happier at that moment than I'd ever seen him, as happy as Cardwell with his trilobites, Jank with his eurypterid—

—King with his ichthyologist.

I suddenly felt so tired. This was the last time, I thought, I don't have another good love affair left in me, or even a bad one. I saw the rest of my life. I'd spend my time drinking and listening to people argue whether or not it was a good idea to use the Paleozoic to keep the twenty-first century clanking and sputtering along. Not that argument would stop it from happening. I'd hear Holiday sing another few hundred or thousand times of how she covered the waterfront, be dazzled anew at every playing of the Shaw or the Goodman "Moonglow," and hum along whenever the morning found me miles away with still a million things to say. The long, quiet Silurian summer would wear on, Laurasia and Gondwanaland would draw inexorably together, and the solar system would continue its circuit of the outer reaches of the Milky Way. I'd do whatever I had to do for Ruth to go on being a hanger-on here, and I wouldn't write, and if ever I found myself *seeing* anyone else whom I'd only been looking at before, I'd throw myself overboard. . . .

"Feel that wind," Chamberlain murmured. His long, thin hair whipped about his skull. "I've been thinking a lot about fetch today."

"Huh? Like with a dog?"

"Idiot. Fetch is the extent of open water a wind can blow across. Here we've got a northern hemisphere that's almost nothing but fetch. Wind, waves could travel right around the planet. Storm comes along, whips together a bunch of mid-ocean waves traveling at different speeds, piles 'em up into big waves. *Big* waves. Back in the nineteen-thirties, a Navy ship in the Pacific sighted a wave over thirty-five meters high."

I was appalled. "You're hoping we break that record?"

"Hm. About time we had some excitement around here." He regarded me with approximately equal parts of amusement and tenderness. "See how quickly your priorities are getting straightened out?"

"Okay," I said, "so there're things that're bigger than the things that're bigger than me."

"Hm. Mm hm." For Chamberlain, that was a gale of laughter.

THE NIGHT WE BURIED ROAD DOG

Jack Cady

▼

Here's a haunting and evocative piece of modern-day folklore, funny and sad by turns, that sends us hurtling at full throttle down the back roads and blue highways of a nighttime, honkytonk world—and deep into the heart of the American spirit. . . .

Jack Cady is at present perhaps better known in the horror/fantasy field than in science fiction, but although he's published horror novels such as *The Well* and *The Jonah Watch*, he has also published one SF novel, *The Man Who Could Make Things Vanish* . . . and it won't take many more stories of the power of "The Night They Buried Road Dog" to establish his name with the SF readership as well. His most recent books are a collection, *The Sons of Noah and Other Stories*, and a short novel, *Inagehi*. Coming up soon is a new horror novel entitled *Street*, and he has a new story collection in the works as well. Cady lives in Port Townsend, Washington.

I

Brother Jesse buried his '47 Hudson back in '61, and the roads got just that much more lonesome. Highway 2 across north Montana still wailed with engines as reservation cars blew past; and it lay like a tunnel of darkness before headlights of big rigs. Tandems pounded, and the smart crack of downshifts rapped across grassland as trucks swept past the bars at every crossroad. The state put up metal crosses to mark the sites of fatal accidents. Around the bars, those crosses sprouted like thickets.

That Hudson was named Miss Molly, and it logged 220,000 miles while never burning a clutch. Through the years, it wore into the respectable look that comes to old machinery. It was rough as a cob, cracked glass on one side, and primer over dents. It had the tough-and-ready look of a hunting hound about its business. I was a good deal younger then, but not so young that I was fearless. The burial had something to do with mystery, and Brother Jesse did his burying at midnight.

Through fluke or foresight, Brother Jesse had got hold of eighty acres of rangeland that wasn't worth a shake. There wasn't enough of it to run stock, and you couldn't raise anything on it except a little hell. Jesse stuck an old house trailer out there, stacked hay around it for insulation in Montana winters, and hauled in just enough water to suit him. By the time his Hudson died, he was ready to go into trade.

"Jed," he told me the night of the burial, "I'm gonna make myself some history, despite this damn Democrat administration." Over beside the house trailer, the Hudson sat looking like it was about ready to get off the mark in a road race, but the poor thing was a goner. Moonlight sprang from between spring clouds, and to the westward the peaks of mountains glowed from snow and moonlight. Along Highway 2, some hot rock wound second gear on an old flathead Ford. You could hear the valves begin to float.

"Some little darlin' done stepped on that boy's balls," Jesse said about the driver. "I reckon that's why he's looking for a ditch." Jesse sighed and sounded sad. "At least we got a nice night. I couldn't stand a winter funeral."

"Road Dog?" I said about the driver of the Ford, which shows just how young I was at the time.

"It ain't The Dog," Jesse told me. "The Dog's a damn survivor."

You never knew where Brother Jesse got his stuff, and you never really knew if he was anybody's brother. The only time I asked, he said, "I come from a close-knit family such as your own," and that made no sense. My own father died when I was twelve, and my mother married again when I turned seventeen. She picked up and moved to Wisconsin.

No one even knew when, or how, Jesse got to Montana territory. We just looked up one day, and there he was, as natural as if he'd always been here, and maybe he always had.

His eighty acres began to fill up. Old printing presses stood gap-mouthed like spinsters holding conversation. A salvaged greenhouse served for storing dog food, engine parts, chromium hair dryers from 1930's beauty shops, dime-store pottery, blades for hay cutters, binder twine, an old gas-powered crosscut saw, seats from a school bus, and a bunch of other stuff not near as useful.

A couple of tabbies lived in that greenhouse, but the Big Cat stood outside. It was an old D6 bulldozer with a shovel, and Jesse stoked it up from time to time. Mostly it just sat there. In summers, it provided shade for Jesse's dogs: Potato was brown and fat and not too bright, while Chip was little and fuzzy. Sometimes they rode with Jesse, and sometimes stayed home. Me or Mike Tarbush fed them. When anything big happened, you could count on those two dogs to get underfoot. Except for me, they were the only ones who attended the funeral.

"If we gotta do it," Jesse said mournfully, "we gotta." He wound up the Cat, turned on the headlights, and headed for the grave site, which was an embankment overlooking Highway 2. Back in those days, Jesse's hair still shone black, and it was even blacker in the darkness. It dangled around a face that carried an Indian forehead and a Scotsman's nose. Denim stretched across most of the six feet of him, and he wasn't rangy; he was thin. He had feet to match his height, and his hands seemed bigger than his feet; but the man could skin a Cat.

I stood in moonlight and watched him work. A little puff of flame dwelt in the stack of the bulldozer. It flashed against the darkness of those distant mountains. It burbled hot in the cold spring moonlight. Jesse made rough cuts pretty quick, moved a lot of soil, then started getting delicate. He shaped and reshaped that grave. He carved a little from one side, backed the dozer, found his cut not satisfactory. He took a spoonful of earth to straighten things, then fussed with the grade leading into the grave. You could tell he wanted a slight elevation, so the Hudson's nose would be sniffing toward the road. Old Potato dog had a hound's ears, but not a hound's good sense. He started baying at the moon.

It came to me that I was scared. Then it came to me that I was scared most of the time anyway. I was nineteen, and folks talked about having a war across the sea. I didn't want to hear about it. On top of the war talk, women were driving me crazy: the ones who said "no" and the ones who said "yes." It got downright mystifying just trying to figure out which was worse. At nineteen, it's hard to know how to act. There were whole weeks when I could pass myself off as a hellion, then something would go sour. I'd get hit by a streak of conscience and start acting like a missionary.

"Jed," Jesse told me from the seat of the dozer, "go rig a tow on Miss Molly." In the headlights the grave now looked like a garage dug into the side of that little slope. Brother Jesse eased the Cat back in there to fuss with the grade. I stepped slow toward the Hudson, wiggled under, and fetched the towing cable around the frame. Potato howled. Chip danced like a fuzzy fury, and started chewing on my boot like he was trying to drag me from under the Hudson. I was on my back trying to kick Chip away and secure the cable. Then I like to died from fright.

Nothing else in the world sounds anywhere near like a Hudson starter. It's a combination of whine and clatter and growl. If I'd been dead a thousand years, you could stand me right up with a Hudson starter. There's threat in that sound. There's also the promise that things can get pretty rowdy, pretty quick.

The starter went off. The Hudson jiggled. In the one-half second it took to get from under that car, I thought of every bad thing I ever did in my life. I was headed for Hell, certain sure. By the time I was on my feet, there wasn't an ounce of blood showing anywhere on me. When the old folks say, "white as a sheet," they're talking about a guy under a Hudson.

Brother Jesse climbed from the Cat and gave me a couple of shakes.

"She ain't dead," I stuttered. "The engine turned over. Miss Molly's still thinking speedy." From Highway 2 came the wail of Mike Tarbush's '48 Road-master. Mike loved and cussed that car. It always flattened out at around eighty.

"There's still some sap left in the batt'ry," Jesse said about the Hudson. "You probably caused a short." He dropped the cable around the hitch on the dozer. "Steer her," he said.

The steering wheel still felt alive, despite what Jesse said. I crouched behind the wheel as the Hudson got dragged toward the grave. Its brakes locked twice, but the towing cable held. The locked brakes caused the car to sideslip. Each time, Jesse cussed. Cold spring moonlight made the shadowed grave look like a cave of darkness.

The Hudson bided its time. We got it lined up, then pushed it backward into the grave. The hunched front fenders spread beside the snarly grille. The front bumper was the only thing about that car that still showed clean and uncluttered. I could swear Miss Molly moved in the darkness of the grave, about to come charging onto Highway 2. Then she seemed to make some kind of decision, and sort of settled down. Jesse gave the eulogy.

"This here car never did nothing bad," he said. "I must have seen a million crap-crates, but this car wasn't one of them. She had a second gear like Hydra-matic, and you could wind to seventy before you dropped to third. There wasn't no top end to her—at least I never had the guts to find it. This here was a hundred-mile-an-hour car on a bad night, and God knows what on a good'n." From Highway 2, you could hear the purr of Matt Simons's '56 Dodge, five speeds, what with the overdrive, and Matt was scorching.

Potato howled long and mournful. Chip whined. Jesse scratched his head, trying to figure a way to end the eulogy. It came to him like a blessing. "I can't prove it," he said, "'cause no one could. But I expect this car has passed The Road Dog maybe a couple of hundred times." He made like he was going to cross himself, then remembered he was Methodist. "Rest in peace," he said, and he said it with eyes full of tears. "There ain't that many who can comprehend The Dog." He climbed back on the Cat and began to fill the grave.

Next day, Jesse mounded the grave with real care. He erected a marker, although the marker was more like a little signboard:

1947–1961
Hudson coupe—"Molly"
220,023 miles on straight eight cylinder
Died of busted crankshaft
Beloved in the memory of
Jesse Still

Montana roads are long and lonesome, and Highway 2 is lonesomest. You pick it up over on the Idaho border where the land is mountains. Bear and cougar still live pretty good, and beaver still build dams. The highway runs beside some pretty lakes. Canada is no more than a jump away; it hangs at your left shoulder when you're headed east.

And can you roll those mountains? Yes, oh yes. It's two-lane all the way across, and twisty in the hills. From Libby, you ride down to Kalispell, then pop back north. The hills last till the Blackfoot reservation. It's rangeland into Cut Bank, then to Havre. That's just about the center of the state.

Just let the engine howl from town to town. The road goes through a dozen, then swings south. And there you are at Glasgow and the river. By Wolf Point, you're in cropland, and it's flat from there until Chicago.

I almost hate to tell about this road, because easterners may want to come and visit. Then they'll do something dumb at a blind entry. The state will erect more metal crosses. Enough folks die up here already. And it's sure no place for rice grinders, or tacky Swedish station wagons, or high-priced German crap-crates. This was always a V-8 road, and V-12 if you had 'em. In the old, old days there were even a few V-16s up here. The top end on those things came when friction stripped the tires from too much speed.

Speed or not, brakes sure sounded as cars passed Miss Molly's grave. Pickup trucks fishtailed as men snapped them to the shoulder. The men would sit in their trucks for a minute, scratching their heads like they couldn't believe what they'd just seen. Then they'd climb from the truck, walk back to the grave, and read the marker. About half of them would start holding their sides. One guy even rolled around on the ground, he was laughing so much.

"These old boys are laughing now," Brother Jesse told me, "but I predict a change in attitude. I reckon they'll come around before first snowfall."

With his car dead, Jesse had to find a set of wheels. He swapped an old hay rake and a gang of discs for a '49 Chevrolet.

"It wouldn't pull the doorknob off a cathouse," he told me. "It's just to get around in while I shop."

The whole deal was going to take some time. Knowing Jesse, I figured he'd go through half a dozen trades before finding something comfortable. And I was right.

He first showed up in an old Packard hearse that once belonged to a funeral home in Billings. He'd swapped the Chev for the hearse, plus a gilt-covered coffin so gaudy it wouldn't fit anybody but a radio preacher. He swapped the hearse to Sam Winder, who aimed to use it for hunting trips. Sam's dogs wouldn't go anywhere near the thing. Sam opened all the windows and the back door, then took the hearse up to speed trying to blow out all the ghosts. The dogs still wouldn't go near it. Sam said, "To hell with it," and pushed it into a ravine. Every rabbit and fox and varmint in that ravine came bailing out, and nobody has gone in there ever since.

Jesse traded the coffin to Old Man Jefferson, who parked the thing in his woodshed. Jefferson was supposed to be on his last legs, but figured he wasn't ever, never, going to die if his poor body knew it would be buried in that monstrosity. It worked for several years, too, until a bad winter came along, and he split it up for firewood. But we still remember him.

Jesse came out of those trades with a '47 Pontiac and a Model T. He sold the Model T to a collector, then traded the Pontiac and forty bales of hay for a '53 Studebaker. He swapped the Studebaker for a ratty pickup and all the equipment in a restaurant that went bust. He peddled the equipment to some other poor fellow who was hell-bent to go bust in the restaurant business. Then he traded the pickup for a motorcycle, plus a '51 Plymouth that would just about get out of its own way. By the time he peddled both of them, he had his pockets full of cash and was riding shanks' mare.

"Jed," he told me, "let's you and me go to the big city." He was pretty happy, but I remembered how scared I'd been at the funeral. I admit to being skittish.

From the center of north Montana, there weren't a championship lot of big cities. West was Seattle, which was sort of rainy and mythological. North was Winnipeg, a cow town. South was Salt Lake City. To the east. . . .

"The hell with it," Brother Jesse said. "We'll go to Minneapolis."

It was about a thousand miles. Maybe fifteen hours, what with the roads. You could sail Montana and North Dakota, but those Minnesota cops were humorless.

I was shoving a sweet old '53 Desoto. It had a good bit under the bonnet, but the suspension would make a grown man cry. It was a beautiful beast, though. Once you got up to speed, that front end would track like a cat. The upholstery was like brand-new. The radio worked. There wasn't a scratch or ding on it. I had myself a banker's car, and there I was, only nineteen.

"We may want to loiter," Jesse told me. "Plan on a couple of overnights."

I had a job, but told myself that I was due for a vacation; and so screw it. Brother Jesse put down food for the tabbies and whistled up the dogs. Potato hopped into the backseat in his large, dumb way. He looked expectant. Chip sort of hesitated. He made a couple of jumps straight up, then backed down and started barking. Jesse scooped him up and shoved him in with old Potato dog.

"The upholstery," I hollered. It was the first time I ever stood up to Jesse.

Jesse got an old piece of tarp to put under the dogs. "Pee, and you're a goner," he told Potato.

We drove steady through the early-summer morning. The Desoto hung in around eighty, which was no more than you'd want, considering the suspension. Rangeland gave way to cropland. The radio plugged away with western music, beef prices, and an occasional preacher saying, "Grace" and "Gimmie." Highway 2 rolled straight ahead, sometimes rising gradual, so that cars appeared like rapid running spooks out of the blind entries. There'd be a little flash of sunlight from a windshield. Then a car would appear over the rise, and usually it was wailing.

We came across a hell of a wreck just beyond Havre. A new Mercury station wagon rolled about fifteen times across the landscape. There were two nice-dressed people and two children. Not one of them ever stood a chance. They rattled like dice in a drum. I didn't want to see what I was looking at.

Bad wrecks always made me sick, but not sick to puking. That would not have been manly. I prayed for those people under my breath and got all shaky. We pulled into a crossroads bar for a sandwich and a beer. The dogs hopped out. Plenty of hubcaps were nailed on the wall of the bar. We took a couple of them down and filled them with water from an outside tap. The dogs drank and peed.

"I've attended a couple myself," Brother Jesse said about the wreck. "Drove a Terraplane off a bridge back in '53. Damn near drownded." Jesse wasn't about to admit to feeling bad. He just turned thoughtful.

"This here is a big territory," he said to no one in particular. "But you can get across her if you hustle. I reckon that Merc was loaded wrong, or blew a tire." Beyond the windows of the bar, eight metal crosses lined the highway. Somebody had tied red plastic roses on one of them. Another one had plastic violets and forget-me-nots.

We lingered a little. Jesse talked to the guy at the bar, and I ran a rack at the pool table. Then Jesse bought a six-pack while I headed for the can. Since it was still early in the day, the can was clean; all the last night's pee and spit mopped from the floor. Somebody had just painted the walls. There wasn't a thing written on them, except that Road Dog had signed in.

Road Dog
How are things in Glocca Mora?

His script was spidery and perfect, like an artist who drew a signature. I touched the paint, and it was still tacky. We had missed The Dog by only a few minutes.

Road Dog was like Jesse in a way. Nobody could say exactly when he first showed up, but one day he was there. We started seeing the name "Road Dog" written in what Matt Simons called "a fine Spencerian hand." There was always a message attached, and Matt called them "cryptic." The signature and messages flashed from the walls of cans in bars, truck stops, and roadside cafés through four states.

We didn't know Road Dog's route at first. Most guys were tied to work or home or laziness. In a year or two, though, Road Dog's trail got mapped. His fine hand showed up all along Highway 2, trailed east into North Dakota, dropped south through South Dakota, then ran back west across Wyoming. He popped north through Missoula and climbed the state until he connected with Highway 2 again. Road Dog, whoever he was, ran a constant square of road that covered roughly two thousand miles.

Sam Winder claimed Road Dog was a Communist who taught social studies at U. of Montana. "Because," Sam claimed, "that kind of writing comes from Europe. That writing ain't U.S.A."

Mike Tarbush figured Road Dog was a retired cartoonist from a newspaper. He figured nobody could spot The Dog, because The Dog slipped past us in a Nash, or some other old-granny car.

Brother Jesse suggested that Road Dog was a truck driver, or maybe a gypsy, but sounded like he knew better.

Matt Simons supposed Road Dog was a traveling salesman with a flair for advertising. Matt based his notion on one of the cryptic messages:

Road Dog
Ringling Bros. Barnum and Toothpaste

I didn't figure anything. Road Dog stood in my imagination as the heart and soul of Highway 2. When night was deep and engines blazed, I could hang over the wheel and run down that tunnel of two-lane into the night.

The nighttime road is different than any other thing. Ghosts rise around the metal crosses, and ghosts hitchhike along the wide berm. All the mysteries of the world seem normal after dark. If imagination shows dead thumbs aching for a ride, those dead folk only prove the hot and spermy goodness of life. I'd overtake some taillights, grab the other lane, and blow doors off some partygoer who tried to stay out of the ditches. A man can sing and cuss and pray. The miles fill with dreams of power, and women, and happy, happy times.

Road Dog seemed part of that romance. He was the very soul of mystery, a guy who looked at the dark heart of the road and still flew free enough to make jokes and write that fine hand.

In daytime, it was different, though. When I saw Road Dog signed in on the wall of that can, it just seemed like a real bad sign.

The guy who owned the bar had seen no one. He claimed he'd been in the back room putting bottles in his cold case. The Dog had come and gone like a spirit.

Jesse and I stood in the parking lot outside the bar. Sunlight laid earthy and hot across the new crops. A little puff of dust rose from a side road. It advanced real slow, so you could tell it was a farm tractor. All around us, meadowlarks and tanagers were whooping it up.

"We'll likely pass him," Jesse said, "if we crowd a little." Jesse pretended he didn't care, but anyone would. We loaded the dogs, and even hung the hubcaps back up where we got them, because it was what a gentleman would do. The Desoto acted as eager as any Desoto could. We pushed the top end, which was eighty-nine, and maybe ninety-two downhill. At that speed, brakes don't give you much, so you'd better trust your steering and your tires.

If we passed The Dog, we didn't know it. He might have parked in one of the towns, and of course we dropped a lot of revs passing through towns, that being neighborly. What with a little loafing, some pee stops, and general fooling around, we did not hit Minneapolis until a little after midnight. When we checked into a motel on the strip, Potato was sleepy and grumpy. Chip looked relieved.

"Don't fall in love with that bed," Jesse told me. "Some damn salesman is out there waitin' to do us in. It pays to start early."

Car shopping with Jesse turned out as fascinating as anybody could expect. At 7:00 A.M., we cruised the lots. Cars stood in silent rows like advertising men lined up for group pictures. It being Minneapolis, we saw a lot of high-priced iron. Cadillacs and Packards and Lincolns sat beside Buick convertibles, hemi Chryslers, and Corvettes ("Nice c'hars," Jesse said about the Corvettes, "but no room to 'em. You couldn't carry more than one sack of feed."). Hudsons and Studebakers hunched along the back rows. On one lot was something called "Classic Lane." A Model A stood beside a '37 International pickup. An L29 Cord sat like a tombstone, which it was, because it had no engine. But, glory be, beside the Cord nestled a '39 LaSalle coupe just sparkling with threat. That LaSalle might have snookered Jesse, except something highly talented sat buried deep in the lot.

It was the last of the fast and elegant Lincolns, a '54 coupe as snarly as any man could want. The '53 model had taken the Mexican Road Race. The '54 was a refinement. After that the marque went downhill. It started building cars for businessmen and rich grannies.

Jesse walked round and round the Lincoln, which looked like it was used to being cherished. Matchless and scratchless. It was a little less than fire engine red, with a white roof and a grille that could shrug off a cow. That Linc was a solid set of fixings. Jesse got soft lights in his eyes. This was no Miss Molly, but this was Miss somebody. There were a lot of crap-crates running out there, but this Linc wasn't one of them.

"You prob'ly can't even get parts for the damn thing." Jesse murmured, and you could tell he was already scrapping with a salesman. He turned his back on the Lincoln. "We'll catch a bite to eat," he said. "This may take a couple days."

I felt sort of bubbly. "The Dog ain't gonna like this," I told Jesse.

"The Dog is gonna love it," he said. "Me and The Dog *knows* that road."

By the time the car lots opened at 9:00 A.M., Jesse had a trader's light in his eyes. About all that needs saying is that never before, or since, did I ever see a used-car salesman cry.

The poor fellow never had a chance. He stood in his car lot most of the day while me and Jesse went through every car lot on the strip. We waved to him from a sweet little '57 Cad, and we cruised past real smooth in a mama-san '56 Imperial. We kicked tires on anything sturdy while he was watching, and we never even got to his lot until fifteen minutes before closing. Jesse and I climbed from my Desoto. Potato and Chip tailed after us.

"I always know when I get to Minneapolis," Jesse said to me, but loud enough the salesman could just about hear. "My woman wants to lay a farmer, and my dogs start pukin'." When we got within easy hearing range, Jesse's voice got humble. "I expect this fella can help a cowboy in a fix."

I followed, experiencing considerable admiration. In two sentences, Jesse had his man confused.

Potato was dumb enough that he trotted right up to the Lincoln. Chip sat and panted, pretending indifference. Then he ambled over to a ragged-out Pontiac and peed on the tire. "I must be missing something," Jesse said to the salesman, "because that dog has himself a dandy nose." He looked at the Pontiac. "This thing got an engine?"

We all conversed for the best part of an hour. Jesse refused to even look at the Lincoln. He sounded real serious about the LaSalle, to the point of running it around a couple of blocks. It was a darling. It had ceramic covered manifolds to protect against heat and rust. It packed a long-stroke V-8 with enough torque to bite rubber in second gear. My Desoto was a pretty thing, but until that LaSalle, I never realized that my car was a total pussycat. When we left the lot, the salesman looked sad. He was late for supper.

"Stay with what you've got," Jesse told me as he climbed in my Desoto. "The clock has run out on that LaSalle. Let a collector have it. I hate it when something good dies for lack of parts."

I wondered if he was thinking of Miss Molly.

"Because," Jesse said, and kicked the tire on a silly little Volkswagen, "the great, good cars are dying. I blame it on the Germans."

Next day, we bought the Lincoln and made the salesman feel like one proud pup. He figured he foisted something off on Jesse that Jesse didn't want. He was so stuck on himself that he forgot that he had asked a thousand dollars, and come away with $550. He even forgot that his eyes were swollen, and that maybe he crapped his pants.

We went for a test drive, but only after Jesse and I crawled around under the Linc. A little body lead lumped in the left rear fender, but the front end stood sound. Nobody had pumped any sawdust into the differential. We found no water in the oil, or oil in the water. The salesman stood around, admiring his shoeshine. He was one of those easterners who can't help talking down to people, especially when he's trying to be nice. I swear he wore a white tie with little red ducks on it. That Minnesota sunlight made his red hair blond, and his face pop with freckles.

Jesse drove real quiet until he found an interesting stretch of road. The salesman sat beside him. Me and Potato and Chip hunkered in the backseat. Chip looked sort of nauseated, but Potato was pretty happy.

"I'm afraid," Jesse said regretful, "that this thing is gonna turn out to be a howler. A fella gets a few years on him, and he don't want a screamy car." Brother Jesse couldn't have been much more than thirty, but he tugged on his nose and ears like he was ancient. "I sure hope," he said real mournful, "that nobody stuck a boot in any of these here tires." Then he poured on some coal.

There was a most satisfying screech. That Linc took out like a roadrunner in heat. The salesman's head snapped backward, and his shoulders dug into the seat. Potato gave a happy, happy woof and stuck his nose out the open window. I felt like yelling, "Hosanna," but knew enough to keep my big mouth shut. The Linc shrugged off a couple of cars that were conservatively motoring. It wheeled past a hay truck as the tires started humming. The salesman's freckles began to stand up like warts while the airstream howled. Old Potato kept his nose sticking through the open window, and the wind kept drying it. Potato was so damn dumb he tried to lick it wet while his nose stayed in the airstream. His tongue blew sideways.

"It ain't nothing but speed," Jesse complained. "Look at this here steering." He joggled the wheel considerable, which at ninety got even more considerable. The salesman's tie blew straight backward. The little red ducks matched his freckles. "Jee-sus-Chee-sus," he said. "Eight hundred, and slow down." He braced himself against the dash.

When it hit the century mark, the Linc developed a little float in the front end. I expect all of us were thinking about the tires.

You could tell Jesse was jubilant. The Linc still had some pedal left.

"I'm gettin' old," Jesse hollered above the wind. "This ain't no car for an old man."

"Seven hundred," the salesman said. "And Mother of God, slow it down."

"Five-fifty," Jesse told him, and dug the pedal down one more notch.

"You got it," the salesman hollered. His face twisted up real teary. Then Potato got all grateful and started licking the guy on the back of the neck.

So Jesse cut the speed and bought the Linc. He did it diplomatic, pretending he was sorry he'd made the offer. That was kind of him. After all, the guy was nothing but a used-car salesman.

We did a second night in that motel. The Linc and Desoto sat in an all-night filling station. Lube, oil change, and wash, because we were riding high. Jesse had a heap of money left over. In the morning, we got new jeans and shirts, so as to ride along like gentlemen.

"We'll go back through South Dakota," Jesse told me. "There's a place I've heard about."

"What are we looking for?"

"We're checking on The Dog," Jesse told me, and would say no more.

We eased west to Bowman, just under the North Dakota line. Jesse sort of leaned into it, just taking joy from the whole occasion. I flowed along as best the Desoto could. Potato rode with Jesse, and Chip sat on the front seat beside me. Chip seemed rather easier in his mind.

A roadside café hunkered among tall trees. It didn't even have a neon sign. Real old-fashioned.

"I heard of this place all my life," Jesse said as he climbed from the Linc. "This here is the only outhouse in the world with a guest registry." He headed toward the rear of the café.

I tailed along, and Jesse, he was right. It was a palatial privy built like a little cottage. The men's side was a three-holer. There was enough room for a stand-up desk. On the desk was one of those old-fashioned business ledgers like you used to see in banks.

"They're supposed to have a slew of these inside," Jesse said about the register as he flipped pages. "All the way back to the early days."

Some spirit of politeness seemed to take over when you picked up that register. There was hardly any bad talk. I read a few entries:

On this site, May 16th, 1961, James John Johnson (John-John) cussed hell out of his truck.

I came, I saw, I kinda liked it.—Bill Samuels, Tulsa

This place does know squat.—Pauley Smith, Ogden

This South Dakota ain't so bad,
but I sure got the blues,
I'm working in Tacoma,
'cause my kids all need new shoes.—Sad George

Brother Jesse flipped through the pages. "I'm even told," he said, "that Teddy Roosevelt crapped here. This is a fine old place." He sort of hummed as he flipped. "Uh, huh," he said, "The Dog done made his pee spot." He pointed to a page:

Road Dog
Run and run as fast as you can
you can't catch me—I'm the Gingerbread Man.

Jesse just grinned. "He's sorta upping the ante, ain't he? You reckon this is getting serious?" Jesse acted like he knew what he was talking about, but I sure didn't.

II

We didn't know, as we headed home, that Jesse's graveyard business was about to take off. That wouldn't change him, though. He'd almost always had a hundred dollars in his jeans anyway, and was usually a happy man. What changed him was Road Dog and Miss Molly.

The trouble started awhile after we crossed the Montana line. Jesse ran ahead in the Lincoln, and I tagged behind in my Desoto. We drove Highway 2 into a western sunset. It was one of those magic summers where rain sweeps in from British Columbia just regular enough to keep things growing. Rabbits get fat and foolish, and foxes put on weight. Rattlesnakes come out of ditches to cross the sun-hot road. It's not sporting to run over their middles. You have to take them in the head. Redwings perch on fence posts, and magpies flash black and white from the berm, where they scavenge road kills.

We saw a hell of a wreck just after Wolf Point. A guy in an old Kaiser came over the back of a rise and ran under a tanker truck that burned. Smoke rose black as a plume of crows, and we saw it five miles away. By the time we got there, the truck driver stood in the middle of the road, all white and shaking. The guy in the Kaiser sat behind the wheel. It was fearful to see how fast fire can work, and just terrifying to see bones hanging over a steering wheel. I remember thinking the guy no doubt died before any fire started, and we were feeling more than he was.

That didn't help. I said a prayer under my breath. The truck driver wasn't to blame, but he took it hard as a Presbyterian. Jesse tried to comfort him, without much luck. The road melted and stank and began to burn. Nobody was drinking, but it was certain-sure we were all more sober than we'd ever been in our lives. Two deputies showed up. Cars drifted in easy, because of the smoke. In a couple of hours, there were probably twenty cars lined up on either side of the wreck.

"He must of been asleep or drunk," Jesse said about the driver of the Kaiser. "How in hell can a man run under a tanker truck?"

When the cops reopened the road, night hovered over the plains. Nobody cared to run much over sixty, even beneath a bright moon. It seemed like a night to be superstitious, a night when there was a deer or pronghorn out there just ready to jump into your headlights. It wasn't a good night to drink, or shoot pool, or mess around in strange bars. It was a time for being home with your woman, if you had one.

On most nights, ghosts do not show up beside the metal crosses, and they sure don't show up in owl light. Ghosts stand out on the darkest, moonless nights, and only then when bars are closed and the only thing open is the road.

I never gave it a thought. I chased Jesse's taillights, which on that Lincoln were broad, up-and-down slashes in the dark. Chip sat beside me, sad and solemn. I rubbed his ears to perk him, but he just laid down and snuffled. Chip was sensitive. He knew I felt bad over that wreck.

The first ghost showed up on the left berm and fizzled before the headlights. It was a lady ghost, and a pretty old one, judging from her long white hair and long white dress. She flicked on and off in just a flash, so maybe it was a road dream. Chip was so depressed he didn't even notice, and Jesse didn't either. His steering and his brakes didn't wave to me.

Everything stayed straight for another ten miles, then a whole peck of ghosts stood on the right berm. A bundle of crosses shone all silvery white in the headlights. The ghosts melted into each other. You couldn't tell how many, but you could tell they were expectant. They looked like people lined up for a picture show. Jesse never gave a sign he saw them. I told myself to get straight. We hadn't had much sleep in the past two nights, and did some drinking the night before. We'd rolled near two thousand miles.

Admonishing seemed to work. Another twenty minutes passed, maybe thirty, and nothing happened. Wind chased through the open windows of the Desoto, and the radio gave mostly static. I kicked off my boots because that helps you stay awake, the bottoms of the feet being sensitive. Then a single ghost showed up on the right-hand berm, and boy-howdy.

Why anybody would laugh while being dead has got to be a puzzle. This ghost was tall, with Indian hair like Jesse's, and I could swear he looked like Jesse, the spitting image. This ghost was jolly. He clapped his hands and danced. Then he gave me the old road sign for "roll 'em," his hand circling in the air as he danced. The headlights penetrated him, showed tall grass solid at the roadside, and instead of legs, he stood on a column of mist. Still, he was dancing.

It wasn't road dreams. It was hallucination. The nighttime road just fills with things seen or partly seen. When too much scary stuff happens, it's time to pull her over.

I couldn't do it, though. Suppose I pulled over, and suppose it wasn't hallucination? I recall thinking that a man don't ordinarily care for preachers until he needs one. It seemed like me and Jesse were riding through the Book of Revelations. I dropped my speed, then flicked my lights a couple times. Jesse paid it no attention, and then Chip got peculiar.

He didn't bark; he chirped. He stood up on the front seat, looking out the back window, and his paws trembled. He shivered, chirped, shivered, and went chirp, chirp, chirp. Headlights in back of us were closing fast.

I've been closed on plenty of times by guys looking for a ditch. Headlights have jumped out of night and fog and mist when nobody should be pushing forty. I've been overtaken by drunks and suiciders. No set of headlights ever came as fast as the ones that began to wink in the mirrors. This Highway 2 is a quick,

quick road, but it's not the salt flats of Utah. The crazy man behind me was trying to set a new land speed record.

Never confuse an idiot. I stayed off the brakes and coasted, taking off speed and signaling my way onto the berm. The racer could have my share of the road. I didn't want any part of that boy's troubles. Jesse kept pulling away as I slowed. It seemed like he didn't even see the lights. Chip chirped, then sort of rolled down on the floorboards and cried.

For ninety seconds, I feared being dead. For one second, I figured it already happened. Wind banged the Desoto sideways. Wind whooped, the way it does in winter. The headlights blew past. What showed was the curve of a Hudson fender—the kind of curve you'd recognize if you'd been dead a million years— and what showed was the little, squinchy shapes of a Hudson's taillights; and what showed was the slanty doorpost like a nail running kitty-corner; and what showed was slivers of reflection from cracked glass on the rider's side; and what sounded was the drumbeat of a straight-eight engine whanging like a locomotive gone wild; the thrump, bumpa, thrum of a crankshaft whipping in its bed. The slaunch-forward form of Miss Molly wailed, and showers of sparks blew from the tailpipe as Miss Molly rocketed.

Chip was not the only one howling. My voice rose high as the howl of Miss Molly. We all sang it out together, while Jesse cruised three, maybe four miles ahead. It wasn't two minutes before Miss Molly swept past that Linc like it was foundationed in cement. Sparks showered like the 4th of July, and Jesse's brake lights looked pale beside the fireworks. The Linc staggered against wind as Jesse headed for the berm. Wind smashed against my Desoto.

Miss Molly's taillights danced as she did a jig up the road, and then they winked into darkness as Miss Molly topped a rise, or disappeared. The night went darker than dark. A cloud scudded out of nowhere and blocked the moon.

Alongside the road the dancing ghost showed up in my headlights, and I could swear it was Jesse. He laughed like at a good joke, but he gave the old road sign for "slow it down," his hand palm-down like he was patting an invisible pup. It seemed sound advice, and I blamed near liked him. After Miss Molly, a happy ghost seemed downright companionable.

"Shitfire," said Jesse, and that's all he said for the first five minutes after I pulled in behind him. I climbed from the Desoto and walked to the Linc. Old Potato dog sprawled on the seat in a dead faint, and Jesse rubbed his ears trying to warm him back to consciousness. Jesse sat over the wheel like a man who had just met Jesus. His hand touched gentle on Potato's ears, and his voice sounded reverent. Brother Jesse's conversion wasn't going to last, but at the time, it was just beautiful. He had the lights of salvation in his eyes, and his skinny shoulders weren't shaking too much. "I miss my c'har," he muttered finally, and blinked. He wasn't going to cry if he could help. "She's trying to tell me something," he whispered. "Let's find a bar. Miss Molly's in car heaven, certain-sure."

We pulled away, found a bar, and parked. We drank some beer and slept across the car seats. Nobody wanted to go back on that road.

*   *   *

When we woke to a morning hot and clear, Potato's fur had turned white. It didn't seem to bother him much, but, for the rest of his life, he was a lot more thoughtful.

"Looks like mashed Potato," Jesse said, but he wasn't talking a whole lot. We drove home like a couple of old ladies. Guys came scorching past, cussing at our granny speed. We figured they could get mad and stay mad, or get mad and get over it. We made it back to Jesse's place about two in the afternoon.

A couple of things happened quick. Jesse parked beside his house trailer, and the front end fell out of the Lincoln. The right side went down, thump, and the right front tire sagged. Jesse turned even whiter than me, and I was bloodless. We had posted over a hundred miles an hour in that thing. Somehow, when we crawled around underneath inspecting it, we missed something. My shoulders and legs shook so hard I could barely get out of the Desoto. Chip was polite. He just yelped with happiness about being home, but he didn't trot across my lap as we climbed from the car.

Nobody could trust their legs. Jesse climbed out of the Linc and leaned against it. You could see him chewing over all the possibilities, then arriving at the only one that made sense. Some hammer mechanic bolted that front end together with no locknut, no cotter pin, no lock washer, no lock-nothin'. He just wrenched down a plain old nut, and the nut worked loose.

"Miss Molly knew," Jesse whispered. "That's what she was trying to tell." He felt a lot better the minute he said it. Color came back to his face. He peered around the corner of the house trailer, looking toward Miss Molly's grave.

Mike Tarbush was over there with his '48 Roadmaster. Matt Simons stood beside him, and Matt's '56 Dodge sat beside the Roadmaster, looking smug; which that model Dodge always did.

"I figger," Brother Jesse whispered, "that we should keep shut about last night. Word would just get around that we were alkies." He pulled himself together, arranged his face like a horse trying to grin, and walked toward the Roadmaster.

Mike Tarbush was a man in mourning. He sat on the fat trunk of that Buick and gazed off toward the mountains. Mike wore extra-large of everything, and still looked stout. He sported a thick red mustache to make up for his bald head. From time to time, he bragged about his criminal record, which amounted to three days in jail for assaulting a pool table. He threw it through a bar window.

Now his mustache drooped, and Mike seemed small inside his clothes. The hood of the Roadmaster gaped open. Under that hood, things couldn't be worse. The poor thing had thrown a rod into the next county.

Jesse looked under the hood and tsked. "I know what you're going through," he said to Mike. He kind of petted the Roadmaster. "I always figured Betty Lou would last a century. What happened?"

There's no call to tell about a grown man blubbering, and especially not one who can heave pool tables. Mike finally got straight enough to tell the story.

"We was chasing the Dog," he said. "At least I think so. Three nights ago over to Kalispell. This Golden Hawk blew past me sittin'." Mike watched the distant mountains like he'd seen a miracle, or else like he was expecting one to happen. "That sonovabitch shore can drive," he whispered in disbelief. "Blown out by a damn Studebaker."

"But a very swift Studebaker," Matt Simons said. Matt is as small as Mike is large, and Matt is educated. Even so, he's set his share of fence posts. He looks like an algebra teacher, but not as delicate.

"Betty Lou went on up past her flat spot," Mike whispered. "She was tryin'. We had ninety on the clock, and The Dog left us sitting." He patted the Roadmaster. "I reckon she died of a broken heart."

"We got three kinds of funerals," Jesse said, and he was sympathetic. "We got the no-frills type, the regular type, and the extra-special. The extra-special comes with flowers." He said it with a straight face, and Mike took it that way. He bought the extra-special, and that was sixty-five dollars.

Mike put up a nice marker:

1948–1961
Roadmaster two-door—Betty Lou
Gone to Glory while chasing The Dog
She was the best friend of Mike Tarbush

Brother Jesse worked on the Lincoln until the front end tracked rock solid. He named it Sue Ellen, but not *Miss* Sue Ellen, there being no way to know if Miss Molly was jealous. When we examined Miss Molly's grave, the soil seemed rumpled. Wildflowers, which Jesse sowed on the grave, bloomed in midsummer. I couldn't get it out of my head that Miss Molly was still alive, and maybe Jesse couldn't, either.

Jesse explained about the Lincoln's name. "Sue Ellen is a lady I knew in Pocatello. I expect she misses me." He said it hopeful, like he didn't really believe it.

It looked to me like Jesse was brooding. Night usually found him in town, but sometimes he disappeared. When he was around, he drove real calm and always got home before midnight. The wildness hadn't come out of Jesse, but he had it on a tight rein. He claimed he dreamed of Miss Molly. Jesse was working something out.

And so was I, awake or dreaming. Thoughts of the Road Dog filled my nights, and so did thoughts of the dancing ghost. As summer deepened, restlessness took me wailing under moonlight. The road unreeled before my headlights like a magic line that pointed to places under a warm sun where ladies laughed and fell in love. Something went wrong, though. During that summer the ladies stopped being dreams and became only imagination. When I told Jesse, he claimed I was just growing up. I wished for once Jesse was wrong. I wished for a lot of things, and one of the wishes came true. It was Mike Tarbush, not me, who got in the next tangle with Miss Molly.

Mike rode in from Billings, where he'd been car shopping. He showed up at Jesse's place on Sunday afternoon. Montana lay restful. Birds hunkered on wires, or called from high grass. Highway 2 ran watery with sunlight, deserted as a road ever could be. When Mike rolled a '56 Merc up beside the Linc, it looked like Old Home Week at a Ford dealership.

"I got to look at something," Mike said when he climbed from the Mercury. He sort of plodded over to Miss Molly's grave and hovered. Light breezes blew the wildflowers sideways. Mike looked like a bear trying to shake confusion from its head. He walked to the Roadmaster's grave. New grass sprouted reddish green. "I was sober," Mike said. "Most Saturday nights, maybe I ain't, but I was sober as a deputy."

For a while, nobody said anything. Potato sat glowing and white and thoughtful. Chip slept in the sun beside one of the tabbies. Then Chip woke up. He turned around three times and dashed to hide under the bulldozer.

"Now, tell me I ain't crazy," Mike said. He perched on the front fender of the Merc, which was blue and white and adventuresome. "Name of Judith," he said about the Merc. "A real lady." He swabbed sweat from his bald head. "I got blown out by Betty Lou and Miss Molly. That sound reasonable?" He swabbed some more sweat and looked at the graves, which looked like little speed bumps on the prairie. "Nope," he answered himself, "that don't sound reasonable a-tall."

"Something's wrong with your Mercury," Jesse said, real quiet. "You got a bad tire, or a hydraulic line about to blow, or something screwy in the steering."

He made Mike swear not to breathe a word. Then he told about Miss Molly and about the front end of the Lincoln. When the story got over, Mike looked like a halfback hit by a twelve-man line.

"Don't drive another inch," Jesse said. "Not until we find what's wrong."

"That car already cracked a hundred," Mike whispered. "I bought it special to chase one sumbitch in a Studebaker." He looked toward Betty Lou's grave. "The Dog did that."

The three of us went through that Merc like men panning gold. The trouble was so obvious we missed it for two hours while the engine cooled. Then Jesse caught it. The fuel filter rubbed its underside against the valve cover. When Jesse touched it, the filter collapsed. Gasoline spilled on the engine and the spark plugs. That Merc was getting set to catch on fire.

"I got to wonder if The Dog did it," Jesse said about Betty Lou after Mike drove away. "I wonder if the Road Dog is the Studebaker type."

Nights started to get serious, but any lonesomeness on that road was only in a man's head. As summer stretched past its longest days, and sunsets started earlier, ghosts rose beside crosses before daylight hardly left the land. We drove to work and back, drove to town and back. My job was steady at a filling station, but it asked day after day of the same old thing. We never did any serious wrenching; no engine rebuilds or transmissions, just tuneups and flat tires. I dearly wanted to meet a nice lady, but no woman in her right mind would mess with a pump jockey.

Nights were different, though. I figured I was going crazy, and Jesse and Mike were worse. Jesse finally got his situation worked out. He claimed Miss Molly was protecting him. Jesse and Mike took the Linc and the Merc on long runs, just wringing the howl out of those cars. Some nights, they'd flash past me at speed no sane man would try in darkness. Jesse was never a real big drinker, and Mike stopped altogether. They were too busy playing road games. It got so the state cop never tried to chase them. He just dropped past Jesse's place next day and passed out tickets.

The dancing ghost danced in my dreams, both asleep and driving. When daylight left the land, I passed metal crosses and remembered some of the wrecks.

Three crosses stood on one side of the railroad track, and four crosses on the other side. The three happened when some Canadian cowboys lost a race with a train. It was too awful to remember, but on most nights, those guys stood looking down the tracks with startled eyes.

The four crosses happened when one-third of the senior class of '59 hit that grade too fast on prom night. They rolled a damned old Chevrolet. More bodies by Fisher. Now the two girls stood in their long dresses, looking wistful. The two boys pretended that none of it meant nothin'.

Farther out the road, things had happened before my time. An Indian ghost most often stood beside the ghost of a deer. In another place a chubby old rancher looked real picky and angry.

The dancing ghost continued unpredictable. All the other ghosts stood beside their crosses, but the dancing ghost showed up anywhere he wanted, anytime he wanted. I'd slow the Desoto as he came into my lights, and he was the spitting image of Jesse.

"I don't want to hear about it." Jesse said when I tried to tell him. "I'm on a roll. I'm even gettin' famous."

He was right about that. People up and down the line joked about Jesse and his graveyard business.

"It's the very best kind of advertising," he told me. "We'll see more action before snow flies."

"You won't see snow fly," I told him, standing up to him a second time. "Unless you slow down and pay attention."

"I've looked at heaps more road than you," he told me, "and seeing things is just part of the night. That nighttime road is different."

"This is starting to happen at last light."

"I don't see no ghosts," he told me, and he was lying. "Except Miss Molly once or twice." He wouldn't say anything more.

And Jesse was right. As summer ran on, more graves showed up near Miss Molly. A man named Mcguire turned up with a '41 Cad.

1941–1961
Fleetwood Coupe—Annie
304,018 miles on flathead V-8
She was the luck of the Irishman
Pat Mcguire

And Sam Winder buried his '47 Packard.

1947–1961
Packard 2-door—Lois Lane
Super Buddy of Sam Winder
Up Up and Away

And Pete Johansen buried his pickup.

1946–1961
Ford pickup—Gertrude
211,000 miles give or take
Never a screamer
but a good pulling truck.
Pete Johansen put up many a day's work with her.

Montana roads are long and lonesome, and along the highline is lonesomest of all. From Saskatchewan to Texas, nothing stands tall enough to break the wind that begins to blow cold and clear toward late October. Rains sob away toward the Middle West, and grass turns goldish amber. Rattlesnakes move to high ground, where they will winter. Every creature on God's plains begins to fat-up against the winter. Soon it's going to be thirty below and the wind blowing.

Four-wheel-drive weather. Internationals and Fords, with Dodge crummy-wagons in the hills; cars and trucks will line up beside houses, garages, sheds, with electric wires leading from plugs to radiators and blocks. They look like packs of nursing pups. Work will slow, then stop. New work turns to accounting for the weather. Fuel, emergency generators, hay-bale insulation. Horses and cattle and deer look fuzzy beneath thick coats. Check your battery. If your rig won't start, and you're two miles from home, she won't die—but you might.

School buses creep from stop to stop, and bundled kids look like colorful little bears trotting through late-afternoon light. Snowy owls come floating in from northward, while folks go to church on Sunday against the time when there's some better amusement. Men hang around town, because home is either empty or crowded, depending on if you're married. Folks sit before television, watching the funny, goofy, unreal world where everybody plays at being sexy and naked, even when they're not.

And nineteen years old is lonesome, too. And work is lonesome when nobody much cares for you.

Before winter set in, I got it in my head to run the Road Dog's route. It was September. Winter would close us down pretty quick. The trip would be a luxury. What with room rent, and gas, and eating out, it was payday to payday with me. Still, one payday would account for gas and sandwiches. I could sleep across the seat. I hocked a Marlin .30-30 to Jesse for twenty bucks. He seemed happy with my notion. He even went into the greenhouse and came out with an arctic sleeping bag.

"In case things get vigorous," he said, and grinned. "Now get on out there and bite The Dog."

It was a happy time. Dreams of ladies sort of set themselves to one side as I cruised across the eternal land. I came to love the land that autumn, in a way that maybe ranchers do. The land stopped being something that a road ran across. Canadian honkers came winging in vees from the north. The great Montana sky stood easy as eagles. When I'd pull over and cut the engine, sounds of grasshoppers mixed with birdcalls. Once, a wild turkey, as smart as any domestic turkey is dumb, talked to himself and paid me not the least mind.

The Dog showed up right away. In a café in Malta:

> *Road Dog*
> *"It was all a hideous mistake."*
> *Christopher Columbus*

In a bar in Tampico:

> *Road Dog*
> *Who's afraid of the big bad Woof?*

In another bar in Culbertson:

> *Road Dog*
> *Go East, young man, go East*

I rolled Williston and dropped south through North Dakota. The Dog's trail disappeared until Watford City, where it showed up in the can of a filling station:

> *Road Dog*
> *Atlantis and Sargasso*
> *Full fathom five thy brother lies*

And in a joint in Grassy Butte:

> *Road Dog*
> *Ain't Misbehavin'*

That morning in Grassy Butte, I woke to a sunrise where the land lay bathed in rose and blue. Silhouettes of grazing deer mixed with silhouettes of cattle. They herded together peaceful as a dream of having your own place, your own woman, and you working hard; and her glad to see you coming home.

In Bowman, The Dog showed up in a nice restaurant:

Road Dog
The Katzenjammer Kids minus one

Ghosts did not show up along the road, but the road stayed the same. I tangled with a bathtub Hudson, a '53, outside of Spearfish in South Dakota. I chased him into Wyoming like being dragged on a string. The guy played with me for twenty miles, then got bored. He shoved more coal in the stoker and purely flew out of sight.

Sheridan was a nice town back in those days, just nice and friendly; plus, I started to get sick of the way I smelled. In early afternoon, I found a five-dollar motel with a shower. That gave me the afternoon, the evening, and next morning if it seemed right. I spiffed up, put on a good shirt, slicked down my hair, and felt just fine.

The streets lay dusty and lazy. Ranchers' pickups stood all dented and work-worn before bars, and an old Indian sat on hay bales in the back of one of them. He wore a flop hat, and he seemed like the eyes and heart of the prairie. He looked at me like I was a splendid puppy that might someday amount to something. It seemed O.K. when he did it.

I hung around a soda fountain at the five-and-dime because a girl smiled. She was just beautiful. A little horsey-faced, but with sun-blonde hair, and with hands long-fingered and gentle. There wasn't a chance of talking, because she stood behind the counter for ladies' underwear. I pretended to myself that she looked sad when I left.

It got on to late afternoon. Sunlight drifted in between buildings, and shadows overreached the streets. Everything was normal, and then everything got scary.

I was just poking along, looking in store windows, checking the show at the movie house, when, ahead of me, Jesse walked toward a Golden Hawk. He was maybe a block and a half away, but it was Jesse, sure as God made sunshine. It was a Golden Hawk. There was no way of mistaking that car. Hawks were high-priced sets of wheels, and Studebaker never sold that many.

I yelled and ran. Jesse waited beside the car, looking sort of puzzled. When I pulled up beside him, he grinned.

"It's happening again," he said, and his voice sounded amused, but not mean. Sunlight made his face reddish, but shadow put his legs and feet in darkness. "You believe me to be a gentleman named Jesse Still." Behind him, shadows of buildings told that night was on its way. Sunset happens quick on the prairies.

And I said, "Jesse, what in the hell are you doing in Sheridan?"

And he said, "Young man, you are not looking at Jesse Still." He said it quiet and polite, and he thought he had a point. His voice was smooth and cultured, so he sure didn't sound like Jesse. His hair hung combed-out, and he wore clothes that never came from a dry-goods. His jeans were soft-looking and expensive. His boots were tooled. They kind of glowed in the dusk. The Golden Hawk didn't have a dust speck on it, and the interior had never carried a tool, or a car part, or a sack of feed. It just sparkled. I almost believed him, and then I didn't.

"You're fooling with me."

"On the contrary," he said real soft. "Jesse Still is fooling with *me*, although he doesn't mean to. We've never met." He didn't exactly look nervous, but he looked impatient. He climbed in the Stude and started the engine. It purred like racing tune. "This is a large and awfully complex world," he said, "and Mr. Still will probably tell you the same. I've been told we look like brothers."

I wanted to say more, but he waved real friendly and pulled away. The flat and racey back end of the Hawk reflected one slash of sunlight, then rolled into shadow. If I'd had a hot car, I'd have gone out hunting him. It wouldn't have done a lick of good, but doing something would be better than doing nothing.

I stood sort of shaking and amazed. Life had just changed somehow, and it wasn't going to change back. There wasn't a thing in the world to do, so I went to get some supper.

The Dog had signed in at the café:

Road Dog
The Bobbsey Twins Attend The Motor Races

And—I sat chewing roast beef and mashed potatoes.

And—I saw how the guy in the Hawk might be lying, and that Jesse was a twin.

And—I finally saw what a chancy, dicey world this was, because without meaning to, exactly, and without even knowing it was happening, I had just run up against The Road Dog.

It was a night of dreams. Dreams wouldn't let me go. The dancing ghost tried to tell me Jesse was triplets. The ghosts among the crosses begged rides into nowhere, rides down the long tunnel of night that ran past lands of dreams, but never turned off to those lands. It all came back: the crazy summer, the running, running, running behind the howl of engines. The Road Dog drawled with Jesse's voice, and then The Dog spoke cultured. The girl at the five-and-dime held out a gentle hand, then pulled it back. I dreamed of a hundred roadside joints, bars, cafés, old-fashioned filling stations with grease pits. I dreamed of winter wind, and the dark, dark days of winter; and of nights when you hunch in your room because it's a chore too big to bundle up and go outside.

I woke to an early dawn and slurped coffee at the bakery, which kept open because they had to make morning doughnuts. The land lay all around me, but it had nothing to say. I counted my money and figured miles.

I climbed in the Desoto, thinking I had never got around to giving it a name. The road unreeled toward the west. It ended in Seattle, where I sold my car. Everybody said there was going to be a war, and I wasn't doing anything anyway. I joined the Navy.

III

What with him burying cars and raising hell, Jesse never wrote to me in summer. He was surely faithful in winter, though. He wrote long letters printed in a clumsy hand. He tried to cheer me up, and so did Matt Simons.

The Navy sent me to boot camp and diesel school, then to a motor pool in San Diego. I worked there three and a half years, sometimes even working on ships if the ships weren't going anywhere. A sunny land and smiling ladies lay all about, but the ladies mostly fell in love by ten at night and got over it by dawn. Women in the bars were younger and prettier than back home. There was enough clap to go around.

"The business is growing like Jimsonweed," Jesse wrote toward Christmas of '62. "I buried fourteen cars this summer, and one of them was a Kraut." He wrote a whole page about his morals. It didn't seem right to stick a crap-crate in the ground beside real cars. At the same time, it was bad business not to. He opened a special corner of the cemetery, and pretended it was exclusive for foreign iron.

"And Mike Tarbush got to drinking," he wrote. "I'm sad to say we planted Judith."

Mike never had a minute's trouble with that Merc. Judith behaved like a perfect lady until Mike turned upside down. He backed across a parking lot at night, rather hasty, and drove backward up the guy wire of a power pole. It was the only rollover wreck in history that happened at twenty miles an hour.

"Mike can't stop discussing it," Jesse wrote. "He's never caught The Dog, neither, but he ain't stopped trying. He wheeled in here in a beefed-up '57 Olds called Sally. It goes like stink and looks like a Hereford."

Home seemed far away, though it couldn't have been more than thirty-six hours by road for a man willing to hang over the wheel. I wanted to take a leave and drive home, but knew it better not happen. Once I got there, I'd likely stay.

"George Pierson at the feedstore says he's going to file a paternity suit against Potato," Jesse wrote. "The pups are cute, and there's a family resemblance."

It came to me then why I was homesick. I surely missed the land, but even more, I missed the people. Back home, folks were important enough that you knew their names. When somebody got messed up or killed, you felt sorry. In California, nobody knew nobody. They just swept up broken glass and moved right along. I should have meshed right in. I had made my rating and was pushing a rich man's car, a '57 hemi Chrysler, but never felt it fit.

"Don't pay it any mind," Jesse wrote when I told about meeting Road Dog. "I've heard about a guy who looks the same as me. Sometimes stuff like that happens."

And that was all he ever did say.

Nineteen sixty-three ended happy and hopeful. Matt Simons wrote a letter. Sam Winder bought a big Christmas card, and everybody signed it with little messages. Even my old boss at the filling station signed, "Merry Xmas, Jed— Keep It Between The Fence Posts." My boss didn't hold it against me that I left. In Montana a guy is supposed to be free to find out what he's all about.

Christmas of '63 saw Jesse pleased as a bee in clover. A lady named Sarah moved in with him. She waitressed at the café, and Jesse's letter ran pretty short. He'd put twenty-three cars under that year, and bought more acreage. He ordered a genuine marble gravestone for Miss Molly. "Sue Ellen is a real darling," Jesse wrote about the Linc. "That marker like to weighed a ton. We just about bent a back axle bringing it from the railroad."

From Christmas of '63 to January of '64 was just a few days, but they marked an awful downturn for Jesse. His letter was more real to me than all the diesels in San Diego.

He drew black borders all around the pages. The letter started out O.K., but went downhill. "Sarah moved out and into a rented room," he wrote. "I reckon I was just too much to handle." He didn't explain, but I did my own reckoning. I could imagine that it was Jesse, plus two cats and two dogs trying to get into a ten-wide-fifty trailer, that got to Sarah. "I think she misses me," he wrote, "but I expect she'll have to bear it."

Then the letter got just awful.

"A pack of wolves came through from Canada," Jesse wrote. "They picked off old Potato like a berry from a bush. Me and Mike found tracks, and a little blood in the snow."

I sat in the summery dayroom surrounded by sailors shooting pool and playing Ping-Pong. I imagined the snow and ice of home. I imagined old Potato nosing around in his dumb and happy way, looking for rabbits or lifting his leg. Maybe he even wagged his tail when that first wolf came into view. I sat blinking tears, ready to bawl over a dog, and then I did, and to hell with it.

The world was changing, and it wouldn't change back. I put in for sea duty one more time, and the chief warrant who ramrodded that motor pool turned it down again. He claimed we kept the world safe by wrenching engines.

"The '62 Dodge is emerging as the car of choice for people in a hurry." Matt Simons wrote that in February '64, knowing I'd understand that nobody could tell which cars would be treasured until they had a year or two on them. "It's an extreme winter," he wrote, "and it's taking its toll on many of us. Mike has now learned not to punch a policeman. He's doing ten days. Sam Winder managed to roll a Jeep, and neither he, nor I, can figure out how a man can roll a Jeep. Sam has a broken arm, and lost two toes to frost. He was trapped under the wreck. It took awhile to pull him out. Brother Jesse is in the darkest sort of mood. He comes and goes in an irregular manner, but the Linc sits outside the pool hall on most days.

"And for myself," Matt wrote, "I think, come summer, I'll drop some revs. My flaming youth seems to be giving way to other interests. A young woman named Nancy started teaching at the school. Until now, I thought I was a confirmed bachelor."

A postcard came the end of February. The postmark said "Cheyenne, Wyoming," way down in the southeast corner of the state. It was written fancy. Nobody could mistake that fine, spidery hand. It read:

Road Dog
Run and run as fast as he can,
He can't find who is the Gingerbread Man

The picture on the card had been taken from an airplane. It showed an oval racetrack where cars chased each other round and round. I couldn't figure why Jesse sent it, but it had to be Jesse. Then it came to me that Jesse was The Road Dog. Then it came to me that he wasn't. The Road Dog was too slick. He wrote real delicate, and Jesse only printed real clumsy. On the other hand, The Road Dog didn't know me from Adam's off ox. Somehow it *had* to be Jesse.

"We got snow nut-deep to a tall palm tree," Jesse wrote at about the same time, "and Chip is failing. He's off his feed. He don't even tease the kitties. Chip just can't seem to stop mourning."

I had bad premonitions. Chip was sensitive. I feared he wouldn't be around by the time I got back home, and my fear proved right. Chip held off until the first warm sun of spring, and then he died while napping in the shade of the bulldozer. When Jesse sent a quick note telling me, I felt pretty bad, but had been expecting it. Chip had a good heart. I figured now he was with Potato, romping in the hills somewhere. I knew that was a bunch of crap, but that's just the way I chose to figure it.

They say a man can get used to anything, but maybe some can't. Day after day, and week after week, California weather nagged. Sometimes a puny little dab of weather dribbled in from the Pacific, and people hollered it was storming. Sometimes temperatures dropped toward the fifties, and people trotted around in thick sweaters and coats. It was almost a relief when that happened, because everybody put on their shirts. In three years, I'd seen more woman skin than a normal man sees in a lifetime, and more tattoos on men. The chief warrant at the motor pool had the only tattoo in the world called "worm's-eye view of a pig's butt in the moonlight."

In autumn '64, with one more year to pull, I took a two-week leave and headed north just chasing weather. It showed up first in Oregon with rain, and more in Washington. I got hassled on the Canadian border by a distressful little guy who thought, what with the war, that I wanted political asylum.

I chased on up to Calgary, where matters got chill and wholesome. Wind worked through the mountains like it wanted to drive me south toward home. Elk and moose and porcupines went about their business. Red-tailed hawks circled. I slid on over to Edmonton, chased on east to Saskatoon, then dropped south through the Dakotas. In Williston, I had a terrible want to cut and run for home, but didn't dare.

The Road Dog showed up all over the place, but the messages were getting strange. At a bar in Amidon:

Road Dog
Taking Kentucky Windage

At a hamburger joint in Belle Fourche:

Road Dog
Chasing his tail

At a restaurant in Redbird:

> *Road Dog*
> *Flea and flee as much as we can*
> *We'll soon find who is the Gingerbread Man*

In a poolroom in Fort Collins:

> *Road Dog*
> *Home home on derange*

Road Dog, or Jesse, was too far south. The Dog had never showed up in Colorado before. At least, nobody ever heard of such.

My leave was running out. There was nothing to do except sit over the wheel. I dropped on south to Albuquerque, hung a right, and headed back to the big city. All along the road, I chewed a dreadful fear for Jesse. Something bad was happening, and that didn't seem fair, because something good went on between me and the Chrysler. We reached an understanding. The Chrysler came alive and began to hum. All that poor car had ever needed was to look at road. It had been raised among traffic and poodles, but needed long sight-distances and bears.

When I got back, there seemed no way out of writing a letter to Matt Simons, even if it was borrowing trouble. It took evening after evening of gnawing the end of a pencil. I hated to tell about Miss Molly, and about the dancing ghost, and about my fears for Jesse. A man is supposed to keep his problems to himself.

At the same time, Matt was educated. Maybe he could give Jesse a hand if he knew all of it. The letter came out pretty thick. I mailed it thinking Matt wasn't likely to answer real soon. Autumn deepened to winter back home, and everybody would be busy.

So I worked and waited. There was an old White Mustang with a fifth wheel left over from the last war. It was a lean and hungry-looking animal, and slightly marvelous. I overhauled the engine, then dropped the tranny and adapted a ten-speed Roadranger. When I got that truck running smooth as a Baptist's mouth, the Navy surveyed it and sold it for scrap.

"Ghost cars are a tradition," Matt wrote toward the back of October, "and I'd be hard pressed to say they are not real. I recall being passed by an Auburn boat-tail about 3:00 A.M. on a summer day. That happened ten years ago. I was about your age, which means there was not an Auburn boat-tail in all of Montana. That car died in the early thirties.

"And we all hear stories of huge old headlights overtaking in the mist, stories of Mercers and Deusenbergs and Bugattis. I try to believe the stories are true, because, in a way, it would be a shame if they were not.

"The same for road ghosts. I've never seen a ghost who looked like Jesse. The ghosts I've seen might not have been ghosts. To paraphrase an expert, they may have been a trapped beer belch, an undigested hamburger, or blowing mist. On the other hand, maybe not. They certainly seemed real at the time.

"As for Jesse—we have a problem here. In a way, we've had it for a long while, but only since last winter have matters become solemn. Then your letter arrives, and matters become mysterious. Jesse has—or had—a twin brother. One night when we were carousing, he told me that, but he also said his brother was dead. Then he swore me to a silence I must now break."

Matt went on to say that I must never, never say anything. He figured something was going on between brothers. He figured it must run deep.

"There is something uncanny about twins," Matt wrote. "What great matters are joined in the womb? When twins enter the world, they learn and grow the way all of us do; but some communication (or communion) surely happens before birth. A clash between brothers is a terrible thing. A clash between twins may spell tragedy."

Matt went on to tell how Jesse was going over the edge with road games, only, the games stayed close to home. All during the summer, Jesse would head out, roll fifty or a hundred miles, and come home scorching like drawn by a string. Matt guessed the postcard I'd gotten from Jesse in February was part of the game, and it was the last time Jesse had been very far from home. Matt figured Jesse used tracing paper to imitate the Road Dog's writing. He also figured Road Dog had to be Jesse's brother.

"It's obvious," Matt wrote, "that Jesse's brother is still alive, and is only metaphorically dead to Jesse. There are look-alikes in this world, but you have reported identical twins."

Matt told how Jesse drove so crazy, even Mike would not run with him. That was bad enough, but it seemed the graveyard had sort of moved in on Jesse's mind. That graveyard was no longer just something to do. Jesse swapped around until he came up with a tractor and mower. Three times that summer, he trimmed the graveyard and straightened the markers. He dusted and polished Miss Molly's headstone.

"It's past being a joke," Matt wrote, "or a sentimental indulgence. Jesse no longer drinks, and no longer hells around in a general way. He either runs or tends the cemetery. I've seen other men search for a ditch, but never in such bizarre fashion."

Jesse had been seen on his knees, praying before Miss Molly's grave.

"Or perhaps he was praying for himself, or for Chip." Matt wrote. "Chip is buried beside Miss Molly. The graveyard has to be seen to be believed. Who would ever think so many machines would be so dear to so many men?"

Then Matt went on to say he was going to "inquire in various places" that winter. "There are ways to trace Jesse's brother," Matt wrote, "and I am very good at that sort of research." He said it was about the only thing he could still do for Jesse.

"Because," Matt wrote, "I seem to have fallen in love with a romantic. Nancy wants a June wedding. I look forward to another winter alone, but it will be an easy wait. Nancy is rather old-fashioned, and I find that I'm old-fashioned as well. I will never regret my years spent helling around, but am glad they are now in the past."

Back home, winter deepened. At Christmas a long letter came from Jesse, and some of it made sense. "I put eighteen cars under this summer. Business fell off because I lost my hustle. You got to scooch around a good bit, or you don't make contacts. I may start advertising.

"And the tabbies took off. I forgot to slop them regular, so now they're mousing in a barn on Jimmy Come Lately Road. Mike says I ought to get another dog, but my heart isn't in it."

Then the letter went into plans for the cemetery. Jesse talked some grand ideas. He thought a nice wrought-iron gate might be showy, and bring in business. He thought of finding a truck that would haul "deceased" cars. "On the other hand," he wrote, "if a guy don't care enough to find a tow, maybe I don't want to plant his iron." He went on for a good while about morals, but a lawyer couldn't understand it. He seemed to be saying something about respect for Miss Molly, and Betty Lou, and Judith. "Sue Ellen is a real hummer," he wrote about the Linc. "She's got two hundred thousand I know about, plus whatever went on before."

Which meant Jesse was piling up about seventy thousand miles a year, and that didn't seem too bad. Truck drivers put up a hundred thousand. Of course, they make a living at it.

Then the letter got so crazy it was hard to credit.

"I got The Road Dog figured out. There's two little kids. Their mama reads to them, and they play tag. The one that don't get caught gets to be the Gingerbread Man. This all come together because I ran across a bunch of kids down on the Colorado line. I was down that way to call on a lady I once knew, but she moved, and I said what the hell, and hung around a few days, and that's what clued me to The Dog. The kids were at a Sunday-school picnic, and I was napping across the car seat. Then a preacher's wife came over and saw I wasn't drunk, but the preacher was there, too, and they invited me. I eased over to the picnic, and everybody made me welcome. Anyway, those kids were playing, and I heard the gingerbread business, and I figured The Dog is from Colorado."

The last page of the letter was just as scary. Jesse took kids' crayons and drew the front ends of the Linc and Miss Molly. There was a tail that was probably Potato's, sticking out from behind the picture of Miss Molly, and everything was centered around the picture of a marker that said "R.I.P. Road Dog."

But—there weren't any little kids. Jesse had not been to Colorado. Jesse had been tending that graveyard, and staying close to home. Jesse played make-believe, or else Matt Simons lied; and there was no reason for Matt to lie. Something bad, bad wrong was going on with Jesse.

There was no help for it. I did my time and wrote a letter every month or six weeks pretending everything was normal. I wrote about what we'd do when I got home, and about the Chrysler. Maybe that didn't make much sense, but Jesse was important to me. He was a big part of what I remembered about home.

At the end of April, a postcard came, this time from Havre. "The Dog is after me. I feel it." It was just a plain old postcard. No picture.

Matt wrote in May, mostly his own plans. He busied himself building a couple of rooms onto his place. "Nancy and I do not want a family right away," he wrote, "but someday we will." He wrote a bubbly letter with a feel of springtime to it.

"I almost forgot my main reason for writing," the letter said. "Jesse comes from around Boulder, Colorado. His parents are long dead, ironically in a car wreck. His mother was a schoolteacher, his father a librarian. Those people, who lived such quiet lives, somehow produced a hellion like Jesse, and Jesse's brother. That's the factual side of the matter.

"The human side is so complex it will not commit to paper. In fact, I do not trust what I know. When you get home next fall, we'll discuss it."

The letter made me sad and mad. Sad because I wasn't getting married, and mad because Matt didn't think I'd keep my mouth shut. Then I thought better of it. Matt didn't trust himself. I did what any gentleman would do, and sent him and Nancy a nice gravy boat for the wedding.

In late July, Jesse sent another postcard. "He's after me; I'm after him. If I ain't around when you get back, don't fret. Stuff happens. It's just a matter of chasing road."

Summer rolled on. The Navy released "nonessential personnel" in spite of the war. I put four years in the outfit and got called nonessential. Days choked past like a rig with fouled injectors. One good thing happened. My old boss moved his station to the outskirts of town and started an IH dealership. He straight-out wrote how he needed a diesel mechanic. I felt hopeful thoughts, and dark ones.

In September, I became a veteran who qualified for an overseas ribbon, because of work on ships that later on went somewhere. Now I could join the Legion post back home, which was maybe the payoff. They had the best pool table in the county.

"Gents," I said to the boys at the motor pool, "it's been a distinct by-God pleasure enjoying your company, and don't never come to Montana, 'cause she's a heartbreaker." The Chrysler and me lit out like a kyoodle of pups.

It would have been easier to run to Salt Lake, then climb the map to Havre, but notions pushed. I slid east to Las Cruces, then popped north to Boulder with the idea of tracing Jesse. The Chrysler hummed and chewed up road. When I got to Boulder, the notion turned hopeless. There were too many people. I didn't even know where to start asking.

It's no big job to fool yourself. Above Boulder, it came to me how I'd been pointing for Sheridan all along, and not even Sheridan. I pointed toward a girl who smiled at me four years ago.

I found her working at a hardware, and she wasn't wearing any rings. I blushed around a little bit, then got out of there to catch my breath. I thought of how Jesse took whatever time was needed when he bought the Linc. It looked like this would take awhile.

My pockets were crowded with mustering-out pay and money for unused leave. I camped in a ten-dollar motel. It took three days to get acquainted, then we went to a show and supper afterward. Her name was Linda. Her father was a Mormon. That meant a year of courting, but it's not all that far from north Montana to Sheridan.

I had to get home and get employed, which would make the Mormon happy. On Saturday afternoon, Linda and I went back to the same old movie, but this time we held hands. Before going home, she kissed me once, real gentle. That made up for those hard times in San Diego. It let me know I was back with my own people.

I drove downtown all fired-up with visions. It was way too early for bed, and I cared nothing for a beer. A run-down café sat on the outskirts. I figured pie and coffee.

The Dog had signed in. His writing showed faint, like the wall had been scrubbed. Newer stuff scrabbled over it.

> *Road Dog*
> *Tweedledum and Tweedledee*
> *Lonely pups as pups can be*
> *For each other had to wait*
> *Down beside the churchyard gate.*

The café sort of slumbered. Several old men lined the counter. Four young gearheads sat at a table and talked fuel injection. The old men yawned and put up with it. Faded pictures of old racing cars hung along the walls. The young guys sat beneath a picture of the Bluebird. That car held the land speed record of 301.29 m.p.h. This was a racer's café, and had been for a long, long time.

The waitress was graying and motherly. She tsked and tished over the old men as much as she did the young ones. Her eyes held that long-distance prairie look, a look knowing wind and fire and hard times, stuff that either breaks people or leaves them wise. Matt Simons might get that look in another twenty years. I tried to imagine Linda when she became the waitress's age, and it wasn't bad imagining.

Pictures of quarter-mile cars hung back of the counter, and pictures of street machines hung on each side of the door. Fifties hot rods scorched beside worked-up stockers. Some mighty rowdy iron crowded that wall. One picture showed a Golden Hawk. I walked over, and in one corner was the name "Still"—written in The Road Dog's hand. It shouldn't have been scary.

I went back to the counter shaking. A nice-looking old gent nursed coffee. His hands wore knuckles busted by a thousand slipped wrenches. Grease was worked in deep around his eyes, the way it gets after years and years when no soap made will touch it. You could tell he'd been a steady man. His eyes were clear as a kid.

"Mister," I said, "and beg pardon for bothering you. Do you know anything about that Studebaker?" I pointed to the wall.

"You ain't bothering me," he said, "but I'll tell you when you do." He tapped the side of his head like trying to ease a gear in place, then he started talking engine specs on the Stude.

"I mean the man who owns it."

The old man probably liked my haircut, which was short. He liked it that I was raised right. Young guys don't always pay old men much mind.

"You still ain't bothering me." He turned to the waitress. "Sue," he said, "has Johnny Still been in?"

She turned from cleaning the pie case, and she looked toward the young guys like she feared for them. You could tell she was no big fan of engines. "It's been the better part of a year, maybe more." She looked down the line of old men. "I was fretting about him just the other day. . . ." She let it hang. Nobody said anything. "He comes and goes so quiet, you might miss him."

"I don't miss him a hell of a lot," one of the young guys said. The guy looked like a duck, and had a voice like a sparrow. His fingernails were too clean. That proved something.

"Because Johnny blew you out," another young guy said. "Johnny *always* blew you out."

"Because he's crazy," the first guy said. "There's noisy-crazy and quiet-crazy. The guy is a spook."

"He's going through something," the waitress said, and said it kind. "Johnny's taken a lot of loss. He's the type who grieves." She looked at me like she expected an explanation.

"I'm friends with his brother," I told her. "Maybe Johnny and his brother don't get along."

The old man looked at me rather strange. "You go back quite a ways," he told me. "Jesse's been dead a good long time."

I thought I'd pass out. My hands started shaking, and my legs felt too weak to stand. Beyond the window of the café, red light came from a neon sign, and inside the café, everybody sat quiet, waiting to see if I was crazy, too. I sort of picked at my pie. One of the young guys moved real uneasy. He loafed toward the door, maybe figuring he'd need a shotgun. The other three young ones looked confused.

"No offense," I said to the old man, "but Jesse Still is alive. Up on the highline. We run together."

"Jesse Still drove a damn old Hudson Terraplane into the South Platte River in spring of '52, maybe '53." The old man said it real quiet. "He popped a tire when not real sober."

"Which is why Johnny doesn't drink," the waitress said. "At least, I expect that's the reason."

"And now you are bothering me." The old man looked to the waitress, and she was as full of questions as he was.

Nobody ever felt more hopeless or scared. These folks had no reason to tell this kind of yarn. "Jesse is sort of roughhouse." My voice was only whispering. It wouldn't make enough sound. "Jesse made his reputation helling around."

"You've got that part right," the old man told me, "and youngster, I don't give a tinker's damn if you believe me or not, but Jesse Still is dead."

I saw what it had to be, but seeing isn't always believing. "Thank you, mister,'' I whispered to the old man, ''and thank you, ma'am,'' to the waitress. Then I hauled out of there leaving them with something to discuss.

A terrible fear rolled with me, because of Jesse's last postcard. He said he might not be home, and now that could mean more than it said. The Chrysler bettered its reputation, and we just flew. From the Montana line to Shelby is eight hours on a clear day. You can wail it in seven, or maybe six and a half if a deer doesn't tangle with your front end. I was afraid, and confused, and getting mad. Me and Linda were just to the point of hoping for an understanding, and now I was going to get killed running over a porcupine or into a heifer. The Chrysler blazed like a hound on a hot scent. At eighty the pedal kept wanting to dig deep and really howl.

The nighttime road yells danger. Shadows crawl over everything. What jumps into your headlights may be real, and may be not. Metal crosses hold little clusters of dark flowers on their arms, and the land rolls out beneath the moon. Buttes stand like great ships anchored in the plains, and riverbeds run like dry ink. Come spring, they'll flow; but in September, all flow is in the road.

The dancing ghost picked me up on Highway 3 outside Comanche, but this time he wasn't dancing. He stood on the berm, and no mist tied him in place. He gave the old road sign for ''roll 'em.'' Beyond Columbia, he showed up again. His mouth moved like he was yelling me along, and his face twisted with as much fear as my own.

That gave me reason to hope. I'd never known Jesse to be afraid like that, so maybe there was a mistake. Maybe the dancing ghost wasn't the ghost of Jesse. I hung over the wheel and forced myself to think of Linda. When I thought of her, I couldn't bring myself to get crazy. Highway 3 is not much of a road, but that's no bother. I can drive anything with wheels over any road ever made. The dancing ghost kept showing up and beckoning, telling me to scorch. I told myself the damn ghost had no judgment, or he wouldn't be a ghost in the first place.

That didn't keep me from pushing faster, but it wasn't fast enough to satisfy the roadside. They came out of the mist, or out of the ditches; crowds and clusters of ghosts standing pale beneath a weak moon. Some of them gossiped with each other. Some stood yelling me along. Maybe there was sense to it, but I had my hands full. If they were trying to help, they sure weren't doing it. They just made me get my back up, and think of dropping revs.

Maybe the ghosts held a meeting and studied out the problem. They could see a clear road, but I couldn't. The dancing ghost showed up on Highway 12 and gave me ''thumbs up'' for a clear road. I didn't believe a word of it, and then I really didn't believe what showed in my mirrors. Headlights closed like I was standing. My feelings said that all of this had happened before; except, last time, there was only one set of headlights.

It was Miss Molly and Betty Lou that brought me home. Miss Molly overtook, sweeping past with a lane change smooth and sober as an Adventist. The high, slaunch-forward form of Miss Molly thrummed with business. She wasn't blowing sparks or showing off. She wasn't playing Gingerbread Man or tag.

Betty Lou came alongside so I could see who she was, then Betty Lou laid back a half mile. If we ran into a claim-jumping deputy, he'd have to chase her first; and more luck to him. Her headlights hovered back there like angels.

Miss Molly settled down a mile ahead of the Chrysler and stayed at that distance, no matter how hard I pressed. Twice before Great Falls, she spotted trouble, and her squinchy little brake lights hauled me down. Once it was an animal, and once it was busted road surface. Miss Molly and Betty Lou dropped me off before Great Falls, and picked me back up the minute I cleared town.

We ran the night like rockets. The roadside lay deserted. The dancing ghost stayed out of it, and so did the others. That let me concentrate, which proved a blessing. At those speeds a man don't have time to do deep thinking. The road rolls past, the hours roll, but you've got a racer's mind. No matter how tired you should be, you don't get tired until it's over.

I chased a ghost car northward while a fingernail moon moved across the sky. In deepest night the land turned silver. At speed, you don't think, but you do have time to feel. The farther north we pushed, the more my feelings went to despair. Maybe Miss Molly thought the same, but everybody did all they could.

The Chrysler was a howler, and Lord knows where the top end lay. I buried the needle. Even accounting for speedometer error, we burned along in the low half of the second century. We made Highway 2 and Shelby around three in the morning, then hung a left. In just about no time, I rolled home. Betty Lou dropped back and faded. Miss Molly blew sparks and purely flew out of sight. The sparks meant something. Maybe Miss Molly was still hopeful. Or maybe she knew we were too late.

Beneath that thin moon, mounded graves looked like dark surf across the acreage. No lights burned in the trailer, and the Linc showed nowhere. Even under the scant light, you could see snowy tops of mountains, and the perfectly straight markers standing at the head of each grave. A tent, big enough to hold a small revival, stood not far from the trailer. In my headlights a sign on the tent read "chapel." I fetched a flashlight from the glove box.

A dozen folding chairs stood in the chapel, and a podium served as an altar. Jesse had rigged up two sets of candles, so I lit some. Matt Simons had written that the graveyard had to be seen to be believed. Hanging on one side of the tent was a sign reading "shrine," and all along that side hung road maps, and pictures of cars, and pictures of men standing beside their cars. There was a special display of odometers, with little cards beneath them: "330,938 miles"; "407,000 miles"; "half a million miles, more or less." These were the championship cars, the all-time best at piling up road, and those odometers would make even a married man feel lonesome. You couldn't look at them without thinking of empty roads and empty nights.

Even with darkness spreading across the cemetery, nothing felt worse than the inside of the tent. I could believe that Jesse took it serious, and had tried to make it nice, but couldn't believe anyone else would buy it.

The night was not too late for owls, and nearly silent wings swept past as I

left the tent. I walked to Miss Molly's grave, half-expecting ghostly headlights.
Two small markers stood beside a real fine marble headstone.

Potato
Happy-go-sloppy and good
Rest In Peace Wherever You Are

Chip
A dandy little sidekicker
Running With Potato

From a distance, I could see piled dirt where the dozer had dug new graves.
I stepped cautious toward the dozer, not knowing why, but knowing it had to
happen.

Two graves stood open like little garages, and the front ends of the Linc and
the Hawk poked out. The Linc's front bumper shone spotless, but the rest of the
Linc looked tough and experienced. Dents and dings crowded the sides, and
cracked glass starred the windows.

The Hawk stood sparkly, ready to come roaring from the grave. Its glass shone
washed and clean before my flashlight. I thought of what I heard in Sheridan,
and thought of the first time I'd seen the Hawk. It hadn't changed. The Hawk
looked like it had just been driven off a showroom floor.

Nobody in his right mind would want to look in those two cars, but it wasn't
a matter of "want." Jesse, or Johnny—if that's who it was—had to be here
someplace. It was certain-sure he needed help. When I looked, the Hawk sat
empty. My flashlight poked against the glass of the Linc. Jesse lay there, taking
his last nap across a car seat. His long black hair had turned gray. He had always
been thin, but now he was skin and bones. Too many miles, and no time to eat.
Creases around his eyes came from looking at road, but now the creases were
deep like an old man's. His eyes showed that he was dead. They were open only
a little bit, but open enough.

I couldn't stand to be alone with such a sight. In less than fifteen minutes, I stood
banging on Matt Simon's door. Matt finally answered, and Nancy showed up
behind him. She was in her robe. She stood taller than Matt, and sleepier. She
looked blonde and Swedish. Matt didn't know whether to be mad or glad. Then
I got my story pieced together, and he really woke up.

"Dr. Jekyll has finally dealt with Mr. Hyde," he said in a low voice to Nancy.
"Or maybe the other way around." To me, he said, "That may be a bad joke,
but it's not ill meant." He went to get dressed. "Call Mike," he said to me.
"Drunk or sober, I want him there."

Nancy showed me the phone. Then she went to the bedroom to talk with Matt.
I could hear him soothing her fears. When Mike answered, he was sleepy and
sober, but he woke up stampeding.

Deep night and a thin moon is a perfect time for ghosts, but none showed up as Matt rode with me back to the graveyard. The Chrysler loafed. There was no need for hurry.

I told Matt what I'd learned in Sheridan.

"That matches what I heard," he said, "and we have two mysteries. The first mystery is interesting, but it's no longer important. Was John Still pretending to be Jesse Still, or was Jesse pretending to be John?"

"If Jesse drove into a river in '53, then it has to be John." I didn't like what I said, because Jesse was real. The best actor in the world couldn't pretend that well. My sorrow choked me, but I wasn't ashamed.

Matt seemed to be thinking along the same lines. "We don't know how long the game went on," he said real quiet. "We never will know. John could have been playing at being Jesse way back in '53."

That got things tangled, and I felt resentful. Things were complicated enough. Me and Matt had just lost a friend, and now Matt was talking like that was the least interesting part.

"Makes no difference whether he was John or Jesse," I told Matt. "He was Jesse when he died. He's laying across the seat in Jesse's car. Figure it any way you want, but we're talking about Jesse."

"You're right," Matt said. "Also, you're wrong. We're talking about someone who was both." Matt sat quiet for a minute, figuring things out. I told myself it was just as well that he'd married a schoolteacher. "Assume, for the sake of argument," he said, "that John was playing Jesse in '53. John drove into the river, and people believed they were burying Jesse.

"Or, for the sake of argument, assume that it was Jesse in '53. In that case the game started with John's grief. Either way the game ran for many years." Matt was getting at something, but he always has to go roundabout.

"After years, John, or Jesse, disappeared. There was only a man who was both John and Jesse. That's the reason it makes no difference who died in '53."

Matt looked through the car window into the darkness like he expected to discover something important. "This is a long and lonesome country," he said. "The biggest mystery is: Why? The answer may lie in the mystery of twins, or it may be as simple as a man reaching into the past for happy memories. At any rate, one brother dies, and the survivor keeps his brother alive by living his brother's life, as well as his own. Think of the planning, the elaborate schemes, the near self-deception. Think of how often the roles shifted. A time must have arrived when that lonely man could not even remember who he was."

The answer was easy, and I saw it. Jesse, or John, chased the road to find something they'd lost on the road. They lost their parents and each other. I didn't say a damn word. Matt was making me mad, but I worked at forgiving him. He was handling his own grief, and maybe he didn't have a better way.

"And so he invented The Road Dog," Matt said. "That kept the personalities separate. The Road Dog was a metaphor to make him proud. Perhaps it might confuse some of the ladies, but there isn't a man ever born who wouldn't understand it."

I remembered long nights and long roads. I couldn't fault his reasoning.

"At the same time," Matt said, "the metaphor served the twins. They could play road games with the innocence of children, maybe even replay memories of a time when their parents were alive and the world seemed warm. John played The Road Dog, and Jesse chased; and by God, so did the rest of us. It was a magnificent metaphor."

"If it was that blamed snappy," I said, "how come it fell to pieces? For the past year, it seems like Jesse's been running away from The Dog."

"The metaphor began to take over. The twins began to defend against each other," Matt said. "I've been watching it all along, but couldn't understand what was happening. John Still was trying to take over Jesse, and Jesse was trying to take over John."

"It worked for a long time," I said, "and then it didn't work. What's the kicker?"

"Our own belief," Matt said. "We all believed in The Road Dog. When all of us believed, John was forced to become stronger."

"And Jesse fought him off?"

"Successfully," Matt said. "All this year, when Jesse came firing out of town, rolling fifty miles, and firing back, I thought it was Jesse's problem. Now I see that John was trying to get free, get back on the road, and Jesse was dragging him back. This was a struggle between real men, maybe titans in the oldest sense, but certainly not imitations."

"It was a guy handling his problems."

"That's an easy answer. We can't know what went on with John," Matt said, "but we know some of what went on with Jesse. He tried to love a woman, Sarah, and failed. He lost his dogs—which doesn't sound like much, unless your dogs are all you have. Jesse fought defeat by building his other metaphor, which was that damned cemetery." Matt's voice got husky. He'd been holding in his sorrow, but his sorrow started coming through. It made me feel better about him.

"I think the cemetery was Jesse's way of answering John, or denying that he was vulnerable. He needed a symbol. He tried to protect his loves and couldn't. He couldn't even protect his love for his brother. That cemetery is the last bastion of Jesse's love." Matt looked like he was going to cry, and I felt the same.

"Cars can't hurt you," Matt said. "Only bad driving hurts you. The cemetery is a symbol for protecting one of the few loves you can protect. That's not saying anything bad about Jesse. That's saying something with sadness for all of us."

I slowed to pull onto Jesse's place. Mike's Olds sat by the trailer. Lights were on in the trailer, but no other lights showed anywhere.

"Men build all kinds of worlds in order to defeat fear and loneliness," Matt said. "We give and take as we build those worlds. One must wonder how much Jesse, and John, gave in order to take the little that they got."

We climbed from the Chrysler as autumn wind moved across the graveyard and felt its way toward my bones. The moon lighted faces of grave markers, but not enough that you could read them. Mike had the bulldozer warming up. It stood and puttered, and darkness felt best, and Mike knew it. The headlights were off. Far away on Highway 2, an engine wound tight and squalling, and it seemed like echoes of engines whispered among the graves. Mike stood huge as a grizzly.

"I've shot horses that looked healthier than you two guys," he said, but said it sort of husky.

Matt motioned toward the bulldozer. "This is illegal."

"Nobody ever claimed it wasn't." Mike was ready to fight if a fight was needed. "Anybody who don't like it can turn around and walk."

"I like it," Matt said. "It's fitting and proper. But if we're caught, there's hell to pay."

"I like most everything and everybody," Mike said, "except the government. They paw a man to death while he's alive, then keep pawing his corpse. I'm saving Jesse a little trouble."

"They like to know that he's dead and what killed him."

"Sorrow killed him," Mike said. "Let it go at that."

Jesse killed himself, timing his tiredness and starvation just right, but I was willing to let it go, and Matt was, too.

"We'll go along with you," Matt said. "But they'll sell this place for taxes. Somebody will start digging sometime."

"Not for years and years. It's deeded to me. Jesse fixed up papers. They're on the kitchen table." Mike turned toward the trailer. "We're going to do this right, and there's not much time."

We found a blanket and a quilt in the trailer. Mike opened a kitchen drawer and pulled out snapshots. Some looked pretty new, and some were faded: a man and woman in old-fashioned clothes, a picture of two young boys in Sunday suits, pictures of cars and road signs, and pictures of two women who were maybe Sue Ellen and Sarah. Mike piled them like a deck of cards, snapped a rubber band around them, and checked the trailer. He picked up a pair of pale yellow sunglasses that some racers use for night driving. "You guys see anything else?"

"His dogs," Matt said. "He had pictures of his dogs."

We found them under a pillow, and it didn't pay to think why they were there. Then we went to the Linc and wrapped Jesse real careful in the blanket. We spread the quilt over him, and laid his stuff on the floor beside the accelerator. Then Mike remembered something. He half-unwrapped Jesse, went through his pockets, then wrapped him back up. He took Jesse's keys and left them hanging in the ignition.

The three of us stood beside the Linc, and Matt cleared his throat.

"It's my place to say it," Mike told him. "This was my best friend." Mike took off his cap. Moonlight lay thin on his bald head.

"A lot of preachers will be glad this man is gone, and that's one good thing you can say for him. He drove nice people crazy. This man was a hellion, pure and simple; but what folks don't understand is, hellions have their place. They put everything on the line over nothing very much. Most guys worry so much about dying, they never do any living. Jesse was so alive with living, he never gave dying any thought. This man would roll ninety just to get to a bar before it closed." Mike kind of choked up and stopped to listen. From the graveyard came the echoes of engines, and from Highway 2 rose the thrum of a straight-eight crankshaft whipping in its bed. Dim light covered the graveyard, like a hundred sets of parking lights and not the moon.

"This man kept adventure alive, when, everyplace else, it's dying. There was nothing ever smug or safe about this man. If he had fears, he laughed. This man never hit a woman or crossed a friend. He did tie the can on Betty Lou one night, but can't be blamed. It was really The Dog who did that one. Jesse never had a problem until he climbed into that Studebaker."

So Mike had known all along. At least Mike knew something.

"I could always run even with Jesse," Mike said, "but I never could beat The Dog. The Dog could clear any track. And in a damn Studebaker."

"But a very swift Studebaker," Matt muttered, like a Holy Roller answering the preacher.

"Bored and stroked and rowdy," Mike said, "and you can say the same for Jesse. Let that be the final word. Amen."

IV

A little spark of flame dwelt at the stack of the dozer, and distant mountains lay white-capped and prophesied winter. Mike filled the graves quick. Matt got rakes and a shovel. I helped him mound the graves with only moonlight to go on, while Mike went to the trailer. He made coffee.

"Drink up and git," Mike told us when he poured the coffee. "Jesse's got some friends who need to visit, and it will be morning pretty quick."

"Let them," Matt said. "We're no hindrance."

"You're a smart man," Mike told Matt, "but your smartness makes you dumb. You started to hinder the night you stopped driving beyond your headlights." Mike didn't know how to say it kind, so he said it rough. His red mustache and bald head made him look like a pirate in a picture.

"You're saying that I'm getting old." Matt has known Mike long enough not to take offense.

"Me, too," Mike said, "but not that old. When you get old, you stop seeing them. Then you want to stop seeing them. You get afraid for your hide."

"You stop imagining?"

"Shitfire," Mike said, "You stop seeing. Imagination is something you use when you don't have eyes." He pulled a cigar out of his shirt pocket and was chewing it before he ever got it lit. "Ghosts have lost it all. Maybe they're the ones the Lord didn't love well enough. If you see them, but ain't one, maybe you're important."

Matt mulled that, and so did I. We've both wailed a lot of road for some sort of reason.

"They're kind of rough," Matt said about ghosts. "They hitch rides, but don't want 'em. I've stopped for them and got laughed at. They fool themselves, or maybe they don't."

"It's a young man's game," Matt said.

"It's a game guys got to play. Jesse played the whole deck. He was who he was, whenever he was it. That's the key. That's the reason you slug cops when you gotta. It looks like Jesse died old, but he lived young longer than most. That's the real mystery. How does a fella keep going?"

"Before we leave," I said, "how long did you know that Jesse was The Dog?"

"Maybe a year and a half. About the time he started running crazy."

"And never said a word?"

Mike looked at me like something you'd wipe off your boot. "Learn to ride your own fence," he told me. "It was Jesse's business." Then he felt sorry for being rough. "Besides," he said, "we were having fun. I expect that's all over now."

Matt followed me to the Chrysler. We left the cemetery, feeling tired and mournful. I shoved the car onto Highway 2, heading toward Matt's place.

"Wring it out once for old times?"

"Putter along," Matt said. "I just entered the putter stage of life, and may as well practice doing it."

In my mirrors a stream of headlights showed, then vanished one by one as cars turned into the graveyard. The moon had left the sky. Over toward South Dakota was a suggestion of first faint morning light. Mounded graves lay at my elbow, and so did Canada. On my left the road south ran fine and fast as a man can go. Mist rose from the roadside ditches, and maybe there was movement in the mist, maybe not.

There's little more to tell. Through fall and winter and spring and summer, I drove to Sheridan. The Mormon turned out to be a pretty good man, for a Mormon. I kept at it, and drove through another autumn and another winter. Linda got convinced. We got married in the spring, and I expected trouble. Married people are supposed to fight, but nothing like that ever happened. We just worked hard, got our own place in a few years, and Linda birthed two girls. That disappointed the Mormon, but was a relief to me.

And in those seasons of driving, when the roads were good for twenty miles an hour in the snow, or eighty under sun, the road stood empty except for a couple times. Miss Molly showed up once early on to say a bridge was out. She might have showed up another time. Squinchy little taillights winked one night when it was late and I was highballing. Some guy jackknifed a Freightliner, and his trailer lay across the road.

But I saw no other ghosts. I'd like to say that I saw the twins, John and Jesse, standing by the road, giving the high sign or dancing, but it never happened.

I did think of Jesse, though, and thought of one more thing. If Matt was right, then I saw how Jesse had to die before I got home. He had to, because I believed in Road Dog. My belief would have been just enough to bring John forward, and that would have been fatal, too. If either one of them became too strong, they both of them lost. So Jesse had to do it.

The graveyard sank beneath the weather. Mike tended it for a while, but lost interest. Weather swept the mounds flat. Weed-covered markers tumbled to decay and dust, so that only one marble headstone stands solid beside Highway 2. The marker doesn't bend before the winter winds, nor does the little stone that me and Mike and Matt put there. It lays flat against the ground. You have to know where to look:

Road Dog
1931–1965
2 million miles, more or less
Run and run as fast as we can
We never can catch the Gingerbread Man

And now, even the great good cars are dead, or most of them. What with gas prices and wars and rumors of wars, the cars these days are all suspensions. They'll corner like a cat, but don't have the scratch of a cat; and maybe that's a good thing. The state posts fewer crosses.

Still, there are some howlers left out there, and some guys are still howling. I lie in bed of nights and listen to the scorch of engines along Highway 2. I hear them claw the darkness, stretching lonesome at the sky, scatting across the eternal land; younger guys running as young guys must; chasing each other, or chasing the land of dreams, or chasing into ghostland while hoping it ain't true—guys running into darkness chasing each other, or chasing something—chasing road.

FEEDBACK

Joe Haldeman

▼

"I may not know art," the old cliché tells us, "but I know what I like!" Just *what* someone likes, though, can vary radically from one person to another—sometimes, as the high-tech shocker that follows will demonstrate, with strange and unforeseeable results. . . .

Born in Oklahoma City, Oklahoma, Joe Haldeman took a B.S. degree in physics and astronomy from the University of Maryland, and did postgraduate work in mathematics and computer science. But his plans for a career in science were cut short by the U.S. Army, which sent him to Vietnam in 1968 as a combat engineer. Seriously wounded in action, Haldeman returned home in 1969 and began to write. He sold his first story to *Galaxy* in 1969, and by 1976 had garnered both the Nebula Award and the Hugo Award for his famous novel *The Forever War*, one of the landmark books of the seventies. He took another Hugo Award in 1977 for his story "Tricentennial," won the Rhysling Award in 1983 for the best science fiction poem of the year (although usually thought of primarily as a "hard-science" writer, Haldeman is, in fact, also an accomplished poet, and has sold poetry to most of the major professional markets in the genre), and won both the Nebula and the Hugo Award in 1991 for the novella version of "The Hemingway Hoax." His other books include a mainstream novel, *War Year*, the SF novels *Mindbridge, All My Sins Remembered, There Is No Darkness* (written with his brother, SF writer Jack C. Haldeman II) *Worlds, Worlds Apart, Buying Time*, and *The Hemingway Hoax*, the "techno-thriller" *Tool of the Trade*, the collections *Infinite Dreams* and *Dealing in Futures*, and, as editor, the anthologies *Study War No More, Cosmic Laughter*, and *Nebula Award Stories Seventeen*. His most recent books are the SF novel *Worlds Enough and Time* and a new collection, *Vietnam and Other Alien Worlds*. Upcoming is a major new mainstream novel, *1969*. He has had stories in our First, Third, Eighth, and Tenth Annual Collections. Haldeman lives part of the year in Boston, where he teaches writing at the Massachusetts Institute of Technology, and the rest of the year in Florida, where he and his wife, Gay, make their home.

This game was easier before I was famous, or infamous, and before the damned process was so efficient. When I could still pretend it was my own art, or at least about my art. Nowadays, once you're doped up and squeezed into the skinsuit, it's hard to tell whose eye is measuring the model. Whose hand is holding the brush.

I'll work in any painting or drawing medium the customer wants, within reason. Through most of my career people naturally chose my own specialty, transparent watercolor, but since I became famous with the Manhattan Monster thing, a lot of them want me to trowel on thick acrylics in primary colors. Boring. But they take the painting home and hang it up and ask their friends, Isn't that just as scary as shit? That's the stylistic association with the Monster, usually, not the subject matter. Most people's nightmares stay safely hidden when they pick up a brush. Good thing, too. If the customer is a nut case, the collaboration can be truly disturbing—and perhaps revealing. A lot of us find employment in mental institutions. Some of us find residence in them. Occupational hazard.

At least I make enough per assignment now, thanks to the notoriety of the Monster case, so that I can take off half the year to travel and paint for myself. This year, I was leaving the first of February to start off the vacation sailing in the Caribbean. With one week to go, I could already feel the sun, taste the rum. I'd sublet the apartment and studio and already had all my clothes and gear packed into two small bags. Watercolors don't take up much space, and you don't need a lot of clothes where I was headed.

I was even tempted to forsake my schedule and go to the islands early. It would have cost extra and confused my friends, who know me to be methodical and punctual. But I should have done it. God, I should have done it.

We had one of those fast, hard snows that make Manhattan beautiful for a while. I walked to and from lunch the long way, through Central Park, willing to trade the slight extra danger for the beauty. Besides, my walking stick supposedly holds an electric charge strong enough to stun a horse.

The man waiting for me in the lobby didn't look like trouble, though you never know. Short, balding, old-fashioned John Lennon-style spectacles.

He introduced himself while I fumbled with overcoat and boots. Juan Carlos Segura, investment counselor.

"Have you ever painted before?" I asked him. "Drawn or sculpted or anything?" Some of the most interesting work I produce in collaboration comes from the inexperienced, their unfamiliarity with the tools and techniques resulting in happy accidents, spontaneity.

"No. My talents lie elsewhere." I think I was supposed to be able to tell how wealthy he was by upper-class lodge signals—the cut of his conservative blue pinstripe, the gold mechanical watch—but my talents lie elsewhere. So I asked him directly, "You understand how expensive my services are?"

"Exactly. One hundred thousand dollars a day."

"And you know you must accept the work as produced? No money-back guarantee."

"I understand."

"We're in business, then." I buzzed my assistant, Allison, to start tea while we waited for the ancient elevator.

People who aren't impressed by my studio, with its original Picasso, Monet, Dali and Turner, are often fascinated by Allison. She is beautiful but very large, 6'3" but perfectly proportioned, as if some magic device had enlarged her by 20 percent. Segura didn't notice the paintings on the walls and didn't blink at her, either. Maybe that should have told me something. He accepted his tea and thanked her politely.

I blew on my tea and studied him over the cup. He looked serious, studious, calm. So had the Manhattan Monster.

"There's half a page of facilitators in the phone book," I said. "Every single one of them charges less than I do." I believe in the direct approach. It sometimes costs me a commission.

He nodded, studying me back.

"Some people want me just because I am the most expensive. A few want me because they know my work, my own work, and it's very good. Most want a painting by the man who released the Monster from Claude Avery."

"Is it important for you to know why I chose you?"

"The more I know about you, the better picture you'll get."

He nodded and paused. "Then accept this. Maybe fifty percent of my motivation is because you are the most costly. That is sometimes an index of value. Of your artistic abilities, or anybody else's, I am totally ignorant."

"So fifty percent is the Monster?"

"Not exactly. In the first place, I don't care to pay that much for something that so many other people have. And I don't like the style. Two of my acquaintances own paintings they did with you in that disturbing mode. But, looking at their paintings, it occurred to me that something more subtle was possible. You. Your anger at being used in this way."

"I have expressed that in my own paintings."

"I am sure that you have. What I want, I suppose, is to express my own anger. At my customers."

That was a new wrinkle. "You're angry at your customers?"

"Not all of them. Most. People give me large amounts of money to invest for them. Once each quarter, I extract a percentage of the profit." He set down the cup and put his hands on his knees. "But most of them want some input. It is their money, after all."

"And you would prefer to follow a single strategy," I said, "to use all their money the same way. The more capital you have behind your investment pattern, the less actual risk—since I assume that you don't have to pay back a percentage—if an investment fails."

"For an artist, you know a lot about money."

I smiled. "I'm a rich artist."

"People are emotionally connected to their money, and they want to do things with it, other than make more money. They want to change the world."

"Interesting. I see the connection with my work. My clients."

"I saw it when I read the profile in *Forbes* a couple years ago."

"And you waited for my price to come down?"

"Your price actually has come down nine percent, because of inflation, since the article. You'll be raising it soon."

"Good timing. I like round numbers, so I'm going up to one-twenty when I return from vacation in August." I picked up a stylus and touchpad and began drawing close parallel lines. It helps me think. "The connection, the analogy, is good. I know that many of my clients must be dissatisfied with abstract smearings that cost them six figures. But they get exactly what they pay for. I explain it to them beforehand, and if they choose not to hear me, that's their problem."

"You said as much in the article. But I don't want abstract smearings. I want your customary medium, when you are working seriously. The old-fashioned hyperrealism."

"Do you want a Boston School watercolor?"

"Exactly. I know the subject, the setting——"

"That's three weeks' work, minimum. More than two million dollars."

"I can afford it."

"Can you afford to leave your own work for three weeks?" I was drawing lines very fast. This would really screw up my vacation schedule. But it would be half a year's income in three weeks.

"I'm not only going to leave for three weeks, I'm going exactly where you are. The Cayman Islands. George Town."

I just looked at him.

"They say the beach is wonderful."

I never asked him how he'd found out about my vacation plans. Through my credit-card company, I supposed. That he would take the trouble before our initial interview was revealing. He was a man who left nothing to chance.

He wanted a photo-realist painting of a nude woman sitting in a conference room, alone, studying papers. Horn-rimmed glasses. The conference room elegant.

The room would be no problem, given money, since George Town has as many banks and insurance buildings as bikinis. The model was another matter. Most of the models in George Town would be black, which would complicate the text of the painting, or would be gorgeous beach bums with tan lines and silicone breasts. I told him that I thought we wanted an ordinary woman, trim but severe-looking, someone whose posture would radiate dignity without clothing. (I showed him *Olympia* and *Maja Desnuda* and some Delacroix, and a few of Wyeth's Helgas that had that quality.) She also would have to be a damned good model to do three weeks of sittings in the same position. I suggested we hire someone in New York and fly her down with us. He agreed.

Allison had been watching through the ceiling bug, part of her job. She came in when he left and poured herself a cup of tea. "Nut case," she said.

"Interesting nut case, though. Rich."

"If you ever took on a charity nut case, I wasn't watching." She stirred a spoonful of marmalade into her tea. Russian style. She does that only to watch me cringe. "So I should get tickets to the Caymans for me and M&M?"

"Yeah, Friday."

"First class?"

"What's it worth to you?"

"I don't know. You want a cup of tea in your lap?"

"First class."

Finding the right model was difficult. I knew two or three women who would fill the bill in terms of physical appearance and sitting ability, but they were friends. That would interfere with the client's wishes, since he obviously wanted a cold, clinical approach. Allison and I spent an afternoon going through agency files, and another afternoon interviewing people, until we found the right one. Rhonda Speck, 30, slender enough to show ribs. I disliked her on sight, and liked her even less when she took off her clothes, for the way she looked at me—her expression a prim gash of disapproval. Even if I were heterosexual, I wouldn't be ogling her unprofessionally. That edge of resentment might help the painting, I thought. I didn't know the half of it.

I told Rhonda the job involved a free trip to the Cayman Islands and she showed as much enthusiasm as if I had said Long Island. She did brighten a little when I described the setting. She was working on her law degree and could study while she sat. That also helped to distance me from her, since I am not a great admirer of the profession.

I called my banker in George Town and described the office that I needed. She knew of a small law firm that was closing for a February vacation, and would inquire.

It had been a few years since I'd painted nudes, and I'd done only two photo-realist studies ever. I didn't want to work with Rhonda any more than I had to, or pay her any more than I had to, so I had a friend with a figure similar to Rhonda's come over and sit. For two days I did sketches and photographs, experimenting with postures and lightings. I took them to Segura and we agreed on the pose—the woman looking up coldly from her papers, as if interrupted, strong light from the desk lamp putting half of her face in shadow. Making the desk lamp the only source of light also isolated the figure from the details of the office, which would be rendered in photorealist detail, but darkly, making for a sinister background.

Then I spent three days doing a careful portrait of the model, head and upper body, solving some technical problems about rendering the glossy hair and the small breasts. I wanted them to look hard, unfeminine, yet realistic.

I took the portrait up to Segura's office and he approved. His only reservations were about himself. "You're sure I'll be able to produce something with this kind of control? I literally can't draw a face that looks like a face."

"No problem. Your hands will be stiff from using undeveloped muscles, but while you're in the skinsuit your movements will be precisely the same as mine. Have I told you about the time I hired a facilitator myself?" He shook his head. "I was curious about how it felt on the other end. I hired a guitarist-composer, and we spent two days writing a short fugue in the style of Bach. We started with the four letters of my last name—which, coincidentally, form an A-minor-seventh chord—and made up a marvelously complicated little piece that was unequivocally mine. Even though I can't play it.''

"You could play it in the skinsuit, though.''

"Beautifully. I have a tape of it, the facilitator sitting beside me playing a silent solid-body guitar while I roam around the frets with brilliant sensitivity.'' I laughed. "At the end of each day my hands were so weak I couldn't pick up a fork, let alone a brush. My fingers were stiff for a week.'' I wriggled them. "Your experience will be less extreme. Using a brush doesn't involve the unnatural stretching that playing a guitar does.''

Segura was willing to part with an extra hundred grand for a one-day demonstration. A predictable course, given hindsight, knowing him to be a man boxed in by distrust and driven, or at least directed, by what I would call paranoia.

He suggested a self-portrait. I told him it would have to be done from photographs, since the skinsuit distorts your face almost as much as a bank-robber's pantyhose disguise. That interested him. He was going to spend three weeks in the skinsuit; why not have a record of what it was like? I pretended that nobody had come up with the idea before and said sure, sounds interesting.

In fact, I'd done it twice, but both times the collaborators produced impasto abstractions that didn't resemble anything. Segura would be different.

By law, a doctor has to be present when you begin the facilitation. After it gets under way, any kind of nurse or medic is adequate for standing guard. A few collaborators have had blood-pressure spikes or panic attacks. The nurse can terminate the process instantly if the biosensors show something happening. He pushes a button that releases a trank into my bloodstream, which breaks the connection. It also puts me into a Valium haze the rest of the day. A good reason to have people pay in advance.

There's a doctor in my building who's always willing to pop up and earn a hundred dollars for five minutes' work. I always use the same nurse, too, a careful and alert man with the unlikely name of Marion Marion. He calls himself M&M, since he's brown and round.

I soaked and taped down four half-sheets of heavy D'Arches cold-press, allowing for three disasters, and prepared my standard portrait palette. I set up the session to begin at 9:30 sharp. M&M came over early, as usual, to have tea and joke around with Allison and me. He's a natural comic and I think also a natural psychologist. Whatever, he puts me at ease before facing what can be a rather trying experience.

(I should point out here that it's not always bad. If the collaborator has talent and training and a pleasant disposition, it can be as refreshing as dancing with a skilled partner.)

The others showed up on time and we got down to business. An anteroom off my studio has two parallel examining tables. Segura and I stripped and lay down and were injected with six hours' worth of buffer. M&M glued the induction electrodes to the proper places on our shaven heads. The doctor looked at them, signed a piece of paper and left. Then M&M, with Allison's assistance, rolled the loose skinsuits over us, sealed them and pumped the air out.

Segura and I woke up at the same instant M&M turned on the microcurrent that initiated the process. It's like being puppet and puppeteer simultaneously. I saw through Segura's eyes. His body sat me up, slid me to the floor and walked me into the studio. He perched me on a stool in front of the nearly horizontal easel and the mirror. Then I took over.

If you were watching us work, you would see two men sitting side by side, engaged in what looks like a painstakingly overpracticed mime routine. If one of us scratches his ear, the other one does. But from the inside it is more complicated: We exchange control second by second. This is why not every good artist can be a good facilitator. You have to have an instinct for when to assert your judgment, your skills, and let the client be in control otherwise. It is literally a thousand decisions per hour for six hours. It's exhausting. I earn my fee.

My initial idea was, in compositional terms, similar to what our nude would be—a realistic face in harsh light glowing in front of an indistinct background. There wouldn't be time to paint in background details, of course.

I made a light drawing of the head and shoulders, taking most of an hour. Then I took a chisel brush and carefully painted in the outlines of the drawing with frisket, a compound like rubber cement. You can paint over it and, when the paint dries, rub it off with an eraser or your fingertip, exposing the paper and the drawing underneath.

When the frisket was dry, I mopped the entire painting with clear water and then made an inky wash out of burnt umber and French ultramarine. I worked the wash over the whole painting and, while it was still damp, floated in diffuse shapes of umber and ultramarine that would hint at shadowy background. Then I buzzed Allison in to dry it while I/we walked around, loosening up. She came in with a hair dryer and worked over the wet paper carefully, uniformly, while I didn't watch. Sometimes a dramatic background wash just doesn't work when it dries—looks obvious or cheesy or dull—and there is never any way to fix it. (Maybe you could soak the paper overnight, removing most of the pigment. Better to just start over, though.)

I walked Segura across to the bay window and looked out over the city. The snow that remained on the shaded part of rooftops was gray or black. Traffic crawled in the thin bright light. Pedestrians hurried through the wind and slush.

Segura's body wanted a cigarette and I allowed him to walk me over to his clothes and light one up. The narcotic rush was disorienting. I had to lean us against a wall to keep from staggering. It was not unpleasant, though, once I surrendered control to him. No need for me to dominate motor responses until we had brush in hand.

Allison said the wash was ready and looked good. It did—vague, gloomy shapes suggesting a prison or asylum cell. I rolled up a kneaded eraser and carefully rubbed away the frisket. The light pencil drawing floated over the darkness like a disembodied thought.

I had to apply frisket again, this time in a halo around the drawing, and there was a minor setback: I'd neglected to put the frisket brush into solvent, and the bristles had dried into a solid, useless block. I surprised myself by throwing it across the room. That was Segura acting.

I found another square brush and carefully worked a thin frisket mask around the head and shoulders, to keep the dark background from bleeding in, but had to stop several times and lift up the brush because my hand was trembling with Segura's suppressed anger at the mistake. Relax, it was a cheap brush. You must be hell on wheels to work for.

First a dilute yellow wash, new gamboge, over the entire face. I picked up the hair dryer and used it for six or seven minutes, making sure the wash was bone-dry, meanwhile planning the next couple of stages.

This technique—glazing—consists of building up a picture with layer upon layer of dilute paint. It takes patience and precision and judgment: Sometimes you want the previous layer to be completely dry, and sometimes you want it damp, to diffuse the lines between the two colors. If it's too damp, you risk muddying the colors, which can be irreversible and fatal. But that's one thing that attracts me to the technique—the challenge of gambling everything on the timing of one stroke of the brush.

Segura obviously felt otherwise. Odd for a man who essentially gambled for a living, albeit with other people's money. He wanted each layer safely dry before proceeding with the next, once he understood what I was doing. That's a technique, but it's not *my* technique, which is what he was paying for. It would also turn this portrait, distorted as it was, into a clown's mask.

So I pushed back a little, establishing my authority, so to speak. I didn't want this to become a contest of wills. I just wanted control over the hair dryer, actually, not over Juan Carlos Segura.

There was a slight battle, lasting only seconds. It's hard to describe the sensation to someone who hasn't used a facilitator. It's something like being annoyed at yourself for not being able to make up your mind, but rather intensi-fied—"being of two minds," literally.

Of course, I won the contest, having about ten thousand times more experience at it than Segura. I set down the hair dryer, and the next layer, defining the hollows of the face visible through the skinsuit, went on with soft edges. I checked the mirror and automatically noted the places I would come back to later when the paper was dry, to make actual lines, defining the bottom of the goggle ridges, the top of the lip, the forward part of the ear mass.

The portrait was finished in two hours, but the background still needed something. Pursuing a vague memory from a week before, I flipped through a book of Matthew Brady photographs, visions of the Civil War's hell. Our face in the skinsuit resembled those of some corpses, open-mouthed, staring. I found the background I wanted, a ruined tumble of brick wall, and took the book back to the easel. I worked an intimation of the wall into the background, dry-brushing umber and ultramarine with speckles and threads of clotted blood color, alizarin muted with raw umber. Then I dropped the brushes into water and looked away, buzzing M&M. I didn't want to see the painting again until I saw it with my own eyes.

Coming out of the facilitation state takes longer than going in, especially if you don't go the full six hours. The remaining buffer has to be neutralized with a series of timed shots. Otherwise, Segura and I would hardly have been able to walk, expecting the collaboration of another brain that was no longer there.

I was up and around a few minutes before Segura. Allison had set out some cheese and fruit and an ice bucket with a bottle of white burgundy. I was hungry, as always, but only nibbled a bit, waiting for lunch.

Segura attacked the food like a starved animal. "What do you think?" he said between bites. "Is it any good?"

"Always hard to tell while you're working. Let's take a look." I buzzed Allison and she brought the painting in. She'd done a good job, as usual, the painting set off in a double mat of brick red and forest green inside a black metal frame.

"It does look good," he said, as if surprised.

I nodded and sipped wine, studying it. The painting was technically good, but it would probably hang in a gallery for years, gathering nervous compliments, before anybody bought it. It was profoundly ugly, a portrait of brutality. The skinsuit seemed to be straining to contain a mask of rage. Something truly sick burned behind the eyes.

He propped it up on the couch and walked back and forth, admiring it from various angles. For a moment I hoped he would say, "This will do fine; forget about the nude." I didn't look forward to three weeks of his intimate company.

"It captures something," he said, grinning. "I could use it to intimidate clients."

"The style suits you?"

"Yes. Yes, indeed." He looked at me with a sort of squint. "I vaguely remember fighting over some aspect of it."

"Technical matter. I prevailed, of course—that's what you pay me for."

He nodded slowly. "Well. I'll see you in George Town, then." He offered his hand, dry and hot.

"Friday morning. I'll be at the Hilton." Allison put the painting into a leather portfolio and ushered him out.

She came back in with a color photocopy of it. "Sick puppy."

I examined the picture, nodding. "There's some talent here, though. A lot of artists are sick puppies."

"Present company excluded. Lunch?"

"Not today. Got a date."

"Harry?"

"He's out of town. Guy I met at the gym."

She arched an eyebrow at me. "Young and cute."

"Younger than you," I said. "Big nose, though."

"Yeah, nose." She poured herself a glass and refilled mine. "So you won't be back after lunch?"

"Depends."

"Well, I'll be back around two, if you need anything." She headed for her office. "Happy hose."

"Nose, damn it!" She laughed and whispered the door shut behind her.

I carried my wine over to the window. The icy wind was audible through the double-pane glass. The people on the sidewalk hurried, hunched over against the gale. Tomorrow I'd be lying on snow-white sand, swimming in blood-warm water. A few days of sunshine before Segura showed up. I drank the wine and shivered.

In the 18th century, George III was sailing in the Caribbean when a sudden storm, probably a hurricane, smashed his ship to pieces. Fishermen from one of the Caymans braved the storm to go out and pick up survivors. Saved from what he'd thought would be certain death, King George expressed his royal gratitude by declaring that no resident of the islands would ever have to pay taxes to the British crown for the rest of eternity.

So where other Caribbean islands have craft shops and laid-back bars, George Town has high-rise banks and insurance buildings. A lot of expatriate Brits and Americans live and work there, doing business by satellite bounce.

I have a bank account in George Town myself, and may retire there someday. For this time of my life, it's too peaceful, except for the odd hurricane. I need Manhattan's garish excitement, the constant input, the dangerous edge.

But it's good to get away. The beach is an ideal place for quick figure sketches, so I loosened up for the commission by filling a notebook with pictures of women as they walked by or played in the sand and water. Drawing forces you to see, so for the first time I was aware that the beauty of the native black women was fundamentally different from that of the tourists, white or black. It was mainly a matter of posture and expression, dignified and detached. The tourist women were always to some extent posing, even at their most casual. Which I think was the nature of the place, rather than some characteristic female vanity. I normally pay much closer attention to men, and believe me, we corner the market on that small vice.

My staff came down on Thursday. M&M tore off into town to find out whether either of his girlfriends had learned about the other. Allison joined me on the beach.

Impressive as she is in office clothes, Allison is spectacular out of them. She has never tanned; her skin is like ivory. Thousands of hours in the gym have given her the sharply defined musculature of a classical statue. She wore a black leather string bikini that revealed everything not absolutely necessary for reproduction or lactation. But I don't think most straight men would characterize her as sexy. She was too formidable. That was all right with Allison, since she almost never was physically attracted to any man shorter or less well built than she. That dismissed all but a tenth of one percent of the male race. She had yet to find an Einstein, or even a Schwarzenegger, among the qualifiers. They usually turned out to be gentle but self-absorbed, predictably, and sometimes more interested in me than her. The message light was on when we got back to the hotel; both Rhonda Speck and Segura had arrived. It wasn't quite ten, but we agreed it was too late to return their calls, and retired.

* * *

I set up the pose and lighting before we went under, explaining to Rhonda exactly what we were after. Segura was silent, watching. I took longer than necessary, messing with the blinds and the rheostats I'd put on the two light sources. I wanted Segura to get used to Rhonda's nudity. He was obviously as straight as a plank, and we didn't want the painting to reveal any sexual curiosity or desire. Rhonda was only slightly more sexy than a mackerel, but you could never tell.

For the same reason, I didn't want to start the actual painting the first day. We'd start with a series of charcoal roughs. I explained to Segura about negative spaces and how important it was to establish balance between the light and dark. That was something I'd already worked out, of course. I just wanted him to stare at Rhonda long enough to become bored with the idea.

It didn't quite work out that way.

We didn't need a doctor's certification in George Town, so the setting up took a little less time. Artist and client lock-stepped into the office where Rhonda waited, studying the pages of notes stacked neatly on her desk.

There were two piano stools with identical newsprint pads and boxes of charcoal sticks. The idea was to sketch her from eight or ten slightly different angles, Segura moving around her in a small arc while I worked just behind him, looking over his shoulder. Theoretically, I could be anywhere, even in another room, since I was seeing her through his eyes. But it seems to work better this way, especially with a model.

The sketches had a lot of energy—so much energy that Segura actually tore through the paper a few times, blocking out the darkness around the seated figure. I got excited myself, and not just by feedback from Segura. The negative-space exercise is just that, an art school formalism, but Segura didn't know that. The result came close to being actual art.

I showed him that after we came out of the buffer. The sketches were good, strong abstractions. You could turn them upside down or sideways, retaining symmetry while obliterating text, and they still worked well.

I had a nascent artist on my hands. Segura had real native talent. That didn't often come my way. The combination could produce a painting of some value, one that I wouldn't have been able to do by myself. If things worked out.

Allison and I took the boat out after lunch—or rather, Allison took the boat out with me as ballast, baking inertly under a heavy coat of total sun block. (She and I are almost equally pale, and that's not all we have in common; I'm also nearly as well-muscled. We met at the weight machines in a Broadway gym.) She sailed and I watched billowing clouds form abstract patterns in the impossible cobalt sky. The soothing sounds of the boat lulled me to sleep—the keel slipping through warm water, the lines creaking, the ruffle of the sails.

She woke me to help her bring it back in. There was a cool mist of rain that became intermittently heavy. A couple of miles from shore we started to see lightning, so we struck sail and revved up the little motor and drove straight in, prudence conquering seamanship.

We dried off at the marina bar and drank hot chocolate laced with rum, watching a squall line roll across land and water, feeling lucky to be inside.

"Photography tomorrow?" she asked.

"Yeah. And then drawing, drawing, drawing."

"The part you like best."

"Oh, yes." Actually, I halfway do like it, the way an athlete can enjoy warming up, in expectation of the actual event.

The next morning I set up the cameras before we went into the skinsuits. The main one was a fairly complex and delicate piece of equipment, an antique 8 × 10 view camera that took hairline-accurate black-and-white negatives. I could have accomplished the same thing with a modern large-format camera, but I liked the smooth working of the gears, the smell of the oak and leather, the sense of contact with an earlier, less hurried age. The paradox of combining the technology of that age with ours.

The other camera was a medium-format Polaroid. Buffered and suited, I led Segura through the arcane art and science of tweaking lights, model, f-stop and exposure to produce a subtle spectrum of prints: a sequence of 98 slightly different, and profoundly different, pictures of one woman. We studied the pictures and her and finally decided on the right combination. I set up the antique 8 × 10 and reproduced the lighting. We focused it with his somewhat younger eyes and took three slightly different exposures.

Then we took the film into the darkroom that M&M had improvised in the firm's executive washroom. We developed each sheet in Rodinal, fixed and washed them and hung them up weighted to dry.

We left the darkroom and spent a few minutes smoking, studying Rhonda as she studied her law. I told her she was free for three days and that she should show up Thursday morning. She nodded curtly and left, resentful.

Her annoyance was understandable. She'd been sitting there naked for all that time we were playing in the darkroom. I should have dismissed her when we finished shooting.

We lit up another cigarette and I realized that it wasn't I who had kept her waiting. It was Segura. I'd started to tell her to go and then he manufactured a little crisis that led straight to the darkroom. From then on I hadn't thought of the woman except as a reversed ghost appearing in the developer tray.

Under the circumstances, it wasn't a bad thing to have her hostile toward us, if we could capture the hostility on paper. But it goes against my grain to mistreat an employee, even a temporary one.

We examined each of the negatives on a lightbox with a loupe, then took the best one back into the darkroom for printing. Plain contact prints on finest-grain paper. The third one was perfect: rich and stark, almost scary in its knife-edge sharpness. You could see one bleached hair standing out from her left nipple.

That was enough work for the day; in fact, we'd gone slightly over the six-hour limit, and both of us were starting to get headaches and cramps. Another half-hour and it would be double vision and tremors. More than that—though I'd never experienced it—you wind up mentally confused, the two minds still linked electrically but no longer cooperating. Some poor guinea pigs took it as far as convulsions or catatonia, back when the buffer drug was first being developed.

M&M eased us out of it and helped us down to a taxi. It was only five blocks to the hotel, but neither of us was feeling particularly athletic. For some reason the buffer hangover hits people like me, in very good shape, particularly hard. Segura was flabby, but he had less trouble getting out of the car.

Back in the room, I pulled the blackout blinds over the windows and collapsed, desperately hungry but too tired to do anything about it except dream of food.

Allison had set up the paper, one large sheet of handmade hot-pressed 400-pound rag, soaking it overnight and then taping it down, giving it plenty of time to dry completely. That sheet of paper, the one Segura would be drawing on, cost more than some gallery paintings. The sheet I'd be working on was just paper, with a similar tooth.

We had set up two drawing tables with their boards at identical angles, mine a little higher, since I have a larger frame. An opaque projector mounted above Segura shot a duplicate of yesterday's photo onto the expensive paper. Our job for the next three days was to execute an accurate but ghost-light tracing of the picture, which would be gently erased after the painting was done.

Some so-called photo-realists bypass this step with a combination of photography and xerography—make a high-contrast print and then impress a light photocopy of it onto watercolor paper. That makes their job a high-salaried kind of paint-by-numbers. Doing the actual underdrawing puts you well ''into'' the painting before the first brush is wet.

We both sat down and went to work, starting with the uniformly bound law books on the shelves behind Rhonda. It was an unchallenging, repetitive subject to occupy us while we got used to doing this kind of labor together.

For a few minutes we worked on a scrap piece of paper, until I was absolutely confident of his eye and hand. Then we started on the real thing.

After five grueling hours we had completed about a third of the background, an area half the size of a newspaper page. I was well pleased with that progress; working by myself I would have done little more.

Segura was not so happy. In the taxi, he cradled his right hand and stared at it, the wrist quivering, the thumb frankly twitching. ''How can I possibly keep this up?'' he said. ''I won't even be able to pick up a pencil tomorrow.''

I held out my own hand and wrist, steady, muscular. ''But I will. That's all that counts.''

''It could permanently damage my hand.''

''Never happened.'' Of course, I'd never worked with anyone for three weeks. ''Go to that masseur, the man whose card I gave you. He'll make your hand as good as new. Do you still have the card?''

''Oh, yeah.'' He shifted uncomfortably. ''I don't mean to be personal, or offensive. But is this man gay? I would have trouble with that.''

''I wouldn't know. We don't have little badges or a secret handshake.'' He didn't laugh, but he looked less grim. ''My relationship with him is professional. I wouldn't know whether or not he is gay.'' Actually, since our professional relationship included orgasm, if he wasn't gay, he was quite a Method actor.

But I assumed he would divine Segura's orientation as quickly as I had. A masseur ought to have a feel for his clients.

The next day went a lot better. Like myself, Segura was heartened by the sight of the previous day's careful work outline. We worked faster and with equal care, finishing all of the drawing except for the woman and the things on the desk in front of her.

It was on the third day that I had the first inkling of trouble. Working on the image of Rhonda, Segura wanted to bear down too hard. That could be disastrous; if the pencil point actually broke the fibers of paper along a line, it could never be completely erased. You can't have outlines in this kind of painting, just sharply defined masses perfectly joining other sharply defined masses. A pencil line might as well be an inkblot.

I thought the pressure was because of simple muscular fatigue. Segura was not in good physical shape. His normal workday comprised six hours in conference and six hours talking on the phone or dictating correspondence. He took a perverse pride in not even being able to keyboard. He never lifted anything heavier than a cigarette.

People who think art isn't physically demanding ought to try to sit in one position for six hours, brush or pencil in hand, staring at something or someone and trying to transfer its essence to a piece of paper or canvas. Even an athletic person leaves that arena with aches and twinges. A couch potato like Segura can't even walk away without help.

He never complained, though, other than expressing concern that his fatigue might interfere with the project. I reassured him. In fact, I had once completed a successful piece with a quadriplegic so frail he couldn't sign his name the same way twice. We taught ourselves how to hold the brush in our teeth.

It was a breathtaking moment when we turned off the overhead projector for the last time. The finished drawing floated on the paper, an exquisite ghost of what the painting would become. Through Segura's eyes I stared at it hungrily for 15 or 20 minutes, mapping out strategies of frisket and mask, in my mind's eye seeing the paper glow through layer after careful layer of glaze. It would be perfect.

Rhonda wasn't in a great mood, coming back to sit after three days on her own, but even she seemed to share our excitement when she saw the underdrawing. It made the project real.

The first step was to paint a careful frisket over her figure, as well as the chair, the lamp and the table with its clutter. That took an hour, since the figure was more than a foot high on the paper. I also masked out reflections on a vase and the glass front of a bookcase.

I realized it would be good to start the curtains with a thin wash of Payne's gray, which is not a color I normally keep on my palette, so I gave Rhonda a five-minute break while I rummaged for it. She put on a robe and walked over to the painting and gasped. We heard her across the room.

I looked over and saw what had distressed her. The beautifully detailed picture of her body had been blotted out with gray frisket, and it did look weird. She was a nonbeing, a featureless negative space hovering in the middle of an almost photographic depiction of a room. All three of us laughed at her reaction. I started to explain, but she knew about frisketing; it had just taken her by surprise.

Even the best facilitators have moments of confusion, when their client's emotional reaction to a situation is totally at odds with their own. This was one of those times: My reaction to Rhonda's startled response was a kind of ironic empathy, but Segura's reaction was malicious glee.

I could see that he disliked Rhonda at a very deep level. What I didn't see (although Allison had known from the first day) was that it wasn't just Rhonda. It was women in general.

I've always liked women myself, even though I've known since 13 or 14 that I would never desire them. It's pernicious to generalize, but I think that my friendships with women have usually been deeper and more honest than they would have been had I been straight. A straight man can simply like a woman and desire her friendship, but there's always a molecule or two of testosterone buzzing between them, if they are both of an age and social situation where sex might be a possibility, however remote. I have to handle that complication with some men whom I know or suspect are gay, even when I feel no particular attraction toward them.

The drawing had gone approximately from upper left to lower right, then back to the middle for the figure, but the painting would have to proceed in a less straightforward way. You work all over the painting at once: a layer of rose madder on the spines of one set of books and on the shady side of the vase and on two of the flowers. You need a complete mental picture of the finished painting so you can predict the sequence of glazes, sometimes covering up areas with frisket or, when there were straight lines, with drafting tape. The paper was dry, though, so it was usually just a matter of careful brushwork—pathologically careful: You can't erase paint.

Of course, Rhonda had to sit even though for the first week her image would be hidden behind frisket. Her skin tones affected the colors of everything else. Her emotional presence affected the background. And Segura's feeling toward her "colored" the painting, literally.

The work went smoothly. It was a good thing Segura had suggested the trial painting; we'd been able to talk over the necessity for occasional boldness and spontaneity, to keep the painting from becoming an exercise in careful draftsmanship. Especially with this dark, sinister background, we often had to work glazes wet-into-wet. Making details soft and diffuse at the periphery of a painting can render it more realistic rather than less. Our own eyes see the world with precision only in a surprisingly small area around the thing that has our attention. The rest is blur, more or less ignored. (The part of the mind that is not ignoring the background is the animal part that waits for a sudden movement or noise; a painting can derive tension from that.)

Segura and I worked so well together that it was going to cost me money; the painting would be complete in closer to two weeks than three. When I mentioned this he said not to worry; if the painting was good, he'd pay the second million regardless of the amount of time (he'd paid a million down before we left New York), and he was sure the painting would be good.

Of course, there was arithmetic involved there, as well as art. *Fortune* listed his income last year as $98 million. He probably wanted to get back to his quarter-million-a-day telephone.

So the total time from photography to finished background was only 11 days, and I was sure we could do the figure and face in a day. We still had a couple of hours' buffer left when we removed the frisket, but I decided to stop at that point. We studied her for an hour or so, sketching.

The sketches were accurate, but in a way they were almost caricatures, angular, hostile. As art, they were not bad, though like Segura's initial self-portrait, they were fundamentally, intentionally ugly. I could feel Manet's careful brush and sardonic eye here: How can a well-shaped breast or the lush curve of a hip be both beautiful and ugly? Cover the dark, dagger-staring face of *Olympia* and drink in the lovely body. Then uncover the face.

That quality would be submerged in the final painting. It would be a beautiful picture, dramatic but exquisitely balanced. The hatred of women there but concealed, like an underpainting.

It was a great physical relief to be nearing the end. I'd never facilitated for more than five days in a row, and the skinsuit was becoming repulsive to me. I was earning my long vacation.

That night I watched bad movies and drank too much. The morning was brilliant, but I was not. M&M injected me with a cocktail of vitamins and speed that burned away the hangover. I knew I'd come down hard by nightfall, but the painting would be done long before then.

Segura was jittery, snappish, as we prepared for the last day. Maybe M&M gave him a little something along with the buffer, to calm him down. Maybe it wasn't a good idea.

Rhonda was weird that morning, too, with good reason. She was finally the focus of our attention and she played her part well. Her concentration on us was ferocious, her contempt palpable.

I dabbed frisket on a few highlights—collarbone, breast, eye and that glossy hair—and then put in a pale flesh-colored wash over everything, cadmium-yellow light with a speck of rose. While it dried, we smoked a cigarette and stared at her. Rhonda had made it clear that she didn't like smoke, and we normally went into another room or at least stood by an open window. Not today, though.

I had a little difficulty controlling Segura: He was mesmerized by her face and kept wanting to go back to it. But it doesn't work that way: the glazes go on in a particular order, one color at various places on the body all at once. If you finished the face and then worked your way down, the skin tones wouldn't quite match. And there was actual loathing behind his obsession with her face, something close to nausea.

That feeling fed his natural amateurish desire to speed up, just to find out what the picture was going to look like. In retrospect, I wonder whether there might have been something sinister about that, as well.

It was obvious that the face and figure would take longer than I had planned, maybe half again as long, with so much of my attention going into hauling in on the reins. His impatience would cost us an extra day in the skinsuits, which annoyed me and further slowed us down.

Here I have to admit to a lack of empathy, which for a facilitator is tantamount to a truck driver admitting to falling asleep at the wheel. My own revulsion at having to spend another day confined in plastic masked what Segura was feeling about his own confinement. I was not alert. I had lost some of my professional control. I didn't see where his disgust was leading him, leading us.

This is hindsight again: One of the talents that Segura translated into millions of dollars was an ability to hide his emotions, to make people misread him. This was not something he had to project: he did it automatically, the way a pathological liar will lie even when there is nothing at stake. The misogyny that seemed to flood his attitude toward the painting—and Rhonda—was only a small fraction of what he must have actually felt, emotions amplified by the buffer drug and empath circuitry. Some woman must have hurt him profoundly, repeatedly, when he was a child. Maybe that's just amateur psychology. I don't think so. If it had a sexual component, it would have felt quite different, and I would have instantly picked up on it. His hate was more primitive, inchoate.

I knew already that Segura was the kind of person who tightens up during facilitation, which was a relief; they're easier to work with. Doubly a relief with Segura, since from the beginning I felt I didn't want to know him all that well.

I might have prevented it by quitting early. But I wanted to do all the light passages and then start the next day with a fresh palette, loaded with dark. Perhaps I also wanted to punish Segura, or push him.

The actions were simple, if the motivations were not. We had gone 20 minutes past the six-hour mark and had perhaps another half hour to go. I had an annoying headache, not bad enough to make me quit. I assumed Segura felt the same.

Every now and then we approached Rhonda to adjust her pose. Only a mannequin could retain exactly the same posture all day. Her chin had fallen slightly. Segura got up and walked toward her.

I don't remember feeling his hand slip out and pick up the large wash brush, one that we hadn't used since the first day. Its handle is a stick of hardwood that is almost an inch in diameter, ending in a sharp bevel. I never thought of it as a weapon.

He touched her chin with his left forefinger and she tilted her head up, closing her eyes. Then with all his strength he drove the sharp stick into her chest.

The blast of rage hit me without warning. I fell backward off the stool and struck my head. It didn't knock me out, but I was stunned, disoriented. I heard Rhonda's scream, which became a horrible series of liquid coughs, and heard the paper and desk accessories scattering as (we later reconstructed) she lurched forward and Segura pushed her face down onto the desk. Then there were three meaty sounds as he punched her repeatedly in the back with the handle of the brush.

About this time M&M and Allison came rushing through the door. I don't know what Allison did, other than not scream. M&M pulled Segura off Rhonda's body, a powerful forearm scissored across his throat, cutting off his wind.

I couldn't breathe either, of course. I started flopping around, gagging, and M&M yelled for Allison to unhook me. She turned me over and ripped off the top part of the skinsuit and jerked the electrodes free.

Then I could breathe, but little else. I heard the quiet struggle between M&M and Segura, the one-sided execution.

Allison carried me into the prep room and completed the procedure that M&M normally did, stripping off the skinsuit and giving me the shot. In about ten minutes I was able to dress myself and go back into the office.

M&M had laid out Rhonda's body on a printer's dropsheet, facedown in a shockingly large pool of blood. He had cleaned the blood off the desk and was waxing it. The lemon varnish smell didn't mask the smell of freshly butchered meat.

Segura lay where he had been dropped, his limbs at odd angles, his face bluish behind the skinsuit mask.

Allison sat on the couch, motionless, prim, impossibly pale. "What now?" she said softly. M&M looked up and raised his eyebrows.

I thought. "One thing we have to agree on before we leave this room," I said, "is whether we go to the police or . . . take care of it ourselves."

"The publicity would be terrible." Allison said.

"They also might hang us." M&M said, "if they do that here."

"Let's not find out," I said, and outlined my plan to them.

It took a certain amount of money. It was a good thing I had the million in advance. We staged a tragic accident, transferring both of their bodies to a small boat whose inboard motor leaked gasoline. They were less than a mile from shore when thousands saw the huge blossom of flame light up the night, and before rescuers could reach the hulk, the fire had consumed it nearly to the waterline. Burned almost beyond recognition, the "artist" and his model lay in a final embrace.

I finished the face of the picture myself. A look of pleasant surprise, mischievousness. The posture that was to have communicated hardness was transformed into that of a woman galvanized by surprise, perhaps expectation.

We gave it to Segura's family, along with the story we'd given to the press: Crusty financier falls in love with young law student/model. It was an unlikely story to anyone who knew Segura well, but the people who knew him well were busy scrambling after his fortune. His sister put the picture up for auction in two weeks, and since its notoriety hadn't faded, it brought her $2.2 million.

There's nothing like a good love story that ends in tragedy.

Back in New York, I looked at my situation and decided I could afford to quit. I gave Allison and M&M generous severance pay, and what I got for the studio paid for even nicer places in Maine and Key West.

I sold the facilitating equipment and have since devoted myself to pure water colors and photography. People understood. This latest tragedy on top of the grotesque experience with the Monster.

But I downplayed that angle. I wanted to do my own work. I was tired of collaboration, and especially tired of the skinsuit. The thousand decisions every hour, in and out of control.

You never know whose hand is picking up the brush.

LIESERL

Stephen Baxter

▼

Stephen Baxter is another of those young British writers such as Paul J. McAuley, Iain Banks, Gwyneth Jones, Ian McDonald, Ian R. MacLeod, and Greg Egan (actually an Australian, but that's Close Enough for Government Work, as they say) who are busily revitalizing the "hard-science" story here at the beginning of the nineties (in parallel, one should add, with American counterparts such as Michael Swanwick, Bruce Sterling, Pat Cadigan, and Greg Bear, and along with older but revitalized writers such as Brian Stableford, Vernor Vinge, and Ian Watson). Like most of the writers mentioned above, Baxter often works on the cutting edge of science—his work bristles with weird new ideas, and often takes place against vistas of almost outrageously cosmic scope . . . but he usually succeeds in balancing conceptualization with storytelling, and rarely forgets the *human* side of the equation.

This balancing act is displayed beautifully in "Lieserl," which introduces us to one of the strangest and most haunting characters you're ever likely to meet. . . .

Stephen Baxter has become one of *Interzone*'s most frequent contributors since making his first sale there in 1987, and he has also made sales to *Asimov's Science Fiction, Zenith, New Worlds*, and elsewhere. His first novel, *Raft*, was released in 1991 to wide and enthusiastic acclaim, and his second novel, *Timelike Infinity* was released in 1992 to similar response. His most recent book is a new novel, *Anti-Ice*.

Lieserl was suspended inside the body of the Sun.

She spread her arms wide and lifted up her face. She was deep within the Sun's convective zone, the broad mantle of turbulent material beneath the glowing protosphere; convective cells larger than the Earth, tangled with ropes of magnetic flux, filled the world around her. She could hear the roar of the great convective founts, smell the stale photons diffusing out towards space from the remote fusing core.

She felt as if she were inside some huge cavern. Looking up she could see how the photosphere formed a glowing roof over her world perhaps fifty thousand miles above her, and the boundary of the inner radiative zone was a shining, impenetrable floor another fifty thousand miles beneath.

Lieserl? Can you hear me? Are you all right?

The capcom. It sounded like her mother's voice, she thought.

She thrust her arms down by her sides and swooped up, letting the floor and roof of the cavern-world wheel around her. She opened up her senses, so that she could feel the turbulence as a whisper against her skin, the glow of hard photons from the core as a gentle warmth against her face.

Lieserl? Lieserl?

She remembered how her mother had enfolded her in her arms. "The Sun, Lieserl. *The Sun . . .*"

Even at the moment she was born she knew something was wrong.

A face loomed over her: wide, smooth, smiling. The cheeks were damp, the glistening eyes huge. "Lieserl. Oh, Lieserl . . ."

Lieserl. My name, then.

She explored the face before her, studying the lines around the eyes, the humorous upturn of the mouth, the strong nose. It was an intelligent, lived-in face. *This is a good human being*, she thought. *Good stock . . .*

Good stock? What am I thinking of?

This was impossible. She felt terrified of her own explosive consciousness. She shouldn't even be able to focus her eyes yet . . .

She tried to touch her mother's face. Her own hand was still moist with amniotic fluid—*but it was growing visibly*, the bones extending and broadening, filling out the loose skin like a glove.

She opened her mouth. It was dry, her gums already sore with budding teeth. She tried to speak.

Her mother's eyes brimmed with tears. "Oh, Lieserl. My impossible baby."

Strong arms reached beneath her. She felt weak, helpless, consumed by growth. Her mother lifted her up, high in the air. Bony adult fingers dug into the aching flesh of her back; her head lolled backwards, the expanding muscles still too weak to support the burgeoning weight of her head. She could sense other adults surrounding her, the bed in which she'd been born, the outlines of a room.

She was held before a window, with her body tipped forward. Her head lolled; spittle laced across her chin.

An immense light flooded her eyes.

She cried out.

Her mother enfolded her in her arms. "The Sun, Lieserl. *The Sun . . .*"

The first few days were the worst. Her parents—impossibly tall, looming figures—took her through brightly lit rooms, a garden always flooded with sunlight. She learned to sit up. The muscles in her back fanned out, pulsing as they grew. To distract her from the unending pain, clowns tumbled over the grass before her, chortling through their huge red lips, then popping out of existence in clouds of pixels.

She grew explosively, feeding all the time, a million impressions crowding into her soft sensorium.

There seemed to be no limit to the number of rooms in this place, this House. Slowly she began to understand that some of the rooms were Virtual chambers— blank screens against which any number of images could be projected. But even so, the House must comprise hundreds of rooms. And she—with her parents— wasn't alone here, she realized. There were other people, but at first they kept away, out of sight, apparent only by their actions: the meals they prepared, the toys they left her.

On the third day her parents took her on a trip by flitter. It was the first time she'd been away from the House, its grounds. She stared through the bulbous windows, pressing her nose to heated glass. The journey was an arc over a toylike landscape; a breast of blue ocean curved away from the land, all around her. This was the island of Skiros, her mother told her, and the sea was called the Aegean. The House was the largest construct on the island; it was a jumble of white, cube-shaped buildings, linked by corridors and surrounded by garden— grass, trees. Further out there were bridges and roads looping through the air above the ground, houses like a child's bricks sprinkled across glowing hillsides.

Everything was drenched in heavy, liquid sunlight.

The flitter snuggled at last against a grassy sward close to the shore of an ocean. Lieserl's mother lifted her out and placed her—on her stretching, unsteady legs—on the rough, sandy grass.

Hand in hand, the little family walked down a short slope to the beach.

The Sun burned through thinned air from an unbearably blue sky. Her vision seemed telescopic. She looked at distant groups of children and adults playing— far away, halfway to the horizon—and it was as if she was among them herself. Her feet, still uncertain, pressed into gritty, moist sand. She could taste the brine salt on the air; it seemed to permeate her very skin.

She found mussels clinging to a ruined pier. She prised them away with a toy spade, and gazed, fascinated, at their slime-dripping feet.

She sat on the sand with her parents, feeling her light costume stretch over her still-stretching limbs. They played a simple game, of counters moving over a floating Virtual board, pictures of ladders and hissing snakes. There was laughter, mock complaints by her father, elaborate pantomimes of cheating.

Her senses were electric. It was a wonderful day, full of light and joy, extraordinarily vivid sensations. Her parents loved her—she could see that in the way they moved with each other, came to her, played with her.

They must know she was different; but they didn't seem to care.

She didn't want to be different—to be *wrong*. She closed her mind against the thoughts, and concentrated on the snakes, the ladders, the sparkling counters.

Every morning she woke up in a bed that felt too small.

Lieserl liked the garden. She liked to watch the flowers straining their tiny, pretty faces towards the Sun, as the great light climbed patiently across the sky. The sunlight made the flowers grow, her father told her. Maybe she was like a flower, she thought, growing too quickly in all this sunlight.

On the fifth day she was taken to a wide, irregularly shaped, colourful classroom. This room was full of children—*other children*!—and toys, drawings, books. Sunlight flooded the room; perhaps there was some clear dome stretched over the open walls.

The children sat on the floor and played with paints and dolls, or talked earnestly to brilliantly coloured Virtual figures—smiling birds, tiny clowns. The children turned to watch as she came in with her mother, their faces round and bright, like dapples of sunlight through leaves. She'd never been so close to other children before. Were these children *different* too?

One small girl scowled at her, and Lieserl quailed against her mother's legs. But her mother's familiar warm hands pressed into her back. "Go ahead. It's all right."

As she stared at the unknown girl's scowling face, Lieserl's questions, her too-adult, too-sophisticated doubts, seemed to evaporate. Suddenly, all that mattered to her—all that mattered in the world—was that she should be accepted by these children—that they wouldn't know she was *different*.

An adult approached her: a man, young, thin, his features bland with youth. He wore a jumpsuit coloured a ludicrous orange; in the sunlight, the glow of it shone up over his chin. He smiled at her. "Lieserl, isn't it? My name's Michael. We're glad you're here." In a louder, exaggerated voice, he said, "Aren't we, people?"

He was answered by a rehearsed, chorused "Yes."

"Now come and we'll find something for you to do," Michael said. He led her across the child-littered floor to a space beside a small boy. The boy—red-haired, with startling blue eyes—was staring at a Virtual puppet which endlessly formed and reformed: the figure two, collapsing into two snowflakes, two swans, two dancing children; the figure three, followed by three bears, three fish swimming in the air, three cakes. The boy mouthed the numbers, following the tinny voice of the Virtual. "Two. One. Two and one is three."

Michael introduced her to the boy—Tommy—and she sat down with him. Tommy, she was relieved to find, was so fascinated by his Virtual that he scarcely seemed aware that Lieserl was present—let alone *different*.

The number Virtual ran through its cycle and winked out of existence. "Bye bye, Tommy! Goodbye, Lieserl!"

Tommy was resting on his stomach, his chin cupped in his palms. Lieserl, awkwardly, copied his posture. Now Tommy turned to her—without appraisal, merely looking at her, with unconscious acceptance.

Lieserl said, "Can we see it again?"

He yawned and poked a finger into one nostril. "No. Let's see another. There's a great one about the preCambrian explosion—"

"The what?"

He waved a hand dismissively. "You know, the Burgess Shale and all that. Wait till you see *Hallucigenia* crawling over your neck . . ."

The children played, and learned, and napped. Later, the girl who'd scowled at Lieserl—Ginnie—started some trouble. She poked fun at the way Lieserl's bony wrists stuck out of her sleeves (Lieserl's growth rate was slowing, but she was still growing out of her clothes during a day). Then—unexpectedly, astonishingly—Ginnie started to bawl, claiming that Lieserl had walked through her Virtual. When Michael came over Lieserl started to explain, calmly and rationally, that Ginnie must be mistaken; but Michael told her not to cause such distress, and for punishment she was forced to sit away from the other children for ten minutes, without stimulation.

It was all desperately, savagely unfair. It was the longest ten minutes of Lieserl's life. She glowered at Ginnie, filled with resentment.

The next day she found herself looking forward to going to the room with the children again. She set off with her mother through sunlit corridors. They reached the room Lieserl remembered—there was Michael, smiling a little wistfully to her, and Tommy, and the girl Ginnie—but Ginnie seemed different: childlike, unformed . . .

At least a head shorter than Lieserl.

Lieserl tried to recapture that delicious enmity of the day before, but it vanished even as she conjured it. Ginnie was just a kid.

She felt as if something had been stolen from her.

Her mother squeezed her hand. "Come on. Let's find a new room for you to play in."

Every day was unique. Every day Lieserl spent in a new place, with new people.

The world glowed with sunlight. Shining points trailed endlessly across the sky: low-orbit habitats and comet nuclei, tethered for power and fuel.

People walked through a sea of information, with access to the Virtual libraries available anywhere in the world at a subvocalized command. Lieserl learned quickly. She read about her parents. They were scientists, studying the Sun. They weren't alone; there were many people, huge resources, devoted to the Sun.

In the libraries there was a lot of material about the Sun, little of which she could follow. But she sensed some common threads.

Once, people had taken the Sun for granted. No longer. Now—for some reason—they *feared* it.

On the ninth day Lieserl studied herself in a Virtual holomirror. She had the image turn around, so she could see the shape of her skull, the lie of her hair. There was still some childish softness in her face, she thought, but the woman inside her was emerging already, as if her childhood was a receding tide. She would look like her mother—Phillida—in the strong-nosed set of her face, her large, vulnerable eyes; but she would have the sandy colouring of her father, George.

Lieserl looked about nine years old. But she was just nine *days* old.

She bade the Virtual break up; it shattered into a million tiny images of her face which drifted away like flies in the sunlit air.

Phillida and George were fine parents, she thought. They spent their time away from her working through technical papers—which scrolled through the air like falling leaves—and exploring elaborate, onion-ring Virtual models of stars. Although they were both clearly busy they gave themselves to her without hesitation. She moved in a happy world of smiles, sympathy and support.

Her parents loved her unreservedly. But that wasn't always enough.

She started to come up with more complicated, detailed questions. Like, what was the mechanism by which she was growing so rapidly? She didn't seem to eat more than the other children she encountered; what could be fueling her absurd growth rates?

How did she *know* so much? She'd been born self-aware, with even the rudiments of language in her head. The Virtuals she interacted with in the classrooms were fun, and she always seemed to learn something new; but she absorbed no more than scraps of knowledge through them compared to the feast of insight with which she awoke each morning.

What had taught her, in the womb? What was teaching her now?

She had no answers. But perhaps—somehow—it was all connected with this strange, global obsession with the Sun. She remembered her childish fantasy— that she might be like a flower, straining up too quickly to the Sun. Maybe, she wondered now, there was some grain of truth in that insight.

The strange little family had worked up some simple, homely rituals together. Lieserl's favourite was the game, each evening, of snakes and ladders. George brought home an old set—a *real* board made of card, and wooden counters. Already Lieserl was too old for the game; but she loved the company of her parents, her father's elaborate jokes, the simple challenge of the game, the feel of the worn, antique counters.

Phillida showed her how to use Virtuals to produce her own game boards. Her first efforts, on her eleventh day, were plain, neat forms, little more than copies of the commercial boards she'd seen. But she soon began to experiment. She drew a huge board of a million squares, which covered a whole room—she could walk through the board, a planar sheet of light at about waist height. She crammed the board with intricate, curling snakes, vast ladders, vibrantly glowing squares—detail piled on detail.

The next morning she walked with eagerness to the room where she'd built her board—and was immediately disappointed. Her efforts seemed pale, static, derivative—obviously the work of a child, despite the assistance of the Virtual software.

She wiped the board clean, leaving a grid of pale squares floating in the air. Then she started to populate it again—but this time with animated half-human snakes, slithering "ladders" of a hundred forms. She'd learned to access the Virtual libraries, and she plundered the art and history of a hundred centuries to populate her board.

Of course it was no longer possible to play games on the board, but that didn't matter. The board was the thing, a little world in itself. She withdrew a little from her parents, spending long hours in deep searches through the libraries. She gave up her classes. Her parents didn't seem to mind; they came to speak to her regularly, and showed an interest in her projects, and respected her privacy.

The board kept her interest the next day. But now she evolved elaborate games, dividing the board into countries and empires with arbitrary bands of glowing light. Armies of ladder-folk joined with legions of snakes in crude reproductions of the great events of human history.

She watched the symbols flicker across the Virtual board, shimmering, coalescing; she dictated lengthy chronicles of the histories of her imaginary countries.

By the end of the day, though, she was starting to grow more interested in the history texts she was plundering than in her own elaborations on them. She went to bed, eager for the next morning to come.

She awoke in darkness, doubled in agony.

She called for light, which flooded the room, sourceless. She sat up in bed.

Blood spotted the sheets. She screamed.

Phillida sat with her, cradling her head. Lieserl pressed herself against her mother's warmth, trying to still her trembling.

"I think it's time you asked me your questions."

Lieserl sniffed. "What questions?"

"The ones you've carried around with you since the moment you were born." Phillida smiled. "I could see it in your eyes, even at the moment. You poor thing . . . to be burdened with so much *awareness*. I'm sorry, Lieserl."

Lieserl pulled away. Suddenly she felt cold, vulnerable.

"Tell me why you're sorry," she said at last.

"You're my daughter." Phillida placed her hands on Lieserl's shoulders and pushed her face close; Lieserl could feel the warmth of her breath, and the soft room light caught the grey in her mother's blonde hair, making it seem to shine. "Never forget that. You're as human as I am. But—" She hesitated.

"But what?"

"But you're being—*engineered.*"

Nanobots swarmed through Lieserl's body, Phillida said. They plated calcium over her bones, stimulated the generation of new cells, force-growing her body like some absurd sunflower—they even implanted memories, artificial learning, directly into her cortex.

Lieserl felt like scraping at her skin, gouging out this artificial infection. "*Why?* Why did you let this be done to me?"

Phillida pulled her close, but Lieserl stayed stiff, resisting mutely. Phillida buried her face in Lieserl's hair; Lieserl felt the soft weight of her mother's cheek on the crown of her head. "Not yet," Phillida said. "Not yet. A few more days, my love. That's all . . ."

Phillida's cheeks grew warmer, as if she was crying, silently, into her daughter's hair.

Lieserl returned to her snakes and ladders board. She found herself looking on her creation with affection, but also nostalgic sadness; she felt distant from this elaborate, slightly obsessive concoction.

Already she'd outgrown it.

She walked into the middle of the sparkling board and bade the Sun, a foot wide, rise out from the centre of her body. Light swamped the board, shattering it.

She wasn't the only adolescent who had constructed fantasy worlds like this. She read about the Brontës, in their lonely parsonage in the north of England, and their elaborate shared world of kings and princes and empires. And she read about the history of the humble game of snakes and ladders. The game had come from India, where it was a morality teaching aid called *Moksha-Patamu*. There were twelve vices and four virtues, and the objective was to get to Nirvana. It was easier to fail than to succeed . . . The British in the 19th century had adopted it as an instructional guide for children called *Kismet*; Lieserl stared at images of claustrophobic boards, forbidding snakes. Thirteen snakes and eight ladders showed children that if they were good and obedient their life would be rewarded.

But by a few decades later the game had lost its moral subtexts. Lieserl found images from the early 20th century of a sad-looking little clown; he slithered haplessly down snakes and heroically clambered up ladders. Lieserl stared at him, trying to understand the appeal of his baggy trousers, walking cane and little moustache.

The game, with its charm and simplicity, had survived through the 20 centuries which had worn away since the death of that forgotten clown.

She grew interested in the *numbers* embedded in the various versions of the game. The twelve-to-four ratio of *Moksha-Patamu* clearly made it a harder game to win than *Kismet's* thirteen-to-eight—but how much harder?

She began to draw new boards in the air. But these boards were abstractions— clean, colourless, little more than sketches. She ran through high-speed simulated games, studying their outcomes. She experimented with ratios of snakes to ladders, with their placement. Phillida sat with her and introduced her to combinatorial mathematics, the theory of games—to different forms of wonder.

On her 15th day she tired of her own company and started to attend classes again. She found the perceptions of others a refreshing counterpoint to her own high-speed learning.

The world seemed to open up around her like a flower; it was a world full of sunlight, of endless avenues of information, of stimulating people.

She read up on nanobots.

Body cells were programmed to commit suicide. A cell itself manufactured enzymes which cut its DNA into neat pieces, and quietly closed down. The suicide of cells was a guard against uncontrolled growth—tumours—and a tool to sculpt the developing body: in the womb, the withering of unwanted cells carved fingers and toes from blunt tissue buds.

Death was the default of a cell. Chemical signals were sent by the body, to instruct cells to remain alive.

The nanotechnological manipulation of this process made immortality simple. It also made the manufacture of a Lieserl simple.

Lieserl studied this, scratching absently at her inhabited, engineered arms. She still didn't know why.

With a boy called Matthew, from her class, she took a trip away from the House—without her parents for the first time. They rode a flitter to the shore where she'd played as a child, twelve days earlier. She found the broken pier where she'd discovered mussels. The place seemed less vivid—less magical—and she felt a sad nostalgia for the loss of the freshness of her childish senses.

But there were other compensations. Her body was strong, lithe, and the sunlight was like warm oil on her skin. She ran and swam, relishing the sparkle of the ozone-laden air in her lungs. She and Matthew mock-wrestled and chased in the surf, clambering over each other like young apes—like children, she thought, but not quite with complete innocence . . .

As sunset approached they allowed the flitter to return them to the House. They agreed to meet the next day, perhaps take another trip somewhere. Matthew kissed her lightly, on the lips, as they parted.

That night she could barely sleep. She lay in the dark of her room, the scent of salt still strong in her nostrils, the image of Matthew alive in her mind. Her body seemed to pulse with hot blood, with its endless, continuing growth.

The next day—her 16th—Lieserl rose quickly. She'd never felt so alive; her skin still glowed from the salt and sunlight of the shore, and there was a hot tension inside her, an ache deep in her belly, a tightness.

When she reached the flitter bay at the front of the House, Matthew was waiting for her. His back was turned, the low sunlight causing the fine hairs at the base of his neck to glow.

He turned to face her.

He reached out to her, uncertainly, then allowed his hands to drop to his sides. He didn't seem to know what to say; his posture changed, subtly, his shoulders slumping slightly; before her eyes he was becoming shy of her.

She was taller than him. Visibly *older*. She became abruptly aware of the still-childlike roundness of his face, the awkwardness of his manner. The thought of *touching* him—the memory of her feverish dreams during the night—seemed absurd, impossibly adolescent.

She felt the muscles in her neck tighten; she felt as if she must scream. Matthew seemed to recede from her, as if she was viewing him through a tunnel.

Once again the labouring nanobots—the damned, unceasing nanotechnological infection of her body—had taken away part of her life.

This time, though, it was too much to bear.

"Why? *Why?*" She wanted to scream abuse at her mother—to *hurt* her.

Phillida had never looked so old. Her skin seemed drawn tight across the bones of her face, the lines etched deep. "I'm sorry," she said. "Believe me. When we—George and I—volunteered for this programme, we knew it would be painful. But we never dreamed how much. Neither of us had children before. Perhaps if we had, we'd have been able to anticipate how this would feel."

"I'm a freak—an absurd experiment," Lieserl shouted. "A *construct*. Why did you make me human? Why not some insentient animal? Why not a Virtual?"

"Oh, you had to be human. As human as possible . . ." Phillida seemed to come to a decision. "I'd hoped to give you a few more days of—life, normality—before it had to end. You seemed to be finding some happiness—"

"In fragments," Lieserl said bitterly. "This is no life, Phillida. It's *grotesque.*"

"I know. I'm sorry, my love. Come with me."

"Where?"

"Outside. To the garden. I want to show you something."

Suspicious, hostile, Lieserl allowed her mother to take her hand; but she made her fingers lie lifeless, cold in Phillida's warm grasp.

It was mid-morning now. The Sun's light flooded the garden; flowers—white and yellow—strained up towards the sky.

Lieserl looked around; the garden was empty. "What am I supposed to be seeing?"

Phillida, solemnly, pointed upwards.

Lieserl tilted back her head, shading her eyes to block out the light. The sky was a searing-blue dome, marked only by a high vapour trail and the lights of habitats.

"No." Gently, Phillida pulled Lieserl's hand down from her face, and, cupping her chin, tipped her face flower-like towards the Sun.

The star's light seemed to fill her head. Dazzled, she dropped her eyes, stared at Phillida through a haze of blurred, streaked retinal images.

The Sun. Of course . . .

The capcom said, *Damn it, Lieserl, you're going to have to respond properly. Things are difficult enough without—*

"I know. I'm sorry. How are you feeling, anyway?"

Me? I'm fine. But that's hardly the point, is it? Now come on, Lieserl, the team here are getting on my back; let's run through the tests.

"You mean I'm not down here to enjoy myself?"

The capcom, in his safe habitat far beyond the protosphere, didn't respond.

"Yeah. The tests. Okay, electromagnetic first." She adjusted her sensorium. "I'm plunged into darkness," she said dryly. "There's very little free radiation at any frequency—perhaps an X-ray glow from the protosphere; it looks a little like a late evening sky. And—"

We know the systems are functioning. I need to know what you see, what you feel.

"What I feel?"

She spread her arms and sailed backwards through the "air" of the cavern. The huge convective cells buffeted and merged like living things, whales in this insubstantial sea of gas.

"I see convection fountains," she said. "A cave full of them."

She rolled over onto her belly, so that she was gliding face-down, surveying the plasma sea below her. She *opened* her eyes, changing her mode of perception. The convective honeycomb faded into the background of her senses, and the magnetic flux tubes came into prominence, solidifying out of the air; beyond them the convective pattern was a sketchy framework, overlaid. The tubes were each a hundred yards broad, channels cutting through the air; they were thousands of miles long, and they filled the air around her, all the way down to the plasma sea.

Lieserl dipped into a tube; she felt the tingle of enhanced magnetic strength. Its walls rushed past her, curving gracefully. "It's wonderful," she said. "I'm inside a flux tube. It's an immense tunnel; it's like a fairground ride. I could follow this path all the way round the Sun."

Maybe. I don't know if we need the poetry, Lieserl. The capcom hesitated, and when he spoke again he sounded severely encouraging, as if he'd been instructed to be nice to her. *We're glad you're feeling—ah—happy in yourself, Lieserl.*

"My new self. Maybe. Well, it was an improvement on the old; you have to admit that."

Yes. I want you to think back to the downloading. Can you do that?

"The downloading? Why?"

Come on, Lieserl. It's another test, obviously.

"A test of what?"

Your trace functions. We want to know if—

"My trace functions. You mean my memory."

. . . Yes. He had the grace to sound embarrassed. *Think back, Lieserl. Can you remember?*

Downloading . . .

It was her 90th day, her 90th physical-year. She was impossibly frail—unable even to walk, or feed herself, or clean herself.

They'd taken her to a habitat close to the Sun. They'd almost left the download too late; they'd had one scare when an infection had somehow got through to her and settled into her lungs, nearly killing her.

She wanted to die.

Physically she was the oldest human in the System. She felt as if she were underwater: she could barely feel, or taste, or see anything, as if she was encased in some deadening, viscous fluid. And she knew her mind was failing.

It was so fast she could *feel* it. It was like a ghastly reverse run of her accelerated childhood. She woke every day to a new diminution of her self. She had come to dread sleep, yet could not avoid it.

She couldn't bear the indignity of it. Everybody else was immortal, and young; and the technology which had made them so was being used to kill Lieserl. She hated those who had put her in this position.

Her mother visited her for the last time, a few days before the download. Lieserl, through her ruined, rheumy old eyes, was barely able to recognize Phillida—this young, weeping woman, only a few months older than when she had held up her baby girl to the Sun.

Lieserl cursed her, sent her away.

At last she was taken, in her bed, to a downloading chamber at the heart of the habitat.

Do you remember, Lieserl? Was it—continuous?

". . . No."

It was a sensory explosion.

In an instant she was young again, with every sense alive and vivid. Her vision was sharp, her hearing impossibly precise. And slowly, slowly, she had become aware of new senses—senses beyond the human. She could see the dull infra-red glow of the bellies and heads of the people working around the shell of her own abandoned body, the sparkle of X-ray photons from the Solar protosphere as they leaked through the habitat's shielding.

She'd retained her human memories, but they were qualitatively different from the experiences she was accumulating now. Limited, partial, subjective, imperfectly recorded: like fading paintings, she thought.

. . . Except, perhaps, for that single, golden day at the beach.

She studied the husk of her body. It was almost visibly imploding now, empty . . .

"I remember," she told the capcom. "Yes, I remember."

Now the flux tube curved away to the right; and, in following it, she became aware that she was tracing out a spiral path. She let herself relax into the motion, and watched the cave-world beyond the tube wheel around her. The flux tubes neighbouring her own had become twisted into spirals too, she realized; she was following one strand in a rope of twisted-together flux tubes.

Lieserl, what's happening? We can see your trajectory's altering, fast.

"I'm fine. I've got myself into a flux rope, that's all . . ."

Lieserl, you should get out of there . . .

She let the tube sweep her around. "Why? This is fun."

Maybe. But it isn't a good idea for you to break the surface; we're concerned about the stability of the wormhole—

Lieserl sighed and let herself slow. "Oh, damn it, you're just no fun. I would have enjoyed bursting out through the middle of a sunspot. What a great way to go."

We're not done with the tests yet, Lieserl.

"What do you want me to do?"

One more . . .

"Just tell me."

Run a full self-check, Lieserl. Just for a few minutes . . . Drop the Virtual constructs.

She hesitated. "Why? The systems are obviously functioning to specification."

Lieserl, you don't need to make this difficult for me. The capcom sounded defensive. *This is a standard suite of tests for any AI which—*

"All right, damn it."

She closed her eyes, and with a sudden, impulsive, stab of will, let her Virtual image of herself—the illusion of a human body around her—crumble.

It was like waking from a dream: a soft comfortable dream of childhood, waking to find herself entombed in a machine, a crude construct of bolts and cords and gears.

She considered herself.

The tetrahedral Interface of the wormhole was suspended in the body of the Sun. The thin, searing-hot gas of the convective zone poured into its four triangular faces, so that the Interface was surrounded by a sculpture of inflowing gas, a flower carved dynamically from the Sun's flesh, almost obscuring the Interface itself. The solar material was, she knew, being pumped through the wormhole to the second Interface in orbit around the Sun; convective zone gases emerged, blazing, from the drifting tetrahedron, making it into a second, miniature Sun around which human habitats could cluster.

By pumping away the gas, and the heat it carried, the Interface refrigerated itself, enabling it to survive—with its precious, fragile cargo of data stores . . .

The stores which sustained the awareness of herself, Lieserl.

She inspected herself, at many levels, simultaneously.

At the physical level she studied crisp matrices of data, shifting, coalescing. And overlaid on that was the logical structure of data storage and access paths which represented the components of her mind.

Good . . . Good, Lieserl. You're sending us good data. How are you feeling?

"You keep asking me that, damn it. I feel—"

Enhanced . . .

No longer trapped in a single point, in a box of bone behind eyes made of jelly.

What made her conscious? It was the ability to be aware of what was happening in her mind, and in the world around her, and what had happened in the past.

By any test, she was more conscious than any other human—because she had more of the *machinery* of consciousness. She was supremely conscious—the most conscious human who had ever lived.

If, she thought uneasily, she was still human.

Good. Good. All right, Lieserl. We have work to do.

She let her awareness implode, once more, into a Virtual-human form. Her perception was immediately simplified. To be seeing through apparently-human eyes was comforting . . . and yet, she thought, restrictive.

Perhaps it wouldn't be much longer before she felt ready to abandon even this last vestige of humanity. And then what?

Lieserl?

"I hear you."

She turned her face towards the core.

"There is a *purpose*, Lieserl," her mother said. "A justification. You aren't simply an experiment. You have a mission." She waved her hand at the sprawling, friendly buildings that comprised the House. "Most of the people here, particularly the children, don't know anything about you. They have jobs, goals—lives of their own to follow. But they're here for *you.*

"Lieserl, your experiences have been designed—George and I were selected, even—to ensure that the first few days of your existence would *imprint* you with humanity."

"The first few days?" Suddenly the unknowable future was like a black wall, looming towards her; she felt as out of control of her life as if she was a counter on some immense, invisible snakes-and-ladders board.

"I don't want this. I want to be me. I want my freedom, Phillida."

"No, Lieserl. You're not free, I'm afraid; you never can be. You have a goal."

"What goal?"

"Listen to me. The Sun gave us life. Without it—without the other stars— we couldn't survive.

"We're a strong species. We believe we can live as long as the stars—for tens of billions of years. And perhaps even beyond that. But we've had— glimpses—of the future, the far distant future . . . Disturbing glimpses. People are starting to plan for that future—to work on projects which will take millions of years to come to fruition . . .

"Lieserl, you're one of those projects."

"I don't understand."

Phillida took her hand, squeezed it gently; the simple human contact seemed incongruous, the garden around them transient, a chimera, before this talk of megayears and the future of the species.

"Lieserl, something is wrong with the Sun. *You* have to find out what. The Sun is dying; something—or someone—is *killing* it."

Phillida's eyes were huge before her, staring, probing for understanding. "Don't be afraid. My dear, you will live forever. If you want to. You are a new form of human. And you will see wonders of which I—and everyone else who has ever lived—can only dream."

Lieserl listened to her tone, coldly, analysing it. "But you don't *envy* me. Do you, Phillida?"

Phillida's smile crumbled. "No," she said quietly.

Lieserl tipped back her head. An immense light flooded her eyes.

She cried out.

Her mother enfolded her in her arms. "The Sun, Lieserl. *The Sun . . .*"

FLASHBACK

Dan Simmons

▼

Dan Simmons sold his first story to *The Twilight Zone Magazine* in 1982, and by the end of that decade had become one of the most popular and best-selling authors in both the horror *and* the science fiction genres, winning, for instance, both the Hugo Award for his epic science fiction novel *Hyperion* and the Bram Stoker Award for his huge horror novel *Carrion Comfort* in the *same year*, 1990. He has since continued to split his output between science fiction (*The Fall of Hyperion, The Hollow Man*) and horror (*Song of Kali, Summer of Night, Children of the Night*) . . . although a few of his novels are downright unclassifiable (*Phases of Gravity*, for instance, which is a straight literary novel, although it was *published* as part of a science fiction line), and some (like *Children of the Night*) could be legitimately considered *either* science fiction or horror, depending on how you squint at them. Similarly, his first collection, *Prayers to Broken Stones*, contains a mix of science fiction, fantasy, horror, and "mainstream" stories, as does his most recent book, the novella collection *Lovedeath*. However eclectic he gets, though (and *Lovedeath* contains an American Indian vagina-dentata pseudo-folktale, a thoughtful mainstream story, a horrific tale of sexual vampires, and a World War I fantasy, in addition to undeniable hard-edged science fiction like the story that follows), his readers seem to like it—and no wonder, because he is a writer of considerable power, range, and ambition. Born in Peoria, Illinois, Simmons now lives with his family in Colorado.

Here he gives us a frightening look at an all-too-plausible future, one that has learned nothing from the lessons of the past, but has certainly not *forgotten* them.

Carol awoke, saw the light of morning—true morning, realtime morning—and had to resist the urge to pop her last twenty-minute tube of flashback. Instead she rolled over, pulled the pillow half over her face, and tried to recapture her dreams rather than let the realtime shakes get her. It did not work. At bedtime the night before she had flashed three hours' worth of the second trip to Bermuda with Danny, but afterward her dreams had been chaotic and unrelated. Like life.

Carol felt the rush of realtime anxiety hit her like a cold wave: she had no idea what the day could bring—death or danger to her family, embarrassment, pain—*unpredictability*. She hugged her arms to her chest and curled into a tight shell. It did not help. The shaking continued. She had unconsciously opened the drawer of the bedside table and actually had the last tube in her hand before she noticed the three collapsed and empty vials on the floor beside her bed. Carol set the twenty-minute tube on the table and went in to drive the cold shakes away with a hot shower, shouting to Val to get out of bed as she turned on the water. She saw her father's open door and knew that he had been up for hours, as he always was, having cereal and coffee before the sun rose and then puttering around in the garage before coming in to make fresh coffee for her and toast for Val.

Her father never flashbacked while the others were in the house. But Carol always found the tubes in the garage. The old man was doing three to six hours per day. Always three to six hours of the same fifteen minutes, Carol knew. Always trying to change the unchangeable.

Always trying to die.

Val was fifteen and unhappy. This morning as he slumped to the table he was wearing a Yamato interactive T-shirt, black jeans, and VR shades tuned to random overlays. He did not speak as he poured milk on his cereal and gulped his orange juice.

His grandfather came in from the garage and paused in the doorway. His name was Robert. His wife and friends had always called him Bobby. No one called him that anymore. The old man had that slightly lost, slightly querulous expression that came from age or flashback or both. Now he focused on his grandson and cleared his throat, but Val did not look up and Robert could not tell if the boy was tuned to the here and now or to the VR flickerings behind his shades.

"Warm day today," said Carol's father. He'd not been outside yet, but most days in the L.A. basin were warm.

Val grunted and continued staring in the direction of the back of the cereal box.

The old man poured coffee for himself and came over to the table. "The school counselor program called yesterday. Told me that you'd ditched another three days last week."

This got the boy's attention. His head shot up, he lowered his glasses on his nose, and said, "You tell Mom?"

"Take the glasses off," said the old man. It was not a request.

Val removed the VR shades, deactivated the telem link, tucked them in his T-shirt pocket, and waited.

"No, I didn't tell her," his grandfather said finally. "I should, but I haven't. Yet."

Val heard the threat but said nothing.

"There's no reason why a young boy like you has to screw around with flashback." Robert's voice was phlegmy with age and brittle with anger.

Val grunted and looked away.

"I mean it, goddammit," snapped his grandfather.

"Tell me about not using flashback," said Val, his voice dripping with sarcasm.

Robert took a step forward with his face mottled and fists clenched, as if he were about to hit the boy. Val stared him down as the old man stopped and tried to compose himself. When his grandfather spoke again, his voice held a forced softness. "I mean it, Val. You're too young to spend your time replaying . . ."

Val slipped out of his chair, grabbed his gym bag, and tugged the door open. "What do you know about being young?" he said.

His grandfather blinked as if he had been slapped. He opened his mouth to speak, but by the time he could think of what to say, the boy was gone.

Carol came in and poured herself some coffee. "Has Val left for school yet?"

Robert could only stare at the door and nod.

Robert looks down, sees his own hands gripping the side of the dark limousine, and knows instantly where and when he is. The heat is intense for November. His gaze moves from the windows above, then to the crowd—only two deep along this stretch of street—then back to the windows. Occasionally he glances at the back of the head in the open Lincoln ahead of him. *Lancer looks relaxed today*, he thinks.

He can hear his own thoughts like a radio tuned to a distant station, the volume little more than a murmur. He is thinking about the open windows and the slowness of the motorcade.

Robert jumps off the running board and easily jogs to his position near the left rear fender of Lancer's blue Lincoln while his eyes stay on the crowd and the windows above the street. His running is relaxed and easy; his thirty-two-year-old body is in excellent condition. Within two blocks the neighborhood changes—no more tall buildings, more empty lots and small shops, the crowd no longer even lining the route—and Robert falls back and steps onto the left running board of the number one chase car.

"You're going to wear yourself out," says Bill McIntyre from his place on the running board.

Robert grins at the other agent and sees his own reflection in Bill's sunglasses. *I'm so young*, thinks Robert for the thousandth time at this instant while his other thoughts stay tuned to the windows on the taller building ahead. He hears himself think about the route as street signs pass: Main and Market.

Get off now! he screams silently at himself. *Let go now! Run up there now.*

He seethes with frustration as he ignores the internal screams. His other thoughts contemplate running up to the rear of the Lincoln, but the low buildings here and thinning crowds convince him to stay on the running board.

No! Go! At least get closer.

Robert's head is turning away from the crowds and toward the blue Lincoln. He braces himself for the sight of the familiar thatch of chestnut hair. There it is. Then Lancer is lost to sight as Robert's gaze continues to track left. There is an open area: a hilly patch of grass and some trees.

Robert knows to the instant when he will step down off the running board, but he tries to tense his body to make himself jump sooner. It does not work. He steps off the same instant that he always does.

It takes only a few seconds to jog up to the Lincoln. Robert's attention is distracted to the right as a small group of women shout something he has never been able to make out. Glen and the others in the car also swivel their heads to the right. The four women are holding small Brownie cameras and shouting at the passengers in the Lincoln. His glance appraises and dismisses them as no threat within three seconds, but Robert knows each of the women's faces more intimately than he remembers his dead wife's. Once, in the mid-nineties, he had seen a bent old woman crossing a street in downtown Los Angeles and knew at once it was the third woman from the right from that curb thirty-two years earlier.

Now . . . get on the Lincoln's running board! he commands himself.

Instead he reaches out, taps the spare tire of the blue Lincoln as if in farewell, and drops back to the following car. Ahead, the motorcycles and lead car turn right off Main onto Houston. The blue Lincoln convertible follows a few seconds later, slowing even more than the lead car so as to make the right-angle turn without jostling the four passengers in the back. Robert steps back onto the running board of the chase car.

Look up!

Glancing left, Robert sees that railroad workers are congregated atop an overpass under which the cars will pass in a moment. He curses to himself and thinks *sloppy, sloppy.* All three cars are making a slow left onto Elm Street now. Robert leans into the open chase car and says, "Railroad bridge . . . people." In the front seat, their commander, Emory Roberts, has already seen them and is on the portable radio. Robert waves to a police officer in a yellow rain slicker who is standing on the overpass, gesturing for him to clear the bridge. The officer waves back.

"Shit," says Robert. *Go now!* he commands himself.

The blue Lincoln passes directly under a Hertz billboard with a huge clock in it. It is exactly 12:30.

"Not bad," Bill McIntyre is saying. "Couple of minutes late is all. We'll have him there in five minutes."

Robert is watching the railroad overpass. The workers are well back from the edge. The cop in the yellow slicker is standing between them and the railing. Robert relaxes a bit and glances to the right at the large brick building they are passing. Workers on their lunch break wave from the steps and curb.

Please . . . dear Jesus, please . . . move now.

Robert looks back at the overpass. The police officer in the slicker is waving, as are the workers. Two men in long raincoats stand on the bridge approach, not waving. *Plainclothes detectives or Goldwater men*, thinks Robert. Beneath those thoughts, his mind is screaming. *Now! Run now!*

"Halfback to Base. Five minutes to destination." Emory Roberts is on the radio to the Mart.

Robert is tired. The night before in Fort Worth he had been up until long after midnight playing poker with Glen, Bill, and several of the others. Today's heat is oppressive. He shakes his right arm to free his sodden shirt from his arm and back. Robert hears Jack Ready say something from the other side of the chase car and he looks across at him. People are waving and shouting happily beyond the curb there. The grass is much greener here than in Washington.

There is a sound.

Go! There's still time!

Christ, he hears himself think, *one of those goddamn workers has fired off a railroad torpedo.*

Robert looks ahead, sees the pink of the woman's dress, sees Lancer's arms rise, elbows high, hands at his own throat.

Robert's feet hit the ground as the echo of the first shot is still bouncing from building to building. He tears across the hot pavement, heart pounding. Behind him, the chase car accelerates and then has to brake hard. Amazingly, incredibly, in the face of all procedure and training, the driver of the Lincoln ahead has slowed the big car. There is another sound. One of the outrider cops glances down at his motorcycle as if it has backfired on him.

Less than three seconds have elapsed when Robert dives for the trunk grip of the Lincoln.

The third shot rings out.

Robert sees and hears the impact. Lancer's head of healthy chestnut hair seems to dissolve in a mist of pink blood and white brain matter. A piece of the President's skull, as surprisingly pink as the inside of a watermelon, arches into the air and lands on the trunk of the Lincoln, trapped there by the ornamental spare tire.

Robert's left hand has seized the metal grip and his left foot is on the step plate when the Lincoln finally accelerates. His foot comes off and he is dragging. Now he is connected to the suddenly speeding vehicle only by the numbed fingers of his left hand. He hears himself think that he will be dragged to death rather than release that grip.

It doesn't matter now, he thinks at himself. *It doesn't matter.*

Incredibly, the woman in pink is crawling out onto the trunk. Robert thinks that she is trying to reach him, to help him onto the car, but then he realizes with a stab of horror that she is reaching for the segment of skull still lodged at the rear of the trunk. With a superhuman effort he swings his right arm forward and grabs her reaching arm. Her eyes seem to glaze, she pauses . . . and helps to pull him onto the trunk of the speeding car.

Too late. All too late.

Robert pushes her down into the spattered upholstery, then shoves her to the floor of the open car. He spreadeagles his body across her and the other form in the backseat. His first glance confirms what he knew at the second of the third bullet's impact.

The car is racing now that it is too late. Motorcycles cut in ahead, their sirens screaming.

Too late.

Robert is sobbing. The wind whips his tears away. All the way to Parkland Hospital he is sobbing.

Carol's Honda was only half-charged this morning, either because of another brownout during the night or some problem with the car's batteries. She hoped and prayed that it was a brownout. She could not afford more work on the car.

There was just enough charge to get her to and from work.

The I-5 guideway was jammed to gridlock. As always, Carol had the impulse to pull the Honda into the almost-empty VIP lane and flash by the traffic jam. Only a few Lexuses or Acura Omegas were using the lane, the chauffeurs' faces stoic, the Japanese faces in the rear seats lowered to paperwork or powerbooks. *It would be worth it*, she thought, *just to get a mile or two at high speed before the freeway cops cut my power and pull me over.*

She crept forward with the inching traffic flow, watching her charge gauge drop steadily. She had assumed that the holdup was the usual bridge or lane repair, but when she got to the Santa Monica Freeway exit she saw the Nissan Voltaire van with the CHP vehicles around it. The driver was being lifted out. His eyes were open and he looked to be breathing, but he was limp and unresponsive as they trundled him into the backseat of the patrol car.

Flashback, thought Carol. More and more, people were using it even while they were stuck in traffic. As if reminded of the possibility, she opened her purse and lifted out the twenty-minute vial. If her Honda had fully charged, she could have stopped at her supplier's on Whittier Boulevard before going to work. As it was, she would have to depend on her stash at work.

Carol was almost thirty minutes late when she pulled into the parking garage beneath the Civic Center complex, but she was still the first of the four court stenographers to arrive. She turned off the motor, considered attaching the charge cable despite the higher rates here, decided to try to get home on the charge she had, opened the car door, and then closed it again.

Her bosses were used to the stenographers being late. Her bosses probably weren't in yet either. No one arrived on time anymore. She probably had half an hour or forty-five minutes before any real work would be attempted.

Carol lifted the twenty-minute vial, concentrated on summoning a specific memory the way Danny had taught her the first time she had used flashback, and popped the lid. There was the usual sweet smell, the sharp tang, and then she went somewhere else.

Danny comes in from the patio and hugs her from behind as she pours juice at the counter. His hands slip under her terrycloth robe. Rich Caribbean light pours through the windows and open door of their bungalow.

"Hey, you'll make me spill," says Carol, holding the glass of juice out over the counter.

"I want to make you spill," Danny murmurs. He is nuzzling her neck.

Carol arches back into his arms. "I read somewhere that men hug women in the kitchen as just another form of male domination," she says in a husky whisper. "A sort of Pavlovian thing to keep us in the kitchen . . ."

"Shut up," he says. He tugs her robe down over her shoulders as he continues nuzzling.

Carol closes her eyes. Her body still carries the memory of last night's lovemaking. Danny's hands come around the front of her robe now, untying the belt, opening it.

"You have to meet the buyers in thirty minutes," Carol says softly, her eyes still closed. She raises a hand to his cheek.

Danny kisses her throat precisely where her pulse throbs. "That gives us a full fifteen minutes," he whispers, his breath soft against her flesh.

Inside the swirl of sensations, Carol surrenders herself to her own surrender.

Under the high span of the railroad bridge, just below where the concrete trusses arced together like the buttresses of some Gothic cathedral, Coyne handed Val the .32-caliber semiautomatic pistol. Gene D. and Sully whistled and made other approving noises.

"This is the tool," said Coyne. "You got to make the rest happen."

"Make the rest happen," echoed Gene D.

"This is just the tool, Fool," said Sully.

"Go ahead. Check it out." Coyne's dark eyes were bright. All three of the boys were white, dressed in the torn T-shirts and tattered jeans of the middle class. Their fuzzy-logic sneakers were not new enough or expensive enough or smart enough to show that the boys were members of any ghetto gang.

Val's hands shook only slightly as he turned the pistol over in his hands and racked the slide. A bullet lay snug in the chamber. Val let the slide slam home and held the cocked weapon with his finger on the trigger guard.

"It doesn't matter who," whispered Coyne.

"Don't matter at all," giggled Sully.

"Better not to know," agreed Gene D.

"But you've gotta do the trash to enjoy the flash," said Coyne. "You gotta pay your dues, babechik."

"Dues get paid, then you get frayed," laughed Sully.

Val looked at his friends and then slid the pistol into his belt, tugging his T-shirt over it.

Gene D. high-fived him and pounded out a rioter's dap on Val's head. "Better check that safety, Babe. Don't want to blow your business off before you do the deed."

Red-faced, Val pulled the pistol out, clicked on the safety, and slid it back in his belt.

"Today's the *day!*" Sully screamed at the sky and slid down the long concrete embankment on his back. The echo of his shout bounced back from concrete walls and girders.

Before they slid down to join him, Gene D. and Coyne slapped Val on the back. "Next time you flash, boy, you'll be the Flash*man*."

Screaming until their echoes overlapped with realtime shouts, the three boys slid down the slippery slope.

Robert lived with his daughter but also had a secret address. Just six blocks from their modest suburban home, set along an old surface street that was rarely used since the Infrastructure Crash, was a cheap VR motel that catered to New Okies and illegal immigrants. Robert kept a room there. It was close to his flashback supplier and for some reason he felt less guilty about replaying there.

Besides, the motel had keyed its telem to nostalgia options for its old-fart patrons and when Robert used the VR peepers—which was rarely now—he called up his room in early-sixties' decor. Somehow it helped the transition.

Robert used the last of his Social Security card balance to score a dozen fifteen-minute vials at the usual dollar-a-minute rate. There were deals on every block between his house and the VR flop. Robert slipped the two bubble-wrap sixpacs in his pocket and moved on to the motel in his old man's shuffle.

Today he keyed the peepers. The room was a set designer's image of 1960 Holiday Inn elegant. A kidney-shaped coffee table sat in front of a low-slung Scandinavian couch; pole lamps and starburst light fixtures spilled light; black-velvet paintings of doe-eyed children and photos of Elvis decorated the walls. Copies of *Life* magazine and the *Saturday Evening Post* were fanned on the coffee table. The view out the picture window was of a park with steel and glass skyscrapers rising above the trees. Huge Detroit-built cars were visible on a highway, their I-C engines rumbling along with a nostalgic background roar. Everything was new and clean and plastic. Only the powerful smell of rotting garbage seemed incongruous.

Robert snorted and removed the peepers. The room was bare cinderblock, empty except for the cot he was lying on and the crude wireform constructs taking up space where the table and couch should be. There was no window. The garbage smell seeped in through the ventilator and under the scarred door.

He set the headset back in place and cracked the bubblewrap. Looking out the window at the Dodges and Fords and late-fifties Chevies driving past, he called back the hot Dallas day and the heat of the car metal under his hands until he was sure that the right memory synapses were firing.

Robert lifted the fifteen-minute vial to his nose and popped the top.

Carol was scheduled to record a deposition in the district attorney's offices at 10 A.M. but the Assistant D.A. who was handling the deposition was in his cubicle flashing on a favorite fishing trip until 10:20, the elderly witness was half-an-hour late, the associate from the defense attorney's office didn't show at all, the video technician had another appointment at 11:00, and the paramedic whom the law required to administer the flashback called to say that he was stuck in traffic. The witness ended up being dismissed and Carol stowed her datawriter keyboard.

"Fuck it," said Dale Fritch, the young Assistant D.A., "the old lady wouldn't agree to flashback anyway. The whole thing is fucked."

Carol nodded. A witness who wouldn't agree to being questioned immediately after flashback was either lying or some sort of religious fanatic. The elderly black woman whom they'd been trying to get a deposition from was no religious fanatic. Even though flashback depos had no legal weight, no jury would believe testimony where the witness refused to replay the event before testifying. Video-recorded flashback depositions had almost replaced live testimony in criminal trials.

"If I call her to testify live, they'll know she's lying," said Dale Fritch as they paused by the coffee machine. "Flash may be habit-forming and hurting our productivity, but we know that it doesn't lie."

Carol took the offered cup of coffee, poured sugar in it, and said, "Sometimes it does."

Fritch raised an eyebrow.

Carol explained about her father's flashbacks.

"Christ, your dad was JFK's secret service guy? That's sort of neat."

Carol sipped the hot coffee and shook her head. "No, he wasn't. That's the weird part. The agent who jumped on the back of Kennedy's car fifty years ago was named Clint Hill. He was thirty-something when the president was shot. My dad was an insurance adjustor until he retired. He was still in high school when Kennedy was shot."

Dale Fritch frowned. "But flashback only lets you relive your own memories . . ."

Carol gripped her coffee cup. "Yeah. Unless you're crazy or suffering from Alzheimer's. Or both."

The Assistant D.A. nodded and sucked on the coffee stirrer. "I'd heard about schizos having false flashbacks, but . . ." He looked up suddenly. "Hey, uh . . . Carol . . . I'm sorry . . ."

Carol tried a smile. "It's all right. The Medicaid specialists don't think that Dad's schizophrenic, but he hasn't responded to the Alzheimer's medication . . ."

"How old is he?" asked Fritch, glancing at his watch.

"Just turned seventy," said Carol. "Anyway, they don't know why he's having these false flashbacks. All they can do is to advise him not to take the drug."

Fritch smiled. "And does he follow their advice?"

Carol tossed her empty cup away. "Dad's convinced that everything in the country's so shitty today because he didn't get between John Kennedy and the bullet fast enough. He figures that if he just gets there a little sooner, Kennedy will survive November twenty-second and history will retrofit itself."

The Assistant D.A. stood and smoothed his tie. "Well, he's right about one thing," he said, tossing his own cup in the recycling bin. "The country's in shitty shape."

Val stood opposite his high school and considered going in to blow away Mr. Loehr, his history teacher. The reasons he did not were clear: 1) the school had metal detectors at all the entrances and rent-a-cops in the halls and 2) even if he got in and did it, they'd catch him. What fun would it be flashing on this trashing if he had to do it in a Russian gulag? Val had never lived in an age where excess American prisoners weren't shipped to the Russian Republic, so the chance of serving time in a Siberian gulag did not seem strange to him. Once, when his grandfather had mentioned that it had not always been that way, Val had sneered and said, "Shit, what else other than prison space did we ever think the Russies had to sell?" His grandfather had not answered.

Now Val adjusted the .32 in his waistband and slouched away from the school, heading toward the shopping strip above the Interstate. The trick was to choose someone at random, do them, drop the gun somewhere it wouldn't be found, and get the hell out of the area. He'd be watching ITV when the evening news told about another senseless killing which the police suspected was flashback-related.

Val keyed his shades to provide nude realtime overlays of all the women he saw as he picked up his pace toward the shopping strip.

Carol is waiting for her high school date to pick her up. She checks her frilly Madonna-blouse to make sure that her antiperspirant is working and then stands on the corner, shifting from foot to foot and watching the traffic. She sees Ned's almost-new '93 Camaro come slashing through traffic and screech to a stop, and then she is squeezing into the backseat with Kathi.

As always on this flashback, Carol marvels at the sight of herself as she checks the rearview mirror to make sure that her makeup is all right. Her hair is shaved and dyed and spiked, she has three fake diamonds in her left ear, and her lashes and eyeliner make her look like a bright cartoon. Along with the shock of seeing herself young and bold, Carol *feels* the energy of youth in herself. She *feels* the lightness in her step, the firmness in her breasts and muscles, and the enthusiasm in her spirit. More than that, she senses the bounding skitter and slide of her own thoughts, as different in their energetic optimism from the daily plod of her thinking in the future-present as her appearance is in the then-now.

Kathi is chattering but Carol tunes out the babel and merely drinks in the sight of her friend. Kathi dropped out of school in her senior year, dropped out of sight shortly after that, and dropped out of Carol's thoughts until the fall of '98 when she heard from a friend that Kathi had died in a car accident somewhere in Canada. As always, Carol feels a flood of warm feeling toward her old friend and has to fight the useless urge to warn the girl not to follow her boyfriend to Vancouver. Instead of warning her, Carol hears her own voice babbling about who wrote whom a note in study hall that day. She feels her quickened heartbeat and flushed skin as she studiously avoids talking to the strange boy in the front passenger seat.

Ned has roared back out into traffic, cutting off a Villager van and switching lanes almost at random. Now he turns around and says, "Hey, Carol babe, you gonna ignore my friend here all day or what?"

Carol raises her chin. "Are you going to introduce your friend, or what?"

Ned makes a rude noise. From the rush of fumes, it seems that he has been drinking. "Carol, this stud muffin is Danny Rogallo. He's from West High. Danny, meet Carol Hearns. She's Kathi's friend and knows our football team, uh, how do you say it? *Intimately*. Oh shit." Ned has to brake hard and change lanes to avoid a truck that slows suddenly.

Carol bobs forward, braces herself with both hands on the back of the new boy's seat, and looks at him. Danny has turned to smile at her, either from the introduction or out of embarrassment at Ned's driving. Carol hears herself thinking that the boy is handsome with his Tom Cruise–like smile, severe athlete's haircut, and diamond ear stud. "Hey there, stud muffin," Carol hears herself say.

Danny's smile broadens.

"Hey there yourself," says the new boy, still twisted in his seat to look back at her.

Carol knows that the flashback is precisely half over and the next big moment is when their hands will accidentally touch as they ride the escalator in the mall.

"Halfback to Base. Five minutes to destination."

Robert glances at the front seat to see Emory Roberts set the radio down and write something in his shift report. Robert shakes his arm to free his sweat-sodden shirt and then glances to his right as Jack Ready says something from the running board on the opposite side of the chase car.

There is a sound.

Go, goddammit! Go! You have almost two seconds. Use it!

His gaze snaps back to the railroad overpass and he hears himself think, *Christ, one of those goddamn workers has fired off a railroad torpedo.*

Lancer's arms rise almost comically. His hands go to his throat so that, from the rear, his arms seem to extend in a direct line from his shoulders and terminate at the elbows.

Robert feels himself jump from the running board. Finally.

He is running hard toward the blue Lincoln. There is a babble in the chase car behind him. Robert has to concentrate during a score of flashbacks to sort out Emory Roberts' voice commanding Jack Ready back onto the running board and the voice of Dave Powers, Lancer's friend who is riding in the Secret Service chase car for no special reason, crying out, "I think the President's been hit!"

It is all unperceived realtime background noise now—indistinguishable from the echoes of the gunshot or the flap of pigeon wings—as he digs hard for the rear of the open Lincoln, his eyes fixed on Lancer's head of chestnut hair.

Lancer begins to slump.

The Lincoln inexplicably slows.

Robert dives for the rear trunk grip.

Another shot rings out.

Lancer's head explodes in a spray of pink mist.

"Goddamn," said Robert. He was weeping. For a second he did not know where he was—the sixties decor, the traffic outside the motel window—but then he raised his hand to wipe the tears away, bumped the VR headset, and remembered.

"Goddamn," he whispered again, tearing off the headset. The almost-bare room reeked of garbage and mildew. Robert pounded the cot and wept.

Val has passed the old malls, all boarded up or converted to prison space now, and then climbed the wooden scaffolding to the strip mall on the freeway.

They were called malls and were the only malls that Val had known in his short lifetime, but even he knew that in reality they were little more than glorified flea markets on the elevated stretches of Interstate Highway that had been abandoned after the '08 Big One. Today a quarter of a mile or more of brightly colored canvas rippled and fluttered in the breeze; the gypsy vendors were out in force. Val joined the midday mobs of shoppers and understood why Coyne and Gene D. had urged him to do his flashback shooting here: he could blend into the mob in a second, there were a score of stairways down which he could escape, and the maze of shattered concrete slabs and support rods on the tumbled section of the freeway was a perfect spot to get rid of the gun.

Val walked the white stripe between canvas booths, checking out the new Japanese and German merchandise and pretending to look at the old recycled Russ and American crap. The Japanese VR and interactive stuff was cool, although he knew it was generations behind the tech toys that Jap and German kids could buy. The problem with TV, especially interactive TV, was that it gave you a taste of how the other half lived without showing you how you could ever get there. Val's mother said that this had always been the case with TV— that when she was a kid way back in the dark ages, Africs and Spanics in the ghetto had felt that way about programs that showed white, middle-class American affluence. Val didn't give a damn what it used to be like in his mother's day; he just wanted some of the new Jap tech stuff.

But not today. Today Val only wanted to use the .32, get rid of it, and get out of there.

Coyne and Gene D. swore that there was nothing in the universe like flashing on doing someone. Sully also swore that, but Val trusted nothing that the taller boy said. Sully used crack, angel dust, and turbometh as well as flashback, and Val had the usual flashbacker's contempt for someone on one of the old drugs. Still, Val could only watch when the three others used a thirty-minute vial to replay their own shootings. Their faces would get lax in that sort of idiot-dreamer's expression flashback-users had, and then they would slump and twitch, their eyes rolling in REM randomness under closed lids. Val had seen Coyne actually get sexually excited as he approached the shooting part of the flashback. Gene D. said that wasting someone was better in flashback than in realtime because you get all the adrenaline rush and physical high while you knew—the you watching behind everything knew—that you weren't going to get caught.

Val touched the pistol through his loose shirt and wondered. He had not enjoyed the flashback of the rape of that Spanic girl the way Coyne had said he would: her cries and the smell of her fear while Sully held her down made him sick each time, so that he felt his nausea *under* his replayed nausea. So after two or three of the gang flashbacks on that gig, Val had taken to remembering something else—such as the time he and Coyne had stolen Old Man Weimart's cash box when they were seven—rather than replay the rape.

But Coyne said that there was nothing like flashbacking on wasting someone. Nothing.

The open-air strip mall was busy with lunchtime shoppers and flashback dropouts. Val had noticed that more and more people were just not going to work anymore; realtime interfered with their flashing. He wondered if that was the reason the garbage was always piled so high along the curbs, why the mails rarely were delivered any longer, and why nothing seemed to get done anymore except when the Japanese were there to supervise.

Val shrugged. It really didn't matter. What mattered now was finding someone to waste, dropping the gun, and getting out of there. Strolling away from the crowded booths selling Jap and German goods toward the Russ stalls, he felt his heart rate accelerate at the mere thought of what was about to happen.

He began to see how it should be done. This section of the shopping strip near the tumbled section of freeway was less crowded than the main area, but still seemed busy enough that Val could do the shooting and get away without being too visible. He noticed the narrow lanes between the booths. Moving into one of these canvas-walled alleys, he could see the shoppers without being watched by them or by the sales people inside the makeshift tents. Val pulled the small automatic out of his waistband and held it loosely by his side. The choice now was who . . .

A woman in her sixties wandered from stall to stall, peering over bifocals at the Russ artifacts and icons on the counters. Val licked his lips and then lowered the pistol again. She looked too much like photos he'd seen of his grandmother.

Two gay dudes in wraparound VR peepers strolled arm in arm, laughing at the crude Russ merchandise and using every laugh as an excuse to hug each other. One of the men had his hand in the hip pocket of the other's jeans.

This seemed good. Val held the pistol higher. Then he saw the poodles. Each of the gays had a yapping little dog on a leash. Something about the thought of those dogs barking and leaping around after he wasted the guy was not sympatico. Val set the pistol behind his back and continued watching.

An older man moved down the line of counters, giving close attention to the Russ junk. This guy was bald and liver-spotted with age, wearing neither VR shades nor peepers, but something about his baggy old-man clothes and his watery old-man eyes reminded Val of his grandfather.

Val lifted the pistol, clicked the safety off, and took a half step beneath the flapping canvas overhang. *Shoot, walk away slowly, toss the gun in the concrete tumble down below, take the J Bus home . . .* he went over Coyne's instructions in his mind. His heart was pounding almost painfully as he lifted the little .32 and sighted down the short barrel.

A shot rang out and the old man's head jerked up. Everyone was looking down the aisle toward where the gays and their poodles had gone. The old man moved away from the counter and stared with the others as the shouting and footsteps grew louder.

Val lowered the pistol with shaking hands and stepped out to look.

The woman with gray hair and bifocals was lying in a tumble on the white-stripe center of the shopping lane. A kid no more than twelve or thirteen was running toward the end of the elevated section, his leather jacket flying. One of the gay dudes had dropped to one knee and was shouting for the kid to stop. The other gay dude was holding a badge toward the crowd and yelling at them to stay back while the dude on one knee gripped a blunt, plastic tube with both hands. Val recognized the black lump from a hundred interactive movies: an Uzi-940 needlegun. He had no doubt that the clownlike VR wraparounds were giving targeting and tactical info. The cop shouted one last time for the kid to stop. Almost at the end of the staircase, the boy did not even look back. The two poodles were straining at their leashes and barking hysterically.

The boy finally looked over his shoulder just as the cop fired. The Uzi made a compressed-air noise much like a tire gauge slipping off a valve and then the boy's jacket seemed to explode into a black cloud of leather strips as several hundred glass and steel microflechettes hit home. The boy fell and tumbled, limbs as loose as a rag doll's, as his own inertia and the impact of the needle cloud carried his body under the rope railing and off the elevated strip. Bits of leather jacket were still coming down like confetti as the crowd rushed forward past the gay cops and the hysterical poodles to goggle at the body thirty feet below.

Val took a breath, slipped the .32 into his waistband, pulled his shirt over it, and walked slowly to another staircase. His legs were only slightly shaky.

Carol came out of her flashback of meeting Danny to find Dale Fritch waiting just outside the door of her cubicle. She had no idea how long he had been waiting. In the past few years, privacy had become an imperative and everyone who used flashback respected other people's need for a time and space beyond interruption. Now Carol used the small mirror in her desk drawer to check her makeup and to quickly run a brush through her hair before opening the door.

The Assistant D.A. seemed uneasy. "Carol . . . ah . . . I was just wondering if you . . . ah . . . might be free for a special project tomorrow."

She raised an eyebrow. She had worked with Fritch on more than a few depositions and had been court reporter for a score of trials that he had appeared at, but until their conversation about her father that morning, she did not think they had ever said anything personal to one another. "Special project?" she said, wondering if this was some sort of come-on. She knew that the Assistant D.A. was married with two small children and had thought that his only passion was one he spoke of occasionally: trout fishing.

Dale glanced over his shoulder, stepped into an empty meeting room, and beckoned her in. Carol waited while he closed the door.

"You know that I've been investigating the Hayakawa murder?" he said softly.

Carol nodded. Mr. Hayakawa had been an important corporate advisor in the L.A. area and everyone at County knew that the investigation was . . . to use a word the D.A. tended to overuse . . . sensitive.

"Well," continued Dale, running a hand through his blond hair, "I have a witness who swears that the shooting wasn't robbery the way the cops pegged it. He swears that it's drug related."

"Drug related?" said Carol. "Coke, you mean?"

Dale chewed his lower lip. "Flashback."

Carol almost laughed out loud. "Flashback? Hayakawa could have scored flashback on any corner in the city. So could anyone else. Why would they kill him for flashback?"

Dale Fritch shook his head. "No, they killed him because he was supplying it and someone disagreed on the amount. Or so my informant swears."

Carol did not hide her skepticism. "Dale," she said, using his first name for the first time, "the Japanese don't allow any use of flashback. It's mandatory death penalty over there."

The Assistant D.A. nodded agreement. "My informant says that Hayakawa was part of a delivery network. He says that the Japanese developed the drug and . . ."

Carol made a rude noise. "Flashback was first synthesized in a lab in Chicago. I remember reading about it before it hit the streets."

"He says that the Japanese developed it and have been foisting it on us for more than a decade," continued Fritch. "Look, Carol, I know it sounds crazy, but I need a good stenographer who can keep quiet about this until I show that this informant's crazy or . . . Anyway, can you do it tomorrow?"

Carol hesitated only a second. "Sure."

"Can you do it during your lunch hour? We need to meet this guy at a café all the way across town. He's paranoid as hell."

Carol smiled only slightly. "Well, if he thinks he's blowing the lid off some gigantic international conspiracy, I can see why. Sure, I usually just brown bag it. I'll meet you in your office at noon."

Dale Fritch hesitated. "Could we make it outside . . . say the corner on the south side of the parking garage? I don't want anyone in the office to know about this."

Carol raised an eyebrow. "Not even Mr. Torrazio?" Bert Torrazio was the District Attorney, a political appointee of the mayor and his Japanese advisors. No one, not even the stenographers, thought that Torrazio was competent.

"*Especially* not Torrazio," said Fritch, his voice tense. "This whole investigation has been off the record, Carol. If Bert gets a whiff of it, Hizzoner and all the Jap money-men downtown will be on me like flies on shit . . . sorry for the language."

Carol smiled. "I'll be on the corner at noon."

The Assistant D.A.'s relief and gratitude were visible on his boyish face. "Thanks, Carol. I appreciate it."

Carol felt like an idiot for thinking that his approach had been a come-on. Nonetheless, she did not think of Danny for the entire ride home. She made it to her garage with her charge dial reading zero.

Robert saw the problem in Val's face as soon as the boy returned home. The teenager was frequently manic, more frequently depressed, and often out-of-focus from the dislocation that flashback gave you, but Robert had never seen the boy quite so distressed as this evening. Val had slammed in while he and Carol were microwaving dinner and had gone straight up to his room. There was no conversation during dinner—which was not unusual—but Val's face held that slick sheen through the entire meal and his eyes continued to flicker left and right as if he were waiting for the phone to ring. The TV was on during dinner, as was their habit, to cover the lack of talk, and Robert noticed the boy watching the local news carefully, which was more than unusual, it was unprecedented.

Robert saw the boy shift in his chair, his head actually jerking up as the local anchorwoman began describing a shooting on the I-5 strip mall.

". . . the victim has been identified as Ms. Jennifer Lopato, sixty-four, of Glendale. LAPD spokesperson Heather Gonzales says that no motive has been established for the shooting and authorities suspect that it is another flashback-related murder. In this case, however, the alleged shooter was caught in the act by two off-duty police officers who responded with deadly force. CNN/LA has obtained official LAPD gun-camera vid footage of the shooting. We warn you, the vid you are about to see is graphic . . ."

Robert watched Val watching the tape. As far as Robert could tell from glancing at the screen, the footage was no different than the nightly gun-camera carnage that filled the news these days. But Val seemed mesmerized by the images. Robert watched the boy staring open-mouthed as a youngster ran through the crowd, refused to respond to the off-screen officers' shouts to stop, and then was blown to fragments by the flechette cloud. His grandson only closed his mouth, swallowed, and turned back to the table after another minute of unrelated news about L.A.'s person-on-the-net responses to the bad war news from China.

Carol did not seem to notice her son's reaction. Her own gaze was turned inward as it usually was these days.

We're all on flashback even when we're not on flashback, thought Robert. He felt a shudder of vertigo as he often did when he thought about his own flashback experiences, followed by a worse shudder of revulsion at himself. At his family. At America.

"Something wrong, Dad?" asked Carol, looking up from her coffee. Her eyes still had that myopic, distracted look, but she was also frowning in concern.

"No," said the old man, lifting a hand in Val's direction, "I just . . ." He stopped himself. While he had been lost in his own reverie, his grandson had left the table. Robert did not even know if he had gone upstairs or out the door. "Nothing," he said to his daughter, patting her hand clumsily. "Nothing's wrong."

Years ago they had caged in the pedestrian overpass to prevent people from dropping heavy objects or themselves on the twelve lanes of northbound traffic below, then—when highway shootings had first reached epidemic proportions in the mid-nineties—they had covered it with a thick Plexiglas that was supposed to stop bullets. It didn't—as evidenced by dozens of bullet holes, both outgoing and incoming, that fractured the warped plastic all along the tunnel—but it threw off the shooters' aim enough that they used other snipers' perches above the Interstate. By then, of course, most of the public figured that anyone driving in an unarmored car deserved a bullet in the ear.

In Val's lifetime, however, wonky vets from the Asian and South American mercenary wars were beginning to drop fragmentation and other types of grenades from the overpasses, and pedestrian bridges were caged-over and sealed up again, this time with welded steel doors at either end to keep people off them altogether. Gangs blew holes in the steel plates and used the long, dark overpasses as meeting places and their own private flashback parlors. It was very dark in there and Val had to use his VR shades as nightvision goggles to find Coyne, Gene D., and Sully among the dark shapes huddling, nodding, selling, and buying.

Val pulled the .32 from his waistband and held it in the palm of his hand.

"Couldn't do it, huh?" Coyne said softly, picking the pistol up. He was a radiant green figure holding a pulsing white tube in Val's amplified night vision.

Val opened his mouth to explain about the kid and the fag cops, but then he said nothing.

Sully made a disgusted sound but the green figure that was Coyne shoved him into silence. Coyne handed the pistol back. "Keep it, Val my man. Like whatshername, the Southern bitch, said in the old movie, 'Tomorrow's another day.'"

Val blinked. Someone had lit a cigarette down the bridge-tunnel and that end of the span blazed in white light. A dozen voices shouted at the figure to douse the fucking light.

"Meanwhile," said Gene D., throwing his arm around Val, "we scored some primo flash . . ."

Val blinked again. "Flash is just flash, asshole."

Sully snorted again and Coyne put his hand on Val's back. Val felt the contact with Coyne and Gene D. pulling him in, like a noose around his chest that made it difficult to breathe.

"Flash is just flash," whispered Coyne, "but this flash has like, I dunno, some sort of pheremone-exciter shit in it, so if you're flashing, like, fucking somebody like that time we did the Spanic bitch, you come harder than you did the first time."

Val nodded although he did not understand. Flash was flash. How could you experience more than you experienced the first time? Also, he had never had an orgasm except when he played with himself, and he did not like to flash on that. But he nodded and let Gene D. and Coyne pull him down to where a bit of light through one of the cracks in the blacked-out Plexiglas spilled across the grimy concrete as bright as liquid metal.

Gene D. produced four one-hour vials. Val tried to think of what he could flash on. Most of his memories were miserable. He would never tell the others, but often—when he said he was flashing on the time they fucked the Spanic kid—he was actually replaying a Little League game he had played when he was eight. That was the first and last year he had played, after finding that none of the guys thought baseball was cool. As far as Val knew, no one played Little League anymore . . . no money. The fucking Reagandebt. Sending the fucking army to fight the fucking Jap wars for them wasn't coming close to paying the interest on the fucking Jap loans.

Val didn't understand any of it. He just knew that everything was shit. He started to take the sixty-minute vial from Coyne, but the bigger boy pulled him close and whispered huskily in his ear, "Tomorrow, Val my man, we'll go with you and help you get your trash so you can flash . . ."

Val nodded, pulled away, and lifted the tube to his nose. The Little League game didn't come when he tried to visualize it. Instead, he found himself remembering a time when he was a tiny little shit—three, maybe two—and his mother had held him on her lap to read to him. He thought it was before she began doing flash. He had fallen asleep on her lap, but not so asleep that he couldn't hear the words as she read, slow and steady.

Feeling like the world's greatest wuss and pussy wonk, Val held the memory and broke the tab on the flashback vial.

Robert did not like interactive TV, but when Carol was in bed and when he was sure that Val was gone, he brought up CNN/LA and accessed the anchorwoman persona. The attractive Eurasian face smiled at him. "Yes, Mr. Hearns?"

"The shooting on tonight's news," he said brusquely. He did not like talking to generated personas.

The anchor smiled more broadly. "Which segment, Mr. Hearns? The news is aired hourly and . . ."

"Seven P.M.," said Robert and forced himself to relax a bit. "Please," he said, feeling foolish.

The anchor beamed at him. "Would that be the shooting of Mr. Colfax, Mr. Mendez, Mr. Roosevelt, Mr. Kettering, the Richardson infant, Ms. Dozois, the unidentified Haitian, Mr. Ing, Ms. Lopato . . ."

"Lopato," said Robert. "The Lopato shooting."

"Yes," said the anchor, disappearing into a box as the video lead-in to the story filled the screen. "Do you wish the original narration?"

"No."

"Augmented narration?"

"No. No sound at all."

"Realtime or slo-mo?"

Robert hesitated. "Slow motion, please."

The gun-camera video began rolling. The CNN/LA logo was superimposed on the lower right corner of the frame. Robert watched the rough-cut jumble of images: first the victim, a woman a few years younger than Robert lying in a pool of her own blood, her glasses nearby, then the gun camera swinging up, a slo-mo jostling of people pointing toward the body and then toward a running figure. The camera zoomed on the figure and targeting data filled the right column of the image. Robert realized that he was seeing what the cops had seen through their telem peepers. It was obvious that the running boy was no more than twelve or thirteen.

Then a fire-confirm light flashed in the right column and the cloud of flechettes, easily visible in the extreme slow motion, expanded like a halo of ice crystals until it all but obscured the running child.

The boy's coat exploded into a corona of leather shreds.

The back of the boy's head expanded in a slow-motion unfurling of hair, scalp, skull, and brain.

The bit of skull on the trunk lid, thought Robert, feeling himself slide away from realtime. He forced himself back.

The boy tumbled, the back of his head gone, flechettes quite visible in his bulging eyes and protruded face; tumbled, slid under a rope railing, and was gone. The gun-camera image froze and faded. The CNN/LA logo expanded until it filled the frame and a copyright violation warning flashed across the screen. A second later the anchorperson persona was back, waiting patiently.

"Run it again," Robert said. His voice was thick.

This time he froze the image five seconds into it, after the gun-camera lens had left the victim but before it had picked up the fleeing boy. "Go . . . stop again," said Robert.

The frozen tableau showed two or three adults pointing. One woman had her mouth open in a shout or scream. It was the shadow-within-a-shadow in an alley between two tents that interested Robert.

"Zoom there . . . no, up . . . there. Left a bit. Stop. Good. Now can you enhance that?"

"Of course, Mr. Hearns," came the anchor's simulated voice.

As the pixels began rearranging themselves into what might be a human shape, sharpening the white blur into a recognizable face, Robert thought, *Jesus, if they'd only had this in 1963 instead of the Zapruder film . . .*

Then all such thoughts fled as the image resolved itself.

"Do you wish further augmentation?" asked the smooth voice. "There will be an additional interactive charge."

"No," said Robert. "Just hold this a minute." He was, of course, looking at his grandson's face. Val was holding a pistol with the barrel vertical, only inches from his own face. The boy's expression of horror and fascination somewhat resembled his grandfather's.

Robert heard the tapping of the rear door's combination lock and the chime of the cheap security system's approval. Val came in through the kitchen.

"Off," said Robert and the screen snapped to black.

Val was back in his own bed by 2 A.M. but the pressure and tension of the day did not let him sleep. He found two twenty-minute vials and flashed on the first one.

He is four and it is his birthday. His daddy still lives with them. They are in the apartment near the Lankershim Reconstruction Projects and Val's friend from across the corridor, five-year-old Samuel, is having dinner with them because it is a special day.

Val is in the tall wooden chair that his mommy bought at the unpainted furniture place and decorated with painted animal designs just for him after he had outgrown his highchair. Even though he is four, he loves the tall chair that allows him to look across the table eye to eye with his daddy. Now the table is littered with the remains of his special dinner . . . the crusts of hot dog rolls, bits of red Jell-O, random potato chips . . . but his daddy's plate is clean, his chair empty.

The door opens and Grandpa and Grandma come in. Val is struck, as he always is during this replay, not only by the fact that his grandmother is alive and unravaged by cancer, but at how alive and young his grandfather appears, even though this flash is only a little more than a decade in the past. *Time sure kicks the shit out of people*, he thinks, not for the first time.

"Happy Birthday, kiddo," says his suddenly-young grandfather, ruffling his hair. His grandmother bends to kiss him and he is surrounded by the scent of fresh violets. Feeling his younger self's happiness and eagerness to get on to the presents, the watching Val knows that the back of his grandfather's closet, where the old man keeps a few of her dresses, still holds a bit of that scent. He wonders if his grandfather ever lifts the dresses to his face to recapture that scent. Sometimes, when the old man is out on a trip to his flashback motel, Val does that.

Val watches his own stubby hands play with the party favors and listens to Samuel's giggles. Hardly noticed at the time but all too clear to Val now is the hurried kitchen conversation that he catches bits of . . .

"He promised to be home on time tonight," his mommy is saying. "He *promised.*"

"Why don't we serve the cake anyway," his grandma says, her voice as soothing as a remembered touch or texture.

"His own boy's birthday party . . ." Robert's voice is heavy with anger.

"Let's serve the cake!" his grandma says brightly.

Val and Samuel pause in their play as the lights go out. Suddenly the world is illuminated by a richer, deeper light as his mother carries in the cake with four huge candles on it. Everyone is singing "Happy Birthday."

Val is old enough to understand that if he makes a wish and blows all the candles out successfully, the wish will come true. His mother has not said it, but he suspects that if he does not blow all of them out on the first try the wish will fail.

He blows them out. Samuel and Grandpa and Grandma and Mommy cheer. They have all just started to cut the cake for him when the door opens and Daddy sweeps into the room, his face flushed and jacket flapping. He is carrying a large stuffed bear with a red ribbon around the neck.

Little Val does not look at the gift. He glances at Mommy's face and even the watching fifteen-year-old Val shares the fear of what he may find there.

It is all right. Mommy's reaction is not one of anger but of relief. Her eyes sparkle as if the candles had been lighted again.

Daddy kisses him and lifts him and puts his other arm around Mommy and the three of them hug there above the littered table, with Grandma and Grandpa singing "Happy Birthday" again as if this time is for real, and Samuel wiggling to get at the toys and play with him, and Daddy's arm strong around him and the tears on Mommy's cheeks being all right because she is happy, they all are happy, and little Val knows that wishes do come true and he sets his cheek against Daddy's neck and smells the sweet blend of aftershave and outdoor air there, and Grandpa is saying . . .

Val came out of the twenty-minute replay to the smell of festering garbage and the sound of sirens. Small-arms fire rattled somewhere in the neighborhood. Police choppers thudded overhead and their searchlights stabbed white through the darkness and spilled through his window like white paint.

Val rolled over and tugged his pillow over his head, trying not to think about anything, trying to recapture the flashback and incorporate it into his dreams.

His face struck something hard and cold. The pistol.

Val sat up with a stab of nausea, held the loaded semiautomatic a moment, then tucked it under his mattress with the *Penthouse* magazines. His heart was pounding. He pulled the second twenty-minute vial from his jeans pocket on the floor and broke the tab—almost too quickly—he had to rush to concentrate on the memory image so the *temprolin* could access the right neurons, stimulate the proper synapses.

He is four and it is his birthday. Samuel is yelling, his mother is preparing the cake in the kitchen, and the table is a mess of half-eaten hot dog rolls, red Jell-O, and potato chips.

The door chimes and Grandpa and Grandma sweep in . . .

Carol is watching Danny come out of the blue water and run toward her up the white-sand beach. He looks handsome, lean, tanned from their five days in the sun, and is grinning at her. He throws himself down on the blanket next to her and Carol feels her heart seem to swell with love and happiness. She takes his wet fingers. "Danny, tell me that we'll always love each other."

"We'll always love each other," he says quickly, only this time, locked away in herself, the more observing Carol sees the quick glance toward her under long lashes, the glance that might have been appraising or slightly mocking.

At the time, Carol feels only happiness. She rolls onto her back, letting the fierce Bermuda sun paint her with heat. Danny has said that they are exempt from worries about the ozone layer and skin cancer on this vacation and Carol has happily agreed. She sets her fingers against the small of Danny's back, feeling the droplets of sea water drying there. Playfully, only slightly possessively, she runs her fingers under the elastic at the back of his trunks. The base of his spine and tops of his buttocks are very cool.

She feels him stir and shift slightly on the blanket. "Want to go up to the room?" he whispers. The beach is almost empty and Carol imagines what it would be like to make love right there in the sunlight.

"In a minute," she says.

Coasting on the tide of her own sensations, the realtime Carol understands a simple fact: men tend to flashback their favorite sexual incidents—Carol knows this from their conversation—while most women travel back to re-experience times when closeness and happiness were at their peak. This does not mean that she avoids sexual incidents—in a moment she and Danny will go up to their room and the next thirty minutes will be passionate enough for anyone to choose to replay—but the moments that beckon her back through time are the instants like this where her sense of being loved are absolute, her sense of closeness almost as palpable as the heat from the tropical sun overhead.

Carol turns her head and lifts a hand to her face, ostensibly to block the fierce sunlight, but actually to steal a glimpse of Danny's face so close to hers. His eyes are closed. Beads of water glisten on his lashes. He is smiling slightly.

The bastard brought along a vial of flashback on this trip. He'll show it to me on the last evening, explain how it works, suggest that we flash back to our first sexual encounters—with someone else! He turned that last night into a sort of double ménage à trois.

Carol tries to stifle these thoughts and her realtime anger as the then-Carol rubs her fingers across her eyes, ostensibly to brush away sand but actually to brush away tears of happiness.

The police officer in the yellow rain slicker is waving at the motorcade and Robert wants to have him fired. Luckily the cop is standing between the workers and the railing, so no one should be able to throw anything. Robert glances to the right at people eating their lunch on the steps of a brick building set right where the road swings left around the grassy plaza toward the railroad overpass. They are waving. Robert sees nothing amiss there and glances back at the approaching railroad bridge.

Go! Now! Get down and run!

He stays on the left running board of the chase car. It is very hot.

"Halfback to base," their commander, Emory Roberts, radios from the front seat. "Five minutes to destination."

Robert imagines the destination, the huge merchandise mart where Lancer is scheduled to speak to hundreds of Texas businessmen. The realtime Robert feels his own fatigue in the heat.

Ignore it. Go now!

A sharp sound sends pigeons wheeling above the plaza.

Christ, one of those goddamn workers has fired off a railroad torpedo. He screams over these thoughts, trying to make himself recognize the threat. All those years of training and experience fucked by these two seconds of incomprehension. But it is not until he looks ahead again, sees Lancer's arms rising in the unmistakable gesture of a gunshot victim, that the young agent moves.

The sprint across the gap that separates the two vehicles could not be faster. Robert is reaching for the metal grip just as the third shot strikes the President.

Jesus. The impact is a fraction of a second before I hear the sound. I've never noticed that before.

Lanier's head dissolves in a mist of pink blood and white matter.

Robert seizes the metal grip and leaps onto the step plate just as the heavy Lincoln roars ahead. Robert's foot slips off the plate and he is being half-dragged behind the accelerating convertible.

Too late. Another two seconds. A second and a half. But I will never close it.

The woman in pink is crawling out onto the trunk in an hysterical effort to retrieve part of Lancer's skull so that no one can see what she has just seen.

Inside himself, Robert unsuccessfully tries to close his eyes so that he does not have to see the next minute or two of horror.

Val was out and gone before breakfast. Over coffee, Carol found herself actually talking to her father for a change.

"Today's your counseling session, isn't it, Dad?"

Robert grunted.

"You're going, aren't you?" Carol heard the parental tone in her own voice but could do nothing about it. *When is it*, she wondered, *that we become parents to our parents?*

When they become senile or neurotic or helpless enough that we have to, came her answering thought.

"Have I ever missed one?" said her father, his voice a bit querulous.

"I don't know," said Carol, glancing at her watch.

Robert made a rude noise. "You'd know. The goddamn therapy program would call you, leave messages, and keep calling you until you got in touch in person. Just like the school truancy program . . ." The old man stopped quickly.

Carol looked up. "Has Val been ditching school again?"

Her father hesitated a second and then shrugged. "Does it matter? The schools haven't been much more than holding pens since I was a kid . . ."

"Goddammit," breathed Carol. She rinsed her coffee mug and slammed it into the dishwasher. "I'll talk to him tonight."

"Busy day?" asked her father, as if eager to change the subject.

"Hmmm," said Carol, pulling on her cape. *Dale Fritch's lunch-time depo*, she thought with a jolt. She had all but forgotten it after the night's flashbacks. Perhaps after meeting him and his crazy informant for lunch she could score some more flashback in the Afric section of town before heading back to work. She was down to a single thirty-minute tube.

The Honda was down to a quarter charge. Enough to get her to work but there was no way she could get home without paying the higher charge rates at the Civic Center. And it would mean more expensive work in the shop.

"Fuck," she said, kicking the dented side of the nine-year-old heap of junk. *Great way to start the day.*

She was pulling onto the guideway before she remembered that she had not said good-bye to her father.

"These tunnels are cool," said Coyne. "Long bus ride to get here, but they're definitely cool. How'd you say you found the entrance?"

"My mom showed me a few years ago when she started working at the Civic Center," said Val. "Used to be a bunch of malls and shit down here. They used to bring prisoners through here before they shut it up after the Big One."

Sully and Gene D. looked impressed and a bit nervous. Their footfalls echoed in the dripping corridors. There were no lights, but their VR shades amplified the slightest glow from the ventilation grills.

"You say it runs all the way from where your old lady works at the Civic Center to Pueblo Park on the other side of the One-Oh-One?" said Coyne.

"Yeah." They stopped at a boarded up storefront to light up cigarettes and pass around a bottle of wine. The matches flared like incendiary explosions in VR amplification.

"I think that you should do a Jap," said Coyne.

Val's head snapped up. "A Jap?"

Coyne, Sully, and Gene D. were grinning. "Zap a Jap," crooned Sully.

Val looked only at Coyne. "Why a Jap?"

The taller boy shrugged. "It'd be cool."

"Jap's are crazy about their security," said Val. "They've got bodyguards coming out the ass."

Coyne grinned. "Makes it cooler. We can all watch you, Val my man. We can all flash on this."

Val felt his heart pounding. "No, I mean it," he said, hoping that his voice did not sound as rattled and full of pleading as he felt. "Mom says that the Jap advisors who come to visit with the mayor or the D.A. are nuts about security. Always traveling around with bodyguards. She says that they shut off all the traffic near the Civic Center when Kasai, Morozumi, or Harada visit because . . ." Val stopped but not before he realized that he had said too much. Much too much.

Coyne leaned closer. The amplification made his lean face a blaze of light and shadows. "Because then no one can get close, right, Val my man?" He gestured toward the tunnel. "But we could get close, couldn't we?"

"Nobody knows when the mayor and his tame Japs would visit," said Val, hearing the whine in his own voice and hating it. "Really. I swear."

"Don't your old lady know?" asked Gene D. His voice echoed in the darkness. "She's hot shit down here, ain't she?"

Val made a fist, but Coyne grabbed him. "She doesn't know," said Val. "Ever. Honest."

"Hey, cryo yourself, Val my man," said Coyne, patting his arm. "We believe you. It's all right. We got all the time in the world, Babe. No rush on nothing." Coyne's face looked demonic in amplified light. "We're all friends here, yeah? And this is a mean place. Our own clubhouse, like without the gang trash, you know?" He patted Val's arm a final time and smiled at the others. "A Jap would be cool, but it don't matter who the bod is as long as we got someone to trash so's you can flash. Am I right or am I right?"

They sat and smoked in the darkness.

Carol scored three vials of flashback from one of the clerks in the D.A.'s office to tide her over and spent the morning doing depositions on civil cases for several of the lawyers who used the offices there. She was always pleased to take depositions for the private firms because it meant extra money selling them copies of the transcripts. Several of the other stenographers were out—which was usually the case—but she learned that one of them, a woman named Sally Carter whom Carol did not know too well, was home because word had just reached her that her husband had been killed in the fighting near Hong Kong. There was the usual clucking and muttering that America had no business fighting wars for Japan or the Chinese warlords, but in the end everyone admitted that the country needed the money and that there were precious few commodities other than American military technology and warm bodies that Japan or the EC would buy.

Sally Carter's absence meant more work and deposition sales for Carol.

At 11:00 A.M. she looked in her desk drawer, ready to steal a muffin from her lunch bag, remembered that she had not packed a lunch today, and then remembered the reason. She smiled at the thought of her cloak-and-dagger rendezvous with the Assistant D.A.

At 11:15 A.M., Danny called.

The phone was obviously a poorly lighted pay phone in a bar somewhere and the video quality was poor: Danny was little more than a pale blur in the shadows. But it was a familiar blur. And his voice had not changed.

"Carol," he said, "you're looking great, kiddo. Really good."

Carol said nothing. She could not speak. It had been eight and a half years since she had last seen or spoken to Danny.

"Anyway," he said, speaking quickly to fill her silence, "I was in L.A. for a couple of days . . . I live in Chicago now, you know . . . and I just thought . . . I mean I hoped . . . I mean, dammit, Carol, will you please have lunch with me today? Please? It's very important to me."

No, thought Carol. *Absolutely not. You don't just leave Val and me, no letter, no explanation, no child support, and then call me up eight years later and say you want to have lunch. Absolutely not. No.*

"Yes," she heard herself say, feeling as if she were in one of her flashbacks and wondering if she *were* flashing on this from some sad future. "Where? When?"

Danny told her the place. It was a downtown bar in which they had eaten when they first moved to L.A. fifteen years ago and used to steal lunchbreaks to be together. "Say . . . ten minutes from now?"

Carol knew that if she took the Honda it might not hold a charge and would leave her stranded in the shitty section of the city. She would have to take the bus. "Twenty minutes," she said.

The pale blob that was Danny nodded. She thought she could see a smile.

Carol hung up but kept her finger on the button for a minute, as if caressing it. Then she hurried to reapply her makeup and get downstairs to the bus.

"Halfback to Base. Five minutes to destination."

Oh, fuck it. Fuck it all to hell. Robert is disgusted. After years of this, he knows what will not happen. It is like self-abuse without a climax.

He keeps his eyes closed . . . or tries to. One cannot shut out flashback visuals without a tremendous effort of will. People are shouting and waving on the green grass to his left.

Robert tried to escape, to return to another time, another memory . . . but once begun, there is no escape from a flashback episode. They glide toward the railroad bridge overpass.

There is a sound. Pigeons wheel into the canyon above the plaza.

No use. Empty. Useless.

Three seconds later he leaps from the chase car and sprints toward the blue Lincoln.

Useless. No exercise of will can make him move more quickly. Time and memory are immutable.

Not even my fucking memory. I am crazy. Kay, I miss you.

The second shot. He dives for the footplate and metal grip. The third shot.

Robert tries not to see, but the image of the President's head exploding is not to be denied.

Twenty years later, fifty percent of Americans polled remembered seeing this live on television. It was never on television. It was almost two years until censored parts of the Zapruder film were released . . . and then only to Life *magazine. Before flashback, memories lied . . . we edited them at will. Shit, Kennedy was elected with only forty-some percent of the vote, but ten years after his death seventy-two percent of the people polled said they had voted for him.*

Memory lies.

He pushes the President's wife back into the vehicle, noticing the insanity in her wide eyes but understanding the urgency in her single-minded ambition to retrieve the bit of skull. To make everything all right again.

I'm going to find Val. Make sure he doesn't do anything stupid.

He shoves the woman back down in the seat and guards her and Lancer's body all the way to Parkland Hospital. The hopelessness flows over him like a rising tide.

Val and his friends watched the I-5 guideway from their perch on the roof of a building abandoned after the Big One. Val was holding the .32, bracing it with both hands along the edge of the roof. The traffic glided by silently except for the rush of tires on wet pavement. It had rained in the past hour.

"I could wait until a Lexus comes along and blast it," said Val.

Coyne gave him a disgusted look. "With that popgun? It's thirty yards to the VIP lane. You couldn't even hit the fucking car, much less the Jap in the backseat. If there *is* a Jap in the backseat."

"Besides," said Gene D., "their cars have the best armorplating there is. A fucking ought-six wouldn't go through one of their fucking windshields."

"Yeah," said Sully.

"A fucking needlegun wouldn't hurt a Jap Lexus from here," said Gene D.

Val lowered the pistol. "I thought that it was the best if the . . . if it was a random thing you did to flash on."

Coyne rubbed Val's short hair with his knuckles. "It *was* the best, Val my man. Now a Jap's the thing."

Val sat back, leaving the .32 on the ledge. Water pooled on the sagging asphalt roof. "But it might take days . . . weeks . . ."

Coyne grinned, swept the pistol off the ledge, and offered it to Val. "Hey, we got time, don't we, my men?"

Sully and Gene D. made noises.

Val hesitated a second and then took the pistol. It started raining again and the boys hurried for shelter. Val did not see his grandfather watching them from across the street. When they left the building a few minutes later, none of the boys noticed the old man following them toward the river.

* * *

It was raining by the time Carol got to the bar on San Julian. She hustled in, holding a newspaper over her hair, and stood a minute blinking in the dark. When the heavyset man approached her, she actually took a step backward before she recognized him.

"Danny."

He took her hands and set the wet newspaper on a table. "Carol. Christ, you look good." He hugged her clumsily.

She could not say the same about her ex-husband. Danny had put on weight— at least a hundred pounds—and his features and familiar body seemed lost in the excess. Much of his blond hair was gone and his scalp was freckled with brown spots like her father's. His skin was sallow, his eyes were dark and sunken over heavy pouches, and he was wheezing softly. What she had assumed were bad lighting and poor video quality on the phone were actually shadows and distortions of Danny himself.

"I've got our old booth," he said. Without letting go of her hands, he led her to a corner near the rear. She did not remember having a special booth here, and she had never replayed this particular memory.

A glass of Scotch sat half-finished on the table. From the way Danny smelled when he kissed her, he'd had more than one.

They sat looking at each other across the table. For a minute neither spoke. The bar was almost empty this time of day, but the bartender and a man in a tattered raincoat near the front were having an argument with a sportscaster persona on an old HDTV above a line of bottles. Carol looked down and realized that Danny was still holding both of her hands in one of his. She felt strange, anaesthetized, as if the nerves in her hands conveyed no tactile information.

"Well, Jesus, Carol," Danny said at last, "you really look great. You really do."

Carol nodded and waited.

Danny swallowed the last of the Scotch, waved the bartender over for a refill, gestured to Carol, and took the slight shaking of her head as a no. Only after a full glass of whiskey was delivered did he speak again. The rush of words flowed over Carol, relieving her of any necessity to speak.

"Well, God, Carol, here I was on a . . . well, a sort of business trip actually . . . and I realized, well, I wondered . . . Does she still work down at the Hall of Justice? . . . and there you were, right on the answering persona's list of options. Anyway, I thought . . . you know, why not? So . . . Christ, did I tell you how great you look? Beautiful, actually. Not that you weren't always a knockout. I always thought you were a knockout. But, hey, you know that.

"Anyway, you probably want to know what I'm up to, huh? Been what? Four or five years since that time . . . anyway, I'm in Chicago now. Not with Caldwell Banker anymore. Sold luxury electrics for a while, but . . . you know . . . the market's really gone to shit on those. Got out just at the right time. So, where was I? I'm in Chicago . . . I'm into some deep pattern counseling . . . thought you might be interested in me getting into some counseling."

Danny laughed. It was an oddly abrasive sound and the two men at the front of the bar glanced back and then went back to their argument with the sportscaster persona. Danny touched her fingers, lifted her hands in his again as if they were a pair of gloves he had forgotten he had, and then set them down on the scarred table. He took a drink.

"So anyway, this deep pattern counseling . . . you've heard of it? No? Jesus, I thought everyone in California would . . . anyway, there's this brilliant guy in Chicago, he's a doctor . . . you know, a Ph.D. in therapeutic flashback use . . . and he had sort of, well, ashram is the word. People with serious things to work out sort of live there and tithe to him . . . well, actually it's a bit more than tithe since it involves power of attorney . . . but what it is, is, that it's not a one-shot-a-week type of thing. We live there and the counseling . . . deep pattern counseling, it's called . . . the counseling is sort of our job like. It's an all day thing . . ."

"Using flashback," said Carol.

Danny grinned as if terrifically relieved and impressed by her depth of understanding. "You got it. Right. Perfect. You probably know all about it . . . there's a million deep pattern type counseling centers out here in sunny California. But, yeah, we're in counseling with it for eight to ten hours a day . . . under the strict supervision of Dr. Singh, of course. Or his appointed therapist-counselors. It's not like, you know, how I used to use the stuff when we were together . . ." He rubbed his cheeks and Carol heard the rasp of his palm on the stubble there. "I know I was fucking around with it then, Carol. I mean, I hardly flash on the teenage sex stuff now. It's just . . . you know . . . it's just not important given the totality of the therapeutic experience, y'know?"

Carol brushed a strand of wet hair off her forehead. "What *is* important?" she asked.

"What?" Danny had finished his Scotch and was trying to get the bartender's attention. "I'm sorry, Babe. What?"

"What is important, Danny?"

He waited for the refill and then smiled almost beatifically. "I've got a chance for a real breakthrough here, Babe. Dr. Singh himself says that I've reached the point where I can turn things around. But . . ."

Carol knew the tone well. She said nothing.

Danny took her hands again and rubbed them as if they were cold. It was *his* hands that were cold.

"But I need some help . . ." he began.

"Money," said Carol.

Danny dropped her hands and made a fist. Carol noticed how pudgy, pale, and weak his hand looked, as if the muscles there had been replaced by fat. *Or creme filling*, she thought. *Like those Bavarian creme donuts he used to eat.*

"Not just money," he rasped at her. "*Help.* I'm ready to take the step to total reintegration, and Dr. Singh says that . . ."

"Total reintegration?" said Carol. It sounded like some new software telem package that Val wanted to buy for his VR shades.

Danny's smile was condescending. "Yeah. Total recall. Complete reintegration of this past life with the soul-knowledge that I've gained during my time at the ashram. It's like . . . you know . . . retrofitting an old gas-burning car for electric or methane. There are some people at the ashram who are actually at the stage where they can reintegrate their *past* lives, but . . . Jesus, you know . . . I feel like I'll be lucky to handle this one." He made the abrasive laughing sound again.

Carol nodded. "You need money for flashback that you use in this . . . therapy," she said. "How much? How long a replay?" Her voice would have betrayed her almost total lack of curiosity if Danny had been paying any real attention.

"Well," he said, excited, obviously thinking that he had a chance, "total reintegration is . . . you know . . . *total*. I've already liquidated what I had . . . the Lakeshore apartment, the Chrysler electric, the few stocks that Wally left me . . . but I'll need a lot more to . . ." He stopped when he saw her expression. "Hey, Carol, this isn't, like, a one-payment thing. It's like . . . you know . . . a mortgage or car payments. It's not really much at all when you look at it stretched out over the period we're talking about, and . . ."

Carol said, "You're talking about flashing back on your whole life."

"Well . . . you know . . . what I mean is . . . yeah."

"Total reintegration," said Carol. "You're forty-four years old, Danny, and you're going to flashback your entire life."

He sat up straight, his chin thrusting out in what Carol remembered as his belligerent posture. As pale, overweight, and soft as he looked now, the sight was a bit pathetic.

"It's easy to make fun of someone who's willing to be vulnerable," he said. "I'm trying to straighten out my life, Carol."

Carol laughed softly. "Danny, you'd be *eighty-eight* when you finished the flashback."

He leaned forward as if he were going to impart a secret to her. His voice was wet and intimate. "Carol, this is just one life on the wheel. The most important thing about it is where we are when we *end* it."

Carol stood up. "There's no doubt where you'll be, Danny. You'll be broke." She walked away.

"Hey . . ." shouted Danny, not rising. "I forgot to ask . . . how's Val?"

Carol went out into the rain, could not remember which way the bus stop was, and began walking blindly toward the Civic Center.

Val and his friends were lounging in the steel viaduct buttresses fifty feet above the concrete riverbed when Coyne suddenly sat up, grabbed Val's shoulder, and said, "Bingo!"

"Don't you have your shades wired to news?" said Coyne, nodding and grinning at something in VR.

"News?" said Val. "Are you shitting me?"

Coyne took his glasses off. "I shit you not, Val my man. We have just been delivered a Jap."

Val felt his heart sink.

"Delivered a Jap, delivered a Jap," crooned Sully.

"What's happening?" said Gene D., coming out of a ten-minute flash. From the look of the bulge in Gene D.'s jeans, Val guessed that his friend had been flashing on the Spanic girl's rape again.

"Newsflash," grinned Coyne. "Big stir at the Civic Center. The mayor's headed over there with his Jap advisor buddy, Morozumi."

"Civic Center," said Val. "My mom works there."

Coyne nodded. "We take that neat tunnel complex you showed us in from First Street. Do the deed there at that VIP plaza on Temple Street. Get our asses out through the tunnel to Pueblo Park and then *didi mau* ourselves away by bus. Leave the fucking gun in the fucking tunnel."

"Won't work," said Val, searching his mind for reasons that it would not.

Coyne shrugged. "Maybe not. But it'll be a mainline rush to check it out."

"It won't work," said Val, repeating the phrase like a mantra as he followed the others.

Robert felt more alive than he had in years as he followed the boys onto a caterpillar bus and slid into the section behind them. His pace was lighter, his vision was clearer, and he felt as if he had cleared his head of cobwebs. He stood at the front end of the second bus section, watching through the accordion doors into Val's section to make sure he did not miss it when the boys stepped out.

Robert wondered if the therapy persona was correct, if his flashback obsession was the result of a sense of failure at not protecting his wife from her final bout of cancer. "You are aware," the program had told him, "that more than fifty years after the death of President Kennedy, there are thousands of people obsessed with conspiracy theories that have never been proven."

"I don't believe in a conspiracy," Robert had muttered.

The bearded persona had smiled on the ITV wall. "No, but you perseverate in this protection fantasy."

Robert had worked hard not to become angry. He had said nothing.

"Your wife died . . . how many years ago was it?" asked the counselor.

Robert knew that the program knew. "Six," he said.

"And how long ago was it that the country was so wrapped up in the fiftieth anniversary of this assassination?"

Robert did feel anger at the simple-minded obviousness of this line of questioning. But he had promised Carol and the Medicaid caseworker that he would undergo the counseling. "Five years ago."

"And the flashback obsession . . ."

"About five years," sighed Robert. He had glanced at his watch. "My time's up."

The bearded persona . . . Robert thought it was a persona, he was never sure . . . showed white teeth through his beard. "Bobby," he said, "that's my line."

The boys got off the bus at the ruins of the old Federal Building and Robert followed.

*   *   *

All the way back to the Civic Center in the rain, Carol looked around her with newly opened eyes. She looked at the ten-foot-high heaps of bagged garbage, the abandoned storefronts, the unrepaired damage from the Big One years ago, the slogans in mock-Japanese touting cheap Japanese recreation electronics, the security cameras, the cheap electrics lining the curb with their security holos pulsing ominously, the people hurrying along with gray faces and averted eyes the way she had remembered seeing vid from Eastern Europe and Russ when she was a kid . . . it all seemed to match Danny's fat characterless face and whining, self-absorbed tone.

I'm going to take Val and Dad and move to Canada, she thought. It was not a whim. It was the strongest resolve she had felt in years. *Or Mexico. Somewhere where half the population isn't zonked on flashback at any given moment.*

Carol raised her face to the rain. *I'm going to quit using that shit. Get Val and Dad to stop.*

She tried to remember what the country had been like when she was a tiny little kid, looking at the kindly, grandfatherly face of President Reagan on the old-fashioned TV. *You bankrupted us forever, you kindly, grandfatherly asshole. My kid's kids will never pay off the debt. For what . . . winning the Cold War and creating the Russ Republic so it can compete with us in buying Japanese and EC products? We can't afford them. And we've all become too stupid and too lazy to make our own.*

For the first time, Carol understood why use of flashback was cause for execution in Japan . . . a nation that had not had the death penalty for sixty years before that. For the first time she understood that a culture or a nation actually had to decide whether it would look forward or allow itself to lie back and dream until it died.

Total reintegration. Mother of Christ.

Carol had walked for more than an hour when she realized that the rain had stopped but that her cheeks were still wet. It was a shock when she turned the corner near the Civic Center and was stopped by security agents. She showed her badge at two points, was frisked by a sniffer, and then approached the north entrance where the mayor's limo and several armored Lexuses sat within a cordon of police motorcycles.

She was already upstairs and had been checked by two more security people before one of the women from the secretarial pool came rushing toward her, tears streaming down the woman's heavy face. "Carol, did you hear? It's terrible. Poor Dale."

Carol pulled herself free, went into her cubicle, and keyed her phone to vid news. The bulletin was repeated a moment later. L.A. Assistant Attorney Dale Fritch, a Japanese national named Hiroshi Nakamura, and five other people had been murdered in a downtown café. There was the usual montage of crime scene video. Carol sat down heavily.

Her urgent-message phone light was blinking. Numbly, Carol killed the news feed and keyed the message.

"Carol," said Dale Fritch, his boyish image only slightly distorted by the poor pay-phone video, "I'm sorry we missed each other, but it's all right. Hiroshi talked more freely with just me here. Carol . . . *I believe him*. I think the Japanese have been feeding this stuff to us since the late nineties. I think there's something here bigger than the EC Payback Scandal, bigger than Watergate . . . shit, bigger than the Big One. Hiroshi has disks, papers, memos, payoff lists . . ." Fritch glanced over his shoulder. "Look, Carol, I've got to get back to him. Look, I'm not coming in this afternoon. Can you bring your datawriter and meet me at . . . uh . . . say the LAX Holiday Inn . . . at five-thirty? It'll be worth it, I promise. Okay. Uh . . . don't say anything about any of this to anyone, okay? See you at five-thirty. *Ciao*."

Carol sat looking at her phone a minute and then recorded the message to a fresh disk, slipped it in her pocket, and keyed the news feed. A live reporter was standing in front of a restaurant where bodies were being removed on gurneys. ". . . police know only that Assistant D.A. Fritch was at the restaurant in an unofficial capacity when three men in black ski masks entered and opened fire with what one witness described as, quote, 'military-type needleguns, the kind you see in the movies.' Assistant D.A. Fritch and the others died instantly. The Japanese Embassy has no comment on the identity of the man with Fritch, but a CNN/LA news source close to the embassy informs us that the Japanese national was one Hiroshi Nakamura, a felon wanted by Tokyo Police Prefecture. Sources within the L.A.P.D. speculate that Nakamura may have been meeting with Assistant D.A. Fritch to sound out Los Angeles justice authorities on a plea bargain in exchange for a promise of no extradition. These same sources inform CNN/LA that the hit bears all the marks of a Yakuza assassination. The Yakuza, as you may remember, are Japan's most lethal crime organization and a rising problem in the new . . ."

"Carol?" said a voice behind her. "Could you step into my office for a moment?" Bert Torrazio was standing there with several security men in plain-clothes.

The mayor and his advisor, Mr. Morozumi, were sitting in leather chairs across from the D.A.'s desk. Carol nodded although no introductions were made.

"Bert," said the mayor, "take me down to Dale's office, would you? I'd like to offer my condolences to his staff."

Everyone left except for Carol, two Japanese security men, and Morozumi. The advisor was impeccable in a Sartori suit, gray tie, and perfectly groomed gray hair. A modest Nippon Space Agency wrist chronometer that must have cost at least thirty thousand dollars was his only concession to extravagance. Mr. Morozumi nodded and the security men left.

"You returned from lunch three minutes too soon, Ms. Rogallo," said the advisor. "The disk, please."

Carol hesitated only a second before handing him the CD.

Morozumi smiled slightly as he slipped the silver disk in his coat pocket. "We knew, of course, that Mr. Fritch had called someone, but the city's antiquated communications equipment succeeded in tracing the call only seconds ago." Morozumi rose and crossed to a rubber tree near the window. "Mr. Torrazio should take better care of his plants," the advisor murmured almost to himself.

"Why?" said Carol. *Why kill Dale? Why feed a nation a drug for twenty years?*

Mr. Morozumi raised his face. Sunlight glinted on his round glasses. He touched a leaf of the rubber tree. "It is a sign of slovenliness not to take care of those living things in one's care," he said.

"What happens next?" said Carol. When Morozumi did not answer, she said, "To me."

The little man dusted another leaf with his fingers and then rubbed his fingertips together, cleaning them. "You live with your child, Valentine, and a father who is currently receiving counseling. Your ex-husband, Daniel, is still alive and . . . I believe . . . visiting your fair city even as we speak."

Carol felt something like cold fingers close around her heart and throat.

"To answer your question," continued Mr. Morozumi, "I presume you will continue doing your fine job here at the Justice Center and that Mr. Torrazio will be pleased with your performance. From time to time I will, perhaps, have the opportunity to chat with you and hear about the continued health and well-being of your family."

Carol said nothing. She concentrated on staying on her feet and not swaying.

Mr. Morozumi pulled a tissue from a dispenser on Bert Torrazio's desk, wiped his dirty fingers, and dropped the Kleenex on the D.A.'s blotter. As if on signal, the mayor, the D.A., and the security people came back through the door. Torrazio looked at Carol and then raised his eyebrows questioningly.

Mr. Morozumi averted his glance as if Torrazio had food on his upper lip. "We had a delightful chat and it is time to get back to business," said Mr. Morozumi. He left with the slim security men. The mayor shook Torrazio's hand, nodded in Carol's direction, and rushed to catch up to the procession.

Carol and the District Attorney stared at each other for a full minute before she turned on her heel and went back to her cubicle. The file cabinet was empty and both her phone and computer had been replaced. Carol sat down and stared at a cartoon she had taped to the frosted glass of her partition four years earlier. It showed a court reporter typing furiously as a witness and lawyer screamed at each other, the judge pounded her gravel, the defendant stood shouting at the witness, the defendant's lawyer yelled at him, and two jurors bellowed at each other on the verge of a violent confrontation. A woman behind the court reporter was saying to a friend, "She's a good writer but her plots aren't very believable."

The underground mall ended at a ventilator grill between the landscaping and the Civic Center. Coyne had brought a crowbar. The boys found themselves standing with a small press contingent bristling with vid cameras and parabolic mikes. Local reporters shouted questions at the mayor and his Japanese advisor as they descended the stairs to the idling limousine. Val was within twenty feet of the VIPs. The ventilator grill was open and waiting twenty feet behind him. The security people ignored the previously searched press group and concentrated on watching the buildings and the crowd being held back across the little plaza.

"Do it," said Coyne. "Now."

Val took the pistol and cocked it.

The mayor paused just long enough to answer a shouted question and then wave at someone in the Civic Center doorway. Obeying protocol, Mr. Morozumi waited by the open limousine door for the mayor to finish.

Val raised the pistol. It was less then fifteen feet to the Japanese man's head. The pistol barrel was just one more lens thrust toward the small knot of VIPs. Val was not aware of Coyne, Sully, and Gene D. sliding away and disappearing down the open grill.

Robert had almost not been able to pull himself up out of the opening. He thought that all of his strength was gone by the time he stood up, brushing rust and dead leaves from his pants, but then he saw Val, saw the gun, saw that he was closer to the target than to his grandson, and then Robert ran forward immediately, without thinking, without hesitating an instant.

Val pulled the trigger. Nothing happened. He blinked and then clicked the safety off. He had just raised the pistol again when one of the cameramen near him shouted, ''Hey!''

Robert ran full tilt at the black limousine. To put his body between Val and the mayor he would have to jump up and over the right rear of the trunk. He did so, forgetting his age, forgetting his arthritis, forgetting everything except the imperative to be there before the boy pulled the trigger again.

Val saw his grandfather at the last second and could not believe it as the old man vaulted to the trunk of the limo, skidded across it, and landed on his feet between the mayor and Mr. Morozumi. Security men leaped on Mr. Morozumi, pushing him down. The mayor stood alone, mouth still open to answer a question.

I made it! thought Robert knowing that he was between Val and the mayor, knowing that any bullet meant for the other man would have to go through him. *This time I made . . .*

Two of the Japanese security agents crouched, braced their weapons, and shot Robert from a distance of fifteen feet. At almost the same instant, a third security man raked automatic weapons fire across the press gallery. Val and three cameramen went down.

The mayor and Mr. Morozumi were pushed into the limo and rushed away before the watching crowd had time to begin screaming. Neither the mayor nor his advisor was hurt.

Val's body was taken to the police morgue but Carol was allowed to visit her father.

''He won't know you're here,'' said the doctor. His voice was disinterested. ''The neurological damage is too great. There is some brain activity, but it is very limited. I'm afraid that it is just a matter of how long the life support can keep things up. Hours perhaps. Days at the most.''

Carol nodded and sat down in the chair next to the bed. She did not touch his hand. The room was illuminated just by the electronic monitors.

The room is illuminated just by the light of the medical monitors. Visitors do not think that Robert can hear what they are saying, but he can.

"He has been like this for some time," says the nurse to the President's visiting daughter and her son.

"My father wants nothing but the finest care for him," says Lancer's daughter. She has grown into a beautiful woman. Her son is three or four and has inherited his grandfather's healthy thatch of chestnut hair. The little boy takes Robert's fingers in his small hands. He is not frightened by the hospital room or the IV drips or the medical monitors. He has been here before.

Lancer's daughter sits by his bedside as she has so many times before. *Do not weep for me*, thinks Robert. *I am not unhappy.*

Carol sits by her father's bed until 3 A.M. when the technicians come to unhook the machines and to take his body away.

When they are gone, she continues to sit in the dark room. Her eyes are open but she does not see. After a while she smiles, takes out a thirty-minute tube, raises it almost reverently to her nose, and breaks the tab.

A CHILD'S CHRISTMAS IN FLORIDA

William Browning Spencer

▼

Here's a strange and blackly funny little story that depicts a very *odd* way to celebrate a very familiar holiday, a holiday you may never be able to look at in quite the same way again. . . .

New writer William Browning Spencer was born in Washington, D.C., and now lives in Austin, Texas. His first novel, *Maybe I'll Call Anna*, was published in 1990 and won a New American Writing Award. His most recent books are a collection, *The Return of Count Electric and Other Stories*, and a new novel, *Resume with Monsters*, and he is currently at work on a fantasy novel entitled *Zod Wallop*.

The week before Christmas, Luke Haliday killed the traditional mud turtle, gutted it, and gave its shell to his oldest son, Hark. Hark painted the shell with day-glo colors and wore it on his head, where it would remain until two days before Christmas when the youngest of the children, Lou Belle, would snatch it from his head, run giggling down to the creek, and fill the gaudy shell with round, smooth stones.

"I miss Harrisburg," Janice Mosely said to her husband. "It should be cold at Christmas. There should be snow." Her husband didn't say anything, but simply leaned over his newspaper like he might dive into it. Well, Al could ignore her if he pleased. She knew he missed Pennsylvania too and just didn't care to talk about it. There was no getting around it: Christmas was for colder climes, everyone all bundled up and hustling from house to house with presents, red-faced children, loud, wet people in the hall peeling off layers of clothing, scarves, boots, gloves, shouting because they were full of hot life that winter had failed to freeze and ready for any marvelous thing. And snow, snow could make the world look like the cellophane had just been shucked from it, was still crackling in the air.

"Barbara says it snowed eight inches last week," Janice said. Barbara was their daughter. Al Mosely looked up from his newspaper and regarded his wife with pale, sleepy blue eyes. A wispy cloud of gray hair bloomed over his high forehead, giving his face a truculent, just-wakened cast. In fact, he had been up since five (his unvarying routine) and regarded his wife's nine o'clock appearance at the breakfast table as something approaching decadence.

"She'll have to get that dodger"—Al always referred to Barbara's live-in boyfriend as "that dodger," an allusion to the young man's ability to avoid matrimony—"She'll have to get that dodger to shovel her walk this year," Al said. "She was the one who was so hot for us to retire to Florida, and we done it and we'll just see if she gets that layabout to do anything more than wait for the spring thaw."

"Oh Al," Janice said, waving a hand at him and turning away. She walked into the living room and stared out the window. Not only had they moved to Florida, they had moved to rural Florida, land of cows and scrub pines and cattle egrets. Her husband had said, "Okay, I'll go to Florida, but not to some condominium on the ocean. I don't want a place full of old folks playing bridge and shuffleboard. If I'm gonna retire, I'm gonna retire right. A little place in the country—that's the ticket."

Janice watched a yellow dog walk out into the road. Its image shimmered in the heat, like a bad television transmission. Christmas. Christmas in Loomis, Florida. Dear God. Why, none of her neighbors had even put up lights. And maybe they had the right idea. Why bother? There was no way this flat, sandy place could cobble up a Christmas to fool a half-wit.

As Janice Mosely stared out the window, three boys, the tallest of them wearing a funny, brightly colored beanie, marched by. A tiny little girl ran in their wake. The boys were carrying a Christmas tree. With an air of triumphant high spirits, they wrestled it down the road, shouting to each other, country boys in tattered jeans and T-shirts and home-cropped haircuts, boys full of reckless enthusiasm and native rudeness. Janice smiled and scolded herself. "Well, it's a perfectly fine Christmas for some, Mrs. Janice 'Scrooge' Mosely," she said out loud. Still smiling, she turned away from the window and walked back into the kitchen. Her husband was listening to the radio, the news, all of it bleak: war, famine, murder, political graft.

"What's the world coming to?" Janice asked her husband.

"Let me think about it before I answer," Al said.

Hark was the oldest boy, but he wasn't right in the head, so Danny, who was three years younger, was in charge. "You don't do it that way," Danny said. "You will just bust your fingers doing it that way. Boy, you are a rattlebrain."

"Shut up," Hark said. "If you know what's good for you, shut up."

"What's the problem here?" their father asked, coming into the backyard. Luke Haliday was a tall, lanky man with a bristly black mustache. There wasn't any nonsense in him and his children knew it. He had been very strict since their mother left. Now he said, "Maybe you would rather fight than have a Christmas?"

"No, no!" shouted little Lou Belle who was so infused with the spirit of Christmas that it made her eyes bulge. The boys, Hark, Danny, and Calder, all shouted: "No, no."

"I was just trying to explain to Hark that you got to tie these traps onto the tree first and then set em. You do it the other way, you just catch all your fingers," Danny said.

Luke laid a hand on Hark's shoulder. "Is this the first tree you ever decorated?" he asked his son.

"No sir," Hark said.

"Well then," Luke said.

"Tie em, then set em," Hark said, kicking dirt.

Luke stood back from his children and regarded the Christmas tree; the boys had dug a hole for the trunk and braced it with wires and stakes. The tree stood straight, tall and proud, the field rolling out behind it. "That's a damned fine tree," Luke said. "You children got an eye for a tree. You take this one out of Griper's field?"

"Yes sir," Danny said.

"It's a good one," their father said. He reached down, picked up one of the mousetraps, and tied it to a branch with a piece of brown string. Then he set the trap and stood back again. The tree already had a dozen traps tied to various branches. "If a tree like this can't bring us luck then we might as well give up. We might as well lie down and let them skin us and salt us if a tree like this don't bode a fine Christmas."

The children agreed.

Their father turned and walked back to the shack, and the children set to work tying the remaining traps to branches. Later they would paint colored dots on them. "I want blue," Lou Belle insisted. "I want mine blue." Her voice was shrill, prepared for an argument, but Danny just said, "Sure. Why not?"

"Hello," Janice shouted, when she saw the little girl again. "Hello, little girl." The child turned and stared at Janice for a long time before finally changing course and toddling toward the old woman.

"Lou Belle," the little girl said in answer to Janice's question. *What a sweet child*, Janice thought, with such full cheeks—they cried out to be pinched—and those glorious, big brown eyes. The girl wore corduroy overalls and a white T-shirt. Her feet were bare.

"What's Santa bringing you for Christmas?" Janice asked.

The girl shrugged her shoulders. "Santa don't come to our house," she said.

"Oh, I'm sure he does." Janice knelt down and placed her hands on the child's shoulders. Lou Belle was a frail little thing. "Santa wouldn't miss a sweet little girl like you."

"Yes'm," the girl said. "He don't come anymore. He left. He and my mommy. They went to live in sin."

"Goodness," Janice said. What an odd child.

Janice stood up. "Would you like to see my Christmas tree? I just finished decorating it, and I thought, 'There's no one around to see it except Al'—that's my husband, and he couldn't care less about such things. And then I looked out the window and there you were, and I thought, 'I bet that little girl would like to see this tree.' "

"Yes'm," Lou Belle said, and she followed Janice Mosely into the house, and she studied the evergreen that Janice had harried her husband into buying and which she had then decorated carefully, all the while listening to Christmas music and ignoring her husband's grumblings and general humbuggery.

Lou Belle touched the glass ornaments. Lou Belle leaned close and blinked at the hand-sewn angels. She even rubbed the styrofoam snowman against her cheek—it made a *skritch, skritch* sound—but finally she stepped back and said, "It won't catch nuthin."

Lou Belle thought about it that night when she couldn't sleep. Silly old lady. What could you catch inside a house, anyway? Even with the best of traps?

Lou Belle couldn't sleep because tomorrow was Omen Day, the third day before Christmas. Last night they had baited the traps, and this morning they would get out of bed while it was still dark out; they would wake their father and he would make them eat breakfast first, while they craned their necks and peered out the back window, trying to squint through the darkness. Father would move slow, especially slow out of that meanness that adults have, and he would fix eggs and toast and talk about everything, as though it weren't Omen Day at all but any normal day and finally, finally, when they had all finished and were watching and fidgeting as their father mopped up the last of his eggs with a bread crust, he would say, "All right, let's see what we've got."

And it would still be dark, and he would grab up the big lantern flashlight and they would run down to the tree.

Who could possibly sleep the night before Omen Day?

And when it finally did come, when Lou Belle could stand it no longer and ran into her brother Hark's room and woke him and then the two of them fetched Danny and Calder and the long, long breakfast was endured, they pushed the screen door open and ran out into the darkness of the yard. Her heart thrummed like a telephone wire in a hurricane. The grass was wet under her feet.

She thought she would faint when her father, moving the flashlight over the tree, said, "There's a lizard. That's a red dot. Calder, that's you." She wanted to cry out, "No! Not Calder! I'm the Chosen!" But before she could scream, her father spoke again, in a low, awed whisper. "Well, would you look at that." And Lou Belle followed the flashlight's beam with her eyes, and there, flapping awkwardly, caught, like a wound-down toy, was a black, furry lump, and her breathing flipped backwards and she said, in a hiccup of triumph, "Bat!" And she knew, before her father called out "Blue, that's Lou Belle" that it was hers.

And she didn't need her father to tell her that bat was best, that bat was the king of good luck. She clapped her hands and laughed.

"Light the tree, Lou Belle," they urged her, and she smelled the kerosene smell that was, more than anything, the smell of Christmas, and her father gave her the burning straw and she thrust it forward, and the whole tree stood up with flame, *whoosh*, and in the brightness she could see the bat, her bat, and she squealed with joy. Then her father started it off, with his fine, deep voice. "Silent night, holy night," he sang. They all joined in. "All is calm, all is bright."

"Listen," Janice said to her husband. "Do you hear that?"

"What?"

"Carolers," Janice said. "Isn't that nice?"

Because Lou Belle was the Chosen, she stole the mud turtle shell from Hark and filled it with smooth stones. And on Christmas Eve, just before twilight, Lou Belle distributed the stones among her brothers, and they each made their wishes on them and solemnly threw them into the lake, and then they all climbed into the back of their father's pickup truck and drove into town and on past the town and down to Clearwater and late, very late at night, with the salt air filling her lungs, Lou Belle fell asleep, her head resting on a dirty blanket smelling faintly of gasoline. When she woke it was dark, thick, muggy dark, and Hark was urging her out of the truck. She ran after them, instantly alert. A bouncing, silver ball on the grass was the orb of her father's flashlight.

They were in a suburb. She heard glass break and then Danny was beside her. "Come on, come on," he was whispering.

Oh. Her father had pushed open the sliding glass door to reveal, like a magician, a treasure of gifts, gaudily wrapped boxes, all strewn under a thick-bodied Christmas tree pin-pricked with yellow lights. Amid all the gift-wrapped boxes, a marvelous orange tricycle with yellow handlebars glowed.

"Oh," Lou Belle said. She pointed a stubby finger at the bike, and her father moved swiftly across the room, lifted the bike and returned to her.

"Shhhhhhhhhhh," her father said, raising a finger to his lips.

Hark and Danny and Calder were busy under the tree. Calder raised both hands, clutching a brand new air rifle, a smile scrawled across his face.

This is the best Christmas, the best, Lou Belle thought. Next year some of the magic would be gone. Other Christmases would bring disillusionment. She would learn, as her brothers already knew, that her father took great pains to discover a proper house, and that it was his vigilance and care in the choosing that was important, not the catch on Omen Day, not how fervently the wishes were placed on the turtle stones.

But for now it was all magic, and as they raced back across the lawn and piled into the truck, as the motor caught with a sound like thunder, as someone behind them shouted, Lou Belle sent a quick prayer to the baby Jesus, king of thieves.

WHISPERS

Maureen F. McHugh and David B. Kisor

▼

Born in Ohio, Maureen F. McHugh spent some years living in Shijiazhuang in the People's Republic of China, an experience that has been one of the major shaping forces on her fiction to date. Upon returning to the United States, she made her first sale in 1989, and has since made a powerful impression on the SF world of the early nineties with a relatively small body of work, becoming a frequent contributor to *Asimov's Science Fiction*, as well as selling to *The Magazine of Fantasy & Science Fiction, Alternate Warriors, Aladdin*, and other markets. In 1992, she published one of the year's most widely acclaimed and talked-about first novels, *China Mountain Zhang*, which received the prestigious Tiptree Memorial Award. Coming up is a new novel, tentatively entitled *Half the Day Is Night*. Recently married, she lives in Twinsburg, Ohio.

David B. Kisor is a composer and musician who used to work at the same company as McHugh, where this story grew out of a discussion between them about how hard it is to be creative and hold a day job at the same time. It was his first professional sale, and their first collaboration.

In it, they give us a harrowing look at a future world ravaged by a strange and devastating plague—a world in which the boundary lines between the Haves and the Have-Nots, between the fortunate and the unfortunate, and between family and strangers, are suddenly being redrawn in some startling and very unexpected ways. . . .

The plague is not the only health problem in the countryside surrounding Tai'an. Shandong is a rural province, the Appalachia of China. Shandong peasants are the hillbillies of China, and have something of the same reputation—apparently not very bright, distrustful of strangers, local boys who let you think you're real smart until they get you out on their own terms. I don't know if they're moonshiners; the clear local sorghum liquor (which we foreigners call "jet fuel" because it smells like fingernail polish and is usually about 150 proof) is probably too cheap to encourage much bootlegging.

Not that it's Lexington or Louisville. A Kentucky girl like me doesn't feel at home; after all, Kentucky isn't particularly famous for its brine-pickled vegetables (not just cucumber; but carrots, and cabbage with hot peppers, too). The land is bare and brown, the hills covered in places with dead grass and a few pine trees, but in other places scratched to bare, baked or frozen earth.

I work in a clinic about an hour south of Tai'an, headed toward Qufu, the ancient birthplace of Confucius. The town is called Lijiazhang, and the clinic is brick and concrete. It used to be a store. I vaccinate for plague, and treat a lot of poverty-related diseases, too. Tuberculosis is rampant because they burn bituminous coal (this part of Shandong is coal country, mountainous like West Virginia). Bituminous coal is soft, high-sulfur coal. Black-lung stuff when they mine it. Here, after they get it out of the ground, they grind it to powder in places with so little regard for workers' health that OSHA representatives would probably have seizures, then they mix it with mud to make dull-black round bricks with holes through them. They burn the bricks in stoves to heat and cook. The bricks burn more slowly than pure coal.

We burn the bricks in the clinic, too. Our stove is a red-brick affair, kind of like an oven. It's got a vent, but the pipe doesn't draw correctly, and it's thick with whatever the stuff is that clogs coal stoves. I thought I read that the stuff is dangerous and can cause explosions, but nobody seems particularly concerned. Much of the smoke from the stove hangs in the clinic. Like everybody else, I've had a chest cold since November, and when I spit into the toilet after working all day, my saliva is laced with black from the smoke. We test ourselves for tuberculosis every sixty days. So far, nobody has tested positive. I wonder what two years in China is going to do for my health. Besides lung damage from the pollution, they still use DDT and pesticides that have been banned in the US for fifty years. It would be ironic to have survived the plague in my childhood only to die a few years from now of cancer that originated in exposure from something in Tai'an.

Particularly since, after an initial burst of enthusiasm, the locals have made it clear that they don't think much of the efficacy of Western medicine in treating EID. The new vaccine is only about 50 percent effective. Furthermore, if the host has already been infected and the virus is latent, vaccination can activate it. It's hard to explain to people that the vaccine doesn't *cause* the disease. It's not what they want—they want Western medicine to provide instant answers, or they'll go back to their own methods.

Surely, at the end of a long day with the lepers, tired out of his mind, even Albert Schweitzer sat on his cot among his chickens and goats and wondered how he had managed to so thoroughly screw up his life.

Terry, Megan, and I are at the clinic by 8:00 A.M. We are medical practitioners, MPs. I hope to go to medical school when I get back to the States and become an MD. I thought that coming to China would give me practical experience, and that it would be a chance to travel. A once-in-a-lifetime chance. Maybe, like Dr. Schweitzer, I would find my calling.

My third patient this morning is a boy about sixteen, whose name is Zhao Lianfeng. Small-boned, with tiny beautiful hard brown hands, dirt ingrained in the knuckles. He has a fever, difficulty breathing, anxiety, and he tells Xiao Cao he hears voices whispering in his blood. Entotic Illusory Disease (EID) means illusions in the ear. Zhao Lianfeng is lucid, despite the whispering he hears. Patients often are. No one has ever been able to explain the whispers, despite all the mumbo-jumbo we rattle off about fever and R-brains and induced dream states.

"What do the voices say?" I ask. I ask a lot of my patients that. I get some strange answers.

"They are whispering in a foreign language," Xiao Cao translates.

Sometimes they are whispering too quietly for the patient to make out the words.

I stroke his forehead, and he looks up at me. The Chinese don't touch much across genders. Boyfriend and girlfriend don't hold hands in public, although a couple of boys can walk down the street with their arms around each other's shoulders and nobody pays any attention. But I touch my patients a lot. Sick people need comforting.

I can't do a lot else for Zhao Lianfeng. The only things I can give him are fluids for dehydration, broad-spectrum antibiotics against secondary infections, and something for his breathing. He will either live or die. So I hold his hand, while his mother, a middle-aged woman with a perm that lays precisely as the rollers were placed in her hair, watches me. After a moment, the inhaler has helped his breathing. *"Shi hao ma?"* I ask, "You good?" in the local version of Mandarin.

He smiles for me. *"Shi haode,"* he says. "Good." His hand is calloused. Peasant boys have calloused hands. In Shandong, peasant isn't a description of what you do for a living. This boy doesn't farm, he works in a village factory. He helps make parts for motor scooters. But he is still a peasant, because he wears quilted navy-blue cotton jackets and pants. Because he lives in a village. Because, at sixteen, he has finished school and says *shi haode* instead of *hen hao*, the way a city boy would. Like saying "ain't," or "pitcher" for "picture."

I smile at Zhao Lianfeng, and I smile at his mother.

His mother doesn't smile. She isn't fooled, she knows my remedies are temporary. For my records, I ask for a history. Has he had a history of illness? I check bronchitis without bothering to ask; here everybody has bronchitis in the winter. How about his family? Xiao Cao translates: the boy's father is dead of EID, which the Chinese around here call the Whispers, his mother had it but recovered, twelve years ago. His sister had it as a child, but survived. Anyone else? His mother shakes her head.

"Didi," the boy says, "little brother."

The mother turns her head away.

I press her through Xiao Cao: what happened to the little brother?

"Baixuebing." Xiao Cao finally translates, "White blood sickness."

Leukemia. The leukemia rate among children in China is one of the highest in the world, the result of years of toxics being dumped into the air, the land, and the water. I put my forms in his folder. At the end of the month, I'll tabulate it all, send my report to someone in Geneva at the World Health Organization. It's all entered into a data file, but nobody pays much attention to the results. There's no pattern, or rather, no particularly surprising pattern. EID is virulently contagious, spread by contact, endemic. It is particularly bad among the impoverished, who are, of course, susceptible because of poor nutrition and health and overcrowding. Although, since EID has killed over a billion-and-a-half people world wide, over-crowding in places like Bangladesh and Mexico City is much less of a problem than it used to be.

I survived because I am an American, and, as a child, I was among the first to get it. I got it in 1996, when hospital care was available that wasn't available a year later, when medical services were completely overwhelmed by the number of cases. My father got it early, too, but died despite great medical care. My mother didn't get it until three years later, when medical care was nearly non-existent, but she survived anyway. Like Zhao Lianfeng's mother survived it.

Zhao Lianfeng does not want to let go of my hand, but I have other patients, so he must. If his mother had brought him in for a vaccination two years ago, he might not be sick now. The disease can lie dormant for years, though, so if he'd had it already, but was asymptomatic, the vaccine might have activated the virus too.

Sometimes they live, I think. And then there's the next patient, there's always a next patient.

Usually part of me is numb. I'm tired all the time from my chest cold, and the number of patients is overwhelming. Patients are all frightened; some are brave, some aren't. I treat toddlers, I treat old people. A lot of them die. A lot of them don't even die of EID; China doesn't need EID to find a way to kill you. Just breathe coal dust all winter, or drink yourself to death on 150 proof sorghum liquor, or die of untreated diabetes, or heart disease, or the astounding cancer rate, or pneumonia. Or get run over by a coal truck out in the country, and die because there's no medical aid at all for most of the villages.

When I come back to the clinic the next morning, Zhao Lianfeng's fever has spiked to 41 degrees Celsius during the night, about 105 Fahrenheit. Now it is down around 39 degrees. His mother has spent the night with him. When I come by his bed, she watches me without reproach. Without much hope, either.

"*Daifu*," Lianfeng says when I lean over him. "Doctor." I sit down for a moment and hold his calloused, dry-hot hand.

Their faces are the pinched angular faces of country people. Square-jawed. For all their differences of race, they are like the faces in the black-and-white photos of people from places with names like Jackson Hollow and Stinking Creek. Or like the Dust Bowl faces of Okies.

I have the strange urge to lean over and kiss Zhao Lianfeng's cheek. It comes over me with patients sometimes; I never tell anyone. It is not an Albert Schweitzer love-of-all-mankind urge, it is just an urge to touch that young and shining skin, those hectic red cheeks. Even dried by fever.

He says something, and I recognize *eryu*, "whisper." They are whispering. "Ssss ssss ssss," he says, trying to mimic the sibilance he hears.

I hold his hand and rub his forehead.

"Kate," Xiao Cao says. Patients waiting. Triage, ignore the dying boy I can do nothing for, concentrate on finding the ones I *can* help.

Xiao Cao doesn't have that pinched look. He is thin, a beanpole of a young man, but he is a city boy. He graduated from the Foreign Languages department in Tai'an Teacher's College, his father is a professor. I like Xiao Cao, he is open and trusting and naïve. Chinese young people seem younger than their peers in the States. Maybe that is simply because he is less sophisticated in *my* culture than he is in his own. Maybe *I* seem simpler, unsophisticated, to *him*.

He is also a tremendous help in the clinic. He has been vaccinated against EID, and is happy to be a model of the efficacy of the vaccine. He preaches western medicine to the patients, thinks of us as the Americans who have developed the vaccine, who will save everyone if they will just come and let us.

I worry about what he tells people; his ideas are a weird mix of what we tell him and local speculation. One day he announced to me that the reason we foreigners get so many colds is that we wear flat shoes. Colds come from the ground, up through your feet, he told me. Wear heels and get your feet off the ground, and there is less surface for the colds to get through.

I wonder what kind of life it is for a young man like him, working with Americans and sick people.

The morning is the usual parade. Most people do not come to us unless they are very sick. We refer some on to the hospital in Tai'an, but most don't go. In China, your health care is paid for by your work unit, that is, your factory or employer. But the peasants don't have work units, and they have to pay for their own health care, up front. If a dying man walks into a Chinese hospital without cash, he dies in the waiting room. I palpitate a man's stomach, find a mass. I tell him he needs to see a doctor in Tai'an, give him a prescription for pain, and he goes home to die.

A woman with tuberculosis I can treat. I start her on a course of antibiotics, tell her to send the rest of the family to be tested in case they have caught it from her.

We stop accepting patients at 11:30; lunch is at noon.

"*Daifu*," Zhao Lianfeng says. His fever is up to 40 degrees Celsius. I take his hot hand. I used to want to clean them up, the rings of dirt on their collars distressed me, but dirt doesn't really hurt or help him now. I sit a moment, give him a new IV bag, go on to lunch.

Lunch is hot and spicy cabbage, clear soup, and rice. It's one of my favorite lunches, but Terry doesn't really care for cabbage.

"You know what I'm really hungry for," Terry says.

It's a game, a kind of torture we inflict on ourselves. Sometimes I've played with tears in my eyes, but one of the unwritten rules is to pretend it's only a game.

Terry's meal is pizza, a big tossed salad with ranch dressing, a two liter bottle of Coke. He swipes his kinky blond hair out of his eyes and throws in a Steelers-Oilers game. Tall, fair Terry is so foreign-looking that I've seen him cause bicycle accidents; most of the locals have never seen a foreigner, and when they see us, they stare. As we walk down the street, the whispers follow us, "*Weiguoren, weiguoren.*" Foreigner, foreigner.

Megan's meal is steak, baked potato, broccoli with cheese sauce, and apple pie.

My meal is skillet-fried chicken, mashed potatoes with milk gravy, and green beans. My mother's, but I don't say that. I'll write it in my next letter. Thinking of my mother makes me think of Zhao Lianfeng's mother, sitting next to her son at the clinic. I bet I know Zhao Lianfeng's favorite meal—Chinese dumplings, potstickers.

I don't want to go back to work. I want to go home.

The next morning, I am surprised: Zhao Lianfeng is still holding on. He does not say *daifu* when I sit down, but he opens his eyes. I take his hand, smile at him. "Hold on, little brother," I say in English.

He closes his eyes.

Xiao Cao comes to tell me I have patients, and Zhao Lianfeng opens his eyes. He says something to the air, to no one in particular.

"They are whispering," Xiao Cao translates.

"What are they whispering?" I ask.

For a long moment, Zhao Lianfeng does not answer. Then he says something ". . . *shi haode.*"

"They say, hold on, you're good, you're okay," Xiao Cao translates.

I smile and nod. "*Shi haode,*" I agree, "you're good."

Zhao Lianfeng doesn't seem to care, he just closes his eyes.

I check on him on and off during the day. We have twenty-seven beds, all filled. Zhao Lianfeng's temperature is back up between 40 and 41 degrees, somewhere around 104 degrees Fahrenheit. He is not really conscious. It is really only a matter of time.

I am hoping that when I come to work the next morning, the bed will simply be empty. But the next morning, Zhao Lianfeng is still there, still suspended between consciousness and unconsciousness, still running a fever that must, by now, be causing brain damage. There are no facilities here for rehabilitation, so if he is brain damaged, he will go back to his village and his mother will take care of him. Or not take care of him.

So I begin to hope that he will die. Maybe I am terrible, maybe Albert Schweitzer would feel differently. I know that there is sanctity in all human life and that I took an oath—even medical practitioners take an oath—but there is sanctity in death, too.

Zhao Lianfeng doesn't die. Not that whole long day.

Nor the next day, although the fever is wasting him nearly down to the bone. I force myself to sit down, to take his hand and brush his hair off his forehead, but long black hairs come away in my hand.

His mother sleeps sitting on the floor, her back to the wall, or wakes and waits.

After three days, I am thinking the unthinkable. There are lots of things I could add to his IV bag and Zhao Lianfeng would slide gently away. I've never done it. Doctors, real full-degree MD doctors do it, although usually not officially. I think Megan has done it, although she says she hasn't. Terry never would. Terry might be from the suburbs of Chicago, but he comes from a conservative family. Terry brought his Bible to China with him, belongs to a Bible Study group at home. Terry really believes in the sanctity of human life and lets God make all the calls on the quality of life.

Albert Schweitzer would leave it to God. Kate Lambert of Lexington, Kentucky doesn't trust leaving things to God, or to other men, either. Maybe we're supposed to make that decision, maybe that's part of being a healer.

But I don't do it because I can't do it in front of his mother. Not that she would know, necessarily; I put antibiotics in his drip, how could she know this is different? But she would be watching and I just can't see myself doing it under her eyes. What if I were wrong? It's not likely that he has a chance of recovery, nothing in my experience indicates that Zhao Lianfeng will ever go back to the little sweatshop run by his village and make parts for motor scooters again. Most likely he will die without my help or, at worst, he will recover from EID and go home to his village with cerebral palsy, or aphasia or paralysis, maybe end up tied in a bed and fed with a spoon.

Most likely, I tell myself, he will die. Eventually I'll forget about him, forget about feeling guilty. Eventually I'll go home to Lexington, Kentucky, and eat skillet-fried chicken and mashed potatoes with milk gravy.

After five days, Zhao Lianfeng's fever begins to drop. It drops to 39 degrees Celsius, spikes 41 again, drops again to 39 by the sixth day. By the seventh day, it is below normal, which is common after a fever. He isn't conscious, although his eyes are slightly open.

His aunt sits next to the bed; his mother has gone home to rest a few days. I keep an IV of glucose going, and antibiotics, of course, and otherwise avoid the bed.

Two days later, he is still not conscious, not truly. His aunt can prop him up in bed, and he'll even take broth, but he's in a vegetative state. Which may be permanent. When he closes his eyes, he looks angelic, his wrists as thin as a child's. I stop to look one afternoon, and he is curled up on his side with his thumb in his mouth.

After that, I ask Megan to take over. She doesn't ask for any explanation; once in a while we just trade patients.

We are done with him, and his family comes with a truck borrowed from the headman of their village, bundles him into quilts, and takes him home.

That weekend, Terry decides that I need R&R. What he really means is that it is his and my turn to spend a weekend in Beijing going to foreign motels in our cheap Chinese coats, looking like the missionaries who come down from the hills to buy supplies. We take the train to Jinan, and then six more hours to Beijing, and eat lasagna at the Jianguo Hotel coffee shop. It's a bland concoction of cheese and meat. So many Chinese are lactose intolerant that they don't eat cheese (which has never explained the popularity of ice cream, but it's true), and every time we go it's been so long since I've eaten western food that it makes me sick, but it's still wonderful. Even in the evening, jagged out on Cokes and crying in the bathroom with the water running so Terry won't hear.

Two days of hot running water, heated rooms, Cokes, and candy bars. It costs half my monthly stipend, but there's not a lot else to spend my monthly stipend on, so I can't really get upset. I use the hotel long distance phones to call home, "How are you, Mom?" "It's eight o'clock in the evening here, what time is it there?" "How are you, how's your cold?" "The cold is doing great, Mom, but I feel terrible, ha ha."

And then, Sunday night, we take the train, soft sleeper berths, back into China. My backpack is stuffed with Cokes and Snickers Bars and two buckets of Kentucky Fried Chicken to share with Megan for manning the store. Hell of a dinner we'll have, Kentucky Fried Chicken and Qingdao beer.

It's all incredible luxury; my monthly stipend is 1600 yuan, less than $400 US. Making parts for motor scooters, Zhao Lianfeng probably made around 200 yuan a month. Good money in China, but it doesn't buy many cans of Coke at 4 yuan a pop.

Just because Zhao Lianfeng can't afford it, does that mean I should forego it all myself? I don't know what Albert Schweitzer's view was on going native, but I suspect he'd find my existence decadent.

"*Daifu*," he says, beaming. It's March, six weeks after Zhao Lianfeng left the clinic, bundled in cotton quilts. The weather is warmer, but he is still bundled up, still painfully thin. His mother has his arm, steadying him. His coordination has been affected by the fever. Still he smiles at me. "*Daifu*," he says.

His mother explains through Xiao Cao that he has been after her to come see the *daifu*. He seems delighted and childlike, a bit simple. He smiles and smiles, eyes squinched in the sunlight.

"Come in, let me look you over," I say.

Underneath his cotton shirt, his collar bones rise like wings, but he seems basically healthy. His chest is clear, his ears and eyes good. His blood pressure is low, but not drastically, his heart sounds strong.

His mother explains that he was like a baby at first, but that he has been "growing up."

"*Daifu*," he says, and then, in Chinese I can barely follow, "Doctor, they tell me, tell you, it's good."

I smile and nod. His speech is childlike. I've no way of testing the amount of damage done.

He frowns, and takes my hand and repeats insistently—Xiao Cao translating—"Tell her, they tell me, it's good."

"*Shi haode*," I agree, in my lame Chinese, "It's good."

He is distressed, though. My response isn't what he wants. He looks thoughtful. Frowns a moment. Finally he says, slowly, "Hold on, little brother."

English. Did he hear me say that? And now he remembers? "Incredible!" I say, delighted. Who knows how the human mind works, what it remembers, what it doesn't?

But he doesn't care about my response. He takes my hand and repeats, in the same slow way, "Hold on, little brother." He is probably even mimicking my inflection, he sounds as if he is trying to comfort me. Of course, I'm vulnerable. We are all living on the edge of nerves, Terry, Megan and I. There's not much left over to comfort each other, and I *want* comfort, so badly. I can feel the tears rising in my eyes.

He nods, thin faced, clear-eyed. He'll come back, he promises.

And he does, every couple of weeks. At first, he comes with his cousin or his uncle, getting off the bus carefully, like an old man. Each time we go through the same ritual, and I check him over. Then he sits and watches me while I work with other patients. In June, Megan's two years are up, and Terry and Xiao Cao take her to Beijing and put her on a plane home. The next time Zhao Lianfeng comes to see me, he gets off the bus alone, no cousin or uncle helping him, and stands in the hot June sun, smiling at his accomplishment. I introduce him to Jeff, Megan's replacement, and I give him a Snickers bar from Beijing. He thinks Snickers Bars are *shi haode*.

In June, one of our EID cases (we average about fifteen a month) goes through the same stages as Lianfeng's. She is a woman in her forties, but after five days of high fever, her temperature comes back to below normal. By the seventh day, she is curled up on her side, sucking her thumb. At the end of the month, I include the information in my report to Geneva.

In July, Lianfeng is still thin, the points of his bare shoulders are sharp under his skin. He wears a bright pink strap T-shirt and baggy, navy-blue pants. His speech improves. He learns a little English. "Hello, Kate-ah *Daifu*," he says when he gets off the bus in August. A miracle, I think. A tribute to the resiliency of the human body. And, despite his fragile look, he remains surprisingly healthy. His lungs stay clear even in this country, where it seems that no one has clear lungs. A little bundle of bone, he sweeps out the clinic one day.

"Do you work, do you have a job?" I ask through Xiao Cao.

He nods. He is making parts for motor scooters again, although he looks like a stiff wind would knock him over. "Okay, Kate-ah *Daifu*," he says, "Lianfeng okay. They tell you, thank you."

My Chinese is getting a little better. "Who are 'they'?"

"*Eryu-de*," he says, and I have to get a translation. He doesn't want to tell Xiao Cao, but he finally does, "Whisperers."

"Do you still hear whispers?" I ask. I've never heard of anyone still hearing whispers after they've recovered, but it could be residual damage.

But he doesn't want to talk in front of Xiao Cao, countryside boy saying foolish things in front of the city boy. He turns his head away and won't answer.

EID cases are on the upswing worldwide. The disease seems to have changed. It's done this periodically over the last twenty years. It doesn't seem to start in one area and travel; when it changes, it seems to change abruptly all over the world, all at once. One of the more peculiar qualities of EID. We have twenty-one cases in August. Seven of our cases exhibit the Lianfeng cycle. Eleven of the more traditional cases die, three recover in a more typical fashion.

In September, Zhao Lianfeng cleans our coal flue. He has quick hands, the hands of a mechanic. My uncle, my father's brother, had those hands, stained around the nails with oil and grime after a Saturday spent fixing the car. My uncle is dead of EID, died when I was nine; the sudden strength of the memory surprises me.

In October, I realize that Zhao Lianfeng is growing. He is seventeen, and it's not unheard of for seventeen-year-olds to grow, but he is still so thin, so fragile-looking. But he's added two inches, he looks me in the eye. Me, the solid, heavy-hipped 5'7" giantess from the west.

I don't give him physical exams anymore, but with this sudden growth spurt, I feel compelled to have him sit on the examining table. He climbs up for me, and I realize that over the last couple of months he has regained all the coordination he lost. His temperature at his monthly exam is 35 degrees Celsius, way below normal. His blood pressure is 85 over 50. I smile at him, pretending not to be concerned. He has bruises under the skin on the insides of his elbows and knees. Anemia? Leukemia? Bruising is a symptom of leukemia, but usually there is a rise in temperature. I've never heard of somebody with leukemia having a low body temperature. Maybe the EID caused heart damage, but his hands are not cold.

I need Xiao Cao for this. "Lianfeng," I say, "I want you to go with me to the hospital in Tai'an."

Xiao Cao knows this is bad, but his face betrays nothing.

"Don't worry about money," I say, "this won't cost you anything." I don't want to alarm him. I want to have blood tests run. I think of the hospital in Tai'an, and cringe, remembering water standing on the uneven concrete floor, spittoons in the corners. They have a heart-lung machine, the only one in the province, but they still give injections with re-usable syringes. Hepatitis? Could this be some odd manifestation of hepatitis?

"Kate-ah *Daifu*," Lianfeng says, "*mei guanxi*." "It doesn't matter."

"*Shi haode*," I say, "it's good."

He shakes his head. "Tai'an hospital, no go," he says. And launches into a torrent of Chinese with Xiao Cao. A conversation in Mandarin sounds like an argument in English. Sometimes I wonder if the Chinese are all slightly hard of hearing. But the upshot is that he says he doesn't need to go, he is not sick. He says that several times, emphatically. Despite the evidence in front of me, despite a chest like a washboard, despite the yoke of his collar and shoulder bones, despite his deer-narrow wrists.

"He says it is 'them,' " Xiao Cao reports. "He says they are just still making some changes."

"What does he mean, 'them'?"

"I think he means demons," Xiao Cao confides. "*Guai-zi ma*?" he asks Lianfeng.

Lianfeng snaps a negative, offended, and launches into a torrent.

I can't follow the rest of the argument. It must be hot, Xiao Cao is angry. When Xiao Cao gets angry or has a beer, his whole face flushes down to his collar, as if he has been washed in watercolor. He is flushed now, and arguing back.

"Enough!" I finally shout. "What?" I say to Xiao Cao.

Xiao Cao has a sense of the enormity of his responsibilities as mouthpiece for western medicine, and he draws himself up. "He says I am calling him a stupid peasant," Xiao Cao explains. "He says he doesn't believe in demons, and that the whisperers are real. It doesn't matter what you call it, though, it is superstition, whether you call it demons or whisperers."

Lianfeng knows he's being slandered, he can see it in Xiao Cao's face. "Kate-ah *Daifu*," he begins, but is immediately defeated by his lack of English vocabulary. In frustration, he turns on Xiao Cao again.

Again I manage to stop it. The important thing is the low body temperature and blood pressure, the bruising at his joints. I think the whispering is a red herring; it's probably residual brain damage from the fever, or even some sort of tinnitus. Maybe he's making meaning out of white noise; I don't know or care.

He argues—the whisperers say he is all right.

"Then it won't hurt to go to the hospital," I say.

Xiao Cao translates with glee, and Lianfeng can clearly think of no counter argument.

But the way he looks at me needs no translation. Betrayed by his beloved Kate-ah *Daifu*.

Wednesday morning, we are supposed to go to the hospital. It is a clear, cold October day, just two weeks after the October first holiday. October first is the Chinese Fourth of July. It and May Day are the only two official holidays. I don't know whether Lianfeng is going to get off the bus or not, but I am hoping. I don't know what village he lives in; if Lianfeng doesn't get off that bus, he could disappear out of my life forever, just slip into the vast pool of humanity in China, and I would never know.

I stand there in my quilted navy-blue coat, with my cap pulled down over my ears, and watch for the red-and-white long-distance bus. Finally, it comes slowly through the little town of Lijiazhuang, slowing to rattle across the railroad tracks, and stopping to let people off at the railway station. I can hear the gears grind a block away, and the blue smoke of the exhaust rises.

It stops in front of the clinic, and two men get off, but neither of them is Lianfeng.

I am not surprised. I am feeling as if I am supposed to be surprised, but I am not. I betrayed Lianfeng's trust in the argument with Xiao Cao, I could tell. I don't know what else I could have done, though.

"Kate-ah *Daifu*?" one of the men says.

It's not Lianfeng. Oh Lord, is the boy sick? If he is sick, what can I do for him in a village in the middle of nowhere? The logistics of getting him to the hospital in Tai'an seem insurmountable. And how would I pay for a hospital visit?

"Come in," I say, "come in," gesturing like a friend for the man to follow. "Xiao Cao. Xiao Cao!"

It is Lianfeng's uncle (mother's younger brother, Chinese is very specific about family relationships). Lianfeng is fine, he explains through Xiao Cao. He could not come today, he is sorry. There is a chance for a big order for motor scooter parts, but Lianfeng must build a machine, a kind of stamp or mold—Xiao Cao's English doesn't include much practice at manufacturing parts. Lianfeng, it turns out, can build machines like no one else. He is making the village wealthy, the uncle says proudly.

"He's sick," I say.

No, the uncle says, Lianfeng said that Kate-ah *Daifu* would be very upset, but she must understand, he is fine. But he will come Friday, and go to the hospital with her.

China. Goddamn China, where you make plans and they say, sorry, not today. No tickets available for the train. Or they come at seven in the morning, unannounced, and say, are you ready?

"You don't understand," I say, searching my smattering of Chinese. Anger, I discover, improves my ability to speak. "He is sick." I grasp for something to make them understand the importance. "I don't know, I think, *baixuebing*." White blood disease. Leukemia. "Maybe," I add in English, for Xiao Cao to translate, "I don't know. I need a hospital to tell me."

The uncle is a young man, in his thirties, a peasant with bad teeth and thoughtful eyes. He listens, and absorbs, and is very still. He looks at me for a long moment. Then he nods, and, through Xiao Cao, he says to tell me that he will bring Lianfeng tomorrow. He cannot bring him today, the bus back to the village doesn't leave until two, it will be too late when he gets home.

He won't stay, he has errands to do in Lijiazhuang.

Watching him walk off through the crisp morning, carrying his string bag for purchases, I am embarrassed by my anger. The man has made a trip that will cost him ten hours out of his day, in order to make excuses for Zhao Lianfeng. Because I'm a western doctor, and western doctors are important, have a certain prestige. Forget that I'm not really a doctor—in China, I have more training than most of the local doctors. If the plague hadn't hit China, maybe there would be a phone, but there is no phone in the clinic, maybe no phone in Zhao Lianfeng's village. Oh, China! Oh, Lianfeng!

At least the uncle understands the importance of getting Lianfeng here.

Thursday morning, we ride the train to Tai'an together. We are riding hardseat for the hour trip to the city. It's a local train, lots of stops, lots of peasants getting on all bundled-up in quilted jackets and layers of pants, women carrying bags the size of suitcases. The men slouch on a seat—if they can get one—and go to sleep. The women tend children, passing out drinks and orange slices to pacify them. The children drink tea out of jars.

Lianfeng has the seat next to the window, and I'm sitting in the middle. He watches out the window. It's his first trip to the city. I don't have enough Chinese, and he doesn't have enough English for us to talk, but the distance between us feels more profound than that. The man sitting across from us leans forward and asks me how old I am.

I tell him twenty-seven, and that I'm American, since that is usually the next question.

He asks me something else. Every trip is like this, a series of questions that would be too personal to ask back home. Fortunately, I can't understand him, so I smile and shrug and say I don't speak much Mandarin. He asks me again, and then smiles at my incomprehension, says "American" in Chinese, and nods.

I glance at Lianfeng, but he is not looking at us. The man asks him something, and Lianfeng answers him reluctantly. The man has found a source of explanation, and Lianfeng is forced to talk. *Daifu*, he explains. American doctor. Albert Schweitzer. Dragging an unwilling boy to Tai'an "for his own good."

Lianfeng is more interested as we pull into Tai'an. It must seem like we go through a lot of city before we get to the train station. What would he think of Beijing? I wonder. Coming into Beijing by train we always pass a big amusement park; Ferris wheel, roller coaster, the works. I could take him to a western hotel, buy him a duck dinner in the restaurant near Tiananmen Square, go to the Great Wall. The trip of a lifetime for a peasant boy.

A trip to the Tai'an hospital will have to do. (Unless he is dying, I think, admitting the thought for the first time. If he is dying, I'll take him to Beijing.)

The hospital is as horrible as I remember. Patients sleep in beds covered with quilts and blankets from home. Women bring food—Chinese hospitals don't provide food, although there are vendors who will sell a patient a dinner. The bathroom is not western: a trench in the concrete floor, washed with water and disinfectant. A man crouches in the hall, his IV on a stand. He wears pants and a T-shirt, and has his jacket slung over his shoulders, so that the sleeve doesn't interfere with the tubing in his arm. He's smoking a cigarette and talking to another man, maybe a friend come to visit. They look up in curiosity as we pass.

"Dr. Lambert." My liaison at the Tai'an hospital is a woman, Dr. Yi. She doesn't speak much English. I have a list of instructions carefully written out for me by Xiao Cao. She reads them and nods, smiles at Zhao Lianfeng, and says something reassuring. I sit while she prods and taps and peers and draws blood. He is embarrassed to death by the request for a urine sample.

"Four o'clock," she says when she is finished, pointing to the clock and then holding up four fingers. Test results at four o'clock.

I promise we'll come back. She nods, smiles at me. Then takes my wrist. "TB test?" she says. "You TB test, yes, no?"

"TB test no," I say. "No TB."

Lianfeng is standing there, happy to be wearing a shirt again, but when I say "no" he looks up, hair in his eyes, and cocks his head, as if listening. His eyes drift left, the way people's eyes do when they are thinking of something. It is activity also common in some types of seizure, and he looks so strange that Dr. Yi and I both stop talking. He says something to Dr. Yi.

She answers him, explaining TB, I guess.

"TB *yes*," he says to me.

"TB no," I say, feeling foolish and ungrammatical. We test ourselves for TB every couple of months, except in the summer. I can test myself at the clinic.

Dr. Yi says something to him.

He shakes his head at me, says in Chinese, "They tell me." I can understand what he is saying.

"Who are 'they'?" But either he doesn't understand or won't answer. "TB yes," he says firmly.

What the hell, I dragged Lianfeng all the way here for his tests, the least I can do is let her stick me for TB. And it will empower Lianfeng, give him back some self-respect.

Of course, in this hospital with spittoons in the corners, the TB sticks are modern, Japanese, efficient. By four o'clock, Dr. Yi will tell me what my TB results are. In the clinic, we still use the old serum test with the injection under the skin and the three day wait to see if there's a reaction.

I take Lianfeng shopping. He has a list from his parents, aunts, uncles, cousins. Prices are too high, he clicks his tongue in disapproval and shakes his head. He buys some tools. The shop girls intimidate him with their ponytails and bracelets of watches (Beijing fashion a year out of date). But he is more himself, animated and full of energy. More energy than I have. It's ironic that he still looks like bone and wire covered in skin and I still have western hips, but he's got twice the energy I do.

He eats pretty well, too. We order half a kilo of dumplings and two dishes of pork and vegetables and a couple of cans of orange soda. He eats three-fourths of it, and even jokes with the waitresses.

Dr. Yi is waiting for us when we get back to the hospital. She is like many doctors with some college training, she reads medical English, and she has copied out test names and test results for me in careful printing. The results make no sense. His white blood count is not high, it's normal. He is negative for hepatitis, TB, and diabetes. His cholesterol count is 66. That's about half mine, and I'm very low. His blood pressure, as I noted, is abnormally low.

She has done a few other tests as well. He is EID positive, of course. I am EID positive, anyone who has ever had the disease is. On the multiphage index, the test of immune capabilities, he scores a chart-shattering thirty-one. The average score in the US is twenty-one, the average score in most Third World countries is around fourteen. On the viral index for a range of cancers, his results are so low that they don't even register. Everybody—*everybody*—has some precancerous cells in their body. If you measure six or below on the scale, that means that a normal immune system is able to handle whatever minor cell breakdown you experience as a result of exposure to sunlight or the normal carcinogens (like coal smoke). Six to ten suggests the need for monitoring, and above ten means that you are either at high risk or already have a malignancy.

"*Shi-haode*," I say, bemused.

He tells me he knows. He is grave.

Then Dr. Yi hands me my test results.

Lianfeng reaches out and takes my wrist. Carefully he says, "Hold on, little brother."

I have TB.

TB is no big deal. I can treat it with antibiotics at the clinic. But it means that I can't work with patients until I've run the treatment course, twenty-one days of antibiotics since I am asymptomatic.

Lianfeng's blood results obsess me. I include them in my monthly report to Geneva. I go through our records until I find a history of the middle-aged woman whose disease went through the Lianfeng cycle in September and who is from Lijiazhuang, and Xiao Cao and I go to see her. She is like Lianfeng was in the first weeks, childish and simple, but I persuade her husband, and the four of us, Mr. Qian, Mrs. Zhang (husbands and wives do not have the same name in China), Xiao Cao, and I take the train to Tai'an, where Mrs. Zhang is given a full blood work-up.

Her results are not as good as Lianfeng's, but they are startlingly better than they should be.

"Do you hear whispers?" I ask her through Xiao Cao. She looks at her husband, who is frowning, and leans forward conspiratorially. Like a little girl with a secret, she tells Xiao Cao that "they" upset her husband, so she doesn't speak of them.

Zhao Lianfeng comes to see me on Sunday, his only day off, and I sit with Xiao Cao and question him about how he feels, about the whisperers. They have taught him to think differently, he says. Sometimes now he can see better ways to make things. They have made him smarter. The village has made a contract to sell motor scooter parts to Guangzhou—which we call Canton—because he has figured out ways to make them cheaper.

"Who are they?" I keep asking, but he doesn't know. He can only shrug.

"Where are they?" I ask.

In him. And then, surprisingly, in me. "In Xiao Cao?" I ask.

He shakes his head and then looks thoughtful, eyes to the left, that sudden-struck look he had in the hospital in Tai'an.

"He says not, because of the vaccine," Xiao Cao reports neutrally.

He can understand a little about me, though, because the whisperers are in me, too.

"Can they make me healthier?" I ask.

No, he says, then hesitates. Then firmly, "No, the mold was not right."

I write it all down.

During the day, I write down lists of things I know about EID. Long and obsessive lists, since at first I do not exclude anything. I write down that it killed my uncle and my father, although not my mother or myself (but it is not gender specific, the World Health Organization's statistics have found no correlation between mortality and gender). I tell Terry and Jeff, show them the test results, and we talk about it long into the night.

On the twentieth day of my course of antibiotics. I take the train to Tai'an alone, although Terry and Jeff have given me instructions that I have to call and tell them how things turn out. At the Tai'an Guesthouse, I pay and make a long distance call to Geneva, Switzerland. The only name I know is Dr. Geuter, the name on the address I use to mail my reports, and it takes over an hour of long distance operators and receptionists in Geneva before I finally get to him. When I tell him what I have found, he transfers me yet again, to a woman named Ilse Erandt, who speaks clear English with the almost British accent of some Germans.

She listens as I pour out my theory. Probably, over the years, she has gotten these kinds of calls before, I think. People who think that the plague is from God, or from Venusians, or from the increase of active cultures in our diet from eating yogurt. When I finish, she is silent, and I listen to the crackle of the open line, not as clear as it would be from Beijing. Maybe I've been in China too long, maybe I'm losing my mind.

"When did he come into your clinic?" she asks.

"March," I say.

"That's the earliest case of Windhouk Syndrome so far," she says. And explains that until I called, the earliest case they knew of was from a camp outside Windhouk, Namibia, back in July. That person was killed in a riot. They have hundreds of cases from August, but the survivors are all still childlike.

"March," she says. "I would like to see this young man."

There are dust storms in Beijing. Sand blown in from the Gobi is turning the sky yellow, even at noon. Sandstorms are not like they are in *Lawrence of Arabia*, they are more like a yellow fog. The Chinese call it ghost weather.

The plane climbs above the yellow, rising out of it until the sky is blue and only the land below is stained yellow. From above, there are thin places and thicker, darker places, as the wind moves the sand in currents.

I have been thinking about the whispers.

It's possible that Lianfeng has anthropomorphized the changes the disease has caused. That his mind, in order to cope with his brain and body, has manufactured a "them" that "tells him." But there are two things that keep coming back to me. The first is his insistence that I get a TB test. Maybe it was just a way for him to turn the tables on me because he was angry at me for making him go to the hospital, a kind of "if I have to, you have to" tit-for-tat. But I feel as if he *knew* I was going to test positive. And he said that it was because the whisperers in *me* had told the whisperers in *him*.

Second is something Terry brought up in one of our late-night discussions; the peculiar way that the disease patterns seem to change worldwide, all at once. Lianfeng had the Windhouk Cycle in March, another patient, thousands of miles away in Southern Africa, demonstrated the same symptoms a couple of months later. And when there was an upswing in the disease, it was worldwide. When that happened before, in '98, '02, and again in '07, there were attempts to link the upswing to everything from magnetic storms and sunspots to the greenhouse effect, and on through to astrology.

What if EID is like the sandstorm, not just the grains of sand individually, but the whole? All interconnected. Then it would make sense that, for the whisperers, what happened in Lijiazhuang, China, and what happened just outside Windhouk, Namibia, could be connected. Lianfeng is the first cell to change in a whole *body* that's changing.

He'd told Xiao Cao that the whisperers couldn't improve me because "the mold wasn't right."

If they have got that right, that's going to cause some real change, because, since the US and EC perfected the vaccine in 2010, most of the industrialized countries have been fully vaccinated. And Lianfeng had told Xiao Cao that the whisperers were in Lianfeng, and were in me, but that they weren't in Xiao Cao, because of the vaccine.

All over the world, in places like the outlying suburbs of Mexico City, and Mozambique, and Bolivia, and all the forgotten countries of the world where the vaccine hasn't come, there are lots of people for whom "the mold is right." People who will be healthier, and smarter, and who, like Lianfeng, may be able to improve their village sweatshops. Maybe there is a whole economic miracle about to unfold in the Third World, while the US, locked out by the vaccine, can only watch.

It's only speculation. And it's hard to imagine, watching Lianfeng sleep beside me in his seat.

Geneva is lightyears—a full century!—away from Beijing, and nothing I have told Lianfeng could possibly have prepared him. He stands in the airport in his new Beijing clothes, looking at the advertisements, the mixture of foreigners, innocent of the West.

Dr. Erandt is a woman my mother's age, wearing a beautiful suit the creamy brown of eggshells. Dr. Erandt's Chinese translator has an earring in his nose. Lianfeng can't stop staring at it (and neither can I). I haven't had a decent haircut in over a year, and I'm still wearing my awful cotton coat from China.

"I am so happy to meet you," Dr. Erandt says, shaking Lianfeng's hand. "You don't have any *idea* how happy I am to meet you."

"Dr. Erandt," I say, "have you ever had EID?"

"No," says Dr. Erandt, "I was lucky."

Lianfeng looks at me. He *couldn't* have understood, I asked in English. But he nods. "*Weiguoren*," he says to me.

Foreigners.

WALL, STONE, CRAFT

Walter Jon Williams

▼

Here's a vivid and compelling bit of Alternate History, in which Lord Byron—in *our* universe a famous poet—opts for a military career instead, and becomes the Hero of Waterloo, and one of the most celebrated men on Earth—but finds that his most significant encounter is yet to be fought, a life-and-death contest of clashing wills and conflicting ideals waged against a frail but determined young woman named Mary Wollstonecraft Shelley, who has greatness inside her, waiting to be born. . . .

Walter Jon Williams was born in Minnesota and now lives in Albuquerque, New Mexico. His stories have appeared in our Third, Fourth, Fifth, Sixth, and Ninth Annual Collections. His novels include *Ambassador of Progress, Knight Moves, Hardwired, The Crown Jewels, Voice of the Whirlwind, House of Shards, Angel Station*, and *Days of Atonement*. His most recent books are a collection of his short work, *Facets*, and a big, critically acclaimed new novel, *Aristoi*.

1

She awoke, there in the common room of the inn, from a brief dream of roses and death. Once Mary came awake she recalled there were wild roses on her mother's grave, and wondered if her mother's spirit had visited her.

On her mother's grave, Mary's lover had first proposed their elopement. It was there the two of them had first made love.

Now she believed she was pregnant. Her lover was of the opinion that she was mistaken. That was about where it stood.

Mary concluded that it was best not to think about it. And so, blinking sleep from her eyes, she sat in the common room of the inn at Le Caillou and resolved to study her Italian grammar by candlelight.

Plurals. *La nascita, le nascite. La madre, le madri. Un bambino, i bambini. . .*

Interruption: stampings, snortings, the rattle of harness, the barking of dogs. Four young Englishmen entered the inn, one in scarlet uniform coat, the others in fine traveling clothes. Raindrops dazzled on their shoulders. The innkeeper bustled out from the kitchen, smiled, proffered the register.

Mary, unimpressed by anything English, concentrated on the grammar.

"Let me sign, George," the redcoat said. "My hand needs the practice."
Mary glanced up at the comment.

"I say, George, here's a fellow signed in Greek!" The Englishman peered at
yellowed pages of the inn's register, trying to make out the words in the dim
light of the innkeeper's lamp. Mary smiled at the English officer's efforts.

"Perseus, I believe the name is. Perseus Busseus—d'ye suppose he means
Bishop?—Kselleius. And he gives his occupation as 'te anthropou philou'—that
would make him a friendly fellow, eh?—" The officer looked over his shoulder
and grinned, then returned to the register. " 'Kai atheos.' " The officer scowled,
then straightened. "Does that mean what I think it does, George?"

George—the pretty auburn-haired man in byrons—shook rain off his short
cape, stepped to the register, examined the text. "Not 'friendly fellow,' " he
said. "That would be 'anehr philos.' 'Anthropos' is mankind, not man." There
was the faintest touch of Scotland in his speech.

"So it is," said the officer. "It comes back now."

George bent at his slim waist and looked carefully at the register. "What the
fellow says is, 'Both friend of man and—' " He frowned, then looked at his
friend. "You were right about the 'atheist,' I'm afraid."

The officer was indignant. "Ain't funny, George," he said.

George gave a cynical little half-smile. His voice changed, turned comical and
fussy, became that of a high-pitched English schoolmaster. "Let us try to make
out the name of this famous atheist." He bent over the register again. "Perseus—
you had that right, Somerset. Busseus—how *very* irregular. Kselleius—Kelly?
Shelley?" He smiled at his friend. His voice became very Irish. "Kelly, I
imagine. An atheistical upstart Irish schoolmaster with a little Greek. But what
the Busseus might be eludes me, unless his middle name is Omnibus."

Somerset chuckled. Mary rose from her place and walked quietly toward the
pair. "The gentleman's name is Bysshe, sir," she said. "Percy Bysshe Shelley."

The two men turned in surprise. The officer—Somerset—bowed as he perceived a lady. Mary saw for the first time that he had one empty sleeve pinned
across his tunic, which would account for the comment about the hand. The
other—George, the man in byrons—swept off his hat and gave Mary a flourishing
bow, one far too theatrical to be taken seriously. When he straightened, he gave
Mary a little frown.

"Bysshe Shelley?" he said. "Any relation to Sir Bysshe, the baronet?"

"His grandson."

"Sir Bysshe is a protegé of old Norfolk." This an aside to his friends. Radical
Whiggery was afoot, or so the tone implied. George returned his attention to Mary
as the other Englishmen gathered about her. "An interesting family, no doubt," he
said, and smiled at her. Mary wanted to flinch from the compelling way he looked
at her, gazed upward, intently, from beneath his brows. "And are you of his party?"

"I am."

"And you are, I take it, Mrs. Shelley?"

Mary straightened and gazed defiantly into George's eyes. "Mrs. Shelley
resides in England. My name is Godwin."

George's eyes widened, flickered a little. Low English murmurs came to Mary's ears. George bowed again. "Charmed to meet you, Miss Godwin."

George pointed to each of his companions with his hat. "Lord Fitzroy Somerset." The armless man bowed again. "Captain Harry Smith. Captain Austen of the Navy. Pásmány, my fencing master." Most of the party, Mary thought, were young, and all were handsome, George most of all. George turned to Mary again, a little smile of anticipation curling his lips. His burning look was almost insolent. "My name is Newstead."

Mortal embarrassment clutched at Mary's heart. She knew her cheeks were burning, but still she held George's eyes as she bobbed a curtsey.

George had not been Marquess Newstead for more than a few months. He had been famous for years both as an intimate of the Prince Regent and the most dashing of Wellington's cavalry officers, but it was his exploits on the field of Waterloo and his capture of Napoleon on the bridge at Genappe that had made him immortal. He was the talk of England and the Continent, though he had achieved his fame under another name.

Before the Prince Regent had given him the title of Newstead, auburn-haired, insolent-eyed George had been known as George Gordon Noël, the sixth Lord Byron.

Mary decided she was not going to be impressed by either his titles or his manner. She decided she would think of him as George.

"Pleased to meet you, my lord," Mary said. Pride steeled her as she realized her voice hadn't trembled.

She was spared further embarrassment when the door burst open and a servant entered followed by a pack of muddy dogs—whippets—who showered them all with water, then howled and bounded about George, their master. Standing tall, his strong, well-formed legs in the famous side-laced boots that he had invented to show off his calf and ankle, George laughed as the dogs jumped up on his chest and bayed for attention. His lordship barked back at them and wrestled with them for a moment—not very lordlike, Mary thought—and then he told his dogs to be still. At first they ignored him, but eventually he got them down and silenced.

He looked up at Mary. "I can discipline men, Miss Godwin," he said, "but I'm afraid I'm not very good with animals."

"That shows you have a kind heart, I'm sure," Mary said.

The others laughed a bit at this—apparently kindheartedness was not one of George's better-known qualities—but George smiled indulgently.

"Have you and your companion supped, Miss Godwin? I would welcome the company of fellow English in this tiresome land of Brabant."

Mary was unable to resist an impertinence. "Even if one of them is an atheistical upstart Irish schoolmaster?"

"Miss Godwin, I would dine with Wolfe Tone himself." Still with that intent, under-eyed look, as if he was dissecting her.

Mary was relieved to turn away from George's gaze and look toward the back of the inn, in the direction of the kitchen. "Bysshe is in the kitchen giving instructions to the cook. I believe my sister is with him."

"Are there more in your party?"

"Only the three of us. And one rather elderly carriage horse."

"Forgive us if we do not invite the horse to table."

"Your ape, George," Somerset said dolefully, "will be quite enough."

Mary would have pursued this interesting remark, but at that moment Bysshe and Claire appeared from out of the kitchen passage. Both were laughing, as if at a shared secret, and Claire's black eyes glittered. Mary repressed a spasm of annoyance.

"Mary!" Bysshe said. "The cook told us a ghost story!" He was about to go on, but paused as he saw the visitors.

"We have an invitation to dinner," Mary said. "Lord Newstead has been kind enough—"

"Newstead!" said Claire. "*The* Lord Newstead?"

George turned his searching gaze on Claire. "I'm the only Newstead I know."

Mary felt a chill of alarm, for a moment seeing Claire as George doubtless saw her: black-haired, black-eyed, fatally indiscreet, and all of sixteen.

Sometimes the year's difference in age between Mary and Claire seemed a century.

"Lord Newstead!" Claire babbled. "I recognize you now! How exciting to meet you!"

Mary resigned herself to fate. "My lord," she said, "may I present my sister, Miss Jane—Claire, rather, Claire Clairmont, and Mr. Shelley."

"Overwhelmed and charmed, Miss Clairmont. Mr. Perseus Omnibus Kselleius, tí kánete?"

Bysshe blinked for a second or two, then grinned. "Thànmásia eùxaristô," returning politeness, "kaí eseîs?"

For a moment Mary gloried in Bysshe, in his big frame in his shabby clothes, his fair, disordered hair, his freckles, his large hands—and his absolute disinclination to be impressed by one of the most famous men on Earth.

George searched his mind for a moment. "Polú kalá, eùxaristô. Thá éthela ná—" He groped for words, then gave a laugh. "Hang the Greek!" he said. "It's been far too many years since Trinity. May I present my friend Somerset?"

Somerset gave the atheist a cold Christian eye. "How d'ye do?"

George finished his introductions. There was the snapping of coach whips outside, and the sound of more stamping horses. The dogs began barking again. At least two more coaches had arrived. George led the party into the dining room. Mary found herself sitting next to George, with Claire and Bysshe across the table.

"Damme, I quite forgot to register," Somerset said, rising from his bench. "What bed will you settle for, George?"

"Nothing less than Bonaparte's."

Somerset sighed. "I thought not," he said.

"Did Bonaparte sleep here in Le Caillou?" Claire asked.

"The night before Waterloo."

"How exciting! Is Waterloo nearby?" She looked at Bysshe. "Had we known, we could have asked for his room."

"Which we then would have had to surrender to my lord Newstead," Bysshe said tolerantly. "He has greater claim, after all, than we."

George gave Mary his intent look again. His voice was pitched low. "I would not deprive two lovely ladies of their bed for all the Bonapartes in Europe."

But rather join us in it, Mary thought. That look was clear enough.

The rest of George's party—servants, aides-de-camp, clerks, one black man in full Mameluke fig, turned-up slippers, ostrich plumes, scarlet turban and all—carried George's equipage from his carriages. In addition to an endless series of trunks and a large miscellany of weaponry there were more animals. Not only the promised ape—actually a large monkey, which seated itself on George's shoulder—but brightly-colored parrots in cages, a pair of greyhounds, some hooded hunting hawks, songbirds, two forlorn-looking kit foxes in cages, which set all the dogs howling and jumping in eagerness to get at them, and a half-grown panther in a jewelled collar, which the dogs knew better than to bark at. The innkeeper was loud in his complaint as he attempted to sort them all out and stay outside of the range of beaks, claws, and fangs.

Bysshe watched with bright eyes, enjoying the spectacle. George's friends looked as if they were weary of it.

"I hope we will sleep tonight," Mary said.

"If you sleep not," said George, playing with the monkey, "we shall contrive to keep you entertained." ·

How gracious to include your friends in the orgy, Mary thought. But once again kept silent.

Bysshe was still enjoying the parade of frolicking animals. He glanced at Mary. "Don't you think, Maie, this is the very image of philosophical anarchism?"

"You are welcome to it, sir," said Somerset, returning from the register. "George, your mastiff has injured the ostler's dog. He is loud in his complaint."

"I'll have Ferrante pay him off."

"See that you do. And have him pistol the brains out of that mastiff while he's at it."

"Injure poor Picton?" George was offended. "I'll have none of it."

"Poor Picton will have his fangs in the ostler next."

"He must have been teasing the poor beast."

"Picton will kill us all one day." Grudgingly.

"Forgive us, Somerset-laddie." Mary watched as George reached over to Somerset and tweaked his ear. Somerset reddened but seemed pleased.

"Mr. Shelley," said Captain Austen. "I wonder if you know what surprises the kitchen has in store for us."

Austen was a well-built man in a plain black coat, older than the others, with a lined and weathered naval face and a reserved manner unique in this company.

"Board 'em in the smoke! That's the Navy for you!" George said. "Straight to the business of eating, never mind the other nonsense."

"If you ate wormy biscuit for twenty years of war," said Harry Smith, "you'd care about the food as well."

Bysshe gave Austen a smile. "The provisions seem adequate enough for a country inn,'' he said. "And the rooms are clean, unlike most in this country. Claire and the Maie and I do not eat meat, so I had to tell the cook how to prepare our dinner. But if your taste runs to fowl or something in the cutlet line I daresay the cook can set you up.''

"No meat!" George seemed enthralled by the concept. "Disciples of J.F. Newton, as I take it?''

"Among others," said Mary.

"But are you well? Do you not feel an enervation? Are you not feverish with lack of a proper diet?'' George leaned very close and touched Mary's forehead with the back of one cool hand while he reached to find her pulse with the other. The monkey grimaced at her from his shoulder. Mary disengaged and placed her hands on the table.

"I'm quite well, I assure you," she said.

"The Maie's health is far better than when I met her," Bysshe said.

"Mine too," said Claire.

"I believe most diseases can be conquered by proper diet," said Bysshe. And then he added,

> "He slays the lamb that looks him in the face,
> And horribly devours his mangled flesh.''

"Let's have some mangled flesh tonight, George," said Somerset gaily.

"Do let's," added Smith.

George's hand remained on Mary's forehead. His voice was very soft. "If eating flesh offend thee," he said, "I will eat but only greens.''

Mary could feel her hackles rise. "Order what you please," she said. "I don't care one way or another.''

"Brava, Miss Godwin!" said Smith thankfully. "Let it be mangled flesh for us all, and to perdition with all those little Low Country cabbages!''

"I don't like them, either," said Claire.

George removed his hand from Mary's forehead and tried to signal the innkeeper, who was still struggling to corral the dogs. George failed, frowned, and lowered his hand.

"I'm cheered to know you're familiar with the works of Newton," Bysshe said.

"I wouldn't say *familiar*," said George. He was still trying to signal the innkeeper. "I haven't read his books. But I know he wants me not to eat meat, and that's all I need to know.''

Bysshe folded his big hands on the table. "Oh, there's much more than that. Abstaining from meat implies an entire new moral order, in which mankind is placed on an equal level with the animals.''

"George in particular should appreciate that," said Harry Smith, and made a face at the monkey.

"I think I prefer being ranked above the animals," George said. "And above most people, too." He looked up at Bysshe. "Shall we avoid talk of food matters before we eat? My stomach's rumbling louder than a battery of Napoleon's daughters.'' He looked down at the monkey and assumed a high-pitched Scots dowager's voice. ''An' sae is Jerome Bonaparte's, annit nae, Jerome?''

George finally succeeded in attracting the innkeeper's attention and the company ordered food and wine. Bread, cheese, and pickles were brought to tide them over in the meantime. Jerome Bonaparte was permitted off his master's lap to roam free along the table and eat what he wished.

George watched as Bysshe carved a piece of cheese for himself. ''In addition to Newton, you would also be a follower of William Godwin?''

Bysshe gave Mary a glance, then nodded. ''Ay. Godwin also.''

''I thought I recognized that 'philosophical anarchism' of yours. Godwin was the rage when I was at Harrow. But not so much thought of now, eh? Excepting of course his lovely namesake.'' Turning his gaze to Mary.

Mary gave him a cold look. ''Truth is ever in fashion, my lord,'' she said.

''Did you say *ever* or *never*?'' Playfully. Mary said nothing, and George gave a shrug. ''Truthful Master Godwin, then. And who else?''

''Ovid,'' Mary said. The officers looked a little serious at this. She smiled. ''Come now—he's not as scandalous as he's been made out. Merely playful.''

This did not reassure her audience. Bysshe offered Mary a private smile. ''We've also been reading Mary Wollstonecraft.''

''Ah!'' George cried. ''Heaven save us from intellectual women!''

''Mary Wollstonecraft,'' said Somerset thoughtfully. ''She was a harlot in France, was she not?''

''I prefer to think of my mother,'' said Mary carefully, ''as a political thinker and authoress.''

There was sudden silence as Somerset turned white with mortification. Then George threw back his head and laughed.

''Sunburn me!'' he said. ''That answers as you deserve!''

Somerset visibly made an effort to collect his wits. ''I am most sorry, Miss—'' he began.

George laughed again. ''By heaven, we'll watch our words hereafter!''

Claire tittered. ''I was in suspense, wondering if there would be a mishap. And there was, there *was*!''

George turned to Mary and managed to compose his face into an attitude of solemnity, though the amusement that danced in his eyes denied it.

''I sincerely apologize on behalf of us all, Miss Godwin. We are soldiers and are accustomed to speaking rough among ourselves, and have been abroad and are doubtless ignorant of the true worth of any individual—'' He searched his mind for a moment, trying to work out a graceful way to conclude. ''—outside of our own little circle,'' he finished.

''Well said,'' said Mary, ''and accepted.'' She had chosen more interesting ground on which to make her stand.

''Oh yes!'' said Claire. ''Well said indeed!''

''My mother is not much understood by the public,'' Mary continued. ''But intellectual women, it would seem, are not much understood by *you*.''

George leaned away from Mary and scanned her with cold eyes. "On the contrary," he said. "I am married to an intellectual woman."

"And she, I imagine . . ." Mary let the pause hang in the air for a moment, like a rapier before it strikes home. ". . . resides in England?"

George scowled. "She does."

"I'm sure she has her books to keep her company."

"And Francis Bacon," George said, his voice sour. "Annabella is an authority on Francis Bacon. And she is welcome to reform *him*, if she likes."

Mary smiled at him. "Who keeps *you* company, my lord?"

There was a stir among his friends. He gave her that insolent, under-eyed look again.

"I am not often lonely," he said.

"Tonight you will rest with the ghost of Napoleon," she said. "Which of you has better claim to that bed?"

George gave a cold little laugh. "I believe that was decided at Waterloo."

"The Duke's victory, or so I've heard."

George's friends were giving each other alarmed looks. Mary decided she had drawn enough Byron blood. She took a piece of cheese.

"Tell us about Waterloo!" Claire insisted. "Is it far from here?"

"The field is a mile or so north," said Somerset. He seemed relieved to turn to the subject of battles. "I had thought perhaps you were English tourists come to visit the site."

"Our arrival is coincidence," Bysshe said. He was looking at Mary narrow-eyed, as if he was trying to work something out. "I'm somewhat embarrassed for funds, and I'm in hope of finding a letter at Brussels from my—" He began to say "wife," but changed the word to "family."

"We're on our way to Vienna," Smith said.

"The long way 'round," said Somerset. "It's grown unsafe in Paris—too many old Bonapartists lurking with guns and bombs, and of course George is the laddie they hate most. So we're off to join the Duke as diplomats, but we plan to meet with his highness of Orange along the way. In Brussels, in two days' time."

"Good old Slender Billy!" said Smith. "I haven't seen him since the battle."

"The battle!" said Claire. "You said you would tell us!"

George gave her an irritated look. "Please, Miss Clairmont, I beg you. No battles before dinner." His stomach rumbled audibly.

"Bysshe," said Mary, "didn't you say the cook had told you a ghost story?"

"A good one, too," said Bysshe. "It happened in the house across the road, the one with the tile roof. A pair of old witches used to live there. Sisters." He looked up at George. "We may have ghosts before dinner, may we not?"

"For all of me, you may."

"They dealt in charms and curses and so on, and made a living supplying the, ah, the supernatural needs of the district. It so happened that two different men had fallen in love with the same girl, and each man applied to one of the weird sisters for a love charm—each to a different sister, you see. One of them used his spell first and won the heart of the maiden, and this drove the other suitor into a rage. So he went to the witch who had sold him his charm, and demanded she change the young lady's mind. When the witch insisted it was impossible, he drew his pistol and shot her dead.''

"How very un-Belgian of him," drawled Smith.

Bysshe continued unperturbed. "So quick as a wink," he said, "the dead witch's sister seized a heavy kitchen cleaver and cut off the young man's head with a single stroke. The head fell to the floor and bounced out the porch steps. And ever since that night—" He leaned across the table toward Mary, his voice dropping dramatically. "—people in the house have sometimes heard a thumping noise, and seen the *suitor's head, dripping gore, bouncing down the steps!*"

Mary and Bysshe shared a delicious shiver. George gave Bysshe a thoughtful look.

"D'ye credit this sort of thing, Mr. Omnibus?"

Bysshe looked up. "Oh yes. I have a great belief in things supernatural."

George gave an insolent smile, and Mary's heart quickened as she recognized a trap.

"Then how can you be an atheist?" George asked.

Bysshe was startled. No one had ever asked him this question before. He gave a nervous laugh. "I am not so much opposed to God," he said, "as I am a worshipper of Galileo and Newton. And of course an enemy of the established Church."

"I see."

A little smile drifted across Bysshe's lips.

> "Yes!" he said, "I have seen God's worshippers unsheathe
> The sword of his revenge, when grace descended,
> Confirming all unnatural impulses,
> To satisfy their desolating deeds;
> And frantic priests waved the ill-omened cross
> O'er the unhappy earth; then shone the sun
> On showers of gore from the upflashing steel
> Of safe assassin—"

"And *have* you seen such?" George's look was piercing.

Bysshe blinked at him. "Beg pardon?"

"I asked if you *had* seen showers of gore, upflashing steel, all that sort of thing."

"Ah. No." He offered George a half-apologetic smile. "I do not hold warfare consonant with my principles."

"Yes." George's stomach rumbled once more. "It's rather more in my line than yours. So I think I am probably better qualified to judge it . . ." His lip twisted. ". . . *and* your principles."

Mary felt her hackles rise. "Surely you don't dispute that warfare is a great evil," she said. "And that the church blesses war and its outcome."

"The church—" He waved a hand. "The chaplains we had with us in Spain were fine men and did good work, from what I could see. Though we had damn few of them, as for the most part they preferred to judge war from their comfortable beds at home. And as for war—ay, it's evil. Yes. Among other things."

"Among other things!" Mary was outraged. "What other things?"

George looked at each of the officers in turn, then at Mary. "War is an abomination, I think we can all agree. But it is also an occasion for all that is great in mankind. Courage, comradeship, sacrifice. Heroism and nobility beyond the scope of imagination."

"Glory," said one-armed Somerset helpfully.

"Death!" snapped Mary. "Hideous, lingering death! Disease. Mutilation!" She realized she had stepped a little far, and bobbed her head toward Somerset, silently begging his pardon for bringing up his disfigurement. "Endless suffering among the starving widows and orphans," she went on. "Early this year Bysshe and Jane and I walked across the part of France that the armies had marched over. It was a desert, my lord. Whole villages without a single soul. Women, children, and cripples in rags. Many without a roof over their head."

"Ay," said Harry Smith. "We saw it in Spain, all of us."

"Miss Godwin," said George, "those poor French people have my sympathy as well as yours. But if a nation is going to murder its rightful king, elect a tyrant, and attack every other nation in the world, then it can but expect to receive that which it giveth. I reserve far greater sympathy for the poor orphans and widows of Spain, Portugal, and the Low Countries."

"And England," said Captain Austen.

"Ay," said George, "and England."

"I did not say that England has not suffered," said Mary. "Anyone with eyes can see the victims of the war. And the victims of the Corn Bill as well."

"Enough." George threw up his hands. "I heard enough debate on the Corn Bill in the House of Lords—I beg you, not here."

"People are starving, my lord," Mary said quietly.

"But thanks to Waterloo," George said, "they at least starve in peace."

"Here's our flesh!" said a relieved Harry Smith. Napkins flourished, silverware rattled, the dinner was laid down. Bysshe took a bite of his cheese pie, then sampled one of the little Brabant cabbages and gave a freckled smile—he had not, as had Mary, grown tired of them. Smith, Somerset, and George chatted about various Army acquaintances, and the others ate in silence. Somerset, Mary noticed, had come equipped with a combination knife-and-fork and managed his cutlet efficiently.

George, she noted, ate only a little, despite the grumblings of his stomach.

"Is it not to your taste, my lord?" she asked.

"My appetite is off." Shortly.

"That light cavalry figure don't come without sacrifice," said Smith. "I'm an infantryman, though," brandishing knife and fork, "and can tuck in to my vittles."

George gave him an irritated glance and sipped at his hock. "Cavalry, infantry,

Senior Service, staff," he said, pointing at himself, Smith, Austen, and Somerset with his fork. The fork swung to Bysshe. "Do you, sir, have an occupation? Besides being atheistical, I mean."

Bysshe put down his knife and fork and answered deliberately. "I have been a scientist, and a reformer, and a sort of an engineer. I have now taken up poetry."

"I didn't know it was something to be *taken up*," said George.

"Captain Austen's sister does something in the literary line, I believe," Harry Smith said.

Austen gave a little shake of his head. "Please, Harry. Not here."

"I know she publishes anonymously, but—"

"She doesn't want it known," firmly, "and I prefer her wishes be respected."

Smith gave Austen an apologetic look. "Sorry, Frank."

Mary watched Austen's distress with amusement. Austen had a spinster sister, she supposed—she could just imagine the type—who probably wrote ripe horrid Gothic novels, all terror and dark battlements and cloaked sensuality, all to the constant mortification of the family.

Well, Mary thought. She should be charitable. Perhaps they were good.

She and Bysshe liked a good gothic, when they were in the mood. Bysshe had even written a couple, when he was fifteen or so.

George turned to Bysshe. "That was your own verse you quoted?"

"Yes."

"I thought perhaps it was, as I hadn't recognized it."

"*Queen Mab*," said Claire. "It's *very* good." She gave Bysshe a look of adoration that sent a weary despairing cry through Mary's nerves. "It's got all Bysshe's ideas in it," she said.

"And the publisher?"

"I published it myself," Bysshe said, "in an edition of seventy copies."

George raised an eyebrow. "A self-published phenomenon, forsooth. But why so few?"

"The poem is a political statement in accordance with Mr. Godwin's *Political Justice*. Were it widely circulated, the government might act to suppress it, and to prosecute the publisher." He gave a shudder. "With people like Lord Ellenborough in office, I think it best to take no chances."

"Lord Ellenborough is a great man," said Captain Austen firmly. Mary was surprised at his emphatic tone. "He led for Mr. Warren Hastings, do you know, during his trial, and that trial lasted seven years or more and ended in acquittal. Governor Hastings did me many a good turn in India—he was the making of me. I'm sure I owe Lord Ellenborough my purest gratitude."

Bysshe gave Austen a serious look. "Lord Ellenborough sent Daniel Eaton to prison for publishing Thomas Paine," he said. "And he sent Leigh Hunt to prison for publishing the truth about the Prince Regent."

"One an atheist," Austen scowled, "the other a pamphleteer."

"Why, so am I both," said Bysshe sweetly, and, smiling, sipped his spring water. Mary wanted to clap aloud.

"It is the duty of the Lord Chief Justice to guard the realm from subversion," said Somerset. "We were at war, you know."

"We are no longer at war," said Bysshe, "and Lord Ellenborough still sends good folk to prison."

"At least," said Mary, "he can no longer accuse reformers of being Jacobins. Not with France under the Bourbons again."

"Of course he can," Bysshe said. "Reform is an idea, and Jacobinism is an idea, and Ellenborough conceives them the same."

"But are they not?" George said.

Mary's temper flared. "Are you serious? Comparing those who seek to correct injustice with those who—"

"Who cut the heads off everyone with whom they disagreed?" George interrupted. "I'm perfectly serious. Robespierre was the very type of reformer— virtuous, sober, sedate, educated, a spotless private life. And how many thousands did he murder?" He jabbed his fork at Bysshe again, and Mary restrained the impulse to slap it out of his hand. "You may not like Ellenborough's sentencing, but a few hours in the pillory or a few months in prison ain't the same as beheading. And that's what reform in England would come to in the end—mobs and demagogues heaping up death, and then a dictator like Cromwell, or worse luck Bonaparte, to end liberty for a whole generation."

"I do not look to the French for a model," said Bysshe, "but rather to America."

"So did the French," said George, "and look what *they* got."

"If France had not desperately needed reform," Bysshe said, "there would have been nothing so violent as their revolution. If England reforms itself, there need be no violence."

"Ah. So if the government simply resigns, and frame-breakers and agitators and democratic philosophers and wandering poets take their place, then things shall be well in England."

"Things will be better in any case," Bysshe said quietly, "than they are now."

"Exactly!" Claire said.

George gave his companions a knowing look. *See how I humor this vagabond?* Mary read. Loathing stirred her heart.

Bysshe could read a look as well as Mary. His face darkened. "Please understand me," he said. "I do not look for immediate change, nor do I preach violent revolution. Mr. Godwin has corrected that error in my thought. There will be little amendment for years to come. But Ellenborough is old, and the King is old and mad, and the Regent and his loathsome brothers are not young . . ." He smiled. "I will outlive them, will I not?"

George looked at him. "Will you outlive me, sir? I am not yet thirty."

"I am three-and-twenty." Mildly. "I believe the odds favor me."

Bysshe and the others laughed, while George looked cynical and dyspeptic. *Used to being the young cavalier*, Mary thought. *He's not so young any longer— how much longer will that pretty face last?*

"And of course advance of science may turn this debate irrelevant," Bysshe went on. "Mr. Godwin calculates that with the use of mechanical aids, people may reduce their daily labor to an hour or two, to the general benefit of all."

"But you oppose such machines, don't ye?" George said. "You support the Luddites, I assume?"

"Ay, but—"

"And the frame-breakers are destroying the machines that have taken their livelihood, aren't they? So where is your general benefit, then?"

Mary couldn't hold it in any longer. She slapped her hand down on the table, and George and Bysshe started. "The riots occur because the profits of the looms were not used to benefit the weavers, but to enrich the mill owners! Were the owners to share their profits with the weavers, there would have been no disorder."

George gave her a civil bow. "Your view of human nature is generous," he said, "if you expect a mill owner to support the families of those who are not even his employees."

"It would be for the good of all, wouldn't it?" Bysshe said. "If he does not want his mills threatened and frames broken."

"It sounds like extortion wrapped in pretty philosophy."

"The mill owners will pay one way or another," Mary pointed out. "They can pay taxes to the government to suppress the Luddites with militia and dragoons, or they can have the goodwill of the people, and let the swords and muskets rust."

"They will buy the swords every time," George said. "They are useful in ways other than suppressing disorder, such as securing trade routes and the safety of the nation." He put on a benevolent face. "You must forgive me, but your view of humanity is too benign. You do not account for the violence and passion that are in the very heart of man, and which institutions such as law and religion are intended to help control. And when science serves the passions, only tragedy can result—when I think of science, I think of the science of Dr. Guillotin."

"We are fallen," said Captain Austen. "Eden will never be within our grasp."

"The passions are a problem, but I think they can be turned to good," said Bysshe. "That is—" He gave an apologetic smile. "That is the aim of my current work. To use the means of poetry to channel the passions to a humane and beneficent aim."

"I offer you my very best wishes," condescendingly, "but I fear mankind will disappoint you. Passions are—" George gave Mary an insolent, knowing smile. "—are the downfall of many a fine young virtue."

Mary considered hitting him in the face. Bysshe seemed not to have noticed George's look, nor Mary's reaction. "Mr. Godwin ventured the thought that dreams are the source of many irrational passions," he mused. "He believes that should we ever find a way of doing without sleep, the passions would fall away."

"Ay!" barked George. "Through enervation, if nothing else."

The others laughed. Mary decided she had had enough, and rose.

"I shall withdraw," she said. "The journey has been fatiguing."

The gentlemen, Bysshe excepted, rose to their feet. "Good night, Maie," he said. "I will stay for a while, I think."

"As you like, Bysshe." Mary looked at her sister. "Jane? I mean Claire? Will you come with me?"

"Oh, no." Quickly. "I'm not at all tired."

Annoyance stiffened Mary's spine. "As you like," she said.

George bowed toward her, picked a candle off the table, and offered her an arm. "May I light you up the stair? I should like to apologize for my temerity in contradicting such a charming lady." He offered his brightest smile. "I think *my* poor virtue will extend that far, yes?"

She looked at him coldly—she couldn't think it customary, even in George's circles, to escort a woman to her bedroom.

Damn it anyway. "My lord," she said, and put her arm through his.

Jerome Bonaparte made a flying leap from the table and landed on George's shoulder. It clung to his long auburn hair, screamed, and made a face, and the others laughed. Mary considered the thought of being escorted up to bed by a lord and a monkey, and it improved her humor.

"Goodnight, gentlemen," Mary said. "Claire."

The gentlemen reseated themselves and George took Mary up the stairs. They were so narrow and steep that they couldn't go up abreast; George, with the candle, went first, and Mary, holding his hand, came up behind. Her door was the first up the stairs; she put her hand on the wooden door handle and turned to face her escort. The monkey leered at her from his shoulder.

"I thank you for your company, my lord," she said. "I fear your journey was a little short."

"I wished a word with you," softly, "a little apart from the others."

Mary stiffened. To her annoyance her heart gave a lurch. "What word is that?" she asked.

His expression was all affability. "I am sensible to the difficulties that you and your sister must be having. Without money in a foreign country, and with your only protector a man—" He hesitated. Jerome Bonaparte, jealous for his attention, tugged at his hair. "A charming man of noble ideals, surely, but without money."

"I thank you for your concern, but it is misplaced," Mary said. "Claire and I are perfectly well."

"Your health ain't my worry," he said. Was he deliberately misunderstanding? Mary wondered in fury. "I worry for your future—you are on an adventure with a man who cannot support you, cannot see you safe home, cannot marry you."

"Bysshe and I do not wish to marry." The words caught at her heart. "We are free."

"And the damage to your reputation in society—" he began, and came up short when she burst into laughter. He looked severe, while the monkey mocked him from his shoulder. "You may laugh now, Miss Godwin, but there are those who will use this adventure against you. Political enemies of your father at the very least.''

"That isn't why I was laughing. I am the daughter of William Godwin and Mary Wollstonecraft—I *have* no reputation! It's like being the natural daughter of Lucifer and the Scarlet Woman of Babylon. Nothing is expected of us, nothing at all. Society has given us license to do as we please. We were dead to them from birth.''

He gave her a narrow look. "But you have at least a little concern for the proprieties—why else travel pseudonymously?''

Mary looked at him in surprise. "What d'you mean?''

He smiled. "Give me a little credit, Miss Godwin. When you call your sister *Jane* half the time, and your protector calls you *May* . . .''

Mary laughed again. "*The* Maie—Maie for short—is one of Bysshe's pet names for me. The other is Pecksie.''

"Oh.''

"And Jane is my sister's given name, which she has always hated. Last year she decided to call herself Clara or Claire—this week it is Claire.''

Jerome Bonaparte began to yank at George's ear, and George made a face, pulled the monkey from his shoulder, and shook it with mock ferocity. Again he spoke in the cracked Scots dowager's voice. "Are ye sae donsie wicked, creeture? Tae Elba w'ye!''

Mary burst into laughter again. George gave her a careless grin, then returned the monkey to his shoulder. It sat and regarded Mary with bright, wise eyes.

"Miss Godwin, I am truly concerned for you, believe else of me what you will.''

Mary's laughter died away. She took the candle from his hand. "Please, my lord. My sister and I are perfectly safe in Mr. Shelley's company.''

"You will not accept my protection? I will freely give it.''

"We do not need it. I thank you.''

"Will you not take a loan, then? To see you safe across the Channel? Mr. Shelley may pay me back if he is ever in funds.''

Mary shook her head.

A little of the old insolence returned to George's expression. "Well. I have done what I could.''

"Good night, Lord Newstead.''

"Good night.''

Mary readied herself for bed and climbed atop the soft mattress. She tried to read her Italian grammar, but the sounds coming up the stairway were a distraction. There was loud conversation, and singing, and then Claire's fine voice, unaccompanied, rising clear and sweet up the narrow stair.

Torcere, Mary thought, looking fiercely at her book, *attorcere, rattorcere, scontorcere, torcere.*

Twist. Twist, twist, twist, twist.

Claire finished, and there was loud applause. Bysshe came in shortly afterwards. His eyes sparkled and his color was high. "We were singing," he said.

"I heard.''

"I hope we didn't disturb you." He began to undress.

Mary frowned at her book. "You did."

"And I argued some more with Byron." He looked at her and smiled. "Imagine it—if we could convert Byron! Bring one of the most famous men in the world to our views."

She gave him a look. "I can think of nothing more disastrous to our cause than to have him lead it."

"Byron's famous. And he's a splendid man." He looked at her with a self-conscious grin. "I have a pair of byrons, you know, back home. I think I have a good turn of ankle, but the things are the very devil to lace. You really need servants for it."

"He's Newstead now. Not Byron. I wonder if they'll have to change the name of the boot?"

"Why would he change his name, d'you suppose? After he'd become famous with it."

"Wellington became famous as Wellesley."

"Wellington *had* to change his name. His brother was *already* Lord Wellesley." He approached the bed and smiled down at her. "He likes you."

"He likes any woman who crosses his path. Or so I understand."

Bysshe crawled into the bed and put his arm around her, the hand resting warmly on her belly. He smelled of the tobacco he'd been smoking with George. She put her hand atop his, feeling on the third finger the gold wedding ring he still wore. Dissatisfaction crackled through her. "You are free, you know." He spoke softly into her ear. "You can be with Byron if you wish."

Mary gave him an irritated look. "I don't *wish* to be with Byron. I want to be with you."

"But you *may*," whispering, the hand stroking her belly, "be with Byron if you want."

Temper flared through Mary. "I don't *want* Byron!" she said. "And I don't want Mr. Thomas Jefferson Hogg, or any of your other friends!"

He seemed a little hurt. "Hogg's a splendid fellow."

"Hogg tried to seduce your wife, and he's tried to seduce me. And I don't understand how he remains your best friend."

"Because we agree on everything, and I hold him no malice where his intent was not malicious." Bysshe gave her a searching look. "I only want you to be free. If we're not free, our love is chained, chained absolutely, and all ruined. I can't live that way—I found that out with Harriet."

She sighed, put her arm around him, drew her fingers through his tangled hair. He rested his head on her shoulder and looked up into her eyes. "I want to be *free* to be with you," Mary told him. "Why will that not suit?"

"It suits." He kissed her cheek. "It suits very well." He looked up at her happily. "And if Harriet joins us in Brussels, with a little money, then all shall be perfect."

Mary gazed at him, utterly unable to understand how he could think his wife would join them, or why, for that matter, he thought it a good idea.

He misses his little boy, she thought. *He wants to be with him.*

The thought rang hollow in her mind.

He kissed her again, his hand moving along her belly, touching her lightly. "My golden-haired Maie." The hand cupped her breast. Her breath hissed inward.

"Careful," she said. "I'm very tender there."

"I will be nothing but tenderness." The kisses reached her lips. "I desire nothing but tenderness for you."

She turned to him, let his lips brush against hers, then press more firmly. Sensation, a little painful, flushed her breast. His tongue touched hers. Desire rose and she put her arms around him.

The door opened and Claire came in, chattering of George while she undressed. Mood broken, tenderness broken, there was nothing to do but sleep.

"Come and look," Mary said, "here's a cat eating roses; she'll turn into a woman, when beasts eat these roses they turn into men and women." But there was no one in the cottage, only the sound of the wind.

Fear touched her, cold on the back of her neck.

She stepped into the cottage, and suddenly there was something blocking the sun that came through the windows, an enormous figure, monstrous and black and hungry . . .

Nausea and the sounds of swordplay woke her. A dog was barking maniacally. Mary rose from the bed swiftly and wrapped her shawl around herself. The room was hot and stuffy, and her gorge rose. She stepped to the window, trying not to vomit, and opened the pane to bring in fresh air.

Coolness touched her cheeks. Below in the courtyard of the inn was Pásmány, the fencing teacher, slashing madly at his pupil, Byron. Newstead. *George*, she reminded herself, she would remember he was *George*.

And serve him right.

She dragged welcome morning air into her lungs as the two battled below her. George was in his shirt, planted firmly on his strong, muscular legs, his pretty face set in an expression of intent calculation. Pásmány flung himself at the man, darting in and out, his sword almost fluid in its movement. They were using straight heavy sabers, dangerous even if unsharpened, and no protective equipment at all. A huge black dog, tied to the vermilion wheel of a big dark-blue barouche, barked at the both of them without cease.

Nausea swam over Mary; she closed her eyes and clutched the windowsill. The ringing of the swords suddenly seemed very far away.

"Are they fighting?" Claire's fingers clutched her shoulder. "Is it a duel? Oh, it's *Byron*!"

Mary abandoned the window and groped her way to the bed. Sweat beaded on her forehead. Bysshe blinked muzzily at her from his pillow.

"I must go down and watch," said Claire. She reached for her clothing and, hopping, managed to dress without missing a second of the action outside. She grabbed a hairbrush on her way out the door and was arranging her hair on the run even before the door slammed behind her.

"Whatever is happening?" Bysshe murmured. She reached blindly for his hand and clutched it.

"Bysshe," she gasped. "I am with child. I must be."

"I shouldn't think so." Calmly. "We've been using every precaution." He touched her cheek. His hand was cool. "It's the travel and excitement. Perhaps a bad egg."

Nausea blackened her vision and bent her double. Sweat fell in stately rhythm from her forehead to the floor. "This can't be a bad egg," she said. "Not day after day."

"Poor Maie." He nestled behind her, stroked her back and shoulders. "Perhaps there is a flaw in the theory," he said. "Time will tell."

No turning back, Mary thought. She had *wanted* there to be no turning back, to burn every bridge behind her, commit herself totally, as her mother had, to her beliefs. And now she'd succeeded—she and Bysshe were linked forever, linked by the child in her womb. Even if they parted, if—free, as they both wished to be—he abandoned this union, there would still be that link, those bridges burnt, her mother's defiant inheritance fulfilled . . .

Perhaps there is a flaw in the theory. She wanted to laugh and cry at once.

Bysshe stroked her, his thoughts his own, and outside the martial clangor went on and on.

It was some time before she could dress and go down to the common rooms. The sabre practice had ended, and Bysshe and Claire were already breaking their fast with Somerset, Smith, and Captain Austen. The thought of breakfast made Mary ill, so she wandered outside into the courtyard, where the two breathless swordsmen, towels draped around their necks, were sitting on a bench drinking water, with a tin dipper, from an old wooden bucket. The huge black dog barked, foaming, as she stepped out of the inn, and the two men, seeing her, rose.

"Please sit, gentlemen," she said, waving them back to their bench; she walked across the courtyard to the big open gate and stepped outside. She leaned against the whitewashed stone wall and took deep breaths of the country air. Sweet-smelling wildflowers grew in the verges of the highway. Prosperous-looking villagers nodded pleasantly as they passed about their errands.

"Looking for your haunted house, Miss Godwin?"

George's inevitable voice grated on her ears. She looked at him over her shoulder. "My intention was simply to enjoy the morning."

"I hope I'm not spoiling it."

Reluctant courtesy rescued him from her own riposting tongue. "How was the Emperor's bed?" she said finally.

He stepped out into the road. "I believe I slept better than he did, and longer." He smiled at her. "No ghosts walked."

"But you still fought a battle after your sleep."

"A far, far better one. Waterloo was not something I would care to experience more than once."

"I shouldn't care to experience it even the first time."

"Well. You're female, of course." All offhand, unaware of her rising hackles. He looked up and down the highway.

"D'ye know, this is the first time I've seen this road in peace. I first rode it north during the retreat from Quatre Bras, a miserable rainy night, and then there was the chase south after Boney the night of Waterloo, then later the advance with the army to Paris . . ." He shook his head. "It's a pleasant road, ain't it? Much better without the armies."

"Yes."

"We went along there." His hand sketched a line across the opposite horizon. "This road was choked with retreating French, so we went around them. With two squadrons of Vandeleur's lads, the 12th, the Prince of Wales's Own, all I could find once the French gave way. I knew Boney would be running, and I knew it had to be along this road. I had to find him, make certain he would never trouble our peace. Find him for England." He dropped right fist into left palm.

"Boney'd left two battalions of the Guard to hold us, but I went around them. I knew the Prussians would be after him, too, and their mounts were fresher. So we drove on through the night, jumping fences, breaking down hedges, galloping like madmen, and then we found him at Genappe. The bridge was so crammed with refugees that he couldn't get his barouche across."

Mary watched carefully as George, uninvited, told the story that he must, by now, have told a hundred times, and wondered why he was telling it now to someone with such a clear distaste for things military. His color was high, and he was still breathing hard from his exercise; sweat gleamed on his immaculate forehead and matted his shirt; she could see the pulse throbbing in his throat. Perhaps the swordplay and sight of the road had brought the memory back; perhaps he was merely, after all, trying to impress her.

A female, of course. Damn the man.

"They'd brought a white Arab up for him to ride away," George went on. "His Chasseurs of the Guard were close around. I told each trooper to mark his enemy as we rode up—we came up at a slow trot, in silence, our weapons sheathed. In the dark the enemy took us for French—our uniforms were similar enough. I gave the signal—we drew pistols and carbines—half the French saddles were emptied in an instant. Some poor lad of a cornet tried to get in my way, and I cut him up through the teeth. Then there he was—the Emperor. With one foot in the stirrup, and Roustam the Mameluke ready to boost him into the saddle."

A tigerish, triumphant smile spread across George's face. His eyes were focused down the road, not seeing her at all. "I put my dripping point in his face, and for the life of me I couldn't think of any French to say except to tell him to sit down. '*Asseyez-vous!*' I ordered, and he gave me a sullen look and sat down, right down in the muddy roadway, with the carbines still cracking around us and bullets flying through the air. And I thought, He's finished. He's done. There's nothing left of him now. We finished off his bodyguard—they hadn't a chance after our first volley. The French soldiers around us thought we were the Prussian advance guard, and they were running as fast as their legs could carry them. Either they didn't know we had their Emperor or they didn't care. So we dragged Boney's barouche off the road, and dragged Boney with it, and ten minutes later the Prussians galloped up—the Death's Head Hussars under Gneisenau, all in black and silver, riding like devils. But the devils had lost the prize.''

Looking at the wild glow in George's eyes Mary realized that she'd been wrong—the story was not for her at all, but for *him*. For George. He needed it somehow, this affirmation of himself, the enunciated remembrance of his moment of triumph.

But why? Why did he need it?

She realized his eyes were on her. "Would you like to see the coach, Miss Godwin?" he asked. The question surprised her.

"It's here?"

"I kept it." He laughed. "Why not? It was mine. What Captain Austen would call a fair prize of war." He offered her his arm. She took it, curious about what else she might discover.

The black mastiff began slavering at her the second she set foot inside the courtyard. Its howls filled the air. "Hush, Picton," George said, and walked straight to the big gold-trimmed blue coach with vermilion wheels. The door had the Byron arms and the Latin motto CREDE BYRON.

Should she believe him? Mary wondered. And if so, how much?

"This is Bonaparte's?" she said.

"Was, Miss Godwin. Till June 16th last. *Down*, Picton!" The dog lunged at him, and he wrestled with it, laughing, until it calmed down and began to fawn on him.

George stepped to the door and opened it. "The Imperial symbols are still on the lining, as you see." The door and couch were lined with rich purple, with golden bees and the letter N worked in heavy gold embroidery. "Fine Italian leatherwork," he said. "Drop-down secretaires so that the great man could write or dictate on the march. Holsters for pistols." He knocked on the coach's polished side. "Bulletproof. There are steel panels built in, just in case any of the Great Man's subjects decided to imitate Marcus Brutus." He smiled. "I was glad for that steel in Paris, I assure you, with Bonapartist assassins lurking under every tree." A mischievous gleam entered his eye. "And last, the best thing of all." He opened a compartment under one of the seats and withdrew a solid silver chamber pot. "You'll notice it still bears the imperial *N*."

"Vanity in silver."

"Possibly. Or perhaps he was afraid one of his soldiers would steal it if he didn't mark it for his own."

Mary looked at the preposterous object and found herself laughing. George looked pleased and stowed the chamber pot in its little cabinet. He looked at her with his head cocked to one side. "You will not reconsider my offer?"

"No." Mary stiffened. "Please don't mention it again."

The mastiff Picton began to howl again, and George seized its collar and told it to behave itself. Mary turned to see Claire walking toward them.

"Won't you be joining us for breakfast, my lord?"

George straightened. "Perhaps a crust or two. I'm not much for breakfast."

Still fasting, Mary thought. "It would make such sense for you to give up meat, you know," she said. "Since you deprive yourself of food anyway."

"I prefer not to deny myself pleasure, even if the quantities are necessarily restricted."

"Your swordplay was magnificent."

"Thank you. Cavalry style, you know—all slash and dash. But I *am* good, for a' that."

"I know you're busy, but—" Claire bit her lip. "Will you take us to Waterloo?"

"Claire!" cried Mary.

Claire gave a nervous laugh. "Truly," she said. "I'm absolutely with child to see Waterloo."

George looked at her, his eyes intent. "Very well," he said. "We'll be driving through it in any case. And Captain Austen has expressed an interest."

Fury rose in Mary's heart. "Claire, how *dare* you impose—"

"Ha' ye nae pity for the puir lassie?" The Scots voice was mock-severe. "Ye shallnae keep her fra' her Waterloo."

Claire's Waterloo, Mary thought, was exactly what she wanted to keep her from.

George offered them his exaggerated, flourishing bow. "If you'll excuse me, ladies, I must give the necessary orders."

He strode through the door. Pásmány followed, the swords tucked under his arm. Claire gave a little joyous jump, her shoes scraping on cobbles. "I can hardly believe it," she said. "Byron showing us Waterloo!"

"I can't believe it either," Mary said. She sighed wearily and headed for the dining room.

Perhaps she would dare to sip a little milk.

They rode out in Napoleon's six-horse barouche, Claire, Mary, and Bysshe inside with George, and Smith, Somerset, and Captain Austen sharing the outside rear seat. The leather top with its bulletproof steel inserts had been folded away and the inside passengers could all enjoy the open air. The barouche wasn't driven by a coachman up top, but by three postboys who rode the right-hand horses, so there was nothing in front to interrupt the view. Bysshe's mule and little carriage, filled with bags and books, ate dust behind along with the officers' baggage coaches, all driven by George's servants.

The men talked of war and Claire listened to them with shining eyes. Mary concentrated on enjoying the shape of the low hills with their whitewashed farmhouses and red tile roofs, the cut fields of golden rye stubble, the smell of wildflowers and the sound of birdsong. It was only when the carriage passed a walled farm, its whitewash marred by bullets and cannon shot, that her reverie was marred by the thought of what had happened here.

"La Haie Sainte," George remarked. "The King's German Legion held it throughout the battle, even after they'd run out of ammunition. I sent Mercer's horse guns to keep the French from the walls, else Lord knows what would have happened.'' He stood in the carriage, looked left and right, frowned. ''These roads we're about to pass were sunken—an obstacle to both sides, but mainly to the French. They're filled in now. Mass graves.''

''The French were cut down in heaps during their cavalry attack,'' Somerset added. ''The piles were eight feet tall, men and horses.''

''How gruesome!'' laughed Claire.

''Turn right, Swinson,'' said George.

Homemade souvenir stands had been set up at the crossroads. Prosperous-looking rustics hawked torn uniforms, breastplates, swords, muskets, bayonets. Somerset scowled at them. ''They must have made a fortune looting the dead.''

''And the living,'' said Smith. ''Some of our poor wounded weren't brought in till two days after the battle. Many had been stripped naked by the peasants.''

A young man ran up alongside the coach, shouting in French. He explained he had been in the battle, a guide to the great Englishman Lord Byron, and would guide them over the field for a few guilders.

''Never heard of you,'' drawled George, and dismissed him. ''Hey! Swinson! Pull up here.''

The postboys pulled up their teams. George opened the door of the coach and strolled to one of the souvenir stands. When he returned it was with a French breastplate and helmet. Streaks of rust dribbled down the breastplate, and the helmet's horsehair plume smelled of mildew.

''I thought we could take a few shots at it,'' George said. ''I'd like to see whether armor provides any protection at all against bullets—I suspect not. There's a movement afoot at Whitehall to give breastplates to the Household Brigade, and I suspect they ain't worth the weight. If I can shoot a few holes in this with my Mantons, I may be able to prove my point.''

They drove down a rutted road of soft earth. It was lined with thorn hedges, but most of them had been broken down during the battle and there were long vistas of rye stubble, the gentle sloping ground, the pattern of plow and harvest. Occasionally the coach wheels grated on something, and Mary remembered they were moving along a mass grave, over the decaying flesh and whitening bones of hundreds of horses and men. A cloud passed across the sun, and she shivered.

''Can ye pull through the hedge, Swinson?'' George asked. ''I think the ground is firm enough to support us—no rain for a few days at least.'' The lead postboy studied the hedge with a practiced eye, then guided the lead team through a gap in it.

The barouche rocked over exposed roots and broken limbs, then ground onto a rutted sward of green grass, knee-high, that led gently down into the valley they'd just crossed. George stood again, his eyes scanning the ground. ''Pull up over there,'' he said, pointing, and the coachman complied.

''Here you can see where the battle was won,'' George said. He tossed his clanging armor out onto the grass, opened the coach door and stepped out himself. The others followed, Mary reluctantly. George pointed with one elegant hand at the ridge running along the opposite end of the valley from their own, a half-mile opposite.

"Napoleon's grand battery," he said. "Eighty guns, many of them twelve-pounders—Boney called them his daughters. He was an artillerist, you know, and he always prepared his attacks with a massed bombardment. The guns fired for an hour and put our poor fellows through hell. Bylandt's Dutchmen were standing in the open, right where we are now, and the guns broke 'em entirely.

"Then the main attack came, about two o'clock. Count d'Erlon's corps, 16,000 strong, arrayed 25 men deep with heavy cavalry on the wings. They captured La Haye and Papelotte, those farms over there on the left, and rolled up this ridge with drums beating the *pas de charge* . . ."

George turned. There was a smile on his face. Mary watched him closely—the pulse was beating like d'Erlon's drums in his throat, and his color was high. He was loving every second of this.

He went on, describing the action, and against her will Mary found herself seeing it, Picton's division lying in wait, prone on the reverse slope, George bringing the heavy cavalry up, the cannons banging away. Picton's men rising, firing their volleys, following with the bayonet. The Highlanders screaming in Gaelic, their plumes nodding as they drew their long broadswords and plunged into the fight, the pipers playing "Johnnie Cope" amid all the screams and clatter. George leading the Household and Union Brigades against the enemy cavalry, the huge grain-fed English hunters driving back the chargers from Normandy. And then George falling on d'Erlon's flanks, driving the French in a frightened mob all the way back across the valley while the British horsemen slashed at their backs. The French gunners of the grand battery unable to fire for fear of hitting their own men, and then dying themselves under the British sabres.

Mary could sense as well the things George left out. The sound of steel grating on bone. Wails and moans of the wounded, the horrid challenging roars of the horses. And in the end, a valley filled with stillness, a carpet of bodies and pierced flesh . . .

George gave a long sigh. "Our cavalry are brave, you know, far too brave for their own good. And the officers get their early training in steeplechases and the hunt, and their instinct is to ride straight at the objective at full gallop, which is absolutely the worst thing cavalry can ever do. After Slade led his command to disaster back in the Year Twelve, the Duke realized he could only commit cavalry at his peril. In Spain we finally trained the horse to maneuver and to make careful charges, but the Union and Household troops hadn't been in the Peninsula, and didn't know the drill. . . . I drove myself mad in the weeks before the battle, trying to beat the recall orders into them." He laughed self-consciously. "My heart was in my mouth during the whole charge, I confess, less with fear of the enemy than with terror my own men would run mad. But they answered the trumpets, all but the Inniskillings, who wouldnae listen—the Irish blood was up—and while they ran off into the valley, the rest of us stayed in the grand battery. Sabred the gunners, drove off the limbers with the ready ammunition—and where we could we took the wheels off the guns, and rolled 'em back to our lines like boys with hoops. And the Inniskillings—'' He shook his head. "They ran wild into the enemy lines, and Boney loosed his lancers at 'em, and they died almost to a man. I had to watch from the middle of the battery, with my officers begging to be let slip again and rescue their comrades, and I had to forbid it.''

There were absolute tears in George's eyes. Mary watched in fascination and wondered if this was a part of the performance, or whether he was genuinely affected—but then she saw that Bysshe's eyes had misted over and Somerset was wiping his eyes with his one good sleeve. So, she thought, she *could* believe Byron, at least a little.

"Well.'' George cleared his throat, trying to control himself. "Well. We came back across the valley herding thousands of prisoners—and that charge proved the winning stroke. Boney attacked later, of course—all his heavy cavalry came knee-to-knee up the middle, between La Haie Sainte and Hougoumont,'' gesturing to the left with one arm, "we had great guns and squares of infantry to hold them, and my heavies to counterattack. The Prussians were pressing the French at Plancenoit and Papelotte. Boney's last throw of the dice sent the Old Guard across the valley after sunset, but our Guards under Maitland held them, and Colborne's 52nd and the Belgian Chasseurs got round their flanks, and after they broke I let the Household and Union troopers have their head—we swept 'em away. Sabred and trampled Boney's finest troops right in front of his eyes, all in revenge for the brave, mad Inniskillings—the only time his Guard ever failed in attack, and it marked the end of his reign. We were blown by the end of it, but Boney had nothing left to counterattack with. I knew he would flee. So I had a fresh horse brought up and went after him.''

"So you won the battle of Waterloo!'' said Claire.

George gave her a modest look that, to Mary, seemed false as the very devil. "I was privileged to have a decisive part. But 'twas the Duke that won the battle. We all fought at his direction.''

"But you captured Napoleon and ended the Empire!''

He smiled. "That I did do, lassie, ay.''

"Bravo!'' Claire clapped her hands.

Harry Smith glanced up with bright eyes. "D'ye know, George,'' he said, "pleased as I am to hear this modest recitation of your accomplishments, I find precious little mention in your discourse of the *infantry*. I seem to remember fighting a few Frenchies myself, down Hougoumont way, with Reille's whole corps marching down on us, and I believe I can recollect in my dim footsoldier's mind that I stood all day under cannonshot and bursting mortar bombs, and that Kellerman's heavy cavalry came wave after wave all afternoon, with the Old Guard afterward as a lagniappe . . .''

"I am pleased that you had some little part,'' George said, and bowed from his slim cavalry waist.

"Your lordship's condescension does you more credit than I can possibly express.'' Returning the bow.

George reached out and gave Smith's ear an affectionate tweak. "May I continue my tale? And then we may travel to Captain Harry's part of the battle-field, and he will remind us of whatever small role it was the footsoldiers played."

George went through the story of Napoleon's capture again. It was the same, sentiment for sentiment, almost word for word. Mary wandered away, the fat moist grass turning the hem of her skirt green. Skylarks danced through the air, trilling as they went. She wandered by the old broken thorn hedge and saw wild roses blossoming in it, and she remembered the wild roses planted on her mother's grave.

She thought of George Gordon Noël with tears in his eyes, and the way the others had wanted to weep—even Bysshe, who hadn't been there—and all for the loss of some Irishmen who, had they been crippled or out of uniform or begging for food or employment, these fine English officers would probably have turned into the street to starve . . .

She looked up at the sound of footsteps. Harry Smith walked up and nodded pleasantly. "I believe I have heard George give this speech," he said.

"So have I. Does he give it often?"

"Oh yes." His voice dropped, imitated George's limpid dramatics. *"He's finished. He's done. There's nothing left of him now."* Mary covered amusement with her hand. "Though the tale has improved somewhat since the first time," Smith added. "In this poor infantryman's opinion."

Mary gave him a careful look. "Is he all he seems to think he is?"

Smith gave a thin smile. "Oh, ay. The greatest cavalryman of our time, to be sure. Without doubt a genius. *Chevalier sans peur et*—well, I won't say *sans reproche.* Not quite." His brow contracted as he gave careful thought to his next words. "He purchased his way up to colonel—that would be with Lady Newstead's money—but since then he's earned his spurs."

"He truly is talented, then."

"Truly. But of course he's lucky, too. If Le Marchant hadn't died at Salamanca, George wouldn't have been able to get his heavy brigade, and if poor General Cotton hadn't been shot by our own sentry George wouldn't have got all the cavalry in time for Vitoria, and of course if Uxbridge hadn't run off with Wellington's sister-in-law then George might not have got command at Waterloo. . . . Young and without political influence as he is, he wouldn't have *kept* all those commands for long if he hadn't spent his every leave getting soused with that unspeakable hound the Prince of Wales. Ay, there's been luck involved. But who won't wish for luck in his life, eh?"

"What if his runs out?"

Smith gave this notion the same careful consideration. "I don't know," he said finally. "He's fortune's laddie, but that don't mean he's without character."

"You surprise me, speaking of him so frankly."

"We've been friends since Spain. And nothing I say will matter in any case." He smiled. "Besides, hardly anyone ever asks for *my* opinion."

The sound of Claire's laughter and applause carried across the sward. Smith cocked an eye at the other party. "Boney's at sword's point, if I'm not mistaken."

"Your turn for glory."

"Ay. If anyone will listen after George's already won the battle." He held out his arm and Mary took it. "You should meet my wife. Juanita—I met her in Spain at the storming of Badajoz. The troops were carrying away the loot, but I carried her away instead." He looked at her thoughtfully. "You have a certain spirit in common."

Mary felt flattered. "Thank you, Captain Smith. I'm honored by the comparison."

They moved to another part of the battlefield. There was a picnic overlooking the château of Hougoumont that lay red-roofed in its valley next to a well-tended orchard. Part of the chateau had been destroyed in the battle, Smith reported, but it had been rebuilt since.

Rebuilt, Mary thought, by owners enriched by battlefield loot.

George called for his pistols and moved the cuirass a distance away, propping it up on a small slope with the helmet sitting on top. A servant brought the Mantons and loaded them, and while the others stood and watched, George aimed and fired. Claire clapped her hands and laughed, though there was no discernible effect. White gunsmoke drifted on the morning breeze. George presented his second pistol, paused to aim, fired again. There was a whining sound and a scar appeared on the shoulder of the cuirass. The other men laughed.

"That cuirassier's got you for sure!" Harry Smith said.

"May I venture a shot?" Bysshe asked. George assented.

One of George's servants reloaded the pistols while George gave Bysshe instruction in shooting. "Hold the arm out straight and use the bead to aim."

"I like keeping the elbow bent a little," Bysshe said. "Not tucked in like a duellist, but not locked, either."

Bysshe took effortless aim—Mary's heart leaped at the grace of his movement—then Bysshe paused an instant and fired. There was a thunking sound and a hole appeared in the French breastplate, directly over the heart.

"Luck!" George said.

"Yes!" Claire said. "Purest luck!"

"Not so," Bysshe said easily. "Observe the plume holder." He presented the other pistol, took briefest aim, fired. With a little whine the helmet's metal plume holder took flight and whipped spinning through the air. Claire applauded and gave a cheer.

Mary smelled powder on the gentle morning wind.

Bysshe returned the pistols to George. "Fine weapons," he said, "though I prefer an octagonal barrel, as you can sight along the top."

George smiled thinly and said nothing.

"Mr. Shelley," said Somerset, "you have the makings of a soldier."

"I've always enjoyed a good shoot," Bysshe said, "though of course I won't fire at an animal. And as for soldiering, who knows what I might have been were I not exposed to Mr. Godwin's political thought?"

There was silence at this. Bysshe smiled at George. "You shouldn't lock the elbow out,'' he said. ''That fashion, every little motion of the body transmits itself to the weapon. If you keep the elbow bent a bit, it forms a sort of a spring to absorb involuntary muscle tremors and you'll have better control.'' He looked at the others gaily. ''It's not for nothing I was an engineer!''

George handed the pistols to his servant for loading. ''We'll fire another volley,'' he said. His voice was curt.

Mary watched George as the Mantons were loaded, as he presented each pistol—straight-armed—and fired again. One knocked the helmet off its perch, the other struck the breastplate at an angle and bounced off. The others laughed, and Mary could see a little muscle twitching in George's cheek.

''My turn, George,'' said Harry Smith, and the pistols were recharged. His first shot threw up turf, but the second punched a hole in the cuirass. ''There,'' Smith said, ''that should satisfy the Horse Guards that armor ain't worth the weight.''

Somerset took his turn, firing awkwardly with his one hand, and missed both shots.

''Another volley,'' George said.

There was something unpleasant in his tone, and the others took hushed notice. The pistols were reloaded. George presented the first pistol at the target, and Mary could see how he was vibrating with passion, so taut his knuckles were white on the pistol-grip. His shots missed clean.

''Bad luck, George,'' Somerset said. His voice was calming. ''Probably the bullets were deformed and didn't fly right.''

''Another volley,'' said George.

''We have an appointment in Brussels, George.''

''It can wait.''

The others drew aside and clustered together while George insisted on firing several more times. ''What a troublesome fellow he is,'' Smith muttered. Eventually George put some holes in the cuirass, collected it, and stalked to the coach, where he had the servants strap it to the rear so that he could have it sent to the Prince of Wales.

Mary sat as far away from George as possible. George's air of defiant petulance hung over the company as they started north on the Brussels road. But then Bysshe asked Claire to sing, and Claire's high, sweet voice rose above the green countryside of Brabant, and by the end of the song everyone was smiling. Mary flashed Bysshe a look of gratitude.

The talk turned to war again, battles and sieges and the dead, a long line of uniformed shadows, young, brave men who fell to the French, to accident, to camp fever. Mary had little to say on the subject that she hadn't already offered, but she listened carefully, felt the soldiers' sadness at the death of comrades, the rejoicing at victory, the satisfaction of a deadly, intricate job done well. The feelings expressed seemed fine, passionate, even a little exalted. Bysshe listened and spoke little, but gradually Mary began to feel that he was somehow included in this circle of men and that she was not—perhaps his expert pistol shooting had made him a part of this company.

A female, of course. War was a fraternity only, though the suffering it caused made no distinction as to sex.

"May I offer an observation?" Mary said.

"Of course," said Captain Austen.

"I am struck by the passion you show when speaking of your comrades and your—shall I call it your craft?"

"Please, Miss Godwin," George said. "The enlisted men may have a *craft*, if you like. We are gentlemen, and have a *profession*."

"I intended no offense. But still—I couldn't help but observe the fine feelings you show towards your comrades, and the attention you give to the details of your . . . profession."

George seemed pleased. "Ay. Didn't I speak last night of war being full of its own kind of greatness?"

"Greatness perhaps the greater," Bysshe said, "by existing in contrast to war's wretchedness."

"Precisely," said George.

"Ay," Mary said, "but what struck me most was that you gentlemen showed such elevated passion when discussing war, such sensibility, high feeling, and utter conviction—more than I am accustomed to seeing from any . . . respectable males." Harry Smith gave an uncomfortable laugh at this characterization.

"Perhaps you gentlemen practice war," Mary went on, "because it allows free play to your passions. You are free to feel, to exist at the highest pitch of emotion. Society does not normally permit this to its members—perhaps it *must* in order to make war attractive."

Bysshe listened to her in admiration. "Brava!" he cried. "War as the sole refuge of the passions—I think you have struck the thing exactly."

Smith and Somerset frowned, working through the notion. It was impossible to read Austen's weathered countenance. But George shook his head wearily.

"Mere stuff, I'm afraid," he said. "Your analysis shows an admirable ingenuity, Miss Godwin, but I'm afraid there's no more place for passion on the battlefield than anywhere else. The poor Inniskillings had passion, but look what became of *them*." He paused, shook his head again. "No, it's drill and cold logic and a good eye for ground that wins the battles. In my line it's not only my own sensibility that must be mastered, but those of hundreds of men and horses."

"Drill is meant to master the passions," said Captain Austen. "For in a battle, the impulse, the overwhelming passion, is to run away. This impulse must be subdued."

Mary was incredulous. "You claim not to experience these elevated passions which you display so plainly?"

George gave her the insolent, under-eyed look again. "All passions have their place, Miss Godwin. I reserve mine for the appropriate time."

Resentment snarled up Mary's spine. "Weren't those tears I saw standing in your eyes when you described the death of the Inniskillings? Do you claim that's part of your drill?"

George's color brightened. "I didn't shed those tears during the battle. At the time I was too busy damning those cursed Irishmen for the wild fools they were, and wishing I'd flogged more of them when I'd the chance."

"But wasn't Bonaparte's great success on account of his ability to inspire his soldiers and his nation?" Bysshe asked. "To raise their passions to a great pitch and conquer the world?"

"And it was the uninspired, roguey English with their drill and discipline who put him back in his place," George said. "Bonaparte should have saved the speeches and put his faith in the drill-square."

Somerset gave an amused laugh. "This conversation begins to sound like one of Mrs. West's novels of Sense and Sensibility that were so popular in the Nineties," he said. "I suppose you're too young to recall them. *A Gossip's Story*, and *The Advantages of Education*. My governess made me read them both."

Harry Smith looked at Captain Austen with glittering eyes. "In *fact*—" he began.

Captain Austen interrupted. "One is not blind to the world of feeling," he said, "but surely Reason must rule the passions, else even a good heart can be led astray."

"I can't agree," Bysshe said. "Surely it is Reason that has led us to the world of law, and property, and equity, and kingship—and all the hypocrisy that comes with upholding these artificial formations, and denying our true nature, all that deprives us of life, of true and natural goodness."

"Absolutely!" said Claire.

"It is Reason," Mary said, "which makes you deny the evidence of my senses. I *saw* your emotion, gentlemen, when you discussed your dead comrades. And I applaud it."

"It does you credit," Bysshe added.

"Do you claim not to feel anything in battle?" Mary demanded. "Nothing at all?"

George paused a moment, then answered seriously. "My concentration is very great. It is an elevated sort of apprehension, very intent. I must be aware of so much, you see—I can't afford to miss a thing. My analytical faculty is always in play."

"And that's all?" cried Mary.

That condescending half-smile returned. "There isnae time for else, lass."

"At the height of a charge? In the midst of an engagement?"

"Then especially. An instant's break in my concentration and all could be lost."

"Lord Newstead," Mary said, "I cannot credit this."

George only maintained his slight smile, knowing and superior. Mary wanted to wipe it from his face, and considered reminding him of his fractious conduct over the pistols. *How's that for control and discipline*, she thought.

But no, she decided, it would be a long, unpleasant ride to Brussels if she upset George again.

Against her inclinations, she concluded to be English, and hypocritical, and say nothing.

Bysshe found neither wife nor money in Brussels, and George arranged lodgings for them that they couldn't afford. The only option Mary could think of was to make their way to a channel port, then somehow try to talk their way to England with promise of payment once Bysshe had access to funds in London.

It was something for which she held little hope.

They couldn't afford any local diversions, and so spent their days in a graveyard, companionably reading.

And then, one morning two days after their arrival in Brussels, as Mary lay ill in their bed, Bysshe returned from an errand with money, coins clanking in a bag. "We're saved!" he said, and emptied the bag into her lap.

Mary looked at the silver lying on the comforter and felt her anxiety ease. They were old Spanish coins with the head of George III stamped over their original design, but they were real for all that. "A draft from Har . . . from your wife?" she said.

"No." Bysshe sat on the bed, frowned. "It's a loan from Byron—Lord Newstead, I mean."

"Bysshe!" Mary sat up and set bedclothes and silver flying. "You took money from that man? Why?"

He put a paternal hand on hers. "Lord Newstead convinced me it would be in your interest, and Claire's. To see you safely to England."

"We'll do well enough without his money! It's not even his to give away, it's his wife's."

Bysshe seemed hurt. "It's a loan," he said. "I'll pay it back once I'm in London." He gave a little laugh. "I'm certain he doesn't expect repayment. He thinks we're vagabonds."

"He thinks worse of us than that." A wave of nausea took her and she doubled up with a little cry. She rolled away from him. Coins rang on the floor. Bysshe put a hand on her shoulder, stroked her back.

"Poor Pecksie," he said. "Some English cooking will do you good."

"Why don't you believe me?" Tears welled in her eyes. "I'm with child, Bysshe!"

He stroked her. "Perhaps. In a week or two we'll know for certain." His tone lightened. "He invited us to a ball tonight."

"Who?"

"Newstead. The ball's in his honor, he can invite whomever he pleases. The Prince of Orange will be there, and the English ambassador."

Mary had no inclination to be the subject of one of George's freaks. "We have no clothes fit for a ball," she said, "and I don't wish to go in any case."

"We have money now. We can buy clothes." He smiled. "And Lord Newstead said he would loan you and Claire some jewels."

"Lady Newstead's jewels," Mary reminded.

"All those powerful people! Imagine it! Perhaps we can affect a conversion."

Mary glared at him over her shoulder. "That money is for our passage to England. George wants only to display us, his tame Radicals, like his tame monkey or his tame panther. We're just a caprice of his—he doesn't take either us or our arguments seriously."

"That doesn't invalidate our arguments. We can still make them." Cheerfully. "Claire and I will go, then. She's quite set on it, and I hate to disappoint her."

"I think it will do us no good to be in his company for an instant longer. I think he is . . ." She reached behind her back, took his hand, touched it. "Perhaps he is a little mad," she said.

"Byron? Really? He's *wrong*, of course, but . . ."

Nausea twisted her insides. Mary spoke rapidly, desperate to convince Bysshe of her opinions. "He so craves glory and fame, Bysshe. The war gave expression to his passions, gave him the achievement he desired—but now the war's over and he can't have the worship he needs. That's why he's taken up with us—he wants even *our* admiration. There's no future for him now—he could follow Wellington into politics but he'd be in Wellington's shadow forever that way. He's got nowhere to go."

There was a moment's silence. "I see you've been giving him much thought," Bysshe said finally.

"His marriage is a failure—he can't go back to England. His relations with women will be irregular, and—"

"*Our* relations are irregular, Maie. And it's the better for it."

"I didn't mean that. I meant he cannot love. It's worship he wants, not love. And those pretty young men he travels with—there's something peculiar in that. Something unhealthy."

"Captain Austen is neither pretty nor young."

"He's along only by accident. Another of George's freaks."

"And if you think he's a paederast, well—we should be tolerant. Plato believed it a virtue. And George always asks after *you*."

"I do not wish to be in his thoughts."

"He is in yours." His voice was gentle. "And that is all right. You are free."

Mary's heart sank. "It is *your* child I have, Bysshe," she said.

Bysshe didn't answer. *Torcere*, she thought. *Attorcere, rattorcere.*

Claire's face glowed as she modelled her new ball gown, circling on the parlor carpet of the lodgings George had acquired for Bysshe's party. Lady Newstead's jewels glittered from Claire's fingers and throat. Bysshe, in a new coat, boots, and pantaloons, smiled approvingly from the corner.

"Very lovely, Miss Clairmont," George approved.

George was in full uniform, scarlet coat, blue facings, gold braid, and byrons laced tight. His cocked hat was laid carelessly on the mantel. George's eyes turned to Mary.

"I'm sorry you are ill, Miss Godwin," he said. "I wish you were able to accompany us."

Bysshe, Mary presumed, had told him this. Mary found no reason why she should support the lie.

"I'm not ill," she said mildly. "I simply do not wish to go—I have some pages I wish to finish. A story called *Hate*."

George and Bysshe flushed alike. Mary, smiling, approached Claire, took her hand, admired gown and gems. She was surprised by the affect: the jewels, designed for an older woman, gave Claire a surprisingly mature look, older and more experienced than her sixteen years. Mary found herself growing uneasy.

"The seamstress was shocked when she was told I needed it tonight," Claire said. "She had to call in extra help to finish in time." She laughed. "But money mended everything!"

"For which we may thank Lord Newstead," Mary said, "and Lady Newstead to thank for the jewels." She looked up at George, who was still smouldering from her earlier shot. "I'm surprised, my lord, that she allows them to travel without her."

"Annabella has her own jewels," George said. "These are mine. I travel often without her, and as I move in the highest circles, I want to make certain that any lady who finds herself in my company can glitter with the best of them."

"How chivalrous." George cocked his head, trying to decide whether or not this was irony. Mary decided to let him wonder. She folded her hands and smiled sweetly.

"I believe it's time to leave," she said. "You don't want to keep his highness of Orange waiting."

Cloaks and hats were snatched; goodbyes were said. Mary managed to whisper to Claire as she helped with her cloak.

"Be careful, Jane," she said.

Resentment glittered in Claire's black eyes. "*You* have a man," she said.

Mary looked at her. "So does Lady Newstead."

Claire glared hatred and swept out, fastening bonnet-strings. Bysshe kissed Mary's lips, George her hand. Mary prepared to settle by the fire with pen and manuscript, but before she could sit, there was a knock on the door and George rushed in.

"Forgot me hat," he said. But instead of taking it from the mantel, he walked to where Mary stood by her chair and simply looked at her. Mary's heart lurched at the intensity of his gaze.

"Your hat awaits you, my lord," she said.

"I hope you will reconsider," said George.

Mary merely looked at him, forced him to state his business. He took her hand in both of his, and she clenched her fist as his fingers touched hers.

"I ask you, Miss Godwin, to reconsider my offer to take you under my protection," George said.

Mary clenched her teeth. Her heart hammered. "I am perfectly safe with Mr. Shelley," she said.

"Perhaps not as safe as you think." She glared at him. George's eyes bored into hers. "I gave him money," he said, "and he told me you were free. Is that the act of a protector?"

Rage flamed through Mary. She snatched her hand back and came within an inch of slapping George's face.

"Do you think he's sold me to you?" she cried.

"I can conceive no other explanation," George said.

"You are mistaken and a fool." She turned away, trembling in anger, and leaned against the wall.

"I understand this may be a shock. To have trusted such a man, and then discovered—"

The wallpaper had little bees on it, Napoleon's emblem. "Can't you understand that Bysshe was perfectly literal!" she shouted. "I am free, he is free, Claire is free—free to go, or free to stay." She straightened her back, clenched her fists. "I will stay. Goodbye, Lord Newstead."

"I fear for you."

"Go away," she said, speaking to the wallpaper; and after a moment's silence she heard George turn, and take his hat from the mantel, and leave the building.

Mary collapsed into her chair. The only thing she could think was, *Poor Claire.*

2

Mary was pregnant again. She folded her hands over her belly, stood on the end of the dock, and gazed up at the Alps.

Clouds sat low on the mountains, growling. The passes were closed with avalanche and unseasonal snow, the *vaudaire* storm wind tore white from the steep waves of the gray lake, and *Ariel* pitched madly at its buoy by the waterfront, its mast-tip tracing wild figures against the sky.

The *vaudaire* had caused a "seiche"—the whole mass of the lake had shifted toward Montreux, and water levels had gone up six feet. The strange freshwater tide had cast up a line of dead fish and dead birds along the stony waterfront, all staring at Mary with brittle glass eyes.

"It doesn't look as if we'll be leaving tomorrow," Bysshe said. He and Mary stood by the waterfront, cloaked and sheltered by an umbrella. Water broke on the shore, leaped through the air, reaching for her, for Bysshe. . . . It spattered at her feet.

She thought of Harriet, Bysshe's wife, hair drifting, clothes floating like seaweed. Staring eyes like dark glass. Her hands reaching for her husband from the water.

She had been missing for weeks before her drowned body was finally found.

The *vaudaire* was supposed to be a warm wind from Italy, but its warmth was lost on Mary. It felt like the burning touch of a glacier.

"Let's go back to the hotel," Mary said. "I'm feeling a little weak."

She would deliver around the New Year unless the baby was again premature.

A distant boom reached her, was echoed, again and again, by mountains. Another avalanche. She hoped it hadn't fallen on any of the brave Swiss who were trying to clear the roads.

She and Bysshe returned to the hotel through darkening streets. It was a fine place, rather expensive, though they could afford it now. Their circumstances had improved in the last year, though at cost.

Old Sir Bysshe had died, and left Bysshe a thousand pounds per year. Harriet Shelley had drowned, bricks in her pockets. Mary had given birth to a premature daughter who had lived only two weeks. She wondered about the child she carried—she had an intuition all was not well. Death, perhaps, was stalking her baby, was stalking them all.

In payment for what? Mary wondered. What sin had they committed?

She walked through Montreux's wet streets and thought of dead glass eyes, and grasping hands, and hair streaming like seaweed. Her daughter dying alone in her cradle at night, convulsing, twitching, eyes open and tiny red face torn with mortal terror.

When Mary had come to the cradle later to nurse the baby, she had thought it in an unusually deep sleep. She hadn't realized that death had come until after dawn, when the little corpse turned cold.

Death. She and Bysshe had kissed and coupled on her mother's grave, had shivered together at the gothic delights of *Vathek*, had whispered ghost stories to one another in the dead of night till Claire screamed with hysteria. Somehow death had not really touched her before. She and Bysshe had crossed war-scarred France two years ago, sleeping in homes abandoned for fear of Cossacks, and somehow death had not intruded into their lives.

"Winter is coming," Bysshe said. "Do we wish to spend it in Geneva? I'd rather push on to Italy and be a happy salamander in the sun."

"I've had another letter from Mrs. Godwin."

Bysshe sighed. "England, then."

She sought his hand and squeezed it. Bysshe wanted the sun of Italy, but Bysshe was her sun, the blaze that kept her warm, kept her from despair. Death had not touched *him*. He flamed with life, with joy, with optimism.

She tried to stay in his radiance. Where his light banished the creeping shadows that followed her.

As they entered their hotel room they heard the wailing of an infant and found Claire trying to comfort her daughter Alba. "Where have you been?" Claire demanded. There were tears on her cheeks. "I fell asleep and dreamed you'd abandoned me! And then I cried out and woke the baby."

Bysshe moved to comfort her. Mary settled herself heavily onto a sofa.

In the small room in Montreux, with dark shadows creeping in the corners and the *vaudaire* driving against the shutters, Mary put her arms around her unborn child and willed the shade of death to keep away.

Bysshe stopped short in the midst of his afternoon promenade. "Great heavens," he said. His tone implied only mild surprise—he was so filled with life and certitude that he took most of life's shocks purely in stride.

When Mary looked up, she gasped and her heart gave a crash.

It was a barouche—*the* barouche. Vermilion wheels, liveried postboys wearing muddy slickers, armorial bearings on the door, the bulletproof top raised to keep out the storm. Baggage piled on platforms fore and aft.

Rolling past as Mary and Bysshe stood on the tidy Swiss sidewalk and stared.

CREDE BYRON, Mary thought viciously. As soon credit Lucifer.

The gray sky lowered as they watched the barouche grind past, steel-rimmed wheels thundering on the cobbles. And then a window dropped on its leather strap, and someone shouted something to the postboys. The words were lost in the *vaudaire*, but the postboys pulled the horses to a stop. The door opened and George appeared, jamming a round hat down over his auburn hair. His jacket was a little tight, and he appeared to have gained a stone or more since Mary had last seen him. He walked toward Bysshe and Mary, and Mary tried not to stiffen with fury at the sight of him.

"Mr. Omnibus! Tí kánete?"

"Very well, thank you."

"Miss Godwin." George bowed, clasped Mary's hand. She closed her fist, reminded herself that she hated him.

"I'm Mrs. Shelley now."

"My felicitations," George said.

George turned to Bysshe. "Are the roads clear to the west?" he asked. "I and my companion must push on to Geneva on a matter of urgency."

"The roads have been closed for three days," Bysshe said. "There have been both rockslides and avalanches near Chexbres."

"That's what they told me in Vevey. There was no lodging there, so I came here, even though it's out of our way." George pressed his lips together, a pale line. He looked over his shoulder at the coach, at the mountainside, at the dangerous weather. "We'll have to try to force our way through tomorrow," he said. "Though it will be damned hard."

"It shouldn't," Bysshe said. "Not in a heavy coach like that."

George looked grim. "It was unaccountably dangerous just getting here," he said.

"Stay till the weather is better," Bysshe said, smiling. "You can't be blamed if the weather holds you up."

Mary hated Bysshe for that smile, even though she knew he had reasons to be obliging.

Just as she had reasons for hating.

"Nay." George shook his head, and a little Scots fell out. "I cannae bide."

"You might make it on a mule."

"I have a lady with me." Shortly. "Mules are out of the question."

"A boat . . . ?"

"Perhaps if the lady is superfluous," Mary interrupted, "you could leave her behind, and carry out your errand on a mule, alone."

The picture was certainly an enjoyable one.

George looked at her, visibly mastered his unspoken reply, then shook his head.

"She must come."

"Lord Newstead," Mary went on, "would you like to see your daughter? She is not superfluous either, and she is here."

George glanced nervously at the coach, then back. "Is Claire here as well?" "Yes."

George looked grim. "This is not . . . a good time."

Bysshe summoned an unaccustomed gravity. "I think, my lord," Bysshe said, "there may never be a better time. You have not been within five hundred miles of your daughter since her birth. You are on an urgent errand and may not tarry— very well. But you must spend a night here, and can't press on till morning. There will never be a better moment."

George looked at him stony-eyed, then nodded. "What hotel?"

"La Royale."

He smiled. "Royal, eh? A pretty sentiment for the Genevan Republic."

"We're in Vaud, not Geneva."

"Still not over the border?" George gave another nervous glance over his shoulder. "I need to set a faster pace."

His long hair streamed in the wind as he stalked back to the coach. Mary could barely see a blonde head gazing cautiously from the window. She half-expected that the coach would drive on and she would never see George again, but instead the postboys turned the horses from the waterfront road into the town, toward the hotel.

Bysshe smiled purposefully and began to stride to the hotel. Mary followed, walking fast across the wet cobbles to keep up with him. "I can't but think that good will come of this," he said.

"I pray you're right."

Much pain, Mary thought, *however it turned out.*

George's new female was tall and blonde and pink-faced, though she walked hunched over as if embrassed by her height, and took small, shy steps. She was perhaps in her middle twenties.

They met, embarrassingly, on the hotel's wide stair, Mary with Claire, Alba in Claire's arms. The tall blonde, lower lip outthrust haughtily, walked past them on the way to her room, her gaze passing blankly over them. Perhaps she hadn't been told who Alba's father was.

She had a maid with her and a pair of George's men, both of whom had pistols stuffed in their belts. For a wild moment Mary wondered if George had abducted her.

No, she decided, this was only George's theatricality. He didn't have his menagerie with him this time, no leopards or monkeys, so he dressed his postboys as bandits.

The woman passed. Mary felt Claire stiffen. "She looks like *you*," Claire hissed.

Mary looked at the woman in astonishment. "She doesn't. Not at all."

"She does! Tall, blonde, fair eyes . . ." Claire's own eyes filled with tears. "Why can't she be dark, like me?"

"Don't be absurd!" Mary seized her sister's hand, pulled her down the stairs. "Save the tears for later. They may be needed."

In the lobby Mary saw more of George's men carrying in luggage. Pásmány, the fencing master, had slung a carbine over one shoulder. Mary's mind whirled—perhaps this was an abduction after all.

Or perhaps the blonde's family—or husband—was in pursuit.

"This way." Bysshe's voice. He led them into one of the hotel's candlelit drawing rooms, closed the crystal-knobbed door behind them. A huge porcelain stove loomed over them.

George stood uncertain in the candlelight, elegant clothing over muddy boots. He looked at Claire and Alba stonily, then advanced, peered at the tiny form that Claire offered him.

"Your daughter Alba," Bysshe said, hovering at his shoulder.

George watched the child for a long, doubtful moment, his auburn hair hanging down his forehead. Then he straightened. "My offer rests, Miss Clairmont, on its previous terms."

Claire drew back, rested Alba on her shoulder. "Never," she said. She licked her lips. "It is too monstrous."

"Come, my lord," Bysshe said. He ventured to put a hand on George's shoulder. "Surely your demands are unreasonable."

"I offered to provide the child with means," George said, "to see that she is raised in a fine home, free from want, and among good people—friends of mine, who will offer her every advantage. I would take her myself but," hesitating, "my domestic conditions would not permit it."

Mary's heart flamed. "But at the cost of forbidding her the sight of her mother!" she said. "That is too cruel."

"The child's future will already be impaired by her irregular connections," George said. "Prolonging those connections could only do her further harm." His eyes flicked up to Claire. "Her mother can only lower her station, not raise it. She is best off with a proper family who can raise her with their own."

Claire's eyes flooded with tears. She turned away, clutching Alba to her. "I won't give her up!" she said. The child began to cry.

George folded his arms. "That settles matters. If you won't accept my offer, then there's an end." The baby's wails filled the air.

"Alba cries for her father," Bysshe said. "Can you not let her into your heart?"

A half-smile twitched across George's lips. "I have no absolute certainty that I *am* this child's father."

A keening sound came from Claire. For a wild, raging moment Mary looked for a weapon to plunge into George's breast. "Unnatural man!" she cried. "Can't you acknowledge the consequences of your own behavior?"

"On the contrary, I am willing to ignore the questionable situation in which I found Miss Clairmont and to care for the child completely. But only on my terms."

"I don't trust his promises!" Claire said. "He abandoned me in Munich without a penny!"

"We agreed to part," George said.

"If it hadn't been for Captain Austen's kindness, I would have starved." She leaned on the door jamb for support, and Mary joined her and buoyed her with an arm around her waist.

"You ran out into the night," George said. "You wouldn't take money."

"I'll tell her!" Claire drew away from Mary, dragged at the door, hauled it open. "I'll tell your new woman!"

Fear leaped into George's eyes. "Claire!" He rushed to the door, seized her arm as she tried to pass; Claire wrenched herself free and staggered into the hotel lobby. Alba wailed in her arms. George's servants were long gone, but hotel guests stared as if in tableaux, hats and walking-sticks half-raised. Fully aware of the spectacle they were making, Mary, clumsy in pregnancy, inserted herself between George and Claire. Claire broke for the stair, while George danced around Mary like an awkward footballer. Mary rejoiced in the fact that her pregnancy seemed only to make her more difficult to get around.

Bysshe put an end to it. He seized George's wrist in a firm grip. "You can't stop us all, my lord," he said.

George glared at him, his look all fury and ice. "What d'ye want, then?"

Claire, panting and flushed, paused halfway up the stair. Alba's alarmed shrieks echoed up the grand staircase.

Bysshe's answer was quick. "A competence for your daughter. Nothing more."

"A thousand a year," George said flatly. "No more than that."

Mary's heart leaped at the figure that doubled the family's income.

Bysshe nodded. "That will do, my lord."

"I want nothing more to do with the girl than that. Nothing whatever."

"Call for pen and paper. And we can bring this to an end."

Two copies were made, and George signed and sealed them with his signet before bidding them all a frigid good-night. The first payment was made that night, one of George's men coming to the door carrying a valise that clanked with gold. Mary gazed at it in amazement—why was George carrying so much?

"Have we done the right thing?" Bysshe wondered, looking at the valise as Claire stuffed it under her bed. "This violence, this extortion?"

"We offered love," Mary said, "and he returned only finance. How else could we deal with him?" She sighed. "And Alba will thank us."

Claire straightened and looked down at the bed. "I only wanted him to pay," said Claire. "Any other considerations can go to the devil."

The *vaudaire* blew on, scarcely fainter than before. The water level was still high. Dead fish still floated in the freshwater tide. "I would venture it," Bysshe said, frowning as he watched the dancing *Ariel*, "but not with the children."

Children. Mary's smile was inward as she realized how real her new baby was to Bysshe. "We can afford to stay at the hotel a little longer," she said.

"Still—a reef in the mains'l would make it safe enough."

Mary paused a moment, perhaps to hear the cold summons of Harriet Shelley from beneath the water. There was no sound, but she shivered anyway. "No harm to wait another day."

Bysshe smiled at her hopefully. "Very well. Perhaps we'll have a chance to speak to George again."

"Bysshe, sometimes your optimism is . . ." She shook her head. "Let us finish our walk."

They walked on through windswept morning streets. The bright sun glared off the white snow and deadly black ice that covered the surrounding high peaks. Soon the snow and ice would melt and threaten avalanche once more. "I am growing weary with this town," Bysshe said.

"Let's go back to our room and read *Chamouni*," Mary suggested. Mr. Coleridge had been a guest of her father's, and his poem about the Alps a favorite of theirs now they were lodged in Switzerland.

Bysshe was working on writing another descriptive poem on the Vale of Chamouni—unlike Coleridge, he and Mary had actually seen the place—and as an homage to Coleridge, Bysshe was including some reworked lines from *Kubla Khan*.

The everlasting universe of things, she recited to herself, *flows through the mind*.

Lovely stuff. Bysshe's best by far.

On their return to the hotel they found one of George's servants waiting for them. "Lord Newstead would like to see you."

Ah, Mary thought. *He wants his gold back.*

Let him try to take it.

George waited in the same drawing room in which he'd made his previous night's concession. Despite the bright daylight the room was still lit by lamps— the heavy dark curtains were drawn against the *vaudaire*. George was standing straight as a whip in the center of the room, a dangerous light in his eyes. Mary wondered if this was how he looked in battle.

"Mr. Shelley," George said, and bowed, "I would like to hire your boat to take my party to Geneva."

Bysshe blinked. "I—" he began, then, "*Ariel* is small, only twenty-five feet. Your party is very large and—"

"The local commissaire visited me this morning," George interrupted. "He has forbidden me to depart Montreux. As it is vital for me to leave at once, I must find other means. And I am prepared to pay well for them."

Bysshe looked at Mary, then at George. Hesitated again. "I suppose it would be possible . . ."

"Why is it," Mary demanded, "that you are forbidden to leave?"

George folded his arms, looked down at her. "I have broken no law. It is a ridiculous political matter."

Bysshe offered a smile. "If that's all, then . . ."

Mary interrupted. "If Mr. Shelley and I end up in jail as a result of this, I wonder how ridiculous it will seem."

Bysshe looked at her, shocked. "Mary!"

Mary kept her eyes on George. "Why should we help you?"

"Because . . ." He paused, ran a nervous hand through his hair. Not used, Mary thought, to justifying himself.

"Because," he said finally, "I am assisting someone who is fleeing oppression."

"Fleeing a husband?"

"Husband?" George looked startled. "No—her husband is abroad and cannot protect her." He stepped forward, his color high, his nostrils flared like those of a warhorse. "She is fleeing the attentions of a seducer—a powerful man who has callously used her to gain wealth and influence. I intend to aid her in escaping his power."

Bysshe's eyes blazed. "Of *course* I will aid you!"

Mary watched this display of chivalry with a sinking heart. The masculine confraternity had excluded her, had lost her within its own rituals and condescension.

"I will pay you a further hundred—" George began.

"Please, my lord. I and my little boat are entirely at your service in this noble cause."

George stepped forward, clasped his hand. "Mr. Omnibus, I am in your debt."

The *vaudaire* wailed at the window. Mary wondered if it was Harriet's call, and her hands clenched into fists. She would resist the cry if she could.

Bysshe turned to Mary. "We must prepare." Heavy in her pregnancy, she followed him from the drawing room, up the stair, toward their own rooms. "I will deliver Lord Newstead and his lady to Geneva, and you and Claire can join me there when the roads are cleared. Or if weather is suitable I will return for you."

"I will go with you," Mary said. "Of course."

Bysshe seemed surprised that she would accompany him on this piece of masculine knight-errantry. "It may not be entirely safe on the lake," he said.

"I'll make it safer—you'll take fewer chances with me aboard. And if I'm with you, George is less likely to inspire you to run off to South America on some noble mission or other."

"I wouldn't do that." Mildly. "And I think you are being a little severe."

"What has George done for us that we should risk anything for him?"

"I do not serve him, but his lady."

"Of whom he has told you nothing. You don't even know her name. And in any case, you seem perfectly willing to risk *her* life on this venture."

Alba's cries sounded through the door of their room. Bysshe paused a moment, resignation plain in his eyes, then opened the door. "It's for Alba, really," he said. "The more contact between George and our little family, the better it may be for her. The better chance we will have to melt his heart."

He opened the door. Claire was holding her colicky child. Tears filled her black eyes. "Where have you been for so long? I was afraid you were gone forever!"

"You know better than that." Mary took the baby from her, the gesture so natural that sadness took a moment to come—the memory that she had held her own lost child this way, held it to her breast and felt the touch of its cold lips.

"And what is this about George?" Claire demanded.

"He wants me to take him down the lake," Bysshe said. "And Mary wishes to join us. You and Alba can remain here until the roads are clear."

Claire's voice rose to a shriek. *"No! Never!"* She lunged for Alba and snatched the girl from Mary's astonished arms. "You're going to abandon me—just like George! You're all going to Geneva to laugh at me!"

"Of course not," Bysshe said reasonably.

Mary stared at her sister, tried to speak, but Claire's cries trampled over her intentions.

"You're abandoning me! I'm useless to you—worthless! You'll soon have your own baby!"

Mary tried to comfort Claire, but it was hopeless. Claire screamed and shuddered and wept, convinced that she would be left forever in Montreux. In the end there was no choice but to take her along. Mary received mean satisfaction in watching Bysshe as he absorbed this reality, as his chivalrous, noble-minded expedition alongside the hero of Waterloo turned into a low family comedy, George and his old lover, his new lover, and his wailing bastard.

And ghosts. Harriet, lurking under the water. And their dead baby calling.

Ariel bucked like a horse on the white-topped waves as the *vaudaire* keened in the rigging. Frigid spray flew in Mary's face and her feet slid on slippery planking. Her heart thrashed into her throat. The boat seemed half-full of water. She gave a despairing look over her shoulder at the retreating rowboat they'd hired to bring them from the jetty to their craft.

"Bysshe!" she said. "This is hopeless."

"Better once we're under way. See that the cuddy will be comfortable for Claire and Alba."

"This is madness."

Bysshe licked joyfully at the freshwater spray that ran down his lips. "We'll be fine, I'm sure."

He was a much better sailor than she: she had to trust him. She opened the sliding hatch to the cuddy, the little cabin forward, and saw several inches of water sloshing in the bottom. The cushions on the little seats were soaked. Wearily, she looked up at Bysshe.

"We'll have to bail."

"Very well."

It took a quarter hour to bail out the boat, during which time Claire paced back and forth on the little jetty, Alba in her arms. She looked like a specter with her pale face peering out from her dark shawl.

Bysshe cast off the gaskets that reefed the mainsail to the boom, then jumped forward to the halyards and raised the sail on its gaff. The wind tore at the canvas with a sound like a cannonade, open-hand slaps against Mary's ears. The shrouds were taut as bowstrings. Bysshe reefed the sail down, hauled the halyards and topping lift again till the canvas was taut, lowered the leeboards, then asked Mary to take the tiller while he cast *Ariel* off from its buoy.

Bysshe braced himself against the gunwale as he hauled on the mooring line, drawing *Ariel* up against the wind. When Bysshe cast off from the buoy the boat paid instantly off the wind and the sail filled with a rolling boom. Water surged under the boat's counter and suddenly, before Mary knew it, *Ariel* was flying fast. Fear closed a fist around her windpipe as the little boat heeled and the tiller almost yanked her arms from their sockets. She could hear Harriet's wails in the windsong. Mary dug her heels into the planks and hauled the tiller up to her chest, keeping *Ariel* up into the wind. Frigid water boiled up over the lee counter, pouring into the boat like a waterfall.

Bysshe leapt gracefully aft and released the mainsheet. The sail boomed out with a crash that rattled Mary's bones and the boat righted itself. Bysshe took the tiller from Mary, sheeted in, leaned out into the wind as the boat picked up speed. There was a grin on his face.

"Sorry!" he said. "I should have let the sheet go before we set out."

Bysshe tacked and brought *Ariel* into the wind near the jetty. The sail boomed like thunder as it spilled wind. Waves slammed the boat into the jetty. The mast swayed wildly. The stone jetty was at least four feet taller than the boat's deck. Mary helped Claire with the luggage—gold clanked heavily in one bag—then took Alba while Bysshe assisted Claire into the boat.

"It's *wet*," Claire said when she saw the cuddy.

"Take your heavy cloak out of your bags and sit on it," Mary said.

"This is *terrible*," Claire said, and lowered herself carefully into the cuddy.

"Go forrard," Bysshe said to Mary, "and push off from the jetty as hard as you can."

Forrard. Bysshe so enjoyed being nautical. Clumsy in skirts and pregnancy, Mary climbed atop the cuddy and did as she was asked. The booming sail filled, Mary snatched at the shrouds for balance, and *Ariel* leaped from the jetty like a stone from a child's catapult. Mary made her way across the tilting deck to the cockpit. Bysshe was leaning out to weather, his big hands controlling the tiller easily, his long fair hair streaming in the wind.

"I won't ask you to do that again," he said. "George should help from this point."

George and his lady would join the boat at another jetty—there was less chance that the authorities would intervene if they weren't seen where another Englishman was readying his boat.

Ariel raced across the waterfront, foam boiling under its counter. The second jetty—a wooden one—approached swiftly, with cloaked figures upon it. Bysshe rounded into the wind, canvas thundering, and brought *Ariel* neatly to the dock. George's men seized shrouds and a mooring line and held the boat in its place.

George's round hat was jammed down over his brows and the collar of his cloak was turned up, but any attempt at anonymity was wrecked by his famous laced boots. He seized a shroud and leaped easily into the boat, then turned to help his lady.

She had stepped back, frightened by the gunshot cracks of the luffing sail, the wild swings of the boom. Dressed in a blue silk dress, broad-brimmed bonnet, and heavy cloak, she frowned with her haughty lower lip, looking disdainfully at the little boat and its odd collection of passengers.

George reassured his companion. He and one of his men, the swordmaster Pásmány, helped her into the boat, held her arm as she ducked under the boom.

George grabbed the brim of his hat to keep the wind from carrying it away and performed hasty introductions. ''Mr. and Mrs. Shelley. The Comtesse Laufenburg.''

Mary strained her memory, trying to remember if she'd ever heard the name before. The comtesse smiled a superior smile and tried to be pleasant. ''Enchanted to make cognizance of you,'' she said in French.

A baby wailed over the sound of flogging canvas. George straightened, his eyes a little wild.

''Claire is here?'' he asked.

''She did not desire to be abandoned in Montreux,'' Mary said, trying to stress the word *abandoned*.

''My God!'' George said. ''I wish you had greater consideration of the . . . realities.''

''Claire is free and may do as she wishes,'' Mary said.

George clenched his teeth. He took the comtesse by her arm and drew her toward the cuddy.

''The boat will be better balanced,'' Bysshe called after, ''if the comtesse will sit on the weather side.'' *And perhaps*, Mary thought, *we won't capsize*.

George gave Bysshe a blank look. ''The larboard side,'' Bysshe said helpfully. Another blank look.

''Hang it! The left.''

''Very well.''

George and the comtesse ducked down the hatchway. Mary would have liked to have eavesdropped on the comtesse's introduction to Claire, but the furious rattling sail obscured the phrases, if any. George came up, looking grim, and Pásmány began tossing luggage toward him. Other than a pair of valises, most of it was military: a familiar-looking pistol case, a pair of sabers, a brace of carbines. George stowed it all in the cuddy. Then Pásmány himself leaped into the boat, and George signaled all was ready. Bysshe placed George by the weather rail, and Pásmány squatted on the weather foredeck.

''If you gentlemen would push us off?'' Bysshe said.

The sail filled and *Ariel* began to move fast, rising at each wave and thudding into the troughs. Spray rose at each impact. Bysshe trimmed the sail, the luff trembling just a little, the rest full and taut, then cleated the mainsheet down.

''A long reach down the length of the lake,'' Bysshe said with a smile. ''Easy enough sailing, if a little hard on the ladies.''

George peered out over the cuddy, his eyes searching the bank. The old castle of Chillon bulked ominously on the shore, just south of Montreux.

''When do we cross the border into Geneva?'' George asked.

''Why does it matter?'' Bysshe said. ''Geneva joined the Swiss Confederation last year.''

"But the administrations are not yet united. And the more jurisdictions that lie between the comtesse and her pursuers, the happier I will be."

George cast an uncomfortable look astern. With spray dotting his cloak, his hat clamped down on his head, his body disposed awkwardly on the weather side of the boat, George seemed thoroughly miserable—and in an overwhelming flood of sudden understanding, Mary suddenly knew why. It was over for him. His noble birth, his fame, his entire life to this point—all was as naught. Passion had claimed him for its own. His career had ended: there was no place for him in the army, in diplomatic circles, even in polite society. He'd thrown it all away in this mad impulse of passion.

He was an exile now, and the only people whom he could expect to associate with him were other exiles.

Like the exiles aboard *Ariel*.

Perhaps, Mary thought, he was only now realizing it. Poor George. She actually felt sorry for him.

The castle of Chillon fell astern, like a grand symbol of George's hopes, a world of possibility not realized.

"Beg pardon, my lord," she said, "but where do you intend to go?"

George frowned. "France, perhaps," he said. "The comtesse has . . . some friends . . . in France. England, if France won't suit, but we won't be able to stay there long. America, if necessary."

"Can the Prince Regent intervene on your behalf?"

George's smile was grim. "If he wishes. But he's subject to strange fits of morality, particularly if the sins in question remind him of his own. Prinny will *not* wish to be reminded of Mrs. Fitzherbert and Lady Hertford. He *does* wish to look upright in the eyes of the nation. And he has no loyalty to his friends, none at all." He gave a poised, slow-motion shrug. "Perhaps he will help, if the fit is on him. But I think not." He reached inside his greatcoat, patted an inside pocket. "Do you think I can light a cigar in this wind? If so, I hope it will not discomfort you, Mrs. Shelley."

He managed a spark in his strike-a-light, puffed madly till the tinder caught, then ignited his cigar and turned to Bysshe. "I found your poems, Mr. Omnibus. Your *Queen Mab* and *Alastor*. The latter of which I liked better, though I liked both well enough."

Bysshe looked at him in surprise. Wind whistled through the shrouds. "How did you find *Mab*? There were only seventy copies, and I'm certain I can account for each one."

George seemed pleased with himself. "There are few doors closed to me." Darkness clouded his face. "Or rather, *were*." With a sigh. He wiped spray from his ear with the back of his hand.

"I'm surprised that you liked *Mab* at all," Bysshe said quickly, "as its ideas are so contrary to your own."

"You expressed them well enough. As a verse treatise of Mr. Godwin's political thought, I believed it done soundly—as soundly as such a thing *can* be done. And I think you can have it published properly now—it's hardly a threat to public order, Godwin's thought being so out of fashion even among radicals."

He drew deliberately on his cigar, then waved it. The wind tore the cigar smoke from his mouth in little wisps. "*Alastor*, though better poetry, seemed in contrast to have little thought behind it. I never understood what that fellow was *doing* on the boat—was it a metaphor for life? I kept waiting for something to *happen*."

Mary bristled at George's condescension. What are *you* doing on this little boat? she wanted to ask.

Bysshe, however, looked apologetic. "I'm writing better things now."

"He's writing *wonderful* things now," Mary said. "An ode to Mont Blanc. An essay on Christianity. A hymn to intellectual beauty."

George gave her an amused look. "Mrs. Shelley's tone implies that, to me, intellectual beauty is entirely a stranger, but she misunderstands my point. I found it remarkable that the same pen could produce both *Queen Mab* and *Alastor*, and have no doubt that so various a talent will produce very good work in the poetry line—provided," nodding to Bysshe, "that Mr. Shelley continues in it, and doesn't take up engineering again, or chemistry." He grinned. "Or become a sea captain."

"He is and remains a poet," Mary said firmly. She used a corner of her shawl to wipe spray from her cheek.

"Who else do you like, my lord?" Bysshe asked.

"Poets, you mean? Scott, above all. Shakespeare, who is sound on political matters as well as having a magnificent . . . shall I call it a *stride*? Burns, the great poet of my country. And our Laureate."

"Mr. Southey was kind to me when we met," Bysshe said. "And Mrs. Southey made wonderful tea-cakes. But I wish I admired his work more." He looked up. "What do you think of Milton? The Maie and I read him constantly."

George shrugged. "Dour Puritan fellow. I'm surprised you can stand him at all."

"His verse is glorious. And he wasn't a Puritan, but an Independent, like Cromwell—his philosophy was quite unorthodox. He believed, for example, in plural marriage."

George's eyes glittered. "Did he now."

"Ay. And his Satan is a magnificent creation, far more interesting than any of his angels or his simpering pedantic Christ. That long, raging fall from grace, into darkness visible."

George's brows knit. Perhaps he was contemplating his own long fall from the Heaven of polite society. His eyes turned to Mary.

"And how is the originator of Mr. Shelley's political thought? How does your father, Mrs. Shelley?"

"He is working on a novel. An important work."

"I am pleased to hear it. Does he progress?"

Mary was going to answer simply "Very well," but Bysshe's answer came first. "Plagued by lack of money," he said. "We will be going to England to succor him after this, ah, errand is completed."

"Your generosity does you credit," George said, and then resentment entered his eyes and his lip curled. "Of course, you will be able to better afford it, now."

Bysshe's answer was mild. "Mr. Godwin lives partly with our support, but he will not speak to us since I eloped with his daughter. You will not acknowledge Alba, but at least you've been . . . persuaded . . . to do well by her."

George preferred not to rise to this, settled instead for clarification. "You support a man who won't acknowledge you?"

"It is not my father-in-law I support, but rather the author of *Political Justice*."

"A nice discernment," George observed. "Perhaps over-nice."

"One does what goodness one can. And one hopes people will respond." Looking at George, who smiled cynically around his cigar.

"Your charity speaks well for you. But perhaps Mr. Godwin would have greater cause to finish his book if poverty were not being made so convenient for him."

Mary felt herself flushing red. But Bysshe's reply again was mild. "It isn't that simple. Mr. Godwin has dependents, and the public that once celebrated his thought has, alas, forgotten him. His novel may retrieve matters. But a fine thing such as this work cannot be rushed—not if it is to have the impact it deserves."

"I will bow to your expertise in matters of literary production. But still . . . to support someone who will not even speak to you—that is charity indeed. And it does not speak well for Mr. Godwin's gratitude."

"My father is a great man!" Mary knew she was speaking hotly, and she bit back on her anger. "But he judges by a . . . a very high standard of morality. He will accept support from a sincere admirer, but he has not yet understood the depth of sentiment between Bysshe and myself, and believes that Bysshe has done my reputation harm—not," flaring again, "that I would care if he had."

Ariel thudded into a wave trough, and George winced at the impact. He adjusted his seat on the rail and nodded. "Mr. Godwin will accept money from an admirer, but not letters from an in-law. And Mr. Shelley will support the author of *Political Justice*, but not *his* in-laws."

"And *you*," Mary said, "will support a blackmailer, but not a daughter."

George's eyes turned to stone. Mary realized she had gone too far for this small boat and close company.

"Gentlemen, it's cold," she announced. "I will withdraw."

She made her way carefully into the cuddy. The tall comtesse was disposed uncomfortably, on wet cushions, by the hatch, the overhead planking brushing the top of her bonnet. Her gaze was mild, but her lip was haughty. There was a careful three inches between her and Claire, who was nursing Alba and, clearly enough, a grudge.

Mary walked past them to the peak, sat carefully on a wet cushion near Claire. Their knees collided every time *Ariel* fell down a wave. The cuddy smelled of wet stuffing and stale water. There was still water sluicing about on the bottom.

Mary looked at Claire's baby and felt sadness like an ache in her breast.

Claire regarded her resentfully. "The French bitch hates us," she whispered urgently. "Look at her expression."

Mary wished Claire had kept her voice down. Mary leaned out to look at the comtesse, managed a smile. "Vous parlez anglais?" she asked.

"Non. Je regrette. Parles-tu français?" The comtesse had a peculiar accent. As, with a name like Laufenburg, one might expect.

Pleasant of her, though, to use the intimate tu. "Je comprends un peu." Claire's French was much better than hers, but Claire clearly had no interest in conversation.

The comtesse looked at the nursing baby. A shadow flitted across her face. "My own child," in French, "I was forced to leave behind."

"I'm sorry." For a moment Mary hated the comtesse for having a child to leave, that and for the abandonment itself.

No. Bysshe, she remembered, had left his own children. It did not make one unnatural. Sometimes there were circumstances.

Speech languished after this unpromising beginning. Mary leaned her head against the planking and tried to sleep, sadly aware of the cold seep of water up her skirts. The boat's movement was too violent to be restful, but she composed herself deliberately for sleep. Images floated through her mind: the great crumbling keep of Chillon, standing above the surging gray water like the setting of one of "Monk" Lewis's novels; a gray cat eating a blushing rose; a figure, massive and threatening, somehow both George and her father Godwin, flinging back the bed-curtains to reveal, in the bright light of morning, the comtesse Laufenburg's placid blonde face with its outthrust, Habsburg lip.

Habsburg. Mary sat up with a cry and banged her skull on the deckhead.

She cast a wild look at Claire and the comtesse, saw them both drowsing, Alba asleep in Claire's lap. The boat was rolling madly in a freshening breeze: there were ominous, threatening little shrieks of wind in the rigging. The cuddy stank badly.

Mary made her way out of the cuddy, clinging to the sides of the hatch as the boat sought to pitch her out. Bysshe was holding grimly to the tiller with one big hand, controlling the sheet with the other while spray soaked his coat; George and Pásmány were hanging to the shrouds to keep from sliding down the tilted deck.

Astern was Lausanne, north of the lake, and the Cornettes to the south; and Mont Billiat, looming over the valley of the Dranse to the south, was right abeam: they were smack in the middle of the lake, with the *vaudaire* wind funneling down the valley, stronger than ever with the mountain boundary out of the way.

Mary seized the rail, hauled herself up the tilting deck toward George. "I know your secret," she said. "I know who your woman is."

George's face ran with spray; his auburn hair was plastered to the back of his neck. He fixed her with eyes colder than the glaciers of Mont Blanc. "Indeed," he said.

"Marie-Louise of the house of Habsburg." Hot anger pulsed through her, burned against the cold spindrift on her face. "Former Empress of the French!"

Restlessly, George turned his eyes away. "Indeed," he said again.

Mary seized a shroud and dragged herself to the rail next to him. Bysshe watched in shock as Mary shouted into the wind. "Her husband abroad! Abroad, forsooth—all the way to St. Helena! Forced to leave her child behind, because her father would never let Napoleon's son out of his control for an instant. Even a Habsburg lip—my God!"

"Very clever, Miss Godwin. But I believe you have divined my sentiments on the subject of clever women." George gazed ahead, toward Geneva. "Now you see why I wish to be away."

"I see only vanity!" Mary raged. "Colossal vanity! You can't stop fighting Napoleon even now! Even when the battlefield is only a bed!"

George glared at her. "Is it my damned fault that Napoleon could never keep his women?"

"It's your damned fault that *you* keep her!"

George opened his mouth to spit out a reply and then the *vaudaire*, like a giant hand, took *Ariel's* mast in its grasp and slammed the frail boat over. Bysshe cried out and hauled the tiller to his chest and let the mainsheet go, all far too late. The deck pitched out from under Mary's heels and she clung to the shroud for dear life. Pásmány shouted in Hungarian. There was a roar as the sail hit the water. The lake foamed over the lee rail and the wind tore Mary's breath away. There were screams from the cuddy as water poured into the little cabin.

"Halyards and topping lift!" Bysshe gasped. He was clinging to the weather rail: a breaker exploded in his face and he gasped for air. "Let 'em go!"

If the sail filled with water all was lost. Mary let go of the shroud and palmed her way across the vertical deck. Freezing lakewater clutched at her ankles. Harriet Shelley shrieked her triumph in Mary's ears like the wind. Mary lurched forward to the mast, flung the halyard and topping lift off their cleats. The sail sagged free, empty of everything but the water that poured onto its canvas surface, turning it into a giant weight that would drag the boat over. Too late.

"Save the ladies, George!" Bysshe called. His face was dead-white but his voice was calm. "I can't swim!"

Water boiled up Mary's skirts. She could feel the dead weight dragging her down as she clutched at George's leg and hauled herself up the deck. She screamed as her unborn child protested, a gouging pain deep in her belly.

George raged wildly. "Damn it, Shelley, what can I *do*?" He had a leg over one of the shrouds; the other was Mary's support. The wind had taken his hat and his cloak rattled around him like wind-filled canvas.

"Cut the mast free!"

George turned to Mary. "My sword! Get it from the cabin!"

Mary looked down and into the terrified black eyes of Claire, half-out of the cuddy. She held a wailing Alba in her arms. "Take the baby!" she shrieked.

"Give me a sword!" Mary said. A wave broke over the boat, soaking them all in icy rain. Mary thought of Harriet smiling, her hair trailing like seaweed.

"Save my baby!"

"The *sword*! Byron's *sword*! *Give it*!" Mary clung to George's leg with one hand and thrust the crying babe away with the other.

"I hate you!" Claire shrieked, but she turned and fumbled for George's sword. She held it up out of the hatch, and Mary took the cut steel hilt in her hand and drew it rasping from the scabbard. She held it blindly above her head and felt George's firm hand close over hers and take the sabre away. The pain in her belly was like a knife. Through the boat and her spine she felt the thudding blows as George hacked at the shrouds, and then there was a rending as the mast splintered and *Ariel*, relieved of its top-hamper, swung suddenly upright.

Half the lake seemed to splash into the boat as it came off its beam-ends. George pitched over backwards as *Ariel* righted itself, but Mary clung to his leg and kept him from going into the lake while he dragged himself to safety over the rail.

Another wave crashed over them. Mary clutched at her belly and moaned. The pain was ebbing. The boat pirouetted on the lake as the wind took it, and then *Ariel* jerked to a halt. The wreckage of the mast was acting as a sea-anchor, moderating the wave action, keeping the boat stable. Alba's screams floated high above *Ariel's* remains.

Wood floats, Mary remembered dully. And *Ariel* was wood, no matter how much water slopped about in her bottom.

Shelley staggered to his feet, shin-deep in lake water. "By God, George," he gasped. "You've saved us."

"By God," George answered, "so I have." Mary looked up from the deck to see George with the devil's light in his eyes, his color high and his sabre in his hand. So, she reckoned, he must have seemed to Napoleon at Genappe. George bent and peered into the cuddy.

"Are the ladies all right?"

"Je suis bien, merci." From the Austrian princess.

"Damn you to hell, George!" Claire cried. George only grinned.

"I see we are well," he said.

And then Mary felt the warm blood running down the insides of her legs, and knew that George was wrong.

Mary lay on a bed in the farmhouse sipping warm brandy. Reddening cloths were packed between her legs. The hemorrhage had not stopped, though at least there was no pain. Mary could feel the child moving within her, as if struggling in its terror. Over the click of knitting needles, she could hear the voices of the men in the kitchen, and smell George's cigar.

The large farm, sitting below its pastures that stretched up the Noirmont, was owned by a white-mustached old man named Fleury, a man who seemed incapable of surprise or confusion even when armed men arrived at his doorstep, carrying between them a bleeding woman and a sack filled with gold. He turned Mary over to his wife, hitched up his trousers, put his hat on, and went to St. Prex to find a doctor.

Madame Fleury, a large woman unflappable as her husband, tended Mary and made her drink a brandy toddy while she sat by Mary and did her knitting.

When Fleury returned, his news wasn't good. The local surgeon had gone up the road to set the bones of some workmen caught in an avalanche—perhaps there would be amputations—but he would return as soon as he could. The road west to Geneva was still blocked by the slide; the road east to Lausanne had been cleared. George seemed thoughtful at the news. His voice echoed in from the kitchen. "Perhaps the chase will simply go past," he said in English.

"What sort of pursuit do you anticipate?" Bysshe asked. "Surely you don't expect the Austrian Emperor to send his troops into Switzerland."

"Stranger things have happened," George said. "And it may not be the Emperor's own people after us—it might be Neipperg, acting on his own."

Mary knew she'd heard the name before, and tried to recall it. But Bysshe said, "The general? Why would he be concerned?"

There was cynical amusement in George's voice. "Because he's her highness's former lover! I don't imagine he'd like to see his fortune run away."

"Do you credit him with so base a motive?"

George laughed. "In order to prevent Marie-Louise from joining Bonaparte, Prince Metternich *ordered* von Neipperg to leave his wife and to seduce her highness—and that one-eyed scoundrel was only too happy to comply. His reward was to be the co-rulership of Parma, of which her highness was to be Duchess."

"Are you certain of this?"

"Metternich told me at his dinner table over a pipe of tobacco. And Neipperg *boasted* to me, sir!" A sigh, almost a snarl, came from George. "My heart wrung at his words, Mr. Shelley. For I had already met her highness and—" Words failed him for a moment. "I determined to rescue her from Neipperg's clutches, though all the Hungarian Grenadiers of the Empire stood in the way!"

"That was most admirable, my lord," Bysshe said quietly.

Claire's voice piped up. "Who is this Neipperg?"

"Adam von Neipperg is a cavalry officer who defeated Murat," Bysshe said. "That's all I know of him."

George's voice was thoughtful. "He's the best the Austrians have. Quite the *beau sabreur*, and a diplomat as well. He persuaded Crown Prince Bernadotte to switch sides before the battle of Leipzig. And yes, he defeated Murat on the field of Tolentino, a few weeks before Waterloo. Command of the Austrian army was another of Prince Metternich's rewards for his . . . services."

Murat, Mary knew, was Napoleon's great cavalry general. Neipperg, the best Austrian cavalryman, had defeated Murat, and now Britain's greatest horseman had defeated Napoleon *and* Neipperg, one on the battlefield and both in bed.

Such a competitive little company of cavaliers, she thought. Madame Fleury's knitting needles clacked out a complicated pattern.

"You think he's going to come after you?" Bysshe asked.

"*I* would," simply. "And neither he nor I would care what the Swiss think about it. And he'll find enough officers who will want to fight for the, ah, *honor* of their royal family. And he certainly has scouts or agents among the Swiss looking for me—surely one of them visited the commissaire of Montreux."

"I see." Mary heard the sound of Bysshe rising from his seat. "I must see to Mary."

He stepped into the bedroom, sat on the edge of the bed, took her hand. Madame Fleury barely looked up from her knitting.

"Are you better, Pecksie?"

"Nothing has changed." *I'm still dying*, she thought.

Bysshe sighed. "I'm sorry," he said, "to have exposed you to such danger. And now I don't know what to do."

"And all for so little."

Bysshe was thoughtful. "Do you think liberty is so little? And Byron—the voice of monarchy and reaction—fighting for freedom! Think of it!"

My life is bleeding away, Mary thought incredulously, *and his child with it.* There was poison in her voice when she answered.

"This isn't about the freedom of a woman, it's about the freedom of one man to do what he wants."

Bysshe frowned at her.

"He can't love," Mary insisted. "He felt no love for his wife, or for Claire." Bysshe tried to hush her—her voice was probably perfectly audible in the kitchen. But it was pleasing for her not to give a damn.

"It's not love he feels for that poor woman in the cellar," she said. "His passions are entirely concerned with himself—and now that he can't exorcise them on the battlefield, he's got to find other means."

"Are you certain?"

"He's a mad whirlwind of destruction! Look what he did to Claire. And now he's wrecked *Ariel*, and he may yet involve us all in a battle—with Austrian cavalry, forsooth! He'll destroy us all if we let him."

"Perhaps it will not come to that."

George appeared in the door. He was wrapped in a blanket and carried a carbine, and if he was embarrassed by what he'd heard, he failed to display it. "With your permission, Mr. Shelley, I'm going to try to sink your boat. It sits on a rock just below our location, a pistol pointed at our head."

Bysshe looked at Mary. "Do as you wish."

"I'll give you privacy, then." And pointedly closed the door.

Mary heard his bootsteps march out, the outside door open and close. She put her hand on Bysshe's arm. *I am bleeding to death*, she thought. "Promise me you will take no part in anything," she said. "George will try to talk you into defending the princess—he knows you're a good shot."

"But what of Marie-Louise? To be dragged back to Austria by force of arms— what a prospect! An outrage, inhuman and degrading."

I am bleeding to death, Mary thought. But she composed a civil reply. "Her condition saddens me. But she was born a pawn and has lived a pawn her entire life. However this turns out, she will be a pawn either of George or of Metternich, and we cannot change that. It is the evil of monarchy and tyranny that has made her so. We may be thankful we were not born among her class."

There were tears in Bysshe's eyes. "Very well. If you think it best, I will not lift a hand in this."

Mary put her arms around him, held herself close to his warmth. She clenched trembling hands behind his back.

Soon, she thought, *I will lack the strength to do even this. And then I will die.*

There was a warm and spreading lake between her legs. She felt very drowsy as she held Bysshe, the effects of the brandy, and she closed her eyes and tried to rest. Bysshe stroked her cheek and hair. Mary, for a moment, dreamed.

She dreamed of pursuit, a towering, shrouded figure stalking her over the lake—but the lake was frozen, and as Mary fled across the ice she found other people standing there, people to whom she ran for help only to discover them all dead, frozen in their places and covered with frost. Terrified, she ran among them, seeing to her further horror that she knew them all: her mother and namesake; and Mr. Godwin; and George, looking at her insolently with eyes of black ice; and lastly the figure of Harriet Shelley, a woman she had never met in life but who Mary knew at once. Harriet stood rooted to a patch of ice and held in her arms the frost-swathed figure of a child. And despite the rime that covered the tiny face, Mary knew at once, and with agonized despair, just whose child Harriet carried so triumphantly in her arms.

She woke, terror pounding in her heart. There was a gunshot from outside. She felt Bysshe stiffen. Another shot. And then the sound of pounding feet.

"They're here, damn it!" George called. "And my shot missed!"

Gunfire and the sound of hammering swirled through Mary's perceptions. Furniture was shifted, doors barricaded, weapons laid ready. The shutters had already been closed against the *vaudaire*, so no one had to risk himself securing the windows. Claire and Alba came into Mary's room, the both of them screaming; and Mary, not giving a damn any longer, sent them both out. George put them in the cellar with the Austrian princess—Mary was amused that they seemed doomed to share quarters together. Bysshe, throughout, only sat on the bed and held Mary in his arms. He seemed calm, but his heart pounded against her ear. M. Fleury appeared, loading an old Charleville musket as he offhandedly explained that he had served in one of Louis XVI's mercenary Swiss regiments. His wife put down her knitting needles, poured buckshot into her apron pockets, and went off with him to serve as his loader. Afterwards Mary wondered if that particular episode, that vision of the old man with his gun and powder horn, had been a dream—but no, Madame Fleury was gone, her pockets filled with lead.

Eventually the noise died away. George came in with his Mantons stuffed in his belt, looking pleased with himself. "I think we stand well," he said. "This place is fine as a fort. At Waterloo we held Hougoumont and La Haye Sainte against worse—and Neipperg will have no artillery. The odds aren't bad—I counted only eight of them." He looked at Bysshe. "Unless you are willing to join us, Mr. Shelley, in defense of her highness's liberty."

Bysshe sat up. "I wish no man's blood on my hands." Mary rejoiced at the firmness in his voice.

"I will not argue against your conscience, but if you won't fight, then perhaps you can load for me?"

"What of Mary?" Bysshe asked.

Indeed, Mary thought. *What of me?*

"Can we arrange for her, and for Claire and Alba, to leave this house?"

George shook his head. "They don't dare risk letting you go—you'd just inform the Swiss authorities. I could negotiate a cease-fire to allow you to become their prisoners, but then you'd be living in the barn or the outdoors instead of more comfortably in here." He looked down at Mary. "I do not think we should move your lady in any case. Here in the house it is safe enough."

"But what if there's a battle? My God—there's already been shooting!"

"No one was hurt, you'll note—though if I'd had a Baker or a jäger rifle instead of my puisny little carbine, I daresay I'd have dropped one of them. No—what will happen now is that they'll either try an assault, which will take a while to organize, because they're all scattered out watching the house, and which will cost them dearly in the end . . . or they'll wait. They don't know how many people we have in here, and they'll be cautious on that account. We're inside, with plenty of food and fuel and ammunition, and they're in the outdoors facing unseasonably cold weather. And the longer they wait, the more likely it will be that our local Swiss yeomen will discover them, and then . . ." He gave a low laugh. "Austrian soldiers have never fared well in Switzerland, not since the days of William Tell. Our Austrian friends will be arrested and imprisoned."

"But the surgeon? Will they not let the surgeon pass?"

"I can't say."

Bysshe stared. "My God! Can't you speak to them?"

"I will ask if you like. But I don't know what a surgeon can do that we cannot."

Bysshe looked desperate. "There must be something that will stop the bleeding!"

Yes, Mary thought. *Death. Harriet has won.*

George gazed down at Mary with thoughtful eyes. "A Scotch midwife would sit her in a tub of icewater."

Bysshe stiffened like a dog on point. "Is there ice? Is there an ice cellar?" He rushed out of the room. Mary could hear him stammering out frantic questions in French, then Fleury's offhand reply. When Bysshe came back he looked stricken. "There is an icehouse, but it's out behind the barn."

"And in enemy hands." George sighed. "Well, I will ask if they will permit Madame Fleury to bring ice into the house, and pass the surgeon through when he comes."

George left the room and commenced a shouted conversation in French with someone outside. Mary winced at the volume of George's voice. The voice outside spoke French with a harsh accent.

No, she understood. They would not permit ice or a surgeon to enter a house.

"They suspect a plot, I suppose," George reported. He stood wearily in the doorway. "Or they think one of my men is wounded."

"They want to make you watch someone die," Mary said. "And hope it will make you surrender."

George looked at her. "Yes, you comprehend their intent," he said. "That is precisely what they want." Bysshe looked horrified.

George's look turned intent. "And what does Mistress Mary want?"

Mary closed her eyes. "Mistress Mary wants to live, and to hell with you all."

George laughed, a low and misanthropic chuckle. "Very well. Live you shall—and I believe I know the way."

He returned to the other room, and Mary heard his raised voice again. He was asking, in French, what the intruders wanted, and in passing comparing their actions to Napoleon's abduction of the Duc d'Enghien, justly abhorred by all nations.

"A telling hit," Mary said. "Good old George." She wrapped her two small pale hands around one of Bysshe's big ones.

The same voice answered, demanding that Her Highness the Duchess of Parma be surrendered. George returned that her highness was here of her own free will, and that she commanded that they withdraw to their own borders and trouble her no more. The emissary said his party was acting for the honor of Austria and the House of Habsburg. George announced that he felt free to doubt that their shameful actions were in any way honorable, and he was prepared to prove it, *corps-à-corps*, if *Feldmarschall-leutnant* von Neipperg was willing to oblige him.

"My God!" Bysshe said. "He's calling the blackguard out!"

Mary could only laugh. A duel, fought for an Austrian princess and Mary's bleeding womb.

The other asked for time to consider. George gave it.

"This neatly solves our dilemma, don't it?" he said after he returned. "If I beat Neipperg, the rest of those German puppies won't have direction—they'd be on the road back to Austria. Her royal highness and I will be able to make our way to a friendly country. No magistrates, no awkward questions, and a long head start." He smiled. "And all the ice in the world for Mistress Mary."

"And if you lose?" Bysshe asked.

"It ain't to be thought of. I'm a master of the sabre, I practice with Pásmány almost daily, and whatever Neipperg's other virtues I doubt he can compare with me in the art of the sword. The only question," he turned thoughtful, "is whether we can trust his offer. If there's treachery . . ."

"Or if he insists on pistols!" Mary found she couldn't resist pointing this out. "You didn't precisely cover yourself with glory the last time I saw you shoot."

George only seemed amused. "Neipperg only has one eye—I doubt he's much of a shot, either. My second would have to insist on a sabre fight," and here he smiled, "*pour l'honneur de la cavalerie.*"

Somehow Mary found this satisfying. "Go fight, George. I know you love your legend more than you ever loved that Austrian girl—and this will make a nice end to it."

George only chuckled again, while Bysshe looked shocked. "Truthful Mistress Mary," George said. "Never without your sting."

"I see no point in politeness from this position."

"You would have made a good soldier, Mrs. Shelley."

Longing fell upon Mary. "I would have made a better mother," she said, and felt tears sting her eyes.

"God, Maie!" Bysshe cried. "What I would not give!" He bent over her and began to weep.

It was, Mary considered, about time, and then reflected that death had made her satirical.

George watched for a long moment, then withdrew. Mary could hear his boots pacing back and forth in the kitchen, and then a different, younger voice called from outside.

The *Feldmarschall-leutnant* had agreed to the encounter. He, the new voice, was prepared to present himself as von Neipperg's second.

"A soldier all right," George commented. "Civilian clothes, but he's got that sprig of greenery that Austrian troops wear in their hats." His voice lifted. "That's far enough, laddie!" He switched to French and said that his second would be out shortly. Then his bootsteps returned to Mary's rooms and put a hand on Bysshe's shoulder.

"Mr. Shelley," he said, "I regret this intrusion, but I must ask—will you do me the honor of standing my second in this affaire?"

"Bysshe!" Mary cried. "Of course not!"

Bysshe blinked tear-dazzled eyes but managed to speak clearly enough. "I'm totally opposed to the practice. It's vicious and wasteful and utterly without moral foundation. It reeks of death and the dark ages and ruling-class affectation."

George's voice was gentle. "There are no other gentlemen here," he said. "Pásmány is a servant, and I can't see sending our worthy M. Fleury out to negotiate with those little noblemen. And—" He looked at Mary. "Your lady must have her ice and her surgeon."

Bysshe looked stricken. "I know nothing of how to manage these encounters," he said. "I would not do well by you. If you were to fall as a result of my bungling, I should never forgive myself."

"I will tell you what to say, and if he doesn't agree, then bring negotiations to a close."

"Bysshe," Mary reminded, "you said you would have nothing to do with this."

Bysshe wiped tears from his eyes and looked thoughtful.

"Don't you see this is theater?" Mary demanded. "George is adding this scene to his legend—he doesn't give a damn for anyone here!"

George only seemed amused. "You are far from death, madam, I think, to show such spirit," he said. "Come, Mr. Shelley! Despite what Mary thinks, a fight with Neipperg is the only way we can escape without risking the ladies."

"No," Mary said.

Bysshe looked thoroughly unhappy. "Very well," he said. "For Mary's sake, I'll do as you ask, provided I do no violence myself. But I should say that I resent being placed in this . . . *extraordinary* position in the first place."

Mary settled for glaring at Bysshe.

More negotiations were conducted through the window, and then Bysshe, after receiving a thorough briefing, straightened and brushed his jacket, brushed his knees, put on his hat, and said goodbye to Mary. He was very pale under his freckles.

"Don't forget to point out," George said, "that if von Neipperg attempts treachery, he will be instantly shot dead by my men firing from this house."

"Quite."

He left Mary in her bed. George went with him, to pull away the furniture barricade at the front door.

Mary realized she wasn't about to lie in bed while Bysshe was outside risking his neck. She threw off the covers and went to the window. Unbarred the shutter, pushed it open slightly.

Wet coursed down her legs.

Bysshe was holding a conversation with a stiff young man in an overcoat. After a few moments, Bysshe returned and reported to George. Mary, feeling like a guilty child, returned to her bed.

"Baron von Strickow—that's Neipperg's second—was taken with your notion of the swordfight *pour la cavalerie*, but insists the fight should be on horseback." He frowned. "They know, of course, that you haven't a horse with you."

"No doubt they'd offer me some nag or other." George thought for a moment. "Very well. I find the notion of a fight on horseback too piquant quite to ignore— tell them that if they insist on such a fight, they must bring forward six saddled horses, and that I will pick mine first, and Neipperg second."

"Very well."

Bysshe returned to the negotiations, and reported back that all had been settled. "With ill grace, as regards your last condition. But he conceded it was fair." Bysshe returned to Mary's room, speaking to George over his shoulder. "Just as well you're doing this on horseback. The yard is wet and slippery—poor footing for sword work."

"I'll try not to do any quick turns on horseback, either." George stepped into the room, gave Mary a glance, then looked at Bysshe. "Your appreciation of our opponents?"

"The Baron was tired and mud-covered. He's been riding hard. I don't imagine the rest of them are any fresher." Bysshe sat by Mary and took her hand. "He wouldn't shake my hand until he found out my father was a baronet. And then I wouldn't shake his."

"Good fellow!"

Bysshe gave a self-congratulatory look. "I believe it put him out of countenance."

George was amused. "These kraut-eaters make me look positively democratic." He left to give Pásmány his carbine and pistols—"the better to keep Neipperg honest."

"What of the princess?" Mary wondered. "Do you suppose he will bother to tell her of these efforts on her behalf?"

Shortly thereafter came the sound of the kitchen trap being thrown open, and George's bootheels descending to the cellar. Distant French tones, the sound of female protest, George's calm insistence. Claire's furious shrieks. George's abrupt reply, and then his return to the kitchen.

George appeared in the door, clanking in spurs and with a sword in his hand. Marie-Louise, looking pale, hovered behind him.

Mary looked up at Bysshe. "You won't have to participate in this any longer, will you?"

George answered for him. "I'd be obliged if Mr. Shelley would help me select my horse. Then you can withdraw to the porch—but if there's treachery, be prepared to barricade the door again."

Bysshe nodded. "Very well." He rose and looked out the window. "The horses are coming, along with the Baron and a one-eyed man."

George gave a cursory look out the window. ''That's the fellow. He lost the eye at Neerwinden—French sabre cut.'' His voice turned inward. ''I'll try to attack from his blind side—perhaps he'll be weaker there.''

Bysshe was more interested in the animals. ''There are three white horses. What are they?''

''Lipizzaners of the royal stud,'' George said. ''The Roman Caesars rode 'em, or so the Austrians claim. Small horses by the standard of our English hunters, but strong and very sturdy. Bred and trained for war.'' He flashed a smile. ''They'll do for me, I think.''

He stripped off his coat and began to walk toward the door, but recollected, at the last second, the cause of the fight and returned to Marie-Louise. He put his arms around her, murmured something, and kissed her cheek. Then, with a smile, he walked into the other room. Bysshe, deeply unhappy, followed. And then Mary, ignoring the questioning eyes of the Austrian princess, worked her way out of bed and went to the window.

From the window Mary watched as George took his time with the horses, examining each minutely, discoursing on their virtues with Bysshe, checking their shoes and eyes as if he were buying them. The Austrians looked stiff and disapproving. Neipperg was a tall, bull-chested man, handsome despite the eyepatch, with a well-tended halo of hair.

Perhaps George dragged the business out in order to nettle his opponent.

George mounted one of the white horses and trotted it round the yard for a brief while, then repeated the experiment with a second Lipizzaner. Then he went back to the first and declared himself satisfied.

Neipperg, seeming even more rigid than before, took the second horse, the one George had rejected. Perhaps it was his own, Mary thought.

Bysshe retreated to the front porch of the farmhouse, Strickow to the barn, and the two horsemen to opposite ends of the yard. Both handled their horses expertly. Bysshe asked each if he were ready, and received a curt nod.

Mary's legs trembled. She hoped she wouldn't fall. She had to see it. *''Un,''* Strickow called out in a loud voice. *''Deux. Trois!''* Mary had expected the combatants to dash at each other, but they were too cautious, too professional— instead each goaded his beast into a slow trot and held his sabre with the hilt high, the blade dropping across the body, carefully on guard. Mary noticed that George was approaching on his opponent's blind right side. As they came to-gether there were sudden flashes of silver, too fast for the eye to follow, and the sound of ringing steel.

Then they were past. But Neipperg, as he spurred on, delivered a vicious blind swipe at George's back. Mary cried out, but there was another clang—George had dropped his point behind his back to guard against just that attack.

''Foul blow!'' Bysshe cried, from the porch, then clapped his hands. ''Good work, George!''

George turned with an intent smile on his face, as if he had the measure of his opponent. There was a cry from elsewhere in the farmhouse, and Claire came running, terror in her eyes. ''Are they fighting?'' she wailed, and pushed past Mary to get to the window.

Mary tried to pull her back and failed. Her head swam. "You don't want to watch this," she said.

Alba began to cry from the cellar. Claire pushed the shutters wide and thrust her head out.

"Kill him, George!" she shouted. "Kill him!"

George gave no sign of having heard—he and Neipperg were trotting at each other again, and George was crouched down over his horse's neck, his attention wholly on his opponent.

Mary watched over Claire's shoulder as the two approached, as blades flashed and clanged—once, twice—and then George thrust to Neipperg's throat and Mary gasped, not just at the pitilessness of it, but at its strange physical consummation, at the way horse and rider and arm and sword, the dart of the blade and momentum of the horse and rider, merged for an instant in an awesome moment of perfection . . .

Neipperg rode on for a few seconds while blood poured like a tide down his white shirtfront, and then he slumped and fell off his animal like a sack. Mary shivered, knowing she'd just seen a man killed, killed with absolute forethought and deliberation. And George, that intent look still on his face as he watched Neipperg over his shoulder, lowered his scarlet-tipped sword and gave a careless tug of the reins to turn his horse around . . .

Too careless. The horse balked, then turned too suddenly. Its hind legs slid out from under it on the slick grass, George's arms windmilled as he tried to regain his balance, and the horse, with an almost-human cry, fell heavily on George's right leg.

Claire and Mary cried out. The Lipizzaner's legs flailed in the air as he rolled over on George. Bysshe launched himself off the porch in a run. George began to scream, a sound that raised the hair on Mary's neck.

And, while Adam von Neipperg twitched away his life on the grass, Marie-Louise of Austria, France, and Parma, hearing George's cries of agony, bolted hysterically for the door and ran out onto the yard and into the arms of her countryman.

"No!" George insisted. "No surgeons!"

Not a word, Mary noted, for the lost Marie-Louise. She watched from the doorway as his friends carried him in and laid him on the kitchen table. The impassive M. Fleury cut the boot away with a pair of shears and tore the leather away with a suddenness that made George gasp. Bysshe peeled away the bloody stocking, and bit his lip at the sight of protruding bone.

"We *must* show this to the surgeon, George," Bysshe said. "The foot and ankle are shattered."

"No!" Sweat beaded on George's forehead. "I've seen surgeons at their work. My God—" There was horror in his eyes. "I'll be a *cripple*!"

M. Fleury said nothing, only looked down at the shattered ankle with his knowing veteran's eyes. He hitched up his trousers, took a bucket from under the cutting board, and left to get ice for Mary.

The Austrians were long gone, ridden off with their blonde trophy. Their fallen paladin was still in the yard—he'd only slow down their escape.

George was pale and his skin was clammy. Claire choked back tears as she looked down at him. "Does it hurt very much?"

"Yes," George confessed, "it does. Perhaps Madame Fleury would oblige me with a glass of brandy."

Madame Fleury fetched the jug and some glasses. Pásmány stood in the corner exuding dark Hungarian gloom. George looked up at Mary, seemed surprised to find her out of bed.

"I seem to be unlucky for your little family," he said. "I hope you will forgive me."

"If I can," said Mary.

George smiled. "Truthful Miss Mary. How fine you are." A spasm of pain took him and he gasped. Madame Fleury put some brandy in his hand and he gulped it.

"Mary!" Bysshe rushed to her. "You should not be seeing this. Go back to your bed."

"What difference does it make?" Mary said, feeling the blood streaking her legs; but she allowed herself to be put to bed.

Soon the tub of icewater was ready. It was too big to get through the door into Mary's room, so she had to join George in the kitchen after all. She sat in the cold wet, and Bysshe propped her back with pillows, and they both watched as the water turned red.

George was pale, gulping brandy from the bottle. He looked at Bysshe.

"Perhaps you could take our mind off things," he said. "Perhaps you could tell me one of your ghost stories."

Bysshe could not speak. Tears were running down his face. So to calm him, and to occupy her time when dying, Mary began to tell a story. It was about an empty man, a Swiss baron who was a genius but who lacked any quality of soul. His name, in English, meant the Franked Stone—the stone whose noble birth had paid its way, but which was still a stone, and being a stone unable to know love.

And the baron had a wasting disease, one that caused his limbs to wither and die. And he knew he would soon be a cripple.

Being a genius the baron thought he knew the answer. Out of protoplasm and electricity and parts stolen from the graveyard he built another man. He called this man a monster, and held him prisoner. And every time one of the baron's limbs began to wither, he'd arrange for his assistants to cut off one of the monster's limbs, and use it to replace the baron's withered part. The monster's own limb was replaced by one from the graveyard. And the monster went through enormous pain, one hideous surgical procedure after another, but the baron didn't care, because he was whole again and the monster was only a monster, a thing he had created.

But then the monster escaped. He educated himself and grew in understanding and apprehension and he spied on the baron and his family. In revenge the monster killed everyone the baron knew, and the baron was angered not because he loved his family but because the killings were an offense to his pride. So the baron swore revenge on the monster and began to pursue him.

The pursuit took the baron all over the world, but it never ended. At the end the baron pursued the monster to the arctic, and disappeared forever into the ice and mist, into the heart of the white desert of the Pole.

Mary meant the monster to be Soul, of course, and the baron Reason. Because unless the two could unite in sympathy, all was lost in ice and desolation.

It took Mary a long time to tell her story, and she couldn't tell whether George understood her meaning or not. By the time she finished the day was almost over, and her own bleeding had stopped. George had drunk himself nearly insensible, and a diffident notary had arrived from St. Prex to take everyone's testimony.

Mary went back to bed, clean sheets and warmth and the arms of her lover. She and her child would live.

The surgeon came with them, took one look at George's foot, and announced it had to come off.

The surgery was performed on the kitchen table, and George's screams rang for a long time in Mary's dreams.

In a few days Mary had largely recovered. She and Bysshe thanked the Fleurys and sailed to Geneva on a beautiful autumn day in their hired boat. George and Claire—for Claire was George's again—remained behind to sort out George's legal problems. Mary didn't think their friendship would last beyond George's immediate recovery, and she hoped that Claire would not return to England heavy with another child.

After another week's recovery in Geneva, Bysshe and Mary headed for England and the financial rescue of Mr. Godwin. Mary had bought a pocketbook and was already filling its pages with her story of the Franked Stone. Bysshe knew any nymber of publishers, and assured her it would find a home with one of them.

Frankenstein was an immediate success. At one point there were over twenty stage productions going on at once. Though she received no money from the stage adaptations, the book proved a very good seller, and was never out of print. The royalties proved useful in supporting Bysshe and Mary and Claire—once she returned to them, once more with child—during years of wandering, chiefly in Switzerland and Italy.

George's promised thousand pounds a year never materialized.

And the monster, the poor abused charnel creature that was Mary's settlement with death, now stalked through the hearts of all the world.

George went to South America to sell his sword to the revolutionary cause. Mary and Bysshe, reading of his exploits in tattered newspapers sent from England, found it somehow satisfying that he was, at last and however reluctantly, fighting for liberty.

They never saw him again, but Mary thought of him often—the great, famed figure, limping painfully through battle after battle, crippled, ever-restless, and in his breast the arctic waste of the soul, the franked and steely creator with his heart of stone.

HONORABLE MENTIONS
1993

Kevin J. Anderson, "Human, Martian—One, Two, Three," *Full Spectrum 4*.
Arlan Andrews, "Day of the Dancing Dinosaur," *SF Age*, March.
Patricia Anthony, "Born to Be Wild," *Aboriginal SF*, Summer.
———, "Gingerbread Man," *Aboriginal SF*, Fall.
———, "Guardian of Fireflies," *Asimov's*, April.
Kim Antieau, "Another Country," *SF Age*, May.
Michael Armstrong, "Everything That Rises, Must Converge," *Asimov's*, Feb.
Eleanor Arnason, "The Hound of Merin," *Xanadu*.
———, "The Semen Thief," *Amazing*, Winter.
Isaac Asimov, "The Consort," *Asimov's*, April.
———, "More Things in Heaven and Earth," *Asimov's*, Nov.
A. A. Attanasio, "Wax Me Mind," *Crank!* #1.
Eric T. Baker, "Uncertainty and the Dread Word Love," *Amazing*, Oct.
Scott Baker, "Virus Dreams," *Omni Best Science Fiction Three*.
Virginia Baker, "Pictures of Daniel," *Tomorrow*, Jan.
Stephen Baxter, "Downstream," *Interzone*, Sept.
———, "Pilgrim 7," *Interzone*, Jan.
———, "The Sun Person," *Interzone*, March.
Chris Beckett, "The Welfare Man," *Interzone*, Aug.
M. Shayne Bell, "The King's Kiss," *Asimov's*, March.
———, "Night Games," *Tomorrow*, Jan.
———, "With Rain, and a Dog Barking," *F&SF*, April.
Gregory Benford, "The Dark Backward," *Amazing*, Feb.
Terry Bisson, "England Underway," *Omni*, July
———, "The Shadow Knows," *Asimov's*, Sept.
James P. Blaylock and Tim Powers, "We Traverse Afar," *Christmas Forever*.
Michael Blumlein, "Hymenoptera," *Crank!* #1.
Mark Bourne, "Being Human," *Asimov's*, Dec.
———, "Brokedown," *F&SF*, March.
Ben Bova, "Re-Entry Shock," *F&SF*, Jan.
Juleen Brantingham, "Tourist Attraction," *Amazing*, August.
Simon Brown, "Brother Stripes," *Aurealis 11*.
Stephen L. Burns, "Showdown at Hell Creek," *Analog*, Mid-Dec.
Pat Cadigan, "Dino Trend," *Dinosaur Fantastic*.
———, "Lost Girls," *Dirty Work*.
Susan Casper, "Betrayal," *Dinosaur Fantastic*.
———, "Coming of Age," *Journeys to the Twilight Zone*.
———, "Windows of the Soul," *More Whatdunits*.
Rob Chilson, "Just for Tonight," *Tomorrow*, Jan.
———, "The Worting's Testament," *Analog*, March.
Lisa R. Cohen, "Rainbone," *F&SF*, April.
Michael Coney, "Sophie's Spyglass," *F&SF*, Feb.
Greg Costikyan, "The Hart," *Asimov's*, April.
———, "The Winter of Love," *SF Age*, Sept.
Tony Daniel, "Aconcagua," *Asimov's*. Feb.
———, "Always Falling Apart," *SF Age*, Jan.
———, "Dover Beach," *Amazing*, March.

————, "God's Foot," *Asimov's*, May.

————, "Sun So Hot I Froze to Death," *Asimov's*, Jan.

Jack Dann, "The Extra," *Journeys to the Twilight Zone*.

————, "The Glass Casket," *Snow White, Blood Red*.

————, "The Path of Remembrance," *Amazing*, Nov.

————, "Vapors," *Amazing*. June.

Avram Davidson, "A Far Countrie," *Asimov's*, Nov.

————, "Sea-Scene, or, Vergil and the Ox-Thrall," *Asimov's*, Feb.

————, "The Spook-Box of Theodore Delafont De Brooks," *Tomorrow*, July.

Pamela Dean, "Owlswater," *Xanadu*.

L. Sprague de Camp, "The Cayuse," *Expanse 1*.

————, "The Mislaid Mastodon," *Analog*, May.

————, "Pliocene Romance," *Analog*, Jan.

Stephen Dedman, "As Wise as Serpents," *F&SF*, July.

Barbara Delaplace, "Standing Firm," *Alternate Warriors*.

Charles de Lint, "The Bone Woman," *F&SF*, August.

————, "Paperjack," *F&SF*, July.

Nicholas A. DiChario, "Extreme Feminism," *Alternate Warriors*.

Paul Di Filippo, "The Horror Writer," *Nova 5*.

————, "Streetlife," *New Worlds 3*.

————, "Walt and Emily," *Interzone*, Nov.-Dec.

Thomas M. Disch, "The Burial Society," *Amazing*, Sept.

Terry Dowling, "Fear-Me-Now," *Crosstown Traffic*.

Gardner Dozois, "Passage," *Xanadu*.

L. Timmel Duchamp, "Motherhood, Etc.," *Full Spectrum 4*.

J. R. Dunn, "Men of Good Will," *Amazing*, March.

Lawrence Dyer, "The Four-Thousand-Year-Old Boy," *Interzone*, July.

George Alec Effinger, "The Ugly Earthling Murder Case," *More Whatdunits*.

Greg Egan, "The Extra," *Asimov's*, Jan.

————, "Transition Dreams," *Interzone*, Oct.

Wennicke Eide, "Stone Man," *Asimov's*, July.

Kandis Elliot, "Driving the Chevy Biscayne to Oblivion," *Asimov's*, March.

————, "Laying the Meridians," *Tomorrow*, August.

Harlan Ellison, "Mefisto in Onyx," *Omni*, Oct.

Carol Emshwiller, "Mrs. Jones," *Omni*, August.

Timons Esaias, "Norbert and the System," *Interzone*, July.

Christopher Evans, "After the Fall," *Strange Plasma 6*.

Sharon N. Farber, "Advice," *Asimov's*, August.

Gregory Feeley, "The Mind's Place," *Full Spectrum 4*.

————, "Thirteen Ways of Looking at a Dinosaur," *Dinosaur Fantastic*.

Eliot Fintushel, "Herbrand's Conjecture and the White Sox Scandal," *Tomorrow*, Oct.

Maggie Flinn, "One Morning in the Looney Bin," *Asimov's*, Feb.

————, "A Present for Hanna," *Christmas Forever*.

Michael F. Flynn, "Great, Sweet Mother," *Analog*, June.

Valerie J. Freireich, "The Prodigy," *Asimov's*, August.

————, "Ice Atlantis," *Asimov's*, Nov.

————, "The Toolman," *Tomorrow*, April.

Esther M. Friesner, "Puss," *Snow White, Blood Red*.

————, "Lowlifes," *Asimov's*, May.

————, "Three Queens," *Asimov's*, Jan.

Gregory Frost, "Some Things Are Better Left," *Asimov's*, Feb.

Neil Gaiman, "Troll Bridge," *Snow White, Blood Red*.

R. Garcia y Robertson, "Down the River," *Asimov's*, Oct.

————, "The Other Magpie," *Asimov's*, April.

————, "The Siren Shoals," *F&SF*, August.
David Gerrold, "Rex," *Dinosaur Fantastic*.
Mark S. Geston, "Falconer," *Amazing*, May.
Lisa Goldstein, "Infinite Riches," *Asimov's*, April.
————, "The Woman in the Painting," *F&SF*, July.
Phyllis Gotlieb, "Among You," *SF Age*, Nov.
Kathleen Ann Goonan, "Kamehameha's Bones," *Asimov's*, Sept.
————, "The Parrot Man," *Asimov's*, March.
————, "When the Grace Note of the Cities Changed,"
  Tomorrow, July.
Ed Gorman, "The Face," *F&SF*, April.
John Griesemer, "Steam," *Asimov's*, May.
Nicola Griffith, "Touching Fire," *Interzone*, April.
James Gunn, "The Futurist," *Amazing*, Nov.
Jack C. Haldeman II, "The Cold Warrior," *Alternate Warriors*.
Elizabeth Hand, "The Erl-King," *Full Spectrum 4*.
————, "Justice," *F&SF*, July.
Peter F. Hamilton, "Spare Capacity," *New Worlds 3*.
Howard V. Hendrix, "At the Shadow of a Dream," *Aboriginal SF*, Spring.
Nina Kiriki Hoffman, "The Skeleton Key," *F&SF*, August.
Simon Ings, "The Black Lotus," *Omni Best SF Three*.
————and Charles Stross, "Tolkowsky's Cut," *New Worlds 3*.
Alexander Jablokov, "Rest Cure," *Aboriginal SF*, Summer.
————, "The Last Castle of Christmas," *Asimov's*, Dec.
Phillip C. Jennings, "A History of the Antipodes," *Amazing*, March.
————, "Mad Maud's Dance," *Amazing*, Jan.
————, "Precarnation," *Asimov's*, August.
————, "Restart," *Analog*, Dec.
Kij Johnson, "Fox Magic," *Asimov's*, Dec.
Gwyneth Jones, "The Mechanic," *New Worlds 3*.
Graham Joyce, "Gap-sickness," *New Worlds 3*.
Astrid Julian, "Irene's Song," *Interzone*. March.
Janet Kagan, "No Known Cure," *Pulphouse 12*.
————, "Christmas Wingding," *Christmas Forever*.
Bonita Kale, "The Saints," *Full Spectrum 4*.
Michael Kandel, "Virtual Reality," *Simulations*.
James Patrick Kelly, "Chemistry," *Asimov's*, June.
John Kessel, "The Franchise," *Asimov's*, August.
Garry Kilworth, "Fossils," *Interzone*, March.
————, "Punctuated Evolution," *Crank!* #1.
Kathe Koja, "Ballad of the Spanish Civil Guard," *Alternate Warriors*.
————, "I Shall Do Thee Mischief in the Wood," *Snow White, Blood Red*.
———— and Barry N. Malzberg, "The Timbrel Sound of Darkness," *Christmas Ghosts*.
Damon Knight, "Not a Creature," *Christmas Forever*.
Nancy Kress, "The Battle of Long Island," *Omni*, Feb.
————, "Martin on a Wednesday," *Asimov's*, March.
————, "Stalking Beans," *Snow White, Blood Red*.
Michael P. Kube-McDowell, "Because Thou Lovest the Burning-Ground," *Alternate Warriors*.
Geoffrey A. Landis, "Beneath the Stars of Winter," *Asimov's*, Jan.
————, "In the Hole with the Boys with the Toys," *Asimov's*, Oct.
Tanith Lee, "Antonius Bequeathed," *Weird Tales*, Spring.
————, "Winter Flowers," *Asimov's*, June.
————, "Unnalash," *Xanadu*.

Ursula K. Le Guin, "Dancing to Ganam," *Amazing*, Sept.
——, "The Poacher," *Xanadu*.
Jonathan Lethem, "A Small Patch on My Contract," *Interzone*, May.
——, " 'Forever,' Said the Duck," *Asimov's*, Dec.
——, "The Precocious Objects," *Asimov's*, Mid-Dec.
——, "Waiting Under Water," *Jejune*.
Rosaleen Love, "The Daughters of Darius," *Evolution Annie and Other Stories*.
Elizabeth A. Lynn, "The Princess in the Tower," *Snow White, Blood Red*.
Sonia Orin Lyris, "A Hand in the Mirror," *Asimov's*, August.
——, "It Might Be Sunlight," *Asimov's*, Nov.
Bruce McAllister, "Moving On," *Omni Best SF Three*.
——, "Southpaw," *Asimov's*, August.
Paul J. McAuley, "Children of the Revolution," *New Worlds 3*.
——, "Dr. Luther's Assistant," *Interzone*, Feb.
Jack McDevitt, "Ships in the Night," *Amazing*, Oct.
Ian McDonald, "Brody Loved the Masai Woman," *Dedalus Book of Femmes Fatales*.
——, "Some Strange Desire," *Omni Best SF Three*.
——, "The Undifferentiated Object of Desire," *Asimov's*, June.
Mark J. McGarry, "The Ghost in the Machine," *Amazing*, April.
Maureen F. McHugh, "A Coney Island of the Mind," *Asimov's*, Feb.
——, "A Foreigner's Christmas in China," *Christmas Ghosts*.
——, "Tut's Wife," *Alternate Warriors*.
Bridget McKenna, "The Good Pup," *F&SF*, March.
Patricia A. McKillip, "The Snow Queen," *Snow White, Blood Red*.
Sean McMullen, "Charon's Anchor," *Aurealis 12*.
——, "The Way to Greece," *Eidolon 13*.
Barry N. Malzberg, "Andante Lugubre," *SF Age*, May.
——, "Fugato," *Alternate Warriors*.
——, "Standards & Practices," *F&SF*, April.
Diane Mapes, "Globsters," *Asimov's*, May.
Daniel Marcus, "Random Acts of Kindness," *Asimov's*, Oct.
Joe Martino, "Paper Virus," *Analog*, Mid-Dec.
David Marusek, "The Earth Is on the Mend," *Asimov's*, May.
Beth Meacham, "One by One," *Alternate Warriors*.
Bart Meehan, "Canals," *Aurealis 11*.
Robert A. Metzger, "Earl's Snack Shop," *SF Age*, Nov.
Pat Murphy, "A Cartographic Analysis of the Dream State," *Omni Best SF Three*.
——, "An American Childhood," *Asimov's*, April.
Linda Nagata, "Liberator," *F&SF*, June.
Jamil Nasir, "The Dakna," *Asimov's*, Sept.
——, "My Informant Zardon," *Interzone*, August.
——, "Sleepers Awake," *Asimov's*, July.
Kim Newman, "The Big Fish," *Interzone*, Oct.
——, "The Blitz Spirit," *The Time Out Book of London Short Stories*.
G. David Nordley, "Hunting the Space Whale," *Tomorrow*, August.
Jerry Oltion, "Course Changes," *Analog*, Sept.
Rebecca Ore, "Farming in Virginia," *Alien Bootlegger and Other Stories*.
——, "Ocean Hammer," *Asimov's*, Jan.
Michael H. Payne, "River Man," *Asimov's*, August.
Tom Purdom, "The Redemption of August," *Asimov's*, March.
David Redd, "The Old Man of Munington," *Asimov's*, Mid-Dec.
Kit Reed, "Like My Dress," *Omni*, April.
Robert Reed, "Blind," *Asimov's*, May.
——, "Fable Blue," *F&SF*, Oct./Nov.

————, "On the Brink of that Bright New World," *Asimov's*, Jan.

————, "Sister Alice," *Asimov's*, Nov.

————, "The Toad of Heaven," *Asimov's*, June.

Laura Resnick, "The Vatican Outfit," *Alternate Warriors*.

Mike Resnick, "The Pale Thin God," *Xanadu*.

Mark Rich, "With Love from the Plague Territories," *Amazing*, Feb.

Carrie Richerson, "The Light at the End of the Day," *F&SF*, Oct./Nov.

Michael Robbins, "Shared Sorrow," *Xizquil 9*.

Frank M. Robinson, "The Greatest Dying," *Dinosaur Fantastic*.

Alan Rodgers, "The Bear Who Found Christmas," *Christmas Ghosts*.

Mary Rosenblum, "Bordertown," *Asimov's*, Dec.

————, "Entrada," *Asimov's*, Feb.

————, "The Rain Stone," *Asimov's*, July.

————, "Sanctuary," *F&SF*, June.

————, "Stairway," *Asimov's*, May.

Kristine Kathryn Rusch, "The Arrival of Truth," *Alternate Warriors*.

————, "Good Wishes," *F&SF*, June.

James Sallis, "Powers of Flight," *Amazing*, April.

Jessica Amanda Salmonson, "The Toad Witch," *Asimov's*, June.

Robert Sampson, "Dead Gods," *Asimov's*, July.

Pamela Sargent, "Outside the Windows," *Journeys to the Twilight Zone*.

Robert J. Sawyer, "Just Like Old Times," *On Spec*, Summer.

Stanley Schmidt, "Johnny Birdseed," *Analog*, July.

Charles Sheffield, "The Fifteenth Station of the Cross," *SF Age*, July.

————, "The Invariants of Nature," *Analog*, April.

Rick Shelley, "Afterwar," *SF Age*, July.

Lewis Shiner, "Secrets," *Asimov's*, Nov.

————, "Voodoo Child," *Asimov's*, July.

W. M. Shockley, "Old Antagonists," *Asimov's*, Mid-Dec.

D. William Shunn, "From Our Point of View We Had Moved to the Left," *F&SF*, Feb.

Robert Silverberg, "The Sri Lanka Position," *Playboy*, Dec.

Dan Simmons, "Death in Bangkok," *Playboy*, June.

————, "The Great Lover," *Lovedeath*.

————, "Sleeping with Teeth Women," *Lovedeath*.

Dave Smeds, "Suicidal Tendencies," *Full Spectrum 4*

Sarah Smith, "Touched by the Bomb," *F&SF*, June.

S. P. Somtow, "Tagging the Moon," *Asimov's*, Mid-Dec.

Martha Soukup, "A Defense of the Social Contracts," *SF Age*, Sept.

————, "The Story So Far," *Full Spectrum 4*.

Bud Sparhawk, "Dad," *Analog*, June.

Norman Spinrad, "Vampire Junkies," *Tomorrow*, August.

————, "Where the Heart Is," *Pulphouse 12*.

Brian Stableford, "Burned Out," *Interzone*, April.

————, "Carriers," *Asimov's*, July.

————, "The Cure for Love," *Asimov's*, Mid-Dec.

————, "The Facts of Life," *Asimov's*, Sept.

————, "The Flowers of the Forest," *Amazing*, June.

————, "Riding the Tiger," *Interzone*, Feb.

Allen M. Steele, "Mudzilla's Last Stand," *Asimov's*, Jan.

Bruce Sterling, "Deep Eddy," *Asimov's*, August.

Sue Storm, "The Last True Story," *Xizquil 9*.

Dirk Strasser, "The Tale of Valkyra and Verlinden," *Aurealis 12*.

M. C. Sumner, "A Handful of Hatchlings," *Asimov's*, Feb.

————, "In Fourteen Hundred and Ninety-Three, Columbus Crossed the Frozen Sea," *Tomorrow*, August.

Michael Swanwick, "Cold Iron," *Asimov's*, Nov.
——, "Picasso Deconstructed: Eleven Still-Lifes," *Asimov's*, May.
Judith Tarr, "Holiday Station," *Christmas Ghosts*.
——, "Queen of Asia," *Alternate Warriors*.
Melanie Tem, "Jenny," *Asimov's*, Mid-Dec.
William Tenn, "The Girl with Some Kind of Past. And George.," *Asimov's*, Oct.
George Turner, "Worlds," *Strange Plasma 6*.
Harry Turtledove, "Down in the Bottomlands," *Analog*, Jan.
——, "Vermin," *F&SF*, March.
Paul C. Tumey, "Toy Chest River," *Christmas Forever*.
Lisa Tuttle, "Lucy Maria," *Xanadu*.
Steven Utley, "The Country Doctor," *Asimov's*, Oct.
Ray Vukcevich, "My Mustache," *Asimov's*, Nov.
——, "Ornamental Animals," *Pulphouse 15*.
Holly Wade, "The Cool Place," *Asimov's*, Sept.
Susan Wade, "Like a Red, Red Rose," *Snow White, Blood Red*.
Howard Waldrop, "Household Words, or, The Powers-That-Be," *Amazing*, Winter 1994.
Sage Walker, "Roadkill," *Asimov's*, April.
William John Watkins, "The Beggar in the Living Room," *Asimov's*, April.
Lawrence Watt-Evans, "The Murderer," *Asimov's*, April.
——, "A Public Hanging," *Pulphouse 12*.
Don Webb, "The Pact," *Asimov's*, March.
——, "The Canals of Mars," *SF Age*, Sept.
Andrew Weiner, "In Dreams," *Asimov's*, Mid-Dec.
Mel. White, "Sam Clemens and the Notable Mare," *Alternate Warriors*.
Rick Wilber, "Being Ernest," *Pulphouse 12*.
——, "With Twoclicks Watching," *Asimov's*, Jan.
Sean Williams, "White Christmas," *Eidolon 11*.
Jack Williamson, "The Ice Gods," *Amazing*, Winter 1994.
——, "The Litlins," *F&SF*, Dec.
Connie Willis, "Close Encounter," *Asimov's*, Sept.
——, "Inn," *Asimov's*, Dec.
Amy Wolf, "All Singing, All Dancing," *Interzone*, Sept.
Gene Wolfe, "And When They Appear," *Christmas Forever*.
——, "Useful Phrases," *Tomorrow*, Jan.
Dave Wolverton, "My Favorite Christmas," *Christmas Forever*.
William F. Wu, "Tinsel Chink," *Pulphouse 12*.
Jim Young, "Microde City," *Asimov's*, June.
Jane Yolen, "The Snatchers," *F&SF*, Oct./Nov.

ALSO AVAILABLE FROM ST. MARTIN'S PRESS

	Quantity	Price
The Year's Best Science Fiction: *Thirteenth Annual Collection* ($17.95) **ISBN: 0-312-14452-0 (trade paperback)**	_____	_____
Modern Classics of Science Fiction edited by Gardner Dozois ($16.95) **ISBN: 0-312-08847-7 (trade paperback)**	_____	_____
Modern Classic Short Novels of Science Fiction edited by Gardner Dozois ($15.95) **ISBN: 0-312-11317-X (trade paperback)**	_____	_____
Those Who Can: A Science Fiction Reader edited by Robin Wilson ($13.95) **ISBN: 0-312-14139-4 (trade paperback)**	_____	_____
Paragons: Twelve SF Writers Ply Their Craft edited by Robin Wilson ($14.95) **ISBN: 0-312-15623-5 (trade paperback)**	_____	_____
Writing Science Fiction and Fantasy edited by the editors of *Asimov's* and *Analog* ($9.95) **ISBN: 0-312-08926-0 (trade paperback)**	_____	_____
The Encyclopedia of Science Fiction by John Clute and Peter Nicholls ($29.95) **ISBN: 0-312-13486-X (trade paperback)**	_____	_____

POSTAGE & HANDLING

(Books up to $12.00 – add $3.00; books up to $15.00 – add $3.50;
books above $15.00 – add $4.00 – plus $1.00 for each additional book)   _____

8% Sales Tax (New York State residents only)   _____

Amount enclosed: _____

Name _____

Address _____

City _____ State _____ Zip _____

Send this form or a copy with payment to:
Publishers Book & Audio, P.O. Box 070059, 5448 Arthur Kill Road, Staten Island, NY 10307.
Telephone (800) 288-2131. Please allow three weeks for delivery.
For bulk orders (10 copies or more) please contact the St. Martin's Press Special Sales Department
toll free at 800-221-7945 ext. 645 for information. In New York State call 212-674-5151.